the *finished* masterpiece

NEW YORK TIMES BESTSELLING AUTHOR

PEPPER WINTERS

Published: Pepper Winters 2019: **pepperwinters@gmail.com**
Cover Design: Ari @ Cover it! Designs
Editing by: Editing 4 Indies (Jenny Sims)

the
body
painter

NEW YORK TIMES BESTSELLING AUTHOR

PEPPER WINTERS

What am I in the eyes of most people — a nonentity, an eccentric, or an unpleasant person — somebody who has no position in society and will never have; in short, the lowest of the low. All right, then — even if that were absolutely true, then I should one day like to show by my work what such an eccentric, such a nobody, has in his heart. That is my ambition, based less on resentment than on love in spite of everything, based more on a feeling of serenity than on passion. Though I am often in the depths of misery, there is still calmness, pure harmony and music inside me. I see paintings or drawings in the poorest cottages, in the dirtiest corners. And my mind is driven towards these things with an irresistible momentum.
—Vincent Van Gogh

Prologue

Gil

-The Present-

SHE'D RUINED EVERYTHING.

She should've heard my warnings, seen my threats, read between the cruel lines I'd given her.

I'd done my best to be a bastard.

To be hateful, heartless, and vicious in my denial of everything that existed between us.

But she didn't walk away.

She ignored my commands like an idiot.

She believed she could *help* me.

She willingly gave me the heart I'd broken when we were just kids.

And just like back then...it was too late.

Too late because what she didn't know had the power to kill her.

Not emotionally. Not hypothetically. But murder...in cold blood.

And now, she knew too much.

Kiss me?

Love me?

Now die for me.

I'm sorry...

Chapter One

Gil

-The Past-

I'D HAD A crush on her for almost two years before fate decided I'd waited long enough, and set things in motion that I wished I could undo.

Olin Moss.

The kinda quirky, slightly rebellious, wonderfully nice girl who sat two rows in front of me in class.

Most days, I slung into my seat exhausted and hungry—fighting to stay awake and learn, hoping to achieve good grades to earn a job but mostly to stay out of the principal's office so I didn't get a hiding at home.

I did my best to ignore her.

I didn't allow her to distract me with her delicate laugh and the annoying way my heart beat harder when she smiled. I didn't have time to be interested in girls—no desire to get close to anyone.

My life was about survival, not fun.

I wasn't like my fellow students.

I wasn't like *her*.

She didn't look hungry or tired.

She didn't seem angry at life or lacking in basic fundamentals of existence.

Her hazel eyes were intelligent. Her popularity impressive. Her acceptance of both good and bad days a lesson I should probably master. However, I was only intimate with the shitty, dark days that made everything else just as depressing.

While Olin hung out with her friends and ate packed

lunches on the field, I'd do whatever it took to keep myself alive another day.

Food at home was non-existent. I'd learned that if I helped in the canteen during break, I had better opportunity to steal enough to eat. Filling my belly to the brim, knowing it would be another twenty-four hours until my next meal.

When the final bell went, I didn't bolt into freedom like the others. I dragged my feet and slinked down alleyways to a neighbourhood Olin Moss wouldn't be caught dead in.

There, I did my best to forget about the mouldy walls, empty cupboards, and the drunkard down the hall. I used earplugs to block the ranting and homework to ignore the constant stream of stoned guests.

Sleep usually found me face down on a textbook, my dirty blankets thrown over me to ward off the midnight chill.

The next morning was wash and repeat: dash from the house before they woke, spray some deodorant over the unwashed clothes I'd slept in, and collapse onto the chair two rows back from a pancake-and-maple syrup smelling Olin Moss.

For two years, our worlds brushed but never collided.

Until that one fateful day.

A day that ought to have been the best day of my life, but somehow, became the catalyst for the worst.

Chapter Two

Olin

-The Present-

"HELLO?" MY VOICE echoed in the large industrial space as my red heels clicked hesitantly across bare, paint-splattered concrete. "Anyone here?"

Two p.m.

I was on time for my interview, but it seemed I was the only one.

Warehouse number twenty-five yawned in welcome, complete with colourful graffiti on its red brick exterior, a massive roller door with rusty chains, and a cleverly painted sign with the name *Total Trickery*.

I was definitely in the right place.

It was Wednesday at two.

The email confirmation matched the calendar.

So…where was the body painter who was meant to be interviewing me? Where were the other hopeful interviewees as I stepped through a small opening beside the large roller door and traded outside for in?

Paint fumes floated with paraffin parachutes on the air. Turpentine, oil, acrylic, and papyrus all added to the recipe.

My fingers itched to check my phone for the fortieth time. To triple, quadruple check the address.

Stop.

The details said today.

With my chin high and heart racing, I strode purposely forward in my red-clicking heels. My interview-acceptable black dress whispered against my skin as I hoisted my small satchel with my resume up my shoulder. "Hello? I'm here for the two o' clock meeting with—"

A masculine groan followed by a curse whipped my head to the gloomy shadows in the corner. A scuffle sounded, something metallic clattered to the concrete, another curse bit in anger.

Goosebumps spread over my arms. "Um, hi? I'm…eh, here for the interview?" I stepped warily toward the noise.

Another curse followed by a loud thump.

"I heard you the first time." A man appeared from the darkness.

A man with shaggy dark hair, five o'clock shadow, and eyes so maliciously green they masqueraded as body parts but were really well-honed weapons.

A man who was bleeding from his temple, limping, and holding his elbow as if it needed reattaching.

"Sorry, I didn't know if—" I gulped as something long ago tugged in remembrance.

No.

It can't be…

Recognition slammed into me as forcibly as it slammed into him.

I stumbled under the weight.

Punched by the unbelievable.

"Gil? Oh, my God. *Gil!*"

Older.

Darker.

More gorgeous than he'd ever been.

I fought every instinct to go to him.

Did my best not to grab him, kiss him, shake him, slap him.

A gust of air blasted through the warehouse as if the winds of fate woke up, felt a tug on whatever linked us together, and clapped its hands in glee, saying, *'Yes, this will be fun. Let's put these two back together again.'*

"Olin? Fuck…it's you." His gaze tore over me as hungrily as mine tore over him.

Time stood still. It reversed. It plopped us right back in the past where this boy had held my heart, and I'd captured his, and together we knew it would always be about us.

Us.

There is no more us.

I stumbled toward him, desperate to be nearer despite so

much pain. "I can't believe this. What are you doing here?"

"What am I? What are *you*?" He tripped in my direction, his face etched with lines I hadn't seen in his youth, his body all angles and threats. As fast as he'd headed toward me, he halted as if yanked back by a rope. His face fell. His shock at seeing me morphed into hardness.

I didn't understand how he could change so much in a few short seconds.

Goosebumps decorated me as coldness settled like a cloak around his shoulders.

"I've been back in Birmingham two years. I—" I stopped talking, unable to share the secrets that followed such a statement. "I…"

He closed his eyes, shutting me out as if battling something deep within him. Deliberately, he took a step back, his chin coming up, his coldness settling into ice.

The silence that'd chased us in our fledgling romance returned, thick and heavy.

My back prickled. My mouth turned dry.

Too much distance existed between us, swelling with memory of how things had ended, why we were strangers now, and just how much heartbreak had been left behind.

Along with silence came shadows, creeping over Gil's expression, shutting down any remaining signs of his shock and gratefulness at seeing me. Heartbeat by heartbeat, he hid any sign that my visit was a welcome one.

I struggled, not knowing what to say.

His gaze no longer held happiness, just aching emptiness and suspicion. "How did you find me?" He didn't give me chance to reply. "You can't be here, Olin. You need to leave. I don't want you anywhere near me."

What?

Ice water gushed down my spine. "I…what are you talking about?"

"I just told you. You need to go. Just turn around and walk out the same way you walked in." He narrowed his weaponized eyes, ready to scold me, scare me, and ruin, not just my chance at employment, but any hope of closure from the past. "You're not welcome here."

His words were daggers but his voice quavered with dismay.

My heart kicked. "What do you mean?"

"Are you deaf?" He shook his head, his body seething with

anger so brutal and out-of-nowhere it seemed fake. "Why the hell are you here, huh? What made you think I'd *want* you here?" His gaze flickered behind me, locking onto the door as if something evil would waltz right through it. "Goddammit, I don't have time for this."

"Time for what?"

"You!"

I stumbled backward just as he tripped to the side, a wince and gasp escaping through gritted teeth. "Fuck."

"Gil." My concern overrode emotional agony. I flew to him, following old patterns of caring for him, protecting him, ready to be everything he needed because that was how it'd been between us.

A partnership.

A vow that we would always, *always* look after the other.

"Are you okay?" I managed to touch his shoulder, just once. A single caress before he reared back as if I'd hurt him worse than anyone. He swallowed a groan, squeezed his eyes, trembled with pain that I knew didn't have anything to do with his physical injuries but everything to do with us.

Us.

There is no more us.

Remember?

"Don't touch me," he snarled.

"But you're hurt."

"I'm fine."

"You're not. Let me help—"

"Fuck, Olin." His head tipped downward, unable to look at me. Unable to fight the draw that still hummed between us. "I need you to leave. I can't...I can't do this."

My heart fell to the floor.

He sounded exhausted.

Cross.

Confused.

"Tell me who did this to you."

He laughed coldly. "It's nothing I don't deserve."

I reached for him again, my fingertips begging to touch. "Gil..."

"Stop. Just...*fuck!*" He growled with rage and backed away. His thick eyelashes framed impossible pain. A blue streak of paint mixed with the red blood on his cheek.

Straightening his spine, any lingering sign of weakness or

historical affection vanished, slipping into irritable stranger, placing a mask of snow upon his features. "I don't know why you're here, but you need to go. I don't want you here. I asked you politely to leave." His body tensed, bracing himself to be cruel. "There's the goddamn door. Use it."

Gil had always been a conundrum. A loner at school. Sweet with me. Horrible to me.

No matter how he'd treated me, I'd always tended his wounds.

Today is no different.

Squaring my shoulders, I said, "I can't leave you in this state."

"You don't have a choice." Our eyes collided and tangled.

In one stare, every gate and wall I'd built from him hurting me came tumbling down. "Gil, I...where have you been? I've wondered so many times—"

"Don't." He tore his gaze away, struggling with the familiarity between us. The sensation of homecoming. The connection that refused to break, no matter how much time had passed.

"I just want to understand." I stepped closer.

He backed up, succeeding in shutting away his emotions and staring at me with heavy disgust and belittling dislike.

The wind that'd shot inside uninvited, swirled around my legs and up my skirt with icy fingers. I shivered, partly from the draft and partly from the frost now glittering on his face.

"Get out." He bared his teeth. "Now."

"But...I came for the interview."

"Interview?" His eyebrows shot skyward. "You think I'd *interview* you?" His laugh was a vicious thing. Forced and brittle, cruel and callous. "You've wasted your time. There's nothing for you here."

I winced. I couldn't help it.

He was here.

As long as he was here, there were a million reasons why I should stay.

Us.

There is no more us.

Remember!?

"I-I didn't know it was you." I swallowed. "The job opportunity. I didn't know you—"

"And I didn't know it was you. Otherwise, the offer to be

interviewed would never have been given. Your email address wasn't in your name."

"I know. I don't like to advertise my personal info. Wait—" I shook my head, doing my best to keep him talking. The longer he spoke, the more his anger cracked. "How did you become a body painter? I mean you were amazing at art in school, but—"

"Stop it." He winced, licking his lip where a split oozed and swelled. "Enough, Olin. This is over."

"Why do you get to decide it's over?" I kept my attention on his hands, unable to meet his stare. "Why did you get to decide it was over seven years ago?" My question sliced my throat on its way out. Spiky and poisonous, something that I'd wanted to ask since he disappeared.

"Stop." He swallowed hard, washing back excuses, answers, maybe even pleas for forgiveness. Any sign of regret at breaking my heart remained hidden as his green eyes turned lethally black. "Get out. You've been here too long already. I want you gone, do you hear me?"

I stepped backward, my legs obeying the bitten command.

I'd always looked up to Gil. Always been terribly dazzled. Always been hopelessly besotted.

He thought I hadn't noticed him before that day in the corridor, but I had. I'd been blisteringly aware of him sitting behind me. Of the way he chewed his pencil when solving questions. Of the way his hands transformed mundane into magic.

I should've known he'd choose art.

Someone with his talent would always be recognised.

But despite his fury, despite my desire to scurry out of his vicinity to nurse the hot wash of tears, undeniable questions swirled in my mind.

So many years.

Such a long eternity.

How had we gone from teenagers to this? How had time stolen our happily ever after?

Staring at him, catching the strain in his face and the worry lines by his eyes, I didn't see an older, wiser version of the boy who'd made me cry. I only saw so many mistakes and a whole chest worth of heartache.

"Gil—"

"*Don't.*" He barked. "You're on private property. Your invitation has been revoked." Skirting around me, he stalked toward the exit.

"We were friends once."

He didn't look at me. "Don't fool yourself. We were never friends."

He was right.

We'd been aware of each other on an instinctual level. We'd been drawn to one another in ways that exceeded our juvenile comprehension. Our bond exceeded petty arguments or stupid misunderstandings.

There was a link.

An awareness.

A pain.

"We weren't just friends. We were more. *So* much more."

"We were nothing." He let his damaged elbow go, spinning to face me with a hiss. His injuries leeched away his power, leaving him feral with the need to kick me out.

I scowled. "Why can't you accept my help? You obviously need it."

His nostrils flared. For a second, utmost yearning flickered. He swayed toward me, victim to the lashing, licking need between us. But then, he shook his head. He pinched his nose as if fighting the simplicity of us.

Us.

There is no more us.

REMEMBER?!

I tiptoed closer, my voice a whisper. "I just…I need to understand, Gil. I get that I no longer have a chance of employment but…" I swallowed, murmuring with strength I didn't have, "I'm happy for you. Truly. So glad that you get to do what you love for work. I've seen your *Total Trickery* webpage. I've watched you online. Those YouTube videos of the hooded man painting naked canvases…I had no idea it was you." I sighed in awe. "Your talent is incredible."

He flinched.

He didn't speak for the longest moment.

I hoped he'd be kind, now he knew I meant no harm. Perhaps too much time had passed for us to go back to what we were, but there might be a chance for a different type of relationship.

Friends.

Co-workers.

Artist and canvas.

I was willing to accept anything if it meant I got to see him again. If I had the slimmest chance to figure out why he'd left me.

But just like before, he chased off the truth and embraced anger instead. His voice thickened with another growl. "Doesn't matter." He raised his hand, pointing at the exit. "Leave." He looked up, trapping me in emerald intensity. "Goddammit, Olin. *Please* leave."

My fingers curled into fists.

That wasn't fair.

I was useless against him when he begged.

I'd let him guide our path when we were younger; happy to let him be in control because I trusted him impeccably. I loved having the honour of being the only one he talked to. The only one permitted to be close to him, to know his secrets, to walk beside him.

Turned out, I was no longer privileged.

Maybe he'd replaced me.

Maybe he truly couldn't stand me.

But here he was.

Bleeding.

Wounded.

And no sign of a lover to tend to him.

He needed someone to love.

He needed someone who loved him.

I tried one last time. "You shouldn't be alone, Gil. Please, let me stay."

He balled his hands, not showing any signs of an emotional war this time. "I'm better off alone, believe me."

"You need medical attention."

"So will you if you don't leave."

I sighed sadly. "Resorting to threats won't work. Not this time."

His eyes flashed with history. Of the time he'd physically hurt me. Of the time his words had the power to stop my heart.

I braced myself for a torrent of anger, but the ghost of regret softened his features. He exhaled heavily, our battle slipping into the depressing aftermath where nobody won. "I don't want to argue with you. I can tend to my own wounds, and you no longer have an interview. You should never have come here."

I nodded, accepting the agonising truth. I would never win

when it came to Gilbert Clark. I'd lost him long ago. "Okay, Gil."

His shoulders rolled as if our fight had stripped his final reserves. He didn't thank me. I didn't think he had the energy to do anything more than nod listlessly.

My heels clicked loudly as I turned and headed toward the exit.

My back prickled with basic instincts, warning me not to retreat from a hunter. Not to show him vulnerability because that might welcome an attack. But I'd already been down this road. I'd fought for his affection only to receive emotional scars as my reward.

I didn't want to leave.

It felt like defeat. It left me with a bad taste of giving in far too easily.

Surely, I should try again? I should honour the past and stay until he'd talked to me.

But when I turned by the door and looked back, he had one hand planted over his eyes and the other balled into a fist by his side. For a moment, he looked broken. But then, his hand dropped, his eyes whipped to meet mine. They narrowed with harsh impatience. "Go. Don't come back."

My heart bruised as if he'd driven his fist directly into it.

I imprinted the image of a tortured, injured body painter.

I gave him a smile laced with old and recent sadness.

"Goodbye, Gil." Kissing my dreams farewell of getting a job today, I crossed the threshold.

Gil had been the boy I'd wanted to marry.

He'd belonged to me like I'd belonged to him.

But then he'd become a monster…and no one knew why.

I closed the door on us.

Us.

There is no more us.

I know.

Chapter Three

Olin

-The Present-

MY MATHS SUCKED.

That couldn't be all I had.

Can it?

I stabbed the numbers into my phone's calculator again, tabulating my everyday cash, my savings, and the small wad of money from my purse.

I winced as I pressed enter, hoping for a much kinder number, only to receive the same painful one.

Four hundred and ninety-seven pounds to my name.

I'd been unemployed for two months and chewed through what little savings I'd had. I'd applied for everything— waitressing, café worker, Heritage Trust cleaner, secretary to some tech studio, and even considered bar-tending at a local strip club.

After the used car yard where I'd worked closed down— sitting in the back office and typing up invoices—I'd put aside my pride and lofty ideas that I was worth more and begged for a job—*any* job.

But no one had wanted me.

Turned out, a failed dancer who'd passed school but had no accolades or recommendations to her name wasn't in hot demand.

Especially after the 'accident' two years ago.

That had been the beginning of the end for me. The end of my dreams. The end of money. The end of pride in my career path.

My eyes trailed to the print-out listing the requirements for a Living Canvas requested by *Total Trickery*.

Must be slim, able to stand for long periods of time, and be impervious to the cold.

Hours are negotiable, pay is minimal, clothing absolutely forbidden.

Able to hold your bladder and tongue, refrain from opinions or suggestions, and be the perfect Living Canvas.

Other attributes required: non-ticklish, contortionist, and obedient. Must also enjoy being studied while naked in a crowd.

Call or email 'YOUR SKIN, HIS CANVAS' if interested in applying.

Gil.

God, even though long hours separated me from the doomed interview, I couldn't stop thinking about him.

I'd needed that job.

I'd gone with such high hopes of employment, and the failure of yet another botched attempt at earning money was just the sugar on top of my already caramelized disappointment.

If Gil had been able to tolerate me, we could've worked well together. I knew how intense he became when he painted. I knew what sort of dedication he'd require from his employee. Besides, I ticked off most of the wanted attributes of his advert: slim, quiet, preferred winter to summer, and was used to skimpy outfits thanks to a history in dance.

In a word, I was an ideal candidate—minus a few things I'd have to disclose if I'd gotten the gig.

It didn't mean I'd seriously contemplated it as an important career move. I did strive to make something of myself, even if I was currently in a rut.

But dreams were costly, and living didn't come cheap.

It was time to grow up.

Time to get a job that paid semi-decent, squirrel some savings, and go back to school to become an adult and not this pretender.

I sighed, slouching on my wooden chair at the scuffed-up table I'd found in a second-hand shop in downtown Birmingham.

When I'd been sixteen, a life coach came to school and asked what we wanted to be when we grew up. I'd envisioned a life drenched in dance. A world with bright lights, beautiful music, and elegant pirouettes as a prima ballerina. I'd pictured Gil beside me. Travelling the world together, both lucky enough to make a career out of our art.

I definitely didn't see me single and struggling in a city that I'd left the moment I'd finished school—doing my best to succeed, all while parents didn't care in the slightest if I ended up homeless or famous.

They'd totally forgotten they even had a child at this point.

My fingers trailed to the ad again.

What happened to you, Gil?

Who'd hurt him today?

Why did he hate me so much?

Rubbing at the ache in my chest, I stood and padded across my small apartment to grab the rest of the wine in the fridge. Taking a chipped coffee mug from the cupboard, I folded back into my chair and poured the rest of the alcohol into it.

All class.

That's me.

Ugh, what am I going to do?

Rent was due next week, and I didn't have it. My body was hungry, and I had nothing to feed it. I'd combed through all the job listings online and in every publication I could think of. I'd door knocked restaurants. I'd dropped my resume into random offices.

I'd exhausted all my options.

You could just leave.

I slugged back three big mouthfuls of tart wine.

Leave?

And go where?

The cost of living would be the same in any other city. I'd left London because I couldn't afford it after losing my dancing position. I'd already run away from my problems.

Just because Gil had upset me and made me question everything, didn't mean I had to tuck tail and run again.

Plus, I needed money to move.

I needed money for *everything*.

Total Trickery was owned by a boy who had completely broken me at high-school, but…it was also owned by someone I *knew*.

The only job opportunity where I had an in. Wasn't that what people said? *It's not what you know but who you know?*

My brain took the idea and bolted, throwing images of marching back to his warehouse and demanding he give me a chance. If I did, maybe, possibly, *hopefully* he might give me a job?

There was no harm in trying, right?

Are you nuts?

He practically threw me out this afternoon. I'd done nothing to hurt him at high-school—or at least I thought I hadn't—yet he acted as if I'd committed a mortal sin.

Why would I have a chance of employment after he'd so eloquently proved he hadn't forgotten our past? That he still held a grudge against something. That I was still...unwanted.

You need money.

I chewed the inside of my cheek. That was true. But I couldn't see him giving me any.

Even if he flat-out refuses to hire you again, he might know of someone who will.

I stopped chewing, hating that my brain made logical sense.

At this point, I was willing to hold a placard on a street corner for a job. I'd even wash cocky businessmen's cars in a bikini if it meant the stress of a dwindling bank account went away.

See? You're prepared to get mostly naked. Better with the devil you know than the devil you don't.

I shook my head, doing my best to stop thinking.

Gil had hurt me today.

He'd hurt me lots of days.

If I had any friends left, they'd all tell me to stay the hell away from him.

But...once upon a time, there had been an us.

Oh, my God, O. There is no us!

I slugged back another mouthful of wine.

I know that.

I knew I was setting myself up for more pain than I could handle by going back. But...I'd always been drawn to people who were less fortunate than me. Always wanted to share my loneliness with other lonely souls because together, we didn't *have* to be lonely.

Healing people's wounds—physical or emotional—was something that gave me purpose. It reminded me that I might not have someone to do the same for me but it didn't mean I couldn't be there for someone else.

Gil was injured.

He might be lonely.

Gulping back the last of my wine, I stood.

I'd seen him seven hours ago.

It was late.

I should stay home.

I should curl up in front of the TV and enjoy it while I could still afford it.

I shouldn't throw on my only jacket.

I definitely shouldn't summon an Uber and meet it at the curb.

It was as if I couldn't stop myself.

My heart hijacked my self-control, and somehow, I went from standing in my apartment to loitering outside warehouse number twenty-five.

You truly are a sucker for punishment.

I scowled.

Sucker or not, no one could say I hadn't fought for a job. That I hadn't been brave in the face of adversity.

The Uber that I couldn't afford drove off, leaving me with my terrible decisions in the dark. I looked left and right, prickles of uneasy forming.

The industrial area was the exact place all parents warned their kids to avoid.

My parents wouldn't care if they knew where I was. They were thousands of miles away.

God, what am I doing?

He didn't want me here.

To be honest, I didn't really want to be here.

But...I missed him.

He was hurt.

Just go. Before it's too late.

Hugging myself against the crisp evening, I looked down the long row of warehouses to the road in the distance. If I left, I would always wonder. If I left, I would never know why.

Why did he leave me?

Why is he wounded?

With my heart in my throat, I marched forward and knocked on the smaller entrance.

Low voices seeped from inside.

I didn't know if Gil lived onsite or if I was about to get in serious trouble with a stranger, but I knocked again, and this time, I tried the door handle.

If it was locked, I'd go home.

If it was unlocked...well...*fortune favours the bold.*

The handle moved, unlatching the door and cracking it open in invitation.

The voices sounded louder. Two males. One rational and doing their best to calm down the less rational one.

"You're not hearing me, Miller. I'm not interested."

"It's easy coin. I don't get why you wouldn't."

My ears easily picked out Gil's gruff growl. "Because I don't have the time to find a suitable model, and I'm done with interviews."

"Done with asking sexy girls to strip for you?" The other guy chuckled. "What a pain in the ass."

Gil didn't laugh; his tone stayed dark and impatient. "Seen one, seen 'em all."

"If you think that, then you haven't seen the right one."

A clatter of something hitting metal bounced around the cavernous warehouse. A strong whiff of turpentine followed.

"All I'm saying is, this deal with *Paradise Advertising* is mega. You do it, and you'll land a hundred more gigs. They're an advertising king and have contracts with so many world-known brands. You'd be set for life, Clark. You follow me?"

Silence reigned as I snuck closer, tiptoeing in my ballet flats. At least I wasn't in high heels, clicking and announcing my uninvited arrival.

Gil sighed loudly. "You know I hate commercial work."

"Who cares when it pays?"

Something else smashed. "Look, I'm not gonna lie and say I don't need the money because I do. I always do. I'll do any number of shitty gigs if it pays decent." His hard chuckle sounded strained. "But the deadline is in two days. I don't have a canvas, let alone inspiration. I can't exactly paint myself." His voice dropped an octave. "Besides, there's something I need to do. I—"

"Whatever it is can wait. Do the commission. Get a damn canvas. It's easy. Just pick a pretty girl from the street and make her sign whatever you need her to sign and get to work. I've seen you create bigger pieces in shorter timeframes. Two days is plenty."

A drawer slammed. "Forget it. I'll figure something else out." The thump of boots gave me precisely two seconds warning before Gil stormed from the back office and raked his hands through messy, dark hair.

He looked even more exhausted than this afternoon; his features tense and shadows contouring him with sadness.

For a moment, he didn't see me. He believed he was alone

as he rubbed his face and dug fingers into his eyes as if begging for rest.

Gil had always been handsome, but now?

God, he might've been a painting himself. A masterpiece of masculinity with his sweeping eyebrows, harsh jawline, and unreadable, unforgiving green eyes.

I ached to wrap him in a hug and offer whatever he needed.

He froze, his head shot up, his gaze whipping around the space, sensing that he wasn't as alone as he thought. "Olin…" Just like before, the first awareness of me echoed with long-ago desire. His forehead remained smooth. His posture gentle.

But then his boots clunked against the paint-splattered concrete, his mouth twisting into denial. "What the fuck are you doing here?"

Bad idea coming back.

Very, very bad.

I had no way of explaining my breaking and entering behaviour. No way to disguise the longing that I was sure glowed upon my face. I said the only thing I could. "I'm sorry. I didn't mean to barge in uninvited."

"What the hell did you mean to do then? Do a bit of cleaning? Maybe cook some goddamn pancakes while you were at it?"

I winced.

Pancakes.

He remembers.

"I didn't mean to surprise you."

He raked a vicious hand through his hair, yanking at the strands as if he could drive me from his mind. "Did you not get the message this afternoon?" He stalked toward me, heavy boots and predator swiftness. "You can't fucking be here." His hand raised as if to grab me and shove me from his warehouse.

"Gil, what the—" Whoever the other male was careened from the office, appearing behind Gil.

Dirty blond hair, two matching dimples, and vibrant blue eyes. Recognition once again whacked me around the back of the head.

Oh, no.

I'd come here hoping for a job. For answers. For Gil to be honest about *us*.

Unfortunately, I'd found not one, but two familiar boys that I'd spent my high-school years entangled with.

It took Justin Miller longer to recognise me than it'd taken Gil.

Longer to recall the kisses we'd shared. The touches we'd experimented. The breakup I'd initiated.

Gil had been the love of my life.

Justin had been my rebound.

And a friend.

Definitely a good friend.

Gil stepped aside, a grimace painting him in blacks and greys. His gaze never left mine. A piercing connection of awareness.

He knew I knew Justin.

He knew I'd dated Justin.

He knew Justin didn't recognise me and was just waiting for the moment he did.

Justin's eyes widened as he looked me up and down. He licked his lips, shaking his head as if seeing the past. "O? Is...is that really you?"

Gil crossed his arms, his face switching from carefully guarded to unreadable. Doing my best to ignore his overwhelming presence and the way my heart quickened, I nodded at Justin. "Hello."

"Oh, my God!" Justin jogged across the huge warehouse and scooped me into a hug. "I can't believe this!" His arms crushed me tight. I dangled like an unwilling hostage in his embrace.

Why couldn't Gil have reacted this way?

I would've welcomed it.

Cried for it.

Kissed him until I'd died of joy.

Instead, Justin's body enveloped my own. He was warm and unwanted. I squirmed a little to be free.

Patting his back, I pulled away with a smile that I hoped was kind but feared it was more of a wince. "Justin. Fancy seeing you here."

"Fancy seeing *me*?" His eyebrows shot into his hair. He was just as confident as he had been at school. The years had decorated him with a sturdier physique and shrewder gaze, but boyhood charm still lingered, complete with easy flirting. "Fancy seeing *you*." He glanced at Gil behind him before looking me up and down again with a grin. "What are you doing here?" His grin fell. "Wait, do you...do you still hang out with Clark?"

Gil stalked forward. Slow and meticulous with the ever-watchful, always condemning gleam in his green eyes. "No. She came here by accident. Haven't seen her in years."

"Oh." Justin wiped his mouth. "So…you're here at nine p.m. on a school night because…?"

I looked at Gil, waiting for him to reply.

He didn't.

He stood as unmovable as stone, his eyes a storm of complexity.

"I came for the interview today. When Gil recognised me, there was no interview." I shrugged, not looking at my old boyfriend but at my current heartbreak. "But I came back."

Gil's throat worked. Something flickered over his face that I wanted to chase and capture. Whatever it was, it tugged at me with truth.

He crossed his arms, flinching a little thanks to his sore elbow. "You came back against my strict instructions to stay away."

"I can't take no for an answer." I let pitiful pleading enter my voice. "I really need a job, Gil. Like really, really. I'm happy to do whatever you need, or, if you know of someone who's hiring, then I'd be very grateful for their details."

I swallowed, shivering a little as Gil continued to stare right into me. I added, "I also came to check on you. I…I wouldn't have been able to sleep if I hadn't."

He reared back. "I'm not your concern."

I swallowed yet more unresolved pain. "You were once."

His jaw ticked with two opposing forces. Part of him recalled our togetherness, remembered our kindness toward one another. The other rebelled against it, slandering such things with a dirty curse. "Fuck, you're still hung up on things that meant nothing."

I couldn't stop my jerk. "You can be mad at me for entering uninvited, but you can't be mean for no reason."

"Reason?" He scoffed. "You gave me plenty of reasons by ignoring my explicit commands not to return."

"Well, you shouldn't have left without a single goodbye—"

"Well, you shouldn't have found me!"

"I didn't find you. I answered your damn advertisement!"

"We're not bloody children anymore, Olin! What happened in the past is obsolete."

"To you maybe!" My skin flushed. I wasn't good at

confrontation. I'd never been one to pick fights. I was more of a peacemaker. A pacifier. It was why I'd never had a frank conversation with my parents that I'd missed them when I was young. That I'd needed them even though I was capable of making my own stupid packed lunches.

"Whoa, quit the shouting, okay?" Justin placed himself between us, his forehead creased with concern. Facing me, he asked softly, "Check on him? Why?"

I laughed under my breath, frustrated beyond belief. "Why? Did you not see his injuries?"

The bruise on his jaw.

The cut on his lip.

Gil stiffened as if I'd given away all his secrets. Shoving hands into his hoodie pocket, he stormed toward a trestle table chock-full of glass jars containing brushes and rags. "She's seeing things. I actually fear for her mental stability. Get rid of her, will you, Miller?"

My heart physically hiccupped as if he'd reached into my chest and squeezed.

It didn't matter that his back rippled with stress. It didn't matter that his body shook or his eyes gleamed with things he refused to say.

He was being undeniably nasty.

And I deserved better.

You should go.

My chin swooped up.

In a minute.

Brushing past Justin, I went to Gil as he grabbed a bottle of paint and shook it violently. His messy hair tangled around his forehead and ears. His harsh eyebrows tugged down over harsher eyes as if he could eradicate me from his life as he'd done in the past.

"I know I did something to make you hate me when we were kids, but...we're adults now." I ducked in front of him, wedging myself against the table.

His height and bulk pressed against me heavily, even though we didn't touch. He shuddered. His hand rose as if to tuck hair behind my ear before falling into a fist by his thigh. "Is that what you think?" His voice roughened with bitterness. "That you did something to make me leave you?"

My knees turned to water. "Wasn't it? I mean...it had to have been my fault. Why else did you—"

"Enough." His tone strangled. He slammed the bottle of paint onto the table behind me. He stalked away as if he was two seconds from either punching me or punching himself.

I spoke to his retreating back. "I didn't come to discuss the past, Gil."

Liar.

"You're looking for a model, and I'm looking for a job. I fit most of the attributes of your ad. How about we both agree to move on and focus on that?"

He spun to face me. His head cocked, causing more rogue hair to cascade over his forehead. A few dark locks tangled with black eyelashes, giving me the incredible urge to brush them away. "I don't need a model anymore."

"You do. I overheard you guys talking."

"You eavesdropped as well as broke in?"

"Doesn't change the fact that you need to start working on a project very soon."

He looked at the paint-speckled concrete as if this conversation had drained him of all reserves. "I don't want the job. Don't need it. So I don't need *you.*"

"You literally just said you needed the money."

"You. Out." His hand rose. "Immediately."

"Okay, I think tempers have gotten a little hot over here." Justin appeared between us, breaking whatever tense bubble that'd formed. "Let me get this straight. Olin offered to be a model, and you turned her down?" He shook his head. "Gilbert, man, what the fuck?"

Gil bared his teeth. "I told you. I'm not doing the commission."

"What does she mean you were injured, by the way?" Justin's tone lowered with worry. "Is that why you're favouring your left arm?"

"I paint with my right. My left doesn't matter."

Justin huffed. "You're a prick."

Gil looked at the ceiling, shielding himself with rage. "Something I finally agree with. Now, can we wrap this up? I have something I need to do."

I cleared my throat, ready to argue, but Justin fought my battle for me. He waved a hand in my direction. "Proportionally, she'd be a very good asset. A perfect canvas."

"Not gonna happen." Gil brushed past both of us, his boots heavy.

"Just take a look at her. Like I said, the money from *Paradise Advertising* is totally worthwhile." Justin trotted after his friend. "It's not gonna kill you to interview her, is it?"

"It might," Gil grumbled.

I sucked in a breath, hating how my stomach fluttered with idiotic butterflies. I shuffled forward, letting my jacket fall off my shoulders, revealing my Lycra leggings and T-shirt.

Gil slammed to a halt, his gaze locking onto me.

Sexual tension sprang from nowhere, hissing in the chilly air.

I shivered as his gaze traced my figure almost unwillingly, as if his temper was protection. Protection from everything I made him feel.

"Just interview me, Gil," I whispered, cursing the slight feather in my tone. The softness that shouldn't be there.

He stiffened as he tore his eyes from my body. His left arm hung stiff and sore—totally obvious to me that he still suffered pain but not obvious to Justin who grabbed it and shook it as if he could shake common sense into a guy who'd never been good with the word.

If Gil had had common sense when he was a teenager, he would've known that I loved him. He would've known that I couldn't just switch it off like he had. That he'd destroyed me when he took that love away.

The urge to shrug back into my jacket made my hands curl around the cuffs.

"Look at her." Justin pointed at me. "Perfect proportion between shoulders and hips. Not too busty. Long legs. I betcha she's flexible. And the best part…" He narrowed his eyes at Gil. "She's available, right now. She's here, ready to work. So…get painting."

"You're not my boss, Miller." Gil pushed him out of the way, prowling past me with a glower. His speed made air lick around my exposed arms, ordering me to hoist up my jacket and protect myself from the frosty chill that surrounded Gil wherever he went.

I zipped my jacket with a heavy sigh.

Justin groaned under his breath. "Don't worry, O. Let me talk to him tonight and—"

"I won't change my mind." Gil headed toward the shadows at the opposite end of the warehouse. "She can't be here."

"I'll make him hire you." Justin smiled. "Either that or I'll help you find a job. Do you, eh, need cash now? You strapped?"

My cheeks flared with heat. "I'm good." I didn't want some boy from school thinking I was days away from homelessness, even if that was true. "I have savings."

"Okay, great." He grinned. "In that case, want to grab a late dinner? My shout? Be good to catch up."

My stomach grumbled at the offer, but I shook my head politely. "Thanks, Justin, but I really should be getting home."

I need to nurse my wounds in private.

"I could always drop you off after—"

A shrill cell phone ring shattered the tension of the warehouse. Gil flinched as his hand shot into his jeans pocket and pulled out the offending device. He froze as another ear-piercing ring sounded. Instead of answering like a normal person, he pressed accept, shot us a guarded look, then jogged to the office and slammed the door.

Justin rolled his eyes. "That guy has privacy issues."

"He do that a lot when the phone rings?"

"Yep. Never takes a call where he can be overheard."

I supposed that wasn't all that strange. I didn't like talking on the phone in public either.

With Gil gone, my desire to leave escalated. "Well, I guess I'll get going, seeing as I got a second refusal." I smiled half-heartedly. "Least I tried."

Justin scowled. "I don't know what his problem is. The commission is definitely worth his while, and you'd be perfect for it."

"Ah, well." Moving toward the exit, I added, "Nice to see you again."

"Yeah, so random, huh?" He walked with me until we got to the roller door and its small pedestrian access to the side. "I can't believe it's been so long since we were all at school together."

"Yeah, me too." Bizarre how life worked and intertwined. I placed my hand on the door handle. However, a question niggled at the back of my mind. "I didn't know you guys were such good friends to work together. I thought you were practically enemies, actually."

Because of me.

Justin lounged against the roller, crossing his arms with a chuckle. "Yeah, he was pissed that we dated. But that's in the past. And we don't technically work together. I check in on him now and again. We bumped into each other a year ago and kinda stayed in touch."

"That's nice."

"Strange really, seeing as you're right. We didn't talk much at school. He's talented, though. And that's what I respect. Even if he is a prick most of the time."

My heart squeezed, remembering a younger Gil.

He'd never been a prick to me.

Until he was.

"You've seen his YouTube channel?" Justin asked, his eyes lingering on me.

I exhaled in a rush. "Yes. I researched him after I saw the ad. I didn't know it was him though, thanks to the hood."

"Bet you wouldn't have come for the interview if you'd known." His gaze travelled to the office where Gil had disappeared into.

"Oh, I don't know. I'm a sucker for pain."

And I've been searching for him ever since he vanished.

Justin laughed gently. "You certainly riled him up tonight."

"Seems just my presence has that power these days." Awkwardness fell, signalling an end to our weird conversation. "Anyway…I better be—"

"Going. Sure. Sorry." He opened the exit for me. "Guess I'll see ya 'round, O."

"I guess." I smiled again and stepped into the chilly darkness.

"Wait!" The loud bark wrenched my head around as Gil jogged from his office. His phone remained clutched in his fist, but the call had ended.

"What's up?" Justin asked.

Gil ignored him, not stopping until he was within touching distance to me. Stress lines decorated his face. A heaviness that wasn't there before lurked in the depths of his eyes, and a barely restrained violence etched his jaw.

He looked defeated.

He looked dangerous.

Instinct ordered me to back away, but I held my ground.

He breathed hard, the bruise on his jaw and cut lip demanding care as he held up his hand, a silent request for me to stay. "Be here. Tomorrow. Nine a.m. sharp."

I blinked. "What?"

"You heard me. I've changed my mind. I'll do the

commission, but I'm running out of time. Be here first thing. I don't know when we'll be done. Depends if I like my concept or not and how long it takes to paint you."

"So…you're giving me the job?"

"You've got work for the next couple of days." He gritted his teeth as if he already struggled with the idea. "We'll discuss any repeats after."

"Not exactly reliable employment."

"Take it or leave it." He crossed his arms gingerly, pain flashed across his features.

My stomach rumbled embarrassingly, reminding me that no money equalled no food, and my heartache was worthless.

For a second, I deliberated disclosing the parts of me that might make me a less than ideal canvas. But this job wasn't given freely; I would keep my secrets until tomorrow.

Holding out my hand for him to shake, I said softly, "I'll take it."

For the longest second, Gil just stared at my hand. He didn't uncross his arms, making nerves thread their way down my spine. He looked trapped between fear and want.

Justin cleared his throat; Gil rushed to capture my offered palm.

The moment his touch met mine, it was as if seven years had vanished and we were hidden behind the school gym, tucked together in the dusk, our bodies aching, our limbs shaking, our hearts gasping to be brave.

I bit my lip as Gil stiffened, squeezing my fingers until they throbbed. He clutched me as if he wanted to brand me. As if he tasted the past and buckled beneath the memories.

Memories of what we'd once shared.

The openness.

The hope.

The beginning of something so much bigger than us.

Us.

There had once been an *incredible* us.

A blistering connection between a privileged girl and a poor boy who weren't from the same existence.

That same power—the force of forever and belonging—burned with a ferocity that turned my insides to ash and heart to flame.

Full-blown star-crossed temptation.

His fingers switched from squeezing to quaking.

I froze as desire bled from my palm and wrapped tendrils around his wrist, binding him to me, wishing I could keep him this time.

His skin was cold.

Icy as a ghost.

Yet he hadn't always been that way.

There'd been a time when his skin had been as warm as the sunshine in the park where we'd sneak after school. Where his touch sent wings of joy through me instead of clouds of dread.

The sensation of unfinished business and complicated truths made pain manifest.

I couldn't bear it.

I tore my hand from his, shoving it deep into my jacket pocket. He must've felt the same agonising bolt as he ripped his fingers away, wiped them on his jeans, and raked them through his unruly hair.

Justin's eyes bored into me, then into Gil; his forehead furrowed as if he could taste whatever we'd conjured.

Awkwardness settled.

A strange kind of embarrassment and fear.

"Tomorrow." Gil nodded curtly, gave Justin a sour look, then turned and stalked back into the shadows.

The shadows that had claimed him for their own.

Chapter Four

Olin

-The Present-

"YOU'RE LATE."

I closed the door to Gil's warehouse, searching for where his voice had come from. Around the trestle tables and paint splatters, over the props and cupboards.

The moment I found him, my sleepless night and tangled heart punched me in the chest. My hands turned cold, my breath became shallow, my entire body switched to high alert.

He stood beside a table full of equipment and paint, all prepared for a long day creating art. His body was stiff and unyielding, like a king accepting homage or a prisoner braced for punishment.

"I'm not late. It's precisely nine a.m."

He kept his eyes unreadable as I moved toward him, my messenger bag with my packed cucumber sandwich and apple juice swinging against my black leggings.

I'd worn dance-clothes again. Lightweight and easy to remove with a sports bra underneath—not that I'd be allowed to keep the bra.

I'd seen how body painters worked. Skin was the canvas, not fabric.

He backed away as I went to him, his eyes skating over me. "That's why you're late. I wanted to start work at nine."

I didn't let his coldness hurt me. The rush of what'd happened between us last night gave me courage. I'd learned how to cope after he'd abandoned me when we were younger.

It'd been a lesson I didn't want to learn—the hardest lesson—but I'd mastered it regardless. The strength it took to survive his indifferent, uncaring face was built brick by brick.

That skill turned steely in its determination not to let him push me away a second time.

I arched my chin. "Well, you should've asked me to arrive earlier so we had time to prep."

He bristled as I shrugged off my bag and placed it on his table of tricks before slipping off my jacket. The warehouse wasn't exactly chilly, but it wasn't warm either. The advert had been honest about not being affected by the cold being a requirement.

He swallowed hard, jerking his gaze from my chest. "I suggest you don't answer back to your boss, especially seeing as you've been employed for less than two minutes."

"Yes, about that." I ran my fingers over the tops of rainbow paint bottles, pleased that he seemed affected by me. "Do you need me to sign a contract?"

"No." He turned to an air gun, fiddling with dials and checking narrow hoses. His jeans looked like he'd already been painting with splotches and splashes of colour. His grey T-shirt had the same graffiti appearance—obviously his uniform when working.

"What about payment?" I asked as bravely as I dared.

"You'll get cash at the end."

"But what about taxes?"

"What about them?"

"Um, death and taxes? The two terrors you can always rely on."

"You're saying you're flush with coin and happy to give some away?"

I shook my head. "I'm saying, I have no choice."

Just like I have no choice how I feel about you.

He gave me a weighty look. A look that spoke of history and hardships but remained professional and distant. "Cash in hand. That's the deal."

"Ah, so it's *you* who doesn't want to pay taxes." I smiled, doing my best to earn a reaction.

He scowled. "I pay my way." A flicker of regret before he clipped callously, "But you're temporary, and I can't be assed with the paperwork."

Ouch.

It seemed he was better at this game than me.

My energy deflated, accepting today wasn't going to be easy.

It's probably going to be the hardest thing I've ever done.

I nodded. "Cash works."

"Course cash works." He dropped his voice like he used to while discussing his shitty living situation when he was a kid. "Least cash will pay your rent."

My heart hiccupped.

He was a master at making me want to hate him, but beneath that stony façade was a gentle, giving soul.

I know it.

I know he can't have changed so much.

I didn't know if my prior history with Gil was a blessing or a curse. If we'd been complete strangers, I would've chalked his attitude up to being a surly boss with temper issues. But because he'd shared his secrets with me, because he'd trusted me over anyone, because he'd let me see him vulnerable and sweet, I knew homelessness was a very real threat to the younger Gil and most likely tainted the older one's outlook as well.

He might be a famous body painter, but apart from the tools of his trade, he had no luxury within his warehouse. No expensive art or designer furniture. The space was barren and untended.

Yet another by-product of living in a condemned building with a father into illegal practices? Or a personal choice by staying sterile and alone?

My shoulders rounded, weighed down by questions I couldn't ask.

He sighed heavily.

I caught his eye and suffered a racing heart.

His lips twisted in the smallest of smiles. A smile I barely caught before it was smothered beneath grim frostbite.

Could he read me as well as he could read me in our youth? Could he see my struggle not to demand answers and the very real threat of launching myself into his arms and kissing him?

If he could read me, he didn't show it.

And I definitely couldn't read him anymore.

He sighed again as if he second-guessed everything about us.

Us.

Could there still be…us?

"Come. I'll show you where the bathroom is. I need to

work."

I crossed my arms over my pink top and followed him. His long legs chewed up the distance far quicker than my shorter ones.

His back rippled beneath the paint-splattered grey T-shirt. His body tense and untouchable. Even though I would treat this arrangement with professionalism and the appropriate employee submission to her boss, I couldn't stop my insides waking up from its self-imposed hibernation.

I'd had other boyfriends since Justin. I'd been with one guy for a year before my accident. I'd had a couple of flings, doing my best to patch up a ruined heart, but Gilbert Clark had always been the one who got away.

The boy I'd never forgotten.

God, please stop.

Stop making me hurt.

Slowing to a halt, Gil waved at a small room next to his office. "In there. Don't be long." He wiped his mouth, dropping his gaze to the floor. "Strip, put on a bathrobe, and return."

Not waiting around, he stalked back to his workstation before I could agree.

I watched him.

I missed him.

Get a grip.

Tearing my eyes away, I entered the bathroom and found a much larger space than I'd anticipated. The shower held streaks of paint from others washing off Gil's artwork. The double vanity held an array of cotton swabs and towelettes to do the same. To erase hours' worth of detail and perfectionism.

After watching his YouTube videos, it seemed wrong that this was the place where his creations went to die. A miserable death for so many outstanding pieces.

One of my favourites he'd done—black-hooded and face-obscured—had been on two women pressed together into one, their arms folded in such a way that their human forms became a hummingbird.

Thanks to Gil's technique with metallic and shadow, their skin transformed into iridescent feathers, shimmering with precision.

How did he stand it?

How did he spend so long making something come to life only to take a few photos then flush it down the drain?

My reflection mocked me as I moved toward the vanity and grabbed my shoulder-length dark blonde hair. Twisting it into a rope, I made a bun at the base of my neck and secured it with an elastic from around my wrist.

Once my hair was tamed, I searched the walls for a bathrobe.

No hooks. No robes.

Where is it?

My eyes danced around the white-tiled space until they came to rest on a pile of plastic-wrapped garments in the corner. I'd expected a bathrobe—as in singular. Something hanging on the bathroom door.

I should've guessed Gil had multiple canvases to paint. Therefore, he'd need multiple bathrobes. Judging by the pile of them, he ordered in bulk.

Sighing heavily, hurting all over again, I grabbed the top package, ripped open the plastic, and shook out a mothball smelling garment.

I stripped from my leggings and top, leaving my black G-string and sports bra on.

Slipping into the robe, I gave my reflection a shrug, then headed back out to the warehouse where scents of fresh paint, thinner, and citrus danced in the air. The smell grew stronger as I moved toward Gil.

He had his back to me as he mixed something, his head tilted to study what his hands were doing. His left arm looked no different than his right today, even though a bruise still marked his jaw.

Stopping by his side, I asked gently, "Who hurt you yesterday?"

He stiffened. "No one."

"It was someone."

Placing the paint bottles onto the mixing table, he turned to face me. For the first time, he studied me. *Truly* studied me.

And I wanted to run back to the bathroom and slip into three more robes for protection. His harsh eyes stripped me as if he had full access to my depressing, unaspiring life. As if he could see my mistakes, my hiccups, my failures.

Deep in his gaze lurked remnants of the boy I'd loved. A silent apology. A wish for more. That damn connection that refused to be ignored.

But he cleared his throat and shoved such softness away.

Cupping his jaw, he cocked his head and moved around me with meticulous slowness.

Somehow, I knew he'd abandoned the realm of humanity and became as brutal and as beautiful as a weapon. A weapon that slashed with paint, murdered with colour, and no longer saw me as a person.

I was just a blank canvas.

A colourless piece of paper, ready for his art. "Take off the robe."

I shivered.

My muscles seized. My belly flopped. I struggled with prim propriety and the curse of starving lust.

His presence seemed to magnify. His citrusy scent drugged me.

He groaned under his breath when I didn't obey, sounding as confused and as hungry as I felt. Clearing his throat, he grumbled in a strictly controlled voice. "Off, Olin."

Commands a lover would make.

Instructions delivered with hail.

I shivered again from the use of my name.

It drenched me in memories of adolescent moments. Of simpler times. Of excruciating times. Where a crush had the power to erase the world and forsake all others. Where affection had the magic to make you believe in fairy-tales.

He cursed something I didn't catch. Marching away, he dragged both hands through his hair while glowering at the ceiling. For a moment, it looked as if he'd rather throw himself off a cliff than return to me, but then his hands fell from his hair, his back straightened, he retraced his steps to stop beside me.

His voice was brittle with tightly reined temper. "Look, if you've gone shy, then leave. It's best you go. I don't know what I was thinking, asking you to come back." His green gaze shot to the door, his shoulders tensing. "I...this was a mistake. You need to—"

"No." Taking a deep breath, I undid the belt and wriggled out of the comfy warmth. "I want to stay." Letting the robe hang off my wrists, it cascaded down the back of my thighs.

My stomach quivered as Gil's eyes stayed resolutely on mine.

He didn't look.

Didn't devour.

We stood at an impasse.

Me desperate for him to want me.

Him desperate to show no signs of caring.

His jaw clenched as he arched an eyebrow, settling his features into cool indifference.

I wasn't half-naked before him for the very first time. I was merely a piece of parchment stretched on a wooden frame.

"You really should have left." His voice became tumbling rocks, heavy and threatening.

"I need the money."

"Some things are worth more than money." His veneer cracked a little. His jaw twitched. Bracing himself, he dropped his gaze from my eyes to my chin, to my collarbone, breasts, belly, thighs, and toes.

He noticed everything.

The slight scar on my kneecap. The belly button ring I'd recklessly done on my sixteenth birthday. The way my hipbones were a little too stark for my otherwise svelte frame.

He stayed in front of me.

Which I was glad.

My back was where my secrets lay.

His body locked down as if he enlisted every muscle not to reach for me. The freezing warehouse suddenly became a furnace. Deceit couldn't exist in the blistering awareness that things weren't over between us.

They could never be. Not when our souls still belonged to the other.

"Gil…" My heart drummed against my ribcage. "I—"

He bit his lip, shaking his head furiously. Backing away, he rubbed his mouth as if giving himself time to get runaway desire under control. Slowly, difficultly, he shoved away all hints of need, shutting himself down.

With his body rigid, he nudged his chin at my sports bra with its highlighter peach crisscross straps. "I can't paint you with that on." He dropped his stare to my black G-string. "Nor that." Swallowing back the gravel that'd appeared in his throat, he turned and yanked open a drawer on his mixing table. Another packet appeared, this one smaller than the bathrobe but just as new and untouched. "Put this on and take the bra off."

"Here?"

He crossed his arms, a tortured lash of need vanishing beneath bleak determination. "Do you have a better place in mind?"

When I didn't answer, he added, "You read my advert. You know what this job entails."

"I know."

Tension etched its way across his face. "I made a mistake asking you to come back. Maybe you made a mistake applying for—"

"Why did you change your mind? You didn't want to do the commission before."

He froze, every hint of him vanished behind a careful wall. "I don't need permission to switch."

"Was it because of the phone call?"

"Don't."

"Don't what?"

"Search for things that don't exist."

"You say that as if you're hiding things you don't want to be found."

"You're right." His face darkened as a flash of agony highlighted his gaze. "If it was up to me, you wouldn't be here. You would be as far away from this place as possible."

"Why?"

"Because it's—" His lips snapped shut.

He made no effort to enlighten me.

"You're acting as if you've been forced into this." I cursed the goosebumps dancing over my skin.

He twitched as if I'd struck him. His temper slipped. "Stop it, Olin."

"Are you in trouble?"

"Enough," he groaned.

"But—"

"But nothing." He vibrated with ruthless energy, grasping onto it after splintering before me. "Make your choice. Stay and do what you're told. Or leave and never come back."

"If I stay will you talk to me?"

"No."

"If I go can I see you again?"

He shook his head.

I fell quiet, shooing away the tension that'd sprung from nowhere, hoping he'd be able to do the same. "I want to stay. If you refuse to talk about what we had in the past then I'm happy to begin again."

His eyes liquefied with pain. For a moment, he struggled to reply. "What we had…it meant nothing." He flinched as if his

---

own words cut him like fatal swords.

"Why did you leave, Gil?" My voice hugged a whisper, my pain bleeding out without permission.

He looked away, his fists clenching. "I had a reason."

"Tell me."

He shook his head again, his temper returning to shield him. "No past. No history. You're nothing more than a canvas and I'm nothing more than a painter. That's it. That's all there can ever be." The way his voice mixed with merciless misery sent curiosity slashing through me. He harboured something that chewed at him. It lived behind his eyes. It thickened his every breath. It begged me to uncover it.

But...I'd already pushed too far.

I teetered on the edge of falling to my knees and begging for answers or slapping his flawless, heartless face.

I needed time to regroup. To come up with a better plan.

Striding wordlessly toward the stage, I climbed onto the small platform. Turning my back on him, I tugged the robe up and over my shoulders for privacy and, with trembling hands, removed my black G-string. Quickly, I ripped open the packet and traded my underwear for the skin coloured one he'd given me.

The plastic bag and my old G disappeared into the pocket of the robe.

I paused.

I sucked in a breath.

I searched for bravery.

This was it.

No going back.

Gritting my teeth, begging my heart to stop being such a traitorous fool, I spun around, shrugged out of the bathrobe, and tossed it to the side. Not giving myself time to second-guess, I ripped off my sports bra and let it fall.

My hands balled as my nipples pebbled from exposure and nerves. I dared look at Gil, bracing for a sneer or some condescending remark, expecting to be broken into pieces by his frost.

However, his eyes blazed as brilliant and as bright as wildfire. He stood frozen in place. Fists curled, body taut, lips pressed together as if he didn't trust himself.

Just like before, lust sprang violently between us.

I was no longer cold.

He was no longer pretending.

In that aching, wanting moment, the truth was vibrant as it was vicious.

With a quiet grunt and monumental effort, he tore his gaze away. He stumbled toward his workstation, rubbing his face as if he didn't have the strength for more torture.

With jerky movements, he dragged the airbrush on its rolling frame toward me, keeping his attention locked on his tools, fiddling with dials and hoses.

I stood bare and vulnerable, waiting, *begging* him to look at me and let go of whatever held him trapped, but he never did.

He acted as if I had the power to kill him with a single touch, doing his best to keep shields high and decorum fiercely in place.

Without a word, he placed a tray of pre-mixed colours beside the podium. Taking his time, he arranged the supplies until they were neatly rowed by my feet. When he had nothing else to occupy himself with, he sucked in a tattered breath and...looked up.

I clenched my tummy, ready for the ricochet of heat and hurt, but his jaw worked and his eyes remained cold, clinical, totally unaffected that I stood before him in just flesh-coloured knickers and bare breasts.

I breathed harder, my chest rising and falling in invitation.

But he didn't crack. He'd buried himself deep within discipline. His gaze slipped over my hardened nipples, his tone snowy and detached. "Some painters use pasties." He followed the curve of my breast. "I don't as I dislike the way it wrinkles the skin and brings more attention to the area than if they were left bare. Do you have a problem with that?"

He kept his stare resolutely on my flesh, as if my body didn't hurt him as much as my eyes.

I'd never felt so naked or so vulnerable.

Never been so confused.

I fought the urge to cover myself. "That's fine."

"Good." Swallowing hard, he commanded, "Now...turn around. I need to know what I'm working with."

Dressed in new goosebumps, I did as he asked.

Secrets or no secrets.

Job or no job.

I couldn't hide my flaws anymore.

For a moment, there was nothing. Then, an explosive curse.

"Holy shit." His voice slipped from detached to drenched in shock. "O…"

My knees buckled. How could one little letter echo with lifetimes of love?

Tears sprang to my eyes. I gasped as he climbed the podium behind me, and a fingertip traced the torn and tattered flesh of my back. "Wh-what happened?" A delicate question. A dangerous question. His voice was bare of all shields and tempers, annihilated into caring. His touch continued to trace, following the ink on top of scars. "What is this?"

I flinched as his breath skated over the lines and designs down my left side.

Staring at the floor, I murmured, "It's a tattoo."

"Why? Why did you not tell me?"

My heart clawed to go to him, recognising the catch in his voice as pain for not knowing. For tossing me to the side without a backward look. For casting me out where accidents had found me instead.

I wanted to tell him everything. I trembled with the pressure. The need to spill it all. The elation of being chosen to work for the London Dance Company. The joy of dancing every day and night. The horror of the moment when it was all taken away. The loneliness of not having anyone to lean on.

But…I had my pride. I had my stupid ego. I didn't want to give him all of me. Not now, not yet. Some part of him missed me, maybe even still wanted me, but if he wasn't brave enough to put down the barriers he'd erected, then I wasn't either.

"I know I should've told you yesterday. I wasn't honest in my interview."

He tore his hand away, laughing brokenly. "That's how you want to play this?"

Yes.

No.

I nodded.

Inhaling hard, he clipped, "In that case, as my canvas, I expected you to be in pristine condition." His voice scratched with sandpaper. "How can I paint you when you're already scribbled on?"

My chin came up. I'd chosen this path. I would defend it. "It's not a scribble."

"What is it?"

"Something very meaningful." I wanted to twist and look at

what he saw. Whenever someone saw my tattoo for the first time, I craved to see it from their point of view. To study it close and appreciate the talent of the artist I'd chosen.

My tattoo wasn't a vanity thing.

It wasn't an impulsive dare.

It was needed—to heal my broken pieces. To cover up the mess left behind.

I'd hated those scars. Hated me. Hated life itself.

Without 'scribbling' on myself, I doubted I'd be whole enough to go to battle with Gilbert Clark. I would've chosen to check out of trying and sink into my mind where I could still dance, still be happy.

His body cast shockwaves of fury and frustration behind me. He touched me again, gingerly, tenderly, tracing the filigree lines and lacework that convened into a large geometric pattern before bleeding into a realism piece of an owl. Imbedded in the owl's feathers were as many creatures as I could name all starting with O.

For me.

Olin.

I shivered as he touched every blemish I knew well.

Would he understand? Would he see just how pathetic I was?

Back at school, I'd surrounded myself with friends. I'd looked after my fellow students because my parents didn't look after me. I earned their gratefulness and friendships but they never patched up the holes inside me.

Until Gil had chosen me for his own.

Until he'd traded his secrets for mine and, in return, stole every piece of my heart.

It'd been a month into our tentative relationship.

A month of hurried smiles and hesitant hellos before he used the first nickname.

He'd always said my name was odd. That he didn't know anyone else called Olin.

I'd said that was a good thing. It meant he would always remember me.

He'd said the letter O was just as unique as my name. Therefore, any animal beginning with O was just as special.

A few days later, he'd passed me my backpack after class. Whispered under his breath so the other kids couldn't hear—a melodic rasp of secrecy. "Otter, don't forget your bag."

The next week, he'd called me owl by the gym, then octopus in the cafeteria.

I'd fallen in love with him after that.

Tumbled and tripped, rolled and cartwheeled, loving him more than I'd loved anybody.

Ocelot, orangutan, ostrich...

They were all there, peeking in the feathers, turning ugly scars into special uniqueness.

Gil sucked in a pained breath, a strangled grunt escaping his lips.

I twisted to look at him, studying the sudden grief painting his eyes and the regret sketching his mouth.

It was enough to make my knees turn week and my arms beg to hold him.

"You used us to cover your scars." His voice vibrated with something I couldn't decipher. His eyes snapped shut, a visible cloak of cruelty smothering his features. When he opened his eyes again, he was back to being a blizzard king. "How am I supposed to hide ink and scars, Olin?"

I swallowed hard.

When the accident happened, I'd forgotten who I was.

I'd been alone in the hospital and alone in rehab and alone in the months after with my dreams shattered by my feet.

I'd searched for something to make me feel worthy again— to stop the aching wasteland my chest had become.

I'd turned to Google, searching chat rooms for advice on moving on from severe accidents and tips on how to turn bad into survivable. I'd learned about the miracle of tattoos. From women with breast cancer to men with missing limbs—they all turned to the undeniable superpower of turning grotesque memories into fresh beginnings, and I'd designed the piece myself.

The day I'd scrimped up enough cash to sit the three full days in the tattooist chair was the happiest I'd been since Gil made me his. I'd found myself—my *real* self—as I embraced the discomfort of needles and pigment, covering the nasty red scars with something pretty.

I loved that piece more than anything.

I refused to let Gil ruin it. "I don't know, but you can cover it somehow."

"It marks half your back."

"It was needed."

He stopped touching me, stepping from the podium as if everything between us shot him with a thousand arrows. "What happened?"

It was a question free from ice. A question that demanded to know.

I didn't give him what he wanted.

He stopped below me, his gaze tearing into mine as if he could yank out my memories, desperate to uncover the ones where he hadn't been there.

His eyes always had the power to bend my will to his.

I'd been weak and totally his to command whenever I'd caught him staring at me as if his love couldn't be contained.

He wasn't allowed to look at me like that anymore.

I wasn't his.

He wasn't mine.

This is no us.

Yet I was trapped in him. Caged by his vexation and prisoner to so many childhood connections.

He swallowed hard as heat and history prickled between us, hissing with past need and a love that hadn't had the chance to die. It had been torn in two. Ripped down the middle the moment he'd left, two ends unable to heal because the knots tying us together refused to let go.

"Olin, I—" He winced, his voice sorrowful velvet. "I'm sorry you went through something so painful."

The genuine dismay on his face reminded me so much of the boy who'd loved me. The boy who'd protected me, walked me home, supported my dancing, and watched me as if I held his moon and stars.

That boy deserved an answer that wasn't curt or cold.

That boy broke my heart all over again.

His hand shook as he swiped hair from his eyes. "You don't have to answer. It's—"

"It's fine." I shrugged with a half-smile. "There's nothing really to tell. Oldest cliché in the book. Just a silly dancer with big dreams."

"You were never silly."

"I had my moments."

He winced. "That doesn't explain how your back is scarred to shit."

"It does if I was dancing at all hours and didn't have a car to get to and from the theatre."

"What happened?" He cocked his head. "Do you…can you still dance?"

Ouch.

I wasn't successful in hiding my flinch, skirting away from the painful memories. Holding my head high and embracing my flaws, I no longer worried my scars were on display. I painted myself in the fake confidence that came from dancing in front of hundreds of people.

The stage, bright lights, and pantomime granted no room for error. That world was a dangerous place for someone with no confidence. This chilly warehouse was no different.

I was on a stage.

Gil was my spotlight.

I merely had to dance this dance until the curtain fell.

"I was overtired, overworked, underpaid, but in love with dance. You know how I was."

He made a sound under his breath. "Addicted. You were addicted to any form of movement."

My heart did a cabriole, ridiculously happy that he remembered.

He rolled his eyes, his voice doing its best to be dark and disinterested but his green eyes gleamed with history. "You never just walked, you—"

"Floated like a leaf in the breeze." I smiled, a true smile tugging after guarding myself from him. "You told me that the day I cooked you—"

"Pancakes in your parents' kitchen."

His gaze snagged mine.

I sucked in a breath.

He swallowed a curse.

Something that shouldn't have happened cut through our protection, cracking open the hard shells of two adults pretending to loathe one another.

"Go on." He crossed his arms, moving away from me as if to give himself space from the overwhelming need to touch. To remember. To say a proper hello after so, so long apart. "Tell me the rest."

I shrugged again, fighting the urge to hug my breasts, my confidence gone again. "I biked to the theatre and home all the time. That night, though, tiredness made me sluggish. A drunk driver took a corner too fast, and I didn't get out of the way in time. She hit me. I ended up on the windshield of her Mazda

Demio as she drove us through the window of a French restaurant." I sighed as memories of hospitals and operations and being told my aspirations of dancing for a living were over.

I was lucky if I'd ever walk normally again, let alone twist or fly.

I'd proven the doctors wrong after two years of physiotherapy and determination. I could walk and do yoga and exercise better than the average person.

But dancing....

No matter how hard I tried, my back just couldn't cope.

I'd cut myself off from my dance troupe because I didn't belong in their world anymore.

I'd lied to myself that I could find something better, only to find destitution instead.

I'd left London where my contract had kept me paid and fed.

I'd ended up back in Birmingham with my tail between my legs.

Gil raked a hand through his hair. "When?"

"Two and a bit years ago."

"I'm sorry."

I blinked, totally dumbfounded to hear such considerate words. "Thanks."

He paced away, walking around the stage to stare at my back again.

I let him, staying still all while his gaze skated up and down my spine. Was he reliving the nicknames he'd kissed into my hair? Was he suffering the history between us?

His voice did its best to scatter the unwanted tenderness and return to stiff formality. "Normally, I'd send you packing. I don't deal with piercings, scars, or tattoos, and you have all three."

I looked over my shoulder. "I'd say I was sorry, but I'm not. They're a part of me."

He scowled. "Luckily, this commission is frontal only. I don't need you to contort or reveal parts of you less...desirable."

I winced at that.

Not desirable?

No woman liked to be told that—regardless of context. Especially from Gil when once he'd been as hungry for me as I'd been for him.

Our eyes caught again.

So many things flew. So many feelings and hurts and

questions.

My mouth went dry. My knees quaked.

Gil's eyes tightened. His hands fisted.

We both didn't have a chance against the lashing, demanding connection.

He rubbed his mouth with a rough hand, cleared his throat as if eradicating a decade of pain, then returned to his paint table with jerky steps. "We do this one commission, but you'll have to find another job afterward. Long term won't work out."

As much as I didn't want to hear such things, I couldn't blame him.

I'd fit so much of his ad attributes…apart from some pretty major ones.

I'd also interrupted his present, reminding him all over again of unfinished business with a girl who never got over him.

I tried to be pragmatic.

A few days of employment were better than none.

Seeing him for an afternoon was better than forever wondering where he was.

Smiling gently, I ordered my body to relax. I was about to spend untold hours in Gil's very close presence; it was time to get used to it. "That's fine, Gil. I'm just grateful for the work you can give me."

My soft tone wrenched his eyes up. Our gazes tangled all over again, hot and lashing, completely different to the ice surrounding him.

My heart stopped beating, hanging onto the fine thread of love-string he'd severed seven years ago. His eyes darkened with torment, his head shaking infinitesimally as if begging me not to be here. Desperate to keep distance between us. Pleading for space…from me.

It hurt.

Hurt that echoed with new and old, and in that tiny moment, we weren't adults with barriers and warnings, we were kids again. Kids who finally found salvation in the other and were courageous enough to pay for that privilege with their hearts.

I couldn't stop it.

He couldn't stop it.

Whatever drew us together was still as vicious as before.

Gil's neck worked as he swallowed. He struggled to tear his gaze away. His shoulders bunched, and I knew I wasn't the only one struggling.

And that knowledge awoke a tiny sliver of hope.

Hope that frantically plaited filaments of broken string, drawing the two ends of our severed love closer together.

Gil groaned beneath his breath, turning away from me.

I gasped as a thousand dormant butterflies stretched their paper wings and flew.

Chapter Five

Gil

-The Past-

"MISS MOSS, WHERE do you think you're going?"

I glanced up from rubbing out an incorrect answer on my math work. Olin flinched, tucking dark blonde hair behind her ear, the rest of the shoulder-length strands messy from running in the field at lunch.

I'd watched her stand-up to Josie Prichard—a bully of epic proportions today.

Josie had cornered a younger student, commanded her to do her chemistry homework, then robbed the poor girl of her lunch money. I'd stayed in the shadows while Olin had dashed across the grass, placed herself bravely in the middle of the bully and victim, and demanded the money back.

No one else had intervened.

No one else had been kind enough to stand up for the weak.

It didn't matter that Olin hadn't won.

Josie just snickered, punched Olin in the shoulder, then pranced away with a smirk. Olin had rubbed the injury while turning to the young girl, then, as if she was some sort of school-ground angel, plucked the girl's hand and dragged her to her circle of friends where she shared her lunch with her.

She had to stop being so sweet.

Had to stop being so courageous because each time she did something selfless, my walls cracked a little.

I didn't trust anyone. Literally *anyone.*

But Olin...she shone with sincerity. She made me wonder what it would be like to trust her. To have the luxury of her friendship, knowing she'd have my back because that was who she was. She wasn't fake. She didn't protect others for recognition or reward.

She helped others because she was *good*.

And being good these days was one of the rarest things in the world.

For God sake's, even the wildlife wasn't safe from her sweetness.

The sparrows got her sandwich crumbs; the squirrels earned nuts bought to school especially for them. Even the scratched, scarred, and ill-tempered tom cat got loved on as she walked home at the end of the day.

Home time was the only moment when her happiness faded. Her dancing gracefulness fell flat. Her positive personality clouding over.

Yet another reason why she intrigued me.

She gave everything she had to those around her, but when it came time to return to loved ones, she dragged her heels and acted as if home wasn't an enjoyable place to be.

I understood that far too well.

"I asked you a question, Miss Moss. Where do you think you're going?"

Olin rolled into herself, intimidated by Ms Tallup's stare.

Couldn't blame her. Ms Tallup had a nasty streak that was deadly intimidating.

"Bathroom?" Her voice pitched with guilt.

The two girls she hung out with snickered beside her. Olin didn't look at them.

She was the opposite of me.

I was the boy everyone left alone.

She was the girl everyone wanted to be with. Girls flocked to her side. Boys beamed whenever she walked by. But I had a suspicion she was lonely beneath the popularity.

I didn't know how I knew but her drive to protect others must come from somewhere, and it usually came from a desire to have someone do the same for them.

I got it.

I wanted someone to look after me, too. I was sick of fighting through life and dealing with punches, kicks, and sleepless nights. But I was far too wary to go out of my way to help like she did. Far too closed off to give the meagre energy I had to others.

Ms Tallup narrowed her cold, grey eyes. "You went to the bathroom ten minutes ago."

"Tiny bladder." Olin dropped her gaze, a blush working over pretty cheekbones.

"I don't believe you." Ms Tallup stomped to her desk and tossed down a notepad. "But I have to let you go, school policy and all." Her head snapped up. "But you're taking another student."

"Oh." Olin wrinkled her nose. "But, I—"

"No buts." Ms Tallup surveyed the congregation of students. "Mr. Clark. You'll accompany Miss Moss and make sure she doesn't get lost on her journey."

"Me?" I coughed.

What the hell?

I was fine nursing my crush from afar.

Happy to watch her good deeds and selfless acts without her ever knowing how much I missed her when she wasn't there. How much I thought about her when I was at home with screaming whores and cursing fathers.

She didn't need to be tainted by me.

Not when she was literally the only good thing in my world.

An addiction really.

Not only did her kindness trigger a hunger deep inside me to be on the participating end of her generosity but she was just so goddamn beautiful.

Inside and out.

However, that didn't mean I wanted her to—

Olin looked over her shoulder, noticing me for the first time. Her nose smoothed from its embarrassed wrinkle, looking me up and down. She took in the grubby T-shirt I hadn't washed in a while and the jeans that should've been recycled rather than cursed to keep covering my overgrown legs.

She smiled a little, her heart pure and perfect.

She didn't grimace or shame me. She didn't act as if having me escort her would be a death sentence like so many of the girls in our grade would do.

I tore my eyes from hers, unable to hold her open, accepting stare.

She sucked in a tiny gasp before turning back to our teacher. "It's okay, Ms Tallup. I think Mr. Clark would prefer I go with someone else. I can take Patty—"

"No. You will take Mr. Clark." Ms Tallup eyed Patty—the

red-haired troublemaker—and smirked. "I don't trust you girls together."

I flinched as Ms Tallup's gaze found mine, freezing me in place. "I trust Mr. Clark. Don't I, Gilbert?"

My flinch became a cower which I tried to hide with a nonchalant grunt. My hand shook as I dropped my eraser and stood.

There would be no arguments.

Ms Tallup had taught me that last year when she'd held me back a grade. And the year before that when she'd decided I was too stupid to advance with the other students.

Two years of repeats.

Two years of living a nightmare.

I was at her mercy if I wanted to stay in school and get the hell out of this life.

"Yes, Ms Tallup."

"Good boy." Turning toward the board again, she waved at the exit. "Run along now and come back to me quickly."

Standing, I moved toward Olin and hesitated beside her. Already whispers and snickers filled the classroom. My back crawled being centre of attention. My temper spiked.

If we were going to do this, I wanted it over with.

Not thinking of the ramifications, I grabbed her wrist, yanked her from her seat, and dragged her from the classroom. I didn't let the fact that this was the first time I'd touched her knot my stomach or the fact that she'd probably never want to be alone with me again stop me.

I just couldn't stand there with so many eyes upon us.

Instead of fighting me, Olin slipped into step, her dainty dancer's feet light and balanced.

Yet another thing that drew me to her.

The way she moved was magic.

A cat-like grace to her every stride.

I'd often hid in the dusty hall when the school squad practiced their dancing. Her feet had wings. Her body could twist and bend like some silky, perfect ribbon.

She truly was my every fantasy, and that terrified me because the girl in my grasp could never live up to the illusion I'd created, and I didn't want to lose her. Didn't want to lose the dream-girl who made my days slightly better just by watching her dance in the field or sneaking home-baked goods to substitute teachers.

I didn't have much, but I did have my version of Olin. I'd daydreamed her into something my heart desperately wanted because I needed an escape from reality.

I couldn't afford to risk finding out the real girl wasn't nearly as good as my creation.

The second we were in the corridor and the door closed behind us, Olin wriggled her wrist gently. She didn't rip out of my hold, just politely cleared her throat and murmured, "You can let go now. No one is watching us anymore."

I tore my hand off her, my fingers trembling.

Goddammit, even her voice affected me.

Soft and lyrical, gentle and calming.

My heart tripped and stumbled, a black temper doing its best to protect me from falling hard and falling forever. "Hurry." I nudged my chin at the bathrooms down the hall. "Be quick."

She sighed sadly. "I'll be as fast as I can." Reaching into her pocket for her cell phone, she didn't move toward the facilities.

"What are you doing?" I crossed my arms.

"I don't really need to go to the bathroom." She gave me another soft, gentle smile. A smile that no longer held light-hearted, bubbly energy she used with everyone, but dripped with unhappiness and truth.

I froze as every instinct to protect her rose viciously and violently.

This girl was invincible in her quest to save, soothe, and help, so why did her shoulders roll and tears gloss her complex hazel eyes?

My heart growled, desperate not to fall for whatever lie this was. Begging me not to reach out and help her for a change.

But that was the problem.

Olin wasn't a walking, talking lie like the rest of this school.

Her many acts of sweetness had proven that over and over again. I'd watched her for two years. I'd lost count how many times she'd restored my hope in humanity just by being her.

If I was brutally honest with myself, I was mostly in love with her and I'd never even said hello.

I stood stupid and silent as her fingers flew over the on-screen keyboard. My chest ached as she sniffed back sadness and bit her bottom lip.

"What are you doing?" The repeated question fell dark and distrusting before I could stop myself.

Her gaze met mine, the liquid receding a little. She didn't

hide this time. "Responding to an urgent text."

I mulled over her reply, not used to conversation with anyone, let alone the girl of my many fascinations.

Rubbing the back of my neck, I forced out. "So urgent you risked detention?"

Olin returned her attention to her phone. "She can't give out detention for having a weak bladder."

Annoyance at her idiocy rose. "She can do whatever she wants. Tallup isn't someone you want to cross."

I knew that from personal experience.

"I know. But..." She blew air up her face, making pretty bangs dance on her forehead. "I won't be able to concentrate unless I send this." She sniffed back another gush of suspicious wetness in her eyes. "Because...well, you see...it's just...very important."

Once again a surge to be nice overwhelmed me. I didn't like her this way. I wasn't used to her showing weakness. She fought for those who needed help. She'd never cried. Not once.

I'd never seen her so...in pain.

Fuck.

I didn't speak again.

I couldn't.

My heart successfully ignored all my warnings and wanted to keep her. I didn't know how a few sentences and the hint of tears could make me sign over my trust, just like that.

She'd successfully done what no one else had before.

She'd made me care.

Made me put my own sorry excuse of a life on the line. Made me want to put her first and always, *always* be there for her.

My entire body ached while Olin ignored me and wrote her text. My heart ached. My belly ached. My head. My arms. They all ached because the fantasy was no longer just a girl I watched from afar.

She was here.

Standing in front of me.

And I didn't know what the fuck to do.

A minute passed.

Then another.

An awful thought harpooned me.

Is she messaging a boyfriend?

I'd never seen her with anyone but that didn't mean she wasn't secretive or seeing someone outside of school.

Was this a breakup text?

Curiosity burned like acid while her fingers tapped softly.

Finally, I couldn't take it any longer.

Shoving hands into jeans pockets, I cleared my throat. "You done?"

"Almost." Her tongue stuck between her lips. With a heavy sigh, she pressed send. "There. Finished."

I fought the urge to ask. I forbid myself from grabbing her and never letting go. I wanted to know everything. I wanted to be the only one she trusted.

What the hell is wrong with me?

Moving toward the classroom door, I did the most logical thing and not the crazy delusion of stealing her from school and never bringing her back.

Reaching for the door-handle, I jumped as Olin pleaded, "Um, wait?" Her shoulders slumped all over again. She looked at me then down the empty corridor as if needing time before facing education again.

I paused, recognising her reluctance. I knew that look. The look of being trapped when all you wanted was to be free.

My prison was made up of drunkards and fears of homelessness.

What bars surrounded her?

I balled my hands. "You…eh, you okay?"

She half-smiled, tucking loose hair behind her ear. "You know what? No, not really." Her eyes widened as if she hadn't meant to say such things. "Sorry. Whoops, I didn't mean to…ugh, forget it." Her smile blinded me, bright and brave—the one I knew because she wore it like armour.

"Don't do that." My heart swelled at her confiding in me, then frosted over at her attempt to hide. "Don't lie."

She flinched. "I didn't lie."

"Want to talk about it?"

She jerked as if I'd offered crack cocaine in the school corridor. I understood why such an offer would seem random and totally out of nowhere but…we weren't total strangers.

She knew me, kind of.

I rubbed the back of my nape, cursing the length and wishing I'd trimmed my hair last week instead of running errands for my old man and his whores.

"Not sure." She gave me a pained smile. "Why would you care what I have to say?"

I deliberately smirked, acting as cool and calm as I could. "Why wouldn't I care?"

"'Cause you don't know me."

"I know you."

"Yeah, but you're not my friend."

"Not yet."

What the hell, Clark?

The funny thing was, friend was too basic a word.

Friend was *nothing* compared to what I wanted from her.

She froze. "You...you want to be my friend?" The lack of confidence in her tone made my eyes narrow. Where had her brave, bubbly fearlessness gone? Why, in this lonely, empty corridor, did she look at me as if I'd offered her the greatest gift after having nothing but empty promises?

Her obvious hunger made my stomach knot tighter and sharp, painful things stab into my chest.

In just a few short seconds, we'd gone from strangers to something more. "Depends if you'd be friends with the outcast." I shrugged, well aware of my scruffiness, my moodiness, everything that I was and could never be.

"You're not an outcast. I'm sure you could have many fri—"

"It's by choice." I cut her off. "I don't like people."

"But...you just said—"

"You're the one exception."

"Oh." She blushed a deep pleased pink. "Well...I mean...I'm honoured. But...um, why would you want to be friends with me? We're not exactly similar." Her eyelashes fluttered. "What do we have in common? You're older than me and—"

"I'm older than everyone in class."

"Why is that?" She tilted her head inquisitively. "You're studying the same things we are. I've always wondered."

You have?

How long have you wondered?

How long had she noticed me?

I kept my voice as level as I could. "Held back."

"By who?"

"Doesn't matter."

Silence fell.

She licked her bottom lip as if deliberating my trustworthiness. "You seem to prefer your own company, you sure you want to hang out with me?"

I raked a hand through my hair. "I think so."

Her head shot up, her forehead creasing into a frown. "You *think* so?"

I coughed, aware I'd just insulted her but not sure how to fix it. "Like you said, we're from totally different worlds. We might not get on at all. In which case, friendship isn't something that will work."

"What sort of world do you come from?"

Hell.

I come from Hell.

I smiled, but I was afraid it came out more like a scowl. "Those sorts of questions are for friends only."

"And I'm not your friend...yet."

Smart, kind, beautiful...*good*. I didn't stand a chance. Not a goddamn chance. "Exactly."

Silence slipped in again. Nerves at getting into trouble dragged my eyes to the closed door a few metres away. If Ms Tallup found us loitering out here, God knew what she'd do. "Look, we, eh...should probably—"

"I was messaging my dad." Olin rubbed her sneaker into the floor. "And it wasn't urgent. I just like to pretend it is."

I froze, aware that this was privileged information. Somehow, I'd been permitted to learn a secret I doubted any of her other friends knew. "I-I don't understand."

Her eyes met mine, sad and resigned. "He sent me a text this morning saying he and Mum are heading away for the weekend. Again." She rubbed her nose with the back of her hand. "He didn't tell me where. Didn't ask if I wanted to go too. His message didn't need a response, but...I like to make believe it did. I fool myself that he's asked about my day, enquired what I want for dinner—basically that he's a parent who cares that his kid will get home safely from school, even if he won't be there."

Ice crept through my veins. "You're saying you're alone most of the time?"

She looked away. She laughed softly, amazement on her face. "I don't know what I'm saying. Why did I tell you that? I've never told anyone." Her gaze met mine, bewildered and a little lost. "Want to know something else? I'm not as young as the other students. I mean, in age I am, but mentally...I feel ancient. You might be two years older, but most nights, I cook my own meals and get myself to bed." She wrapped her arms around herself. "Oh my God, why can't I shut up around you? I don't even *know* you."

I didn't reply for the longest moment, struggling with the urge to drag her close. To erase her loneliness.

But that would be too much, too fast.

She wasn't invincible like I'd believed. She wasn't endlessly brave and selfless. She was hurting.

Just like me.

And that could never be permitted.

"You can tell me things," I said softly. "I won't betray your trust."

She studied me. Carefully. Intensely. Her hair slipped over her shoulder as she tilted her head. "I believe you." A blush decorated her cheekbones again. "Ditto. I mean...you can tell me things too. I'm trustworthy."

"I know you are."

We stared at each other.

Both aware something had happened.

Something special.

Something strong and scary and not entirely explainable.

We were different.

But similar.

And she'd just become mine in this dingy, depressing corridor all because she was brave enough to share a secret with me.

I wanted to touch her. I'd never wanted anything more.

But I didn't.

Because there would be time for that.

And I wouldn't do a damn thing to jeopardise this one perfect, brilliant thing in my life. "Sharing a secret makes us friends...Olin."

Her name.

Fuck, it kicked my heart and tainted my lips.

She sucked in a breath as I stopped achingly close to her. So close I could pick out the green and brown swirls of her hazel eyes and smell the sweetness of her hair. "I suppose I owe you now." My voice thickened with gravel.

I did my best to pull back.

To rip my eyes from hers and smother the hunger in my tone, but her body softened, welcomed, and a current of power, stronger than electricity, more dangerous than lightning crackled from her heart to mine.

She blinked, her cheeks flushing. "Owe me? Owe me what?"

My eyes hooded. "A secret. I owe you a secret."

And a kiss.

And someone who cares if you're home at night.

And someone to protect you after you've protected everyone else.

"Oh." She looked at my chest, then back to my eyes. "You don't have to."

"I want to. You're special."

"I am?"

"You are." My fingers burned to touch. To tuck aside the strands of hair dangling by her jaw and trace the sharpness of her cheekbone. To pull her into me. To tell her how rare she was. To ask how she'd stayed so good in a world drenched in darkness.

But I kept my hands to myself even as my voice betrayed me. "I like you, Olin. That's my secret. And that's a pretty big deal for me to admit."

I could've given other secrets, but I wasn't ready. Not yet. My other secrets were the kind that would scare off a girl like Olin.

And I didn't want to scare her off.

Ever.

She locked in place, a catch in her voice that undid me. "You *like* me?"

I stepped back so I didn't do something reckless like kiss her.

"You *like* me like me, or just like me?"

I chuckled. "There's a difference?"

"Of course." Her heart-shaped face etched with seriousness. "Definitely. I need to know exactly how you feel—"

The classroom door swung open, interrupting our moment as Ms Tallup stuck her head into business that didn't belong to her—just as she always did. "What on earth is going on? Get back in here. Both of you. Immediately."

My heart bucked for all new reasons, filling with resentment.

Olin jumped with guilt. "Yes, Ms Tallup."

She ducked under the teacher's arm and dashed into the room.

I schooled my face into a mask of insolence and waited until Ms Tallup dropped her barricade before swaggering into the student-filled space.

My façade was back.

My temper hiding the truth.

Olin was the only one allowed to know how fragile I was beneath the barbwire I used to keep everyone at bay.

I didn't know why she was different.

But she was.

And I'm keeping her.

Olin kept her eyes on her math workbook as I passed by, but her gentle whisper met my ears, timid and slightly shocked, but resonating with honesty. "I like you too, Gilbert Clark."

No one else heard her in the babble of commotion.

No one else knew just how much she'd changed my life.

My legs turned shaky, plummeting me into my hard seat.

My heart pounded.

My palms sweated.

And a grateful smile remained hidden beneath a frown.

Chapter Six

Olin

-The Present-

WHO KNEW TIME had the power to drive me insane? Two hours Gil had been within touching distance.

Actually, that isn't true.

For two hours, he'd been *closer* than touching. Kissing distance really.

Yet he hadn't said a word to me.

Not a single syllable.

It was as if conversation was banished so he could forget it was me he painted, make-believing I was a faceless, nameless model instead.

I got why he'd want to ignore the pain I caused him.

But it didn't mean I was immune from the pain he caused me.

Time slowed and ensured I was vibrantly aware of *everything*.

His masculine smell of citrus and paint. The weight of his shallow, controlled breathing. The way his eyes flashed and noticed every blemish and smudge on my skin, diligently brushing over my imperfections with his talent.

The impenetrable quietness that had fallen the moment Gil sprayed the first lash of paint only grew thicker.

If I wobbled, I earned a growl. If I twitched, I earned a pinch.

I wasn't permitted to move a fraction without reprimand.

And not being allowed to move only made the urge unbearable.

I grew claustrophobic in the middle of his chilly warehouse with just him for company.

It cost everything to stay still and obey.

Not that Gilbert cared how I was coping. The intensity I'd witnessed taking him over when he was younger was even more potent now. His art replaced everything. His concentration was his master, making him a slave to colour.

I might've been jilted by the way he no longer saw me as Olin.

I might've been offended by the impertinent way he dismissed me, even while we stood so achingly close.

But because I knew him. Because I knew the savagery of his talent, I didn't mind that his eyes stayed focused on a design I couldn't see. I didn't shy away when his cool fingers traced my inner thigh, branding me with a wake of fire. I didn't complain when the soft lickings of his brush ensured I ached with things I had no right to feel.

I might have flaws but I had courage, and I hid every tingling, tangling, clenching reaction from his methodical painting.

I was the perfect human canvas.

Silent.

Abiding

Aloof.

I bit my lip as he ducked close. His messy hair that followed no law flopped over his forehead in strands of glossy dark. He stayed crouched by my lower belly, his breath heating my flesh, his brushstrokes cursing me.

With a low, displeased grunt, he straightened and tossed the fine bristled brush on his worktable. He swiped at the roguish strands of hair on his forehead, leaving a streak of mottled colour behind.

"What is it?" I asked quietly, knowing to keep my tone soft around a creative person so deep in their craft. I'd been the same way when I'd practiced new chorography. Noise sounded different when you were in the tight embrace of your calling. A voice was a shotgun. A demand a cannon.

Gil raked both hands through his hair, uncaring about the smears he left behind. He ignored me, hastily mixing new pigments with a feverish intensity that erupted goosebumps beneath the paint on my skin, disrupting the smoothness of his lines.

The longer I stood in his empty warehouse, the more I remembered our childhood. How his smile imprinted itself on my heart for always. How his laugh had been so hard earned— his true laugh and not the cynical, detached one he gave in class. I also remembered what it was like to tend to his injuries that he did his best to keep secret.

He'd been beaten up last night. By who, I didn't know. But seeing him with a split lip and blackened eye wasn't new.

He'd come to school with a few colourful shiners. I'd wiped away blood from his chin. I'd slipped him painkillers for his ribs.

I'd seen enough of the results of his home life to understand without him telling me: abuse rained under the roof where he slept.

But…he did tell me.

One day, when he'd gotten to school late with a bowed head of contrition and a hiss of agony as he slid into his seat, I'd known something was wrong. Something worse than normal.

After the bell rang and we'd walked far enough from school not to be seen holding hands, I'd gripped his comforting palm with both of mine and tugged him up my street.

For the first time in my life, I was glad my parents weren't home. Because that night, I led Gil into my house and refused to let him leave. I ran the bath for his aching muscles. I waited with a fresh towel for when he finished. I stared at his naked chest rivering with warm bubbles and gasped at the horror of what he'd lived.

Bruises upon bruises.

Smudges and splodges, scars and slices. His body was a portrait of violence, and when tears came to my eyes and I'd walked into his shaking embrace, all I'd wanted to do was tell him I loved him. To take him to bed. To lie with him. Hug him. Kiss him. Give him what he'd given me: a friend. A person who cared. A person who could become our new family because the current ones we had had failed us.

Stop it!

I couldn't relive such things.

Couldn't welcome such sadness.

The memory of the boy who'd stolen my heart made me soften toward the man who was winter itself. I returned to the present with its slightly chilly warehouse, mostly pretty paintwork, and eternally arctic overseer. "What design are you working on?" I looked down at my naked breasts, unable to see past my arm wedged between them to the picture slowly coming to life on my stomach and hips.

"Nothing." Gil finished mixing whatever shade he required and climbed onto the podium beside me. "Stay still." His lips thinned with demand, but I smiled gently.

"Okay, Gil."

He stiffened at his name, reminding me all over again that there were so many unresolved things between us.

He'd made my school life a sanctuary, then jammed it full of misery. He'd twisted me up in ways I still hadn't unravelled.

Sighing, I slipped back into the strained silence as Gil forgot about me and returned to his art. For the next hour, he focused on my legs. I hissed a couple of times as his air gun tickled between my toes and hid my sudden gasp when his brush traced between my legs like a lover's caress.

I stared at him, my pulse gushing so fast it deafened me. I waited for another stroke, another whip of colour, but he carefully worked on the outside of my hip instead; his jaw locked and motions jerky.

Twisting a little, I did my best to rid the complicated desire he'd left me with. His fingertips instantly latched around my semi-painted hip. "Did I say you could move?"

He didn't look up, and I was glad. Glad because I couldn't stop the truth burning that his fingers were corrosive, sinking through my flesh, slicing through nerves, until he'd reached into my very body and held bone. My heart struck a match, burning itself, sending blood-red smoke to lick around my ribs.

What is going on with me?

Gil made me weak and violent. He made me want to cup his cheeks and demand answers all while slapping his currently cool face and screaming at him for leaving me.

Gritting my teeth hard enough to ache, I jerked my head up and focused away.

I didn't follow his tangled hair as he continued to brush, shadow and light. I didn't care that he studied my body in a way that was illegal for most bosses yet perfectly acceptable in this studio.

He hadn't mentioned my tattoo or scars again since manhandling me into a pose against his black painted wall. He'd removed the offending ink by keeping my back hidden and directed one arm to twist around my waist while the other was placed between my breasts, framing my assets while my fingers locked tight around my nape for purchase.

There'd been no battling lust or buckling beneath desire when he'd touched me.

He'd successfully locked that part of himself away, leaving me at his mercy.

I moved to scratch my nose. The grumbling growl emitting from Gil as he mixed paint at my feet was enough for me to hastily resume the position.

Three hours was an eternity with no conversation when bodies constantly brushed against each other. My muscles turned stiff and achy. My patience quickly overshadowed by hunger.

When a muscle twitched involuntarily, I didn't make a peep. When I trembled, Gil merely steadied me and kept on painting.

Our dealings with each other were as sharp and silent as knives.

Gil's fingers brushed over my lower torso, teasing with the only piece of clothing covering me. He delicately drew a line of vibrant turquoise right along the ridge of my underwear. The brush tickled and made me suck in a breath, but worse, it made my belly clench and nerve endings spring into starving life.

His fingers feathered over my upper thigh as he sketched an outline. His minty breath skated over the tops of my breasts as he leaned closer to add detail. The outside of his hand brushed my nipple as he angled himself to airbrush my cleavage with a vibrant slash of magenta.

Holy…

I bit down on my bottom lip, doing my best to remain stiff and silent.

Time once again intruded on us. I steadily turned from a person into whatever he wanted me to be.

I'd been kidding myself that I could survive him. Years might've flowed between us but whatever it was that drew, linked, and bound us in school was still there. Only this time…it was stronger than a hum, deeper than a puddle, darker than any nightmare.

The warehouse shivered in silence, both of us too afraid to break the oppressive stillness as Gilbert traded his air gun for small bottles and brushes. Enlisting sponge-tipped tools, he added further flourishes.

I locked my knees as he migrated his way up my body. The sensation of paint covering my lower part kept the chill at bay, but it didn't stop my nipples from pebbling as Gil stopped at my chest and made a strange noise.

My heart raced but his face hid any sign of being anything but professional as he reached out with a small sponge and dabbed my breasts with blackened purple.

I stiffened as the wet intrusion of colour made my skin hyperaware of him. It took everything I had to pick a dirty spot on the ceiling and keep my eyes locked on it.

I hoped he'd move onto other areas like he had before, but I wasn't given a reprieve. He stayed painfully close, his frame huge and hulking, his eyes narrowed and calculating, his energy casting waves every time he touched me with his medium.

My eyes closed despite my command to stay open. My chest heaved while he worked so close he could've pressed his nose into my cleavage. An utterly, miserably long eternity passed while he painted flesh that hadn't been touched in a very long time, unwittingly wrapping me up in barbwire desire until I could barely think, let alone remain standing.

The longer he bowed over my breasts, tracing the arm looped between them, the shallower his own breathing became. His Adam's apple bobbed as he swallowed hard. The careful cruelty on his face flickered with seconds of barely restrained violence.

Violence for me? For us? Our past? His work? His injuries? His business?

I didn't know.

I'd probably never know.

All I knew was my body didn't care what Gil had done to me in the past. It wanted him, and this was a new level of unbearable torture.

I'm glad this is a one-time deal.

If I had to stand like this again for him, I'd burn through my self-restraint and end up pushing him to the floor with need. I'd ruin everything all because being with him brought the past to life and nullified the worries of my future.

I breathed him in, learning his scent of citrus, paint thinner, and moody colours. I exhaled just as quickly. He drugged me. Confused me. Hurt me.

He stopped breathing altogether as he swapped his sponge for a delicate brush and did his best to make me collapse with the fine bristles. At one point, self-preservation took over and my chin dropped and shoulders rolled to inch away from his artist's touch.

But he clucked his tongue, pressed paint-smeared fingers under my jaw and coerced me back into place. "Never break the position."

His voice was odd. Thick as oil and dark as charcoal. He cleared his throat as our eyes met. The undercurrent of electricity made me burn alive and freeze to death in equal measure.

"Okay," I strangled as he dropped his fingers and cocked his head, utterly regal and terribly callous. His gaze darted down my mostly painted form with a frown. In a flash, his heavy hand angled my hip closer to him, twisting me this way and that like some store-bought mannequin with plastic in her veins instead of blood.

"Don't move again." With his bitten command, he resumed painting as if fire hadn't sparked and crackled between us. The hair on my arms prickled beneath his colours. My scalp tingled. My tummy clenched. All because I found him beyond attractive as he worked in his element.

His face slipped a little, revealing a wash of lust. Then it was gone again, drowned by the impenetrable artist. "Arch back. I can't get a part of your ribcage."

I shuddered as his knuckles nudged my shoulder, pushing me. "Do what I say."

Trembling, I called on muscles to brace me as I reclined backward, feeling my breasts rising, my arm slipping, my stomach flattening—every part of me elongating to balance.

It felt like a dance.

A frozen in time chorography.

My heart leapt for joy.

My back twinged with agony, warning me not to go too far.

A black noise rumbled in his chest as I settled into this new back-breaking position. For a second, no brush or sponge touched me. Gil stood beside me, his body heat scorching, and I wondered...just for a moment...if he'd snap.

If he'd give into the fog of desire that'd grown so thick around us.

I wanted him to throw down his tools, wrap his fist in my hair, and yank me into a murderous kiss.

But he cleared his throat again and stepped closer, searing me as he dabbed paint on the underside of my breasts.

It didn't take long.

Merely a few seconds, but in those few seconds, my heart was visible beneath my rainbow-hued skin. It pounded for freedom. It thudded for more. Gil ceased to be the boy who broke me. The boy who vanished without a whisper and became the most skilled chemist—blending colours and chroma, somehow using both to infiltrate my very being.

He jerked back, wiping his mouth with the back of his hand as he stormed to his worktable with slightly shaky steps. He kept his back to me as he mixed and diluted his next layer of pigment. "Stand up straight," he ordered over his shoulder as a flash of silver and navy blended with something metallic in his hands.

I did as I was told, maintaining the original pose as he attached the air gun to a new compressor and returned to me.

He refused to meet my gaze as he tested the trigger with a quick press into his palm, frowning at the consistency and coverage.

After a few tweaks of the pressure valve, he crowded me again.

Strength ran from my limbs. I was wobbly and weak and woefully unprepared to continue. I wanted to ask how much longer this nightmare would last, but he ducked to his haunches, his face between my legs, his unruly hair tickling my thigh as he held the gun over my knee and pressed the trigger.

God...

I jolted at the tickle.

He dragged the hissing sensation up my leg, higher and higher until the puff of air found the part of me throbbing for attention. He was too close, too near, too *much*.

I couldn't do it.

I stumbled.

My arm fell from around my breasts, automatically seeking purchase to stop my fall.

My prettily painted fingers landed on his head for balance, those same fingers sinking into his thick, messy hair.

A flashback of running my fingers over his scalp when we were teenagers assaulted me. The texture of his strands hadn't changed. Still coarse but silky. Soft but strong. The heat of his head and the sudden menacing glower of his eyes made my heart relocate into my palms and skip a beat.

"Sorry." I tried to pull away, yet I couldn't seem to order my fingers to let go.

He didn't move—frozen on his haunches before me, his very presence lashing around me.

Shoving aside heavy want, I managed to untangle my fingers

and raise my arm into position. My chin soared up, and my gaze locked onto a poster across the room promoting the benefits of a particular type of latex for prosthetic work.

For an eon, Gil didn't move.

He breathed hard and shallow. His teeth clenched audibly.

Then, slowly, methodically, he leaned forward and pressed the trigger as if nothing had happened.

The burst of air and stream of paint made me shudder. My stomach leapt as he slipped over the tiny scrap of underwear hiding me and worked on my inner thighs.

I *throbbed.*

I wanted, wanted, *wanted,* but somehow, I kept the pose.

It took all my willpower not to arch away, but my mind filled with images of tongues licking me, tasting me, leaving behind sticky coverage in the form of colour that masked my own.

The room stayed deathly silent as Gil gradually covered every inch. He switched his method from soft shading to slashing me with ribbons of paint and harsh bursts of air.

The sensation teased me, made me wet.

I bit my lip.

I locked my toes onto the smoothness of the podium and pressed my arm tighter to my chest, giving my body something else to think about.

The whir of the compressor and the faint hiss of the air gun decorated the stretched silence.

I could've come from the airbrush alone.

But then he was gone, moving onto more tolerable areas, adding finishing touches.

I tried to relax, did my best not to flinch each time he came close with a new colour or suck in a breath when he brushed parts of me normally reserved for lovers.

My nakedness disappeared under a cloud of blended artwork.

"Don't move," he muttered as he tossed his tools down and grabbed his fine brush again.

He drew calligraphy lines and highlighted parts of whatever he'd painted, stepping away and scowling only to storm back and torture me with another lick of bristles.

Once he was happy with my body, he turned to my hair and face.

I'd thought having him focus on my body was hard.

It was *nothing* compared to having Gil's fingers tilting my chin this way and that, his teeth sinking into his bottom lip in concentration, his steady talent transforming my cheeks into art and my hair teased with whatever shade he'd chosen.

At one point, he tugged my hair into a tighter bun and the wash of passion made me jerk with need. His breath caught; the air gun faltered.

I swayed as held my jaw, carefully sponging colour over my forehead and eyebrows.

"Close your eyes." His fingers dug into my skin as if such a command affected him as much as it did me.

I obeyed, grateful to cut him from my vision when he was all I could see. The softness of his paint and the heat of his presence magnified, adding another dimension to my troubles.

But then, it was over.

He stepped away.

Coldness returned, and aloneness resettled.

My first time as a canvas, and it was finished.

Tossing his brushes away, he jumped off the podium and stared at me from a few feet away. His head cocked, assessing each angle and curve, not looking at all happy with his creation.

With me.

He didn't inquire if the pose was comfortable or if the foreignness of being covered in paint was acceptable.

I wasn't Olin.

I was merely his.

With the scent of paint in the air and hunger pangs growing more insistent in my belly, Gilbert came back, added a splatter of rhinestones across my hip bone and brow, then towered over me to paint an area of my shoulder in glue before dabbing turquoise and black glitter over my collarbone.

He leaped off the platform with nimble grace and cupped his chin with paint-speckled hands. He didn't just cock his head this time, he pinned me to the podium with his assessment. His eyes were never still, judging, deliberating.

He stared at my breasts, hips, and legs with more intensity than any man before him.

He only saw flaws and areas of improvement.

Having him a few metres away instead of a few centimetres allowed me to breathe for the first time since I got naked. My knees quaked, and I thanked every star above that he'd only painted my front. I didn't know how I could've coped with him behind me. His breath on the back of my neck. His fingers on my ass. His palms skating down my spine.

Stop it.

It's done.

When the silence became too much, I murmured, "Now what?"

My voice broke the spell.

He jerked as if I'd dragged him away from something painful. He cleared his throat all over again from the crackling tension. "I'm not happy, but it will have to do." Marching away to a cupboard in the shadows, he ordered, "Stay there."

I did as he said, waiting as he pulled open a drawer and came back with an expensive-looking camera. Depositing the camera by my feet, he stalked toward the large spotlights and other photography equipment tucked out of paint's reach and rolled them around the podium.

With no warning to guard my eyes, he turned them all on, blinding me in white intensity.

I winced, squeezing my eyes shut as the heat of the lamps instantly warmed the chill in my bones. The thud of Gil's boots paced around me as he prepared things. Slowly, I cracked open my gaze, getting used to the brightness.

He stood with the camera in his hands and a haughty, hungry look on his face. "Don't move unless I tell you to." Bringing the camera up, he framed me in a picture and pressed the button. The soft click sent another wash of goosebumps over me.

Time slipped into nonsense again as Gil took a copious number of photos from every angle, all with the black matte bricks behind me as the backdrop. Some he came in for a close-up on specific areas on my skin, others he took from far away. He even climbed up a ladder and took some from above.

Through it all, I stayed the perfect mannequin, doing my best to keep my face impassive, breathing light, and muscles smooth.

By the time he clicked the last photo, my stomach wasn't just grumbling for food it was growling, and my feet ached from standing so long.

Gil didn't say a word as he returned the camera to the cupboard, turned the spotlights off, and raked a hand through his hair, smoothing back the roguish strands. He didn't care he had as much paint on his fingers as I did on my body, just like he didn't care I was still there, trapped in his instruction and not permitted to move.

He caught my eye.

Something powerful and ancient throbbed between us.

Something we couldn't control.

I was wrong.

He *did* care.

He cared a great deal.

His forehead furrowed as he drank me in. His shoulders fell as he sighed. "It's over. Go take a shower. I'll get cash for you." Turning away, he marched into his office without a backward glance.

* * * * *

"Holy mother of mercy," I whispered under my breath.

The mirror reflected me.

But it wasn't me.

I'd vanished and left behind some storybook empress.

This magical creature drenched in reds and blues, purples and shadow could never be me.

Wow.

Just...wow.

Gil's bathroom hid me from the cold warehouse. I'd intended to rush into the shower and rid myself of the strange sensation of being wrapped in something foreign.

But that was before the full-length mirror trapped my gaze and I was hypnotised.

I'd seen his talent on YouTube. I'd studied the complicated designs he'd done and always known he was a wizard with paint.

But now?

Now, I had a whole new appreciation for why people called him the Master of Trickery.

Inching forward, I didn't focus on my nudity. How could I when I wore something so much more than mere clothes?

I wore Gilbert's mark. His time and energy and skill.

My torso no longer held breasts or ribs or muscle. It was an underwater cavern with spiels of light illuminating black pockets where eels and crustaceans hid in the gloom. But in the bright sunlight shining from my chin, down my clavicle, and dappling my chest, krill and multi-coloured gemstone fish frolicked, almost as if my ribcage had become an aquarium for such incredible sea life.

Twisting a little, my eyes widened in amazement as I studied a glowing crystal ball depicting a scene of a shipwreck with glittery rhinestones on my hip. Flowing over my shoulder was a perfect waterfall. It puddled in my collarbone before spilling free with blue glitter and silver thread, as lifelike and as wet as any liquid down my arm.

It was magic—pure and simple.

The commission must've been for an aquarium or travel advertisement or something that inspired nature and adventure.

It inspired me.

I felt like I could swim underwater and summon all manner of wildlife.

I felt *royal.*

The photos he'd taken would no doubt be sent to whoever requested this piece, and somewhere out there, in some busy shopping complex or some glossy magazine, people would stare at my naked body and not see a woman but an entire underwater kingdom with me as its ruler.

I'd thought he didn't see me as a person.

I was wrong.

He'd seen past that simple illusion and shown me that even my own perception was too narrow.

Wearing his paint made me stand taller, act prouder, move smoother. I posed as if I wore an expensive gown, custom made and agonisingly tailored to perfection.

I wasn't human.

No way.

I was more.

So, so much more.

And for the first time in a very, very long time…I was happy.

Chapter Seven

Olin

-The Present-

"HERE'S YOUR CASH."

I dragged fingers through my damp hair, slightly tangled from towel drying and not having a brush. "Thanks." I moved toward him, hoisting my bag up my shoulder. My clothes were back in place, and my skin returned to bland—vacant of rhinestones and illusions.

I gingerly reached for the envelope enclosing money that would buy me a few more days of roof and walls. "Appreciate it."

He grunted something and turned away. Just like me, he was clean from any paint, apart from a single streak of navy on his jawline.

My stomach did a little flip.

Stop it, O.

Just stop it.

He looked up as I shoved the envelope a little too firmly into my bag.

"Don't you want to count it?"

I shook my head, unable to hold his gaze. "It's fine."

"You don't even know the going rate."

"No, but I trust you."

"You really shouldn't."

I smiled softly, keeping my eyes on the concrete floor and begging my cheeks not to flame.

I shouldn't trust him?

He *shouldn't trust* me.

I'd done something in that bathroom. In the twenty minutes it'd taken me to shower, I'd dabbled in a fantasy that had seemed too real. I'd pretended Gil kissed me that night in my house. I envisioned years of togetherness instead of distance.

And now, I was ashamed because I'd been tempted to deal with the coursing desire he'd left me with by delivering an orgasm by my own hand in *his* shower.

I hadn't.

Of *course*, I hadn't.

But the urge had been almost undeniable.

Standing in front of that mirror, total awe had shoved aside my wariness and twisted my feelings into something I daren't contemplate.

I didn't have a name for the surging complexity of emotions.

Pain.

Hope.

Forgiveness.

I doubted I ever would. But I *could* admit that I admired him. Greatly. And any wariness and hurt were now shadowed by utmost appreciation.

And a fair amount of regret.

Regret for the past. Regret for not trying to find him when he disappeared.

"You're incredibly talented, Gil," I murmured, finally mustering the courage to look at him.

He seemed to have aged since I'd left him to shower. Exhausted smudges under his eyes. His five o' clock shadow making him angular and unforgiving. "Just lines and fading."

"It's a lot more than that, and you know it."

He looked away, moving to lean against his mixing table as if he needed the support. His body language blocked off conversation as bluntly as possible. "At least the commission is done."

"So you don't need me to come back?"

"No." He shook his head. "I don't."

I forced a smile again. "I understand."

He narrowed his eyes, glaring directly into me. "You need to leave now, Olin."

I glanced at the exit, then back to him.

I could leave.

I *should* leave.

And yet…

"Is it painful? To see all that time and effort disappear?"

How did he do it? How did he stand creating design after design, never to see or touch it again once the canvas had showered?

"Excuse me?" His face covered in dark clouds, warning I wasn't welcome with my hardships and heartaches.

"That masterpiece you did. I struggled to wash it off." I laughed gently, even though I didn't find it funny. More like sad. And a little heart-wrenching. "You invested so much time and energy into something unbelievably magical. Only for it to vanish."

I didn't mean for the past to enter this chat, but somehow it did, licking around us like mist, making him stiffen and frost to feather over his features.

Gil was beyond talented, and that sort of craftsmanship ought to be recognised—even if the boy ran away and left behind a man with the bad manners of a hardened aristocrat.

I meant what I said. It'd seemed barbaric to wash so many minutes of his life away, eradicating something so beautiful.

"Where did you learn to paint like that?" I asked quietly, doing my best to hide my trembles.

The link I'd had with him was gone. He'd successfully pushed me away so he no longer seemed affected by me.

He sighed heavily.

I tasted impatience.

Felt his annoyance.

The impertinent dismissal.

The closed off heart.

Just like before.

Exactly like before

My mouth turned dry.

My heart curled around itself in safety.

Before he could reply, my pain exploded outward. I'd asked gently. I'd waited patiently. If this was the last time I'd see him, I needed to know.

I need to know so I can move on.

"Why did you walk away?" I swiped at my cheek. "Without a single word? Why did you let me fall in love with you if you knew you didn't want me?"

The air turned instantly oppressive.

The warehouse was no longer a building but a prison, and I was trapped with Gil as he slowly unwound his legs and arms and pushed off predator-slow from his table. His eyes flickered with truth but his lips delivered lies. "I decided I didn't like school."

"You were almost finished. You managed to stay an extra two years. You could've—"

"Enough." Coming toward me, he kept his chin down, shading his eyes with dark eyebrows. His untidy hair licked his eyelashes, slicing his forehead with black strands. "Leave, Olin. You've been here too long already."

I backed toward the door like a coward. I would never have run from him before. I'd even fought some of his battles for him. I'd stuck up for him with Ms Tallup—the teacher from hell. I'd snuck money into his backpack when he wasn't looking so he could buy groceries.

I'm not afraid of him.

Are you sure about that?

"Gil...I just want to understand."

"There's nothing to understand." He herded me toward the exit, efficiently, ruthlessly. For every step I took, he took one, hunting me down. His hands remained balled at his sides, his jaw tight and body tense.

He would've been insanely handsome if it hadn't been for the harsh edge that warned this wasn't a game for him. I was a threat, and he wouldn't hesitate to deal with that threat with whatever means necessary.

"I tried to move on." I held my chin higher, glad my voice didn't wobble. "I almost succeeded. But seeing you again? It's just reminded me that so much didn't make sense. You were the one who chased me, remember? You were the one who—"

"I remember." He kept stalking me, smooth and unruffled—nothing like the wild boy in school. I didn't think this version knew how to smile or laugh. He'd mastered the scowl and guarded walls to the point it was a physical reprimand.

"If you remember, then *talk* to me. Let's go for a drink. Catch up. Tell me what you did for the past few years and how you started *Total Trickery*."

"I'm not interested in talking." The way his voice thickened like a river churning gravel made me hesitate.

My heart raced. I tilted my head. "What *are* you interested in?" It was a breathy question. A gambling question. Technically, I knew what he was interested in.

Throwing me from his warehouse.

But there was something else.

Something just beneath the surface.

Something he didn't have the strength to acknowledge.

"Nothing you can give me. Not anymore." He stopped an arm's length away. I stepped back, only to slam against the large metal roller door. The clang vibrated through my bones, making me wince.

He seemed bigger, blacker, more determined to scar me forever. "I've paid you. Our deal is done. I need you to go now."

I couldn't tear my eyes from his. "Can I come by sometime…just to say hi?"

"No." He opened the pedestrian access beside me. "Like I warned you before, you are no longer welcome here. I appreciate your help today. I'm grateful for your time. But you're not permitted to visit. Forget about me because I have nothing to give you."

"Forget about you like you forgot about me?"

His jaw worked. "I didn't forget you."

"You left me."

"We were kids. It meant nothing." His voice sounded like scissors, sharp and deliberate, slicing through my attempt at talking. "I won't reminisce with you, Olin. I'm not trying to be cruel. I just…I really need you to go and promise me you won't ever come ba—"

"You've moved on. I get it." I clutched my bag to my side. The crinkle of the envelope inside reminded me I'd fulfilled why I was here. Trying to talk to him was utterly pointless, and I had groceries to buy so I didn't starve tonight.

Common sense tried to bow me into surrender. My eyes flickered to the door.

But…

But.

I squared my shoulders, speaking my thoughts aloud rather than keeping them silent. "You know…if I walk out of here now, without trying, I'll forever wonder. So…here it goes." I forced myself to smile kindly—to let him know I didn't hold grudges or hate.

I might forgive him, but I would never settle unless he talked to me…just once.

He owed me that.

Surely, he owes me that.

"Olin, stop—" He held up his hand, but it was too late.

"I was in love with you. Did you know that? Of course you knew that. I told you. So many times. And even if I didn't, it was obvious. I was totally, stupidly besotted in only the way a silly teenage girl can be. I had fantasies of saving you. Moving you into my house. Making you my family to replace those we didn't want. And I know you loved me too. You told me with every touch, Gil. Every nickname."

His gaze flew to my shoulder, no doubt thinking of the tattoo hidden on my back. Then his eyes landed back on mine, lashing me in place with unyielding insolence.

"That day…the day I invited you to my place. I wanted to give you everything." I blushed. "So many times, we came close to kissing. So many times, we were *this* close. In fact, we kinda did kiss if you count a quick brush a kiss. We both wanted it. But then…you cut me out with no explanation. You broke up with me so easily. You humiliated me. You ignored me from that point on. You—"

"It's in the past." His teeth bared between indignant lips. "I can't change what I did. Just like I can't change a great number of things, no matter how much I wish I could."

I stilled. "What things?"

He sighed, rubbing his eyes with harsh fingers. "Doesn't matter."

"It obviously does."

He groaned, a tormented sound deep in his chest. "You need to go now."

"Do you…do you wish you hadn't broken up with me?"

His eyebrows tugged down, annoyed at his slip. "What do you want from me, Olin? I'm being as courteous as I can, but you're not listening to me. I need you to leave." His eyes battled with hot and cold. "Never come back."

"I need to know why."

"You don't need to know. I had my reasons, and those reasons still stand. That's enough."

"For you maybe. But not for me. You have to see it from my point of view."

"No, I don't." He stood tall, a heavy weight crushing him even while he grew angry. "I don't owe you anything. All of this was a big mistake. The past was a mistake. Working with you…fuck." His clipped delivery broke, his eyes flashing at the door. "Please, Olin, I'm so fucking sick of asking. Don't keep making me repeat myself. I need you to leave and never step foot in here again. It's better if you forget you ever knew me and move the fuck on."

His words stung like wasps.

Before I could retaliate, he added, "Besides, why do you think I actually had a reason you would accept? A reason I could give you that would absolve what I did?" His gaze glowed with misery—deep, deep, endless misery, but he slammed shutters over his unexplainable sadness and embraced calculated, withering rage instead. "I didn't *need* a reason to break off a teenage fling. I owe you nothing. *We* meant nothing." His body leaned into mine, bringing frost and snow. "*You* meant nothing."

I swayed, banging against the roller door again. He had me trapped. It was up to him to let me go, yet he didn't move aside. Didn't look away. Didn't stop his hand landing on the door by my ear, clanging with a heavy bell of disgust and dismay. "Stop asking questions I can't answer. Stop looking at me as if I'm responsible for destroying your life. Stop making me fight with—"

"I don't play games, Gil." I pushed off the door, shoving him back. "I'm not here to throw insults or act as if things that I *know* meant something were meaningless. If you knew me at all in high-school, you'd know I have no patience for cruelty."

Sucking in a breath, I reached out and cupped his cheek. "Besides, I don't believe you."

He reared back, a guttural noise falling from his lips.

My fingers seared from touching him. My heart cried for the way he reacted.

I dropped my hand. "I tried to have an honest, adult conversation with you, and you tried shaming it with lies." I shook my head, disappointed and distraught that the boy I'd never gotten over had turned into such a short-tempered, unbreakable male. "I'll go. I won't annoy you with my presence anymore. You're not telling me the truth, but I've got the message. Don't worry."

I brushed past him, my spine tense and knees quaking. "You won."

A swift hand shoved me back against the door; a palm splayed over my sternum, holding me in place against the musical metal. "I haven't won. I never fucking won."

"Let me go."

"You act as if you're the only one in pain here. You look at me as if it was all my fucking fault." His hand burned me—not from heat but dry ice. His touch was worse than any brushstroke from before. Then, it had teased and reminded. Now, it sank past my ribs, deep into the chasm of me, and stabbed a heart that still had bruises. "You don't get to judge me, Olin. You don't get to judge what I do to protect—" His eyes snapped closed, his head twisting to the side.

"What aren't you telling me?"

His eyes opened again, blackened with history and lost to whatever secrets he refused to share.

My heart skittered away, afraid of him. Afraid of the cavern of agony inside him. "Gil…"

"Goddammit, don't." His forehead crashed on mine, breathing hard. Our eyes locked, stare to stare, noses almost touching. His anger cracked, revealing a jagged splinter of fragile vulnerability.

I trembled.

How could a man who surrounded himself in barricades suddenly leave himself wide open for attack?

His gaze glittered with two opposing forces even as his throat worked as if swallowing pure rage.

But beneath the rage burned lust.

A lust that had only grown instead of diminished.

A lust that was an infectious, insidious disease.

I froze.

Breath vanished.

Time stood still.

"Goddamn you to hell." His fingers slipped up my neck, holding me captive as his body pressed into me and his lips smashed painfully onto mine.

The second his mouth captured mine, all ethics, willpower, and rationale fled. Normal behaviour scurried like scared little mice as the claws of violence and desire snatched us both.

His fingers tightened on my neck at the same moment his tongue sliced through my lips, invading me, tasting me, taking the kiss he hadn't taken in the past.

For a second, I was his to command. Totally pliable and shocked.

Then, I grew angry. *Furious* that he'd refused to take a kiss I'd welcomed years ago, but now, when there was no such offer, he snatched it from me so callously.

I bit him as he smothered me, his breath catching with a snarl.

"Let me have this." He kissed me harder. "Before I can't."

I should teach him he couldn't touch me without permission. I should knee him in the balls and hurt him as badly as he'd hurt me.

But his voice throbbed with pain. A pain that wasn't flimsy or easily cured. A pain that brought tears to my eyes with its rawness.

Our attraction exploded.

Our togetherness ruptured.

It burned.

It ached.

It wanted.

Whatever connection he'd tried to deny, beat him into acceptance.

His lips opened wide; his tongue dove deep.

My bag slipped from my shoulder, smacking against the concrete floor as I rose in his arms, plastering myself against him, placing more of my throat into his control.

His groan was the headiest, sexiest thing I'd ever heard. Rich with longing and deadly with fury.

I opened my lips, inviting him to plunge and suffocate. I answered his groan with a moan that strangled my stomach.

My excuse was I was lonely. I'd *always* been lonely.

His excuse?

He'd lost.

Lost to me, to him, to us.

There is *an us.*

Reaching up, I tangled my fingers in the hair that'd fascinated me since finding him. Sinking to his scalp, I deliberately dug my nails into his skin as punishment.

He snarled, kissing me savagely.

I wasn't prepared for the wave of aggression. He kissed me so hard our teeth clacked and tongues duelled. His taste was everywhere. Mint and sin and something that woke up long ago memories.

He was everywhere. All around me. In me.

I kissed him back, fast and wet, not caring about the hungry noises I made. Not embarrassed that I let myself go. This was the kiss he owed me. And if he wanted more than a kiss…I'd give it to him.

His answering growl sent kerosene licking across my flesh as he hoisted me off the floor and once again slammed me hard against the twanging metal door.

Instinct made me wrap my legs around his waist, trapping him as surely as he trapped me.

I shivered as his hips shot forward, thrusting against me, revealing he was no longer a boy but a fully-grown man with heat and hardness straining against his jeans.

"*God*, Gil…" I kissed him harder, faster, tongues and teeth and temper.

We were evenly matched in speed and lack of finesse, nipping and licking, sucking and plunging. I squirmed against his body to get closer, demanding, inviting.

I stopped thinking.

I didn't wonder what caused this explosion.

I just accepted it because that was what my accident had taught me.

Any illusions of a future had been wiped away the moment I felt restaurant glass slice me to ribbons. All we had was *now*, this moment, this very precious second.

Grabbing a fistful of his hair, I let my other skate down his body, tracing the rigid strength of him, the unyielding power until I found the only hot piece of him.

He stiffened as I fisted him, telling him explicitly what I wanted and was prepared to do.

I wasn't embarrassed.

I wasn't second-guessing.

This was the boy who got away, and if I could have a taste—a single afternoon where he was mine…I would take it and suffer the consequences later.

Kissing him with a tongue seeking his with determination, I squeezed his erection.

His taut stiffness instantly became liquid lust, driving both his cock and my hand against me, rubbing against my clit, turning it into a fireball of sensation.

Crying out, I locked my ankles together at the base of his ass, pulling him deeper into me, wanton and blatant and far too bold.

But it didn't turn him off.

It only struck a match, and the heat between us was nothing compared to the fire that blazed in the moment it took me to tug at his belt and unzip his jeans. His flesh scalded me through his boxers.

His hand dropped to fist my breast, squeezing the very flesh he'd ignored only an hour before. Pinching the nipple he'd clinically painted, he growled the most deliciously needy, dangerous snarl.

I stroked him in reward, in invitation.

Clothes had no place anymore.

None.

My skin prickled with sweat. My heart raced with urgency. We both sped up until our kisses were replaced with one violent mess of melted mouths and rabid teeth.

I scrambled to get my hand into his tight underwear, desperate to have him, completely irrational with need.

But then…his phone rang.

The shrill, hated little ring.

Slicing.

Shredding.

Slaying.

As quickly as Gil had attacked me with passion, he dropped me with ice.

Ring.

My feet splatted to the floor as he unlocked his arms.

Ring.

My body wobbled as he stepped away.

Ring.

My heart cried as he yanked the phone from his pocket and looked at the screen.

Instantly, any heat I'd caused in his bloodstream returned to glaciers and avalanches, killing any sign of desire for me with a rush of smoke.

Wiping his mouth, he glanced at me with crazed, glowing eyes. Partly manic but mostly resigned to making yet another mistake.

Ring.

With a deliberate breath, he wrapped himself in a suit made from nasty unkindness. "You were just skin to paint today, Olin. This meant nothing. Just like you meant nothing to me in our youth. *Nothing.* Do you hear me?" Holding the phone, ready to accept the call, he pointed at the door. "Forget me. Forget this. Get out, and never come back. I mean it."

Ring.

Slightly tripping in his haste to get away from me, he hissed, "I never want to see you again. Trust me on that."

Giving me his back, he marched into his office, his only purpose to answer his phone.

Ring.

He didn't care his jeans and belt were undone.

He didn't care his mouth still glistened with my kiss.

Ring.

He didn't care...

About me.

The office door closed, and the ringing stopped.

Chapter Eight

Olin

-The Present-

NO WINE.

I have no wine in my stupid apartment.

And I needed wine.

Desperately.

My lips sang from Gil's the entire Uber ride home. My body ached and my mind—well, my mind was drunk already. Drunk on finally knowing what it felt like to be kissed by Gilbert Clark.

But my heart?

The useless thing was in tinkling pieces.

That damn phone.

Who the hell interrupted us? Why did they have the power to stop something that had felt so unbelievably *real?*

Throwing myself onto the tatty couch with its threadbare yellow cushions, I closed my eyes.

Stop thinking about it.

It was over.

Gil had kicked me out of his place.

He'd bit me, licked me, devoured me, and ordered me to never go back.

But he's hurting...

I grabbed a cushion and curled around it.

Don't, O. Don't torture yourself—

My mind threw images of Gil in my face. Of the way his anger slipped, revealing bone deep need. Of the way his temper cracked, showing a man gasping for help.

He doesn't need help.

I squeezed my eyes shut.

That was the problem with me.

I read into things.

Alone and with no one to talk to, my mechanism at coping was to solve other people's problems. At least my life wasn't so empty if I focused on them and granted them happiness, even if I couldn't achieve the same results for myself.

He isn't like the kids from high-school.

No, he was worse.

A thousand times worse.

Back then, the worst pain a student could carry was caused by a parents' divorce or the death of a pet. I knew how to help with that. Knew how to be there for them until they were ready to talk and heal.

But Gil...

He harboured something monstrous.

Something that cannibalised him from the inside out. Something so black and vicious, it had twisted him into two versions of himself.

The Gil I knew was generous, protective, and kind.

The Gil I didn't was violent, distraught, and full of malice.

He needs—

It doesn't matter what he needs, I'm not allowed to go back.

I screamed into the cushion, pressing my mouth to the yellow fabric and exhaling my fear and frustration. I couldn't just accept his command to forget about him. I'd never been able to walk away from something so inexplicably broken.

He was Gil! The boy who chose me above anyone.

I couldn't just—

You don't have a choice.

Memories of our kiss interrupted my internal argument. He'd kissed me as if he'd been drowning—as if I was untainted air, free from the filth around him. He'd claimed me as if he'd been dreaming of such a thing since he'd walked away from me.

A kiss like that couldn't be given and then taken away.

A kiss like that demanded further investigation.

You. Are. Not. Allowed. Back. There. Remember?

Scowling, I plotted a way to disobey Gil and tried not to be carried away with daydreams of *us*.

You truly are a sucker for—

My stomach snarled, reminding me I hadn't eaten my cucumber sandwiches and adrenaline from kissing Gil had burned through all my reserves.

My plan had been to buy groceries.

And that is what I shall do.

New task. New purpose. No more worrying about Gil. No more torturing myself if I should stay away or go back.

Hauling myself from the soft couch, I padded barefoot toward my bag where I'd thrown it onto the kitchen table. Rummaging inside, I pulled out the envelope of cash Gil had paid me and opened it for the first time.

My legs promptly deleted all bone and became useless.

I slammed onto a wooden chair, clacking my teeth at the force.

No.

This can't be right.

Shaking hands pulled out a wad of fifty-pound notes. A pile far too thick to warrant the few hours I'd spent being his canvas.

One, two, three, four, five…fifteen *hundred* pounds.

Holy shit.

Was that the going rate for a model, or had he—?

He never wants to see you again. It's bribery to make sure you stay away.

Don't read into this!

Oh, who was I kidding?

My heart raced, tumbling down the rabbit hole of why he'd given me so much.

I hadn't been able to earn this sort of cash in an entire month doing other jobs. It meant I had rent and utilities covered. I could eat semi-decent food. I could—

I can't accept this.

My shoulders rolled, fisting the cash with possessiveness.

It might be the correct rate for all you know!

If it was…why didn't it feel right? Why did it feel far too much for the tiny role I'd played?

If we'd discussed payment beforehand, and I knew this was what he paid others, then maybe. But now, it just felt dirty. Wrong. I didn't know why, but it reeked of charity from a boy who couldn't stand the sight of me.

And that made my hungry tummy knot because he'd cheapened me. He'd added yet another sensation of not being worthy. He'd bought my silence and my obedience to stay the hell away so he never had to set eyes on me again.

Tears prickled.

You're making this stuff up. Don't jump to conclusions.

It didn't stop pain lancing through me, remembering our kiss. Reliving the way his tongue touched mine, his taste in my mouth, his groan in my ears.

How could he kiss me as if I was utterly priceless and then fob me off with heartless cash?

He paid you for being a canvas! He didn't pay for the kiss, O.

How could I be so sure? How could I be sure he didn't give me far too much to ease his guilt over destroying everything?

I might be making up tales. I might be totally blowing things out of proportion, but Gil was the only one who made me irrational.

All I wanted was him. Yet he'd pushed me away, his money a firm goodbye.

Well, I had a good mind to give it all away.

To prove a point that I might be destitute and made a total mess of my life, but I wasn't a charity case and I couldn't be bought by a man who'd gone out of his way to confuse, ridicule, and condemn me.

I wanted to march back there and throw the money in his face.

I wanted to kiss that face and—

You can go back.

I stroked a fifty-pound note, a plan rapidly unfolding.

This was my reason to return.

This was my excuse to knock on his door, stare him right in the eye, and demand to know what the hell was going on.

But what if he doesn't ask me to leave next time?

What if he threw me out physically? What if he hurt me like he had when I'd pushed him too far at school?

Ripping my fingertips off the money, I couldn't be alone with my chaotic thoughts anymore.

Kisses and curses, hopes and fears.

I was hungry.

I was angry.

Today had been a cocktail of past and present, sex and shame.

I needed wine.

* * * * *

Sipping on my second mug of cheap supermarket pinot, I

winced as I logged onto the laptop that I'd hammered to death looking for work. Instead of going to familiar websites and trolling for employment, I clicked on the icon of my least favourite location.

Facebook.

Ever since my accident, I hardly went on there.

It was too painful.

I wasn't mentally ready to look at the photos of my fellow dancers, see their scheduled performances, read posts of friends complaining about early morning practices and late-night curtain calls.

Eventually, I would be happy for them.

But right now…it was a pitchfork to the heart.

Tonight, I managed to ignore my newsfeed and the urge to click on my dance troupe's page, and instead became a sleuth, stalking the Master of Trickery himself.

I sipped another mouthful as I typed in Gil's name, bracing myself for the search results.

Nothing came up.

Other Gilbert Clarks appeared—one in Scotland and a few overseas—but none that sounded, looked, or came close to the one I knew.

Strange but not really.

Gil had never been one for company.

Topping up my mug, I tried another angle.

Gil might not use Facebook personally, but I had no doubt he'd use it for business.

Total Trickery.

The second I pressed enter, his page popped up, complete with fifty thousand likes, hundreds of comments on his photos, and an overall gush fest on his talent.

For a while, I lost myself in the haze of colour and creation, studying the girls he'd painted, the animals he'd brought to life on their bodies, the landscapes he'd painstakingly used to camouflage human flesh.

Not one image was subpar.

And not one image showed it was Gil painting.

In each one, he kept his back to the camera, his black hoodie obscuring his face and messy hair, turning him nameless—a god of pigment and nothing more.

There was no mention of his biography, where he learned to paint, or his accolades or aspirations. He was as incognito online as he was in his photos; no hint he was the virtuoso that conjured such beauty.

There was also no photo of me from today.

Why?

I clicked on the little message icon, tensing as the bubble popped up to send him a note.

What the hell are you doing, O?

I honestly couldn't answer that.

The entire time I'd been in the supermarket, I'd flip-flopped over being so grateful for the fat wad of money in my purse and so annoyed at it. No matter what I did, I couldn't stop thinking about Gil.

Gil.

Gil.

I needed to talk to him.

I needed to be around him, to be near him, to look into his eyes and tear his secrets out one by one.

My fingers hovered on the keyboard. Opening sentences flew behind my eyes.

Gil, I miss you.

Gil, you paid me way too much.

Gil, what are you hiding?

I slouched.

An emotionless message would never work. He'd just ignore me, block, me, or never even see it. A conversation with him needed to be face to face, so he couldn't hide what he battled.

With another sip of wine, I left Gil's page and navigated to another man's profile.

A man I'd kissed in my youth after another broke my heart.

Justin Miller's Facebook was littered with after work drinks, pretty girls taking selfies with him, and a confident, friendly man who seemed successful.

I was happy for him.

Glad he hadn't messed up his dreams like I had.

With liquid courage and a flush of excess energy, I clicked on a new message bubble.

Gil consumed me.

I needed a distraction.

Olin Moss: *Hey, Justin. It was nice to see you at Gil's last night.*
I...

My fingers paused, searching for something appropriate. I hadn't planned to write. I had no script to follow.

Another sip of wine, and I added:

Olin Moss: *I wanted to thank you for standing up for me and encouraging Gil to use me as a canvas. He finished the design today. It was amazing to be part of his process.*

I chewed my cheek in worry.

What am I doing?

Justin probably didn't want to hear from me. There was a reason school friends drifted apart—especially exes.

I'd been mean to him in the end. Shattered beyond repair when Gil just vanished. I hadn't been able to keep up the pretend anymore—couldn't let Justin try to help me when I no longer wanted to be helped.

Dance had been the only thing that'd granted any peace.

I clicked on the icon to add to my text. To tell him how grateful I was for his help in the past. How stupid I'd been to turn that help away.

But a chime sounded, delivering his reply.

Justin Miller: *Hey, O! Great to hear from you. He wasn't too much of a brooding artist, I hope.*

I smiled.

Olin Moss: *No, he was perfectly professional.*

Justin Miller: *I'm glad. Do you have to go back tomorrow to finish?*

Olin Moss: *No. All done.*

And banished for life.

Justin Miller: *He pay you for your time? He has a bad habit of forgetting.*

My heart picked up its pace.

Olin Moss: *No, he paid me.*

In cash and kisses.

My thoughts returned to the thick envelope.

I shouldn't do it. I knew I shouldn't. But I couldn't stop my fingers typing:

Olin Moss: *Random question, but do you know the going rate for a living canvas?*

I liked torturing myself.

Liked justifying my crazy conclusions.

Liked chasing rabbits that had no right to make me worry.

Justin took a few minutes to reply.

Justin Miller: *Eh, I think it's about three to five hundred per commission. Why?*

I froze.

Oh, no...

I'd been right.

Gil had overpaid me.

Paid me triple.

Over triple.

Why?

Not only had Gil kissed me while trembling with things he couldn't survive, but he'd tarnished that kiss with money.

He'd ruined it.

Successfully hurt me all over again.

Will he ever stop?

I suddenly didn't want to talk after all.

I wanted to finish my wine and sleep. To run away from scars and body painters, money and heartbreak.

Olin Moss: *No reason. Hope you have a good night!*

Without waiting for his response, I closed Facebook in a rush.

I went to shut the laptop, but an email icon showed I had a reply from an office position I'd forgotten I'd applied to.

Some sterile building with its depressing cubicles and mind-numbing tasks. But at least a steady paycheque that meant I get to keep my clothes on and heart intact.

From: Static Enterprises
Subject: Interview for receptionist

Dear Ms Moss,

Thank you for your interest in our company and your resume. We are pleased to invite you to an interview tomorrow at three p.m. at our downtown location.

Please advise if this is convenient.

I didn't hesitate to reply.

A steady job.

A ticket out of bankruptcy.

Something to focus on so I didn't lose myself in the labyrinth that was Gilbert Clark.

If my interview went well and they offered me the job, I would visit Gil and give him his money back.

I'd look into his eyes and demand answers.

I would fight one final time for *us*.

Chapter Nine

Gil

-The Past-

"HEY." I SHOVED my hands deeper into my tattered jeans pockets and smiled, pretending I hadn't run here from home or stolen a bottle of deodorant to ensure I smelled semi-decent.

Olin jolted, one hand flying to her throat, the other clutching her messenger bag with white fingers. "Oh...hey." Her eyes switched from shock-wide to suspicious-narrow. "Where did you appear from?"

I smirked. "Somewhere."

She glanced over my shoulder at the mostly empty field behind me. Early bird students straggled in, but the majority of the school were still shoving toast and jam down their throats at home.

Tilting her head against the sun's glare, she said quietly, "You're early."

"So are you."

She shrugged, still not totally at ease with me even though we'd professed a mutual liking of each other last week. That corridor used to hold nasty memories. Now, it held the best one of my life.

A small smile tilted her lips. "I'm always early."

"I know." I realised my mistake too late.

"You do?" Her forehead furrowed.

Shit.

"Um..." I raked a hand through too-long hair. "I mean..."

Words flew out of my brain. Lies weren't possible. Truth was too hard. My heart crashed against my ribs in panic. "I've...watched you." I couldn't look at her. "I don't mean that in a stalkerish way. I mean...I've noticed you." I swallowed hard. "For a while."

Her pretty blush was back, pink and innocent. "You *noticed* me?"

I nodded, catching her stare. "You're the kindest person at school. I like watching you."

She blushed deeper. "I'm not kind."

"No one else carries Millie's bag to class because it's too heavy. No one else brings a newspaper from home for Mr. Scoot to read with his coffee in the staff room."

I waited for her to run away screaming. To file a restraining order. To tell me to stop being a creep watching her from the bushes.

Instead, she studied me in a way that stripped me bare, gave me no place to hide, and made me so grateful I'd been honest. "Is that why you liked watching me? Because I help where I can?"

I'd never had such intense conversations with anyone. Never been trapped wanting something so fucking much all while petrified of losing it. "Everyone needs help sometimes."

"Do you need help?" Her gaze dropped to my scruffy T-shirt and the patches on my jeans. She didn't sneer at my poverty. She didn't back away at my bad luck. She was the only student to look at me without any biased opinion or expect me to be violent just because I preferred my own company.

"In what way?" I did my best to keep my voice neutral and not echo with warning.

Out of anyone, Olin deserved to know who I was. But I wasn't ready to share. Not yet.

"You're very guarded, anyone ever tell you that?"

"I don't talk to other people."

"Just me."

"Just you."

We shared a smile, tension slipping away and leaving us on equal footing again.

"Life isn't just about survival, you know," she whispered softly.

I reared back. "I didn't say it was."

"I know." She chewed the inside of her cheek before

adding, "I just...I told you things I've never told anyone the other day. It made me feel so much better. Crazy really how sharing something I've been keeping inside suddenly didn't make me so sad." She shielded her eyes from the sun. "I guess all I'm saying is, I owe you."

"Don't *I* owe *you*?"

"No. You gave me a secret. You said you...um, liked me."

I looked away. "That doesn't really count."

"It does." Her smile turned softer. "Besides, I don't expect to know more unless you really want me to."

"Why did revealing your secret make you feel better?" I deflected the subject off me, striding toward the yawning entrance of our school, stupidly pleased when Olin kept pace.

The building with its red bricks was weathered and its glass smudged, but the institutional box with its no-nonsense architecture had a sense of sturdiness that said, for the hours of education, I was safe within its walls.

Tension from a sleepless night and a cuff around the back of my head at two a.m. this morning slid down my spine as the shadows of the foyer welcomed us back.

Tuesday.

A good day.

Four full days within a classroom where the mess of my world couldn't find me.

I sighed heavily, annoyed that my thoughts had darkened while Olin walked by my side. It wasn't fair to her goodness to be thinking of the cesspit I lived in.

Olin took her time answering, her face determined as if her answer was important. Which it was. Everything about her was important.

I wanted to ask every question and steal every answer. I wanted to know what her favourite drink was. What did she do after school? Did she have any hobbies? Did she have a dog or a goldfish? What did she think about late at night in bed?

I trembled with the need to skip past the awkwardness and find comfort in each other. I wasn't cut out for honesty and ripping scabs off emotional wounds. I was drawn to her because she was safe. Telling her who I was didn't feel safe.

It could ruin our friendship. And friendship with Olin had the power to be the most valuable thing in my life.

Entering our classroom, Olin finally said, "I think it made me feel better because it doesn't sound so bad out loud. Sure, I miss my parents. Sure, they're not home a lot and I'm an only child. And sure, compared to my friends who have mums and dads who cook for them and scold them for not doing their homework, I'm a little lonely. But…I'm also so much luckier than most."

My heart once again swelled for this incredible, forgiving girl.

"I have a house. A bed. Blankets. There's electricity for heating and TV. There's a kitchen to make pancakes. There's even space in the garden that's a perfect place to dance." She sighed happily. "So you see, I might not have everything, but I have so much too. So that's why I feel better. It made me focus on what I do have and not what I don't."

"That's why you help others…'cause you're grateful?"

"Isn't that why anyone helps? Because of empathy and the knowledge that someone out there has it way harder than you? Even on those bad days, we're still alive and—"

"It's not that simple." I walked away, tossing my bag beneath my desk. Kicking it farther into the shadows, I didn't want her to see the ketchup stains or rips. I'd pulled it from a dumpster behind a local fast food joint a few months ago because I had no money to buy one and my father would never dream of providing for me.

I supposed she was right.

I might not have much, but I had a bag. I had a bed to sleep in—when I wasn't being abused. I had school.

I have her.

My hackles dropped as I turned to face her.

"Life can be as simple or as complicated as we make it." Olin slipped her bag off her shoulder, letting it slouch onto the floor by her desk. "But I'll shut up now. I get the feeling you don't really want to talk about this."

I scowled. "What gave you that impression?"

She made no move to sit. The empty classroom echoed a little, the sterile walls and lack of decoration making it seem as if we didn't belong without a teacher present.

What would Ms Tallup say if she knew we were here alone?

I shuddered a little.

I loathed Ms Tallup. I loathed her as much as I feared her, and I had a healthy dose of fear. I'd lived through far worse people than a strict woman with a stick up her ass, but instinct was a powerful thing in my world.

And instinct told me to be careful of her.

"You're shutting down on me." Olin smiled gently.

"How can you tell?"

She laughed. "The clenched fists are a dead giveaway."

I looked down, deliberately spreading my fingers. "Oh...sorry."

"Don't be."

Awkwardness settled again. Silence thick and filled with nervous heartbeats.

The quietness grew too painful. I blurted, "If your parents are absentee, what do you do after school?" At the same time, she rushed, "You know, you smell like oranges."

We froze, letting our voices tangle together.

We smiled hesitantly.

We laughed softly.

The tension cracked and ebbed away.

I relaxed, tasting the ease that could be between us. What would that be like? To trust her above all others? To care for her? To protect her? To...love her?

I knew what connection was supposed to be like thanks to books and the occasional glimpse of TV, but I had nothing to compare it to in my own life. No role model to copy. No guidelines to follow.

All I had was the undying, unselfish desire to be whatever Olin needed, and it drove me mad that I didn't know what that was yet.

"The smell is my deodorant." I shrugged. "It's overpowering."

She leaned closer, inhaling deep.

My heart literally exploded.

Her eyes glowed. "I like it. Whenever I think of oranges, I'll think of you."

"You think of oranges often?"

"I will now." Her gaze dropped to the floor as another blush dusted her cheeks. "I mean...um, of course not. Who thinks of fruit? That's just weird." A strained chuckle fell from her lips.

Her reaction to innocent flirting made me tremble. Made me want to keep her.

I'd never kissed anyone.

I wanted her to be my first.

To taste those pretty lips and feel her delicate body against mine.

I swallowed hard as my heart thundered and body swelled.

I thought I could handle just being her friend until I made her mine, but I hadn't factored in the insane amount of affection I already had for her and the hunger that had been building for years.

I want you, O.

More than you can ever know.

Once again, silence squeezed between us, making everything so damn difficult.

What came next? What should I say that would be articulate, funny, and hide just how desperate I was to have her be mine?

"You know…" I squeezed the back of my neck. "Your name starts with O. Like oranges. Maybe I'll associate you with fruit too, and we can both think of each other when—" I cut myself off with a groan. "Forget I said that. Super cheesy."

She giggled; silence once again banished to the empty corners of the room. "You're not at all like I expected."

Our eyes locked. "What did you expect?"

"Oh, I dunno." She waved her hand. "Brooding, sarcastic…mean. You skulk into class and don't talk to anyone. You have a reputation for being dangerous."

"Dangerous?" I grinned, enjoying the fact that she'd been aware of me more than I realised. "Do *you* think I'm dangerous?"

She looked me up and down, raking heat along my skin with her stare. "Maybe. I don't know you yet."

"You know me better than anyone in this school."

"How is that possible? This is our second conversation."

"I'm selective."

"I heard you were a loner."

"That too."

"Why?" She cocked her head, sending dark blonde hair scattering over her baby blue top.

"Because I don't trust easy."

"Can you trust me?"

I pinned her to the spot with honesty. "I *already* trust you."

She frowned. "And what did I do to deserve such an honour?"

My heart fell and the simpleness of our conversation veered into tricky territory. Moving toward her slowly, I dared reach out and, with a slightly shaking hand, cupped her cheek.

The second I touched her, whatever remaining pieces of

myself that were still mine switched owners.

I was hers.

Totally.

Undoubtedly.

My mouth went dry as my heart crashed around my ribcage.

She froze. Her teeth sank into her bottom lip. Her eyes turned wide. "Um, Gil?"

I swallowed hard, unable to tear my gaze from her mouth.

I couldn't reply.

I put all my attention into not clutching her close and kissing her. My self-control almost snapped, my fingertips bruising her beautiful skin, but she didn't pull away.

She didn't believe the rumours to avoid the surly, argumentative bad boy.

She gave me the benefit of the doubt and that made me so damn grateful that she trusted me.

Trust.

You're mine, O.

You just don't know it yet.

My thumb traced her cheekbone. I stepped closer until we were inches apart. My voice was as heavy as my heart as I whispered, "Who said anything about it being an honour?"

She gasped as I pulled her into me, deleting the space between us. I didn't know what the hell I was doing, but I couldn't stop.

Her gaze travelled from my eyes to my lips to my jaw. And the raw desire on her pretty innocent face shadowed with dismay.

Swaying backward, she slipped from my touch.

I let my arm fall, jerking in surprise when she touched me in return.

I couldn't breathe as the softest fingers traced my jawline, dancing over stubble I couldn't quite shave, sending my pulse hammering in my ears.

I'd never been touched so kindly before. Never had blood gush around my body in such a frenzy.

"Olin...what—" I cleared my throat, cursing breathlessness and crazed heartbeats. "What are you doing?"

Leaning into me, she ran her finger by my ear, a frown replacing tentative desire. "You're hurt."

Her voice no longer hypnotised me but brought me back to reality with a painful crash. "What?"

She held up her hand, revealing a streak of blood between

her fingers. Her eyes widened with concern. "Oh, no. You're bleeding." She moved to come closer, to investigate the wound she should never have found.

I backed up instantly, rubbing at the streak of violence I hadn't seen.

So he *did* break the skin last night.

I'd felt the pain of his old class ring whack into my skull.

I'd swallowed stolen aspirin to dull the throb.

"Gil…are you okay?" Olin wiped the redness on her jeans, not caring it smeared on the denim. "Come here, I'll care for you. We'll go to first aid and—"

"I'm fine." My voice no longer held any teasing or tenderness. It was cold and sarcastic—the same tone I used with every student and teacher.

I refused to let her think I was weak.

That I couldn't protect her just because I couldn't protect myself.

I needed to leave.

"Don't worry about it." Not bothering to grab my backpack, I rushed from the classroom just as Ms Tallup arrived.

Chapter Ten

Olin

-The Present-

"THE JOB IS yours, Miss Moss. If you'd like to join our team, of course."

Sitting on the bus, travelling from downtown to the industrial area, I ran through the interview in my mind. The women's nasally voice repeated in my brain. *"The job is yours, Miss Moss. The job is yours."*

It was a good thing they'd offered employment.

A *great* thing.

However, I couldn't quite get excited, which made me feel like a terrible human being.

I'd accepted graciously, gratefully, and taken the contract to read overnight. They wanted me to start tomorrow. The salary was shockingly terrible, but the job didn't demand highly skilled people—merely desperate ones to answer the phones, troubleshoot the website, and be a general 'fetch-it girl'.

I had nothing against office culture or cubicles, but it didn't inspire me. It didn't make me use the gifts I'd been given…and lost. It didn't grant the right nutrition I needed for my damaged dancer's soul.

Ah, well.

I was lucky. Extremely so.

I had a job.

I had security.

And I was ten minutes away from seeing Gil one last time.

* * * * *

Nerves bubbled and popped as I approached Gil's

warehouse.

The graffiti with his business name reminded me of the artwork he'd shown me one night so many years ago. The closed roller door symbolic of his talent at shutting me out when I was so, so sure he'd felt just as strongly for me as I'd felt for him.

I'd been wrong then and made a spectacle of myself chasing after him.

I hope I'm not making the same mistake.

I hadn't slept much last night—our kiss on repeat in my brain. If I'd blown it into something more than what it was, then that was my fault. But if I remembered it correctly, then there had been *something* between us.

Something worth fighting overpayment, angry curses, and a closed off painter who could no longer stand the sight of me.

Approaching the building, I sucked in a breath and squared my shoulders. My office skirt and pale pink blouse seemed out of place when I'd stood naked only yesterday.

My modest heels clicked as I slowed to a stop outside the pedestrian access.

I hesitated.

Should I knock? Enter with no announcement?

Masculine voices sounded inside.

I narrowed my eyes against the animosity bleeding through the door.

Was Justin here? Were he and Gil fighting again?

I leaned closer, pressing my ear to the door. A curt command garbled, followed by the heavy thud of violence.

A grunt exploded, but no shout followed.

Gil.

Instincts roared into life, old habits of caring, annoying impulsions to fight for those in trouble.

Rapping my knuckles on the door, I tried the handle. "Hello?"

Locked.

Another curse. Another thud.

"Gil?!"

I backed up, looking for another way in. Hoisting my handbag higher, I spun on my heel, seeking anyone close by for assistance.

No people to enlist. All alone.

In front of me sat a dinged-up black van. A large scratch marred the glossy paint while a dent on the driver's door hinted the owner didn't care it wasn't pristine.

Justin drove a sedan, I was pretty sure, so who—

The clang of metal whipped my head around as the pedestrian door swung open then crashed shut, spitting a man from Gil's warehouse.

I froze.

It definitely wasn't Justin.

The man scowled at his knuckles, smearing a line of blood glistening on them. His scowl snaked into a smirk then a nasty chuckle. The blood vanished as he wiped the back of his hand on his jeans.

Not his blood.

My heart rate skyrocketed. Was this the man who'd hurt Gil last time? The reason for his cut lip and sore arm? And if so, why was he here and walking without injury? Gil wasn't exactly someone you could pick on and not earn a severe beating in return.

The man looked up as I inhaled sharply.

His face might've been considered handsome if he didn't have such a heartless sneer in his grey gaze. In his early fifties, his thin lips and square jaw weren't off-putting, but the brown, untended to hair hanging over his collar was. Just a mess of grease.

"Who the hell are you?" He watched me closely as if he'd stumbled onto something interesting.

Chills broke out over my arms. Chills that had nothing to do with the Birmingham weather and everything to do with the cold-hearted specimen in front of me.

My chin tilted regally. "I don't see how that's any of your business."

The guy chuckled. "You're in the middle of no-man's land, sweetheart. I'd just answer my question like a good girl." He grinned like a snake, stepping closer. "You lost? All alone?"

I ignored the way my kneecaps jumped, my legs tingling to run. "I'm not lost. I know my way around."

"Do you just?" He licked his lips, that damn smirk grating on my nerves. "Know your way around other things too, I bet."

I didn't stoop to his level to answer that.

I'd wasted enough time on this cretin. Moving toward Gil's warehouse, I paused as the guy muttered, "I wouldn't go in there if I were you." He laughed coldly. "Not unless you like seeing blood."

My insides turned to lead. "What did you do?"

"Nothing that wasn't deserved."

"Who are you?"

"A friend."

The longer I stood there, the louder my instincts became. They didn't just dapple me in worry, they hijacked my nervous system.

Something wasn't right.

Something wasn't safe.

Gil.

Skirting past him, I held my head high, estimating twenty steps before I could tumble into Gil's warehouse and be free.

But I'd made a mistake.

I should never have gotten so close.

He let me walk past, then a hand clamped over my shoulder from behind. All five fingers dug into my flesh with punishment that should never be used, especially on a complete stranger. "Not so fast, sweetheart."

I spun in his hold, whipping my arm up and breaking his hold on me. "Don't you *dare* touch me."

My speed shocked him; his fingernails left hot tracks on my flesh. Our eyes locked, hunter to victim. I glowered back with far more ferocity than I felt.

His face shadowed with rage before clearing with a slightly manic laugh. "You know...I like fighters. Always turn out to be the most fun."

I wanted to stand my ground, but I couldn't override adrenaline. Stumbling back, my handbag bashed against my side. "Just go away. Leave us alone."

"Us?" His eyes narrowed to slits, his gaze shooting from me to Gil's warehouse. "You two together?" Hazy sunlight highlighted his cheek, showing a silver scar running from his eye to the corner of his mouth. "Has that naughty boy been hiding you from me?"

I didn't know what he meant.

I didn't care.

Fumbling in my handbag, I searched for my cell phone. "Leave now or I'm calling the police."

He shook his head, still wrapped up in the idea that Gil had someone to stand beside him, that he wasn't so alone. Slowly, an evil conclusion soaked into his grey gaze. "He knows what's his is mine." Looking me up and down, he snapped, "Get in the van."

"Excuse me?"

"Get in the fucking van. Now."

"No way." I found my phone, ripping it out with quaking limbs. My thumb trembled as I unlocked the screen and tried to dial the emergency number.

He launched forward, reaching for it.

I held it out of his reach, only for it to tumble to the gravel thanks to my slippery fear.

"Stay away from me." I back-peddled out of his reach.

"Get in the van, sweetheart. Your pathetic body painter doesn't want visitors right now."

"How would you know?"

"I know him better than you think." His voice held the melodic rasp of an older person who should be wiser and kinder than most. If it wasn't for the malicious stare and dirty hair, he could've been the sweet neighbour or family friend.

My eyes flickered to his van, then back to his gaze. For a second, I wondered if this was a sick joke. Surely, this couldn't be real.

It was daylight.

It was England.

But the lack of humour and deadly seriousness of his intention made ice tumble down my spine. "I'm not going anywhere with you. Leave and I won't press charges."

He nodded as if I'd made a valid point. He laughed as if my point was utterly ridiculous. "See, that's where we have differences of opinion." His attention shot to the warehouse behind me, then slithered over my body. "If you're his, he knows better. You're coming with me. I won't ask again."

"Don't come near me."

He ignored my warning, prowling closer, assessing my escape routes.

I literally only had one option.

Run.

Run as fast as I could to Gil's and bang on his door and hope to God whatever this man had done to him left him conscious and in some capacity to help.

The long length of warehouses with its aura of downtrodden-ness and alleyways wouldn't save me at all.

Run!

Despite my injuries and surgeries, I was still strong. Strong and swift from all the years of dancing and discipline at not giving in.

I wasn't afraid of hurting someone if they hurt me. I'd never been a wilting flower. I was vicious if enemies tried to hurt me and mine.

But I also knew when to fight and when to flee.

I ran.

Gravel scattered beneath my heels as I turned and bolted.

My handbag swung against my side. I left my phone abandoned.

I pushed as much energy and speed into my legs as possible and chewed up distance. "Gil!"

Footsteps raced after me.

Slithering arms wrapped around me from behind, locking tight.

"Let go of me!"

His breath gushed harsh in my ear as he dragged me backward, despite my struggling. His hands were claws, his embrace a shackle, his strength far greater than mine.

"No!" I squirmed and stomped on his foot. "Gil!" My screech echoed off the warehouses, bouncing back to me unanswered.

His grunt was loud as he clutched me closer, kicking my legs out from under me and hauling me backward. His palm fumbled over my mouth, trying to silence me.

I raised my head to the sky, and screamed at the top of my lungs. *"Help!"*

"Quiet," he hissed in my ear, dragging me another foot.

I fought and scrabbled, scratching and clawing, but despite his age and slim build, his wiry strength bit into me like painful barbwire.

Gil's warehouse grew farther away as the van's shadow came closer.

If he got me into that van, it was all over.

My handbag swung uselessly down my arm, bumping heavily with resume folders, keys, and a large aluminium water bottle.

Throw it.

The command came from basic survival. I had no weapon. No hope. I had one chance.

Eyeing up the roller door, I caught my bag strap as it tumbled from my shoulder.

I didn't aim for my attacker.

I aimed for Gil's warehouse.

He tried to stop me—his arm whacked against mine and he kicked at my legs again.

But it was too late.

I let the bag loose. It sailed forward.

My heart plummeted as the bag arched and fell toward earth—without touching the door. Its spilled contents went flying, cartwheeling everywhere, the heavy water bottle was my saving grace.

It crashed against the door.

The loud *twang* as it bounced off the metal echoed around us.

Hope flared.

Triumph heated.

But my attacker merely pulled me harder. "You'll pay for that."

Sucking in a breath, I twisted sharply in his arms. He narrowed his eyes as our noses almost brushed. "I'm not going anywhere with you." Bracing myself for pain, I arched back and whacked his head with mine.

Agony blinded me with a mushroom cloud of torment. Red haze claimed every sense.

He stumbled back, still holding me. I stumbled with him, deaf and struggling from the pressure I'd struck him with.

I tried to slam my knee between his legs.

I was too woozy and missed the vitals.

A noise sounded behind me.

A noise from a wild animal provoked from its den.

Something bowled into both of us. A loud growl ripped through the blood pounding in my ears as Gil launched himself at the man, tackling me in the process.

We all tumbled to painful gravel, legs knotted, lungs empty of air, arms and hands grabbing anything they could.

A pair of strong arms ripped me from the attacker, tossing me to the side as the fight increased in violence.

Rolling to my knees, sucking in hungry breaths, I gasped as Gil managed to get the guy flat on his back in a matter of seconds. With an angry huff, he pinned his shoulders to the floor as easily as if the guy had been a mere pest and not a threat to my life.

He'd always been strong.

But this—the way his nostrils flared, and his teeth clenched with aggression—he was a demigod with unlimited power. He could kill him with a single squeeze.

My head pounded as my fists curled, wanting to hit the guy myself. Why wasn't Gil hurting him? Why was his temper so controlled?

The longest moment ticked by before Gil suddenly punched the gravel by the stranger's head, then leapt to his feet.

What the hell? He's letting him go?

Gil shook out his hand with a grimace, his anger hot and volatile, yet he didn't deliver his wrath on the guy who deserved it.

I scrambled to my feet, shaking away the rest of the stars. "Gil…wh-what are you doing?"

He held up his hand, silencing me with a snarl. "Shut up, Olin. Just shut up. This doesn't concern you."

The rage that'd been directed at the attempted kidnapper found a new target. I trembled with fire and ice. "*What* did you just say? This doesn't *concern* me?" I threw my hands up, blood trickling from my palms from grappling on gravel. "He just tried to *kidnap* me!"

The guy smirked, slowly climbing to his feet. He snickered under his breath as he kept his gaze on Gil's. "You didn't tell me you were with someone, *Gilbert.*"

Gil squeezed his eyes for a second, his jaw working as if he chewed tough meat. "I'm not. She's nobody. A mere inconvenience."

I wanted to curl around the explosion he caused in my chest.

"She said to leave *us* alone." The guy's eyes narrowed. "Us implies together."

"There is no us." Gil's hot, livid gaze found mine. "She's just a model who won't obey a simple instruction to stay the fuck *away* from me."

I stumbled backward.

What?

"You know I don't put up with liars," the guy muttered. "And I think you're lying."

Gil's hands curled by his sides, turning snowy white he clenched so hard. "There is no us. I promise you."

What the hell is going on?

"I also don't put up with arseholes who don't keep their side of the bargain." The guy cracked his knuckles. "You know that, don't you, Gilbert."

Gil chewed some more, his throat working as he swallowed back words that strangled him. His eyes flashed with soul-deep hatred, but he looked at the ground, his head bowing in submission. "I know."

What is *this?*

"Do you?" The guy rubbed his chin. "I'm not so sure you do."

"I know. Believe me, I know. You've ensured I know explicitly."

"Prove it." The guy raised his chin with challenge.

Gil turned on me, fury dripping from his trembling body and agony glowing on his face. "Leave, Olin. I told you I wasn't interested. I paid you for your time. What more do you fucking want from me, huh?"

"Leave? You want me to *leave?*" I shook my head, pointing at my belongings strewn on the ground. "I'm not leaving you, Gil. I'll grab my phone. We'll call the police and have this bastard arrested."

"There is no *we!*" Gil snarled like a wolf.

I flinched, backing up as his rage became a physical slap.

"Go. I'm done with this." Ripping his gaze from mine, he turned his attention to the guy. Gil was twice the man this wannabe kidnapper would ever be. His arms were double the size; his waist chiselled from granite compared.

With the two so close, it was laughable to think Gil couldn't kill his opponent with a single, well-placed punch.

But every threat and warning vanished from Gil's body. It no longer hummed with power. It hunched in humbleness.

The way he stood with such suffocation and submission brought tears to my eyes.

With a broad smile, spreading blood over white teeth, the kidnapper pulled back his arm, then slammed his fist with every ounce of strength into Gil's belly.

Gil groaned, but he didn't go to his knees. He didn't wrap arms around himself. He merely stood there and accepted the torture.

I couldn't stop myself.

Dashing in front of Gil, I pushed the guy away. "Don't touch him! Just go. *Leave!*" I glanced at his van, quickly memorising the number plate. The second he was gone, I'd call the police. He'd be tracked down and imprisoned so no one else had to deal with his level of crazy.

Gil tossed me to the side, forcibly removing my protection. "For fuck's sake, Olin." His eyes flashed, reminding me all over again of the nastiness he was capable of. "I told you to go! Don't make me hurt you."

You already did.

His face shadowed with agonising things.

The love he hid.

The hate he nursed.

I was lost.

Utterly, totally lost.

"Whatever is going on, Gil...walk away. Don't stand there while he punishes you. At the very least, fight back!"

His voice cracked with things I couldn't understand. "You don't know what you're talking about."

"I know enough to understand this isn't right."

Shoving me away—just like he had when we were younger—he bared his teeth. *"Go."*

His face was blank, pure ice.

No sign of salvation. No beg for help.

I spread my hands helplessly. "Gil...come with me."

He shook his head and, pushing me resolutely to the side, bared himself to the kidnapper.

With a savage smile, the man pounced on Gil as if they had a standing arrangement. Gil grunted as another blow landed.

I shouted, "Stop it!"

Neither man listened to me.

I tried to protect Gil, but I wasn't quick enough as another punch landed on his jaw. He didn't retaliate. Didn't flinch. He stood stoic and broken even as fresh blood trickled from his cheekbone. He kept his head high as the man spun and kicked him in the stomach.

This time, he did fall.

"Stop it!"

Slamming to one knee, he looked like a knight waiting for a sword to complete the sentence. But even on the ground before his attacker, he was undefeatable. He might not retaliate with violence, but his entire demeanour shouted invincible.

Why is he doing this?

Tears once again burned my eyes as the guy bent down and grabbed a fistful of Gil's unruly hair. "You have three days." He spoke with anger, spraying spit over Gil's face.

He flinched but didn't try to get free. "Three days." He nodded as if he'd struck a bargain written by the devil.

The guy let him go, wiping his hands on his jeans. "Don't fuck up, Gilbert. You know what happens if you do."

Gil shut his eyes as if the consequences were too much to bear. "I know."

The guy sniffed as if annoyed at Gil's obedience, swung another punch into his temple, and laughed as Gil crashed to the ground, unconscious.

Chapter Eleven

Olin

-The Present-

I RAN.

The second the guy stepped away, I bolted to Gil's unconscious form and fell to his side. "Don't you *dare* come near us again," I hissed, cradling Gil's head on my lap, my knees on fire from skidding on gravel, my heart a drum in every extremity.

The guy shook out his sore knuckles from punching the one person I'd do anything for. "There's that dangerous word again." He grinned. "Us."

"Fuck off," I spat.

I didn't care that he might try to kidnap me again. I didn't stop to think about my safety. All I cared about was helping the boy I'd always helped. Patching up his wounds and repairing his injuries. The boy who'd always helped me in return.

This was a role I was used to.

This was a man I would defend until the end.

"I'd be careful if I were you, sweetheart." The guy backed toward his vehicle. "Those associated with Gilbert always have a habit of getting hurt." Blowing me a kiss and looking at Gil with a sneer, he chuckled. "I'll be seeing ya."

Turning his back on both of us, he swaggered to his van, slammed the door, and drove off with a squeal of tyres, kicking up dust and a swirl of exhaust.

I didn't move until the van vanished at the bottom of the warehouse driveway, turning into traffic and leaving us alone.

Bastard.

My gaze dropped to Gil's slack, blood-smeared face. "Gil."
Brushing his messy, dark hair from his eyes, I expected a fierce command to stop touching him. A snap to leave. A grumpy slur asking why I'd disobeyed him. Again.

But he didn't move.

And that terrified me worse than any shout he could deliver.

I stroked his stubble-covered cheek. "Come on. He's gone. Let's get inside."

Still no response.

His body lay sprawled on the ground. One arm covered his chest while the other lay awkwardly beneath him.

"Gilbert..." I rocked his shoulder gently, looking up to see if anyone working in the neighbouring warehouses had seen and could offer aid.

At no point did I think about leaving. I could never in good conscious walk away from Gil even if he didn't want me in his life. Even if he'd told me in no uncertain terms to stay away.

I'd been the only one he'd trusted to nurse him.

That probably hadn't changed.

"Why did you let him beat you up for goodness' sake?" I brushed his arm away, exposing his throat, searching for a pulse. I struggled with unhappiness, not able to accept mindless violence or acts of stupidity.

And this was both.

Gil had been so *stupid* to allow such a thing. No reason on earth could justify letting someone beat you unconscious.

My thumb found his pulse, relief shooting through me.

"Why didn't you fight back, huh?" I whispered, running my finger over his bottom lip, checking he still breathed, not quite trusting the throb of blood in his veins. "Was he the one who hurt you the first day I came here?"

I knew my questions would remain unanswered but my voice seemed to soothe him.

The tension in his body faded. His chest rose and fell with a deeper breath.

"Are you in some sort of trouble, Gil?" I kneaded his shoulder, doing my best to wake him gently. "What are you involved in? Why are you so determined to make me hate you, all while I know you don't...not truly."

If I truly believed in the icy monster he did his best to portray, my heart wouldn't prod me to stay. It would accept the truth and move on. But Gil was hiding something. Something scary and secretive and the weight was too much for him to bear.

"Come on, time to wake up." I bent and brushed away a piece of gravel on his forehead. "Please, open your eyes."

He moaned under his breath.

My stomach knotted with heavier relief.

Once again, I felt that string. Knitting together, doing its best to tie its broken ends back together again.

As much as Gil would like to deny it, an unbreakable chain bound us.

It always had.

Ever since we'd stood in that school corridor and I'd told him the truth about my parents, I'd been tied to him.

He hadn't judged me.

He hadn't pitied me.

He'd just shrugged as if it didn't matter. Like I was strong enough to survive without them because he was now my friend.

He'd saved me then.

And he saved me now.

If he hadn't come out, I'd probably be gagged and trussed in the back of the van heading to who the hell knew where.

He'd rescued me reluctantly.

It was my turn to repay the favour and save him.

"I'll give you another minute." Placing his head carefully on the ground, I climbed to my feet and quickly gathered up my belongings scattered on the ground. Shoving them into my handbag, I used my phone to email myself the license plate of the van before my memory played tricks on me.

I didn't care what arrangement Gil had with him. That guy was a menace and deserved to rot in jail.

With the email sent, I slipped my phone into my bag, checked that the envelope with Gil's cash was still inside, and headed back toward him.

He didn't move as I ducked to my haunches and pressed shaking fingertips to his temple, running my fingers through his hair.

So soft.

So warm.

So real and familiar and alive.

I swallowed back another wash of untenable heartache. I missed touching him. I missed having that privilege.

My touch roused him enough for him to groan. Licking his lips and the blood staining them, he moaned as pain took over.

"Hey, I'm here. You're okay."

He pushed off from the ground, his forehead furrowed. I helped him into a sitting position, wedging my shoulder under his arm. "Come on. We need to get inside."

"Wh-what are you still doing…here?" he grunted, testing parts of his bruised body as he clambered to his feet. He tried not to put weight on me, but he swayed and shook his head, giving me a chance to wrap an arm around his waist.

He was solid and strong, and my heart skipped a beat.

His eyes narrowed once the vertigo left him. "Don't touch me, O. I told you to go."

"Yet I'm still here."

"A blatant disregard of my command."

"I'm helping you."

"I don't want your help. How many times do I need to tell you?"

"Too bad. You've got it." Tugging him in the direction of his warehouse, my temper steadily rose. My question wasn't so gentle this time. "What were you thinking, huh?"

He didn't reply, half trying to shove me away, half doing his best not to show he needed my support.

"You wouldn't understand." His legs were stable, even if his mind still swam with unbalance, and it didn't take long to step through the pedestrian access and close the door behind us.

"Try me. I might understand more than you think."

"I already know you can't." He winced, rubbing his belly where that arsehole's foot had connected.

The familiar warehouse welcomed me back as I walked its painting master over the large work area, unsure where to take him. "Do you have a bed here?"

"None of your business."

I shook him. "Answer me. The sooner I find you something soft to rest on, the sooner I can leave."

"As if that will ever happen."

I pinched his side. "Save your energy for healing, not answering back."

His eyebrows settled low over frustrated eyes. "I have a small apartment in the back." He pointed the way with a tilt of his head. "Through the office."

"See? Was that so hard?"

He huffed, dark and miserable. "Harder than you'll ever know." He looked away, not letting me catch his gaze.

My heart beat painfully as I held him tight, and we shuffled through his office together. Papers scattered the only desk. No chair. No filing cabinets. His method of records archaic.

Reaching the door to his apartment, he froze. His hand landed on my shoulder, pushing me resolutely away. "I'm not an invalid."

"You might fall."

"I won't."

I let go, even though it felt like needles of coldness without him close.

He swayed, catching himself against the wall. I gritted my teeth to prevent saying 'I told you so' as he wedged a palm into his temple, blinking back stars. We had a lot of messiness between us, we didn't need petty quips too.

"You'll feel better when you sit down." I followed him as he pushed off the wall and led me into a tiny lounge. My eyes skittered over the space. A TV that'd seen better days, a couch that looked recycled, and a kitchen that held no clutter or signs of being used.

The industrial tone of the warehouse flowed into his residential abode with harsh brick, exposed metal, and no-nonsense decorations.

The only thing brightening up the space was the back wall where two doors remained closed, bordered with graffiti I had no doubt Gilbert had done.

It had his signature all over it.

A vibrant wash of reds and greens, purples and blues. A tropical rainforest with palm trees, heliconias, and parrots flying in the fronds.

"Wow." I stopped, noticing where the spray paint ran a little to give the illusion of muggy humidity, where he'd feathered the colour to give parrot wings depth and flight.

My voice barely registered as I said, "You always were amazing with a can of spray paint."

He'd shown me some of his work when we were younger, proudly revealing his after-dark hobbies. He'd almost kissed me while pinning me against one. I'd almost offered him my virginity, all because I couldn't stand to be so in awe and so in love with him and not claim every inch of him for my own.

He muttered something under his breath, something harsh and cutting.

I was glad I didn't hear it as he inched toward the fake

leather couch with holes in its cushions and lay down. His eyes closed, his forehead furrowing with deep tracks.

My heart squeezed unbearably as I ghosted forward. "What can I do for you?"

His lips thinned as I stopped by his side. Keeping his eyes resolutely shut, he murmured, "Go home, Olin. I'm fine."

Ducking to my haunches, I laid a hand on his head, my fingers slinking through his hair. "Please…don't turn me away."

He turned to stone. His teeth sank into his bottom lip. His entire body vibrated as if he broke beneath my touch. A giant fissure through his chest. An earthquake in his soul. The couch creaked as he jerked his head away, trying to free himself from my touch.

I let my hand trail down, fingertips crying for more.

"Just lie there. I'll look after you." A phrase I'd uttered before. A phrase he knew I meant. No matter what'd happened between us, I would *always* look after him.

Gil didn't say a word as I moved around the small lounge and into the kitchen. Opening wooden cabinets, I searched for a glass. Instead, I found bare essentials. Only a couple of each item, mostly chipped and well-worn, a couple of plastic cups and bowls only suitable for children. Splodges of dried paint decorated them, signalling they weren't used as utensils but for means of holding pigment.

Sighing, I grabbed the least chipped glass and filled it with water. Taking it to Gil, I placed in on the low coffee table, shoving aside an unfinished sketch of a blue whale. "Where do you keep your painkillers, Gil?"

This time no argument or angry commands. His throat worked as he swallowed. "Medicine cabinet. In the bathroom."

I didn't ask for permission to enter a more personal part of his home just off the kitchen. I didn't need to second-guess why there were multiple boxes of different pain relief hidden behind the mirror above the pedestal sink.

I doubted the habit of having such drugs close by would stop anytime soon, especially seeing as he'd allowed that bastard to hurt him.

He'd done nothing to protect vitals. Nothing to prevent damage.

He could have internal bleeding from being kicked in the stomach or a concussion from being knocked out.

He should see a doctor.

But he won't.

Gil didn't have a fond relationship with doctors, thanks to his past. He said he didn't want his dad to be arrested for what he did to him, but I knew he didn't want to be taken away from me and put into foster care.

I hadn't wanted that either, but not a day went by that I didn't beg him to tell someone, reveal what sort of hellhole he lived in, so he was no longer used as a punching bag.

Grabbing a box, I sighed heavily. Gil wouldn't have managed most days at school without relying on popping a few pills. No matter his injuries, he'd only ever let me tend to him— no matter if they were far above my basic skills.

I had a terrible case of déjà vu.

Spinning to leave, I frowned as a whiff of synthetic strawberry shot up my nose. The sweet scent didn't match the masculine bareness of the bathroom with its grey linoleum and white tile walls.

Glancing into the shower, I scanned the bottles on the glass shelf. Nothing—just a block of cream-coloured soap.

No sign of strawberry anything.

Sniffing the air again, nothing sweet teased me.

Not wanting to snoop, I returned to the lounge and found Gil sitting upright with his phone in his hands. The back of his neck strained. The muscles of his back visible beneath his grey T-shirt.

With a heart-wrenching groan, he raked a hand through his hair, threw his phone to the floor, and rocked over the injuries in his stomach. He trembled as if he wanted to tear apart every piece of furniture all while he almost crumpled to his knees.

My heart tripped all over again—falling over an invisible obstacle, derailing my future all because I was still in love with a man who seemed totally destroyed.

With the lightest footsteps, I padded closer and sat beside him. My hand landed gently on his thigh.

He reared back, his head soaring up, his eyes flipping open. For a second, I worried he'd strike me. I braced myself for something horrible.

But he leashed himself, his eyes bleeding pain. His voice cracked with rage and confusion. "I'm running out of strength, O." His head bowed. His heavy palm landed over mine and squeezed.

As quickly as he'd touched me, he plucked my hand from

his thigh and placed it onto mine with a firm rebuff. He shuddered, inching away from me with a faint, agony-filled hiss. "You can't be here."

I didn't ask why. I didn't offer to be his strength. That wasn't how our friendship worked. I merely offered a place of sanctuary. No questions. No demands. Because I'd learned as a young girl that Gil didn't need someone to tell him what to do. He just needed someone who cared.

Sniffing back years' worth of emotion, I said, "No matter what's happened, I care about you. I'm staying until you're not so in pain."

He groaned with torment, too exhausted to answer back.

Cracking open the painkillers, I popped three for him and two for me. My head hurt from being used as a weapon against that madman. "Here."

His gaze tracked to my upturned palm. "We're not kids anymore. I don't need you to play nursemaid."

I didn't reply, reaching for the glass I'd filled for him and stealing a mouthful to swallow my own pain relief.

Comprehension darkened his face. "Did that fucking bastard hurt you?"

"I'm okay."

His large hands landed on my shoulders, spinning me to face him. "Olin."

His eyes trapped mine and he could no longer hide the truth. His amazing, incredible heart that held galaxies worth of love, despite his upbringing. His kindness, his concern, his—

Shutters slammed down, blocking me from seeing anymore. His fingers spasmed on my shoulders before tearing away as if I was made of flame and I'd just scorched him to his very core. "Goddammit."

Pretending my lips weren't on fire to kiss him and doing my best to hide my sudden trembles, I held out the pills for him again. "Take these."

He stared at them as if he didn't know what they were and he was no longer human. His thoughts trapped within whatever prison he'd wrapped himself in.

I waited. I stayed.

Finally, he reached out and flinched as our skin kissed, his fingers on my palm, taking the offered painkillers. With a tight jaw and tighter muscles, he tossed them into his mouth and reached for the glass.

His throat worked fast, gulping back the liquid before slamming the glass down and standing. "Thank you. I'll walk you out."

I stood too, feeling far too small and weak on the couch with him towering over me. I sucked in a breath, ready to fight for what I wanted. "I won't ask what happened out there, not again. But I am going to ask if you're in trouble."

His eyes narrowed. "The only trouble I'm in is because you refuse to obey me."

"Is it because he thinks we're together?"

He flinched. "No."

That was a yes.

"Are you with someone else? Does he think he can beat you up because you're betraying—"

"No." He raked a hand through his hair. "This has nothing to do with you and everything to do with me." His head bowed. "I just need you to go. I need you to go and never come back."

"Come with me. We'll go to my apartment and I'll—"

"Olin." His snap glued my lips together, embarrassed heat glowed in my heart. "Our past means nothing, okay? Walk away."

"How can I when I know something isn't right?"

"Because I don't want you here."

Rejection prickled along my spine and over my scalp. "You never used to enjoy hurting me, Gil. Now, you're an expert at it."

The blackest shadow swallowed his features, as if he'd been sucked into another dimension where only horrors lived, seeing things I couldn't, surviving things I feared.

He balled his hands, fury unfurling. "Maybe you're having trouble remembering our past correctly. Fine, I'll help with your memory, seeing as you think I've lost my manners."

Winter well and truly welcomed him back, his voice pure frost. "I was a master at hurting you. I hurt you all the goddamn time. I made you fall in love with me, only to dump you in that classroom. I made you believe we had a future, only to walk away without a goodbye."

The frost melted, his voice sounding strange, strangled. With a remorseful glare, he forced relentless malice into the tone. "I didn't want you then, and I don't want you now. You're embarrassing yourself, Olin. Chasing after a man who has no intention of ever being with you again."

A tear escaped my control, rolling over my eyelash and

gliding down my cheek. "Thank you for reminding me, Gil, of your perfect indifference toward me." I arched my chin, hugging myself. "But allow me to do the same. For years, I told myself the same thing. I went over and over what happened between us because there were no signs that you hated me until that day. No hints that I annoyed you. No instincts that you were only toying with my heart. You're right though, I *am* embarrassing myself. I'm doing exactly what I promised I'd never do if we ever saw each other again. I'm making a fool out of myself trying to make you remember just how perfect we were for each other."

Swiping at another lonely tear, I shivered with anger as well as grief. "But it wasn't me who ruined it this time, Gil. I would've stayed away after you'd painted me, resigned to losing you seven years ago and strong enough to move on with my life, seeing as you made it abundantly clear you'd moved on with yours. But, here's the thing…" I moved toward him, standing on my tiptoes so we were almost eye-to-eye. "Then you went and kissed me and the lies fell apart."

He sucked in a haggard breath. "That kiss meant nothing."

"That kiss meant *everything*."

"Get away from me."

Electricity crackled. Chemistry hissed.

"Why did you pay me triple the amount you normally pay canvases?"

"*What?*" He bared his teeth. "I don't know what—"

"You kissed me and paid me far too much money." My gaze locked onto his mouth. "Why?"

"You're driving me insane."

"Answer me."

His eyes flashed emerald. "Leave." His nose brushed mine as he bent, forcing the command into my lungs.

I snapped.

My arms swooped up, wrapping like vines around his neck. I yanked him into me, uncaring of his injuries.

He grunted as my lips slammed onto his.

I kissed him as hotly and as fiercely as he'd kissed me. I let him taste the difference between desire and lies. I let him sample my heart all over again.

He broke his tightly reined leash.

His fingers dove into my hair, tangling and knotting, jerking my head back to plunge his tongue past my teeth.

My legs buckled, but it didn't matter. He scooped me into

his arms, squeezing me against him, plastering us together as if he could never bear to be apart.

A savage snarl echoed in his mouth as he kissed me so, *so* hard.

I forgot about my headache, about this afternoon, about him leaving, vanishing, our jilted love story.

I kissed him with apologies and promises. I opened wide and gave him everything.

And he took.

Ruthlessly and with no finesse, he kissed me as if we were teenagers again, possessed by hormones, in love with the idea of forever.

His head tilted, kissing my mouth, my jaw, back to my mouth. His tongue was a spear, conquering inside me—forcing me to yield to his complicated desire.

I gave in. I wanted him to—

"Fuck!" He roared like a beast, ripping himself away.

I tripped at the sudden emptiness of my arms, wincing at the licking lust that'd turned into a snake inside my belly, devouring every butterfly, sinking venomous fangs into every hope.

He stumbled away as if he had to put distance between us in case he did something unforgivable.

Touching burning lips, I was breathless around tattered heartbeats. "Gil."

He didn't reply, tripping his way into the kitchen and gripping the countertop with both hands. White knuckles and braced legs, his head hung between his shoulders as if bowing at the feet of whatever demon who'd trapped him.

I wanted to go to him.

I wanted to hug him, help him, heal him, but...that kiss had ripped out my insides. I was seconds away from bursting into tears. I was lost and hurting, and if I touched him now, I didn't know what would happen.

Didn't know if we'd find our way back together or if I'd break everything.

I didn't want to take that chance.

I wasn't *brave* enough to take that chance.

With tears blinding me, I bolted from his lounge, through his office, and into the warehouse. With jerky steps, I fast-tracked to my handbag, grabbed my phone and winced as the envelope of cash cut my finger.

He'd looked horrified that I'd figured out he'd paid me too much. Guilty for paying me for a kiss.

Well, I'd stolen a kiss this time.

We were even.

Placing the envelope on the painting table where his air compressor and paint vials lived, I looked over my shoulder.

Part of me begged him to chase after me. To have vindication that this blinding connection was real. But as my heartbeats grew wilder instead of calm, and my body shook from everything that'd happened, Gil didn't appear.

He didn't chase.

He let me run.

He wanted me to leave.

I'll come back.

I nodded to my promise.

I'll come back…when I'm strong enough.

When I had the power to break Gil into admitting the truth. When I had the courage to ask him to keep me.

I had nothing.

I had no dance. No family. No friends.

Once upon a time, I'd had Gil.

And I would fight with everything I had to have him again.

Keep him safe.

With shallow breaths, I slung my handbag onto my shoulder and unlocked my phone.

Keep that bastard away from him.

Dialling the police, I hadn't gotten two steps before the line connected with a brusque female, "What's your emergency?"

Protect him.

"Hi, um, I'd like to report an attempted kidnapping?"

The operator tapped something in the background. "Time the incident occurred?"

"About an hour ago. Outside *Total Trickery*—a warehouse down in the industrial area in Birmingham. He…he attempted to drag me into a van."

Help him.

"Okay, we're sending officers right away."

"Oh, no need. He's gone. I was able to escape."

"Do you have a description? A license plate number?"

Heal him.

"Yes." Opening the pedestrian door to leave, I recited. "I got his plate. It's XT8—"

Something slammed me into the metal roller.
My phone tumbled from my hand.
I slipped quick and deep into darkness.

Chapter Twelve

Gil

-The Past-

"YOU DON'T HAVE to walk me home every day, you know." Olin flicked me a smile.

A smile that held a few months of history. A smile that said we were friends based on time and not just want.

"I know." I hoisted her bag higher along with mine, carrying both like a gentleman should. I wasn't a gentleman. But I went out of my way so she never figured that out.

"It's on the opposite side of town where you live."

I stilled. "How do you know where I live?" Ever since the incident with the blood a few months ago, I'd been careful to keep everything about my home life a mystery. I liked Olin too much to let her know I wasn't a straightforward kid like the others in our class. I liked that she liked me for *me*. I liked that there was no pity in her eyes. No sorrow. No charity.

"I don't." She sighed, used to me withdrawing on topics of my health and home. "But I'm not blind and I'm not stupid, Gil." Coming toward me, she slipped her hand into mine.

Just like the first time she'd done that, I jumped and sucked in a breath, not used to such kindness from touch. Not prepared for the feral need to demand more.

Having Olin touch me soothed something broken inside me, but it also condemned me to more pain imaginable.

Schooling the churning confusion in my belly, I squeezed her fingers with propriety.

We walked for a time, strolling through quaint

neighbourhoods and beneath manicured trees before she murmured, "I know you don't have it easy, Gil. I wasn't going to ask but…" She tugged me to a stop on the curb of some pretty white house with its pretty white fence. "I'm worried about you. Who hurts you? Your dad? Your mum? You know you don't have to put up with it, right? We can tell someone. Get you help."

I yanked my hand from hers, stalking forward with two bags banging against my rigid frame. "It's late. Your parents will be wondering where you are."

She laughed sadly, trotting to keep up with me. "You know they don't wonder. They're in Italy again this week."

I kept my gaze locked on the horizon. In the few months I'd been walking Olin home from school, I hadn't once met her parents.

She hadn't been lying about living alone.

"Just leave it, Olin."

We didn't speak again until I opened the small iron gate and marched up the path to her front door. Her home would've been the postcard for any perfect family if it hadn't been as tainted as my hovel on the other side of town. Mine gave no illusions about being destitute in both love and kindness, but Olin's lied with its silver sashes and white render.

It said a daughter lived here with parents who made her healthy dinners and helped her with her homework. It convinced its neighbours that the rooms were full of laughter not loneliness.

My heart hardened, hating her parents more each day as Olin danced to my side and slipped her key into the lock. Slipping her bag off my shoulder, I held it out to her. "See you at school tomorrow."

She turned in the foyer, ignoring the side table with its fake orchids and the plush cream carpet on the staircase leading to bedrooms above. She only had eyes for me as she took her bag, threw it against the coat rack, then grabbed my wrist and yanked me inside.

She knew the rules.

I walked her home.

I left her the moment she was safe.

I hadn't stepped foot into her house.

I didn't belong there.

"Olin, stop."

"Come in, Gil. It's not going to kill you." Fighting against my reluctance, she leaned into her invitation, dragging me forcibly into the living room complete with sectional couches, a large flat screen, and white sparkly kitchen.

It couldn't be more different to the place I lived in if it tried.

My skin crawled to leave. To hide all the bad pieces of me that Olin didn't know about. I wanted her to continue not knowing, despite wanting to tell her everything.

"I'm hungry." She jerked me toward the kitchen, grabbed my dirty backpack and tossed it onto a barstool, then pressed my shoulders for me to sit in a matching one. "You're going to sit there and entertain me while I cook us something. Okay?"

My jaw worked as I fought against her push, eyeing up the front door. "I shouldn't be here."

"You should. You are." Her gaze softened. "Please, Gil. Stay…for me?"

I groaned, slouching on the stool. "That's warfare."

"War? You want a war between us?" Her fingers latched onto my shoulders.

"No. I said asking me to stay that way. It's not fair."

Playfulness entered her voice as she fluttered dark eyelashes. "Oh, have I finally found a weakness? If I say please, does that mean I get to command *you* for a change?" She laughed, her hands sliding from my shoulders to cup my cheeks.

"I don't command you." I gulped as the heat of her fingers made my heart pound.

"Oh, yes, you do." She leaned in and brushed her nose with mine. "But I'm not complaining."

Everything froze.

Our lips were so close.

Our hearts so fast.

All I wanted to do was drag her onto my lap and kiss her. I'd wanted so fucking long to kiss her.

And that was why I didn't trust myself in her house.

Standing quickly, I shoved her back.

Hurt flashed in her gaze, but she recovered quickly. "I'm making pancakes, and you're not going anywhere." Her voice was confident, but it lacked bravery to force me to obey. I could walk out the door, and she would forgive me tomorrow.

But the thing was…*I* wouldn't forgive me because how could I ever walk out on this girl? How could I ever tell her just how much I liked her, wanted her, craved her?

Sighing, I raked a hand over my face and begged my body to

stop driving me crazy. Olin wasn't just someone I wanted to sleep with. She was the future I would do anything to claim.

And that meant I couldn't have her until I knew I had her heart.

Which was a terribly selfish thing to do because until I knew she was in love with me she would know nothing about me. Because once she knew…she wouldn't want a future with me.

Who would?

I had no money, no security. I didn't even have absentee parents. I had abuse and drug use and the mixed bloodlines of whores and thieves.

Olin had to love me for me…only then could I be free.

I sat back down.

As my thoughts raced, Olin danced around the kitchen. I would never grow tired of watching her move. Even when she reached for a pen in class or skirted around students in the hall, she danced.

She couldn't stop it.

Dance was in every droplet of her blood. Every limb elegant, every motion flawless.

I'd sneaked into the ballet recital a few weeks ago to watch her perform. She didn't know I'd been there, and I couldn't tear my eyes off her. I'd always found Olin beautiful, inside and out, but seeing her on that stage? Witnessing how a girl could become light as a feather and perfect as swirling snowflakes, I lost the final barricades around my heart.

I was in love with her because she was pure grace.

She had a way of hypnotising me, calming my dismal thoughts, and anchoring me firmly in the moment. She was so fucking good for me. A medicine I needed to take for the rest of my life. She had no idea the power she held over me just by being her.

I feared the day when she learned how deep I'd fallen.

Would she fall with me…or would she pirouette into a future I wasn't permitted to join?

Companionable silence fell as she pulled ingredients from the pantry. Her feet glided, her head swayed to an unheard beat, her wrists and fingers twitched and arched like delicate swans.

My heart pounded with affection, lust, and a terrifying amount of awe as she cracked eggs, beat batter, and spooned indulgent sized pancakes into a sizzling pan.

She put on a performance just for me.

The second the sweet scents of dessert met my nose, my mouth watered profusely.

It was embarrassing how my body reacted around food.

I was used to the gnawing emptiness in my belly, followed by the over fullness of stuffing my face once a day.

I'd eaten a few hours ago. I was used to not eating again until tomorrow, but what Olin created was fluffy maple syrup magic, and I swallowed thickly as she placed a plate with two round discs covered in icing sugar and dripping in syrup before me.

Her eyes lingered on me as she nudged a knife and fork in my direction.

I did my best not to snatch them like a rabid animal.

All I wanted to do was devour the food she'd cooked for me. The first meal *anyone* had ever cooked for me. But I forced myself to keep my hands locked on my lap, smile stiffly, and ignore the plate. I did my best to be like the other boys, nonchalant and lazy, as if being fed by the girl I wanted more than anyone wasn't a big deal.

It's a big fucking deal.

"You're like a leaf." I looked up, cursing the long hair catching on my eyelashes. "When you move, you look like a leaf caught in a breeze."

She sucked in a gasp.

Our eyes snagged and held. Something endlessly painful sucker-punched me in the chest. An emotion that bypassed teenage flirting and went straight into forever claiming.

I scrambled to delete the sudden awkwardness. "I just meant, watching you cook was the highlight of my day. You're so pretty."

She beamed; the pretty blush that always appeared around me turned her cheeks rosy. "You like watching me?"

I laughed darkly. "You know I do."

I'd told her that. Plus, she'd caught me gawking at her more than once. My fascination with her was obvious.

Her eyelashes fluttered. "Why do you like watching me?"

It was my turn to blush. "Eh, no reason."

"No reason?" She pouted adorably. "Come on, there *must* be a reason." Her lips turned up as her eyes sparkled. "How about I go first?"

My muscles seized. "Y-you watch *me?*"

Shit, what had she seen? How bad had I been?

She bit her bottom lip, nodding. "All the time. I can't stop looking at you."

Fear crawled down my spine. "If you've watched me, why are you still here? Why haven't you run away screaming yet?"

Her face fell. "You act as if I won't want to be your friend the more I get to know you."

"You won't."

She sighed softly. "You're wrong, you know. That can't ever happen."

I looked at my plate, unable to hold her stare. I daren't indulge in the quick kick of hope in my heart. Could she feel a tenth of what I did? Could I keep her, regardless of who I was?

More batter sizzled in the pan as Olin murmured, "You can't scare me away, you know. I see more than you think. I like watching you, Gilbert Clark, because everything you do is assessed, deliberated, and completed with utmost dedication. You don't waste energy on things that aren't important. You're precise and concentrate harder than anyone I know. And if I'm honest, you're kind of scary with how focused you are when you put your mind to it."

"I scare you?" My heart no longer nursed hope but hurt.

"Not anymore. Not now I know you." She looked at me pointedly. "The more I get to know you, the more I like you, so you might as well get used to having me around."

"I *love* having you around." I froze.

Shit.

She smiled. "I'm glad."

Our eyes locked again, and goosebumps shot beneath my clothes. I wanted to go to her. To ask if she liked me enough to kiss me. But I lived with whores. Kisses weren't given willingly most of the time. And I would never, *ever* take something from Olin that she didn't want me to have.

Olin looked away first, her voice wobbling a little. "Anyway, tuck in." She flipped the pancake, expertly landing it in the centre of the pan. A skill that said she'd cooked far more than other kids, from necessity not because of hobbies. "Eat while it's hot."

"I'll wait for you."

"Don't." Her gaze met mine again, this time not with naked vulnerability but concern and far too much knowing. She knew what food meant to me. She knew more about me than I'd told her because that was who she was, empathetic and intelligent, putting pieces together to make a whole.

I shifted uncomfortably on the stool, wishing I was better for her.

"Please, Gil…eat. I know…I know you don't get many meals."

The sugary smell suddenly made me feel sick. "I'm not hungry." I didn't know why pride raised its ugly head. Why it made me so short-tempered.

It made me all too aware of how little I had to offer her. Maybe her friendship was charity, after all? She'd do that. She'd be nice enough to hang out with me if she thought I was lonely.

Bullshit. She likes you, Clark. You just have to man up and accept that, instead of looking for ways to sabotage it.

Flipping the pancake one last time, she turned the element off, then selected a plate for herself. Her motions were smooth and dancing-sensual, but her face shadowed with worry.

Bringing her own snack to sit beside me at the breakfast bar, she cut into the fluffy circle and placed a small bit on her tongue.

She chewed for a moment before turning to face me.

I wanted to run. I wanted to tell her she didn't know me when she obviously did. I needed the pity in her eyes to go away.

Icing sugar dusted her bottom lip as she hesitantly reached across and placed her hand on my thigh.

I stiffened.

My blood heated.

My body hardened.

I squeezed my eyes and fought back a tattered groan.

She didn't speak for the longest moment. A moment where I struggled not to grab her. A moment where I lived in a fantasy of carrying her upstairs, finding the closest bed, and learning how sweet her tongue was after eating delicious pancakes.

"I know you might hate me for saying this…but I know, Gil."

I kept my eyes closed, unable to meet her stare.

Her fingers dug deeper into my thigh. "I know you're beaten at home. I know you don't eat much. I know you don't like leaving school. I know—"

My hand landed over hers, squeezing the delicate bones of her fingers. "Stop."

"I can't," she whispered. "I can't because if I do, I don't know if you'll come back. And I really, *really* want you to come back." She didn't complain as my hand crushed hers. She just continued in her melodic, perfect voice. "You said the first day we talked in the corridor that telling a secret makes us friends. I told you mine, and you've become so important to me these past few months. Do you….perhaps…want to share another one with me?"

I struggled to open my eyes and look at her. My heart flew like a wounded bird, crashing against my ribs, breaking a wing, desperate for help but terrified of it at the same time.

I diverted her attention away from my secrets. "Why…why am I important to you?"

She smiled shyly. "Many reasons."

"Because I walk you home from school?"

"One of them."

"What are the others?"

With her voice soft, she answered, "You're important because you look after me even when you don't think you are. You carry my bag, you sharpen my pencil, you give me cookies from the canteen, you make up silly nicknames for me."

I scowled. "The nicknames are a stupid idea."

"Don't you dare stop, they're the best!" Her eyes glittered. "You make my days better just knowing you're waiting for me to start class together."

I forced myself not to react, even though she'd just given me every gift I ever wanted. "That's why you like me? Because you don't feel so alone? Any boy could do that."

She slipped off her barstool and pressed herself against me. "Any boy isn't you." Her head fell on my shoulder. "I have friends. I have company. But…none of them fills up the holes inside me like you do. It's like…I only need you. And that's terrifying because I know you hide so much, and I don't know if you'll decide that one day—"

"Stop."

"But you'd tell me, right? If I pried too much or annoyed you enough to push you—"

"*Olin.*" My voice was fierce. "Enough."

"I like you, Gilbert, not because of what you do for me, but because of the secrets you refuse to share. You think they'll change how I care about you." She pressed a fleeting kiss on my cheek. "You couldn't be more wrong."

I clenched every muscle I possessed so I didn't clutch her close and kiss her back. Kiss her mouth this time. Kiss her until I couldn't stop.

With my eyes closed, I asked quietly. "You like me?"

"So much."

"How do you like me?" I opened my eyes, forcing a smile and repeating what she said to me that first day we talked. "Do you *like* me like me or just—"

"I *like* you like you." Her gaze fell to my lips. "I want to like you forever."

I froze, even as my heart went wild. "Forever is a long time."

"It's not long enough."

I fell deeper into her gaze, feeling the tug to spill everything. Drowning beneath the need to have her know me. Truly, *truly* know me. To accept me. To no longer fear she'd leave me when she found out everything. To take away her fear that I would ever leave her in return.

Because that would never happen.

Ever.

I would slit my own wrists if I ever thought of abandoning her.

Then you'd leave her in death, you moron.

Okay, I would just have to find a way to be immortal, so Olin would forever be mine.

My hand shook as I reached out and cupped her cheek. She gasped as I ran my thumb over her cheekbone. "Friends isn't enough anymore."

Her tongue licked at the icing sugar on her bottom lip. "What does that mean?"

Twisting on the stool, I dropped my hands to her hips and positioned her between my legs. The softness of her blue pinstripe dress that was the school's summer uniform warmed beneath my touch. I checked my self-control was in full affect, hoping she didn't look down because I couldn't hide my reaction to her. Couldn't pretend I escorted her home because I was a gentleman who kept her safe.

I was the boy who wanted to tear off her clothes and have her beg my name.

I was my father's son and my father liked his women subservient, submissive, with only money forming a foundation between them.

I was afraid that that was me. That I would fight to deserve Olin only to do something unforgivable.

That was a secret I would never be able to tell her, but it helped make my other one not so dangerous. So what I came from a bad beginning? It didn't define me. I had no intention of making Olin live such a life.

"It means that I want you to know who I am, so you can decide if you want me." I sucked in a thin breath. "I live in a whore house. My father is an alcoholic and a pimp. I don't know which of his whores is my mother. She's probably dead from overdosing. My room is next to a whore's whose clients make it impossible to sleep. There's never any food in the house. My father hates me and loves to prove it."

There was only one other person who might've guessed what I survived at night and that was Ms Tallup. And that was only because I'd bled over my homework more than once and she'd sent me to the principal with the threat of Child Protective Services taking me away.

It was probably why I hated and feared her.

As long as I played nice and hid my frequent injuries, I was permitted to stay in her class. If I didn't, I would be removed from school, from hope...from Olin.

Before Olin could speak, I rushed, "I'm not telling you this to make you pity me. I'm telling you this because you guessed, and I don't want to discuss it again. It is what it is, but it won't be for too much longer. I'm gonna graduate, get a good job, and have my own place soon. We'll be together on our own terms and none of that shit will matter."

My tone softened as she stared at me. "And then...when I have my own place, I'll have you round every day. And every night. In fact, we might as well live together because I'll never want you to leave."

She sucked in a breath. "*Live* together?"

I smirked. "Might as well. Isn't that what families do?"

"You want to be my family?" She gasped adorably.

"Family have each other's backs. They're there for each other no matter what." I brushed aside her hair, caressing her ear. "I want to be there for you, and you're already there for me. That makes us family. More so than the ones we have right now."

"I-I...guess." She blushed as I ran my thumb along her jaw.

"It's settled then." I dropped my hand and captured her hip again, holding her tight between my legs. "After school, we'll be together."

"And during school?" Her voice was achingly timid. "What about now?"

Pulling her forward and caging her with my body, I

murmured, "We *are* together."

"Are we?" She blushed again, a tease glowing in her gaze. "I mean…you've never tried to kiss me."

I narrowed my eyes, allowing flirtation to fade in favour of seriousness. "A kiss isn't something I can take back. Once I kiss you, you're mine."

She shuddered. "Well, you might as well get it over with because—"

"Not yet." I rose and kissed her forehead, inhaling her scent of orchids and talc. "Soon."

"You don't have to wait. I don't care about your background. Nothing about you could turn me off, Gil."

I sighed as my ribcage tightened. "I'm sure there are some things."

Her eyes searched mine nervously. "Don't ever doubt us, okay?"

Her concern was one of the things I loved about her. She literally held my heart in her dainty dancer hands. She had more power over me than Ms Tallup or my father. I would do anything for her and it was getting harder and harder not to tell her.

But until I felt worthy of telling her that I belonged to her, I would wait.

Because the promise of *us* was far too precious to rush.

"I'll never doubt us, little orangutan." I tickled her, deliberately erasing the intense connection and welcoming light-hearted ease.

"Ugh." Her nose wrinkled, a laugh tumbling from her lips. "I think I prefer octopus over being called a monkey."

I pushed her away, closing my legs and facing the first meal anyone had ever made for me. The pancakes were more than just pancakes. Eating them was basically marriage in my eyes. I was saying I do to a question she hadn't even asked.

My hands shook as I grabbed the knife and fork. "That's just made me determined to find more monkeys that start with O."

"You wouldn't." She sat back down on her barstool; her cheeks happily flushed.

Slicing into a pancake, I didn't reply until I'd placed the delicious, home-cooked meal onto my tongue and savoured it.

Sweet like O.

Soft like O.

Perfect like O.

Taking another bite, I mumbled, "And you said you knew me."

I'd meant it as a joke, but for some reason, Olin froze. She didn't say anything for the longest time, giving me far too much space to worry in. "You're right. I *do* know you. I like you, Gil. I like you regardless of the people we were born to. You're stuck with me now. The annoying meddling new family."

I longed to press a kiss directly on the lips she bit in nervousness. I wanted to give her the same pleasure she'd just given me by being so damn sweet. But I couldn't move because if I did, I wouldn't be able to stop.

My voice lowered. "That's probably the worst thing you could ever say to me."

Her gorgeous hazel eyes pinned me in place. "Why is that a bad thing to know I have your back? To know I like you...no matter what?"

Taking a risk, I swapped my knife for a handful of her silky hair. Tugging her toward me, I whispered, "It's almost a challenge to see what else I can make you put up with."

"Go ahead. I'll still be here."

Struggling to pull away, I swallowed hard. "You know...I actually believe you."

"Good, because it's true."

"That might be." I let her go, busying myself with cutting another mouthful. "But it does mean I can never let you go. Ever."

Chapter Thirteen

Olin

-The Present-

"SHIT, SHIT, *SHIT.*"

Comprehension shot back, wrenching my eyes open as a wash of pain throbbed in my skull. New pain compounded on top of old pain, wrenching a groan from my lips and a full body seize. I hissed under my breath, pressing palms against my temples, trying to rub the ache away.

What the hell happened?

I seemed to be asking that question a lot lately.

The rainforest mural framed Gil as he paced a few metres away, his back to me, both hands hidden in his hair. His own injuries from before seemed non-existent as he prowled with anxiety.

My eyes trailed from him to the rainforest graffiti, noticing an orangutan in the shadows and an otter playing in the river glistening by the floor.

My heart kicked with remembrance then thudded with panic.

Police.

Kidnapping.

Nothing...

He buried his face into his hands. "Fuck, what have I done?" He looked at the ceiling as if in prayer, then growled as if cursing the lack of guidance. *"Fuck!"*

Spinning around, his gaze landed on mine, his hands tumbled to his sides. "Oh, thank God." Bolting toward me, he skidded to his knees where I lay on his couch. "You're okay." He gathered me tight, crushing me in a bone-crunching hug. His lips brushed my aching temple, his breath fast and worried. "Thank fuck you're okay." His entire body shuddered as if holding me unlocked every gate and smashed every wall between us.

I willingly paid for the privilege of his hug with my headache. I could've lived in that moment forever—the moment where only truth existed. The truth of us. The truth that he *did* care. And deeply.

I tried to move in his arms. To hug him back. To pull him close.

But he fell backward, ripping his hold away, taking his warmth and safety. His eyes met mine, chaotic with monstrous things. "I thought I'd lost you." His voice held a mutiny of self-hatred and decade's worth of regret. "Again."

"Wh-what happened?" I licked my lips, wincing as another throb of pain found me.

He jerked as if I'd slapped him. "You slipped."

I'd woken in a total role reversal.

I'd taken his place, and he was the one nursing me.

But why is he being nurse in the first place?

I swallowed back a wash of nausea, blinking until my vision restored. "I slipped? How?" I looked down at my hands, expecting to see my phone in them. I'd been leaving. I'd been talking to the police.

I didn't slip. I was slammed into the door.

Gil came closer, his face a riot of pain. He ducked by the couch, fumbling to take my hand; cupping it in both of his, he pressed cool lips to my knuckles. "I'm so, *so* sorry, O."

"Wait…" I swallowed hard. "*You* did this to me?" I ripped my hand away. "You knocked me out?"

He hunched, his green eyes flashing. "I didn't mean to. I only meant to unbalance you. I just wanted your phone. But…I pushed too hard. You tripped and fell against the door." His throat worked as he swallowed back self-loathing. "You hit the handle. It…it knocked you out." His eyes squeezed shut. "Fuck, I could've killed you."

I couldn't make sense of anything. "Why…why did you want my phone?"

Swooping to his feet, he backed away from me. His chin came up, an element of frost inching over his features. "I couldn't let you speak to the police."

"The police?" I scooted upright, hating the way the room

spun. "Why not?"

His face fell into darkness. "I just couldn't."

"So, you thought it would be better to maim me?"

"I deserve everything you have to say to me." His hands curled into fists. "But…first, I need you to do something for me." The lines by his eyes were harsher, the colour of his skin ashen. He'd aged ten years in just a few minutes.

"Do something for you? Why the hell would I want to do you a favour after you *knocked me out*?!" I couldn't understand. Everything about Gil confused me to the point of a migraine. "I know I upset you, Gil, but I didn't think you'd actually *hurt* me."

Swinging my legs to the floor, I stole the rest of his water left on the coffee table. I wanted more pills. An entire handful of them to wash away the pain.

Gritting my teeth, I pushed upward. My legs struggled to hold my weight, my brain still recovering from being smashed into a door.

How could he do that?

Tears sprang to my eyes. How had I gotten everything so wrong?

Gil stepped closer as I swayed, his arms wide to catch me.

But I held up my hand, baring my teeth. "Don't you *dare* touch me."

He flinched as if I'd shot him in the heart. His arms fell, he backed away silently.

He'd gotten his wish. He'd won. Kiss or no kiss. Us or no us. I had no intention of ever coming back.

Physical violence was not acceptable, under any condition.

"I wish I never answered your damn advertisement," I hissed, looking around for my handbag and phone. "You haven't changed. You hurt me when we were younger and you've hurt me now." Tears that I couldn't stem flowed wetly down my cheeks. "Congratulations, Gilbert, you're successfully the only man who's broken my heart. Twice."

Stumbling forward, I commanded my legs to work. I didn't care if they were shattered or in pieces, I would use them to walk away. I'd run as fast as I could so I never had to see Gilbert Clark again.

Old injuries twinged from the car accident, reminding me I'd been strong enough to heal from that. I could heal from this, even if he had just ripped out everything vital inside me. "Where's my phone? Give it to me."

A loud fist banged on the roller door of his warehouse, vibrating through the entire space.

"Ah, shit." Gil drove hands into his hair again, pacing frantically. He no longer watched me as if I'd murder him with my bare hands, but acted like a trapped animal, unpredictable and very, very dangerous.

I weaved, backing up a little as another loud knock shattered the silence. A shout followed with authority. "Police. Open up!"

What the—

Gil deleted the space between us with a swiftness that terrified. He crowded me. His large palms landed on my shoulders, squeezing me painfully, not letting go. His green gaze shot right into me, ripping and tearing, not caring how much he hurt me. "Olin, this is incredibly important. I need you to tell the police a fake licence plate number."

"What? Why?" I squirmed in his hold. "Let go of me."

His fingers only bit harder. He shook me, no consideration to my throbbing head. *"Olin."* Temper painted his face with the blackest of colour. His eyes turned into weapons again, freezing me to the spot. "You must tell them a fake number."

I'd never been afraid in Gil's presence.

Not once.

Not even when he'd pushed me away when we were younger.

That'd changed.

Now I had more wariness than hope. More discomfort than familiarity. "Let me go."

His hands swept from my shoulders to my cheeks, his touch raw and violent. "Do you understand? I need you to lie. Stare into their goddamn faces and *lie*."

I braced myself in his imprisonment. "I'm not lying. That bastard needs to be in prison."

His forehead crashed against mine, bruising me all over again. I winced as he rolled his head on mine, our eyes so close, our breaths shared. There was something dangerously intimate and shockingly threatening about the way he had me trapped. "Lie."

"No."

His fingers dug into my cheeks. *"Lie."*

"I'm not letting him beat you senseless again."

"It's not your choice."

"It is if you won't help yourself!"

"Goddamn you, Olin." His eyes snapped shut, his aggression slid from his fingers and he let me go. Stroking my hair with utmost softness, he murmured, "You're so good. So kind. You've always fought for those who needed to be fought for. I understand why you did what you did. I get that you called the police for my sake." His lips twitched in an agonising smile. "You did it to protect me. But, O…" Any sign of softness vanished under another avalanche of suffocating snow. "I need you to lie." The glisten of something heart-breaking flickered in his gaze. "Lie and you save my life. I *beg* you."

I sniffed back more trembles, more tears. "What on earth are you involved in?" I wanted to cry for him, to hug away his hurt. But I was afraid. Terrified to my bones. "What's going on?"

Another fist pounded. "Police! Open this door immediately!"

Gil shuddered. With a heavy shake of his head, he collapsed to his knees before me. He flinched as his own pain from the previous beating drained him of his reserves, but his face was open, imploring, desperate. "You have to trust me on this. I can't say why, but I can say it's a matter of life and death."

"Tell me."

"I can't."

Another pounding on the door. "Last warning!"

Gil made a sound of a man knowing he was about to suffer, his gaze flying over his shoulder to the door. The door that would any minute now be broken down by law enforcement.

I reached for him, unable to see him on his knees.

He grabbed my hands, soared to his feet, and once again trapped my cheeks with calloused palms.

My breath caught as his fingertips branded me. Our eyes locked, and I forgot how to speak, how to think, how to argue. Deep within him, I saw a war that'd been raging for years. A war he'd kept hidden. A war that didn't make sense.

He was losing.

He was almost defeated.

I sucked in a painful breath as he nudged his nose with mine, once again the master at breaking me. "I'm *begging* you, otter."

My knees buckled. Tears pooled faster. I tried to get away, but he only held me tighter. "Don't do that. Don't you dare use old nicknames now."

Those nicknames were sacred from a happier time.

They were not his to use.

Not anymore.

"I need you to trust me." His breath was a vicious kiss on my lips.

"You broke that trust years ago."

"I know." His eyes squeezed shut. He wobbled against me, revealing just how much this crippled him. "Just give them a false description and wrong number. That's all I ask." His fingers fell away as his shoulders slouched with despair. Bone deep, soul ripping, end of the world despair.

I backed up, studying him through my tears as the police knocked one last time. "Open this door or we'll break it down!"

With a grimace that tore out my heart, Gil marched through the office and into the warehouse. He didn't know if I'd do as he asked. He didn't try to force me into obeying. He merely left his life in my hands, his plea still echoing around me.

Lie.

I beg you.

I gave into a sob, clamping a hand over my mouth to stifle more.

I'd called the police to protect him.

I'd thought I'd done the right thing.

But what if...what if I'd condemned him to something worse than I could ever imagine?

Help him.

Sucking in a deep breath, I shoved away my tears. I swallowed my sobs. I locked down my pain and confusion.

Defend him.

I curled my hands against the pounding in my head and put one step in front of the other. I left his small apartment, cut through his office, and entered the permanently chilly warehouse.

Lie for him.

Gil stood frozen by the door, one hand outstretched to open the handle, the other opening and closing by his side. His entire aura rippled with agitated entrapment. Blood decorated his jeans and T-shirt from his fight. His hair tangled and as wild as his current frame of mind.

He stiffened as I stepped quietly toward him. My cheeks still slicked with wetness, but I kept wiping, kept hiding what I could.

"Police!" The knocking turned vicious. "Open this goddamn door!"

Our eyes once again found each other.

Time stood still; I managed to find a steadier breath. His stare glowed with gratefulness. He bowed his head in reverence, his lips moving wordlessly. "Thank you."

I nodded, straightening my spine and looking past him at the door.

He owed me.

He'll tell me why…he will.

With a deep breath, he pressed the handle and opened it wide.

We weren't in any state to be seen by police. I had no ability to lie. Gil was obviously not of rational mind. Yet, he painted himself in a perfect camouflage as he stepped to the side and opened his arm in invitation. "Sorry for the delay. Big place." His voice was steady and cool—a direct contrast to the manic moments of before. "Come in."

I smoothed my skirt and blouse, feeling guilty for no reason as two police officers stepped into Gil's workspace.

A young man with slicked back black hair and an older woman with a short red bob wore matching uniforms and scowls, inspecting the studio as if we'd hidden body parts in the paint bottles.

The woman's stare landed on my whitewashed face. "You okay, ma'am?"

I tried to see it from her point of view. The delay in answering the door. The woman shell-shocked behind it. The man barricading entry into his establishment.

If I were her, I'd ask me if everything was all right, too.

The problem was, things *weren't* all right.

But I'd committed to protecting Gil.

From things I don't understand.

I smiled weakly, not having to fake the discomfort in my voice. "Sorry, I'm a little in shock. It's my fault we didn't open the door sooner."

Gil never took his eyes off me, granting silent support, watching my every move.

The woman flicked him a suspicious look before coming closer to me without an invitation. She looked me up and down. "Were you hurt in the altercation?"

I nodded, the key to lying was to take the truth and embellish, just a little. "Yes. I'm okay though. Nothing serious."

She didn't look as if she believed me, her gaze travelling over my gravel-dusty office outfit. "Were you the one who called about the attempted kidnapping?"

"Yes."

"Why did you hang up before giving more details?"

"I—" I gulped. "I dropped my phone. It hung up by accident."

Gil winced, understanding the mammoth problem he'd dumped me with.

I'd never been good under pressure. And this was a hell of a lot of pressure. I'd also never been a good liar. Not even at school when all teenagers were flexible with the truth about where they were and who they hung out with.

The woman huffed under her breath. "Do you know who tried to take you?"

"No."

"But you said you managed to get the license plate number?"

I looked quickly at Gil.

His throat worked, but he kept an aloof, almost uninterested look on his face. Striding forward to stand by my side, he remained stoic and icy—nothing more than a boss supporting a troubled employee.

I stiffened as the male officer joined us, looking at me and then Gil. He scribbled notes onto a small pad, his forehead furrowed.

"You're Gilbert Clark? The owner of *Total Trickery*?" the man asked.

Gil nodded curtly. "I am."

"Did you see what happened?"

"I did."

"And?" The guy waved his pen in the air, fishing for information.

"I fought the guy off." He gestured to the blood on his clothes, bringing in evidence that could be used against him as evidence of being a Good Samaritan. "I helped Ms Moss escape."

"And you two know each other how?" the female officer enquired. "Working relationship?" Her eyes narrowed, waiting for our answer, almost as if she could taste our lie.

I stepped away from Gil, arching my chin. "We used to know each other at school, but currently, our only relationship is a working one."

Gil looked directly ahead; his jaw clenched.

"I see." The woman nodded.

More scribbling from the man with black hair.

I shivered, doing my best to look innocent when I felt so damn guilty. I couldn't stop it. I'd done nothing wrong. I'd called them in good faith of protecting Gil and society.

So why did I have to lie?

Why did I have to do the opposite of good when all I wanted to do was keep Gil safe?

My head pounded, reminding me of what he'd done. He'd thrown me into the door all to keep me silent. He'd been willing to concuss me to protect himself...*from what?*

My hurt morphed into anger, quickly slipping into disappointment.

I was disappointed in him. In me. In this whole crazy fiasco.

"You're Ms Moss?" the woman pointed at me.

"Yes. Olin Moss."

"Originally from Birmingham?"

"Yes."

"And you have no idea who tried to take you?"

I clasped my hands together, seeking strength. "Like I said, I don't know who he was."

Gil stiffened; his gaze locked resolutely on the police.

"It still doesn't explain why you didn't call back if you dropped your phone. Reporting a crime and then vanishing before the call is completed normally hints that a crime is still in progress." The man scratched his jaw with his pen. "So...want to tell us the real story?"

Goosebumps scattered over me, chased quickly by fear.

I didn't want to do this.

I wanted to tell the truth.

But...Gil hadn't breathed properly since the police arrived. His eyes might be shuttered from emotion, but that damn string that tied us together vibrated with so many dangerous things.

"Sorry." I did my best to smile. "I did tell the operator I escaped. It wasn't really an emergency anymore. I figured I wouldn't waste your time any more than necessary."

"You didn't finish reporting the license plate number. We need that if we're to investigate further."

"Ah." I swallowed hard. "Yes, that makes sense."

You suck, O.

You might as well hold out your wrists for handcuffs.

Gil made a noise in his chest, pinching the bridge of his

nose.

The woman noticed, pinning him with a ruthless stare. "Do you want to enlighten us, Mr. Clark?" She smiled thinly. "After all, this man hurt your employee and is still on the loose. Don't you want him apprehended so other young women don't suffer such a fate?" Her voice lowered conspiratorially. "They might not be as lucky as Ms Moss here. They might not have someone to help them escape."

Gil seemed to grow taller and darker all at once. His eyebrows came down over shadowy eyes. He looked at her as if he despised her. As if she'd failed him in every aspect of his life.

I froze, reading the past in the arctic way he glowered. The lack of care when he was younger. The violence he'd suffered because no authority had noticed. But there was something new too. Something that said he blamed her. Blamed her for every misery he'd recently endured.

"I am not responsible for the protection of every girl in England." His voice stayed clipped and cold.

"That might be, but any help you can provide—"

"He was young," Gil snapped. "Had dirty blond hair and a hooked nose. Tall. Taller than me."

The male officer scratched his pen across his notepad, scribing Gil's description.

"That true, Ms Moss?" The woman locked me in her stare, giving me no place to hide.

No.

It's a lie.

He was older, had dark hair, and a square nose. And he was short. Shorter than Gil.

I shuffled on my feet. "Yup. Hu-huh, that's exactly him."

Gil looked at me out the corner of his eye. His phone screamed, splitting the tension with an angry ring.

His skin lost its darkness, shocking to snow white. Dipping his hand into his pocket, he read the caller ID. His eyes closed with barely concealed distress.

Ring.

Ring.

Ring!

He nodded politely at the officers. "If you don't mind. This is important." Not waiting for their reply, he backed away and stormed toward his apartment through the office.

I stared until he'd disappeared.

The ringing stopped

I sighed and turned to the police, alone and swimming in fib-filled quicksand.

"Anything else I can provide?" I asked softly. "I'm tired and would like to go home to rest."

"Yes, you must be feeling the effects of your ordeal," the woman said.

I nodded, rubbing my temple, trying to ease my headache but also to amplify her empathy.

"Seeing as Mr. Clark provided a description of your assailant, can you add what sort of vehicle he was driving? Toyota? Vauxhall? Any recognisable features? Also, please give us the rest of the number plate, and we'll be on our way."

"Of course." My brain raced, doing its best to recite a believable lie, but all I could think about were the scratches and dents of the black van. They weren't blaringly obvious, but it would work like a fingerprint amongst thousands of others.

Gil reappeared, moving in my peripheral. His hand dragged over his mouth, his eyes vacant with grief. He didn't look at me but his phone, shaking his head as if he couldn't believe how such an innocuous device could deliver such heartache.

Who called?

What was said?

"Ms Moss?" the man prompted. "The vehicle and license plate?"

Every part of me wanted to go to Gil. To shake him back to the world of the living and demand to know what he was hiding. He almost crippled beneath the weight of whatever he carried. I could forgive him for what he'd done to me just from the way he stared helplessly into nothing.

Stared as if he had no one. No one to lean on. No one to help.

I'd been the one he could turn to once upon a time.

I would be her again.

Help him.

My spine straightened, my headache faded, and I said in a clear, crisp voice, "The van was older. White with blue stripes. A Mazda, I think. And the license plate was XT867ND."

The stream of fibs flowed seamlessly.

Gil jerked as if I'd yanked him back from Hell. His gaze met mine, holding far longer than he should in the presence of police.

My skin prickled with the utmost gratefulness that shone

there. My heart broke for the way he stared at me, as if he couldn't stop loving me even though he wished he could.

He made me believe in us.

He made me cling to decaying hope.

Forcibly looking away from him, I focused on the police. "Is that everything?"

The two cops looked at each other, lack of belief on their faces but unable to do anything about it.

I'd answered their questions.

We weren't the criminals.

He was out there. In a black van. Making Gil's life an utter nightmare.

I hate this.

I hated feeling so trapped. So alone. So afraid.

Gil moved to stand beside me, his hand twitching as if fighting the urge to touch me.

A habit from our youth.

A desire to touch and reaffirm that the other was safe.

The police didn't move for a moment, studying us closely.

The four of us stood there, waiting for someone to back down.

Finally, the man coughed and tucked his notebook into his front pocket. "We'll be in touch."

The woman never took her intense gaze off Gil. Distrust once again flickered over her features. "You sure you're all right, Ms Moss?"

I answered her question, all while she stared Gil down. "Yes, I'm very lucky Gilbert was there. I'm safe with him."

Are you?

Are you truly?

The cops pursed their lips as if sensing my lack of conviction. One final stare and they nodded. "Okay, then."

"I'll walk you out." Gil strode with long legs to the exit and wrenched it open for them. He didn't say goodbye as they stepped through it.

With a grunt, he slammed it closed. Hard. So hard it rattled the entire roller door, echoing around the warehouse with fury.

Silence chased the twang, filling all the corners, suffocating all the air.

We stayed in that soundless cocoon for ages, Gil bracing himself on the door as if unable to stand unassisted, me soothing my aching head and trying to delete my confusion.

I honestly didn't know what was expected or what would come next.

All I knew was I was tired.

Exhausted.

And I wanted to be alone.

I'd been on my own so much of my life that it was the only way I could relax. The only way I truly felt safe...with only my thoughts and worry for company.

I'd lied for him. I'd drained myself of everything at his request.

I was spent.

Go.

Stepping toward the exit, my motion snapped Gil back into awareness. He flicked the lock on the door, preventing anyone from entering or leaving. Turning to face me, he let go of the coldness in his eyes, sighing heavily. "I know you have no right to trust me. I know I've been nothing but a bastard since you walked back into my life. But...I can never repay you for what you just did." He moved toward me, stiff and sore. "Thank you...from the bottom of my heart."

My body wanted to collapse in relief. My heart wanted to scream for everything.

I shivered as he closed the distance between us, predator slow, as if he didn't know if I'd run or strike.

Hugging myself at the sudden chill in my blood, I asked quietly, "Why did I just lie to the police?"

"Because I asked you to." He gave me a complicated, grief-stricken smile.

"Because you begged me to."

He nodded gravely. "Because I begged you to."

"Will you tell me why?"

"No."

"Don't you think you owe me an explanation?" My arms wrapped tighter around me. "Don't you think I deserve to know why you let that arsehole beat you up? Don't you think I deserve to know why you knocked me out? Don't you think I deserve—"

"You deserve all those answers and more." He raked a hand through his wild hair, only making the mess worse. "It doesn't mean I can give them to you." Brushing past me, he headed toward the trestle where I'd placed the thick envelope of cash.

His jaw worked as he plucked it with fingers meant to paint and create. His shoulders tensed as he turned to face me, holding the money up, offering it to me all over again. "You earned this. Take it."

I fought the hiccup in my heart and arched my chin. "I took what was owed. The rest you overpaid."

"I just said I can never repay you for what you did. There is no such thing as overpayment. Take it."

"No."

"Isn't it up to me to pay a canvas what I think she's worth?"

My voice cracked with residual pain. "You cheapened me."

His eyes darkened; his forehead furrowed. "*Cheapened* you? How?"

"You paid me for a kiss. You—"

"That's what you think?" He threw the money down as if it was contaminated. "What an idiotic thing—"

"Gil."

His nostrils flared, anger glowing on his tortured face. "You'll take a kiss, you'll goddamn *lie* for me, yet my money isn't good enough for you?"

I stepped toward him, carefully, fearfully. "Pay me in answers. I'll accept those."

His chest heaved as he sucked in a breath. "That's a currency I can't afford."

"Why? What's happened to you, Gil? What's going on? What are you so afraid—"

"I'm not afraid."

I smiled sadly. "You are. It's painfully obvious."

He crossed his arms, forming an impenetrable barrier around him. "Stop."

"But if I do, you'll still be dealing with this nightmare…alone." I dropped my arms, spreading my hands in surrender. "I found you again by some crazy twist of fate. Our connection is still there, even if you deny it. I'm willing to help you, Gil, just like we helped each other in the past. I forgive you for hurting me. I'll be patient if you need time. But…I can't walk away when I know—"

"You know nothing."

"I know enough that you're alone in this and I made a promise a long time ago that you'd never be alone again."

He flinched. "Promises are easy things to break."

"Not mine."

"I broke plenty." His voice trespassed on bitterness. "I left you."

"You said you had reasons."

He laughed icily. "You're willing to forgive me for that too? Fuck, what do I have to do to you to make you hate me?"

I smiled forlornly, remembering a simpler time in my kitchen, the sweet scent of pancakes around us, the joy of having Gil in the place where I'd been so alone.

We'd agreed to be together—to always have each other's backs.

"It's almost a challenge to see what else I can make you put up with."

His voice echoed in my head as if it'd been only a few hours, not years, between that moment and this one.

I didn't know back then that he would honour that joke-given threat. That he would hurt me worse than anyone and push me away again and again, and yet...

"Go ahead. I'll still be here."

My own voice sounded young and innocent, dragged from the past, threading with his inside my mind.

I'd made a promise that day.

I intended to keep it...until Gil no longer needed my help.

"I'm going home, Gil." I dropped my hands. "I'm going home to rest, but I will come back."

"Don't. Don't ever come back."

"Why?"

His temper acted like a shield, a suit of chainmail cold and heavy around his heart. "I can't enlighten you, O. No matter how many times you ask."

"I won't ask. I'll just pop by and offer support."

"You can't. I owe you a debt for today, but that's where this ends." Snatching the money again, he held it out. "Take it. It's the least I can do."

"I'll be seeing you, Gil." I turned to go, to somehow make my way home when my entire body was in pieces. To nurse my bruises and tend to my wounds alone.

"Wait." The command was a snap, a grenade.

His teeth ground together, making his jaw tight and veins thread visibly down his neck. "The phone call...I need..." He grunted as if talking about such things drove splinters into his mind. "I wasn't going to ask. I would...prefer to use another canvas, but...I need to do another commission."

I paused, hiding my hurt. "You'd prefer another canvas because of my tattoo?"

"I'd prefer another canvas who isn't you."

I stumbled at the force of such a nasty phrase.

His face flickered with untold things. "I didn't mean..." The contrition in his voice punished him worse than I ever could. "I..." He rubbed his eyes, seeking truth but battling lies. "I should have the strength to stand here and tell you that the ridges of your scars are hard to hide. That your ink isn't worth the time it takes to camouflage. That you have flaws I'm not prepared to fix."

"I see." Tears prickled my eyes as anger settled in my stomach. "How stupid of me. The Master of Trickery would never paint flaws."

He stepped toward me. "You don't have flaws, O. You never have." The way his tone thickened with remorse made my anger falter.

"Don't." I held up my hand. "It's fine. I knew when I applied for the job that I wasn't perfect."

He swallowed a groan. "Fuck." Dragging hands through his hair, he bared his teeth at whatever had him cornered before breaking its hold and swooping toward me. His hands captured my cheeks, shaking and full of tenderness. "I promised myself I'd be as cruel as necessary to keep you away. That I'd hurt you all over again if that's what it took. But...I'm too fucking weak. You're perfect. You've *always* been perfect."

His lips crashed onto mine, kissing me swift and true.

My mouth opened under his, shock and surprise making me totally his.

His taste was dark and distressing. His tongue violently claiming.

He kissed me as if this was all my fault—as if he blamed me for making his life ten times harder when I'd only tried to help.

His arms shuddered around me, clutching me close.

He kissed me until I was breathless from his pain. Only then did he let me go, drop his touch, and back away as if distance could somehow erase what he'd just done.

Clearing his throat, he balled his hands. "He knows you're here now. You made him think there is an us." His gaze caught mine in a fatal web. "You should never have seen what you did, but I can't change that and now..." He stopped talking, his body stiffening to steel. "Now, everything is all fucked up and you can't keep disobeying me. Be my canvas once more, have a reason to be here, accept my money and keep business our only reason for meeting, and then..." He stood taller as if facing an execution. "Walk away and never come back."

I licked my lips where his taste still lingered. "Is that what you want? For me to never come back?"

He looked away; rage imprisoned in his gaze. "Yes."

"Liar."

"It's what I need."

I didn't bother asking why.

There were only so many times I could ask an unanswerable question. Instead, I asked something I hadn't verbalised, even to myself. A question that'd been haunting me. "Are you so determined to give me your money, because you think you owe me—"

"I *do* owe you."

"Not for today, but for all the times I hid money in your backpack so you could get something to eat."

His eyes snapped shut, his body quaked. He rubbed his mouth as his green eyes reopened with shame. "No. But by the end, I did owe you more than I could ever give you."

"You owed me nothing. It was given with love. A gift."

He flinched with ghosts of our past. We balanced on words—words that could heal the history between us and pave our future. But Gil rearranged his face from pained to impatient, and he was no longer the boy I was in love with but the body painter I couldn't figure out. "Talking about the past won't change anything. It's over between us. It was over seven years ago. All I can offer you is money. Come back tomorrow and—"

"I can't." I cut him off. "I just agreed to work for another company. I start tomorrow."

His face stayed carefully blank. "I can paint you in a few hours. Come by after work."

The thought of being in his presence again so soon? The energy it would take to survive him? I honestly didn't know if I had the strength.

I opened my mouth to push the commission back. To plead exhaustion and beg for time to put my pieces back together again. To be whole enough to help him, even when he was adamant he didn't want such a thing.

But Gil stood frozen, a raincloud of torment overhead, a crack of lightning forking right through his chest. He smiled gravely, tasting my reluctance and hurting because of it.

He nodded. "It's for the best. I won't ask you again." Stalking toward the exit, he murmured, "Please don't come back here, Olin. I mean it."

I followed him, waiting while he unlocked the door, and sucking in courage when he opened it.

Stepping over the threshold, I twisted to face him and raised my hand to cup his jaw.

He winced. His face was a torn mask, cold indifference slipping to reveal passionate concern.

"I'll be your canvas, Gil." Dropping my touch, I slid into the dusk. "I'll help you in whatever way you need."

He shuddered.

Looking back at him, imprinting him, I added softly, "See you tomorrow."

Chapter Fourteen

Olin

-The Present-

MY PHONE VIBRATED in my handbag.

I heard the vibration even as it tickled my foot beneath my desk where I'd tossed it. I did my best to ignore it. After all, this was my first day at my new job.

I hadn't slept.

I couldn't stop thinking about Gil.

But I'd made a commitment and did my best to be a model employee.

The first hour had been spent being dragged around the whole floor, smiling and nodding, knowing I would never remember the names of all the people Shannon—my new manager—introduced me to. She'd shown me the coffee break room, the balcony where smokers and vapers hung out, and the glass walled boxes where the bosses kept the cogs running.

Afterward, she sat me down in a bare cubicle that would become my home and showed me, with her sparkly pink pen, how to log into their servers, answer the phones, and what my job entailed.

I'd focused on her red lips and bouncy blonde hair. I'd jotted notes on her advice and mentally did my best to be present.

But Gil still lurked in the back of my mind.

I could never be free of him.

Only a few hours before I would see him again. A few more hours of calmness before my heart careened off my ribs and my insides tied themselves into knots.

I'd agreed to be his canvas for two reasons.

One, I would stand by my promise to be there for him.

Two, I couldn't bear the thought of him painting another, laughing with another, letting down his walls with another.

Being happy with another.

I'd never really seen him happy.

Even at school when we'd been close, sadness always shadowed his happiness.

He's in danger.

Until he'd solved his mysterious predicament, I doubted he would ever be happy, regardless of the company.

Stop thinking about him.

That was an impossibility.

My mind switched from worrying about him to worrying over the design he'd paint me with tonight.

What was the commission?

Who was the client?

He seemed in high demand. He could command untold riches if he wanted. So why did he still come across as the boy from a penniless beginning? A lonely man living in an empty warehouse that whispered of destitution instead of richness?

Stop it, O.

You'll drive yourself insane.

I was already insane.

There was no other explanation for my going back to him or my tolerance of his behaviour. My head still ached from what he'd done. My body still flighty from the kidnapping attempt.

My work computer pinged, announcing a new email.

I sighed, clicking on it and reading the generic request for warranty terms and conditions of our product.

My fingers flew over the keyboard, typing a scripted response that Shannon had given me.

My phone buzzed again.

I forced myself to finish the email before bowing to pressure to check. I didn't receive many messages these days. After cutting myself off from my friends and dance troupe, no one bothered to reach out. Even my parents never texted to tell me where in the world they were.

Ducking down, I fumbled in my bag. Grabbing my phone, I swiped it on and clicked on the messenger app.

One new message from someone I didn't expect.

Justin Miller: *Hi, O. Hope you're good. Quick question. Is Gilbert with you?*

What?

Why would Gil be with me?

I bit my lip, looking over my partition as if Gil would magically appear. Staff milled about as sunshine beamed into the high-rise building. Some people had pulled blackout blinds to prevent direct light on their computer screens. The babble of voices and scents of coffee and warm machinery were a total contrast to Gil's chilly, unwelcoming warehouse.

And he wasn't anywhere to be found.

Not that he has any clue where I work.

Olin Moss: *Hi Justin. Nope. Haven't seen him since yesterday. Why?*

A phone call came in on the office line, making me jolt. Placing my personal mobile on the desk, I did my job and answered the work one. The entire time I dealt with a customer requiring a new battery for a computer that was ten years out of date, I waited for Justin to reply.

The little dots bounced beside his name, signalling he was typing.

By the time I hung up, a message popped onto my screen.

Justin Miller: *I'm at his place, and he's not here. He's ALWAYS here. I've literally never come here and he's not. It's just odd is all.*

My heart picked up a strange beat.

Olin Moss: *Why would you think he's with me?*

Justin Miller: *Come on. It's obvious you guys have unfinished history.*

I had no response to that. He was right.

Olin Moss: *He's probably at the supermarket or something.*

Justin Miller: *He gets food delivered. Doesn't like people, remember?*

Olin Moss: *Maybe he needed some fresh air?*

Justin Miller: *In the year since we've kinda been friends, he's never needed anything but his art.*

I didn't reply straight away.

What does he want me to say?

Justin had been friends with Gil far longer than me these days. I'd entered Gil's life and he'd promptly tried to shove me out of it. Why would I know his schedule?

Olin Moss: *Sorry, Justin. I don't know where he is. Wish I could be more help.*

Justin Miller: *No worries. It was a long shot. I'm just...jumping to conclusions. He's a grown man. I'll call him again tomorrow if I haven't heard from him. Cheers.*

I sighed, ready to lock my phone and return to work, but a final message popped up.

Justin Miller: *I haven't forgotten about dinner by the way. Let me know what night works and I'll pick you up!*

Shannon caught my eye from across two cubicles. She had another trainee who probably wasn't on their phone like I was.

She waved and flounced over to me in her floaty skirt and cream blouse.

I quickly locked my phone and shoved it into the desk drawer.

"Hey, Olin. Everything going okay so far?"

I nodded. "Yes. Great."

"Awesome." She grinned. "Well, you know where I am if you need any help."

"I do." Turning to my computer, I placed my fingers on the keyboard, doing my best to seem a worthwhile employee and not one with her head full of things she shouldn't be thinking about.

A head full of *someone* she shouldn't be thinking about.

Another email chimed. Shannon looked at me expectantly.

I gritted my teeth, shoved Gil and Justin from my mind, and did my best to enjoy my new job.

Chapter Fifteen

Olin

-The Present-

I KNOCKED.

It was the polite thing to do.

No crazy kidnapper lurked outside. No sounds of fists and curses came from inside. The normal, brisk Birmingham evening boasted typical background noises of pigeons and traffic.

My knock went unanswered.

My second knock was ignored too.

I looked at my phone. Nine p.m.

I'd taken longer than I wanted, what with a new job, going home to shower and change, I'd borrowed more time by eating a sandwich and gathering the courage to spend an entire night with Gil while he painted me.

I would admit I'd been weak. I'd dragged my heels, searching for strength.

I was late.

But Gil should be here.

Checking he hadn't messaged me to postpone our arrangement, I put my phone away before I gave into the temptation to message Justin.

He might know where Gil was…or he might not. Either way, I didn't want to enter a messaging flurry while standing on Gil's doorstep in the dark.

Knocking again, I called, "Hello?"

Deep, dark silence.

"Gil?"

Nothing.

I tried the handle, expecting it to open.

It didn't.

I paused, chewing my lip.

What do I do?

Go home? Wait?

What if Justin was right?

What if Gil wasn't just missing...but taken?

My heart exploded into gear, taking that question and drowning me in terrible scenarios. Of him inside, beaten and bleeding. Of him in the van, tied up and gagged. Of him dying—

"Gil!"

Backing up, I studied the large brick warehouse. The *Total Trickery* graffiti didn't hide any other entrances: no fire escape ladders, no back-alley sneak-ins. The only other way was the large roller door used for trucks reversing to empty and pick up supplies.

My thoughts grew evermore gruesome.

I didn't stop to think. I didn't tell myself to calm the hell down.

This was Gil.

This was *important.*

I'd handle his temper if he'd just changed his mind and didn't want to paint me. I'd allow him to kick me out if he just wanted to forget I existed.

Those I could get over.

I could never get over failing him if any of the awful images my head turned out to be true.

My handbag slid off my shoulder as I ducked and tested the roller door.

It moved a fraction.

I froze.

I'd expected it to be padlocked to the ground, but either it wasn't chained down or it was loose.

Dropping to my haunches, I squirreled my fingers under the metal and pulled. It screamed and squeaked, creeping slowly from the ground.

A large chain clanked by the pedestrian access, jangling in place and preventing the door from going any higher than a foot and a half.

It wasn't exactly a method of welcome, but I'd never been afraid of unconventional entries. Gil had taught me the allure of going to places we weren't supposed to be at night. The park, the local swimming pool, even the school.

We'd broken in one evening when my parents forgot I'd danced at the school hall as Beauty from a ballet rendition of *Beauty and the Beast.* They'd never turned up—even though I'd pinned their invitations to their pillows every night for a week.

I hadn't even told Gil that I'd danced as Belle, too shy to tell him about the performance. But somehow, he'd found out and waited for me outside my house when I got home. No one was inside. Just him sitting on the stoop with his sad smile and knowing gaze.

I'd given him a shrug, fighting back tears. I'd wanted so badly for my mum and dad to watch me.

He'd looked at my dangling ballet slippers and my still-painted face and hugged me close. "You were amazing, owl. Absolutely spectacular."

I pulled away, shock making my heart skip. "You saw?"

"I saw."

"How?"

"I broke in." He kissed my forehead, took my hand in his, and walked me all the way back to school. "I want to watch you again." He brushed away the strands of hair that'd come loose from my bun. "Would you do that for me? Give me a private dance?"

I no longer needed my parents' approval or smiles.

I only needed his.

I wanted to dance for him more than anything in the world. "Yes."

The minute I agreed, he climbed the storeroom behind the gym to the roof, jumped the distance to the main building, slipped through a skylight into the science lab, and made his way through dark and empty corridors to unlock the main door for me.

With a secretive smirk, he'd led me to the school hall, picked me up and placed me on the stage that still held the backdrop of a magical castle where a beast was trapped by a curse, then commanded I put my ballet slippers back on and dance.

To start with, I'd been so nervous I could barely walk, let alone dance.

Dance was my special place; my vulnerable place.

But his pride and affection soon became the music I needed

to lose myself in my art.

I didn't need other dancers.

I didn't need the guy who played the Beast to hold me, spin me, throw me.

I only needed Gil as he held his breath, devoured me with his eyes, and after—when I breathed hard and my body hummed with an endorphin rush—he'd climbed the steps to join me on the stage. "I've watched you dance a thousand times, but this...you stole my heart, O."

I'd thought he would kiss me.

I'd hoped he'd make love to me.

I believed he would have with the way his eyes glowed with love and pure desire etched his face.

I'd never known lust had a recognisable mask.

But it did.

Gil wore it that night.

Lust so deep and powerful, he didn't have to touch me for my body to burn, my nipples to harden, my core to dampen.

With our eyes locked and starlight our only illumination, it was the best foreplay I'd ever had. The only foreplay. We were two teenagers desperate to become adults, hungry to share, not just our hearts, but everything else too.

The air sparked with electricity as he'd breathed my name. My hair prickled. My heart flurried. We stumbled into one another, only to scatter as a torch swung into the hall, and the grouchy voice of the groundskeeper complained about rats scurrying in the corners.

I shook my head, dispelling the memory. My body still sang from that night. My toes still pinched from my ballet slippers. My heart still ravenous to claim Gil's.

Gil had always held such a raw power over me. I'd never gotten over what could've been between us because the almost-was was unbelievably special—the reality of it would've been our undoing.

Hurry.

I lay down on the ground and scooted under the door, dragging my handbag with me. The heavy metal clanged and banged as I let it fall to the floor, effectively announcing to every turpentine bottle and air compressor that a stranger had entered uninvited.

Find him.

Leaving my handbag by the door, I stood and brushed off

dust and grime. "Gil?"

My voice echoed in the unfurnished area.

No response.

"Gil, are you okay?" I kicked off my high heels and jogged in my stockings toward his office. The air hung heavy and still as if trying to convince me no one was there. But something tugged me forward. The silence was a pretender because my skin prickled the way it did whenever I was in Gil's company.

He's here.

Somewhere.

His office was empty, the door slightly open as I pushed through and kept my shoulders braced. Even though I'd been in his home before, I couldn't shed the sensation I wasn't welcome.

"Hello?" My voice fell to a whisper as I entered his apartment.

Nothing.

No sounds, no smells, no Gil.

I stood by the couch, noticing the bottle of painkillers and the glass of water we'd shared.

The clutter hadn't been moved.

Surely, he would've cleaned up after himself. His place seemed tidy. His warehouse was paint-speckled, but his equipment was clean and put away after use.

"Are you here, Gil?" I strode toward the bathroom. The longer I stayed, the more uncomfortable I became. What was I thinking breaking into his place? Why did I think I'd have better luck finding him over Justin who'd been part of his life for the past year?

Ego.

That's what this is.

I thought I'd find him because there was something unexplainable between us. Because every word he gave me, no matter how harsh, begged me to keep coming back.

The rainforest mural glittered in the glow of a single lamp, this time I spied an owl on fern branches, a symbol of me—just like my tattoo was a symbol of him.

He'd never forgotten me. Never stopped wanting me.

"Gil?" My chest hurt as I turned, taking in the space.

A soft snick of a door opening behind me made me spin around at super speed.

My hand flew to my throat as Gil tripped out of one of the rooms hidden in the graffiti rainforest I'd just admired.

No lights illuminated behind him. I couldn't see into the space he'd just vacated, but the faint whiff of strawberry followed him.

My insides tangled.

Strawberry.

Like in his bathroom yesterday.

I backed up as Gil turned around and closed the door. He locked it with a key that vanished into his pocket a moment later. He didn't turn to face me; he didn't show any sign of realising I was there.

Pressing his forehead against the door, his hand stayed glued to the handle as if he couldn't face life outside the room.

My heart physically ached to touch him. To do something, *anything*, to eradicate the sorrow cloaking his shoulders.

I was trapped.

I'd found him, but I wasn't meant to see this.

I wanted to vanish, but if I moved, he'd notice me.

I had no idea what to do, so I just stood there, blushing and afraid as he inhaled a shaky breath and turned slowly.

It took him longer to move than normal, his senses dulled and reactions compromised. His gaze fixated on a mostly empty vodka bottle on the kitchen countertop. He made to move toward it, his eyes hazy and body loose from drinking.

But then, he froze.

His head whipped to me, his lips pulling back in a snarl. "Olin."

His eyes shot to the door behind him as if afraid of what I'd seen. "How shlong have you been standing…there?" His voice dripped with alcohol.

He swayed; his face shadowed with fury.

Out of everything that could've happened tonight, seeing Gil drunk was the hardest.

Not because I feared he'd be violent and a threat to my safety but because of the many moonlight conversations we'd had about his father's drinking.

He'd been fiercely adamant he would never drink like him. The smell and taste of liquor repulsed him. He never wanted to ruin his life with a bottle.

Yet seven years later, he was slurring and swaying before me.

"Gil…what happened?"

He stumbled to the side, shaking his head as if trying to

eradicate the drunkenness he swam in. "You're not meant to be here."

"You told me to come, remember? You were going to paint me."

"Ah…" His eyes unfocused as something brutal and damaging cast over his features. His breath hitched in such a helpless way, tears confiscated my vision. "It's too late."

I rubbed at the liquid in my gaze. "What's too late?"

"Everything." His face tried to settle on furious but just kept melting back into grief. His jeans and grey hoodie were grass stained and muddy. An area by his elbow was torn while blood marked the neckline. Green, taupe, and black paint speckled his skin.

Needing to touch him. Crippling with the need to soothe, I dashed forward and wound my fingers with his.

I couldn't *not* touch him. I couldn't not *care*. "Gil…what's going on? Where have you been? You're hurt. You're filthy."

Yanking his fingers from mine, he groaned, "Get out."

"I can't."

"Go."

"I'm staying."

He narrowed his eyes. *"Leave."*

We'd had this conversation far too many times. I should honour his wishes. This was his place. There was no law about drinking alone.

But…

But.

"I'm not leaving. No matter what you say or do, I'm not going anywhere. Not while you're like this."

"Like what?" His eyes clung to mine, icy green winter.

Dirty.

Hurt.

"Drunk."

"What I do or don't do is none of your conshern."

"It is when I know this isn't you."

"You don't know me." He stormed off, beelining for the kitchen as a thread of strawberry scent followed him, along with a trail of mud from his boots. "If you knew me, you'd run from me." His voice thickened. "You should run. Please, God. *Run.*"

I balled my hands and chased. "I'm not running, Gil. I'm going to help you."

"You can't."

"Let me try."

He reached for the vodka bottle, but I beat him to it.

"Don't." I held it out of arm's reach. "Alcohol can't cure your problems."

His face twisted. "But it can drown out the pain."

"No," I said sadly. "It only amplifies it when it wears off."

"The reprieve is shworth it." He swayed as he pounced on me, pressing me against the kitchen bench, trying to reach the bottle behind my back.

I sucked in a breath as the air crackled like it always did when we touched.

He stiffened.

The outside world vanished.

His focus slipped from the bottle to my lips in a heartbeat, imprisoning me in a different type of hell.

I stopped breathing as his gaze darkened, hiding any vulnerabilities and secrets, turning him into an angry, intoxicated stranger.

A stranger whose nostrils flared and hands landed on either side of my hips, trapping me all while his body pressed indecently into mine.

"Gil…"

"Don't." He shook his head fast, his lips twisting into a grimace.

I shivered as he ducked his head and nuzzled his nose against my neck. The way we fit together, the way he knew instinctually what made me come apart said we'd done this a thousand times. As if it was acceptable, normal, *real.*

The bottle clattered out of my fingers, banging against the tile and spilling its crystal liquor around our feet.

Gil didn't stop.

His fingers dug into my hipbones, yanking me into him. His teeth grazed my neck, and the world erupted in fire.

I moaned as he bit me.

I melted as his tongue licked my neck and his hips thrust hard into mine.

"Fuck, O…" His tongue became his lips, kissing me, decorating me in nips and worship as he worked his way from my throat to my collarbone. I shuddered as he unsheathed his teeth and bit me harder, making me liquefy.

My hands landed in his hair, sinking deep.

He wasn't the only one drunk.

Suddenly, my brain swam. My mind shut down. My very chemical makeup drugged me.

I should push him away and run.

I should remember what he did to me the last time I was here.

I should scream and tell him to stop.

I *couldn't* stop.

I couldn't stop what I'd fantasised about for so long. Even if it was the biggest mistake of my life.

His hands climbed my body—heavy and dangerous. His touch was not gentle or kind as he thumbed my nipples and captured my jaw in both hands.

Pulling away, he blinked with vodka-hazy eyes. "Tell me to stop."

I licked my lips, begging for common sense to answer him, but only lust replied. "I can't."

He squeezed his eyes together, his face a tortured mask. "You should."

I nodded in his imprisonment. "I should."

"But...you won't." His eyes met mine again, misery and heartbreak mixing in the frosty green.

"No." I struggled in his hold, arching my chin up, giving him every permission to kiss me.

My pulse pounded in my ears, matching the drumming of his in his neck. We stood there, snapping in chemistry and drowning in need, both of us desperate but so afraid.

There were things we should say. Rules we should discuss. Futures we should protect.

But with alcohol stealing his power and desire stealing mine, we were both ruined.

"Fuck," he groaned. His mouth descended on mine. Swift and sudden, sharp and sinful.

My eyes snapped shut as our lips bruised each other, our bodies breakable things beneath the hunger quickly consuming us. We'd played a dangerous game when we were younger. We'd denied ourselves. We'd fallen in love and let life steal us apart without ever indulging.

We were about to pay the price of that war.

Gil wrapped a fist in my hair, yanking my head back, bending me into pain as he kissed me deep. His tongue broke my lips apart, plunging into my mouth, possessing me.

I couldn't get free.

My only option was to open wide and let his tongue own mine. The kiss was explosive, like drinking pure dynamite. Our tongues were matches, striking fire, blistering every neuron.

He thrust against me, pressing my back into the bench.

I squirmed as my fingers clawed at his nape, holding on and sinking deep at the same time.

Every lash of his tongue licked into my belly. My flesh swelled. My blood heated. Every part of me grew heavy and demanding.

He crawled into me, almost breaking me in two as he held the back of my neck and kissed me so hard I struggled to breathe.

I didn't need oxygen.

I kissed him back. Violence for violence. My body spinning itself into an aching mess, shivering and sick with the unbearable need to have him inside me.

Our passion was lightning quick.

A bolt of energy that turned us into animals.

Tearing me from the kitchen bench, Gil stumbled toward the couch with me in his arms. He swayed to the side, dropping me to my feet. We didn't make it to the furniture.

We wrapped ourselves around each other, balancing in our drunken, lust-drenched world. Our lips found each other in another manic kiss that made my eyes roll and core clench.

I'd never had such a crazy connection with another.

Never wanted to hurt someone as much as I wanted to love them.

His fingers scratched my nape as he held me tight and kissed me deep.

Kissed me and *kissed* me.

Kissed me as if making up for all the times he hadn't kissed me in the past.

My lips burned. My tongue ached. And my body was jealous.

It wanted him everywhere, not just on my mouth.

Gil dropped to his knees.

For a second, I couldn't figure out what happened. My lips smarted and turned cold. But then a loud moan fell from them as he fumbled at the zipper on my skirt, ripping it down to my feet.

Cool air licked around my garter belt and stockings. After I'd showered, I'd put on fresh office clothes. I stupidly didn't want him knowing I'd been home, when I should've come here straight from work.

Perhaps, if I'd come here straight away, he wouldn't be drunk.

Maybe, if I hadn't delayed, I could've saved him whatever new pain he suffered.

I'd failed him.

Gil sat back on his heels, his eyes hot and black with undiluted lust. "You're killing me, O." His hand trembled as he ran a finger right over my lingerie-clad pussy. "*Killing* me."

My legs buckled.

He caught me, dragging me to the floor, pressing me onto my back as I kicked my skirt from my ankles.

He didn't ask for permission as he shot down my body and knelt between my spread legs. His jaw clenched as he pulled my knickers down and tossed them over his shoulder.

My cheeks blazed as his gaze fixated on my bareness. The part of me he'd never seen, never touched, never tasted.

And I had no shame as I spread my legs even wider, arching my back, begging him to finish what he started.

His eyebrows knitted together. He swallowed hard and shook his head as if trying to convince himself this wasn't a dream. This was real. So, so real.

Without a word, he bowed over me and latched his mouth onto my heated pussy.

I lost myself.

My head dug into the floor as I writhed under his tongue.

There was nothing slow or tentative about him.

Gil licked me as if he'd wake up any second. He spread my folds and plunged his tongue inside me as if he'd owned that part of me his entire life.

Every nerve ending combusted. Every cell shot down my body and gathered on my clit. And when Gil's teeth found me, biting the nub with a thinly veiled punishment, no other part of me existed.

"Oh, God!" I squirmed as he buried his nose into me. Licking and nipping, a feral noise of ownership rumbled in the back of his throat.

His fingers clawed their way up my inner thigh, finding my heat, then driving one deep inside me.

I bowed off the floor.

His free hand landed on my belly, pressing me down as his tongue swirled and his finger hooked with pleasure. A groan clawed through his chest as he bit my clit, inhaling and sucking.

He didn't give me time to adjust or accept.

He merely took.

"Do you know how long I've wanted to do this?" His voice was thick and rich, velvet and sandpaper.

I broke out in goosebumps as his one finger became two. Both drove into me as far as they could go. His hand on my belly moved to dig under my ass, hoisting me up, pulling my pussy harder against his mouth. His tongue battled to enter me all while his fingers thrust with a possession that made everything else inconsequential.

My body responded. How could it not? My stomach twisted, heart raced, and my core invited Gil's invasion with droplets of silky desire.

I didn't care he was paint and dirt covered.

I didn't care this was a terrible, terrible idea.

All I cared about was *this*.

"So many times," Gil groaned as he licked at my moisture. His fingers kept stroking, sending shockwaves through every limb. "So many fucking times I wanted you."

I panted as the mixture of me and his saliva tickled the insides of my thighs.

I couldn't reply, too caught up in his assault.

"Olin…" Another finger joined his two, stretching me, plunging deep.

I cried in bliss as he rocked his hand, his teeth punishing my clit. My heart bucked in a frenzy; the ground didn't feel solid anymore. All I wanted to do was fall into him, onto him.

I wanted his cock inside me.

Tugging at his shoulders, I begged, "Gil…now. I need you. *Now*."

His glowing, furious eyes met mine. His mouth remained on my pussy, his fingers inside my body. Mud marked his cheekbone; a bruise shadowed his temple.

His gaze kept me captured as he arched his fingers and sucked me hard. The painful, exquisite beginnings of an orgasm brewed in my belly. It teased down my legs, throbbing around Gil's fingers.

I bit my lip, fighting it off.

But Gil smiled savagely and drove his fingers deeper. His breathing rasped as we never looked away from each other. He looked wild and untamed, totally unhinged with sex.

And I couldn't stop it.

I couldn't balance on the knife's edge. Not when he looked into me. Not with his touch inside me.

I gave in, throwing myself headfirst into the ricocheting bands of pleasure.

I cried out as it ripped me apart.

Each wave, Gil sucked me harder, thrusting his fingers, sending me higher, adding to the bliss. The power of it echoed in my teeth, stole my vision, and distorted my breath.

On the final pulse of release, Gil soared up my body. His mouth glistened from licking me, his lips swollen with heat. He kissed me, slamming my head against the floor with the force.

I kissed him back, loose and lost, swimming in the aftershocks.

"I missed you." He kissed me deeper. "Missed you every goddamn day."

My eyes flew wide.

I struggled away from his kiss even as his fingers drove into me again, punishing oversensitive nerves.

I searched his face, but his eyes held barriers, trapping his demons. His lips twisted as if he hadn't meant to say such vulnerable things all while his fingers dominated me.

He kissed me again, his mouth pressing hard, bestowing sensual affection layered with dark complication.

He didn't just kiss me.

He poured devotion and bitterness down my throat. He wrapped us in history even while smashing apart time that had distanced us.

"Why did you leave?" I whispered. The question was for a younger Olin. The one who'd been so happy and then so heartbroken by the boy who said he loved her.

The hitch of his breath sent my heart roaring and the same sort of hunger he'd attacked me with sat up nasty and needy in my veins. It didn't matter why he left. Only that he did.

Old anger and agony rose, and my fingernails scratched down his back, grabbing the hem of his hoodie and tugging it up his body.

I trembled with the undeniable need to finish this. To have him naked and glued to me while he took everything that had always belonged to him.

"Off," I hissed. "I need this off."

Thoughts raced in Gil's eyes, totally tangled and

undecipherable. Why couldn't I figure him out? Why couldn't I learn his secrets all while he lay in my arms?

His fingers withdrew from my body as he climbed to his feet. He stood over me, his blood still swimming with liquor, his clothing still filthy. Without a word, he tore his hoodie off, removed his T-shirt, and unbuckled his jeans while kicking off his boots.

He didn't waste time, shedding the items as if they were a hindrance he wanted to burn. His paint-speckled boots clattered by the couch as his zipper came apart and his jeans were torn from his legs.

I sat up slowly, unbuttoning my blouse with trembling fingers.

I couldn't blink, drinking him in.

It'd been a lifetime ago that I'd seen his naked chest, and he'd filled out since then. He rippled with etches and shadows, his stomach flat and carved with ridges. He didn't have much hair; just a splattering between his pecs and a dark line disappearing into his black boxer-briefs, but it wasn't the perfection of his body that entranced me.

It was the wounds.

Old scars, new bruises, ancient injuries, and fresh cuts.

He looked as if he'd stepped through time and off a battlefield. His eyes matched the illusion, heavy with sorrow and hard with remorse.

My heart kicked, wanting to protect him all while wanting to bow to him.

Scrambling to my knees, I reached back and unhooked my bra. Gil sucked in a groan as I threw the lace away, revealing myself to him. He'd seen my breasts. He'd painted my nipples and airbrushed my cleavage.

Yet the way he watched me made me feel like the most powerful creature in the world.

Rubbing his mouth, he shook his head as if he still couldn't believe this was real. His hand dropped to his cock. With a bite of his lip, he squeezed his erection, proud and encased in underwear. "I've dreamt of this, did you know that? Fantasied about fucking you so many times."

I didn't move, panting as his thumbs hooked into his boxer-briefs and pulled them down.

His mouth lined with regret. "I've had nightmares of losing you...hating myself for walking away."

My body broke out in hot desire. "You didn't need to walk away."

"I did." He hung his head as his cock sprang free, hard and long.

"It doesn't matter. We're together now."

"There can't be an us." His voice twisted. "I shouldn't do this. I should fucking have the strength not to do this."

"Maybe you're right." I swallowed. "But you don't have a choice. *We* don't have a choice." Another orgasm spindled, heated and wet, just at the sight of Gil stripping. His unwanted boxers slid to his ankles, only to be kicked away to join his boots and socks.

For the longest moment, he didn't move. As if afraid I'd judge him, not want him.

Terror filled me that he'd stop this. That whatever freedom he'd found thanks to alcohol wasn't enough for us to finish this.

But then, he closed the distance between us. Two swift, determined strides even as condemnation sketched his face. "Fuck, I want you." He ducked and captured my cheeks, kissing me.

Instead of accepting the kiss, I tore my face away. My hand shook as I reached for his cock, shivering at the hard steel of him as I tugged him closer.

He grunted and tripped into me.

His mouth opened to speak.

But it was too late.

His velvety heat was a trigger on my self-control.

My lips encased his tip. I sat higher on my knees squeezing his hot length with my hand. My fingers latched tight and unforgiving, not asking for permission—just like he'd done to me.

He'd owned me. Tasted me. Controlled me.

It's my turn.

My eyes skated up over the furrows and hills of his stomach until I met his gaze. Gil shuddered as I pumped him into my mouth. The winter frost of his eyes blazed like wildfire, hinting that what I took as annoyance and anger were actually tightly reined need.

He buckled with a will of iron.

He didn't give in to the urges beating him to submit—the urges between us. The urges that had always been there, despite our tempers.

I stroked him again, sucking him deep.

His head fell back, and his fingers threaded through my hair. He didn't just hold me steady, he pulled me forward, pressing more of his cock into my mouth.

Everything inside quivered. My wetness would've been embarrassing if I didn't know Gil wanted me as much as I wanted him. I knew it in the tension in his muscles, the groan in his chest, the violence in his fingers.

I opened wider, sucking his girth. My tongue lapped underneath as my fingers corkscrewed around him.

I dared scrape my teeth along sensitive flesh, testing him.

He thrust into me, rocking my body back. Tears flooded my eyes as his savage grunt made my insides clench on emptiness.

Sucking him made me feel powerful. But I needed him inside me. Otherwise, I was going to lose my mind and never be able to function again.

Pressing my legs together, I bobbed my head as my heated flesh made me moan. My jaw ached at his size, saliva trickling from the corner of my mouth as I continued to worship him.

"Fuck—" He thrust harder as desperation to come bunched his thighs, and the salty taste of release grew stronger. He tugged my hair, his eyes tightly closed as his cock rippled in warning.

I wanted to make him unravel. To come apart so I might have some chance at understanding him. I threw myself into pleasuring him, sucking him deeper still. Keeping my lips glued tight, I stroked, massaging my spit into his heat.

Gil gasped, stumbling back as his ass clenched under my free hand. "Stop. *Shit.*" He grabbed his cock, pressing his thumb into the tip as if doing his best to prevent an orgasm.

His eyes squeezed tight as his body shuddered. He bowed over himself, panting and tense.

I waited.

I fought against the urge to stroke myself and relieve the throbbing second release. I did my best not to be consumed by the very image of Gil naked with his cock in his hand.

Time ticked strangely, my heartbeats tattered as Gil slowly straightened and towered over me. His face was furious, eyes blazing, his cock spearing upright from his gorgeously damaged body.

I wanted to capture the moment. To remember it for always.

Because who knew if I'd ever see him this way again.

My hand migrated between my legs on its own accord. I moaned as I touched myself, teasing the pounding need for more.

Gil's attention snapped onto my display. His forehead furrowed as his chest rose and fell. "Christ, you truly want me to die."

I licked my lips. "I need you."

Our eyes locked and the viciousness of sex was replaced by the tenderness of love. He tensed. His head shook. He looked as if he'd rather rip out his heart than touch me in anger.

But then the clouds gathered again, shoving him into blackness—a place of protection from his pain.

Whatever this was, it wasn't making love.

This was darker.

Gil swallowed back tender things, and pounced on me. "Get on all fours." Slamming to his knees, he threw me around until I braced myself on four points. He deliberately faced me away so he didn't have to see how much I cared. Didn't have to fight the never-ending bond we shared.

I understood.

I accepted.

I *wanted*.

His hands caressed my spine and ass, massaging me, spreading me. His touch slid to my tattoo and scars. "This goddamn ink. These awful scars." His heady groan made me shiver as he dragged his nose along the base of my back. "To think of you hurt—" His teeth snapped together, silencing whatever else he wanted to say.

His fingers kept stroking my tattoo, running along owl feathers and ostrich plumes. His touch wasn't gentle, more like a fiery brand flaying me alive. "You're not safe with me," he hissed. "I'm putting you in danger."

My teeth bared in frustration, leaning back into his control. "I don't care."

"*I* care."

"Just finish this, Gil." A full body clench made me beg. *"Please."*

"Tell me to stop." His breath scalded my back as he reared up behind me. "Please, God, tell me to stop." His thighs met mine. His heat burned me. His cock wedged against my ass as he grabbed my hips and ran his length up my crack. "Tell me. Fuck, *tell* me."

My head hung between my shoulders. I dug fingers into the floor, rocking backward into him. "I won't."

"I don't have a condom."

"I'm on the pill."

He cursed under his breath. "I haven't been with anyone in…a long time."

My heart squeezed. "Neither have I."

"I…I won't put you at risk." His teeth chewed the words as if conversation was getting harder and harder to manage.

"Me either." I rocked again, gasping at the temptation of having him so close to taking me.

"You'll regret this in the morning." He groaned, pulling away and lining his cock up with my entrance. "I tried to warn you. Too bad you didn't fucking listen."

He thrust.

He entered me.

He split me in two, condemned me, consumed me, sank deep, *deep* inside me.

My arms buckled at the overwhelming euphoria of having Gilbert Clark—the boy who I'd dreamed about, cried over, wanted, and needed—finally fill me like he was born to do.

The world spun on its axis, blending colours, bleeding futures, hurling us together.

Gil snarled as he withdrew and thrust again. "Why do you have to feel so good?" He drove himself as deep as he could go. His voice traded human for monster. "Why the fuck did you have to come back into my life?"

My tongue was too tangled and useless for words. I was nothing more than sin and sensation, riding him, tempting him, encouraging him to ignore boundaries and tear me apart.

I needed him to fuck me.

Truly, aggressively *fuck* me.

Gil pulled back, then shoved into me so hard, I scooted forward. The sweet bliss of being entered, expanded, and owned sent another depth to the orgasm building in my core.

"I can't believe I'm inside you," Gil grunted. Driving into me, he set a punishing pace. He eradicated all space between us, his thighs rigid and slapping against mine with every impale. "Can't believe you're here. With me."

My pulse shot skyward as I arched my back, giving him unfettered access.

"Fuck, don't." He bowed over me, biting my shoulder as he

drove every inch inside me. The broken despair in his voice knotted with breathless wonderment. As if he'd spent his life, just as I had, trying to understand the compulsive connection between us.

It'd gone past teenage crush. It'd grown even while apart.

No words could describe our strange bond. No common sense could understand why I felt the way I did about him but wanted him to use me so completely.

Gil's fingers dipped between my legs.

I teetered on my knees as he rubbed my wetness around my clit.

"Holy mother of—" I moaned as his touch sent more pressure gathering inside, suffocating me, hurting me to let go.

I soared my ass back, driving him so deep his tip hit the top of me, and we both groaned like animals.

I didn't recognise myself.

I didn't recognise him.

All I knew was I had to come. Again. Now. *Immediately.*

Gil grabbed my hips, hauling me higher so he could thrust at a different angle. Each drive, he hit me in the most perfect, piercing way.

I jolted, unable to bear it. "Gil. God—"

"Don't move." He pulled me back each time he dived forward. No space. No gentleness. "I'm going to fuck you, do you understand?"

My eyes rolled at the dripping darkness in his tone.

Didn't he realise he was already doing that?

"I'm going to fuck you and then you're walking out that door and never coming back." The lace of alcohol in his tone didn't slur but added a cruelty that only sent more fire into my already bleeding need.

"This is the first and only time." His voice was an aphrodisiac as he bent over me, pressing me into the floor as his hips worked hard and fast. "Once." His forehead crashed on my spine as if convincing himself that we could walk away after this. "Just once. That's all this can ever be."

His nails imprinted marks into my flesh as he clawed to get closer. His own words terrifying him into harsher aggression.

I didn't bother replying. I focused on clutching at the floor and giving everything I had.

"Jesus Christ." Gil wrapped a hand around my loose hair, forming a messy ponytail. He rutted into me, staying true to his word to use me.

With a jerk, he yanked my head back, arching my spine, plunging inside me with a roar.

Deep.

Hard.

Bestial ownership.

I opened my mouth to scream, but he clamped a hand over me, riding me, containing my cries. "Quiet. He can't know you're here again."

He thrust quick and dominant.

I didn't know this Gil. No remnants of the teenage boy existed. This man was lethal and I came apart for him. I transcended human form and felt him on a feral level. There was no beginning or end. No choice or conclusion. My orgasm could no longer be denied, working its way up my belly into my spine and teeth. The swirling, twisting warning was my only hint before I shattered outward.

I combusted with pleasure.

I plummeted into pulses.

My entire body contracted and melted.

Gil followed me.

His thrusts grew shallow and fast, dipping into me with a single-minded purpose.

He came with an unbearable noise of heartache and suffering, making tears prick my eyes. His release lasted a while, drenching me with heat.

His body twitched and jerked, his breath short and sharp.

Slowly, our haze receded, depositing us back into the living. My knees screamed and wrists bellowed, and Gil's cock still rippled inside me from his orgasm.

Piece by piece, cell by cell, we returned to our bodies and a chill cloaked me as Gil pulled out and stood.

He stumbled as if the vodka in his system returned full force, making him drunker than before. He didn't bother scooping his clothes from the floor. He just walked naked into the kitchen.

There, he yanked open a cupboard and ripped a glass from the shelf. He poured himself a drink from another bottle of vodka stolen from his pantry. Only once he'd shot the liquor down his throat did he look at me sitting dishevelled and used on his floor.

Our eyes met.

Our souls said goodbye.

I forced back tears as he said, "Get dressed. I'll walk you out."

Chapter Sixteen

Gil

-The Past-

"MR. CLARK, PLEASE stay after class."

I stiffened at my desk as Ms Tallup pinned her grey eyes on me. Olin twisted a little in her seat to look at me, but I shook my head slightly, hiding any sign of the trepidation inching down my spine.

Olin would wait for me to walk her home. I had no doubt about that.

It'd become a tradition. Just as it'd become tradition for her to slip me painkillers if my father had been particularly ruthless with his fists. Just as it'd become the norm for her to bring baked goods and hide money in my backpack so I could eat regularly.

She looked after me as much as I looked after her, and it made my heart suffocate with pain. We were in a relationship. A family-ship.

Yet, I still hadn't kissed her.

I'd been sure only to touch her platonically.

I bit my tongue on what I truly wanted to tell her.

How much I truly cared.

Since the pancake revelation a month ago, we'd been careful to keep some distance. We didn't discuss it; it'd just happened. Happened in a way that said we both felt the intensity of whatever existed between us and weren't quite ready to unleash it.

"Mr. Clark, did you hear me?" Ms Tallup crossed her arms, her nose in the sky.

My hands curled into fists. "Yes, Ms Tallup."

The bell rang.

Students shot to their feet.

Olin cast me a look as she shuffled out with the rest of the class, leaving me alone with the teacher from hell.

What the fuck does she want?

My father had avoided painting my face with bruises lately. My body was a different story, but at least nothing was visible to those who didn't need to know.

Standing slowly, I made a show of stuffing my workbook into my bag and sauntering toward the front where Ms Tallup waited. A marker in one hand and a piece of paper in the other.

My test from the other day.

With a giant F written in red.

Great.

Just fucking great.

"You're flunking me again?" I couldn't hide the contempt in my voice.

She tutted under her breath. "If you don't do the work, I can't reward you with the grades."

"I'm doing the work." I knew my grades were good because Olin helped me. We helped each other. I'd gotten over my aversion to being in her empty house, and we regularly had study sessions together. Her text pages were always so much cleaner than mine. Her bedroom so much warmer than mine. But I kept up with her in the intelligence department, and I trusted myself a little more. Trusted I was just as good as the other students and didn't deserve to be held back.

"That's not what I see." She crossed her arms again, crushing the paper against her body. "I see two students fraternising when they should be focused on school."

"What did you say?" Everything inside me went cold.

"You heard me." She looked at the door as if a pupil might walk by and overhear. Fat chance of that. They were all halfway home by now.

Apart from Olin.

She would wait for me.

She'd wait for me because I'd wait for her.

Always.

"It's none of your business which students hang out together."

She smiled thinly. "It is my business if it's affecting their academic progress."

"You've affected my academic progress by holding me back two years."

"I merely suggested to the headmaster that you weren't at the same level as the others. That's all. If he didn't agree with me, you would've graduated by now."

"I'm just as good as the rest of them." My temper boiled, and I understood partially why my father beat me when he was angry. The urge to punch Ms Tallup sent pins and needles racing into my fists. It would feel so nice to hurt her like she was hurting my future.

"Why are you doing this?" I did my best to speak normally, but it came out like a snarl.

Her eyebrows shot into her mousy hairline. "I don't know what you're talking about. I'm merely a concerned—"

"You're not. You want something. Something from me."

How the fuck didn't I see it before?

The thought was a lightning bolt. Hot and scary and lethal as hell. My head cocked, staying arrogant but quickly sliding into terror. "Tell me. What do you want?"

For the first time, a flicker of truth showed in her steely gaze. She wasn't old—pushing mid-thirties—but a vindictive streak in her said she hated teenagers.

Especially me.

I'd never done anything to her. I was always punctual, polite, hard-working.

But no matter what I did, nothing was ever good enough.

"What makes you think I want something from you, Mr. Clark?"

I leaned toward her, not caring if anyone saw. "I don't think. I know. Call it instinct."

She cocked her head with a gleam in her gaze. "Well, your instincts are wrong."

"They're never wrong."

Backing away, making it seem like she needed to put the marker back on the whiteboard, she said, "I'm merely advising you not to spend so much time chasing after Olin Moss. Now run along, Mr. Clark. Best behave yourself if you want to finish school sometime this century."

I wanted to kill her.

Honest to God murder her with my bare hands around her evil throat.

Instead, I nodded, and with tightly leashed fury, muttered,

"Thank you, Ms Tallup."

It took everything I had to stalk from the classroom, bolt down the corridor, and suck in a breath as green grass and late afternoon sunshine welcomed me.

Olin.

I needed Olin.

I needed the one girl who made my world bearable even while making it that much harder.

Chapter Seventeen

Olin

-The Present-

"SO…" GIL SHOVED his hands into his jeans pockets as we stood beneath the faded stars outside his warehouse.

"So." I licked my lips, smoothing down my skirt, very aware that I hadn't rinsed off and a combination of him and me made my thighs sticky.

His face shadowed with night and emotional darkness. Only one street light existed this far down the warehouse precinct, and its light was futile at chasing back the gloom. The moon was no help, tucked into bed behind wispy clouds where only brave stars peeked from behind.

He sighed as if struggling with what to say.

How did we discuss what happened in there? How did we walk away?

I slung my handbag over my shoulder and leaped into conversation for him. "What just happened, Gil….It was—"

"A mistake." He dragged a shaky hand through his hair. "I don't know how I could let that happen."

Temper heated me. "It wasn't just you, you know."

He glowered at the ground.

"And how dare you call it a mistake." I tried to curb my frustration. "It was amazing. Exactly like I knew it would be between us. It—"

"Won't happen again."

My heart fell. I'd stupidly thought we'd gotten past whatever was keeping us apart. I'd hoped…

I'd stupidly hoped things would magically fix themselves just because we had sex.

I'm an idiot.

"We can discuss this another day." I shrugged, wincing as my hair tugged under my handbag strap. "When you're not so..."

His gaze met mine, narrowed and guarded. "Not so drunk?"

"I wasn't going to bring it up, but yes. You're drunk and dealing with things that you refuse to tell me." I crossed my arms. "You asked me to be your canvas tonight, but instead of finding a professional painter, I found you intoxicated."

"You were late."

My chin flew up. "You were somewhere else."

"How the fuck do you know where I've been?" He pinched the bridge of his nose, groaning under his breath. "Sorry. I just...shit." He shook his head as if doing his best to dispel the tainting liquor.

"Where have you been, Gil?" My question was as quiet as the silver moon peeking from the wisps. My gaze travelled to the paint splatter on his hands and the combination of grass and dirt on his clothes.

Maybe Justin was right to be worried about him. Maybe he needed more help than I could provide.

What made him turn to a bottle today?

Why didn't he turn to me?

"Why were you drinking? You said you'd never be like—"

"Don't." He held up his hand. "Don't ask questions I can't answer."

Guilt squeezed that I hadn't been there for him. Hadn't been able to find him sooner.

He wasn't my responsibility. He'd knocked me out and been nothing but complicated since we'd found each other.

But it didn't change facts.

I would always have feelings for this man.

A kaleidoscope of them.

Undeniable and not fading anytime soon.

"You know I won't judge you for anything, right?" I shifted closer. "You can trust—"

"Stop." He bared his teeth, backing up. The alcohol made him harsher, eradicating the decorum he'd done his best to cling to. "It's time for you to go, Olin."

I ignored him. "Do you still need to paint me tonight?"

His half-smile tangled with a sneer. "Do I look capable of painting you?"

I didn't want to answer that.

Didn't want to admit that he looked as destitute in his soul as he did in possessions. His eyes were vacant but crowded at the same time—a haunted expression blending with depression. The mess on his clothing made him unsuitable for normal society. The twig knotted in his hair depicted him as something wild. The mud contouring his cheekbone said he'd either gone for a hike in the wilderness or fought a monster.

The only problem was, he acted as if the monster was *him*.

The one who didn't deserve kindness and togetherness—the one who did his best to ruin what'd just happened between us because he didn't know how to accept the inevitable.

We'd *always* been made for each other.

Time had ripped us apart, but fate had brought us back.

Too bad he couldn't accept such a gift.

"Do you want to reschedule for tomorrow?" I asked softly.

His eyes flashed. "You're not allowed back here."

"But what about the commission?"

His entire body shuddered as if unable to brace against colossal pain. "Doesn't matter."

"Why?" My stomach churned. "Surely, a day's delay won't make a—"

"It's over." His lips snapped shut, stark fear seeping into his face. Coughing, he straightened his shoulders and hid any trace of terror. "It had to be done today. This afternoon." Anger tinged his tone. "I couldn't deliver because my canvas was off earning minimum wage working for someone else."

I froze. "The alcohol is making you crueller than normal."

"Or allowing me to be honest."

"I don't believe that. I also don't believe you're truly blaming me for this."

"If you'd been here sooner, I might've—"

"I had commitments, Gil," I snapped. "I told you that."

He growled under his breath, burying his face into his hands.

I promised I'd be there for him.

No matter what.

Not able to bear the tension between us, I touched his shoulder. "Do you need money? I don't have much. In fact, I barely have anything, but it's yours if you need it." My rent was due tomorrow. My electricity bill the next day. My pantry was empty and my fridge might as well be switched off to save on power because it never held much these days.

I wouldn't be able to help much monetary wise, but I would share whatever I had.

He jerked away and shook his head, dropping his hands to stare down the long expanse of warehouses and their looming façades. His lips pressed together as if holding back so many awful things. His hands balled as if wanting to fight imaginary beasts. "Even now, you're willing to offer me everything you have." He didn't make eye contact, talking to the night. "You'd give me your last penny without hesitation."

I nodded. "Only because you'd do the same for me."

"Are you so sure?" He laughed coldly. "I'm not as good as you, Olin. I never was."

"It's not a matter of being good or bad. It's a matter of helping those you lo—" I snapped my mouth closed.

His gaze caught mine, endless and aching. "Please, don't."

My heart squeezed, scrambling to hide my almost-confession. "Tell me what you need the money for and I'll get as much as I can."

I'd loved him as a girl.

I'd loved him while apart.

And I still loved him, even though I wasn't sure he deserved it.

He snorted as if I'd asked the saddest, hardest question in the world. "Your money is worthless."

"Why?"

"Because it can't buy what I need."

"What do you need?"

He looked at the stars, his biggest lie slipping from his lips. "Nothing. I need nothing."

Too bad the truth echoed in the void, howling with the opposite of what he'd just said. Gil needed something. He needed *everything*.

Money.

Safety.

Help.

I pressed against him, hurt to my core when he sidestepped away before I could hug him. My fingernails dug into my palms as I did my best not to cry. "You forbid me from talking to the police, but you're in trouble, Gil...you need to tell them. They can help—"

"Help?" He rolled his eyes, the haze of alcohol evaporating a little. "They're about as much help as I am."

"What's that supposed to mean?"

"It means I'm fucking *useless*."

I sucked in a breath. "Why would you say that?"

"Because it's true." He sighed with his entire body. "Anyway, it doesn't matter now. It's too late."

Gil had always been a melancholy type of boy. At school, his smiles were few and far between. His laughter was priceless because it was so rare and whatever reaction he gave was always overshadowed by a taut wariness and cloudy distrust.

But tonight, thanks to alcohol blurring his walls, he struggled to hide.

"What's too late, Gil?" Worry sat thick and cloying in my chest. I wanted to touch him. To hug him. To hold him in my arms and tell him he could tell me because if he didn't, the poison inside would ruin him.

"Everything." He sighed again, swaying a little as tiredness mixed with drunkenness. "Go home, O. Time to forget about me."

I swallowed back my urge to tell him that was an impossibility. That I couldn't stop thinking about him before. Now that we'd had sex, I was doomed to being his forever.

My voice was level and kind as I said, "I'm sorry I couldn't help you with the commission earlier."

He sniffed, glowering at the dark world around us. "Yeah, me too."

Looking toward the empty street, I clutched my handbag closer. The thought of leaving him like his sent warning bells all over my skin. Turning to face him again, I did my best to change the subject. "Was it hard painting me? Did you…want me like you wanted me tonight?"

His face hardened. "I'm many things, Olin, but lusting after a canvas when I'm working is beneath even me."

"Can I be honest and say having you paint me was one of the hardest things I've ever done? Being with you tonight? God, I needed that so much."

My admittance did what I'd intended. It wrenched him from black thoughts, painting his features in surprise. He cleared his throat. "Having me paint you was hard?"

"Very much."

His muscles tensed for all new reasons. "Because…"

"Because you were so close, after being gone for so long. Because your brush felt like a kiss and your airbrush felt like…" I blushed. "Like your tongue."

He swallowed, his throat working. "I…" His eyes glowed as if he wanted to confess a thousand things, but those awful shutters slammed down again and he muttered, "Tonight only happened because I had compromised self-control and you had pent-up need from the previous commission. That's all it was. Basic instinct to find a release."

He effectively threw cold water in my face, slapping away yet another attempt to drag him from the darkness.

He's lost, O…

No, he's just being a jerk.

And frankly, I'd used up my quota of kindness tonight.

There was only so much patience I could offer. I wasn't a saint. I was hurt. I'd been hurt for seven long years. And that hurt became harder to ignore the more he fought me. "Time truly did scar you, Gil. I'm trying so hard to bring you back, but no matter what I do, you just keep pushing me away."

His eyebrows turned into jagged lines. "I grew up, O. We both did. Whoever you knew is no longer a part of me."

"It's so easy for you? To shove aside the parts of you that made us family?"

He shuddered as if I'd stabbed him in the heart. "Nothing about this is easy. You're not *making* it easy because you refuse to listen to me."

"I'm listening now." I didn't look away. "And I think you're forgetting *why* I refuse to obey you. Last time I did, you broke up with me. Last time I didn't fight with everything that I have, you just…disappeared. You keep acting as if you're trying to protect me by keeping me away, but in reality, I think you're just trying to protect yourself."

"I *am* trying to protect you."

"Do it some other way. Don't push me away this time, Gil. Don't be that selfish."

"Selfish?" he roared. "You think I'm being selfish by doing everything I can to keep you safe?"

"I think you're choosing the easy way out—"

"I never had it easy. Fucking ever!"

My voice rose to meet his, uncaring if people heard our domestic. "*You* broke it off with *me*. That was the easy option.

You moved on. You made the choice to leave. I was never given that option."

Why did I say that?

What's wrong with me?

I'd forgiven him for everything. I didn't want to punish him by bringing up the past when it was nothing compared to what he dealt with now.

"Look, I'm sorry, I—"

He crowded me until our chests touched. "You think I *chose* to leave you?"

I couldn't breathe properly. "You did a pretty good job of making it seem that way. You walked out of my life then vanished from school. No one had a clue where you'd gone."

"I didn't have a choice."

My anger rose again, ignoring my desire to stay calm. "Of course, you did! You could've talked to me instead of ripping out my—"

"I told you." His chest rose and fell with agony. "I had my reasons."

"And those reasons weren't good enough." Pain bolted through my blood, unravelling my will to keep this fight from happening. I couldn't stop myself from spilling everything I'd held inside. "Nothing you could tell me would excuse you breaking my heart."

I'd done what I could to stop blaming him. I'd focused on helping him, not on fixing what went wrong.

But...I'd reached my limit.

He was too wrapped up in secrecy.

Too isolated in misery.

I had to know.

I had to understand at least *something* before I went insane.

We'd slept with each other tonight. We'd let our bodies do the talking and it'd been the first honest conversation we'd had.

I wanted more of that.

Gil's gaze landed hotly on my lips. "You broke mine too. I'd say we're fair."

"What?" The starlit darkness crackled with instant electricity. My nipples pebbled and my breath caught as his hand lashed out, looping around my throat.

"You heard me. You went out with Justin. You flaunted your relationship in my goddamn face. Tell me why I should've stuck around at school to watch that?"

I tried to break from his hold, my fingers scratching at his arm. "You're seriously going to make me the bad guy? You pushed me away! You wouldn't speak to me! I spent every night crying, wondering what I'd done wrong. You wouldn't even *look* at me."

"I had reaso—"

"*No*, you didn't!" I ducked and twisted from his hold. "No reason you could have ever given me would justify the coldness you delivered."

"Apparently, you were justified enough to kiss Justin in our spots, though. I saw you. He had his hand up your shirt behind the gym." He punched his chest. "That was *our* spot, O. Ours. No one else's." His eyes glistened with agony. He spun and stormed away, both hands digging through his hair. *"Fuck!"*

With his overwhelming heat and power gone, I sucked in oxygen. How had this fight happened? Why were we tearing each other to ribbons?

I spread my hands in surrender, exhaustion crushing me fast. "Look, none of that matters now. You and Justin are friends, and we're...we're—" I smiled even though my heart felt like shattering. "We're friends, too...even if you'd rather not be."

"You can't be friends with someone who doesn't deserve it." The light went from his eyes, any softness from before deleted from his mouth. He turned to stone as he pointed into the darkness. "I don't deserve you, O. And you don't deserve to suffer. You need to leave. You need to obey because it's the only way I can keep you safe. Leave and never come back." His gaze danced around the open, empty night. "Promise me."

"You don't need to be afraid of him."

I expected him to growl. Instead, his response sent glaciers oozing down my spine.

"I do, and...I *am*." He nodded with conviction, causing my tummy to flip. His voice echoed with uncurable disaster. "Deathly fucking afraid."

"Of what?"

"Of everything."

I reached for him. "Gil—"

He stepped away. "Go." Gritting his teeth, he gave the industrial area a searching, scathing look as if warning goblins and night terrors to leave me the hell alone before stepping through the pedestrian access to his warehouse. "Goodbye, O. For the last time."

With a final splintering look, he slammed the door and locked it.

Chapter Eighteen

Olin

-The Present-

FOR TWO DAYS, life tried to convince me things were normal.

I ate, showered, went to work, and travelled home each night. All the mundane tasks of living alone and fending for yourself in a large city dragged me along in some resemblance of normalcy.

Only, it wasn't normal.

My body knew that. My heart knew that. Even my mind knew it, because it struggled to stop thinking about Gil for a moment, let alone switch off to sleep.

Starting a new job and falling into bed with the boy I never stopped loving weren't a good combination.

I caught Shannon's eye as she smiled at me from across the floor. Even though my thoughts were far from work, I did my best to perform well. The phone was always answered politely, my emails replied to promptly. I'd learned my role fast, so no one had to breathe down my neck.

Yesterday, when I'd messaged Justin that Gil was back at his warehouse, I'd bit my lip in case he went over there and figured out that we'd slept together. My cheeks heated as Justin replied, asking if I knew where Gil had been and what state I'd found him in.

Luckily, I'd had to duck into a team meeting, so I brushed him off and told him to go see Gil if he had any more questions.

That was over twenty-four hours ago, and I was tired. The

clock showed just past four, and I begged for the rest of the time to disappear so I could go home, drink some cheap supermarket wine in a futile attempt to stop reliving the delicious, emotionally-dangerous sex we'd indulged in, and plead for sleep.

"Hi, Olin." The guy from the coffee room who'd flirted with me on my first day smiled over my cubicle wall. His dark skin and darker eyes were highlighted by a white shirt and silver tie. He held a bunch of papers under his arm and his gaze travelled over my similar attire of cream blouse with navy pinstripe skirt. "You up to much this weekend?"

I stopped typing an email about a laptop that needed a factory reset and shook my head. "Not really. You?"

He grinned. "Not much."

"Cool." I smiled awkwardly. "Well, I hope you find—"

"I was gonna see if you wanted to do something, actually." He interrupted me in a rush. "I mean…if you're not doing anything."

I stilled. My roller chair creaked as I sucked in a harsh breath. "Oh. Um…"

"We could do lunch? Or a movie? Even just a walk. I'm easy." He hoisted the papers higher. "Say, Saturday?"

My heart bumped into ribs in its haste to refuse. It'd been a while since I'd been on a date. I didn't think I'd even remember the rules and etiquette required.

You had sex two days ago.

I scowled. Yes, I did. But that couldn't be classified as a date.

Sex with Gil was the opposite of a date. Unplanned, ill-advised, and stupidly spontaneous.

The guy inhaled, waiting for me to puncture his hope.

I fiddled with my pen on the desk. "I don't even know your name."

He slouched in relief that I hadn't shot him down straight away. "It's Hamish."

"Hamish." I nodded with a small smile. "Nice name."

"Olin is nice too."

I tilted my head. "It's strange."

"Strange is always better than normal."

"I'm not so sure about that." I sighed, mainly to myself but smiled brighter as Hamish cocked an eyebrow. "Look, Hamish, I—"

His entire body deflated. "You're busy, after all?"

I couldn't exactly lie after I'd told him I had no plans, but I didn't know what else to say. Lying had never come easy to me, and I'd used up what little talent I had lying to the cops on Gil's behalf. And besides, I didn't want to fib to a new colleague who I might end up working with for a long time. "I can't go out with you because…"

I don't want to date work friends.

I don't mix business and pleasure.

I'm…eh…a lesbian.

Good one, O.

"She's in a relationship with me. That's why."

My head shot up at the chilly, commanding voice as Hamish spun around.

I blinked, not believing who stood in my cubicle.

My heart instantly sat up and glowed. Gratefulness that he'd sought me out after our fight. Insane relief that it wasn't truly over, no matter the fierce words we'd thrown at each other two nights ago.

I'd done my best not to contact him. I'd forced myself to give him space.

It worked.

Hamish scowled, looking Gil up and down. "You're her boyfriend?"

Gil stood tall and impenetrable, hands balled by his sides, hair cascading over his forehead. His black T-shirt and tan jacket held no paint, mud, or blood for once, and his jeans were semi-presentable. His boots, on the other hand, were a colourful, dirty mess.

Gil looked at me, then back at Hamish, his jaw working hard as if chewing his lies, doing his best to make them sound believable. "Yes. Since high-school. She's the love of my life."

My chest ached at the way his voice gruffed with honesty, even while masquerading as falsehoods.

Hamish looked at me. "You didn't say you were with someone."

To be fair, I'd only worked here a few days. And I wasn't the type of person to share such personal details with strangers. I smoothed my minor annoyance away, saying kindly, "I'm rather private about stuff outside of work."

"Which is why she kept me a secret." Gil strode forward, broaching the smallness of my cubicle and placing a possessive hand on my shoulder.

My skin instantly conducted electricity, sprouting goosebumps as if lightning forked from Gil's touch. I hadn't slept in days, yet all my sleepiness vanished just having his hand on me.

My legs bunched to haul me upright. I didn't want to be sitting while Gil towered over me, but his fingers latched into muscle, pressing me firmly down.

I shot him a dirty look as I smiled as normally as I could at Hamish. "Anyway, thanks so much for the offer. I hope you have a great weekend."

Hoping Hamish got the clue that he was dismissed, I kept my smile pasted on my face, waiting for him to go.

He licked his lips, then looked one last time at Gil holding me prisoner before sighing and heading back to his desk. The second he was gone, I swatted Gil's hand from me and swooped to my feet. "What on earth are you doing here?"

My whisper sounded far too loud in the suddenly quiet space. Colleagues pretended to work but kept their attention on the new girl and her uninvited beau.

"I'll tell you back at mine." He grabbed my wrist, tugging me with urgency and strictness. "We need to leave. Right now."

"What, why?" I twisted my arm, dislodging him. "I can't go anywhere with you. I'm at *work*, Gil. I have a commitment to—"

"Olin? Everything okay?" Shannon stretched an annoyed smile with bright pink lip gloss, her hair tied back with a matching coloured ribbon. Her shrewd gaze flew from me to Gil and back again. "You know company policy. Friends and family have to be signed in and approved by management."

"Approved by management?" Gil coughed. "You can't prevent me from seeing her."

Shannon's lips pursed. "I can if you're disrupting other employees."

"I'm not disrupting anyone. Olin needs to leave. I've come to take her—"

"I'm staying," I whispered harshly. "I finish work in less than an hour. I'll come to yours when I'm done."

"I'm not going anywhere without you." His voice darkened with warning. Looking frostily at Shannon, he added, "Don't penalize her for this. Blame me. Blame me, but it won't change the fact that I'm taking her."

My mouth hung open. I rushed to do damage control. "I can't take time off. I literally just started here. I told you, I'll come to you when I'm finished, and not before."

His gaze flashed, his body rippling with energy. "You're not leaving here on your own."

My mind tangled the past with the present. He'd always escorted me home. Always there to chaperon and guard. I'd always felt so safe in his presence, knowing he'd never let anything or anyone hurt me.

Despite Shannon watching us, a twinge of pain left over from our fight made me whisper, "You were fine letting me walk home in the dark the other night."

His face turned to grey ash. "I know. It was the hardest and shittiest thing I've done in a very long time. I'm so sorry, O."

I wasn't expecting that, nor the sincere anguish on his face. It gave me nothing to argue against. It made me see the seriousness of his request.

Not that it's a request.

I sighed, glancing furtively at Shannon. "Sorry about this, Shannon. I value my employment and won't jeopardise—"

"It's fine." She nodded. "I'm sure there's an explanation."

"There is. An exceedingly simple one." Gil raked a hand through his unruly hair. "I need Olin to come with me—"

"I'm *staff*, Gil." I cut in. "I have an obligation to stay until it's time to go home."

Couldn't he see he was messing up my chances for long-term employment?

I need this job!

I needed to pay my bills, so I no longer had to stare at my ceiling late at night and fear the words 'bankruptcy' and 'homelessness'.

"Olin." His big hand captured my cheek, erasing the outside world.

It was just us.

Us.

In a sea of people who no longer mattered.

His thumb caressed my cheekbone. His breath caught. And my heart answered his. My need matched his. I—

"You need to come with me." His voice shattered the illusion of aloneness. Bringing his lips to my ear, he added, "Please, don't argue. I don't have the strength today."

I pulled away, shivers still dancing over my skin. "I'm not being difficult, Gil. I truly can't leave." I pointed at the bank of elevators. "Go home. I'll come by after work and we'll talk."

He crossed his arms, bracing himself against the many curious stares we'd invited. "Like I said before, you can't leave this building alone."

"What? Why?"

His jaw clenched. "He knows where you work."

My heart tripped. The rush of adrenaline from unsuccessful kidnappings and Gil's subsequent punishment sent worry-filled fire through my blood. "That arsehole? How the hell does he know where I work?"

"Look…I'm going to leave you guys to it." Shannon cleared her throat. "This is obviously private. I'm sure if this is a family emergency, the company will understand if Olin leaves a little earlier than normal."

"It is an emergency." Gil never looked away from me while answering her coolly. "And she's family. So it fits both criteria."

I sucked in a breath.

Family.

I thought I was the only one who remembered that promise.

Family.

You've slept with this man.

Family.

You've loved this man.

Family.

Yet right now, you can't understand this man.

"Okay, not a problem." Shannon waved and tottered quickly away on her heels. The second she was gone, I repeated my question, my breath thin. "How does he know where I work, Gil?"

"Same way I do." His body tensed. "Your contract with all your work info must've fallen out of your bag when he…when he tried to take you. He paid me a visit today…he showed me."

So that's where it went.

I'd looked highly incompetent when I'd arrived on my first day missing my signed contract.

My heart sank, two anchors of terror dragging it down. "He'll know where I live too. My address was on there."

He nodded.

Fear for myself was quickly overshadowed by fear for him. Placing a hand on his forearm, I did my best not to be hurt when he twitched and acted as if I'd stabbed him with my pen. "Are you okay? Did he hurt you?"

His gaze snapped to mine. "I tell you I've put you in mortal danger and you *still* ask if I'm the one okay?" He backed away, rubbing his mouth with his hand. "Olin, you really need to stop caring about others and put yourself first. Your goddamn goodness is going to get you killed."

"I'm sorry if my ethics annoy you."

"They don't annoy me, they're just not wise. Worry about yourself for fuck's sake."

"Don't you think it's up to me who I worry about?"

"All I'm saying is, don't waste your concern on me."

"Ha!" I rolled my eyes. "I've literally worried about you my entire life."

"Did I ask you to?" His temper thickened.

"No. It's just what someone does when they care—"

"Stop." He sighed heavily, torment cloudy in his gaze. "Shit...why are we fighting?" One hand opened and closed by his side, the other reached for me despite himself. Once again, he fought the familiar urge to touch, to connect, to bond. "I'm sorry for causing you stress, O. I—"

"It's fine—"

"No." He shook his head. "I never deserved you. Not even when I had you. I definitely don't deserve your concern."

His hand dropped.

He went to shove it into imprisoning pockets.

I reached out and stole it, wrapping our fingers together, binding us tight. Power ignited between us—something pure and transparent, honest and true. It hummed from his palm to mine, tingling and kissing its way up my arm and down my spine. "Just answer my question. Did he hurt you?"

Gil pulled away with a grimace. "No."

That was a yes.

He glanced at the elevators, his desire to leave obvious. "Please...just trust me." His eyes flickered with the past, with a younger Gil who I very much used to trust.

Before he'd broken my heart.

My questions and worry could wait.

"Okay." Snatching my handbag, I logged off the work system and brushed past him with quick steps. He didn't say a word, following me like a queen's guard, waiting possessively close for the elevator to arrive.

My heart beat skipped and tripped having Gil so near. My body steadily betraying me, filling with desire, remembering what it was like to be with him, to kiss him, to have him inside me.

By the time the elevator scooped us up and swallowed us from the curious stares of employees, my knickers were damp and blouse far too tight.

I struggled to catch a proper breath.

I leaned forward to press the button for the ground level, but Gil beat me to it. Our fingers brushed on the button, sending a bolt of lust through my blood.

I didn't know what it was about elevators, but it seemed all great romances had an epic kiss in the claustrophobic transportation. Our tale wasn't exactly a romance, but Gil's hand cupped my cheek, his thumb feathering over my bottom lip. "I'm sorry about the other night."

I moaned under my breath as his thumb dipped into my mouth.

His emerald gaze darkened, his body pressing into mine until he crowded me against the mirrored wall. My spine crashed against the coolness, my breasts and belly tingling as he imprisoned me with his weight.

He trembled, his hips tight on mine, one arm braced on the mirror. "I'm sorry for being so rough with you. What I did...wasn't right. I wasn't...myself."

My heart galloped as his voice caught with something dark and dismal.

My mind was useless, already drunk on his almost-kiss, but temper flared with coherency. "Wait...you're apologising about having *sex* with me?"

He frowned, his stare fixated on my lips. "I was rough with you."

"I liked it."

"I fucked you like an animal." His forehead furrowed as he shut his eyes. "I never wanted to treat you that way. I made a promise when I was younger to always treat you with—"

"With silk gloves?" I moved, trying to push his heavy weight off me. He didn't let me, trapping me harder against the wall.

"With *respect*." His eyes locked on mine. "Men are monsters, O. I learned that lesson right from childhood."

The whorehouse of his youth.

The screams of sex.

The howls of men.

For the first time, comprehension bowled into me. "Is that why you never attempted to sleep with me when we were younger?" I didn't know how I felt about that. In awe? In pain?

Grateful? Frustrated? "You knew how much I wanted you, yet you never touched—"

"How could I touch you when I was that bastard's son?" His mouth bracketed by strain. "I didn't know if I could control myself, and judging by the other night, I was right to keep my dick in my pants."

"Wow." I went to push him away but wrapped my hands behind his neck instead. "You're an idiot." Jerking his head down, I kissed him.

He convulsed as my tongue broke the seam of his lips, tasting him, claiming him. His hands dove into my hair, holding me still as he opened his mouth and kissed me exquisitely hard.

The hushed world of the elevator, the weightlessness of falling—it became a tinderbox. A mirrored prison where lust was a scalpel and desire a blade. Need sliced at my skin, blood bubbled with want.

Our lips slipped and glided, our teeth clacked, our tongues tangled.

His hips thrust into mine. His hands dropped to my ass, squeezing me, massaging with animalistic paws, wrenching me against the hard steel in his jeans.

The elevator pinged.

The doors opened.

The architecturally light-drenched lobby ripped apart our hushed, erotic world.

Gil tore himself from me, stumbling backward with his hands shaking and lips wet. I swayed on my heels, swallowing hard, smoothing my skirt down with trembling fingers.

I managed to walk off the elevator and ignore the amused stares of two security guards, my body still clenching for Gil.

What the hell just happened?

Pulling me to the side, wrapping us in shadows of a corridor leading to the washrooms, Gil gritted his teeth. "That shouldn't have happened."

"I kissed you. I started it."

"Yeah, but I—"

"Don't worry, Gil. I wanted you to maul me. I like it when you lose control. The only thing I don't like is when you apologise for it."

"It can't happen again."

"I'm getting tired of hearing that." I sniffed. "It's repetitive."

"It's the truth."

A dagger slipped through my ribs and found my heart. "Why are you so determined to stop this?"

His eyes sought mine, empty but depthless at the same time. "Because I only destroy those I love. And I fucking refuse to destroy you."

I rubbed at my aching chest. "But what about us?"

He exhaled hard, his tan jacket creaking a little. "There *is* no us."

"There's *always* been an us."

"It's because of *us* that you're in danger!"

"What does he want from you, Gil?"

His face shut down, his features unreadable. "Nothing."

I walked away, my heels condemning and loud on the travertine floor.

"O." His fingers wrapped around my arm, dragging me to a stop. "I can't let you leave. You can't be alone. Not until I figure this out."

Annoyance trickled with previous passion, creating a cyclone of unresolved emotion. "You're forgetting I've lived alone for most of my life. I've managed perfectly well without you. "

I aimed for that to bruise just like he'd just bruised me, but I wasn't prepared for the way sorrow painted his body with tragedy. "I know."

My fight faded as fast as it had arrived. "You can't keep what you're hiding a secret. Not anymore. I deserve to know what's going on. You can tell me. You know I won't judge you. I'll help—"

"Stop." His eyes darkened, glinting like chiselled stone. "You want to know? Fine. He wants you because he knows you mean something to me. That you'll ensure I'll obey." He snarled as if he could deny it. "He's right."

"Gil, I—"

"I didn't want this to happen. I tried to keep you away so this *wouldn't* happen. But it has and…"

"And?"

His muscles locked in place. "And now we both have to pay."

Chapter Nineteen

Gil

-The Past-

"OLIN MOSS, WHAT have I told you about talking in class?"

I looked up from the pop test Ms Tallup had assigned us. Olin's shoulders hunched, her head slid to the side, her gaze catching mine.

My fingers tightened around my pen.

The class was silent.

It'd *been* silent since the test began.

My hearing was acutely attuned to Olin's every noise, and she hadn't made a peep.

My eyes narrowed to blades as Ms Tallup snapped her fingers with a sniff. "Detention, Miss Moss. This afternoon."

"Wait. But I—" Olin held up a hand. "I wasn't talking—"

"Arguing won't help your case." Ms Tallup sat in her chair and ignored the class as Olin threw me a disbelieving look.

I wanted to tell her not to worry. That she didn't have to do detention because she hadn't done anything wrong. But I couldn't because I knew why this had happened.

Last week, the deputy principal had found Olin and me hiding behind the school gym after hours. I'd had a rough night. My ribs were sore from being punished for not getting payment from some john at three in the morning.

My father decided to take payment in blood.

My blood.

After he'd finished, I'd walked out of the house—if that was even a word for the hellhole I lived in—and wandered (stumbled) the streets. At dawn, I'd found an old sketch pad abandoned on the footpath a block away from school. Some of the pages held doodles of dogs and flowers, but the rest were blank, offering a distraction from my pain.

I'd always liked to sketch, but I hadn't attempted anything in years.

But as the sun rose and I waited for Olin to arrive at school, I drew the building, the street, and the tree outside our classroom. I even drew Olin—or what I could from memory.

All day at school, I deliberated whether to show her. The work wasn't very good, but it'd made all the other shit in my life fade knowing I could create art from nothing.

The magic it gave me while dragging a pen over paper had been life-changing.

As life-changing as Olin.

Despite my lines being rudimentary and my skill lacking, I decided to show her, picking a spot where we wouldn't be seen by other students behind the gym. She'd been so happy to share in my newfound hobby, so grateful that I'd given her another piece of myself, and we'd hung out for far longer than we planned.

And of course, we'd been caught.

Caught at the exact moment Olin put her hand on mine and our eyes locked while we sat against the brick wall. My mouth watered. My heart galloped. My stomach churned for the taste of her lips.

We'd been *so* close.

So fucking close to our first kiss.

But then the gruff command from the deputy ripped us apart.

I'd been furious.

But in an awful way, I was grateful.

Furious to have the perfect almost-kiss ruined, but thankful that I didn't lose control and ravage her.

If I touched her.

When I touched her.

She deserved to be pampered and adored. To be given sweet and softness. Not devoured and mauled like I was desperate to do.

I'd thought keeping my distance physically would be easier as time went on, knowing we could be with each other when I was sure she loved me and could never take that back.

But…it only grew harder.

So damn hard it was a physical ache every second of every damn day. I couldn't breathe some days. I woke up at night with an unbearable pain to run over to her house and climb through her window.

To crawl into her bed, to kiss her as hard as I could, to take everything she offered me.

And that sort of desperation terrified me.

I'd have nightmares about making her scream like the whores inside my home.

I'd wake in full sweats at the thought of making her cry with my inherited savagery.

As the weeks went on, more and more fear layered my fraying self-control.

I was afraid to kiss her more than ever now.

Afraid I'd hurt her with the naked violence coursing in my blood.

Olin shrugged helplessly.

I shook my head, commanding her to stay quiet. I'd deal with Ms Tallup after class.

She gave me a grateful smile, blew me a kiss, then returned to her test with tense shoulders.

For the remaining twenty minutes, I scribbled answers as best I could while my brain focused on more important things. The deputy obviously told Ms Tallup he'd caught us. Therefore, she'd done this to punish me.

But why?

What the hell does she want from me?

The bell rang, signalling chairs to squeal away from desks and papers to be gathered in a fast rustle. The mass exodus of students was good because it meant I could speak to Ms Tallup and get far away before my temper exploded.

Olin stood, slinging her messenger bag over her shoulder. She caught my fingers as I walked past, but I pointed at the corridor. "Go."

She bit her lip. After a second, she obeyed, disappearing with the throng of other teenagers.

The second she'd gone, I looked at Ms Tallup.

She stood at the front with her arms crossed and a sick smirk upon her lips. "Mr. Clark. Not rushing off to spend time with your girlfriend today?" She cocked her head. "Does this mean the allure has finally worn off? Are you going to focus on your studies instead of your..." Her gaze dropped down my front, locking on my crotch.

She licked her lips.

Thick disgust rippled down my back.

I knew that look.

It was the look of grotesque hunger when a man looked at a whore he'd bought for the night.

I wasn't a whore.

Yet my teacher looked at me as if I was one.

Thick fear filled me, whispering answers to why Ms Tallup picked on me. Why she watched me more than any other student. Why I felt so on edge around her.

She wanted something from me.

Something sickening.

Something she would never fucking get.

I marched toward her and punched my test onto her desk. "Olin doesn't deserve detention. Tell her it was a mistake."

Her face darkened; she laughed coldly. "A student telling a teacher what to do?" She shook her head, clucking her tongue. "Now, that will never do."

My nostrils flared, doing my best to control my rage. "I'll do it. I'll serve the detention."

"You weren't the one talking."

"Don't care. Olin wasn't either."

"Punishment is given to those who deserve it."

I shivered. Her words were a little too close to the thoughts in my own head. I got it rough at home, but maybe...I deserved it.

Maybe I wasn't as good as I strived to be. Maybe my dad knew something about me that I didn't, and his beatings were part of a punishment I did deserve.

I shook those thoughts away. If that was the case, I would weather the storm. But I wouldn't let Olin be hurt. She'd never done anything wrong in her life.

Removing my fist from her desk, I backed up a step and lowered my voice. "Why do you hate me so much?"

Her eyes widened. "Hate you? Why on earth do you think I hate you?"

"Oh, I dunno. A few reasons."

"None that are real." She waved her hand, her gaze once again landing on my body. "Now, run along."

"I'm not a child. I don't 'run along'."

She smiled coyly. "Oh, believe me. I know you're not a child, Gilbert Clark."

I crossed my arms against the sudden chill. "I should be done with school if it wasn't for you. I think the least I deserve is the truth. You don't like me. I get it. I'm fine with it. But don't take it out on Olin. She's one of your best students."

"She was." She sniffed. "Until she started hanging out with you."

"Her grades are still excellent."

Ms Tallup leaned over the table, casting a subtle glance at the door and empty corridor. "It's not her grades I'm bothered about."

I swallowed hard as her eyes once again skated down my front, lingered on my jeans, then snaked their way back to my face. "I'm worried what you're doing to her. She's underage. You could be arrested."

"Arrested?" I backed up. "For what?"

"For sleeping with your innocent little girlfriend."

I swallowed hard. I didn't like this conversation at all.

The dynamics were off. The subjects all wrong. No way should a teacher discuss a student's love life. No way should the power she held be used to condemn and control me.

Terror slicked down my spine. "Why do you care what Olin and I do outside of school hours?"

She stilled. Her eyes flashed as she made a show of fluffing papers into a neat pile. "I don't. But you should."

"Why?" Goosebumps dotted my arms as her face sharpened, dropping the pretence she'd held for years.

With a short, tight chuckle, she whispered, "You're a smart boy. You'll figure it out."

She left me standing wordless and disgusted as she swept from the classroom with her hips swaying and a sly smile on her lips.

Chapter Twenty

Olin

-The Present-

"WHAT DID YOU mean we both have to pay?"

My question hung in the air as I stepped into Gil's warehouse. He'd driven us here in a small hatchback that'd seen better days with chipped white paint and ripped upholstery. It didn't smell like him nor had any sign of regular use.

I'd held my tongue the entire journey.

He hadn't let me grab any clothes or asked if I needed to check on my apartment. He'd just bundled me into his run-down vehicle and squirreled me away in the same place he'd kicked me out of two days prior.

I tried to be rational.

I tried to be patient.

But I'm running out of restraint.

Gil didn't answer my question, moving through the cavernous space with stormy steps. He looked angry. Angry at having me back in his space.

Well, that makes two of us.

The poise that'd been drilled into me by my dance master fissured a little. My composure that ensured no one ever knew just how lonely I was, frayed.

Gil wanted me.

That was undeniable.

Gil would protect me.

That was tried and tested.

But...when it came to enlightening me about things

happening in his life, he'd always been tricky. It'd always taken an argument for him to be honest. Always been me who'd had to push and push for answers.

If only I'd pushed harder when he'd broken up with me, we might've salvaged what he'd broken.

Don't let him get away with secrets this time, O.

He'll shut down.

Disappear.

Again.

Chasing after him, my determination not to let him ruin our second attempt overcame my need to be considerate of his pain. "Gil…you can't just drag me here and then ignore me, you know."

He kept walking, his shoulders bunching as if my reprimand physically hurt him.

"Gil." I jogged after him, my heels clicking with each dainty step. My pinstripe skirt wasn't exactly meant for quick strides. "You can't avoid this. I deserve an explanation."

His hands fisted as he stopped beside a metal cabinet holding bottles upon bottles of paint. A rainbow of colour, all waiting to be smeared on some woman's skin and photographed.

I didn't like the brushes waiting in their glass jars. I didn't like the fresh sponges or neat nozzles of his air gun. I didn't like anything to do with his art because it hurt so, so much that he'd evolved into someone immensely talented after sharing the first origins of that talent with me.

No one else had known.

And I'd been too stupid to understand just how important it was to him.

My frustration smoked into something with sharper claws. Anger I hadn't dealt with returned. Anger that'd settled deep inside, churning, hurting, demanding answers I could never earn.

He'd only stolen my heart when I was younger, but this time, he'd stolen my body too. He'd shown me just how good we were together. Just how deep that lust and longing went, only for him to slam a door in my face.

Literally!

"You're a master at hurting me these days, Gil," I whispered with stilted, snowy words. "But I'm not young anymore, and I'm not going to let my mind run riot with wonder—not like when you rejected me at school. I refuse to lie to myself like I did back then…constantly believing you'd come back. Do you know how empty I felt as the months went by and you never returned? How hard it was to be honest and admit that you'd just had enough of me? I constantly came up with excuses for you: maybe your dad needed help with the family business. Maybe you suddenly didn't have time for virgin girls anymore when you had whores living in the next room. It broke me, Gil, and I refuse to let you break—"

"Don't." His eyes snapped to mine. "Don't you fucking dare. Is that what you've thought of me?"

I shrugged helplessly. "What? That you were sleeping with whores? It was one scenario."

"There were others?" His nostrils flared.

"There were many. Some better, some worse." I let truth be my weapon. "No answers leads to awful conclusions. You gave me nothing, so I thought the worst. And now, you're doing the same and all I can think about is terrible, gruesome things. My mind is once again making up painful hypotheticals."

His shoulders tightened, face etching with despair. "Your conclusions will be better than any truth I can give you. I'd rather you think the worst of me than learn what I'm truly capable of."

I stilled. "It can't be that bad."

He laughed, his tone empty. "It's worse."

"Well…" I moved toward him slowly, keeping my own pain hidden. "Let me be the judge. Tell me and I'll help in any way I can."

He held up his hand, trying to prevent me from encroaching on him. "You can't help with this, Olin. No one can."

"That's not for you to decide."

"It is. And I have." He ran a hand over his mouth, his eyes narrowing in vexation. "You shouldn't even be here. I don't know what I was thinking bringing you back."

"Then let me go home." I crossed my arms. "I'm perfectly capable of protecting myself—"

"You're not leaving."

"You can't keep me here against my will."

He stepped into me, his powerful presence crushing air from my lungs. "I can if it means you stay safe."

"Safe?" I blinked, staring into menacing green eyes. "How will you keep me safe when that arsehole has been in here? He's probably beaten you up in this very room. You can't keep me safe if you won't raise a hand against him."

A flicker of something painful appeared and disappeared in his gaze. "You don't know what you're saying." His brow scrunched and shadowed his face. "You don't know what you've stumbled into." His own anger soared past his control, raising his cold voice to a blizzard. "Why did you have to see my advertisement, huh? Why couldn't you have stayed away? Stayed far away from me—a forgotten piece of my past? He wouldn't care then. I wouldn't be walking this goddamn tightrope."

"You can't blame me for finding you. Life happens in mysterious—"

"Life is the hardest fucking thing to endure. And you—" His chest rose and fell as if he suffocated for a proper breath. "You made it so much better when we were younger. But now...you're making it a thousand times worse."

My heart broke, bleeding through the cracks. "That isn't my intention, Gil. I'm trying to *help*—"

"And I'm trying to keep you safe! Can't you permit me to do that, seeing as I'm fucking useless at everything else?"

His shout echoed around the warehouse, licking with rage.

He pinched the bridge of his nose, his head bowed. "Look, I'm sorry. I—"

"It's fine." I sighed. "I don't know why I expected you to finally trust me."

His eyes whipped up. "What's that supposed to mean?"

"It means you never told me stuff in the past, so why would you start now?" I ignored the drip, drip, dripping of my bleeding heart.

We were going around in circles.

Gil looked at the ground, effectively shutting me out.

He might be talented with a brush, but he was also talented at keeping people at arm's length. A glacier that refused to melt or yield.

Moving around him, I plucked a bottle of paint from the metal shelf. His attention followed me, locking onto my hands as I rolled the deep blue from left to right.

"Can you at least tell me about the phone calls?" I looked up, catching his stare as I slowly unscrewed the cap.

"Phone calls?" He frowned, distracted enough by my seemingly unconnected topic.

"The one you answered when you refused to give me the job. The night Justin argued on my behalf."

Anger flushed his neck; he growled. "Just a phone call."

"I don't think it was." Dabbing a spot of blue onto my fingertips, I rubbed them together, smearing the pigment. "It made you change your mind about painting me."

"I decided I needed the money."

"Money for blackmail." My fingers kept smearing paint, my stomach a churning mess. I was glad I had something to focus on, rather than freezing in Gil's frost.

"Stop trying to connect dots that aren't there, Olin." He never took his eyes off me as if he hated me touching his things.

"I think there is a connection." I looked up briefly, studying how close I was to pushing him over the edge.

Push harder.

Earn answers.

Be prepared to run if he snaps.

"Doesn't matter what you think." His body vibrated with tension, his eyes heating with a faint wisp of lust. Lust for my hands as I rolled my wrists and danced my blue-smeared fingers in the air.

He'd watched me enough when we were younger that my dancing was foreplay for him. The heavy focus of his desire, the erotic target of his want.

Dancing for him drenched me in a spotlight of forbidden, sinful things.

My tummy somersaulted as he sucked in a breath, unable to tear his eyes away from my painted hands.

"And the phone call that interrupted our first kiss?" I touched the sleeve of my cream blouse with blue tipped fingers, switching topics, marking myself. "Was that unimportant too?"

His jaw locked as hotter desire pooled around us. Sensuality suddenly threaded with frustration.

"That's a trick question," he grumbled.

"How is it a trick question?"

"If I say it was unimportant, then I make our kiss seem as if it meant nothing. But if I say it was the most important phone call of my life, then you're vindicated in chasing this topic."

I smiled gently, even as my heart fell over. "So which is it? Did our kiss mean something? Or was it merely a mistake?" I ran out of paint. I didn't want to stop seducing him, ruining him. Grabbing the bottle, I tipped a puddle of rich royal blue into my palm.

I willingly vandalized my own clothes when I didn't have disposable income to buy more. The craving to touch his paint. To wield it like he did. To prove a point that what he valued could be borrowed, sampled, taken.

And through it all, Gil stood frozen like a hunter. A hunter who would very much like to pounce.

The rapidly thickening need between us drove me to recklessness.

His voice gruffed with gravel. "I can't answer that."

"You can."

"No, I can't." He groaned under his breath as paint slowly oozed through my fingers.

Plop.

Plop.

Plo—

His hand shot beneath mine, catching blue droplets, his gaze never leaving mine. "I don't like wastage, O."

Such a simple, curt sentence, yet it sizzled with something potent and passionate.

I shivered as I deliberately tipped my palm, sending a thick river of blue into his. "And I don't like being left in the dark."

He looked at the paint in his hand. His jaw worked. His eyes flashed. "You don't have a choice."

Our argument twisted with something dangerous.

My gaze landed on his handsome, exhausted face, an invitation husky in my throat. "I choose not to lose you for the second time."

In a flash, he reached for my throat, his skin slippery and cold with blue.

I gasped as his fingers latched around me, squeezing the pigment into my flesh. It bled between us, thick and rich, dribbling down my chest and into my cleavage.

Gil followed every track, his gaze hypnotic and hazy. "You can't lose what you don't have."

My nipples pebbled; time stood still. "I've *always* had you."

Breathlessness tortured me as his fingers unlocked from my neck and smeared heavy and possessive down my chest. He cupped my breast, ruining my blouse with sapphire streaks. "That's what you believe?" His nose grazed mine. "That I belong to you?"

"Yes." My heart hammered against my ribs. "Just like I belong to you."

Darkness clawed over his face. "I can't own what isn't mine to take." His thumb feathered over my pulse, his lips thinning as my rapid heartbeat revealed just how undone I was.

My head grew heavy, my body swaying under his touch. "I

was yours the very first day we spoke."

His fingers kneaded my breast even as he shook his head. "I only borrowed you…I didn't claim you."

I bit my lip as his thumb circled my hardened nipple, drawing a crescent blue moon around it. I couldn't look away from the smeared graffiti or the way Gil's jaw locked with fury.

Desire didn't just whisper between us.

It positively set fire to us.

Fireworks of need.

Explosions of lust.

"We're family, Gil." My eyes hooded. "Family isn't temporary. It's forever."

"Stop." His fingers slicked over the column of my throat, pushing me into the metal shelves behind me. "Please fucking stop." A cloud of rage and rapture twisted his voice—two opposing colours mixed with a sharp palette knife.

My spine bruised as he pinned me to the many bottles and apparatus behind me.

The things Gil hid weren't ordinary, simple secrets. They cast a shadow over everything. An ominous skulking demon that he pretended wasn't real. They devoured him from the inside out. They left him the ghost of the boy he'd once been.

But standing there, with his fingers latched on me in possession, his paint on me in ownership, and our chests panting to the same erratic beat, there was simplicity instead of complication.

"Stop?" I arched into him, no longer caring about secrets and safety. No longer brave enough to fight for answers.

This was important.

This was needed.

Him.

Me.

Us.

"Are you sure?" I whispered.

His entire body shuddered. For a moment, I hoped he'd spill everything. It was all there, swimming in his gaze. Dreadful, grim things he'd endured without telling me. Hard, painful things he'd buried, deep, deep inside. But then he broke eye contact and embraced the ice he'd mastered. "I can't do this again."

I leaned into his hold, pressing my neck into his control. I wanted to nuzzle him—to rub against his cheek like a cat. "It's just us, Gil. No one else."

His groan sent goosebumps scattering over me. "There's always someone else. *Something* else."

"There doesn't have to be."

He caged me tighter against the shelves. "I've already put you in enough danger." His power and heat rippled in waves. His hips pressed mine into submission. The hard hotness in his jeans said I wasn't the only one unravelling, even though he fought it. "I can't touch you again."

His words and body were enemies. His body vibrated with sexual hunger; his voice condemned with denials.

He fought me.

He fought *us*.

I grew wet as well as furious. "You already touched me." I looked pointedly at my blue-smeared breast, his fingers preventing my chin from tipping too far. "Your hand is on me, listening to my pulse, knowing how much I want you."

His forehead furrowed. His fingers loosened around my neck.

Piece by piece, breath by breath, he did his best to control himself.

I couldn't let that happen.

Couldn't let him shut me out again.

Reaching blindly behind me, I snatched another paint bottle. Ripping off the cap, not looking at what colour I held, I bit my lip against massive ramifications and tipped the entire thing on his head.

Seconds screeched to a halt.

Gil turned to stone.

Happy, vibrant yellow licked through his messy hair, slithering to his temples and cascading down his cheeks. The contrast of sunshine pigment crowning his depressive dark splintered what was left of my heart.

He didn't move as yellow trickled down his forehead, danced in his left eyebrow, and dripped off his eyelashes.

A sunshine droplet landed on my blouse, smearing over the blue. I rubbed it with my fingertip, blending the two together until a vibrant green formed.

Green.

Like Gil's eyes.

Green.

Like the school field we used to walk over.

Green.

For the trees we'd hang out beneath.

He sucked in a breath as I looked up. My body no longer invited him to take what he wanted, it liquefied just like the paint, moulding to him, warming against him, changing its molecules the longer he stared.

I was pure hunger.

Undiluted desire.

He didn't speak, his teeth puncturing his bottom lip.

My heart hammered as he reached behind me. Selecting a bottle, he twisted off the cap and, without a word, tipped a generous dollop onto my chest.

Cold.

Pink.

A rich fuchsia that glowed with femininity and fun.

Throwing the bottle to the ground, his hands tore at my blouse until my buttons popped and the fabric gaped open.

"Fuck." His lips landed on my neck, his hands cupping my breasts and kneading pink into my skin and bra.

My skin broke out in chills as the icy, pretty colour stained me, conjuring old memories of a similar shade.

"Flamingos," I murmured as his teeth scraped my jaw.

He jerked back. "What?"

Pink meandered down my belly, teasing with my skirt's waistline.

"Your first mural that you showed me." I panted, needing him to touch me, to fix me. "The graffiti flamingos."

"Goddammit, you remember." His eyes snapped shut. Another curse fell from his mouth as his entire features teetered between acrimony and despair. "It was the easiest colour to steal."

I didn't want to sink into history. I didn't want anything to sneak in and ruin this.

Gil's self-control had frayed.

Mine was in ribbons.

Two tattered pieces of string that just needed to be knotted together to be whole.

"Kiss me, Gil."

There would be time to reminisce.

Later.

"Kiss me...please."

His eyes locked on mine.

Sadness wept there for things we'd lost and couldn't fix.

Starvation glittered for all the aches and hungers we endured. But most of all love glowed, despite Gil doing his best to suffocate it.

Tears raced up my spine. Tears for him and me and everything in between. "Kiss—"

"Goddamn you." His lips slammed over mine. His fingers cupped my cheeks as his tongue entered my mouth, swift and violent. He kissed me as if we hadn't kissed in decades. He kissed me as if it was the last kiss he'd ever give.

The metal shelving behind me wobbled as Gil glued himself to me. His thigh went between my legs, thrusting up, hoisting my skirt up my stockings.

When it didn't move high enough, he reached down and tore the fabric, ripping through pinstripe and satin.

My one outfit. I had nothing else here—nothing else to wear.

But I didn't care.

I didn't care about anything.

I moaned, encouraging him to take everything with a deep, lingering kiss. His hips rocked forward, his cock heavy and hot against my knickers, teasing my clit.

A bottle tumbled over my shoulder, wedging between us. Without breaking our kiss, I reached for it, uncapped it, and used whatever colour lived inside to drench my hands.

Icy, silky paint on my palms.

Sexy, slippery paint on Gil's face as I ran my fingers over his cheeks and down his throat, tracing the Master of Trickery with the tools of his trade.

His eyes snapped open. He pulled back, grabbing my wrists and yanking my touch away.

But it was too late.

Black.

Deep, rich ebony glistened over his features. Yellow smeared within it, setting a dangerous combination. A wasp with a sting. A sting I probably wouldn't survive.

His lips were wet, his eyes wild. "I told you I don't like wastage."

I shivered. "Guess you should finish the masterpiece we've started then."

Creative sparks ignited in his gaze. He assessed my ruffled, ruined outfit. "You're right." Snatching my wrist, he dragged me toward the same podium where he'd painted me. The matte black bricks dampened all other colour and texture, setting alive the flares of vibrancy on our skin.

Whipping me around, he made me leap onto the stage.

He climbed behind me, tearing my blouse off from behind. Dragging it down my arms, he kept it bunched around my wrists, forcing my back to arch and breasts to jut out.

His nose ran along the contour of my shoulder, smelling me, breathing me.

The difference in this moment to the one where he'd painted me couldn't be compared. Previously, he'd been snowflakes settling on blue ice. Now he was smoke billowing from red fire.

Kicking my ankle, he spread my legs. "You're driving me insane." Wrenching my torn skirt up, he formed a belt with the broken material. With a groan, he dived his hand between my legs and cupped me hard. "Why can't I stop myself around you?"

My head flopped back as he kissed and nipped his way along my exposed shoulder all while his fingers moved my knickers aside and plunged two inside me.

I cried out.

He cursed.

My wetness was as slippery and intoxicating as the paint gluing us together.

My hips thrust into his hand, seeking more, while he thrust against my ass, rubbing his erection against me. We stumbled and slammed together, violent and unapologetic.

Just like our first time, there were no requests or assurances. Nothing sweet or tame.

Just dark and desperate, crippling beneath years of denial.

Tearing his fingers from my body, he spun me around, yanked my blouse off my wrists and unhooked my bra. Leaving me half-naked, he dropped to his knees, taking my skirt and bra with him to the floor.

In a single heartbeat, I stood in just my stockings, garter belt, and knickers, breathing hard, glassy-eyed, smudged and sullied with his paint.

His arms banded around my thighs, dragging me closer. His mouth captured my pussy, his tongue licking me through my knickers.

My knees buckled, my black pigmented hands landing on his wet yellow hair.

He bit me.

I almost collapsed.

He was gone as quickly as he'd grabbed me.

"Don't move." He growled.

Tripping off the podium, he rubbed at his blackened cheeks as he yanked open the drawer where his expensive camera lived. Removing the lens cap and fiddling with a setting, he pointed the thing directly at me.

Instinctually, I covered my breasts.

Gil smouldered below. "Drop your arms."

"You can't— I'm half-naked."

"You were mostly naked last time I took photos."

"I was painted then."

"You're painted now." He snapped a few pictures, angling left and right. "Remove your arms, O." His eyes latched on mine. "Strip…for me."

I blushed. "I'm not letting you take photos of me mid sex."

"I haven't been inside you yet. Sex hasn't occurred."

My stomach bottomed out, making me impossibly wetter. "You've had your fingers inside me. Your tongue was just—"

"Tasting you. I know." His stare licked me up and down. "You're in my mouth, up my nose, in my fucking blood. I need to see you. I want you as broken as you've made me."

My knees quaked. I hesitated.

"I won't sell them." His voice danced with darkness. "No one will ever see."

"Why do you want them then?" I couldn't catch my breath, light-headed and achy.

"Because I have no photos of you from the past—no way of immortalizing just how fucking stunning you are."

"Oh." My entire body clenched.

"My memories never did you justice." He grimaced, his throat working as if he didn't want to admit such things but unable to stop himself. "Night after night, I'd think about you. I'd jerk off to hazy images. I'd come with your name in my heart. I never stopped missing you…never stopped wanting you. And I fucking want this. I want something to remember you by." The image of Gil masturbating over me. The thought of him in his bed with his cock his hand and his face grimacing mid-release—

"I'm right here; you don't have to remember me." My arms tumbled from my breasts, tears once again glossing my vision. "You can look at me whenever you wish."

He just gave me the saddest smile with an infinitesimal shake of his head.

Then his camera rose. The shutter clicked, capturing me forever.

My skin was hypersensitive, my heart a smoking mess, but some reason, I had the unbearable urge to cry. This felt like goodbye. A permanent farewell to all my dreamings of us.

Why would he need photos when I had no intention of leaving…unless, he planned to push me away and never look back.

His eyes glistened with grief but his voice still teased with need. Taking photos with one hand, his other dropped to his jeans. Rubbing himself, he groaned, "I'm so fucking hard for you."

I lived on the threshold of a release just from his voice. "And I'm wet for you."

He shuddered, his gaze trailing over my body. His teeth sank into his bottom lips as his face once again glowed with creation. Creation that had no rhyme or reason when it struck. Creation that couldn't be ignored.

Swaying, he put the camera down.

His hands went to his T-shirt hem, yanking it over his head. His belly pulsed with breath, the ridges of muscle making my mouth dry and pussy wet.

I fought the snarling, sensual spindle of thick desire. "Gil…"

His hands unbuckled his belt, unzipped his jeans, and removed both his trousers and underwear in one swipe, just like last time. With a kick of his boots and tug of clothing, he stood beautifully naked and utterly sinful before me.

I drank him in, goosebumps prickling at his powerful perfection. I stepped toward him as a trickle of lust dampened my underwear.

"No." He bared his teeth, stopping me from going to him. "I want to see you. Every inch." His paint-smeared hand went to his cock, heavy and hard between his legs.

He didn't care yellow still trickled down his chest or that black, pink, and blue streaked his fingers, marring his erection the longer he pumped.

He didn't see anything but me.

He didn't *want* anything else but me.

And that was the headiest, most potent aphrodisiac.

With shaky hands, I unclipped my garter belt and let it fall. My skin glowed pink from paint and hot with needy blush.

He smirked with tight lips and turbulent eyes, fisting himself. His forearm pulsed with corded muscle as he granted pleasure I wanted to give. "Keep going."

I flushed. Sweat prickled beneath the colours and I wobbled as I slowly rolled a stocking down my leg, never taking my eyes off his.

He groaned long and low as I reached my foot and stepped daintily from the sheer garment. "Fuck, I could come just watching you."

A full body quake hinted how close I was to an orgasm myself. I could come from nothing else but his eyes and breath. Eyes that drank me, ate me, devoured me. And breaths that spoke the truth. That he couldn't survive without having me. Even though he'd survived for years without me by his side.

Removing my other stocking, I stood as elegantly as I could and hooked my fingers in my underwear. If I did this, he'd see how desperate I was. How wet. How needy.

But I wasn't the only one. His cock jutted out, thick and engorged. His thumb pressed into the slit at the top, his jaw locked and body rippling with yearning.

With a quick inhale, I slipped my knickers down, almost embarrassed by the glisten of desire on the fabric. But a guttural, curse-filled groan came from Gil, and I was no longer embarrassed.

I was pleased.

Thankful that he knew just how much I wanted him. Wanted him for most of my life.

Without tearing his eyes from my nakedness, he marched to the trestle table holding more paint. Grabbing a few bottles, he marched toward me, his cock bouncing between his legs with each ground-eating stride.

Standing at the base of the podium, he passed me the colours, his eyes lingering on my body. Hesitatingly, I took them from him as he backed up with visible hardship.

"What do you want me to do?" My voice mixed air with need.

"Paint." He swallowed hard. "You're the one who wanted to waste my supplies." He bowed mockingly. "So play."

Placing the bottles by my feet, I selected a royal purple with glitter flecks. "Is it safe...for, um, personal places?"

He chuckled with a strained groan. "Yes." His skin flushed as I uncapped the lid and held out my arm. Wincing against the coolness, I locked eyes with Gil as purple cascaded over my forearm and fell in glittering droplets to the floor.

Stepping in the mess, I smeared my toes, covering my feet with purple just like my arm rained in it.

A long ago melody of elegance and ballet nudged awake muscles that'd been torn and stitched in the accident.

This was a dance.

A dance of colours and need.

And I didn't fight the flow of sensuality as I tipped the bottle again, standing on tiptoes, moving to the silent beat of my heart. My arms soared upward, losing myself in the magic of movement. Purple drizzled from above.

"Fucking hell." Gil froze. The camera remained forgotten by his feet as he stood transfixed, hypnotised by the paint and my nakedness.

By the private dance I gave him.

Twinges reminded me I wasn't the perfect ballerina anymore. Healed scars restricted certain skills. But my audience didn't care. His hand found his cock again, squeezing brutally hard.

My core clenched with every heartbeat, imploring him to stop wasting time and join me.

I no longer wanted to dance alone.

I wanted a partner.

Everlasting.

My heart raced faster and faster, sending blood and oxygen through my veins as well as colour. Bending as swan-like and regal as my back would allow, I selected another bottle from the stage.

Metallic silver.

So perfect and luminescent it looked like pure starlight.

This was too special to waste. The colour too pure.

But Gil looked like he stood in Hell, all while I teased him from Heaven. And I wanted to erase the misery inside him. I embraced debauchery and tipped the silver starlight over my breasts.

Sterling perfection rivered over me, pebbling my nipples as it turned my skin from pink to priceless.

I followed its path with my fingers, biting my lip as it trickled through my trimmed pubic hair, dripping lazily down my thighs to my feet. It tickled and teased, more erotic than anything I'd ever done.

"Gil…" I moaned as my finger strayed between my legs, touching how hot I was, how drenched. I flinched at the sensitivity, turned on to the point of pain.

He snapped.

In one leap, he cleared the step, grabbed me, and swung me off my feet.

A second later, he sat on the stage, moved me until my thighs were spread over his lap, then fisted a hand in my hair. Yanking my head back, he kissed me before I could speak.

He kissed me savagely, deeply, forcing my every sense to lock onto him.

While his lips corrupted me, his other hand dove between us. He thrust two fingers inside me, testing, making sure I was ready.

I convulsed in his arms.

With a feral groan, he withdrew, grabbed his cock and angled it at my entrance. He stopped kissing me, sucking in air and pressing his forehead to mine. Our eyes snapped together, wild and wanting.

Our souls spoke. Our bodies commanded.

He never looked away as he thrust inside me, plunging deep, taking everything.

I cried out.

He snarled, his chest rumbling with vicious greed, spreading me, taking me.

My mouth opened wide beneath his as he kissed me again and again. My body stretched and yielded to his sudden invasion. I moaned as he thrust upward, pushing my body onto his.

He gave me nowhere to run, no space to wriggle away from the oversaturation of his possession, no way of easing into his violence.

His brow came down, casting shadows. His entire body vibrated with everything I wasn't allowed to know. Terror shone in his gaze, ravenous longing coloured his lips, and a bone-deep depression painted him better than all the other colours I'd marked him with.

Gil had sad eyes.

He always had.

But with him driving into me, my arms slung over his shoulders, and our gazes stitched together, I understood something I hadn't before.

Gil had lost his way.

While life had dragged me along, stealing my dancing dreams and gracing me with scars, he'd endured his own hardship. And it wasn't physical. It was emotional.

He couldn't tattoo over the wounds on his heart. He couldn't pretty up the defects and craters left by whatever nightmares he'd walked through.

My pulse pounded as his body ravaged mine and tears prickled for him. I would've been there for him if he'd let me. I would've held his hand in the dark and raised a sword in his defence if only he'd kept me by his side and not tossed me away.

I hated him for that.

Hated him as much as I wanted him, blending two opposite emotions into a treacherous one.

I was vulnerable in that moment.

I was angry in that moment.

Nuzzling his nose with mine, I kissed him.

Kissed him sweet and soft to combat the harsh, hard way he took me.

Kissed him gentle and loving to combat the violent unhappiness within his soul.

He stiffened.

Our skin slipped together, spreading silver, pink, and black. The yellow crowning him dappled his shoulders, dressing him in a sunshine cape.

Halcyon.

The word swept into my mind from an English lesson at school. Gil had sat behind me, whispering the new word as Ms Tallup showed how to spell it on the board.

Halcyon.

It meant peaceful, tranquil, harmonious.

A serene, balmy day that had no worries, stress, or strife.

That was what Gil needed.

What a shame the yellow in his unruly hair couldn't grant such things.

I kissed him harder, cupping his cheeks as he thrust into me particularly deep, almost in punishment, almost as if he sensed my pity for whatever pain he'd lived through.

He growled as his pace increased. My breasts bounced, shining in quicksilver.

His head tilted as his hands swooped up my back and into my hair, kissing me viciously, switching the softness into savagery once again. I gave myself over to it, catching his tongue with mine in a swirly, ancient dance.

Unsheathing my teeth, I bit his bottom lip.

And that was the end of whatever gentleness existed between us.

Our eyes snapped closed as our kiss grew wet and hot and fierce. Our bodies matched the thrusting, hunting tempo of our tongues. Our hips rocked and rolled, never satisfied, even as the sharp sizzle of a release made his fingers bruise my skin and a plea hiss through my teeth.

"You should never have found me," he grunted, driving upward.

My body rejected his length, squeezing tight around him.

"What the fuck am I supposed to do now, huh?" he groaned with another consuming thrust. "How am I supposed to survive this?"

I had no answers, so I gave him none. I just let him take what he needed.

Falling backward, he pulled me with him.

We tumbled to the stage where he'd stood and painted a hundred different women. Paint bottles rolled around us as Gil twisted and placed me on my back.

We lay on his place of employment, naked and vibrant, and connected in the basest of ways.

He reared up on his hands, his hips pistoning into mine as the paint on our skin smeared the floor where other droplets had dried. Where other art had been created and destroyed. Where he'd painted me the first time and almost ruined me.

His hand slicked down my body, pressing between my legs while he drove deep. His fingers found my clit, swirling in time to the rhythm he set. Consuming, possessing, heart-stealing.

My back bowed as he conjured every heated, hungry nerve ending to focus on his touch. The way his cock spread me wide. The way his fingers soared me high. It stole every ability to think and I belonged entirely to him.

My pussy clenched around him, demanding the release he teased me with.

His lips slammed on mine again, pinning my head to the stage. His tongue speared into my mouth, tasting me, making me drunk on the fiery desire he poured down my throat.

My back slid against the smooth podium as we fought against each other. With each thrust, I grew heavier, hotter, drowning in the delicious thrill of a steadily building orgasm.

"Gil—" I clawed at his lower back, pulling him deeper into me. "Now, please...I want—"

"Not yet." His fingers ripped from my body, reaching for a bottle tangled in my hair. My orgasm faltered. My lips pressed together with impatience.

Ripping the cap open with his teeth, he smiled grimly as he upended the brightest, deadliest red into the hollow of my throat.

I flinched as the cool fingers of liquid puddled over and cascaded on either side of my neck, feeling as if he'd slit me from ear to ear.

Instead of attacking me with more feral urgency, Gil froze.

His cock pulsed inside me. Horror filled his eyes.

I didn't know how the paint looked blending with silver, pink, and blue but the whiteness beneath the black on his cheeks spoke of death and decay.

My death.

"Fuck." A tormented groan fell from his lips as he swiped away the pool of crimson. Again and again, he smeared my skin, turning my individual colours into a muddy, metallic gleam.

His hand dove into my hair, painting the strands while his forehead crashed on mine.

The weight of his body increased, the rattle of his breathing quickened, and I stroked his back with shaking fingers. "It's okay—"

"It's not fucking okay," he snarled, rearing up onto his elbows and thrusting into me so viciously, I scooted away from him.

But he followed; his knees locked between my legs, driving his cock into me with single-minded determination—a rutting, debasing need to finish, because whatever lived between us had shown far too many flaws to be allowed.

"Jesus Christ," he groaned, buckling over me as his anger added a new element to the lust between us. His cock throbbed and thickened inside me, dragging my unrequited orgasm from the depths of my belly and into my pussy.

My body rippled, milking his length, testing permission to explode.

His eyes narrowed to wicked weapons as he dropped his head and kissed me.

The moment his tongue entered my mouth, I couldn't stop it.

My release wrapped tight spindles around my spine and legs,

crippling me with intensity as it ricocheted outward.

Gil grabbed my breast mid-pulse, making me groan and shudder. His fingers pinched my nipple as his teeth bit my lip, and my mouth went slack beneath his, totally obsessed with the quaking, toe-curling pleasure he smothered me with.

He kissed me deeper, trying to crawl inside me. I opened wider, submitting to his crude commands.

His hips never stopped pumping, pounding into me as he wrung every ripple of release from my blood. Only once I was floppy and swimming in ecstasy did his body stiffen and his cock pulse inside me.

Hot jets of his pleasure filled me as his head crashed to my shoulder, mixing his yellow and black with my red and silver. He jolted in my arms, again and again as he fed me every drop.

And I was allowed to stroke him.

Allowed to show tenderness after such a fiendish display.

Slowly, his head rose, his face a wash of colour but his eyes dull and exhausted as if he'd given me his last remaining heartbeats.

We stared at each, trying to see each other's secrets but only finding roadblocks and confusion.

Gil gave me a bitter smile, looking like some god born to a demon.

Two personalities.

Two tragedies.

Two men.

And I didn't know either of them.

He withdrew and stood, towering over me, painted and sated but still totally tormented.

With a gruff whisper, he bent over and offered me his hand. "Come on."

Placing my fingers in his, I marvelled at the swirls and shades of our multihued skin. "Where are we going?"

He hauled me to my feet, granting balance as I stepped from the stage. "To wash."

I padded naked and barefoot beside him as we left his studio and entered his apartment.

To wash away our lovemaking.

To wash away our art.

To wash away...us.

Chapter Twenty-One

Olin

-The Present-

STEPPING INTO GIL'S personal bathroom for the second time was no stranger than the first.

Then I'd been searching for painkillers for his unretaliated punch-up. Now, I stood awkward and naked as Gil turned on the shower and waited until steam curled behind the grey and white shower curtain.

His back held streaks of paint, his ass toned and muscular with my handprint on his left cheek. His cock still hung hard and heavy as if his orgasm hadn't given him the same level of release mine had.

Hugging my colourful breasts, I backed up as he stepped into the shower and held his head under the stream. The thick yellow in his hair instantly diluted to water colours, flooding his chest and face in liquid lemon.

Rubbing his eyes clear of the sluice, he looked past the steam to where I stood by the vanity. I waited my turn, very aware of my nudity and the remnants of sex between my legs.

I wanted to be by myself. To piece myself back together and harden my heart after being shattered all over again.

I need to be alone.

A by-product of being lonely for so many years.

But he held out his dripping hand, his skin slick and delicious. "Get in."

I shook my head. "I'll wait."

Not wasting words, he climbed from the shower and

marched toward me. His footprints left colour-swirls dancing on droplets as he grabbed my wrist and pulled me into the warm embrace of the spray.

The moment the water hit my face, I sighed, rubbing at the stickiness of pigment, running hands down my body to remove any trace.

Gil stood behind me, his looming presence growing ever more intense the longer I stayed under the heat.

I jerked as his heavy hands landed on my shoulders, kneading me, slowly cascading down my spine. His fingers traced the lines and shadows of my tattoo, following the bumps of scar tissue and valleys of torn muscles.

My body locked in place as he took his time, touching and learning.

I wished I could see his face. I wanted to spin in his embrace and study whatever emotion he felt.

But I didn't.

I stayed bound beneath the comforting water, goosebumps contradicting the heat as he continued to inspect the most personal part of me. The part that was almost a shrine to our childhood.

He cleared his throat as if heavy painful things lodged there, making it impossible to swallow. "There's even an ocelot in here." His finger worshipped me as he followed an owl's feather and found the tiny wild cat.

I squeezed my eyes against the memory, slipping back into the past.

He'd slowly started running out of things to call me starting with O. One day, in the library during lunch, while we hid from other students, he'd claimed a dictionary and sat beside me while I'd nibbled my ham and mustard sandwiches. He hadn't taken a sandwich, saying I fed him too much already.

As I swallowed a mouthful, he'd smirked and stabbed the pages with a finger. "Ocelot. You're an ocelot."

"I'm a what now?"

"A feral spotted cat."

I took another bite. "I suppose that's better than a fruit or a monkey."

He leaned closer, tucking a strand of hair behind my ear. "Does this mean you have claws, my fuzzy little ocelot?"

I grinned, pretending to swipe at him like a cat. "The sharpest."

"I'll remember that." He captured my hand, kissed my knuckles, and continued reading the dictionary as if nothing had happened. All the while, my heart soared, fluttered, and plummeted deeper into love.

Gil's touch dragged me back, making me shiver.

He stole the air right out of my lungs, and I couldn't do this anymore.

"Stop." Twisting in his hold, I faced him with water plastering my hair to my shoulders and paint still staining us. I said what he'd said to me, begging him for space. "Please, don't."

Our eyes caught.

I sucked in a breath.

How could I admit that he was the soul-mate who got away?

I can't.

Pure and simple.

The boy I was in love with wasn't the same as the man, and my heart sank. It sank to the shower floor and slithered down the drain because I didn't have the courage to tell him to either commit to us or leave me alone.

He didn't utter a sound.

Utmost silence apart from the hissing shower as his hands cupped my hipbones, his fingers bruising me.

He stopped breathing as heat and history flared between us. So many things lurked beneath the surface. So many things trapped us from truth and stopped us from being honest, and it hurt.

It hurt way, way too much.

It hurt him too.

Pain glimmered in his eyes the longer he stared.

Standing in the cramped shower with the faint hint of strawberry on the steam, we washed in vulnerability and fragility. Two very breakable things because we were two very breakable people.

We did our best to seem unconquerable and brave, but in that moment, that heart-stopping, life-ceasing moment, we were the same.

Doomed.

His features shadowed with confliction and a heavy dose of self-loathing. With aching tenderness, he slipped his touch up my waist, caressed the sides of my breasts, and cupped my throat. His thumbs stroked me with irreparable reverence.

I didn't want to.

I fought against the pull.

But I tripped a little.

I fell into him.

Literally and figuratively.

My body into his body; my heart into his heart.

I fell out of sanity and into lunacy because I had no right to feel this way. He had no right to *make* me feel this way.

His lips captured mine in the sweetest, softest kiss. His fingers braided through my hair, cupping the back of my neck. With our mouths touching, he paused as if giving me the chance to pull away.

I tried to.

I tried to stop loving him.

But my lips parted and the tip of my tongue requested more. A butterfly-inducing *more*.

His fingers tightened, holding me firm. He deepened the kiss, touching his tongue to mine, tasting me, dancing with me, slowly, gently, lovingly.

The shower disappeared.

The past and present blended, and I kissed him back.

I kissed him like he kissed me…with devotion, idolization, and a cold gust of fear.

This was truth.

This was authentic and legitimately real.

We kissed forever.

Our heads choreographed in their seduction, our mouths a perfect fit, our tongues meant for each other.

My hands swooped up his naked chest.

He flinched and kissed me harder as my palms felt his thundering heartbeat beneath the mixture of paint and flesh.

We couldn't stop.

We couldn't end whatever spell cast around us, dragging us deeper, confusing us, ruining us. I'd slept with Gil twice. I'd loved him for years. Yet there was something singular about this kiss.

Something unique and special and absolutely *terrifying*.

This wasn't about sex.

It wasn't about power or passion.

This was deeper and darker and dangerously raw.

His soft groan made my heart bloom like a rose, its petals straining for whatever sustenance he could offer. All while the tangle of thorns in my stomach warned me not to fall. Not to put myself through the pain of Gilbert Clark again.

His body tensed as he tried to pull away. His tongue retreated and his lips thinned, and I prepared to withdraw from the most spectacular kiss of my life.

Only...as space encroached on our togetherness, he pulled me back. He jerked me into his arms as if he couldn't bear to let me go, and I moaned in agony.

Couldn't he see neither of us were equipped for whatever fallout would follow?

Locking our lips together, he kissed me with a desperation that burned. Our sex had been explosive and almost angry. Both times. But this...this was totally different. It wasn't playing games with our lust but with our hearts.

And I was unbelievably scared.

A snarl built in his throat as his tongue lashed mine. Then, with a haggard groan, he forcibly pulled away.

Keeping his eyes downcast, he scrambled from the shower and ripped a black towel off the rail on the wall. Wrapping it around his waist, he stalked from the bathroom without a word.

* * * * *

"You can wear these," Gil muttered as I stepped from the bathroom in a matching black towel. "Seeing as your clothes are, eh..."

"Torn and painted?"

He nodded sharply. "Yeah."

"Thanks." My voice was soft and quiet as I took the offered clothes while we stood in his living room. Licks of colour still baptised us from our lack of cleaning and too much kissing in the shower.

His eyes met mine.

Any sign of an emotional connection was gone. Snow and ice decorated his features, placed there by self-preservation. "I'll show you where you'll sleep." Turning on his heel, his white T-shirt and grey sweatpants looked delectable with his bare feet and damp hair.

I clutched the clothes and towel and followed him as he opened the door to the right in the graffiti artwork of jungles and wildlife. My eyes strayed to the left door. The door I'd caught him exiting the night vodka and lapsed decisions ensured a memorable event on my hands and knees.

What's in there?

My curiosity clawed to find out as I stepped over the

threshold into Gil's bedroom. I paused, studying the dark slate-grey walls and the simple king mattress on the floor. No bedframe. No side tables. No lamps or art or sign of habitation.

An impersonal box with no hint of the complex man standing beside me.

I frowned, sensing a pattern with his belongings. Either he didn't have time for the typical stuff an ordinary person did or he lived frugally.

Peering deeper into the shadows, I noticed indents in the beige carpet where a tallboy would've stood. There were signs of a rug at the bottom of the bed. Hints that this room wasn't always so sparse.

"Did you always live this simply, or is it a new lifestyle choice?" I asked, feeling as if I'd once again trespassed and wasn't welcome.

Gil raked a hand through his yellow-streaked hair. Polite decorum camouflaged barely leashed sorrow. "Over the past year, I've sold some stuff."

"Why?"

He winced as a tidal wave of pain washed through his eyes. "Doesn't matter."

My stomach twisted.

That response was getting old.

I wanted to ask if it was related to his regular bruises, beatings, and mysterious secrets, but I bit my lip and stayed silent.

What was the point when I already knew?

Heading toward the small wardrobe in the corner, he pulled out fresh sheets and blankets. Tossing them onto the mattress, he stood and shrugged as if he was as lost as I was about all of this. "I'll, um, leave you to rest."

"We haven't even had dinner."

He grimaced as if I'd announced he had to fight a hundred wolverines and battle for his life instead of eating a meal with me.

His reaction bruised me. His tension made me fake a yawn. "You know what? Doesn't matter. I'm not hungry."

He gave me a grateful nod. "Good."

"Okay, then…" I moved toward the bed, uncomfortable and desperate for my own space.

I wanted to go home.

I wanted to be alone…so I could come back when I was calmer and tell Gil once and for all that he had to choose.

Choose me.

Choose help.

But Gil gave me a tight smile and bowed his head. "Goodnight, Olin."

Olin.

No more nicknames. No more thawing.

Hugging the clothes he'd given me, I nodded as he stepped from the room. "Goodnight, Gil."

Chapter Twenty-Two

Gil

-The Past-

I'D BEEN PAINTING a lot.

Ever since Ms Tallup hinted at what she wanted from me, I couldn't outrun the terrible sensation of sickness. Each class we had with her, I was repulsed. Each look she gave me, I was petrified Olin would guess something was wrong.

I despised Ms Tallup for taking the one place where I found sanctuary and turning it into yet another cesspit. I was no longer safe there. I was as hunted in those corridors as I was at home, and the stress steadily increased my sleepless nights, giving me a temper toward Olin when she didn't deserve it.

The only thing that helped was when I lost myself in a drawing. Sketching had been the Band-Aid I needed, but when I stole some spray paint and decorated the side of an industrial building one night while everyone slept, I found a drug I needed to eradicate the symptoms of my life.

If only temporarily.

I hadn't told Olin I'd been breaking the law.

I hid the overspray on my fingers and didn't show her my sketchbook again in case the images I drew scared her—images of violence and gore and people being tormented by circumstances outside their control.

But tonight, Olin's parents had been particularly cruel to her. She'd shown me a text her mother had sent during school. Some short sentence about going to a gala and for her to fend for herself. It wasn't anything unusual apart from the gala was for the children of the employees who worked for their telecom company.

Her parents were hanging out all night with their employees and *their* children and didn't even want to take their own.

Arseholes.

The second the class ended, I'd stolen her hand while throwing a loathsome look at Ms Tallup, and yanked Olin from school grounds. We used the small amount of money her parents gave her for dinner and shared a burger and fries, then blew the rest on some game parlour in downtown Birmingham, playing air hockey and racing car games, earning a few tokens to win a silly stuffed ostrich which became Olin's new nickname for the evening.

Afterward, licking sugar from our fingers and wandering empty streets, I pulled a can of spray paint from my dirty backpack and shook it. The mixer inside clicked against the metal. "Fancy doing something not exactly legal, little ostrich?"

I waited for her to shake her head in shock, but instead, a dainty smirk twisted her lips. "With you? I'd do anything."

And I fell head over heels.

No one else could compare.

No one else meant this much to me.

Of course, I'd known for a while now that I was in love with her.

I knew it each time my heart flipped when she wriggled in her seat in front of me in class. I tasted it every time she touched me, smiled at me, cooked for me, and studied with me.

But right there, I knew I loved her to my very core while standing beneath a streetlamp on a dreary English night.

I loved her.

I wanted to keep her.

My life would be infinitely better the moment it was just the two of us.

No matter how much time passed. No matter what shit I put her through, I would always love this girl because she owned me heart and soul.

"So...you're a secret rebel?" I chuckled under my breath. "Who knew."

"I'm a rebel if *you're* a rebel." She plucked the can from my fingers and shook it. The rattle made my heart pick up speed. "You've done this before?"

"Done what?" I crossed my arms, feigning innocence.

"Graffitied some innocent building."

I laughed cynically. "No building is innocent. Most of them house monsters. I'm just making them pretty."

"So you *have* done this before."

"Maybe."

"Show me?" Her sneakers scuffed the pavement as she came closer. So close the gold in her hair glittered beneath the streetlamp and her eyes were more green and stars than hazel and reality.

Without a word, I grabbed her hand, looped my fingers in hers, and together, we jogged to the last place I'd 'decorated'.

It didn't take long to get there, but excitement coursed through me to show her how my art was improving. Always improving. And improving fast with the amount of time I dedicated to it these days.

I barely slept. I hardly went home.

I focused on a talent that'd been hidden from me but I never wanted to lose again.

"Oh, wow. Gil..." Olin broke away from my touch, running toward the wall where the trio of colours I'd been able to steal blended together to form a monochromatic landscape of flamingos.

Pink, red, and black were the only colours in snatchable distance when I'd gone to the warehouse that housed art supplies.

I didn't like stealing, but I had no cash to my name.

I'd pay them back...when I started earning.

Olin's fingers traced the feathers of the largest flamingo. "This is so good, Gil." She spun in place, her face alight and eyes full of pride.

I smiled, enjoying her response. "Glad you like it."

"Like it? I *love* it."

"Next time, I'll try to get browns and fawny colours."

She nodded in excitement. "To do woodland creatures?"

I shook my head, crowding her against the pink splashed wall. With a hand on either side of her, I trapped her.

I didn't mean to. It just happened.

But with her imprisoned, my system drenched with hunger that I'd been ignoring for way, *way* too long.

"Not woodland creatures." My eyes locked on her lips as she licked them.

Her chest rose and fell, brushing mine with her rapid

inhales. The silence of the evening thickened until it hummed with energy. Energy that electrocuted me.

The chemistry that constantly burned between us scorched my veins.

She moaned a little. Her eyelids fell to half-mast, becoming as drunk as I was. "What then?"

Fuck, I needed her.

I couldn't stand the pain anymore. The self-imposed celibacy when all I wanted was her mouth on mine and my hands all over her.

Bending closer, my brain fogged with lust. My body clawed for more. I leaned against her, her frame flush with mine. I shivered with how goddamn good she felt. "Owls. Lots and lots of owls."

"Oh." Her voice was just breath.

"Owls for O. For you. I'll do an entire portrait with every animal starting with O."

She melted into my touch as I cupped her cheek and held her still. We stared at each other. Our senses turned primitive...only taste and touch remained.

Her hands landed on my chest, bunching fistfuls of my T-shirt as her head fell back against my graffiti. "Gil..."

"Yeah?"

"Do you think...would you...I mean—"

"You want me to kiss you?"

She shuddered; her eyes closed.

She nodded weakly.

I closed the final distance, her breath so delicate and sugary on my lips. Her skin so soft and her body so intoxicating.

I'd waited so fucking long for this. I'd reached the end of my control.

"O..." I brushed my lips on hers.

Just once.

A simple graze.

But it was enough to punch through my ribs and drag a gasping, bleeding heart out of me.

I groaned.

She moaned.

I struggled to stay the gentleman she knew and not the bastard she didn't.

Her chin tilted upward, seeking my mouth.

I went to kiss her.

To give in to her.

But then, her phone rang.

Shrill and demanding, it sliced through the thick intimacy that'd bubbled around us, kicking us back into the world like a bucket of ice water.

I cleared my throat, stepping away and adjusting the constant agony in my jeans.

Olin stomped her foot, her face wild and eyes annoyed as she jerked the offending device from her pocket. She paused. "That's strange. It's my dad."

"Answer him."

It would give me time to get myself together.

What the hell had I been *thinking*?

Kissing her in a dark alley, alone in the middle of the city? *Anything* could've happened. What if I couldn't stop? What if I'd done something as horrendous as all the johns who visited my father's whore house?

I hadn't even told her I was in love with her.

She hadn't told me.

I'd promised not to touch her until I was sure she was mine in every way.

"Hey, Dad." Olin answered the call on the fourth ring. "Yep, I'm good. Uh-huh. Nope. Oh, really. Ah, okay. Yeah, I guess."

I couldn't make out what her father said, but by the time she hung up, the strained pressure in my jeans had faded enough for me to be semi-coherent. "Everything okay?"

She shook her head, shock and trepidation on her face. "They want me to join them at the gala."

"What? Now?" My eyebrows rose. "It's late. And…you're not exactly dressed."

She smoothed down her grey hoodie and jeans. "I know, but he said they feel awkward not having me there. They've probably been asked a lot why I'm not there, seeing as it's kids related, you know?"

"I understand." I raked a hand through my hair, forcing a bright smile for her. "See? They're finally realising the benefits of having a daughter."

She laughed sadly. "Yeah, right."

Scooping up the forgotten spray can from the ground, I held out my hand for her to take. "Come on. Let's get you to that gala, little ostrich."

I held her hand while we waited for a taxi.

I kissed her knuckles as she stepped from the vehicle and climbed the stairs of the large convention hall.

I paid the fare with money she'd given me and made my way back home.

But I didn't enter the house of horrors.

Instead, I crept through my neighbourhood with a half-empty can of spray paint and partook in my new form of medicine.

Chapter Twenty-Three

Olin

-The Present-

A HAUNTED NOISE echoed through the warehouse and into Gil's bedroom.

I jolted upright, ripped from whatever dream I'd been having.

I blinked with disorientation, brain hazy and eyes fuzzy. The nest of blankets around me were warm and cosy, but whatever woke me came again, launching me from the covers.

What the hell is that?

Scrambling upright, I dashed to the door and cracked it open. Darkness yawned deep and endless, hiding familiar and unfamiliar things. The borrowed clothes hung on my slim frame. Gil's size wasn't exactly in keeping with my own, and I hoisted up the waistband of the black sweatpants he'd loaned me, retying the strings tighter around my hips.

I'd struggled when I'd slipped his belongings on. They'd smelled of him. Smelled of comforting washing powder and the citrusy paint smell that permeated his skin. It was a scent that hurt my heart.

After he'd left me, I'd dressed and made the bed, then sat and stared at the door, trying to decide what to do. I hadn't meant to fall asleep. I'd been trying to come up with an excuse of going home. But after so many sleepless nights and a paint-smeared evening, I couldn't fight the fatigue anymore.

A cool breeze nibbled at my bare feet.

How long have I been asleep?

A warbled grunt came from the warehouse. My protective instincts sent adrenaline flowing.

Gil!

Rushing from his room, I padded through the night-shrouded lounge. The too-large T-shirt wafted around me as I crept toward the warehouse.

A curse shattered the silence followed by a thud.

I ran.

Bolting through the office, I skidded to a silent stop as my eyes locked on Gil fast asleep on a tatty couch by the wall. Moonlight and the faint stirrings of dawn highlighted his strained face.

No one was hurting him. No one else was here.

Just Gil and his nightmare.

His legs were tangled in a plaid blanket while he lay on his back. One hand rested on the paint-speckled floor while the other was balled into a fist on his belly. His brow tugged over shut eyes while his chest rose and fell as if he'd run from a monster in his dreams.

Another groan vibrated through his body, tortured and broken, almost wet with tears.

I froze.

Chills scattered down my back with the utmost knowledge I was not supposed to see this.

"O. God...I'm so sorry." His face switched from distraught to fury. "Don't! No—"

My knees threatened to buckle.

Did he dream of me?

Was I the O he pleaded with or did he know another?

"Olive—" He thrashed as if fighting mercenaries of cruel illusions. "I'll save you...I-I promise."

Olive.

He'd never called me Olive in our youth. Oatmeal, Oreo, Oregano, yes. But never Olive.

His limbs seized with nightmare-induced energy, twisting the blankets tighter around his thighs. His hand thumped on the floor, indicating the thud I'd heard was just Gil struggling in his sleep.

I'd had my fair share of night terrors.

For months, I'd dreamed of tumbling through the restaurant window while glass sliced me to shreds. I'd woken up crying with imaginary blood on my fingers.

But those weren't the worst ones.

The worst were the happy dreams where I flew into my dance partner's arms—lithe and limber and forever graceful.

Gil's lips pinched together as he grunted, sounding less coherent and sucked back into unconscious horrors.

I stood there a little longer—a watcher in the dark as he calmed and quietened. I didn't move to wake him. I doubted he'd take kindly to my interruption, nor appreciate that I'd seen him at his most vulnerable.

I wanted to reassure him. I wanted to curl into his side and kiss away his troubles.

But I'd already pushed hard enough.

He needed to rest.

So do I.

Hugging myself from the cool emptiness in the warehouse, I backed away and headed through his office.

Entering his apartment, I padded to the kitchen and opened his equally empty cupboards. The sparse collection of glasses and the plastic cups meant for a child looked hauntingly sad.

Selecting one, I filled it with water and took it to the couch.

As much as I needed to rest, sleep was no longer an option for me. The clock above his cooker said dawn was only an hour or so away. I would wait to ensure Gil slept soundly and safely, and then I would go to work.

I had bills due.

I needed time to think.

And no amount of disgruntled, argumentative body painters could stop me.

* * * * *

Tiptoeing around Gil's warehouse, gathering my stuff while he still slept an hour later, made my heart race.

I felt as if I was letting him down by leaving. I worried about him and his nightmares.

But I couldn't stay—not with being such a new employee.

I had no choice but to borrow the clothes he'd given me, scoop up my belongings—no matter how paint-splattered and destroyed they were—and force myself to be an adult with responsibilities rather than a girl with useless wishes.

Staying as quiet as I could, I tucked my underwear, blouse, skirt, and stockings into my handbag, and dangled my high heels from my fingertips as I surveyed the carnage we'd left behind.

Unscrewed bottles lay forgotten on the floor. Paint splashed up the shelves and stage. A visible red handprint from Gil as he'd thrust into me on the floor was a perfect scarlet letter. A noticeable outline of my back and hair as I'd writhed beneath him the hint of exactly what we'd been doing, and a mix of yellow, black, silver, pink, purple, and blue created a story of violent need.

I blushed.

Blushed and wondered if I should clean up the mess, but Gil shifted on the couch, hinting that my time of escape was now or never.

Holding my breath, I turned from the colourful chaos and padded barefoot toward the exit. The door squeaked a little as I opened it. Throwing Gil a worried glance, I waited for him to soar off the couch and demand to know where the hell I was going.

Instead, he slung an arm over his eyes and stayed where he was.

Goodbye, Gil.

Stepping through the pedestrian access, I turned to quietly close the door behind me.

"Olin? Hi! What are you doing here so early?"

I stiffened, spinning around to face Justin Miller.

The man who seemed to have the worst possible timing in the world. He climbed from his car, his keys clinking in his fingers.

Hiding my heels behind my back and wishing I wasn't in Gil's baggy borrowed clothing, I smiled. "Good morning, Justin."

He narrowed his eyes, looking me up and down. "Morning." Coming closer, he stuffed his keys into his pocket before reaching for a red-stiff strand of my hair. "Gil do a commission today?"

"You could say that." I rocked out of his reach, cursing the fact that I hadn't showered properly and washed evidence away. Streaks of silver and crimson still decorated my chest beneath Gil's T-shirt.

"He's normally meticulous about clean up."

"Yeah, well, not this time." I shrugged. "I'll get rid of the paint at home—"

The door ripped open behind me, gusting with air as Gil's imposing presence pressed against my spine. A blizzard whipped around me as I turned slowly to face the man I'd seen in so many naked ways. Physically naked. Nightmare naked.

Yet I still couldn't figure out a single secret he kept hidden.

"O." His eyes pinned me to the spot. "Justin." He looked at his friend. "Nice morning for a chat on my doorstep."

Justin sniffed, eyeballing the yellow threads in Gil's messy hair. He raised an eyebrow, dropping his inquisitive stare to the black smudge on Gil's cheek and the red rimming his fingernails. "Had a busy morning, Gilbert?" His face twisted with mirth. "What have you two been—"

"Nothing." I stuck out my chin. "We've been doing nothing." Looking at an imaginary watch on my bare wrist, I chirped, "Oh, look at the time. Gotta go. See ya!" Tripping away, I tasted freedom before Gil's dominating hand latched around my elbow and yanked me back. "Not so fast."

I glowered. "I have to go to work, Gil."

His nostrils flared as he shook his head. "Not today." Pulling me back into his warehouse, he scanned the industrial area as if my mere appearance had encouraged the evil in the world to gather outside and plot their takeover.

Justin didn't speak as he followed us inside and closed the door.

"So…" Justin rocked on his heels. "What did I interrupt?"

"Like Olin said, you interrupted nothing." Gil stalked toward the couch where the blanket he'd used lay discarded on the floor as if he'd launched from sleep the moment he'd heard my voice outside.

Picking it up, he tossed it over the armrest before crossing his arms and facing his friend.

Justin's friendly gaze danced around the space, landing on the paint smears, the wonky shelving, the handprint, the body print, the aura of sex still lurking on the stage. The camera waited where it had been abandoned, its casing dabbled with colours.

It was obvious what'd happened.

So *embarrassingly* obvious.

I prickled with heat, flicking Gil a furtive look.

He held my stare with dark, angry eyes. Not angry that we'd been caught. Angry that I'd tried to slip away while he slept. His biceps clenched as he rippled with tension, berating me in that silent, serious way of his, ensuring I knew I'd screwed up and would pay.

Tearing his eyes from mine, Gil looked at Justin. "Why are you here, Miller?"

Justin swallowed a chuckle, knowing exactly what we'd done thanks to the evidence of our activities. He cleared his throat, seriousness replacing his amusement. "Swung by to see what you think of the news."

"News?" Gil crossed his arms. "What news?"

"Another girl has gone missing."

I froze.

What?

Gil turned equally frosty and unmovable. "I didn't know."

"Yeah, painted again. Poor thing was tied and gagged. Couldn't make a sound even while the cops patrolled the same area she was trapped in." Justin brushed lint off his blazer. "She was painted to match the treetops where he'd hidden her. The killer is talented like you, Clark. I'm guessing the cops will be knocking soon to ask your opinion on how he managed to do the camouflage artwork while she was still alive."

Gil sucked in a harsh breath.

"Guess there's a body painter out there with murdering tenancies." Justin sighed. "Fucked up world we live in."

"Wha-what are you talking about?" I whispered, stepping toward Justin.

He shrugged sadly. "Another murder. Third girl this year. All the same motive. Body painted and left to starve, all while she was right in front of the police's noses—"

"Stop." Gil threw me a hunted, haunted look. "Don't upset Olin with the graphic details." His face became unreadable as he opened his arm in invitation. "Coffee first. Then we'll talk."

"Think the bastard could be tracked down by the paint he's using?" Justin asked, moving forward, falling into step with Gil.

Gil didn't reply, vanishing into his apartment with Justin by his side.

The door closed.

I was alone.

My feet moved to follow. The topic was too harrowing not to know every detail.

But...I paused.

I'm alone.

I needed to go to work. I had responsibilities.

Gil was distracted, and the exit was unpatrolled and unlocked.

I'm sorry.

Sending Gil a silent goodbye, I hoisted my handbag higher

and walked out of *Total Trickery's* warehouse unobstructed.

Chapter Twenty-Four

Olin

-The Present-

"GOOD TO SEE you, Olin. Everything okay at home?" Shannon asked as I plonked at my desk, yanked my phone from my bag, and turned on the work computer.

My breath was choppy from running, and my hair still damp from my very rushed shower, but at least I'd made it home, removed any remaining paint, changed into suitable office attire, and hoofed it over to Status Enterprises only twenty minutes late.

However, twenty minutes was an eternity when it came to being a new employee. I wasn't exactly giving them the best impression.

"I'm so sorry I'm late. I'll stay twenty minutes behind so I—"

"It's fine." Shannon waved her hand, sipping on a thick mug of coffee. "Don't worry about it. We all have a life that gets in the way now and again. As long as things are good, don't stress." Her eyes caught mine pointedly. "So...are they good?"

I plucked a muesli bar from my blazer pocket—my quick fix for breakfast—and nodded. "Yes, all sorted."

"And that sexy man who dragged you out of here is satisfied the 'family emergency' is all defused?"

"Yes." I opened the wrapper. "He knows not to interrupt me at work again."

I hope.

"Great!" A broad grin spread over her cherry-glossed lips.

She leaned over my cubicle wall with a wink. "He was rather yummy. Got a good catch there, girl."

I bit into my muesli bar. "I'm very lucky."

Or very unlucky.

Depending on my mood.

Chuckling, she pushed off from the cubicle. "Happy working. There's a staff meeting at three. See you there."

I waved her away and logged into my emails. Nibbling on my breakfast—wishing it was a large plate of pancakes and syrup—I replied to the questions and queries that had come in overnight, all the while Justin's voice echoed in my mind.

"Another girl has gone missing."

Why did I not know about these murders?

Why did my heart sink with dread at the very mention of a killer with body painting skills?

Clicking on an email, I did my best to focus all while worry gathered in my belly.

* * * * *

By four p.m., my self-restraint snapped.

Justin's voice was a loop inside my head. *"Another murder. Third girl this year."*

My thoughts were awash with gruesome killings of pretty girls camouflaged in paint. I didn't know if I felt a kindred calling to them because I'd been painted or because I was in love with a body painter.

Either way, my instinctual drive to protect Gil demanded I know more.

Gil.

He had issues and complexities; he was prickly and hiding something monstrous beneath his icy façade.

But he was gentle.

Kind.

And mine.

Mine to guard against new and old horrors.

Chewing on my bottom lip, I opened a new internet search: *Murdered painted girls in England.*

My lungs stuck together as page results flickered over my screen.

Clicking on a link, I trembled as I read something normally reserved for other places, other counties, other populations.

Tragically, another young woman was found early last night by a dog walker in Nottingham forest. The girl appears to have died from dehydration and starvation while being restrained and gagged in the treetops. The police searched the area a few days prior, thanks to an anonymous tip, but were unsuccessful in locating her due to the significant paintwork over her skin mimicking the branches where she was tied. Because of the camouflage, she was effectively invisible to law enforcement and most likely saw them searching for her before she died.

Today, police have been criticized for their lack of use of sniffer dogs.

This is the third death of similar methods, which leads law enforcement to believe a serial killer is loose in the Garden of England. Two previous girls (Shelly King (22) and Moira Jonston (27)) where found in the shrub garden at Wightwick Manor and Cannon Hill Park. Shelly King was painted to match the undergrowth she was tucked beneath, and Moira Jonston was lashed to a tree with her skin the same texture and shadow of bark.

Both women were already dead upon discovery.

Police urge anyone who might know anything about these murders to call their emergency hotline. They also advise that young women avoid unnecessary travel alone until further notice.

No arrests have been made.

My stomach roiled.

What sort of sick bastard tied up women, silenced them, then made them invisible to the people trying to find them? What sort of killer left his victims to *starve* to death? Why bother killing at that point? It wasn't like he got the thrill of taking someone's life. He had to wait to read about their demise in the local paper, just like the rest of us.

Those poor girls.

Murders happened all the time. The world had turned into a dark, violent place. I'd heard about other crimes far worse…but those dead painted girls wriggled into my bones and scraped out my marrow.

A blizzard howled in my chest.

Gil…

Would he be able to help the police track down who'd done this? Could he even have met them? Did body painters share their tips and tricks? Attend seminars of talent?

There wasn't any doubt that the killer had to be severely deranged.

Psychotic without a doubt.

He had to have transport.

Perhaps a van like the guy who tried to kidnap me?

I turned into a statue.

No...

I couldn't stop it. Couldn't outrun the runaway train my brain became.

That guy is a bastard.

He hurt Gil.

He has something over him.

He wasn't...normal.

Could it be?

If he was the killer, did that mean Gil was involved? What if he was next? What if he was trapped in something even worse than I thought?

The incessant whispers slithered and snaked. I couldn't stop the what if, what if, *what if.*

What if Gil has something to do with this?

My heart stopped beating.

He was bleeding and dirty the night he was drunk.

Goosebumps scattered over my flesh as my mind unfolded the night I'd slept with him. How he'd poured alcohol down his throat as if running from something. As if he drank pure regret.

He'd smelled of earth and paint.

He'd looked beside himself with rage and despair.

Could he—

Stop it.

Just stop it.

He is no way involved in this.

He can't be!

You know him.

You've known him since he was a boy.

But I *couldn't* stop it.

It was a knife in my side; a pebble in my shoe.

It was stark fear that Gil was silenced by the devil and stuck in a torturous hell.

With my heart lodged in my throat, I grabbed my phone and opened messenger. Pulling up the conversation I'd had with Justin over Gil's disappearance around the time the third girl was kidnapped, I froze.

What do you think you're doing?

You're seriously going to ask Justin if he believes Gil is involved?

Could I really think such atrocious things and ask his best friend to prove me wrong?

Gil saved me from the guy with the van!

Yes! Therefore, he couldn't be the murderer.

But why did he make me lie to the police…?

I gasped at the barbed, thorny thought.

Why didn't Gil beat that bastard into the ground?

What did that guy have over him as blackmail?

The air became thin and sour. I unbuttoned a few pearl clasps on my grey blouse, prickling with sweat.

I swiped at my hair again as my eyes fell on the awaiting message bubble. A fleck of silver paint fell from my strands, landing on the desk.

If I didn't ask, I'd go crazy.

Olin Moss: *Those murdered girls you mentioned this morning…do you think…and this is NUTS, but is there any way Gil could be wrapped up in…whatever is going on? I don't know what I'm asking…but do you think he's in trouble?*

I squeezed my eyes and tapped send, unable to breathe.

Thirty seconds ticked past before his response blared across my screen.

Justin Miller: *Wow. I know it's been a long time since you've seen the guy but seriously?*

Olin Moss: *I know. I hate myself for even asking. I'm just worried about him. He's hiding something, Justin. Something huge.*

Justin Miller: *He is not a killer. No matter what he's hiding.*

I wanted to leave it at that. I believed Justin. I trusted Gil. I knew in my heart he could never be capable of hurting *anyone.*

But…

But!

Olin Moss: *The girls were painted. He went missing around the same time that last girl was kidnapped.*

Justin Miller: *He said he had family business to deal with. You know the jackass that was his father. His disappearance probably had something to do with that. And there are other body painters, O. Countless others.*

He had a point.

The same wonderfully valid point my own mind had thrown at me.

A hundred other artists existed just like there were a hundred other office workers, authors, and politicians. And he was also right about Gil's father. I hadn't even factored that in.

Justin Miller: *Your turn to answer a question. Do YOU think Gilbert Clark is a serial murderer?*

The black and white finality of the words cut into my eyes and bled into my soul. A kaleidoscope of memories, recent and past, swirled together with the same vibrant colours Gil wielded so effortlessly.

A man with smiling sad eyes.

A man desperately trying not to kiss me.

A boy promising to never drink because he was better than his father.

A boy walking me home every day to keep me safe.

That boy was not a killer.

And just because age had weathered him, hurt him, harrowed away at his heart, he was still that person.

I knew that.

I knew it in the way he kissed me so reverently in his shower. Knew it in the way he stared at me with history and hope in his eyes.

He had his secrets. He had his insecurities and problems and a complicated vein of mystery, but...*he is not a killer*.

Relief blanketed me with grateful warmth as my fingers tapped the screen.

Olin Moss: *Gil is many things. But he is not a murderer.*

"All right, everyone. Staff meeting in five!" Shannon yelled across the office floor. Employees stuck up their hand to signal they'd heard; others stood with pen and paper for note taking.

I went to turn off my phone, wishing I could delete the entire conversation and any sign of my doubt about Gil, but Justin sent one last reply.

Justin Miller: *He's had it rough, O. I don't know what, and he refuses to confide in me, but something happened to him. Whatever it was did a real number on him. You only have to look past the cold exterior to see how much the guy suffers. His ability to keep people away is his coping mechanism, you know? You and me...we've been through stuff that changed us. But Gil...he's been through shit that I can't even imagine. Be nice to him. He needs all the friends he can get.*

Chapter Twenty-Five

Olin

-The Present-

CRADLING MY PHONE in my palm, I stepped from the elevator into the lobby. I hadn't heard from Gil all day. I'd left his protection when he'd specifically told me not to, and I'd had no angry messages or inconvenient visitors.

I couldn't unscramble how I felt about that.

"Olin."

His gruff, sorrowful voice ripped my head to the comfy, velvet chairs by the security desk. Gil stood slowly, unwinding his powerful frame and standing on long, strong legs. Shadows decorated under his eyes, and his usual aura of tragedy hung heavier on his shoulders.

How could I ever think he was a killer? Even for the tiniest of moments. No killer would hold remorse and regret the way he did. No killer could look so full of despair.

I didn't think.

I didn't pause.

My feet broke into a run. I threw myself into him. "I'm sorry." I hugged his firm waist, snuggling into his citrusy, earthy chest.

"Sorry for what?" He didn't hug me back. His arms stayed by his sides. His hands balled tight and unyielding. "For leaving when I told you not to?"

I placed a kiss right over his heart. "For that and…other things." Pulling away, I backed up and slipped my phone into my bag. No way did I want him to see the messages between Justin and me. I never wanted to hurt him in that way—to know my trust in him had wavered.

Gil didn't move, his eyes narrowed and suspicious. "I expected you to run in the opposite direction, not into my arms."

"Why?"

"Because I demanded you stay with me." His spine stiffened. "Of course, my request was denied…and you left without a goodbye."

"I didn't leave because I was angry at you for forbidding me." I fought the urge to touch him again. "I left because I have a job."

His jaw clenched. "It wasn't safe to go without me. If I knew you were that damn stubborn about menial labour, I would've escorted you."

I ignored his deliberate zing. "I can take care of myself."

He sighed, his entire body forlorn. "That's the thing, O. In this…you can't."

My pulse picked up pace. "What's that supposed to mean?"

"It means…" He looked away, shedding off the truth. "Doesn't matter. You're okay. We're together again."

My heart flipped. "Are we?"

His eyes narrowed. "Are we what?"

"*Together* together?"

"No." He shook his head. "Not in that way."

Not yet.

I smiled weakly, doing my best to change the subject. "Would you believe me if I said I missed you?"

He scowled. "Not in a million years. Why would you? I've been an arsehole."

In a crystal moment of absolute vulnerability, I murmured, "Would you believe me if I said I missed hugging you? We've kissed and connected in ways we never did as teenagers, but we haven't hugged."

He sucked in a breath.

I braced myself for a warning—a scathing telling-off. Instead, his knuckles nudged my chin, bringing my gaze to his. I froze as he stared into me, seeing my fears, my guilt, my endless need for him, and he closed his eyes as if he couldn't survive what he saw. "I keep saying this, and you keep ignoring me, but…*please* stop. I can't take much more."

My lips tingled for his. My body warmed. My heart raced. "I can't stop what I feel."

"You shouldn't feel anything for me."

"I've *always* felt something for you." A couple of colleagues walked past, reminding us we were in public. This wasn't private. And yet, the intensity that'd sprung between us was visceral.

Gil sighed heavily. His knuckles dropped from my chin. "Just...don't."

I winced at the plea in his voice, the aching, quaking request not to tangle emotion with whatever physical chemistry we shared.

I'd asked him the same thing in the shower when he'd traced my tattoo.

Don't.

Please don't.

Don't make me fall.

Don't make me hurt.

The last thing I wanted to do was cause him more pain.

Clearing his throat, doing his best to return to callous and cold, he said, "You need to pack a few things. You're coming back to my place. No arguments."

"Eh, excuse me?"

"You refused to stay longer than a night—even though I've been explicit about the danger—"

"You haven't told me anything—"

"Let me finish." He scowled. "I get that I came off...overbearing. So, I'm *asking* you to stay with me until I can fix this." Rubbing the back of his neck, he sighed, "And if you're going to stay, you'll need clothes."

I blinked. "How long are you suggesting?"

"I don't know." His shoulders slumped. "I've failed in every way to resolve it quickly, but it has to end...soon."

"Why?"

His face etched with shadows. "Because there's only so much a person can tolerate before they're pushed too far."

I froze. The need to touch him overrode all other function. Moving closer, I cupped his cheek. "You can tell me what—"

Arching his face out of my reach, his forehead furrowed with impatience at himself, at me, at whatever he battled. "You're living with me until I say otherwise."

"And if I don't like sharing a home?"

"You don't really have a choice."

"I *always* have a choice, Gil."

His eyes shot black as memories sucked him deep. "*No one*

has a choice."

The softness between us vanished into thick smoke, leaving behind the charred remains.

He raked a hand through his hair. "Three nights, okay?" His eyes jumped over suited men and women, assessing for threats. "That's all I'll ask for."

Three nights were an eternity.

An eternity for all new romances.

Time took on a different depth at the beginning of a fledgling love affair. An hour wasn't just an hour when love and lust were involved. A minute wasn't just a minute when hearts had countless of opportunities to fall.

There would be no more places to hide. No more lies we could tell ourselves. Only the stark truth that both of us were in danger and had been for years.

Couldn't he see that?

Couldn't he taste the hypocrisy?

Three nights would destroy us both.

Gil fought against my silence, saying, "Pack a bag with clothes for three nights. If I haven't fixed the problem…then you'll probably have to move countries because you won't be safe anywhere."

I snapped out of my worry. "I never took you for being dramatic."

"I'm being deadly serious." His voice was flat and cold.

Ice slithered down my spine. I shivered, pointing to the sunny evening, needing warmth and open air. "Let's go. We can talk about living arrangements later." If we were ever to have an honest conversation, I wanted to be anywhere else but here, surrounded by strangers.

"Fine." Gil bowed a little, letting me lead the way.

My back prickled as he fell into step with me—not submissive in my leadership but wary and watchful. I understood why he'd placed himself behind me. He'd done it out of protection. Even in my office building, he acted as if the devil himself was going to crawl through the floorboards and claim me.

Pushing open the glass doors, I turned to face him as he stepped into the late afternoon sunshine. "How long have you been waiting for me?"

He kept his eyes on the men and women leaving for the day. "Since I kicked Justin out and came directly here." He glanced at me. "I saw you arrive. I got here before you did."

"You've waited all day for me?"

"I told you I wasn't going to let you out of my sight."

"I *was* out of your sight, though." Striking off into a walk, my black kitten toe heels clicked on the pavement.

"You were in the office building all day. I was satisfied you'd be safe up there."

"You were *satisfied?*"

He nodded, ducking behind me to let a man stride past talking loudly on his cell phone.

"So, you decided not to drag me from my place of employment even though you did such a thing yesterday?"

"I was wrong." He walked beside me with firm, even steps. "You were right."

I slammed to a stop, my temper rising for no other reason than sexual frustration and star-crossed heartaches. "Wow. I never thought I'd see the day."

"Sarcasm isn't becoming on you, O." Grabbing my elbow, he pulled me back into motion. "Where do you live?"

I studied him, unable to take my eyes off his thick eyelashes or the way he still had black smudged on his cheek and yellow decorating his hair. He'd told the truth. He'd raced to my work the moment Justin was gone.

His desire to protect me wasn't just some pantomime but a deep-seated drive.

Once again, guilt crushed me for the awful, awful thought I'd had and my messages with Justin.

How could I be that cruel? That distrustful?

Tilting his head, he caught me staring.

I blushed but didn't look away. "You're just the same as before...but different too." I hated how my cheeks burned, giving away my heart's truth all over again. "I always found you very handsome."

His face darkened. "What the hell has gotten into you?" Pulling me forward by my wrist, he grumbled something undeterminable under his breath. "Don't mistake me being here for anything other than what it is. We aren't dating. We aren't together. There is no us or we." He winced. "Got it?"

"I get that you're fighting what *could* be."

"I'm accepting what *is*." He strode forward, dragging me along. "Enough."

I ignored the fresh pain, the rampant confusion. Why did he

care about keeping me safe if he was determined to keep me away? "Maybe we *should* go on a date. We never wined and dined when we were younger. We've slept together...it makes sense that we at least go to a movie."

His eyes flashed. "I can't."

"Why?"

"Because."

"That isn't a good enough reason, Gil." I tried to tug out of his grip. "I'm tired. I'm doing my best to be patient and understanding but there's only so much—"

"For fuck's sake." Yanking me to a stop, we created a little island in a sea of people. His gaze was bare, turmoil clouding the wintery green. "No movies. No dinners. *Nothing.* Don't ask me to hurt you any more than I already have. Don't ask me why I can't keep you."

"Why can't you keep me?" My voice was small, the tiniest mouse in a world of predators.

He groaned, low and tortured.

I whispered, "Why touch me if you can't explore even the slimmest notion of—"

His arm banded around my waist, yanking me into him. His lips cast hot breath against my ear. "I want you. I've always fucking wanted you. I've been honest about that. You know what you mean to me and I can't deny that there are things between us that will never go away." He pulled back, pinning me with darkness, allowing finality to fill his voice. "But whatever we shared, ends here. Whatever you thought was happening, is over. Touching you was the worst mistake of my life. I refuse to do it again."

Jerking me forward, he weaved around a pack of pedestrians, glaring at the buildings looming over us as if he could guess which apartment was mine. "Where do you live?"

I couldn't answer him.

My tongue had turned useless. My voice mute.

I'd been hurt by this man over and over again.

But that? Here, now...

"Touching you was the worst mistake of my life."

A silent tear fell down my cheek, more liquid blurring the world around me. I went loose in his grip, following meekly all while I broke inside.

His fingers fisted tight, his own pain leeching into me. "I'm...sorry." He kept his stare straight ahead. "I didn't mean it like that. I—" He groaned again, sounding as if he'd just cut out his own heart. "I just mean…I can't be with you. I should never have—" He cut himself off.

I bit my lip to staunch more tears, swallowing them back. He didn't need to know how hurt I was. Didn't need more power over my emotions.

"O?" He slowed, still not looking at me. His voice went toneless. "Where is your apartment?"

Straightening, I pushed away the catastrophe that'd just happened. I was a dancer. We were used to agony and pushing forward. The show must go on, after all. "I don't need you to walk me home." My voice was empty. I'd fought to win him. I'd done my best to stay friendly and kind—despite all my questions and heartache from our past. I'd given what little strength I had to heal the hurt inside him…unable to see him so lost.

I'd fallen in love with the idea of not being alone anymore.

Loneliness was my one true companion. While I accepted it as my bedfellow, confidant, and lover, life couldn't scar me too badly because loneliness was the most painful of curses. Nothing else could compare—not destitution, not car accidents, not even the death of my dreams.

But Gil…he'd always been the one that'd promised a cure to my loneliness.

The *only* one.

I'd felt it when we spoke that first time in the corridor.

I'd felt it each time we fell a little deeper.

He was different to the others because he didn't just patch up the lonely holes inside me, he filled them until they never even existed.

He completed me by just *being* there.

I didn't need much.

I'd never asked for anything.

Yet on that busy street, the truth finally shattered my final dream.

Of us.

I stumbled as the hot, lacerating blade punctured my heart and the rest of my hope.

Gil's hold kept me from falling, his gaze landing on my tears. He jerked to a halt. Once again, we were an island in a sea of pedestrians, but this time…our island was cracked and cratered by unfixable earthquakes.

I rolled my wrist, doing my best to be free of him. "I need

to be alone, Gil." I kept my gaze on the pavement, allowing fallen tears to dry on my cheeks. "Please…let me go."

His hand fell away, his fingers curling into fists. "Olin, I—"

"No." I shook my head, striding forward with my arms wrapped around myself. "Just…leave me alone."

Each footstep was eternally heavy. All I wanted to do was go home, curl up on my couch, and forget I'd ever found Gilbert Clark and his painful box of colours.

We didn't speak as I followed familiar streets, crossed roads, and bypassed buildings.

Gil trailed after me.

He didn't leave me alone like I'd asked…escorting me to my door in silence.

* * * * *

Gil didn't leave, standing stiff and protective while I fumbled in my handbag for my keys. His eyes skated over the grunge-covered walls and the cobwebs in the corners. The stairwell of my building wasn't exactly five stars, but at least the tenants kept to themselves, and it was mainly a quiet place to live.

Slightly depressing, but affordable.

Inserting my key, I turned the lock but didn't open the door. "You can go now," I murmured, not turning around to look at him. "I'm safe here."

He shifted, his clothing rustling with a harsh breath. "You're not safe anywhere."

I shrugged. "That might be, but I want to be alone."

His large palm landed on my shoulder, shooting heat and dazzling need through me. "Olin…" His fingers squeezed in both affection and frustration. "Hate me. I deserve it. I would rather you hate me than forgive me. But…you have to let me inside."

The thought of letting Gil trespass on my private sanctuary made my body tremble. "Please, Gil…not tonight."

He reached around me, his front scorching my back as his hand dropped to cover mine on the handle. "He knows where you live. I can't let you stay here."

"This is my *home*." Temper once again infected me.

"And I've destroyed it." His voice was endlessly sad. "But it doesn't change the fact that I can't let you be here your own." Pressing down on my hand, he worked the handle to unlatch the door then gently pushed me over the threshold.

I tensed as he followed me inside then closed the door

behind him, flicking the lock back into place. Once secure, he sucked in a deep breath as he surveyed my home.

Strange that the last place he'd seen of mine was technically my parents. He'd watched me while I'd cooked in a fancy kitchen. He'd thanked me with his sad eyes when he'd soaked in a bath after a severe beating. He'd tiptoed through that two-story house as if he wasn't welcome—and the reality was, he wasn't because it wasn't mine. It'd belonged to my parents who didn't even know he existed.

This apartment, however.

This is mine.

I'd moved into it when my dancing dreams died, and I'd had to relocate from London. I'd had no one to couch surf on. No parents to ask for support. While my body healed from slashes and surgeries, I'd sourced it, signed the lease, paid my bond, and sparsely furnished it all on my own. It'd been hard but filled me with triumph that I'd succeeded.

I'd expected no hand outs; I'd asked for no short-cuts. I'd accepted that my life path had changed forever. What little I had, I guarded with a fierceness that knew what it felt like to lose what was most important.

I've lost him.

He was precious and I'd lost the war.

All over again.

Forcing myself to stay proud of my rag-tag achievements rather than dash around and try to improve on what couldn't be improved upon, I said, "You can see no one is here. No monsters in the corners. No kidnappers in the kitchen." I looked at the door behind him. "You don't need to stay."

He didn't respond; his jaw gritted as he glanced at my threadbare couch, scruffy dining table, and the kitchen that barely fit a fridge and oven. Compared to his impressive warehouse with its industrial shelving and priceless painting equipment, my tiny one bedroom was depressingly sad.

Stalking through the small space, he didn't say a word as his fingers traced the bench top that still held my dirty coffee cup and empty wine bottle.

I would've been embarrassed if I wasn't so emotionally exhausted.

His boots carried him over the ugly carpet as he peered into the postage stamp-size bathroom and the bedroom next to it. The cream and navy floral bedspread I had was rumpled and needed making, but the gauzy fabric I'd hung from the ceiling to drape on either side gave it a slight Moroccan feel.

Marching back toward me, he muttered, "There's no art anywhere."

I scanned my walls, noting the bareness, the barrenness after the huge graffiti in Gil's place.

I shrugged. "I'm not an artist."

"You were with dance."

I flinched. "*Were* being the keyword in that sentence."

He studied me. His green eyes so piercing it was as if he could see the rehabilitation and surgeries I'd endured. The fact that I'd just been thinking about the loss of something so dear made the pain all the more acute.

His voice hovered around a whisper. "Do you miss it?"

Breaking eye contact, I kept my scarred and tattooed back straight as I kicked off my heels and padded into my bedroom. "Would you miss painting if you couldn't do it?"

I made the mistake of looking at him, standing on the threshold of my room. He leaned against the doorframe with his ankles and arms crossed. His nonchalant pose couldn't disguise the wash of unease and quick slip of horror.

I waited for him to make some flippant comment. Instead, he glowered at my carpet. "I wouldn't survive. Pure and simple. It's the only thing that keeps me going these days."

My heart bucked in my chest. I struggled with something to say, but in the end, I had nothing. All I wanted to do was tumble to my bed and close my eyes.

"Gil...I—"

He moved toward me, backing me up until I was trapped against the wall and him. His gaze caught mine so intensely, the hair on the back of my neck pricked and instincts screamed on high alert.

His hands cupped my hipbones, his thumbs tracing small circles. "How did you survive, O?" he breathed. "How did you pick yourself up after what happened?"

I froze, my insides melting from his touch and my heart fracturing from his question. "What do you mean?"

He shrugged as if he didn't really understand himself. "Your parents basically disowned you since you were a child. Your dreams of being a dancer were destroyed. You don't seem to have stayed in touch with people from school...you're alone. Yet you're not fucking up your life like I am."

"How do you know what I'm doing with my life?"

"You're so strong. Strong enough to push me away, even when I tell you you're in danger. Strong enough to give me everything you have, all because you're selfless. Strong enough to forgive, even though I'm the reason you're in trouble." His nose nuzzled mine. "I need to know how you can do all that, endure everything you have, and still be good...because I...I'm really fucking struggling."

My heart restarted, defibrillated from its forlorn fatigue all because I was stupid when it came to this man. Stupid and flawlessly forgiving. "Whatever you're dealing with...you don't have to do it alone."

"God, there you go again." His chest rose and fell as his breathing turned shallow. His eyes darkened, and the tiny space of my bedroom vibrated with connection. "You're *still* willing to offer me salvation after everything I've done."

"It's okay."

"No, it's not." His teeth bared. "You coped on your own."

"Yes."

"So why the fuck can't I?" His eyes blazed, locking onto my lips. His temper dragged lust into the mix, swirling two potent chemicals in my bloodstream. "I'm useless. I'm failing everyone I love. I—" His forehead pressed onto mine. "I'm failing you...just like always."

My stomach dropped and my core clenched, answering his summons, dragged into his need despite myself. Just as I knew it would. Just like it always would.

"Gil..." I shook my head as he placed one hand on my wall, caging me by my wardrobe, leaving the other one digging into my hip.

"You were so popular at school." His fingers pulsed with ownership. "Until I stole you from them."

I couldn't heal the agony glowing in his gaze but I could offer a tiny bit of redemption. Pressing a hand over his heart, I whispered, "Until I *chose* you over them."

He swallowed hard. "Why are you so alone now?"

God, what was the point of these agonising questions? "I'm not alone. You're here."

"And all I'm doing is making shit worse." His hand caressed the side of my waist, over my breast, and settled above my heart—just like I touched him. "I wish I could be different. I wish *we* could be different."

"We can be…if—"

"Stop."

I didn't like the weakness he conjured in me. I didn't like the endless torment in his stare. What changed from the cruel body painter who'd said touching me was a mistake to this broken man unable to let me go?

Why did he care all of a sudden? Why did I grow angry that he did?

Steeling myself against his touch, I said, "I think it's best if you go. We can talk later, when we're both a bit more stable."

He flinched. "Was it hard?"

I blinked, unable to keep up with his subject changes. "Was what hard?"

"Earning money. Keeping this place after your accident?"

Okay, this is too much.

Whatever was happening between us wasn't the white-hot chemistry that'd gotten us into trouble with paint and orgasms yesterday. It wasn't the raw, vulnerable truth that appeared when we'd kissed in the shower.

This was different.

This was…*conversation.*

This was learning about one another, discovering secrets, sympathising with past struggles.

This was *talking.*

And talking was so much more dangerous than any sex or kiss.

Ducking under his arm, I padded toward my bed, sucking in a shallow breath. He spun to face me, spying the duffel I used to use for my dance practices. Grabbing it, he tossed it on the bed.

I frowned. "What are you doing?"

"Packing."

"I told you I'm staying here."

Bending to open the middle drawer of my tallboy, he selected a pair of pyjama bottoms, a hoodie, and fluffy socks before moving to my sparse selection of office clothes in the wardrobe.

I chased after him, yanking a black blouse out of his grip. "Stop it."

"Three days. I'll figure this shit out by then…I promise." He snatched a skirt from a hanger.

I snatched it back. "I can't afford to spend three days at your place."

"Why the hell not? It's not like I'm going to charge you rent." He reached for a shell pink shirt with cream piping.

Ducking in front of him, I stopped him from stealing yet another garment of mine. "I can't be in your space, in your *bed* without being seriously hurt."

He froze, his gaze snapping onto mine. "You're afraid I'll raise a hand against you?"

"No." I laughed sadly. "You'd never hurt me in that way...apart from the other day with the police." I sighed. "I'm talking about other kinds of pain. We've only been back in each other's lives for a few days, and look at the mess we're already in."

He stiffened. "It's a mess I can fix by not touching you anymore." The words seemed to choke him.

"It's a mess that will only get more complicated the longer we spend together." It physically tore out my heart but I forced, "You don't want to be with me—you've told me over and over again—so it's not fair of you to demand I spend time with you...not when I can't stop wanting—"

His lips crashed on mine, silencing me. His tongue dove past my lips, consuming me.

Unbridled angst and energy flowed between us.

I kissed him back—weak and hungry.

His fingers shot through my hair, keeping me pinned as he leaned into me, squashing me against the wall. His hips rocked into mine, wedging his erection against my belly.

God, I didn't stand a chance.

"How are you this brave when you have no one?" He kissed me vicious and deep. "How does loneliness not eat you alive?"

I arched my mouth away from his, breathing hard. My lips tingled, my body damp and ready for anything he wanted to give me, but his question had been horribly cruel.

My hands balled. "I'm not lonely."

"I am." His eyes searched mine. "I'm dying a little every day because of it."

"You can't say things like that."

"Things like the truth?" He traced his thumb over my cheekbone. "Tell me how you did it. Tell me what I should do. Fuck, O...tell me how to stop—" He leaned to kiss me again, but I slipped under his arm and pushed his weight away.

He was a master at making me care. A magician at making me believe he cared in return.

I'd once again lost all my power because Gil had kissed me when I'd wanted space. He'd encroached on my home when all I wanted was time apart.

He sucked up all the air and suffocated me of all my choices.

And *still* I couldn't say no.

My chin tipped up as true anger filled me. Anger at not knowing a thing about him, his past, his present, his secrets. Anger that was done waiting for answers.

Questions crawled up my throat and burned my tongue. I spat them out as if we'd been having a fight, not indulging in an explosive kiss. "Enough. No more." I slashed my hand through the air. "You don't get to ask a single thing about me...not unless you're prepared to trade."

"Trade?" His nostrils flared. The passion between us slipped into something lethal.

"You say I'm lonely." I looked him up and down tauntingly. "Yet you're the saddest person I've ever met."

His entire body tensed, filling with threats. "Olin...be careful."

"You ask if I struggled. But you won't tell me what *you* struggle with."

His throat worked as he swallowed. "I'm warning you."

"Justin said something happened—"

"Justin?" His snarl made me slam my lips together. "What the fuck did Justin say?"

Shit.

"Nothing. Only that—"

"Justin doesn't know anything about me."

"He knows something happened. Just like I know—"

"Neither of you have a fucking clue."

"You say that as if you're proud that you've kept two people who care about you in the dark."

"Proud, no. Grateful, yes." His eyes flashed. "You don't need to know. You *can't* know."

"You're right. I don't need to know. No one *needs* to know anything about someone. But we were friends once, and we're playing with fire now. The logical step is to learn about each other."

"It's not logical. Nothing about this is logical."

"I agree." I winced from the pain in his voice. "There's nothing logical about you knocking me out for calling the police on a legitimate crime. There's nothing logical about why I keep forgiving your attitude. There's nothing *logical* about asking me to stay with you for three days without any other explanation other than my life is in danger."

"That's the best reason to obey me."

"But not the easiest."

"You used to trust me." His voice was measured and cold.

"Yeah, and look where that got me!" My anger soared, pushing my voice up an octave.

His deepened into danger. "What the hell is going on here?"

"What do you mean?"

"How did this happen?" He waved his hand back and forth between us as if he could physically touch the burning, bleeding battle we'd created. "How did we go from kissing to being at war?"

"I've reached my limit. I want to know what you're hiding."

He cocked an eyebrow in a measured, chilly move. "You're crazy if you think I'm going to tell you anything—"

"You think *I'm* the crazy one?"

He nodded, crossing his arms. "Certifiable."

My mouth fell open.

He wanted to play that game? Name-call and ridicule to avoid discussing topics about himself?

Fine.

"Who's Olive, Gil?"

I braced myself for an explosion. I willingly poured gasoline on the fire. I was jealous of his dream. Jealous of another O. An O he obviously cared about, adored, loved, *missed*.

He missed that girl with every molecule of his body, and if I wasn't that girl he dreamed about, then I was wasting my time.

I refused to put myself through the agony. I utterly prohibited myself from falling any further if there wasn't the tiniest, *slimmest* chance that I might win in the end.

That I might crack Gil's arctic shell.

That I might earn his complicated love.

But I wasn't prepared for the lashing, slicing silence that cloaked him, shutting him down piece by piece. His face went dead. His body carved from glaciers. Only his eyes glowed, and they glimmered with a thousand poisonous emeralds. "Where did you hear that name?" His voice was measured and methodical, terrifying in its iciness.

I'd faced his wrath. I'd fought his passion. I'd submitted to his commands.

But standing before him while the temperature plummeted and his jaw ticked with snow, I didn't know how to breathe. Didn't know what to say or how to fix this.

I'd screwed up.

Majorly.

And I didn't fully understand why.

Goosebumps darted all over me as I sidestepped toward the living room. "Forget it. I made a mistake."

He stared at me as if I was a stranger, letting me inch away from his frigid fury.

But then, he stalked toward me.

I raised my hands in surrender, backing away. "Gil...don't."

His brow tugged over furious eyes. "Where did you hear that name?"

"You had a nightmare. The night I stayed at your place." I dodged around the dining room table. "I overheard you."

For a second, sheer relief shone on his face, but it was followed swiftly by more rage. "You spied on me?"

"You kidnapped me." My fingers latched around a scruffy wooden chair, using it as a shield.

"I'm *protecting* you."

"I don't want protecting."

"Well, too fucking bad!"

My head cocked. "What are you protecting me from?"

He shuddered as if I'd asked the hardest question in the world. "Everything."

"Not everything." My heart pounded as I studied his unreadable pose. Give him a sword and he looked ready to smite me down.

He froze, predator still and ready to pounce. "What the hell does that mean?"

I'd picked this fight. I couldn't back down even though my knees trembled. "You might be protecting me from things I don't know, but you're doing a terrible job of protecting me from *you*."

His teeth gnashed together. "I'm not the dangerous one."

I laughed cynically. "You've *always* been the most dangerous one. To me."

"What do you want from me, Olin?" His sigh was endlessly heavy. "You push me until I snap. You taunt me until I retaliate. You're not supposed to be in my life, yet you barged in anyway."

His eyes flashed. "This is your fault. You made it all so fucking complicated."

"You're blaming *me* for all of this?"

He nodded, moving forward and stopping in front of my chair-shield. "All of it."

"Including the mess you're in with the guy who beats you up?"

His eyes snapped closed while he inhaled patience as his shoulders slouched in defeat. "No. That's on me."

"What's on you?"

He smiled sadly. "A punishment I can't bear."

I stopped breathing. "What punishment, Gil?" Inching out from behind my chair, I dared put my hand on his rigid forearm. "You know you can talk to me, right?" I wanted to ask him if I was the O he dreamed of. If I still haunted him like he haunted me.

But I was a coward.

He shrugged me off. "Like I told you before, I can't." He looked at the ceiling with the most distressing, heartsick look. The melancholy wrapping around him slithered from apartment corners and sank painful fangs into his soul.

I couldn't stand to see him so broken. Because that was what he was. His anger and arguments scared me, but it was what lurked beneath his threats that scared me more.

Gilbert Clark was almost at his wits' end.

He was exhausted and drained and living in misery, and I had no idea how to help him.

"I'm still here for you, Gil." I stepped into him, wrapping my arms around his tense frame. "Even if you try to push me away. Even if we fight or say things we don't mean. If you truly need help...I'm *always* here."

He remained unmovable; his frost decorated my flesh with snowflakes, making me shiver.

"I abandoned you." His voice was barely audible, quiet as mist.

"You did."

"I hurt you."

I nodded. "So much."

"I physically hurt you."

"Multiple times."

"But you forgive me?"

I sighed. "I do."

"Why?"

"Because…we're family."

He sucked in a harsh breath. "We're not. We never were."

I squeezed him hard. "Blood doesn't make family. Choice and connection make family. Family is forgiveness."

"Don't." He flinched in my embrace. "Don't forgive me."

I wriggled closer. "It's too late."

"I don't want it."

"Too bad."

"I don't deserve it."

"You don't. But it's done."

His heart drummed against me where I held him. We stood on the precipice of a strange kind of truce. I could taste it—taste his willingness to stop being a bastard—but that softness wasn't strong enough to win over the torment inside him.

"You're determined to destroy everything." His fist swooped into my hair, tugging my head back so his eyes pinned mine from above.

The dark damage in his depths undid me. I'd gone from wanting to keep my distance to wanting no distance at all.

"I guess I'll have to do something unforgivable. Perhaps then you'll see me for what I am." His lips crashed down on mine, bruising me, claiming me.

This kiss was different to the last.

This kiss ended all other kisses. It smited them, annihilated them, killed any memory of softness.

My back bowed in pain as he pressed me hard against the dining room table. His hand cupped the back of my nape, holding me in place as his mouth ravaged mine. His tongue dove deep, pushing mine out of the way and possessing me with angry strokes.

I trembled as his kiss turned as violent as his moods.

I tried to breathe, to kiss him back, to be a participant in this.

But he was too far gone.

Ripping me around, he pushed me to face the table. With a fierce command between my shoulder blades, he folded me in half.

I didn't fight.

If he thought he could take me against my consent, he was wrong. Sex with Gil would always be something I wanted. Sex with Gil gave me a power over him because he dropped barriers he couldn't control.

Spreading my legs before he could kick them apart, I deliberately arched my back and moaned. I told him in every explicit way that I was equal in this. He couldn't steal something that was already his.

His frustrated groan sent goosebumps along my flesh.

Thanks to my rebellious willingness, I prevented him from taking on anymore sin.

"Goddamn you, Olin Moss. Goddamn you for all of it."

I didn't speak as he hoisted my skirt up over my hips and yanked my underwear down.

The floor thudded beneath my feet as he slammed to his knees.

I bit my lip as his teeth tracked a path up my inner thigh, his mouth hot and wet against my skin. I cried out as his tongue found my centre, pushing inside me with no teasing or hesitation. He consumed me, and my legs buckled at the dark pleasure he granted.

His fingers latched around my thighs, keeping me pinned against the table as he sucked me from behind. Breath was no longer fundamental to my existence.

Only Gil was.

He was my air and lifeline. I'd never suffered such a blistering connection with anyone else. Never been so linked to another or so forgiving. Perhaps we were star-crossed—linked and bound by forces outside our control.

Fate.

I sank my teeth into the table as Gil inserted two fingers into me, all while sucking on my clit.

Holy mother of...

An orgasm that hadn't existed three seconds ago shot into being. The bliss spiralled around his finger as he thrust inside me and suckled.

A guttural grunt fell from him as he tongued me hard. His touch was too intense. Too treacherous. Gil had always had the ability to strip me bare and leave me with nothing.

"O..." Gil nuzzled between my legs, eating me, inhaling me, dominating me.

The air crackled and wept around us, full of regret and remorse.

Regret for what?
Remorse for who?

He drove such thoughts from my mind with another body-clenching lick. My heart pounded with lust. My blood sang and shot through my veins, laced with something scarier and much more profound than just desire.

I wanted to come. Desperately. But I was also terrified because I knew the moment my body plummeted, my heart would too.

And I can't survive it.

Almost as if Gil heard my plea, he soared from his knees. Looming behind me, the clink of his belt buckle and the hiss of his zipper were my only warnings as his hot, hard cock speared between my legs and straight into me.

He ducked to fill me deeper. His erection bruised me, hurt me, ploughing me from my feet and onto the table.

I was totally at his mercy.

My fingernails clawed at the wood, searching for grip as he pulled back and slammed into me again and again.

Gil was complex. He had secrets and tempers and love that didn't make sense, but beneath all that complexity was utter simplicity.

He needed me as much as I needed him.

He always had.

And that broke me into a million pieces because he'd torn us apart to survive without each other and look at what we'd become.

Rutting, fucking animals intent on destroying each other because we couldn't cope with the alternative.

The sweet happily-ever-after alternative.

His thrusts vibrated with violence. His brutal, unforgiving hands squeezed and spread my ass cheeks. And through it all, my core wettened and welcomed, letting him treat me as callously as he wanted.

Because *God* it felt good.

Unbelievably *good.*

"Gil…" The table squeaked and screeched as he pounded into me, driving me with each thrust toward the kitchen. The wood groaned as if the fixings would come apart and send me straight to the floor.

But Gil didn't stop.

And I didn't ask him to.

He fucked me.

His hard cock plunged again and again, and each time he

filled me, I arched up to encourage him to take more.

He grunted with pleasure and pain, matching the bruises he graced me with. His hands left my ass, clawing their way up my spine to rip at my blouse and tug it over my shoulder.

His hips pistoned harder while he feasted on my tattoo.

I didn't know what animal he looked at or why he studied something of innocence when debasing me in the worst possible way, but his voice tangled with emotion as he growled with each thrust.

"Otter."

Thrust.

"Ocelot."

Thrust.

"Orangutan, oregano, ostrich." *Thrust, thrust, thrust.*

"Owl."

I waited for more. I waited for Olive.

But his forehead crashed against my spine and he gathered me up, wedging me off the table until my hips lay on his arm. "I'm sorry. So fucking sorry."

His apology had no direction, and I had no time to guess which memory he wanted absolution for. His speed increased until we both cried and groaned together, growing wilder, fiercer, chasing the razor-sharp release just out of reach.

Fear swelled alongside my orgasm, making me sensitive in both body and soul. I was terrified of letting go. Petrified of how I'd feel afterward.

But I couldn't stop it.

Gil drove me to the pinnacle, and I tumbled over the edge.

Gasping, I rode the deep internal waves of rapture. Milking him, thanking him.

My slipperiness added another element to his need, and he took me as brutally as he could. His roar echoed in my ears as he followed me.

Curling over me, he smothered my back as he sank teeth deep into my tattoo. I moaned as he thrust again, filling me completely.

Hot, pulsing streams spurted inside me.

And when it was over, his tattered breathing turned into a breathless curse. "Fuck." He withdrew, backing away from me and buckling his jeans. His entire body shook as he raked both hands through his hair and looked at me with wild, green eyes.

I didn't speak as I slipped off the table and twisted to face him, shimmying my skirt down and pulling together the ends of my torn blouse. His cum trickled down my thigh, staining my pantyhose the longer we stood and stared.

It became unbearable.

The silence.

The stress of what'd happened.

He looked like he was about to jump out of my four-story window. Needing to touch him, to heal him, I tripped into his arms and sucked in a shivery breath as his arms threaded around me and squeezed.

A hug.

So simple and normal but it ripped out my heart better than any sex or orgasm.

Tears glossed my eyes as I pulled away and tried to catch his stare.

He didn't let me, turning away and wiping his mouth with a shaking hand.

Things were fragile now. Terribly delicate and the vulnerability between us didn't have a cure.

My stomach growled, snarling through the quietness.

Gil threw me a half-hearted smirk. "Hungry, O?"

I grinned, grateful for the embarrassing noise. "I haven't eaten properly in days." A plan rapidly unfolded in my head. A plan that could patch up the wounds left behind. "Let's get takeaway and eat here. Then…if you're so determined to babysit me, I can finish packing. I'll stay…for one night."

Ignoring my concession to sleep over, he frowned. "You want to eat…together?"

"Don't worry. It's not a date." I moved toward the fridge where takeout numbers and menus waited under ugly magnets. "Just a necessity of life."

He sighed, muttering something I didn't hear under his breath.

"Sorry?" I grabbed a Thai menu and found my cell phone. "What was that?"

He grimaced. "Nothing you need to hear." Heading toward the bathroom, he added, "We'll eat. But it's not a date."

As the bathroom door closed and my cell phone connected with the Thai restaurant, I whispered, "It's all a date, Gilbert Clark. Every word, every stare, every argument. It's all a dangerous game with no winners."

"Pardon me? You want what?" A Thai-accented voice

sounded in my ear.

I tore my eyes from where Gil had vanished. "Sorry. Can I order a lemon grass chicken and Pad Thai beef? It's date night."

Chapter Twenty-Six

Olin

-The Present-

"WHAT THE FUCK do you want from me? I've done everything you've asked. I have nothing left. Do you get that? Fucking *nothing*. You've bled me dry and—"

Sleep dissolved; the world grew solid. I sat up from my bed as Gil's shadow paced in the dark living room.

"Goddammit, it's too soon. I just—" Whoever he spoke to cut him off, making him growl under his breath. He paced faster. "No, fuck, I'm not saying I won't—"

He stormed to the window where city lights and moonlight painted him in silvery, buttery illumination. "You're not listening to me—"

He punched the windowsill. "Christ, don't. I'll—"

Whirling around, he looked at the ceiling as if he could find divine intervention and support. His nostrils flared, and his eyes were suspiciously wet. Finding no salvation on the ceiling, he hung his head and pinched the bridge of his nose. All fight siphoned out of him. He nodded dully. "Fine. Yes. I'll get the money."

My hands fisted around my covers.

Is that the guy who beats him up?

Gil sighed heavily. "Yeah. Give me a couple of days. Just don't..." He cut himself off before adding, "*Please*, don't."

The sound of Gil begging made me want to burst into tears.

He nodded again at something before terminating the call. His arm bunched behind his back as if to throw his cell phone against the wall. But he stopped himself. Dropping his hand, he placed his phone carefully into his pocket.

And then he turned to my bedroom and caught me sitting upright in bed.

"Ah, shit." He bit the words into pieces.

I didn't speak. What the hell was there to say? He'd been caught in a trap. I'd witnessed him being puppeteered by someone who controlled him with something. Something important with the way his skin had turned to ash and his eyes darkened with helplessness.

"How long have you been awake?" He moved tired and exhausted to lean against my doorframe. We'd ended up staying at my place after a dinner of shared Thai, some Netflix, and the agreement that the kidnapper might know where I lived but I was just as safe here with him on my couch as I was at his place in the same arrangement.

I'd deliberated offering him to sleep in my bed.

But I couldn't quite make myself as we'd said goodnight and I'd thrown him a spare blanket for the threadbare settee.

"How long, O?" He crossed his arms, his biceps bunching.

"Long enough."

He nodded dejectedly. "Great."

"What's the money for?"

He shook his head. "Don't ask questions I can't answer."

"What happens if you don't pay?"

His laughter etched with dismal damnation. "You don't want to know."

"I do. I *do* want to know."

"Yet you're not going to."

"Are you in danger?"

"*You're* in danger."

I waved a hand. "Forget about me. I've just stumbled into this. You've been dealing with this for a long time I'm guessing."

He flinched.

"How long, Gil? How long has the blackmail been going on for?"

His lips thinned as he crossed his arms tighter. "Doesn't matter."

"It does if it's running you into the ground."

He shrugged.

"Did you sell some of your furniture? To pay this arsehole?"

His eyes shot to sniper. "Again. You're trying to connect

dots that—"

"That fit together." I sat on my knees. "I'm not going to ask anything else. I'm just going to ask if I can help you. Again. Seeing as all my previous offers have been ignored."

"You know…" He kept a watchful stare on me. "Ever since Justin interrupted us and announced the news about a body painting murderer, I've waited for you to ask if I'm involved."

My heart literally skipped a beat. "Um…ar-are you?"

His forehead furrowed. "Aren't you even a little bit worried I might be?"

I looked at my duvet, plucking it with worried fingers. "I won't deny that the thought did cross my mind…for a second." I forced myself to glance up. "But…I *know* you. I know you're not capable—"

"How can you be so sure?" With the swiftness of something supernatural, he flew from my door to my bedside and cupped my cheeks. His eyes locked on mine for an eternity. He dropped his guards and let me swim through his sins.

I didn't understand any of them. I couldn't grasp what they were.

But there was no death inside him.

No psychotic tendencies or murderous urges.

Placing my hands on his, I smiled gently. "I'm sure."

"I can't decide if you're a saint or delusional."

I winced. "I think I'm a little bit of both."

Letting his hands drop, he paced away, raking fingers through his hair, unable to stay still. "I stand by what I said; I don't know how I ever deserved you in the past. I definitely don't deserve you now."

I let him stalk the shadows for a bit before whispering, "It's not about deserving, Gil. It's about family."

"Even family have their limits."

"Not us."

Silence fell for a moment.

I broke it, whispering, "I've asked you this before, but…do you need money?"

I'd offer the contents of my empty bank account if it would wipe away the horror from his eyes.

"Goddammit, O." Gil slowly turned to face me, his gaze tortured. "How do you do it? How do you forgive and forgive? How do you have such power over me to make me forget…even for a little while…the utter shit in my life?" He groaned. "I hate you for that, you know. Hate that being with you cures my continuous pain."

I trembled. "Why is that a bad thing?"

"Because I can't be cured. I could never fucking forgive myself if I—" He cut himself off, sucking in a breath. "I don't want your money. But I do need your help. Be my canvas. Tomorrow. I have a commission that came in. I'd refused it, but...I don't have a choice."

I ignored the wounds caused by his previous admission, shrugging sadly. "I would. Of course, I would. But I have work."

He stiffened, looking out the window with layers of grief. "I'll pay you triple what they are."

"You can't. You need the money for whatever this guy has over you."

"I won't let you work for free."

"I can't work for you at all. But I'll help you find—"

"Not enough time." Sitting on the side of my bed, he took my hand in his. He squeezed it until my bones scrunched together, and I winced. "I'm not a begging man, but when it comes to you, I seem to kneel often." He looked at my hands, stroking my knuckles with his thumb. "I have no dignity left. I have no honour or self-respect. I will do whatever it takes to pay my debts. I will hurt and steal to ensure every penny is paid. Do you hear what I'm saying?" His gaze flashed violent and honest. "I would sacrifice anything, anyone. I'm the lowest of the low." He slid off the mattress and onto his knees.

Before, he'd knelt between my legs to grant me angry pleasure. Now, he knelt at my side pleading for things I couldn't understand. Just like he'd knelt and begged me to lie to the police.

"Call in sick. One day. I'll paint fast. I'll do the commission and get the money, and you can go back to your cubicle."

I sniffed. "I'm not embarrassed of my cubicle, Gil. It's a steady paycheque. I'm grateful for it."

"And I'd be forever grateful if you help me earn a paycheque too."

I wanted to say no—not out of vindictiveness but out of loyalty to an employer who allowed me to keep my apartment and food on the table.

But...

Gil.

He looked at me like he used to at school when he'd hidden

a bruised rib or bleeding nose from class but trusted me to keep his wounds secret and heal them. He'd trusted me not to pity him. He'd trusted me to love him regardless of his actions and backstory.

My heart raced as I touched his cheek. "You're not the lowest of the low."

He chuckled, dark and empty. "You don't know what I've done."

"I know what you *are*." I bent to kiss him.

He accepted the sweet kiss with a flinch.

He didn't kiss me back.

"I'll help you, Gilbert Clark." I pulled away, his lips glistening in the shadows from mine. "One day. For tomorrow only, I'll be your canvas."

He nodded as if I'd just sentenced everyone he ever loved to death. Standing, he pulled out his phone and texted whoever he'd previously denied. Once he'd accepted the commission, he turned to me in the darkness. "There are many things between us, O. Things you'll never understand. But I need you to know…you're saving my life tonight. You've saved it before…recently with lying about the license plate, and previously when we were younger. Every injury you bandaged, every painkiller you administered, I knew I could never repay you." His voice roughened. "I can never give you what you've just given me. Thank you isn't enough, but I'll say it anyway."

His eyes captured mine, and he bowed low and eternally grateful. "Thank you. Thank you, Olin Moss…for being you."

Chapter Twenty-Seven

Gil

-The Past-

ANOTHER WEEK OF discomfort.

Another week of watching Ms Tallup pick on Olin in class: two detentions and a trip to the principal's office. Each reprimand I did my best not to leap from my desk and punch the bitch-teacher in the face.

Olin didn't have a clue why she was being targeted.

But I did.

I was the reason.

I knew it every time Ms Tallup glanced my way.

I knew it every time I felt her eyes on me in the cafeteria and school hall.

I knew it with utmost certainty when I hung back from class on Friday and prepared to fight for Olin's future.

Mine might be fucked but Olin's...I wouldn't let anything destroy it—let alone a teacher who wanted things she could never have.

"Gil." Olin snuggled into my side as our fellow students packed up their school bags. "My parents are away all weekend." Her voice lowered. "Stay. Sleep over."

My eyes shot wide, looking down at her. This wasn't the first time her parents had stayed away for days, but it was the first time she'd asked me to sleep there. To slip into her bed. To touch her in the dark. To strip her, kiss her, take her.

I squeezed my eyes against the images, cursing the sudden tightness in my jeans. Why did she have to choose today of all days to break me?

I had a plan.

A script to follow.

Outside of school, it was no secret things were burning between us. She wanted me as much as I wanted her. Her touches were different. Her stares more heated. We could barely be around each other without jumping when we touched and breathing hard for forbidden things.

Our bodies had been patient.

Our hearts had swapped and no longer belonged to us but to each other.

Sex was the natural evolution of our connection.

And I wanted it.

Wanted her.

So fucking much.

All I wanted to do was nuzzle her nose with mine and whisper yes.

Yes to taking her.

Yes to love.

Yes to making her mine.

But Ms Tallup watched my every move. Her eyes made me sick. Her concentration made me shake. And right now, her gaze sent poisoned arrows into my flesh.

I couldn't let Olin keep paying for my mistakes.

I had to guard her...forever.

Swallowing hard, I prepared myself to hurt the one person I adored more than anything, all in the name of protecting her. "I don't think that's a good idea, do you?"

Olin sighed with impatience, but she didn't click to my betrayal. Her tongue licked her bottom lip, not taking my snark for an answer. "We'll talk about it. But it's happening. You're sleeping over tonight, Gilbert Clark. I can't wait another day."

Ms Tallup couldn't hear us, but our protection of other students had gone, and her stare was ever more venomous. Pushing Olin away, I withdrew from her, doing my best to seem cold-hearted and annoyed. "Go home, Olin. We're done here."

Her eyes flared with hurt, studying me helplessly. "Wait...what...?"

"Go on. You know the way." I raised my voice to ensure a certain teacher heard. "Leave me alone." I crippled inside for being such a heartless liar.

I wanted to cuddle her close and whisper that it was all just an act. An act that I hoped Ms Tallup bought. An act that would buy her freedom from the wickedest teacher in this school. My voice glittered with ice as I bled deep inside. "We're through."

One of the girls who Olin hung out with before me slung her bag on and tugged Olin's hand. "Come on. He's being a jerk. I'll walk you home."

I forced myself not to shake with gratefulness with how loud she spoke. I'd pre-arranged this pantomime. I'd asked Olin's friend to call me names, put me down, slam and shame me.

All for an audience of one.

Olin's shock and heartbreak had to be real, but she did too good a job as her eyes watered and she looked at me as if I'd suffocated the love right out of her.

I crossed my arms and clenched my teeth, wrapping myself in as much frost as I could. "Go away, O."

"You don't mean this. Why are you doing this?" Tears spilled from Olin's hazel gaze.

"I do mean it. We're done."

"I don't understand. This can't be real. What are you—"

Olin's friend dragged her toward the exit. "Come on, O. He's such a prick. You can do so much better, you know. No one likes him, anyway. Such a *loser.*"

I flinched as Olin twisted to keep her eyes on mine, searching for some sign that this was a cruel joke.

Cruel, absolutely.

A joke, definitely not.

I would *never* hurt her this way if there was another alternative.

"Gil, please. *Talk* to me."

I hid my trembles as her friend jerked her into the corridor then slammed the classroom door.

I was the only one left.

The only student, anyway.

I pinched the bridge of my nose, doing my best to get my heart rate under control and not bolt after Olin with the biggest apology. My knees burned to slam to the ground and beg for her forgiveness.

And I would.

I would apologise all night at her place. I would gather her close and kiss her deep. I would release my fears and make love to the girl I adored with all my heart. And I would tell her the truth about why our teacher—who was in charge of grooming our future—was doing her best to destroy it.

The soft snick of a door locking ripped my eyes open and head up.

Ms Tallup stood with her back to the now-locked door, her eyes narrowed on me.

I braced myself, balling my hands and staring her down.

We didn't speak.

There weren't words that could be used. Somehow, humans had the ability to hold entire conversations, put forth arguments, plead for help, and understand they were trapped, all without making a sound.

Ms Tallup gave me a tight smile before pushing from the door and clipping in her heels to the supply closet at the back of the room. "Come along, Mr. Clark."

My thighs trembled to run in the opposite direction. To chase after Olin this very second and ease the pain I'd caused in her heart. Tonight was too far away. The tears she'd cry in the meantime. The agony she'd have to endure.

It *killed* me.

But...I'd bought this opportunity. I'd created this hell for a reason.

Balling my hands until nails sliced into my palms, I turned from the exit and followed Ms Tallup with stiff legs and unwilling steps to the storage area where class paraphernalia grew dusty on shallow shelves.

In there, no one would see us. No one would hear us.

I swallowed hard as I stepped into the dark room, and Ms Tallup grinned like a soul-sucking succubus we'd learned about in mythology. "I wondered when you'd break that silly girl's heart."

My teeth ground together.

The power dynamic between us did its best to keep me in my place as her underling. I was her student. My job was to be subservient, polite, and grateful.

But in this dark, dangerous place, I was her equal. I was her oppressor.

Inhaling sharp, my anger overflowed, gushing from my mouth with clipped vowels and harsh consonants. "Let's get one thing straight. I might be your student, but you aren't God. You don't get to play with our lives. You don't get to make us miserable." My hand came up, slicing through the air like a guillotine. My head came down, glowering at her under my brows. "If you *ever* mess with Olin's future again, I'll hurt you."

She didn't look ruffled by my outburst. Instead, she

chuckled condescendingly. "Quite a display for someone who supposedly just broke up with her."

Shit.

Shit.

I dropped my hand, deleting all sign of emotion from my voice. I embraced the freezing cold that'd helped me cope so many times in my life. "I'm bored of her. Bored of you. Bored of this school."

"Bored is a serious accusation to say to your teacher," she murmured with a hungry gleam. "Are you saying I'm not teaching you to the best of my ability?" She licked her lips, her gaze dancing down my body to my groin. "Because there are other subjects I can teach you. Lots and *lots* of subjects."

A full body heave tried to take control, but I shoved it back, breaking out in goosebumps. "Your current teaching is fine."

"But you just said you were bored." She moved toward me, hips swaying too much, lips glistening from her tongue. "Perhaps we can discuss extra lessons. Make sure you aren't held back for the third time."

Her threat was obvious.

Her hint was disgusting.

I backed up, knocking into a shelf holding markers and glue sticks. They tumbled to the floor, clattering loudly.

"Jumpy little thing," she whispered, placing her hand on my chest.

Sickness oozed from her touch. Horror layered my heart, making it beat thick and wrong.

Swiping at her hand, I sucked in a breath, looking into the empty classroom. No sounds of students in the corridor. No laughter of teachers leaving for the weekend.

We were alone.

Utterly, totally alone.

There'd been many times in my life when I'd been trapped. Trapped by fists. By walls. By rules. By blood. But this was the first time I'd been trapped by love.

Ms Tallup wanted me.

She wanted me enough to destroy Olin in the process.

If I was selfish, I would step aside and not get involved. I would keep Olin for myself, all while knowing it was because of me that her education and future suffered.

But when it came to the girl I loved, I couldn't stand by. I would commit murder for her. I would do whatever it took to protect her.

"You're thinking about her." Ms Tallup touched me again, her fingers tracing my chest.

Steeling myself against her touch, I looked down into her older face. She was the adult here, and I was the kid, yet my body dwarfed hers. My strength could kill her. My physical power so much more than her emotional one.

But Olin…fuck, she was my greatest weakness, and I didn't have a choice. I had to make Tallup believe. Had to make this god-awful child molester buy the story that I was just a guy fucking his way through the girls in his grade.

Girls who meant nothing.

Holding my head high, I hissed, "Like I said, I'm bored of Olin. I'm bored of all the girls in this fucking school. I'm focused on graduating, and that's all. If you've got a problem with me, take it out on me. No one else." I bowed until our noses almost touched. "Unless you're too afraid."

The threat dangled between us.

I didn't worry she'd expel me. I didn't fear she'd hold me back yet again.

I knew in the depths of my being, I was a challenge to her. A conquest she had to have. She wouldn't send me away because where was the fun in that?

For the longest second, she stared at me, assessing my truth and weighing all scenarios. Finally, she ran a hand over my pec and laughed softly. "You know…your first mistake was thinking I'd believe you didn't love her." She pinched my nipple, making me jump. "Your second mistake is thinking you can threaten me when I hold your life in my hands." Reaching up, she captured my stubble covered chin with her sharp fingers, holding me firm. "And your third mistake was stepping into this supply room with me." Her lips spread over sharp teeth.

I ripped my face from her hold and shoved her backward. "Get off me."

"Want to know why you just made the biggest mistake of your life, Gilbert Clark?"

I shuddered, unable to stop my fear showing. "Fuck off. Just leave Olin alone and I won't hurt you."

"*Hurt* me?" She cackled. "You can't hurt me."

My hands curled into fists. "I could hurt you right now."

"Physically, yes." She nodded sombrely all while her fingers went to her breasts and kneaded them through her thin baby blue blouse. "But then you'd be arrested. I'll say you've always been violent, and I fear for society's safety. You'll be lost in the system. A criminal with a record for the rest of his godforsaken life." She licked her lips as she pinched her own nipples, a flush warming her cheeks. "Does that sound like the career path you had planned?"

I couldn't speak as rage choked me.

She nodded as if this was a normal lesson. Her hands left her breasts, trailing to her hips. She stood with her strict educator pose and delivered the worst teaching of my life. "No one will ever believe that you didn't touch me, fuck me, do unwanted things to me. Want to know why?"

Again, my silence vibrated with hate.

She chuckled. "Because you're a nobody. You come from an alcoholic father who has whores in his house. You're beaten, so you have the motive to be violent. You live in a sex environment, so you're more likely to fuck around. And you've had no boundaries, so you're an understandable statistic when it comes to thievery, murder...rape." She shook her head sadly. "All because you don't know right from wrong."

I grunted, doing my best to untangle my voice from fury.

But she crept toward me, locking me against the shelving as she pressed her body flush to mine. Every inch of me was repulsed. I shut down. No hint of interest to the warm breasts wedged against me. No shiver at the invitation of blatant sex.

I wanted nothing to do with this.

Nothing.

"Get. The. Fuck. Off. Me." My voice wasn't human.

She smiled, pushing away all while her hand shot down my front and squeezed my flaccid cock.

I jerked, bile scalding my throat.

Before I could snatch her hand from my body, she fisted me hard, making me wince and eyes water. "How about we make a deal, Gilbert Clark?"

I choked as she squeezed again, sending confused shockwaves down my legs.

"Are you a virgin?"

Blinking, I did my best to focus on her and not the pain she delivered. My jaw worked as I growled. "Get your fucking hands *off* me."

"Not yet. Not until you answer a few questions." She twisted my cock, dipping down and grabbing my balls in the same hand.

"Holy—" I bent over, trying to shove her away, but it only added more agony as she pulled and didn't let go.

"Are you a virgin? Yes or no?" She pinched my balls vindictively. Fireballs of pain made my gut roil. Sweat broke out on my forehead.

"Yes or no." She squeezed again. "I can keep hurting you, or you can answer my question and I'll let you go."

Dark spots danced in my eyes as she drove her hand upward, squishing my balls, making me gasp with nausea. "Yes!" I gasped. "Fuck, yes. Okay."

"Yes, what?"

"Yes, I'm a virgin."

"So you didn't sleep with sweet little Olin?" Her lips sneered. "Not once?"

My head shook wildly, my hands grasping her wrist, desperate to free myself from the vise-like torture of her hold. "No. We…never. We're waiting—"

Her torment vanished.

She let me go.

"Good boy." Shaking out her hand, she smiled.

My cock and balls were mine again—on fire and throbbing, but mine. Cupping them, I shook back the light-headedness and fought the urge to drop to the floor.

Ms Tallup stepped back, giving me some breathing room while she rubbed one hand over the front of her skirt, right over her pussy. Her grey eyes blackened with lust. The entire storeroom fogged with it. Hurting me had turned her on.

I'm in deeper shit than I thought.

"Here's how your future is going to go, Gilbert Clark." She smiled, rocking her body into her hand as if chasing an orgasm just out of reach. Her lips twisted as she sucked in a gasp, forcing her arm to drop and stop touching herself. "You are never to speak to Olin again."

"What?" That hurt worse than any fist on my cock. "That's not possible—"

"It is if you want her to continue being one of my best students with a good enough recommendation to get into any university she chooses. I hear dancing is her dream…it would be such a shame to kill her wish."

I bit my lip, holding back a retort.

She continued, "Second, you are never to speak of this…to

anyone." Her eyes flashed as she pointed a finger in my face. "If you do, let me share how that conversation will go for you. You'll claim I molested you in the storeroom. You'll declare sexual abuse, and I'll be asked for my side of the story." Her head tilted. "Who do you think they'll believe? The teacher who's done charity work at the local reform house for the past six years, who's dedicated her life to the enrichment of her students, and who lives with her elderly mother? Or the angry, aggressive teen who sleeps with whores and is the offspring of an alcoholic pimp?"

The darkness of the storeroom swallowed me whole.

She was right.

In a war of words, she'd win.

No one would believe me. Not in a million years.

I hung my head, raking a shaky hand through my hair.

She tasted my defeat, laughing with cold-hearted joy. "There is a way out of this, you know."

I squeezed my eyes. I didn't want to look at her. I didn't want to hear anymore.

I already knew the way out. I'd known it for years—I'd just been too goddamn afraid to face it.

With breath trapped in my lungs, I forced myself to stand tall and grunt, "You want to fuck me."

She trembled on the spot. "Well, aren't you a naughty boy."

I glowered. "I didn't say *I* wanted to fuck you. I want to kill you. I'd rather have sex with a rabies-infected dog than get anywhere near you."

She licked her lips, her cheeks a deep red with need. "And that just makes this all the more delicious."

My nostrils flared. I looked at the empty classroom.

My virginity was Olin's. We hadn't discussed if she was a virgin or how we would plan our first time. All I knew was sex could be bought, stolen, and dirty, but sex with Olin promised to give me every freedom I sought.

Sex would give me her body, heart, and soul. She'd belong to me as surely as I belonged to her. It would bind us together. For fucking ever.

And now...I'd lost that.

That special hope of a better future had just been torn out of my reach and pissed all over by the one woman who was supposed to have my back.

Ms Tallup came closer, her perfume sickly and far too

sweet. "Meet me at the rear entrance of Motel Gardenia on Sunday at six p.m. I'll let you in so no one sees you. There, I'm going to take your virginity and make you a man." Her voice turned husky. "And you're going to fuck me until I say stop. You are mine to do with as I please. If I want you to fuck me all night, you will. If I want you on your knees begging, you will. You are not allowed to wear a condom—"

"*What?* No way am I—"

"Don't interrupt. I'm on birth control and clean. You're a sweet little virgin, and I want you bare. I want you to always remember the woman who stole your youth. I'll be your first. I'll always be a part of your life." She sighed as if her proposition was romantic and heartfelt and not the most diabolically disgusting thing I'd ever heard. "After a night together, you're free. I'll let you graduate if you stay true to your word never to speak to Olin or any other girl in this school again. Your cock is mine and will stay mine until you walk from these grounds. Just one night, little Gilbert. One night of fucking for a lifetime of freedom." She ran her fingertip along my bottom lip. "Not such a bad deal…is it?"

I fought the insane urge to bite her finger into pieces.

Ripping my face out of her reach, I snarled, "And how do I know you'll leave me alone? How do I know you won't go straight to the police after and—"

"Because I could go straight to the police right now." Her eyes glittered with madness. "If you don't turn up on Sunday night, I'll say you assaulted me. I'll say you held me down and forced me. That you're a minor with the aggressive nature of a murderer, and I escaped just in time. I'll make sure you never see the sun outside of a prison again. You're already screwed, Mr. Clark. I have all the ammunition I need to bury you, so you might as well accept my deal."

She laughed quietly. "After all, it's better to be with an older woman who knows how to please a man, rather than with a little girl who doesn't. You won't hate what I do to you." She blew me a kiss. "You'll love it. You'll be begging for another night."

"I will never beg for anything from you."

"You already did." She smirked. "You begged for Olin's future. And I'm giving it to you. If you give yourself to me."

I couldn't stay there anymore.

I couldn't listen to another twisted, poisoned word.

Lurching from the storeroom, Ms Tallup's voice chased me

as she purred, "Six p.m. on Sunday, Gilbert. Don't be late."

Chapter Twenty-Eight

Olin

-The Present-

I WAS BORROWING tomorrow's happiness.

I knew that.

I knew this wasn't real and wouldn't last.

I knew Gil would kick me from his life the moment he'd dealt with whatever issues he struggled with.

But it didn't change a thing.

Is it naïve to accept the upcoming abandonment? Is it even called abandonment when you know it's inevitable?

My thoughts rushed and raced as Gil drove us in his white hatchback that I suspected was a cheap alternative to another vehicle he might've sold to pay whatever debt he owed.

He didn't seem comfortable driving it. Then again, he didn't seem at ease with anything.

We didn't speak as we arrived outside a large department store in downtown Birmingham. I helped him carry boxes of paint, glitter, and rhinestones from the car. He carried the heavier stuff like air guns, gas bottles, and an entire wooden box of brushes and sponges.

Pedestrians watched us with mild curiosity. The city wasn't too busy thanks to most of the workers already ensconced in their places of business, toiling through a long day.

I squinted against the sun as Gil dumped his armful against the wall of the huge store. Motioning for me to do the same, he marched back to the car and pulled out a foldable trestle table along with a few other artwork requirements.

I waited until he'd set up the table and placed what he needed into logical positions before asking, "What exactly is the commission?" My eyes scanned the milling people, hoping I didn't recognise anyone from Status Enterprises. Calling in sick after only being employed a few days had chipped away at Shannon's supportive welcome. Her tone had turned cooler, and she'd asked for a doctor's certificate if my symptoms went on longer than forty-eight hours—company policy.

I'd screwed up.

I'd willingly put my income on the line to help Gil.

Am I stupid or sweet?

At this point, I was going to go with stupid.

"The department store." Gil cocked his chin at the hulking retail shop where we'd placed his gear.

"Kohls?" I peered at the name of the store. It was hard not to miss with its large lime letters glowing against the dark grey façade.

K.O.H.L.S.

Each giant letter shouted at would-be shoppers to enter and spend. I had no idea how Gil would incorporate them into a painting—they loomed huge from the pavement like ships sailing through concrete.

"Yeah." Gil continued doctoring his supplies. "They want an image they can use in their upcoming catalogues and billboards. Something recognisable to their brand but unique." He rolled his eyes. "I don't like commercial stuff. Never have. I'd much rather do natural."

"Natural?"

"You know...woodlands and beaches. A waterfall or two with humans all hidden with paint."

I stiffened. "So...you like doing camouflage pieces?"

He hooked up the air gun hose to the gas bottle. "Yes. I find natural shadows and textures much more satisfying than manmade."

Moving closer to him, so I didn't have to speak too loudly, I murmured, "The girls who were murdered...the ones painted and left to starve while the police couldn't see them.... Do you know who would—"

"Paint corpses?" Gil interrupted with an icy stare. "No, I can't say I hang out with such creatures."

"I'm just asking if you think whoever painted those girls is talented."

"Talented?" He laughed morbidly. "Talented at killing, you mean?"

"No, talented at shading and disguising."

His eyes narrowed with annoyance. "Sorry to disappoint you, Olin, but I didn't exactly inspect them up close and personal."

"True. Sorry." I pulled back. "Stupid question."

"Very stupid." Turning his attention back to his paints, his hands trembled a little as he worked out the colour palette and placed bottles of his chosen pigment in a row.

Did he shake from hunger? We hadn't had time for breakfast.

Did he shake from cold? The sun was out and warm.

Did he shake from nerves? Surely, he didn't get performance anxiety. Not with skills like his.

Touching his forearm gently, I studied him. "You okay?"

He froze, his gaze locking on my fingertips resting on his bare arm. His T-shirt choice today already held streaks and spots of paint from other work. His jeans were just as paint-decorated, and his boots would be welcome on a building site if it weren't for the orange and highlighter green mixing with dirt and grime.

Slowly, he moved away, dislodging my hold. "I'm fine." Pulling a familiar packet of skin-toned lingerie from his pocket, he artfully switched the conversation from him to me. "Are *you* okay?"

I swallowed nervously as he passed me the packeted G-string. "God, do I have to stand on a busy street at ten in the morning in just a flesh-coloured G?"

"Not just a G-string. I'll let you wear pasties today." His lips twitched a little. "Least your nipples won't be on display."

"Oh, gee. That's so generous of you."

"I thought so."

Pushing past me, he stalked to his car again and returned with a white robe. "Come on."

"Where are we going?"

"To get my canvas prepped."

I trailed behind him as we entered the large department store. Men's, women's, and children's merchandise were all on offer. Silver escalators led to more floors full of stuff. Toys, home-wares, and clothing. A treasure trove for the shopaholic, and a place I hadn't had much reason to enter in a while with no disposable income.

A pretty caramel and cream skirt caught my attention as Gil stormed down the centre aisle, guiding me toward the women's changing rooms.

"You seem to know your way around here."

His eyes trailed over the racks and shoppers. "I've been in a couple of times."

"You don't seem the kind to frequent retail stores."

"Yeah, well." He massaged the back of his neck, wincing as a kid sprinted past, screaming with joy as he headed toward the toy section. Reluctance layered his voice as if he didn't want to admit he'd had a love life before I'd inconveniently waltzed back into it. "Eh, I didn't come in here for me."

Ouch.

If that didn't cure me of my stupid insanity, nothing would.

My heart relocated into my throat as another question poised on my tongue.

Don't ask.

Do. Not. Ask.

"I, um, should probably have checked before this, but…eh, do you have a girlfriend, Gil?"

Every part of him locked into place. His face darkened; his eyes turned chilly. "Do you think I'd sleep with you if I did?" He leaned toward me. "I'm not a cheater, Olin."

I fought the urge to stumble back. "Okay, just thought I'd check." I waited for him to ask me the same question. Normally, that was how these things went. The desire to know if you're both free to pursue whatever magic brewed.

However, Gil already admitted he didn't want what was between us, and he most likely already knew how unlikely it would be for me to be romantically involved with another while he'd always owned my heart.

Justin danced on the edges of my thoughts.

Gil had watched me date him in high-school. He'd seen me overplay the act of happy, contented girlfriend all while my shattered heart remained in pieces. Back then, I'd hoped he'd confront me about it and demand for me to break up with Justin because I was always meant to be his.

But he never had.

He'd vanished instead.

And now, he'd insinuated at previous entanglements where he went shopping with lovers and spent time with them as a generous boyfriend, not this grumpy body painter who bruised me in the dark and couldn't stand me in the light.

Sighing, I brushed past him and continued into the changing rooms alone.

Reaching a stall, I slipped inside and closed the door in Gil's face.

He grunted something under his breath before tossing the robe over the top of the door. A packet of pasties flew to land by my feet. "Let me know if you need help with those."

I didn't reply.

Trying to push away the sudden ache in my chest, I stripped and ripped the skin-tone G from its packet before stepping into it. The mirror revealed my naked breasts and tiny scrap of lingerie between my legs.

It wasn't exactly sexy attire, but shadows of Gil's fingers still marked my hips and ass from last night's dining table action. My body didn't feel the same pain as my heart, and melted at the memories of being taken so roughly and thoroughly.

Jealousy burned like wildfire.

He'd been with others. Had he been that rough and thorough with them? Did he prefer them to me?

Stop it.

Stop torturing yourself.

Picking up the pasties from the floor, I opened the packet and prepared to stick something alien to my boobs. The double-sided tape wouldn't unpeel. The circle was too hard to handle. My fingers weren't dexterous enough to apply.

My patience was nil. Tiredness made me short-tempered, the strain of fighting with Gil pushed me to breaking point. He hadn't given me space to patch up my holes, which meant I was precariously close to snapping at the slightest thing.

I glowered at myself in the mirror.

It's not important who he's been with.

My heart did not believe that.

Knowing Gil had been shopping with other women was the most important, painful thing I could endure.

He might have slept with me.

He might say things that made my soul sing with second chances, but today, I was nothing. He didn't want to date me, love me, keep me.

I was just his employee.

I'm no one—

Gil's knuckles rapped the door. "You done? I've got to get

started."

"Give me a sec." My voice wobbled with tears and temper. He heard.

"Olin." The lock rattled as he tried to open the door. "Let me in."

"I'm fine."

"I said...let me in."

"No. I can do—"

"O, unlock the goddamn door." His angry tone slipped into sympathetic soothe. "Please...let me help."

I didn't want his compassion, but I couldn't stop whirling around and wrenching open the door. I stood with breasts out and body pebbled with goosebumps. A woman perusing the same skirts I'd eyed up gasped at my nakedness.

Gil shot her a glower before shoving me deeper into the changing room and joining me.

The door slamming behind him made guilt throb and wishes that things were different suffocate.

His eyes locked onto my breasts.

My nipples instantly hardened.

He groaned under his breath. "If I had time, I'd bend you over right here, right now."

"Your willpower not to touch me again is abysmal."

His lips twisted. "I know."

"Touching me is a mistake, remember?" I deliberately poked at my wounds.

"The biggest mistake." He nodded. "But it's also the only thing that's keeping me from giving up."

All thoughts of the commission and his past love life vanished under a wave of love and lust. I licked my lips, my breath turning papery. "You can use me to keep going...to keep fighting whatever it is you're battling."

His fingers latched around my throat, pushing me against the full-length mirror. "Stop being so goddamn good."

I shivered as my naked flesh met the cold surface.

"Fuck, O." His head dipped down; his eyes turned hazy. "I have no control around you."

I waited for a kiss.

A kiss that would probably end with him inside me and us banned from the shop for life. But as his lips grazed mine, he groaned and pulled away.

His struggle to ignore the blazing chemistry and desire

between us laced his voice, turning it rich and rough. "Give me the pasties." He held out his hand. The same hand that'd been on my body. His fingers twitched—the same fingers that had been *inside* my body.

I sucked in a needy breath as I dropped the hated pasties into his palm.

"After I've painted you, I'm going to peel these bastards off and fuck you."

I trembled. "How long will the painting take?"

He sighed heavily. "A while."

"And you've made me wet for what purpose?"

His eyes flashed. "You're wet?"

"I'm trapped in a tiny cupboard with you. You're talking about fucking me. You were seconds away from kissing me. What do you think?"

His voice lowered to a thick whisper. "I think I'm fucking hard for you and wish I could put us both out of our misery." Ripping off the double-sided tape from the pasty that I'd struggled to use, he crowded me against the mirror. "But…time is our enemy."

"As always."

His gaze dropped to my breasts. "At least your nipples are hard. Makes putting these things on a bit easier."

My lust instantly switched into resentment. "You have a lot of experience applying these?" My jealousy flared again, turning my voice sharp and sullen.

He studied me coldly. "A little."

"For your canvases?"

He nodded. "If you're not used to them, it's hard to apply with minimal wrinkling. I don't want my painting ruined, so I…offer to help."

"Did you enjoy touching them?" Prickly self-pity raced down my spine.

His temper billowed, etching his face. "You know, you've chosen a strange time to get possessive."

"It's a by-product of sleeping with one's boyfriend."

"*Ex.* Ex-boyfriend." His nostrils flared. "I'm not yours, O."

My stomach twisted painfully.

You don't have to remind me.

I know.

Believe me…I know.

I didn't speak. Tilting my chin, I stuck out my chest.

"You're running out of time. Let's get this over with."

His teeth ground together. For a second, it looked like he'd either attack me or make love to me. But then barriers shuttered his gaze, and he dropped his attention to my left breast.

I sucked in a gasp as his cool fingers pinched my nipple. His head bent, and he placed a dry kiss right on the tip before covering the highly sensitive, tingly sensation with the pasty.

I wasn't expecting sweetness mixed in with the sour.

My enviousness of other women swept back into blistering obsession. "I hate you right now. I hate that I'm tired and tetchy. I hate that I keep letting you confuse me when I should have the balls to tell you to either commit or leave me the hell alone. I hate—"

"*Finally.*" He sucked in a harsh breath, squeezing my breast painfully. "Finally, you're doing something sensible. Hate me. Fuck, out of anyone, you're the most entitled." His eyes glittered. "Hate me, Olin. Hate me...but don't leave me. Not yet."

My limbs turned to water as he pressed my nipple, smoothing out the pasty around my areola.

"It's you who'll leave," I murmured. "Just like before."

He flinched.

The mirror never warmed behind my inked back, reminding me that out of all his canvases, I wasn't the most ideal.

Unresolved anger made me mutter, "My scars and tattoos...will they be an issue with this commission?"

I didn't know why I brought up my flaws. Self-sabotage? A cry for help? A final attempt to push him away so I could be free?

He skimmed his nose down my throat. "They're a pain in the ass. But I can work with them."

Our conversation was all over the place, but I chased him regardless. "How? How will you work with them?"

"I'll keep that part of you facing away from the photo."

"You'll hide who I am?"

"My paint hides who you are." Guarded eyes met mine. "I know what that tattoo represents, Olin. I'm not stupid."

"I never said you were."

"Yeah, well." He sneered. "I get it."

"I don't think you get anything."

His eyes heated to green fire. "Really? You think I don't know that tattoo represents us. Our past. Our love—"

"Love that you walked away from."

He planted a palm on my sternum, keeping me locked against the mirror. "You can't do this."

"Can't do what? Protect myself from you? Speak the truth?"

"Yes...all of it."

"How about telling you how I feel? How about how pathetic I feel for still being in love with y—"

"Don't." His hand immediately fell away as if the feeling of my heart thrumming beneath his hold terrified him. "Stop it. You don't. I don't have the right to—"

"You know how much I lov—"

"*Quiet.*" He slapped his palm against my lips, hushing me. "I don't *want* to know."

The tiny changing room swirled with mistrust and intolerance, quickly slipping back into our safe place.

Sex.

Bodily connection rather than soul belonging.

And instead of suffering the painful knots in my heart, I threw myself into our chemistry. Chemistry that burned so hot it charred away our past and incinerated our pain.

This was what we had.

We had magic.

That part was undeniable.

And if it was all I would earn, then I intended on taking as much as I could.

Pulling away his hand, I said, "I want you, Gil."

His eyes snapped closed. "Stop. Fuck, please...don't make—"

"I'm wet and pissed off and seconds away from either kissing you or slapping you. You get to choose which."

"I choose work." With shaking hands, he fiddled with the second pasty, tearing off the double-sided tape. "Enough."

"Fine." Sticking my breasts almost in his face, I whispered, "Touch me. See what happens."

His entire body stiffened from my angry invitation.

I trembled for aggressive connection. I didn't care we were in a public place. I didn't care I wanted to hurt him as much as help him. I didn't really care about anything apart from deleting the jittery, slithering envy that still lived inside me.

His fingers skimmed my bare nipple, making it diamond hard. He placed the pasty over me with a thick grunt. "I don't know why I'm covering you up when you deserve to be naked."

My head fell back against the mirror as my belly clenched. I wanted to puddle to the floor by his feet. "Don't use them then. You said you don't like painting with them."

"I don't." His nose skimmed my collarbone, inhaling me as if he couldn't stop himself.

"Then why…"

"Because I don't want other men seeing you." His growl hit my cleavage with heavy gusts. His teeth nipped me before he swayed back. With hungry eyes, he pinched the pasty into place, squeezing me cruelly as if to punish me for his reaction.

For our fight.

For everything.

Instinct took over.

Retaliation was my downfall.

My hand shot forward.

I grabbed the throbbing length in his jeans.

He buckled against me, trapping me against the mirror. His hips rocked into my grip as his teeth caught the top of my ear and bit. Hard. "Jesus Christ."

My heart rate exploded, flying free from everything wrong between us.

My other hand fumbled for his belt, furious and fast, needing him with a ferocity that scratched skin from bone.

He bit me again, his teeth sharp before grabbing my chin and wrenching my head to the side.

His mouth crashed on mine, and our tongues immediately met in a war of touch and heat. I moaned as he thrust against me, pushing my hands away from his cock to wedge directly between my legs. The mirror stuck to my back as we rocked and fought, dry-thrusting, fake-fucking, trembling with intoxication and insanity.

I ruined the skin-coloured G-string. I'd never been wetter as he scooped me off my feet and drove his hips into mine with such brutality every bead of my spine cried out in pain.

My fingers dove into his hair, tugging the messy strands all while our lips sucked and kissed, our teeth clacked, our breaths caught.

Our desire turned us messy and manic—clawing body parts and thrusting want.

I needed him naked.

I needed him inside me.

Now.

We acted as if a war went on outside the door and this was

our last chance to be together. Our last chance to be honest—to let our bodies tell the truth while our words spread only lies.

"Fuck, O." He drove his hardness against my clit, sending fireworks up my belly.

Wriggling a little so I had space, I wedged my hand between us, doing my best to undo his zipper.

He kissed me harder, and blood mixed with our flavour. Feral hunger infected both of us as our lips smashed and tongues duelled. I could come just from his kiss.

I was empty.

Empty and angry and lost.

"I need you inside me." Frustration bubbled and lust made me growl. "Ignore the commissions. Screw the money. Take me home, Gil. Screw me instead. God, *please*—"

I expected him to attack me with rage and relief. To give into the delirious desire between us.

Instead, my voice acted like ice water.

He dropped me instantly.

His lips tore from mine.

His chest pumped as he sucked in oxygen and raked hands where my fingers had tangled his hair. "Meet me outside." Turning around, he manhandled the impressive erection in his jeans into a less obvious angle before unlocking the door.

I hugged myself as he stepped out. "Wha-what just happened?" Shivers caught me, partly from the air-conditioning and mostly from his snowy rejection.

"I need this commission." He refused to look at me, his jaw working hard. "I can't forget it. I'll *never* forget it. This commission. *All* the commissions are more important than anything." He whirled on me, fury replacing any sign of weakness. "Do you understand? They come before anything. They come before you and me and everybody. Do. You. Understand?"

"I understand." I backed away from his rage. "You need the money."

"I need it more than you know."

"Tell me, Gil. Tell me what happens if you don't pay—"

A guttural, god-awful grunt fell from his lips. "I'll pay. I'll *always* pay."

"Pay for what?"

His eyes snapped closed as if he couldn't tolerate the question. Anguish replaced any sign of lust from before, dragging him into dark, woeful places he couldn't escape.

Dragging a hand over his face, utter exhaustion and despair caught him all over again. "You're destroying everything. I shouldn't be doing this—I can't forget what's important. I can't let you—*fuck*!"

He punched the changing room wall. "I can't do this. You don't get to come first. No matter what you do to me, no matter what you mean to me, you do *not* get to come first. Not anymore."

"I-I'm not asking to come—"

"Just put on the goddamn robe, O. I've wasted enough time. I'll see you outside."

He left with a melancholy groan that once again shattered my heart.

Chapter Twenty-Nine

Olin

FOUR HOURS OF tense silence.

Four hours of wondering what the hell went wrong.

After he'd left me, I'd bent in half in the changing room and sucked in air. I'd begged my heart to stop jumping around like a fool and willed my body to stop crying for sex.

I had no idea what made Gil switch so completely.

I didn't know why I'd become so belligerent. To be honest, I didn't know myself anymore and I couldn't say I liked who I'd turned into.

I'd always been so careful of who I was and who I wanted to be. I never wanted to be the girl people pitied because of my accident. I definitely didn't want to be the girl who got trampled on time and time again and didn't have the backbone to stand up for herself.

If Gil was just an arrogant bastard, I would've walked away by now.

It was the fact that he *wasn't* an arrogant bastard that kept me imprisoned. I couldn't walk away because he was drowning and I was the rope keeping his head above water.

After gathering my pieces into the best order I could, I left the changing room with a white robe wrapped tight around me. I didn't speak when I found Gil outside with the manager of Kohls, going over the vision for his company.

The squat manager had already arranged tape to be strung around the company's logo and Gil's workstation to keep pedestrians away, along with four life-sized mannequins with bald heads, pert boobs, and willowy limbs.

Next to them, I felt dumpy and un-elegant.

While Gil and the manager arranged the mannequins to match the huge logo letters, I hugged my robe tighter and did my best not to catch the eyes of half-interested shoppers. Each plastic figure was guided into different postures. Some with their arms up, some with legs kicked. They stayed within the lines of the large letters, adding depth to the brand.

English sunshine kept shadows at bay, and Gil finally shook the hand of the manager and waved at me to come closer.

"Where do you want me?" I asked quietly.

"Sit for a while. I've got to paint the mannequins first."

I shrugged and went to rest in the car.

From my vantage point, I'd spent two hours watching Gil turn skin-toned plastic mannequins into multihued extensions of the Kohls logo. One for each letter with their arms angled to match and their stiff, perfect bodies blending effortlessly into the building.

When it came time for Gil to paint me, he positioned me on the O.

Of course.

Manhandling my arms and legs so I curved with the base of the letter of my first name, electric shocks sparked from his skin to mine. It seemed we'd forever be cursed to suffer such connection.

Our eyes avoided each other, both trapped in apologies.

Once Gil had me positioned, I stayed sandwiched between fake models, doing my best to be as elongated and as flawless as them.

"Why the mannequins?" I tensed as the first tickle of Gil's brush licked over my shoulder—the shoulder clear of scars and ink.

"Because I don't have enough real-life canvases."

"Oh." I squeezed my eyes shut as he traded his brush for his air gun, hissing paint and coldness over my flesh, quickly staining me lime, mint, and forest green, ensuring I vanished into the Kohls logo—a complete osmosis of design.

I opened my mouth to ask what exactly the brief had been, but Gil gave me an exhausted shake of his head. "Please don't talk. Don't move. Don't do anything until I'm done. I won't be able to work if you do."

I closed my mouth.

He nodded in thanks before forgetting I was alive and focusing on his craft.

I did my best to keep my twitches and gasps to a minimum as the air gun switched to a sponge and the sponge became a fine-tipped brush, adding depth and reality, mimicking the flaws of the logo and the scars of time.

A crowd steadily gathered, pointing at the already camouflaged mannequins and then at me as I slowly disappeared. Gil worked fast; his technique faultless as he layered me with paint. The sun changed angles, and he added deeper shadows. The breeze picked up, and he cupped his hand around his air gun nozzle to keep the spray correct.

I fell into the lull of his talent once again. Awed at how he shut out the world while he painted. There was no me or them or us. Just him and his creation.

But even in his creative zone, his face held mountains of snow-capped stress.

He wasn't happy.

He wasn't pleased or proud of his work.

Each time he ducked to paint around my throat or swallowed hard when he drew a brush under my breast, I wanted to kiss him. I wanted him to apologise as equally as I wanted to apologise. I needed to assure him that no matter what happened between us, I would *never* ask him to put me above his work.

For two long hours, he wouldn't let me catch his stare, keeping his concentration on the area of my body he was painting. When his brush trailed between my breasts and over my pasty-covered nipple, the sensation wasn't nearly as erotic as being bare.

My back ached from twisting. My arms went dead from being above my head. And my legs trembled from staying in position.

Gil worked fast but not fast enough, and by the time the last detail reached my toes and the crowd clapped with how well I'd morphed into the branding of the department store, I was ready for food, space, and a shower.

Before the paint was dry, Gil turned his attention to the other part of his brief. Halfway through his painting, the manager had arrived with a box of merchandise and requested Gil find homes in his design to show the range of what they stocked.

Now, Gil selected an ebony scarf that he draped over my

fingertips, a glossy blue handbag that he placed by the feet of the K mannequin, a toy train on the upturned palm of the H figurine, a silver toaster balanced on the upturned foot of the S model, and a golf club speared through the hands of the L dummy.

All of us held something, but Gil didn't use a fraction of the stuff provided, preferring to keep the simplicity of four fake and one alive female illusion hidden in the letters as his masterpiece.

The scowl on his face and temper in his shoulders yelled he hated everything about this commission.

To be honest, I didn't like it either.

It felt contrived and commercial. Lacking in originality and imagination.

My stomach growled as Gil stood and rubbed his chin with green-speckled hands. His lips twitched, reminded of my appetite last night. "I'll feed you soon."

The gentleness in his voice was polar opposite to the frost that had been there before.

The stiffness and suffering that had grown while he'd painted me dissolved in an instant. "I'm so sorry, Gil."

He flinched. "No apology needed." Gathering up his brushes, he added, "I'm the one who's sorry. I'm not…I'm not usually so quick tempered. I didn't mean to get so cross." He smiled sadly while he touched up an area of shading on my cheek. His lips were so close to mine all while his face tightened in concentration.

Our eyes locked.

Our hearts pounded.

He stepped back with a sigh.

Throwing the used brush into his supply container, he murmured, "You just found me at the wrong time, that's all."

With that cryptic comment, he hoisted the box beneath his arm and turned to place it on the trestle table.

My eyes followed him, widening in fear at the two police officers who appeared as if from thin air.

"Are you Gilbert Clark?" one with salt and pepper hair asked.

Gil tensed, flinching at the police badge shoved in his face. "Depends who's asking."

"I'm Officer Hoyt, and this is Officer Marlow."

Marlow nodded brusquely with shiny brown hair. "Hello."

Gil didn't return the greeting. His muscles tensed as if ready to pummel them both into the concrete.

Officer Hoyt placed his badge back into his blazer pocket. "We would like to have a word with you."

Gil threw me a look over his shoulder. He tried to make it seem exasperated and impatient, but I'd spent too much time with him. I'd learned how to read him again. I saw the truth.

In his gaze was pure terror and the undeniable desire to run.

I gave him a brave smile, very aware I couldn't move. I wanted to tell him not to be afraid.

I'm sure it's just routine.

He nodded slightly as if he'd heard my silent encouragement. Shifting the box to his other arm, he muttered to me, "Don't move. I still need to take pictures."

His lips thinned as he marched toward his car.

Terrible foreboding filled me.

Why did the police want to talk to him? As a consultant or because they had evidence—

They can't have evidence because Gil didn't do anything.

My heart fluttered as the police hunted Gil's every step.

All I wanted to do was chase them to the curb and fight for his innocence.

Because he *was* innocent.

He's not a killer.

Sweat prickled beneath my painted skin.

I'd been afraid. Afraid of falling for him. Afraid of being hurt. Afraid of what might happen. Now I was afraid they would take him and I'd never see him again.

The cops waited as Gil opened the back door and placed the box inside. "We'd like to ask you a few questions, Mr. Clark."

"What about?" Gil's voice lost any sign of emotion. Cold and as clinical as ever. His form of armour against those he didn't trust.

"Your paints match the paints used on the victims recently found."

What?

Gil stayed unruffled. "That's entirely possible. Not many stores stock paint safe enough for long exposure to the skin. There isn't a large market to choose from. Even online choices are minimal."

"That might be. But with you being a body painter and the murders heavily based on such a hobby, not to mention being committed within our city, we want you to come to the station for questioning."

The other cop added, "Protocol, you see. Won't take long."

"If it's merely protocol, ask me here. I have work to do." Gil's temper sliced through his coldness.

"We have an audience," Officer Hoyt muttered. "Best to discuss such things in private, don't you think?"

God, I wished I wasn't stuck against this stupid letter.

I was seconds away from breaking posture and running to Gil's side.

But Gil seemed to sense my rapidly fraying self-control as he raised his voice. "Don't you dare move, Olin. I'm grabbing my camera."

"Mr. Clark. We've asked you to come—"

"I've just spent four hours of my life painting this commission. I'm not walking away before taking photos that pay my bills." A murmur from the crowd rose as Gil shoved past the cops and opened the boot. Reaching in, he pulled out his expensive camera.

The police followed him again but stayed quiet.

I had no choice but to stay locked in a colourful prison while Gil defied law enforcement and fiddled with the functions on his tools.

With an arrogant look, he stormed away from the police and angled the lens at me. He started snapping. One after another from where he stood, then more from across the street, then more to the sides, up close, front on, and every other angle applicable.

All I had to do was hold the pose that was crippling after so long.

I supposed he'd Photoshop out the crowd and other noise. He'd somehow make it seem as if I'd magically become one with the store logo—floating in the letters, defying all laws of gravity.

With every camera click, the police stalked him. Their patience slowly waning the longer he postponed their chat. He'd probably taken over a hundred pictures, and to them, it most likely seemed as if he delayed their conversation deliberately.

To me, I knew Gil would take a copious number of photos so he would have more than enough to turn in a great commission. He took no chances that the purchaser wouldn't be happy and refuse to pay—especially on a job he hadn't enjoyed doing.

Finally, one of the officers put their hand on his camera and forced him to lower it. I couldn't hear what they said, but I didn't need to.

The cop pointed at the official vehicle parked across the street. Hand gestures said they wanted him to go with them.

That they were done waiting.

Gil nodded sharply and turned off his camera. Walking with them, his steps were short and unwilling.

But he went.

He went because he had no choice.

With his hand on the roof of the cop car, he turned to look at me.

No.

Don't go.

I no longer wanted him to cooperate. What if they pinned it all on him? What if he didn't come back?

What if he's the most talented liar in history and he did *do it?*

What happens if I'm in love with a killer and stupid enough not to see?

With a groan, I forced atrophied muscles to move and stumbled from the illusion that I was one with the logo. "Gil, don't—"

He curled a hand around his mouth to amplify his voice. "Pack up my stuff. Do you have your license?"

I nodded, wanting to hug myself.

"Good. Drive back to the studio with my gear. The key to the warehouse is in the car." His eyes remained unreadable, shoving me deeper into the cold. "I'll see you later."

The crowd murmured loudly. Rumours and questions. Side looks and suspicious glances.

I knew what they were thinking.

Was Gil the body painting murderer?

Was that why the police were taking him?

Arresting him?

I didn't have time to reply before an officer opened the car door, motioned for him to slip inside, then slammed it closed.

Gil didn't look back as they drove him away.

Chapter Thirty

Olin

-The Present-

SOMEONE HAS BEEN in my apartment.
I froze, my key in hand, a foot across the threshold.
I didn't know how I knew, but I *knew*.
Something was off. Something wasn't right. Yet…nothing was missing.

Inching forward, I breathed shallowly as if monsters might hear and attack from behind cheap furniture. The kitchen still held the takeout containers from when Gil stayed over. The couch still decorated with his tossed-aside blanket. The dining room table still askew from our ruthless sex.

If someone had been here, surely something would've been moved?

I'm making stuff up.

No one had been here while Gil painted me on the street. No one had entered my privacy and sneaked around uninvited.

Only…

My eyes fell on a small ballerina figurine that was one of the few gifts my parents had ever given me. When they'd finally understood how serious I was about dance, they'd paid for my lessons but not bothered to take me.

I hadn't cared.

I would've hitchhiked across town to dance, and the fact that they'd recognised that? It meant so much to me. And for them to give me a ballerina? Well, it was my most treasured belonging from them.

It normally sat beneath my TV by the remote.

Now, it stood in a perfect pirouette on my windowsill.

I froze.

Goosebumps shot down my arms.

Had Gil moved it?

Had I forgotten I did?

What the hell is going—

"Miss Moss. Is that you?" A strict voice wrenched the breath from my lungs and sent me whirling to face the door. A fist landed over my thudding heart as I tried to make sense of what I saw.

Two uniformed police stood framed in the open entrance.

Police I'd seen at Gil's warehouse when I'd called and reported the guy with his kidnapping van.

"Wh-what are you doing here?" I asked, cursing how wavy my voice was.

The woman cop stepped into my apartment. I silently swore for leaving the door open. Her gaze skimmed over my still very green and camouflaged skin, mostly hidden beneath the thick, white robe. I'd obeyed Gil's wishes and packed up his gear. I'd stored it in his car, told the Kohls manager Gil would be in touch with the photos and invoice, and climbed into his hatchback still fully painted.

I'd intended to drive to Gil's place like he'd asked. I intended to shower, dress, and head downtown to where Gil had been taken.

But I'd never packed an overnight bag and left my previous outfit in the changing room. If I'd headed to Gil's place, I would've ended up without clothes once I'd washed off his latest creation.

I'd only meant to pop home for five minutes.

I hadn't expected to find the aura of evil still lurking in my safe zone. And I definitely hadn't been prepared to find yet more police on my doorstep after watching Gil being carted away only an hour before.

It's a busy day for them.

Appearing unannounced and ruining both our lives.

"We wanted to follow up with you about your report on the man who tried to kidnap you."

"Oh." I forced myself not to look at the clock with impatience. "Okay. What can I help you with?"

"The license plate number you gave us is incorrect." The

woman narrowed her eyes.

"Oh, I'm sorry. I must've remembered it wrong."

"And you're sure it was a white van with blue stripes?" The male officer came forward, encroaching on my space. "Because nothing checks out. No other reports. No suspicious sightings. It wasn't another colour, and you remembered that wrong, too?"

Standing taller, I did my best to seem unfrazzled. My lack of lying ability almost crippled me. If I didn't get them away soon, I'd slip. I'd stumble on a lie, and Gil would be sentenced to life because of something idiotic I said.

"No, I remember the van. But you're right. I'm obviously not reliable in my recollections." I crossed my arms. "Besides, you ought to know better than me. That's your job, after all."

The cops threw each other a glance.

The female officer sighed at my unhelpfulness. "Regardless, we believe the man who tried to abduct you might be involved with the recent murders." She eyed up my body paint again. "They were painted...like you. We were hoping your memory might be better refreshed today. Give us new information that could aid us."

"Better refreshed?"

"No audience, as it were." Her gaze gleamed with an obvious hint. "Free to say what you want."

"You think I kept things to myself because I was with Gilbert last time?"

"Speaking of Mr. Clark. Where is your boss?" the guy jumped in.

I narrowed my eyes, answering his question and ignoring the rest. "At Status Enterprises. Behind a desk."

"Your other boss." His voice tightened with frustration. "Gilbert Clark."

What was the right answer here? Tell them I didn't know or that he'd been shoved into a police car? Then again, I couldn't exactly say I hadn't seen him, seeing as I wore his brushstrokes. "We just finished a commission for Kohls department store. He was invited to help the police about the body paint used on the murdered girls."

There, that sounded good and not guilty at all.

"Do you believe he could be involved?" The woman walked around me, her eyes never still as she took in my messy apartment.

"No."

"How can you be so sure?" She circled me again, her buttons flashing on her uniform. "He's a body painter—same as the murderer. He has no alibi for the days the girls went missing."

I scowled. "How do you know he has no alibi?"

"We can't disclose that information, miss," the male cop muttered. "What we are interested in is your opinion. Can you shed any light on Mr. Clark's recent whereabouts? Did he go missing for a time? Do anything out of the ordinary?"

My throat closed up.

He went missing.

He came back filthy, bloody, and speckled in paint.

He drank himself into a stupor for something he did.

My kneecaps danced with nerves as I stared him right in the eyes. "He's my boss. What he does with his free time is none of my concern."

The female cop smirked. "You entertain much, Olin?" She pointed at the two forks in the sink and the two glasses on the coffee table.

"None of your business."

She smiled and didn't reply.

I'd just walked into her trap, and I didn't fully understand how.

"If that's all…I really need to shower and—"

"How well do you know Gilbert Clark?" the female interrupted rudely.

I mulled over my answer. What would be better? Admit I was in love with him or lie and say our relationship was strictly professional.

My heart picked up its pace, drowning in fibs.

"Well?" She placed her hands on her hips. Somehow, I knew she waited to catch me in a lie. They'd found out where I lived without me telling them my address. They had records and ways of finding out stuff. That was their job—to uncover the truth.

Letting my arms drop, I allowed honesty to answer for me. "Gil and I go back to high-school—like I told you last time. We dated when we were younger." Even I heard the historical pain in my voice as I added, "We broke up and went our separate ways. I found him again purely by chance, thanks to a job advertisement." I held up my arm, revealing the green exoticness of my flesh. "A job to be a living canvas."

"Interesting." She nodded, her eyes gleaming. "And you can work together amicably after a teenage breakup?"

"It's in the past. It means nothing."

"How would you describe Gilbert Clark at school?" The man opened his notepad, a pen hovering over the pages. "Quiet? Hard-working? What was his family life like?"

Anger rose, followed swiftly by the undeniable need to protect Gil.

His family life would always work against him. Always make people judge—make them believe he was capable of atrocities because that was what he was born into.

"I think you should figure that out for yourself." I nudged my chin at the door. "Now, if you don't mind. I really must—"

"People change, Miss Moss." The woman once again cut me off. "What you think you know about your high-school fling might be hiding the truth staring right in your face."

I grimaced. "What exactly are you implying?"

"I'm not implying anything. I'm just saying be careful." For once, her eyes softened with kindness rather than condemning me with accusation. "Monsters walk amongst us. They wear the same skin. They just hide who they are. Almost like the paint that's hiding you."

She paused as if her speech was all I needed to confess everything.

I sniffed and waited out the silence.

"Okay, then." The two officers moved toward the exit.

The male nodded and stepped into the hallway while the female paused and passed me her card again. "If you happen to recall the correct license plate or want to change your statement, call me."

I took her card and shoved it deep into my robe's pocket. "Thanks."

"You're welcome." With a smile I couldn't decipher, she added, "I wouldn't trust him, Miss Moss. A man who earns money by turning others into a chameleon might also be a chameleon himself. Three girls have lost their lives. Don't lose yours, too."

Chapter Thirty-One

Gil

-The Past-

I'D BEEN LIVING in hell.

The past two days had torn out my heart and made me beg for a solution.

The breakup at school was meant to be fake, but somehow, it had become entirely too real. I needed to take it back. To explain. But the more time that passed, the more horrendously true it became.

"You're never to speak to Olin again."

Ms Tallup's threat repeated incessantly in my brain.

That ultimatum was harder to swallow than knowing what she wanted from me. It made my stomach churn with corrosive acid; nervous anxiety wrapped a noose around my throat.

I *had* to talk to Olin.

I had to see her, touch her, love her.

If I couldn't have Olin…shit, life wasn't worth the pain it cost to live.

Despite Tallup's threat, I'd stumbled over to Olin's the moment I'd left school on Friday. I'd stood on her stoop with tears in my eyes and a broken fucking heart in my hands, trying to get up the guts to ring her doorbell and apologise.

To tell her everything.

To beg her to help me.

But she wasn't home.

For the first time in a very time, I was alone and unwanted.

Not entirely true.

I was wanted.

Just by the devil in female clothing.

I'd lingered outside Olin's place until hunger drove me away. I didn't know who she'd turned to thanks to my betrayal, but I only hoped she was warm and safe.

Just knowing her future hung in the balance because of me and my actions forced my feet to carry me back to the hovel I was born in and tumble into a dirty bed.

That night, my dad beat me brutally—thanks to one of his bourbon-induced rages, and I spent Saturday nursing my wounds. Olin was once again somewhere else when I stumbled to her house in pain.

By Sunday, the bars of my prison had tightened so much, I couldn't see any alternative.

I needed to talk to Olin desperately.

I couldn't bear the thought of never sharing a conversation or having her hand touch mine again. I'd always kept my emotions locked away—better to seem heartless than weak—but where Olin was concerned, I was pathetic.

I fought the urge to tear apart the neighbourhood looking for her.

I waited until dusk, sitting on her street like a homeless stray.

I watched the sun creep apologetically over the horizon, leaving me to a fate worse than any death combined.

Olin was avoiding me.

I couldn't blame her.

She hated everything about me, and I was the only one to blame.

But...it was Sunday.

And Ms Tallup had backed me into an unwinnable corner.

No matter what I did...I was fucked.

Literally.

I could leave school, but that would mean leaving Olin. I could tell the headmaster, but that would mean risking who would be believed. I could tell Olin everything and run away with her, but that would mean her parents—no matter how absentee—would track us down and throw me in jail for kidnapping.

No matter what option I chose, there was always only one conclusion.

Me in prison.

Because of my teacher's word against mine and the god-awful accusation of assault.

Assault?

She was the one assaulting *me*.

And I couldn't tell anyone because who the hell would believe me?

Guys weren't forcibly taken advantage of.

It was physically so much harder. But I'd felt violated in that storeroom. I'd felt hunted all weekend. And now, as I left Olin's street and travelled stiffly toward the back entrance of Motel Gardenia, I felt denied of any and all my choices.

Ms Tallup was waiting for me, holding open the fire escape door and ushering me in the second I was in grabbing distance.

We didn't speak as she clutched my wrist like a runaway schoolboy and dragged me up a level and down a long corridor. Slipping a keycard through a lock on a door, she tugged me inside and slammed it closed.

I exhaled hard as she slid the chain across and drew the curtains closed with a snap. The room already showed signs of use with an overnight bag on the small desk, a grey jacket thrown over the chair, and wrinkled white bed linen as if she'd lain there, picturing what she'd do to me.

The room was gloomy, even with three lights around the space. The carpet was brown, the furniture brown. It reeked of bad decisions and hard situations.

Ms Tallup ran a finger along my back as she bypassed me. She laughed as I leapt out of her way.

"Always so jumpy." She headed to her bag, rummaging inside. Pulling out handcuffs, ropes, a bottle of lube, and a gag, she turned to me with a grin. "I'm proud of you, Mr. Clark. You came. You chose the right option. And, because of that, I'm assuming you will continue to choose wisely." Waggling the bondage toys, she added, "These are if you don't behave. I will have no qualms using them. In fact, it would turn me on to tie you down so perhaps we might play with these, after all."

I cleared my throat as panic raced through my blood. "I'll behave." There was no way I wanted to be restrained. Already the desire to run almost overshadowed my need to protect Olin.

I was willing to run to the police and tell them what happened. I'd risk being charged with assault if it meant I never had to sleep with this psychopath.

But if I was in jail, how the hell would I ever love Olin?

How could our future come true? How could she stay mine when I wasn't there to care and cherish her?

She'll become someone else's.

My heart cracked, blood pouring from torn vessels.

Ms Tallup threw the bottle of lube at me. "I brought that, just in case. But honestly, I'm so wet, we won't need it. Unless we decide to put something in you. Ever experimented with that area of your body, Gilbert?" She cackled. "It could be fun."

I almost vomited on the carpet.

I threw the lube into the shadows of the room.

How the hell did she think I could do this? I couldn't have sex with her because I was as soft as overcooked spaghetti. She repulsed me. No way would I get hard for her.

I lifted my head, slightly braver. Perhaps this wouldn't happen. Maybe I could survive the attempt and then accept the ridicule of being a cockless teen who couldn't get it up.

With a flick of her mousy brown hair, she headed toward the mini bar. With her back to me, she poured two shots of amber liquor, then carried both toward me. "Here."

"No." I shook my head. "I don't drink."

I had a perfect role model in my father of *why* you should never drink.

I couldn't stand the smell because it permeated the entire house I lived in. I couldn't stomach the effects because it made me bleed on a regular basis.

"You don't have sex either, but you're about to." She shoved the shot glass into my hand. "Drink it."

My eyes narrowed as she clinked my glass with hers. "Here's to a night of debauchery. You do know that word, don't you? Don't worry. If you don't, you'll be fully educated by the end of my lesson." She winked and threw the alcohol down her throat.

My fingers squeezed the glass, wishing it would break so the liquid would splash onto the carpet. She stole the untouched shot from me, marched me backward to the bed with a hand on my chest, and pushed me when the back of my knees hit the mattress.

I sat down heavily, heart pounding, pulse throbbing as she walked into me, spreading my thighs and tipping my head up. "I said...drink."

I didn't have a choice as she tugged my chin and poured the liquor past my lips.

The burn disgusted me, and I grimaced, swallowing the

obnoxious alcohol.

"Good boy." She patted my cheek, then ducked to kiss me.

I jerked away, but she threw the shot glass to the floor, grabbed two handfuls of my hair, and held me captive while she planted a wet kiss on my mouth.

Everything inside me froze.

Her tongue shot past my lips, bringing another fresh hell of rum and misery.

I choked, shoving her backward and shooting off the bed.

She merely laughed, wiping her mouth with heat in her eyes. "My own little virgin to teach. Do you know how long I've thought about this? Standing in front of that class, reciting English and Math all while I watched you scribbling notes to a test, imagining you deep inside me."

I shivered from ice and revulsion. "You're sick."

"And you're going to be so much fun." Holding my gaze, she unbuttoned her white shirt, making quick work of the buttons.

I dropped my eyes as she yanked off the material and stood in her lacy white bra.

"Don't look away. Watch."

Her command ordered my eyes up, and I gritted my teeth as she shimmied out of her skirt, undid her bra, and slipped her knickers off until she was bare before me.

No hair on any part of her.

Shaved and smooth.

I didn't like it. I didn't like the falseness. The fake innocence of such a thing.

Nausea was a real problem as I struggled not to be ill.

She moved toward me.

I couldn't control my body's reaction.

I stumbled backward, tripping in my haste. She chased me. I found my footing and crashed against the wall. Just as she'd trapped me in the storeroom, she trapped me in the motel room. Her hands scorched my skin as she tugged at my black T-shirt hem. "Off, please."

Her politeness teased that perhaps someone sane lurked beneath her sexual deviancy. If I could appeal to that side of her—

"Please. Let me leave. We can forget this happened and—"

"T-shirt. Off. *Now.*" Her eyes narrowed. "I won't ask again."

Olin.

I was doing this for her.

Don't think about her.

The thought of her in this place.

God.

If she knew what I was doing?

Fuck.

My eyes squeezed tight as my teacher tore my T-shirt off and undid my belt. I didn't open my eyes as she unbuckled me, unzipped my jeans, and dragged both my underwear and pants to the floor.

I groaned in torture as she ducked before me, untying my boots and easing them off my feet before pulling my trousers off.

Her hot breath skated over my flaccid cock.

I flinched as her hand cupped me, pinching the tip and tutting under her breath. "Well, this is a disappointment."

My eyes squeezed tighter as she inserted me into her mouth. I jolted against the wall, pushing her head away. "Stop."

She merely swatted at my touch and hissed around my cock. "Cooperate, or I'll tie up those pretty wrists and play with you anyway I see fit, okay?"

My hands slowly dropped to my sides.

If it was possible, my cock shrunk inside me, cowering from her mouth.

I tensed for a strike, a slap—for some sort of abusive punishment.

Instead, she stood, laughed a little, and returned to her bag.

Sucking in lungfuls of air, my mind turned dizzy with adrenaline as she lifted two things from the depths.

The first item punched a hole in my chest: a class picture of Olin with her hair neat in a ponytail, her smile conservative, her eyes bright and intelligent.

The second dug my own grave: a box of blue tablets that ensured tonight wouldn't just break me but would shatter apart any future I hoped to give the girl I loved.

Viagra.

Ms Tallup beamed in her nakedness as I groaned and dropped my head into my hands.

"That's right. I hid one in the rum that you so sweetly drank for me. In less than an hour, you'll be as hard as stone and desperate for relief." She tossed the box back into her bag but put the photo of Olin on the side table. "Might as well place your little girlfriend here, so she doesn't miss the show."

The innocent eyes of the girl I loved mocked me while I stood naked in a motel room about to do something unforgivable.

I couldn't look at her.

Keeping my eyes on the floor, I moved to the bed and collapsed on it.

All my fight dissolved. My anger exhausted me. My refusal to accept this stole all my energy.

Slinging an arm over my eyes, I slammed onto my back, not caring I was stark naked. Not caring my goddamn teacher feasted her eyes on me.

All I cared about was getting this over with so I could go home and forget it ever happened.

Now I knew how my father's whores felt like.

Something worthless—their only purpose to be hired, abused, then tossed aside with no thought to the emotional aftermath.

For a while, the room was silent and still. Ms Tallup kept her distance.

Time carried us forward, condemning me with every ticktock.

At one point, she visited the bathroom. Another, the minibar opened and closed again. Minutes passed, heartbeats pounded, and slowly but surely, my body was no longer my own.

Blood gathered outside of my control. Heat and hardness slowly building.

I kept my eyes closed and teeth clenched as the bed shifted and Ms Tallup lay beside me. "Let's help that Viagra along, shall we?"

I flinched and sucked in a breath as her lips once again surrounded my cock.

I didn't push her away. I just locked down my heart and endured purgatory.

My world stayed dark as I kept my eyes shut. Repulsion licked through me. Her tongue was vile. Her touch repugnant. At no point did my thoughts betray me. I found no pleasure in her loathsome touch.

But thanks to the magic of chemicals, what I felt inside no longer matched the outside. My cock swiftly swelled in her mouth. My balls gathered tight. My belly knotted.

My arm stayed tight over my face as every muscle bunched.

Repellent desire crept through my blood, tangling with the righteous nausea.

For long, torturous minutes, she sucked me.

And I let her.

For eternal, horrendous moments, she coaxed my body into forsaking me.

And I didn't stop her.

The quicker she fucked me. The quicker she'd grow bored of me. The quicker I was free.

The bed creaked again as she climbed on top of me. Her thighs spread over my hips, straddling my cock.

Fuck.

This was really going to happen.

I groaned under my breath, sounding like a trapped animal waiting for slaughter as she speared up my cock and sank down slowly.

The first sensation of her body claiming mine was the cruellest thing in the world. Cruel because my virginity was Olin's. Cruel because I was supposed to want this, enjoy this, remember this. Cruel because no matter how wrong and revolting this was, my body was no longer mine but an enemy, and it felt good.

Horribly, disgustingly good.

Fuck. Fuck. *Fuck.*

I trembled so much the bed rocked as my goddamn teacher inserted every inch of me inside her. She didn't say a word until I was fully sheathed. Her body was hot and tight, and I was trapped. Totally fucking trapped.

"You're big. Anyone ever tell you that?" Her breathy voice throbbed with sex. Her hips rolled, welcoming me deeper. "Long and thick. You were made to fuck, Gilbert Clark." She rocked on top of me, dragging an unwilling grunt from my chest. "I'll teach you everything you need to know." Her fingernails raked down my chest as she sat higher on her knees and thrust against me.

Stars exploded behind my eyes. A snarl of lust ricocheted down my legs.

But I never removed my arm. Never looked at her. If I didn't see, I wouldn't remember. I wouldn't have to look at my body in my most hated enemy.

She gathered speed, using me, fucking me. Her ass slapped against my thighs every time she sat on me, shoving me deeper, making me twitch and tense.

Primitive nature demanded I drive my hips upward. The instinctual motions of mating fighting against my control to just lie there.

I was not a willing partner.

I did not want this.

I fucking hated her.

I want to kill her.

Yet my body no longer listened to me.

Sweat broke out over my skin as I struggled, but Ms Tallup just bent over me and licked the salt from my flesh, making my nipples pebble and breath catch.

"You've been a good student at school, Gilbert." She thrust again. "But you're not being a very good one now." Her fingers tugged at my arm blindfolding me—the one thing barricading me from the truth of what was happening. "Look at me. Watch me fuck you. I'll show you things those whores you live with don't know how to do."

I turned my head, keeping my eyes locked tight as she dragged my arm from my face.

Her breathing turned to panting as she rocked over me, again and again. My ears pounded with my erratic pulse. My body hardened to the point of pain.

It wasn't a natural erection.

It was forced. Just like this sex was forced. Just like all my choices had been forced.

And I *hated* her. I detested every sound, every thrust, every touch.

Anger mixed with the rapidly growing hunger in my blood. I wanted to wring her neck and throw her body in the river.

She deserves to die.

She slapped me.

I grunted as my eyes flew open of their own accord, snapping onto her flushed face just as a gush of wetness made her slide deeper over me.

The act of violence turned her on.

Her gaze glittered with malice and lust, riding me with her hands flat on my belly and nails digging into my skin.

Being forced to witness what she did to me broke something inside me. Something I'd always prided myself on. A gentleness that I'd nursed and protected even while my father tried to beat it out of me. I kept people at arm's length, but those I let close got everything I had.

Olin owned every part of me.

She always would.

But thanks to this bitch, I could never have her.

That dream was gone.

That future destroyed.

Stolen from me.

Forever.

Fuck.

My anger slipped up a notch, licking with flames.

Ms Tallup rode me faster, her breasts bouncing, her thighs spread and hairless pussy devouring my cock.

She'd taken everything good in my world and annihilated it.

She'd decided my fate.

She'd sullied me, defiled me, and ensured I was no longer good enough for someone as pure as Olin.

She's murdered my one chance at happiness.

My fists curled.

The flames in my heart incinerated my anger, turning it into ash and rage.

How dare she?

How fucking *dare* she steal everything from me?

How dare she take Olin?

How dare she snuff out my life before I'd had a chance to improve it?

"Fuck me, Gilbert. Don't just lie there. *Fuck me.*" Her cheeks glowed a violent red. Her body clutched mine deep inside her, seeking a release.

My own rage answered hers, tightening with sickening hunger for everything to be over.

To stop.

To end.

And the ash and rage switched into black, dripping savagery.

I was past the point of humanity.

Past the point of rationality.

This woman had murdered my only hope and dream.

She'd stolen Olin.

She'll pay.

Jack-knifing up, I grabbed her and smashed her onto her back.

My cock stayed lodged inside her as I slammed a hand over her mouth, pressing her skull into the mattress with barely restrained fury. "You want me to fuck you, Jane Tallup? Fine. I'll fuck you." My hips soared into hers, painfully, mercilessly. "I'll fucking drive you into the goddamn ground." The bedframe screamed as I let loose.

Every hatred and depraved, disgusting thought I'd ever had poured out of me as I tried to kill my teacher with sex.

She gasped behind my palm. Her eyes wide and watering with lack of air supply.

I didn't care.

I honestly didn't care if she died beneath me.

My flesh crawled as pleasure darted down my back the harder I screwed her. My teeth bared as I dug my knees into the bed and thrust, thrust, *thrust*.

No thoughts, no barriers, no boundaries.

I *hated* her.

And that hate was a brutal, blinding thing.

Her breasts jerked with each of my impales.

Her hair tangled beneath her.

Her teeth scraped my palm as her arms fought me.

Her gaze turned chaotic with lust and fear, and even that didn't stop me.

I pressed her head harder into the mattress, doing my best to crush her. To break her. To crack her skull and be done with it.

She moaned and thrashed, clawing at my wrist.

I merely attacked her harder. "You wanted me. You don't get to stop me now that you've destroyed me." I buried my face into the crook of her neck as my hips pistoned, over and over. My hand suffocated her as my body squashed hers.

She fought me. She wriggled and squirmed, but I didn't let up.

I wasn't myself anymore.

I was the creature she made me, and that filthy knowledge made me want to roar with tragedy.

I was dead already.

I might as well take her with me.

My balls tightened as the first wash of an orgasm ripped into me with needles. Every instinct and sane part of me bellowed to withdraw.

To stop this.

To walk out the door and run.

Run!

But she'd broken me.

She'd turned all the good pieces of me into the thing I'd been terrified of all my life.

I was my father, after all.

And this was a whore.

Just a whore.

Bought and paid to accept a bloodthirsty assault by a brutal beast.

I was no longer human as I drove ever faster, harder. My heart pounded, sweat slicked, and my soul vanished beneath contaminated filth.

And then, I felt it.

Felt the final condemning, life-stealing thing. The sentence to my future, ensuring I would forever walk alone because I didn't deserve anyone.

Especially Olin.

Fuck...

My fingers dug into my teacher's cheeks, hoping to draw blood as I stopped fighting the inevitable.

Tallup gasped behind my hand. Her eyes wild. Her face almost purple. But her body jerked and quaked with frenzied release. Her pussy clutched and clenched. Her limbs stiffened. Her back bowed. Her entire body came apart because of what I'd done to her.

She was in ecstasy.

I was in utmost hell.

I was almost sick.

Almost.

But I was lost.

Lost to the rampaging onslaught I reaped.

Lost to the chemical intoxication of Viagra and despair.

And I couldn't stop.

My own release shot with the most agonising mixture of pleasure and abhorrence. A firing line of grenades and shrapnel, tearing me apart, stripping me into pieces.

Between my legs, up my cock, spilling with fire and brimstone.

Wave after wave of sick, debilitating lust. Spilling into a traitor. Sharing pleasure with an adversary.

I hadn't finished coming before a wave of bile shot up my throat.

Ripping my body from hers, I barrelled off the bed and barely made it to the bathroom before spewing my guts into the sink.

My body purged.

My cock dripped more cum on the tiles as my stomach rid itself of Viagra and rum all while my heart flogged itself, maimed itself, sought salvation for the destruction I'd caused.

Sliding to my knees, I hugged the vanity as shock began.

My teeth chattered as the full consequences of what I'd done crippled me.

I'd spend my life in jail.

I'd never see Olin again.

I'd always be known as a rapist.

"Get up."

I hunched, fighting another wave of sickness as Tallup tapped me on the shoulder.

"Get up," she repeated, stepping into the shower and turning on the hot water.

I didn't move while she soaped and rinsed, fighting to put myself together again so I could stand and face the police.

Her bare wet feet appeared in my line of vision on the floor as she wrapped a towel around her well-used body. The body I'd tried to suffocate. The vessel I'd tried to murder for what she'd made me become.

Her hand landed on my head, and in some twisted, disgusting way, I looked up to her for guidance. She was my teacher. She was supposed to teach me, help me grow, guide me into adulthood.

Instead, she made me into this.

Tears pricked my eyes as I noticed the red marks I'd left on her mouth from holding her down. Her lips were swollen, and blood glowed from where she'd bitten through.

But instead of horror on her face; instead of marching to the phone to call the police, she smiled loose and satisfied. "Turns out, I didn't need to teach you how to fuck, Gilbert Clark. You're a master all on your own."

I froze.

More bile churned in my belly.

She turned and dropped her towel, striding toward the bed and sitting on it with the slyest, nastiest grin on her face. "Now you know what I like, get back here. We have all night before that Viagra stops working." She patted the bed. "Come here."

I shook my head, cursing the burn in my belly. The hunger to obey. The need to come again. And again.

Her eyes narrowed, her temper fizzing in the space. "We agreed on one night. Not one fuck. Obey and you're free. You have my word I won't harass Olin Moss. I'll let you graduate. You can pretend none of this ever happened."

Her hand trailed between her legs, spreading them, revealing exactly where she put her finger. "But if you don't crawl on your hands and knees to me this very second, our deal is void, and I'll call the police." Her finger dipped inside herself. "They won't treat you kindly, Gilbert. They won't have any reason to doubt my claims. I have the bruises to match the accusations. You'll never see Olin again. Never be free." She tutted with a sad shake of her head. "Poor, innocent Gilbert Clark. What a terrible predicament you're in."

Her lips spread into an evil smile. Her eyelashes fluttered as she fingered herself. "Now, *crawl*."

I crawled.

Chapter Thirty-Two

Olin

-The Present-

"COME ON, GIL. Pick up the damn phone."

I cancelled the call as it dropped from ringing to his answer machine for the fourth time. I understood why he wasn't answering. I doubted being interviewed at the police station allowed personal calls to interrupt. It had only been a couple of hours since he'd been 'borrowed' for questions. I was probably overreacting.

I knew all of the above, but it didn't change the fact I *desperately* needed him to pick up.

Something isn't right, Gil.

And...I'm not sure what to do.

Tossing my useless phone onto my lap, I clutched the steering wheel with both hands and focused on the road. My foot rocked on the accelerator, inching over the speed limit, testing the black van tailing me.

My heart raced as the van matched my increase, gliding like a threatening shadow about to swallow me whole.

Shit.

I should've stayed in my apartment.

Then again, the bastard Gil was trying to protect me from had definitely been there. I didn't feel safe knowing his hands had touched my stuff, walked my carpets, and investigated my home.

After the police had left, I'd tiptoed through the rest of my place, doing my best to untangle superstition from fact. I'd almost managed to convince myself it was just crazy imagination, lack of rest, and Gil's ominous 'you're in danger' talk that made me second-guess the privacy of my home.

However, that false hope popped the second I entered my bedroom and found my pillows on the floor. Strange but perhaps not too strange. Gil could've tossed them from my bed while I made us coffee before we left. He could have a weird need to do something odd—to mess up the bed I'd slept in and not offered him to join.

I could've spun a tale that far-out, if it hadn't have been for the symbolism of blood smearing the linen.

Gil was a painter, but I doubted he'd ever take a bottle of red nail varnish and dribble it over my bedding and pillows, staining them with acrid crimson, turning fluffy comfort into fabric corpses.

He wouldn't do something that reeked so pungently of death.

Instinct had kicked in, telling me to flee.

I snatched some clothes, stuffed them into my duffel, and shot from the building. I'd hoped the cops might still loiter outside. They wanted clues to apprehending a criminal? I had clues.

Gil had an airtight alibi this time. Nothing could beat being in police custody while an obvious threat to my life was left uninvited in my apartment. I could tell them about the kidnapper—give the right license plate. I could do my part in protecting Gil for a change.

But no cruiser sat at the curb. No badges and protection were there to jot down my sudden willingness to talk. Only a young couple strolling arm in arm kept me safe as I bowled from my building and almost tripped into them.

Their eyes widened at my bright green skin then snickered as I stumbled in my haste.

My hands shook as I unlocked Gil's hatchback, threw my bag in the back, and buckled in. My driving skills were rusty. But I shoved aside trepidation and tore into gear, my mind careening with scenarios and solutions. Gil wanted me to go to his warehouse. But the guy knew where Gil lived. He'd beaten him up and tried to kidnap me right outside—I daren't go there on my own.

I'd driven down my street, joined the main road, and chewed my lip while contemplating answers. Then I'd looked behind me and spotted company. Company that had never left my tail since leaving my building.

Maybe it's just a coincidence.

My eyes flickered to the rear-view mirror again, studying the black van. The late afternoon sun glinted on scratched paintwork, revealing a dent that matched the one I'd seen when Gil had been on his knees accepting unretaliated abuse.

It wasn't a coincidence, and for the first time, Gil's warnings of danger were no longer an inconvenient threat but a very real concern.

One hand dropped from the steering wheel as I once again scooped up my phone and pressed redial. I hopped into a new lane, haphazardly turning left with no indicator.

I studied my follower as frustrating ringing filled my ear.

The black van mimicked me, earning a honk from some motorist in his rush to chase me around the corner.

My heart stopped.

This was real.

He wasn't just going in my direction. He was hunting me.

The call once again didn't connect, and I was done being the scared mouse. It'd been a while since I'd driven—thanks to using public transport on a budget—but I didn't let that stop me as I stomped on the accelerator and shot forward.

Veering into another lane, I overtook the blue sedan in front of me and ran the amber light while others pulled to a stop.

The van raced forward, cutting the light as it turned red.

Prickles of foreboding galloped over my skin. My eyes flickered to the fuel gauge.

Quarter tank.

How far would that get me before I ran out of ability to run? Where the hell could I go? My parents weren't in the country. Gil was otherwise engaged. My dance friends wouldn't know what to do with me after my vanishing act and lack of communication the past few years.

I literally had no one to turn to and nowhere to go.

I sped up, shooting down a side street that led to a quaint cobblestone lane.

Bad move.

Pedestrians clogged the space as well as food carts spilling from the curb.

Flattening my palm on the horn, I earned a few one finger salutes as I inched my way forward. The van followed, our chase turning from quick to crawl.

With my elbow, I locked the doors, grateful that this uninspiring hatchback at least had central locking. At this speed, the guy could jump from his vehicle and walk to get me.

Come on!

I honked again, ducking low from people's glowers.

My phone slid from my thigh into the crook of my lap as I feathered my foot from brake to gas pedal. I scooped it up again, redialling for the sixth time.

Ring.

Ring.

Answer machine.

I hung up.

Reaching the end of the lane, I looked behind me. The van hugged my bumper, crowding me into traffic.

I'd run out of options, and I didn't have the driving skills of a stunt car operator to lose him. I hadn't wanted to turn to Justin. I hadn't wanted to replay the past by leaning on Justin because Gil wasn't there for me. Gil *was* there for me—he was just incapacitated currently.

But...I don't really have a choice.

The van nudged me, shuttling me forward as I pulled to yet another crawl at a zebra crossing with a mum pushing a pram.

I threw him a nasty gesture, allowing my anger to hide my fear. No way would he make a murderer out of me by running her down all to save myself.

With trembling hands, I pulled up Justin's details and shot forward as the woman reached the pavement. I hesitated a few seconds before pressing call, wincing at what Gil would say, knowing that I'd once again used Justin for my own devices.

Swallowing hard, I activated the speaker and placed the ringing phone on my lap. Planting both hands on the steering wheel, I crept over the speed limit again, trying to put some space between me and the van.

"Miller speaking."

The line crackled a little, but relief shot through my heart. "Justin, it's Olin."

"O? Everything okay?"

"Um. Not really." I took a corner sharply, cursing as the van managed to manoeuvre the same path.

"What's going on?" Justin's tone slipped from casual to sharp. "You in trouble?"

That was Justin.

He might've been the boy everyone liked at school, but it wasn't because of some misplaced popularity contest or ego. He genuinely cared. He was thoughtful and sweet, and it'd been my broken heart over Gil that had drawn him to me.

I hadn't actively tried to date another person. But Justin had seen my tears and offered a shoulder to cry on. He tried to make me happy.

Justin was like me.

It made him feel good to help others. And even though we were too similar to date long term, I'd allowed Justin to soothe me and hid my cringes when he'd kissed me. I'd ignored the fact that I had no romantic interest in him because I'd missed Gil so, so much.

Also, knowing Gil saw me with him...well, the vindictiveness was sweet after heartbreak.

Guilt rose.

Guilt for hurting Justin as well as Gil.

Guilt for hurting myself.

"Olin...you can tell me. If you need help, you know I'm always—"

"There for me. I know." My knuckles turned white on the steering wheel. God, how could I betray Gil's confidence? How much could I spill without telling everything—including the parts I didn't know myself?

I accelerated, taking another corner too fast. "I don't have time to explain, but I'm being chased by someone Gil was protecting me from. I don't have anywhere to go and daren't go to Gil's on my own."

"Where's Gilbert?" Justin demanded. "He isn't with you?"

"He's, um...elsewhere."

"Where are you?"

"Driving around, trying to lose unwanted company."

Justin sucked in a breath. "What do you need from me?"

"I don't really know. I just need somewhere I can be safe."

"Come here."

"Where's here?"

"My work. I'm the CFO of Abacus Accounting. We're on the main drag downtown."

"I don't think I can get there. How would I park? Where would I get out without this arsehole grabbing me?"

He went silent for a second, then strict control entered his voice. "Go to Gil's."

"But I just said—"

"Go to Gilbert's. I'll meet you there."

"I don't think the two of us will scare this guy away. He hurt Gil last time—" I shut myself up. How much did Justin know of Gil's life?

But Justin didn't ask for more details; his mind already on other distractions. "Keep driving for ten minutes, then get to the warehouse. I'll bring reinforcements."

He hung up.

Reinforcements?

I slipped through another orange light and looked at the clock.

I had no idea what that meant, but I had ten minutes to kill.

Ten minutes until this ended—for better or for worse.

I shot forward, doing my best to vanish.

* * * * *

The van shadowed my every move as I turned into the warehouse precinct and followed the long drive past other used and derelict buildings to Gil's painting empire.

I'd done my best to shake my shadow, but I wasn't quick enough, and he was determined.

I'd waited fifteen minutes before driving to Gil's, knowing that it was a one-way entrance, and once I was outside warehouse twenty-five, there was no going back.

With my heart thrumming, I inched farther from public view, begging Justin to have a decent welcome committee. My shoulders slouched in gratefulness when I spotted three cars parked outside Gil's place. Four men in black suits with arms crossed loitered against their expensive sedans.

Thank God.

The van that'd ridden my ass the entire trip, slowed and fell back.

I sped up, putting distance between us as I shot to where Justin stood, and parked swiftly. Launching out of the hatchback with my phone in hand, I jogged to him and turned to face the van.

It hulked in the middle of the road with warehouse debris on either side and evening light dappling it in softness. Standing next to Justin and his friends, I felt like an idiot—as if I'd made up the seriousness of the threat.

Justin reached out and squeezed my hand, giving me a quick

smile. "You all good?"

I nodded, unable to take my eyes off the van but equally unable to leave my hand in his. Tugging away slightly, I returned his smile with a huge sigh of gratefulness. "Thanks so much for helping me."

"Not at all." He nodded at his friends. "Let's go pay our unwanted guest a visit, shall we?"

The men, who looked as if they regularly attended a gym but their natural habitat was behind a desk, moved forward in a black-suited crowd with Justin in the middle.

I trailed behind them, peering into the windshield of the van, trying to see past the window's glare to the driver beyond.

Is it the same guy?

Was Gil being blackmailed by a single person or multiple?

Passing the hatchback with its engine still running, the men balled their hands in an obvious threat. Justin cocked his chin, his profile harsh and cutting in the early evening shadows.

The van didn't move. A black stain on the horizon. It sat and accepted their threat until only a few metres existed between vehicle and man.

I shook with adrenaline, trembling at confronting the very person who terrified me and made Gil's life a living hell. I wanted him arrested. I wanted him dealt with so he could stop hurting Gil so badly.

But as Justin struck into a jog and his friends followed, the van's engine squealed. It shot into reverse, zooming down the road, too fast to be caught.

The guys slowed to a walk. One of them took a photo of the van's license plate while another chucked a rock in the vehicle's direction.

The van swerved at the end of the drive and disappeared into traffic.

It happened so fast, I once again felt like an overreacting idiot.

I fell back as Justin spoke to his friends.

The murmur of masculine voices blended well with the buzz of the city and hum of whatever other industries were alive in the unassuming warehouse buildings. I looked down at my phone, moving away.

Should I call Gil again? How much longer could the police keep him?

With my thoughts on Gil, I didn't look up until the snarl of engines stole my attention, signalling Justin's mates were leaving. I waved in thanks, wishing I'd been more sociable than worrying over Gil.

I owed them the biggest thank you.

My heart skipped a beat as Justin threw a hand up in farewell, then headed toward me. His eyes held lines of stress, but his mouth quirked into a smile. "You sure you're okay?"

I nodded, slipping into step with him. "Yes. Thanks again for all your help."

He shrugged. "That's what friends are for."

"Were those guys your friends?"

"I work with them. All good blokes even if they are accountants. One holds a championship in amateur boxing."

"Impressive."

"It's handy when you have someone threatening you." His gaze narrowed. "Want to tell me what's going on?"

I bit my lip, throwing a look at Gil's warehouse. "I don't know if I can."

"What are you caught up in?"

A huge exhale escaped me. "Honestly...I don't know."

"Your problem or Gil's?"

I eyed him. "Not my problem to tell."

"Okay, so it's Gil's."

"I didn't say that."

He crossed his arms, a scowl darkening his face. "Let me put it another way. Did you have this stalker before you found Gil again, or is it a recent development?"

"He's not a stalker."

"You sure about that?"

"I'm not sure about anything these days."

Looking at the sky, Justin huffed. "Look, it's none of my business what goes on between you and Gil. I don't expect you to tell me, but you did reach out to me, O. You know I'd never betray you—"

"And I can't betray him."

He sighed, visibly calming himself. "Okay, fine. I get it. I'm just glad you're past thinking he's a murderer, so I won't pry." Fumbling in his pocket, he pulled out a key chain. "Come on. Let's at least get behind a locked door in case that bastard comes back."

I padded beside him in my bare feet, green skin, and white robe. "You have a spare key?"

He shot me a grin. "I'm his only friend. Who else would he give a spare to?"

I hugged myself as he unlocked the pedestrian door and moved aside to let me enter. "I still don't understand how your friendship works."

Gil had accepted Justin into his life…but I doubted he'd shared his troubles.

"Guess he'll have to fill you in on that." He stepped inside, turning to close and lock the door.

The hulking warehouse was dark and chilly. The large expanse turned footsteps echoey and the sense of comfort from a home was missing thanks to sparse soft furnishings.

Justin flicked a switch, drenching the space in illumination. "You've obviously seen Gil at some point today." He moved toward the thermostat, turning on the heat to remove the icy lace on the air. It was as if Gil's space stayed as cold as its owner, waiting for the king of snow to return.

"If you're talking about the body paint I should have washed off hours ago, then yes, I've seen Gil today."

"Commission?" He kept moving through the office and into Gil's apartment. I had no choice but to follow him, even though it was awkward being in Gil's space alone with Justin.

I was old fashioned when it came to loyalties.

Gil hadn't exactly made me feel welcome, and we hadn't discussed our relationship, but there *was* a relationship, and this was an overstep of boundaries.

"Yes. For Kohl's department store." The residual jealousy that would forever be linked with that shop and the knowledge that Gil had gone there with other women fired hotly.

Justin stopped, turning to face me with a frown. "He hates those. Normally turns all commercial stores down."

He needed the money.

I saw him beg.

I heard him on the phone with tears in his eyes.

I shrugged. "He changed his mind."

He laughed quietly. "He seems to do that a lot around you."

Hiding my wince, I wrapped my robe tighter. "His prerogative."

"It is." A stagnant pause fell. He squeezed the back of his neck, his immaculate suit whispering with fine fabric and money.

He looked so different to Gil with his paint-splattered clothing. They were from different paths, different pasts, different futures. Yet…somehow, they'd become friends.

I relaxed a little.

I might have been in Justin's life when we were at school, just as I'd been in Gil's, but…I'd shared a small fraction of time compared to what they had in the past year.

The knowledge that I was the third wheel these days actually gave me peace of mind.

Arching my chin at the bathroom door, I said quietly, "I can't thank you enough for coming to my aid again. But now that I'm safe, I might take a shower…if that's okay?"

"You don't need to ask me. Not my place."

"True." I smiled. "Well, in that case." I snapped my fingers. "Oh, no. I left my bag in Gil's car. Along with all his painting gear and the engine running." Turning reluctantly, I went to return outside. "I'll be right back."

Justin moved to cut me off, holding up his hand. "Take a shower. I'll get everything."

My eyes widened. "You sure? Will you be safe on your own?"

He chuckled. "I'm sure I'll be fine."

"Okay…" I blushed. "My overnight bag is in the back. Would you mind leaving it outside the bathroom door?"

He nodded. "Of course." Striding back through the office and into the warehouse, he didn't ask why I had an overnight bag. He didn't ask why I was driving Gil's car. He acted as if whatever was going on with me and Gil was perfectly acceptable. As if he'd known all along this would happen if we ever found each other again.

And perhaps, he knew better than anyone.

After all, he'd nursed my tattered heart and then patched up Gil's.

He'd been the glue to our shattered pieces.

Maybe he could fix what was broken between us.

Maybe.

Chapter Thirty-Three

Olin

-The Present-

I CAUGHT JUSTIN'S stare as our eyes once again trailed from the TV to the clock in the kitchen.

1:13 a.m.

And still no Gil.

I gave Justin a weak smile, burrowing deeper into the blanket surrounding me on the couch. I did my best to focus on whatever show we'd pretended to watch, but I couldn't stop worrying.

My phone rested beside me. Silent and empty of messages. Whenever I tried to call Gil—and I'd called a fair few times—none of them connected.

"I'm sure he's fine," Justin murmured, his voice loud to my overstrained hearing.

"Uh-huh." I nodded, running a hand through my washed and dried hair. My pyjama bottoms and hoodie kept me warm and modest after the green body paint had siphoned down the drain.

Having a shower in Gil's space without him had been wrong.

Having a shower in the same place where he'd kissed me and couldn't stop made my heart squeeze and concern magnify the longer Gil didn't come home.

I missed him.

I needed him.

I'm worried.

I hadn't told Justin that the police took him. Hadn't told him any of it.

We'd kept our conversation to small talk and busied ourselves by making toast with the bare essentials of Gil's kitchen for dinner—neither of us keen on leaving, just in case Gil returned.

"You don't have to stay." I stifled a yawn, once again looking at the clock.

Justin stretched his arms above his head, his spine cricking from sitting down for so long. "If you're in danger, I'm not leaving you until Gil gets back."

"But don't you have someone missing you at home?"

He sighed softly. "Nope. Not for a while now unfortunately."

"What happened?" I blushed. "I don't mean to pry—"

"It's fine. Her name was Colleen. We dated, but then she decided she didn't like me enough to stick around and moved out."

I slouched with empathy. "I'm sorry."

He wiped his face with both hands before chuckling. "Don't be. We weren't right for each other."

"I'm sure you'll find someone who is."

He nodded. "I know. Just like you found Gil again."

I huddled into my blankets. "I don't know if we're right for each other. And besides, reconnecting was entirely by fluke."

"Fluke...fate." He shrugged. "Coincidence has many names. Doesn't change the fact there's something special about you two when you're together."

I didn't speak for a while. My thoughts back in the past when Gil had vanished without an explanation. How he'd hurt me worse than anyone. How I'd forgiven him for all of it so blindly.

Last week, I'd been fumbling through interviews all alone. Now, I burned through concern while waiting like an unwanted wife for a man who said he'd never be mine.

I huffed under my breath. "Special or not, it didn't work the first time. Nothing to say a second chance won't have the same conclusion."

Silence fell for a moment while Justin stared at the TV. "Did he ever tell you why he left?"

Every muscle froze with utmost attention. "No. Do you know why?"

Would I finally get that answer? Would years of wondering be solved right here, right now?

Justin gave me a sad smile. "No."

"But you know something about it?"

"Not really."

"He didn't say anything when you guys started hanging out?"

He snorted. "We don't exactly hang out."

"What do you do?"

"I'm there. That's all."

"There for what?"

"For whatever he needs." He stood. Grabbing his empty glass from the coffee table, he went to fill it with water in the kitchen.

"Is he there for you in the same way?" I asked.

The sound of running water filled the space as Justin answered, "He's had my back. Yes."

"What do you think he's hiding?"

Justin narrowed his eyes as he returned to the couch and sat. "Not really my business."

"But you've wondered."

"I've wondered."

"Any ideas?"

He sighed. "I think you should ask him if you—"

"He wouldn't tell me. Just like he hasn't told you."

"That's true." He sipped his water before placing the glass on the coffee table. "I'm guessing it's something big. Like I said to you on messenger, there's something in his past that screwed him up. He's *still* screwed up."

"Screwed up in what way?"

"The worst possible way."

Goosebumps scattered over my arms. "What's that supposed to mean?"

"It means shut the fuck up and stop discussing my problems." The harsh growl wrenched my head to the office door.

Gil stood on the threshold, arms crossed, face murderous.

Justin leapt to his feet. "Hey, mate. Where the hell have you been?"

Gil's jaw worked as he struggled to rein in exhaustion and temper to reply nicely. He gave up, his fiery green eyes meeting mine. "Hanging out with old friends, Olin?"

Anger prickled, shooting me to my feet. "Don't you dare."

He rolled his eyes and stormed toward the kitchen. "Get out. Both of you."

Justin turned on the spot, chasing him with his gaze. "What happened to you? Why are you so filthy?"

With Gil rummaging in a cupboard, my attention was no longer held hostage by his stare, giving me a chance to study him.

He still wore the paint-splattered clothing from this morning, but he looked as if he'd crawled through a hedgerow, scaled a mountain, and bushwhacked through a forest. Dirt smeared his T-shirt and jeans, mud decorated his arms and hands, and muck clung to his boots, leaving little trails of debris from his march.

A case of déjà vu hit me.

Gil had been just as dirty the night we'd had sex for the first time. He'd been beaten, bloody, and drunk.

He's not drunk this time.

I spoke too soon as Gil found what he wanted and spun to face us defiantly. A fresh bottle of vodka hung in his fist. With a lethal look, he unscrewed the lid and swigged straight from the bottle.

With his head tipped back, injuries not visible came to light. A cut followed the line of his jaw. A bruise bloomed on his collarbone. A dried river of blood trickled from his hairline.

Shit.

Standing, I tossed my blanket to the couch and moved toward him. "Give me the bottle, Gil."

He snarled like a feral animal. His teeth sharp and bared. His eyes wild and haunted. "Leave, Olin. I'm not in the mood for company."

"She can't leave, Clark." Justin cut in. "She was almost abducted today."

Gil froze. "What?" He pinned me with a fierce stare. "What happened?"

"He was in my apartment. When I left to come here, a black van tailed me." Coldness settled into my bones as Gil took another healthy swig.

And another.

His body vibrated with tension but he didn't flock to protect me or demand to know every detail. He acted as if he couldn't care less.

As if his protective routine was over and done with. That

his need for me was finished.

I struggled to keep my tone level and not wobble with sudden sadness. "I tried calling you, Gil. Countless times. But when you didn't pick up, I didn't have anyone else to call…so I asked Justin for help."

He wiped his mouth with the back of his hand. "Yeah, well. I was otherwise indisposed."

"I know." I shot Justin a quick glance. "I get why you couldn't answer to start with, but you've been gone all night. Where have you been?" My voice softened with concern. "I couldn't stop thinking about you. I was so worried."

I risked vulnerability.

I put everything on the line so I didn't have to stare at such an indifferent, frosty face.

Gil's temper blended with exhaustion as if my sign of caring was all too much. His spine rolled, and he rubbed at his eyes.

The coldness I'd read on him slipped into liquid regret. His eyes returned to fiery emeralds as his body became soft and caring.

Tripping toward me, he held the vodka bottle in one hand and cupped my cheek with the other. Not caring Justin watched, he pulled me forward and kissed me swift and deep.

I gasped at the affection. Buckled at the need.

He kissed me as if he was seconds away from killing me or taking his own life.

His tongue laced with sharp alcohol. His breath faint. His energy drained. And not drained from a long day of paint commissions, police interviews, and whatever else he'd been doing, but drained from something that ate him alive.

Something monstrous that sucked on his soul, gnawed his heartbeats, and left him with just enough dregs in which to survive.

My arms trembled to hug him. To give him a safe harbour in which to rest.

But his kiss was over as quickly as it had begun, and his eyes shuttered with fury. "I told you to stay away. I begged you." He swayed back and tipped the bottle to his lips. He sucked down four big mouthfuls before laughing, cold and heartbroken. "I'm sorry, Olin. For everything. But I need you to leave. I…I can't do this anymore. I don't know what the fuck I was thinking." He narrowed his eyes at Justin. "Keep her safe, Miller. Please." Shoving his hand into his pocket, he stalked to the door that was always locked beside his bedroom and inserted a key.

Without another word, he vanished into graffiti rainforests and rooms filled with secrets…with the alcohol.

The door slammed with finality.

I didn't move for the longest moment.

Shell-shocked and war-kissed, my lips tingled and heart smoked with every layer of pain Gilbert had just fed me. In his kiss, he'd shared something explicitly real and inexplicitly complicated. With his mouth on mine, he'd commanded me to go, all while he'd begged me to stay.

And now, I was torn between everything.

Justin's hand landed on my shoulder. "Come on, O. Let's leave."

I shrugged him off almost angrily. "I can't go, Justin." Turning to face him, I sucked in a breath. A breath I'd need for the fight I was about to endure. "I'm not going anywhere. Not tonight." Tears glossed my eyes even as my hands curled into fists. "Can't you see? Don't you understand?"

His eyes danced over mine. "See what?"

"He's breaking."

"He wants to be alone."

"I leave him alone now, and he won't be the same tomorrow."

He shook his head. "I know I said you guys have something special, but…O. This is not the time to try and help."

"This is the perfect time. The *only* time."

"He's not going to come out of that room sober."

"I know."

"In all the time I've known him, he's always kept that door locked." He threw a worried glance at the barred door. "I don't know what's in there. I suggest you're not here to find out."

"I'm not afraid of him."

"You sure about that?" He leaned closer. "You're the one who asked me if he was capable of killing someone."

"That was a mistake."

"I'm all for you guys working shit out, but come on, Olin. Wake up. Just because you've been back in his life for a few days, you think you're the magic pill to cure him?" He laughed sharply. "I wish it was that easy. But the fact is, he's not some school project for you to fix. He's not gonna appreciate you staying. And…I don't think it's safe. He's not a killer, but he has something warring inside him—let him fight that battle on his own."

I crossed my arms, hugging myself for strength. "Yeah, because that method has been working *so* well so far."

"You don't know that. He actually did something other than paint and mope around the past week…he might be dealing with—"

"He had me. That's why. I've been here helping him—"

"Distracting him, you mean."

"Maybe, but is that such a bad thing?"

He sighed as if our argument drained him. "Look, it's late. We both have a life we have to deal with in the morning. Come crash at mine where it's safe and come back tomorrow…when he's had time to cool off."

"I can't leave."

"Yes, you can." He smirked almost cruelly. "He left you pretty easily as I recall. You're just repaying the favour."

My heart hiccupped.

I didn't reply. I wouldn't stoop to pointless ridicule or petty fights.

"Shit, sorry." Justin held out his hand in surrender. "I didn't mean that."

"I know." My skin pebbled with goosebumps. "But I think you better go."

"I don't want to leave without you."

"But you're going to."

He stared at me and then the locked door, his eyes narrowed as if he could see Gil and the vodka he currently poured down his throat. "Don't do this, O."

"Please go."

"I'm not comfortable leaving you here alone with him in his current condition."

"It's none of your concern."

"You *made* it my concern when you asked for my help! I mean, you were in a car chase today! Doesn't that mean anything to you? Worry about yourself, rather than him. If he's the reason you're in danger, then it makes sense to put distance between you until—"

"Justin…" I waited until his shoulders slouched. "I appreciate all your advice and what you've done for me. Truly, I'm ever so grateful. I'm very glad to have you back in my life, and I owe you a huge debt, but…I'm not going to ask again. Gilbert pushed me away once. He succeeded back then, but this time…he won't."

He paced with a sigh. "What if his disappearance is tied with the guy harassing you? What if this mess is only going to get worse and Gil can't protect you—"

"I have no doubt it's connected." I tipped my chin up. "And that's why I'm staying. He's been dealing with this on his own for too long. He can scream at me, get drunk, hurt me, yell at me, and call me every name he can, but until he tells me exactly what the hell is going on, I'm not leaving. I deserve to know. I'm owed answers. And he's going to give them to me. Tonight."

Our argument screeched to a standstill. Justin's arms hung loosely by his sides, his defeat obvious. "You never stopped loving him, did you?"

I stiffened. "What did I know of love? I was a teenager. We all were."

He gave me a depressing smile. "You knew." Backing up, he grabbed his black blazer from where he'd tossed it on the back of the couch. "And I knew, even while we dated. I hope he deserves you, O. I truly do. I hope he has answers that give you peace."

"Me too."

"I'll have my phone on me at all times. Call me if there's anything you need. And I do mean anything, okay?"

"Okay." I smiled, unwilling to let him walk out angry. "Thanks again, Justin. Truly."

"You're welcome." With another grim look, he saluted me as if I'd been drafted into battle. "Please be safe."

I nodded.

He let himself out.

He left me alone with a man who didn't want me.

All because I'd commanded him to.

Chills etched my skin with frosty lace as I inched toward the closed door. My knuckles rapped softly as I pressed my forehead on the unforgiving wood. "He's gone, Gil. It's just me."

No sound.

No murmur.

Nothing.

I sighed heavily, twisting around to lean against the door. An owl perched above me and an otter played in the stream by my feet. The rainforest graffiti did its best to twist lies with truth…just like the painter who'd created it. "You haven't just been with the police tonight…have you?" I looked around his living room, searching for clues on the dark mystery surrounding

Gilbert Clark.

But there was nothing.

Just like there was nothing from Gil barricaded in the locked room.

Sliding to the floor, I wrapped arms around my knees. "I think you're hurting, Gil." I kept my voice lower than a whisper. Too low for his ears behind the door. Almost too low for mine.

Instead, I spoke to his apartment—to the bare kitchen and barren lounge. I asked the shadows to help me understand.

"I think you're caught up in something so much bigger than you or me. I think you've been dealing with it for a very long time. I think…"

I swallowed hard as tears prickled and escaped the prison of my eyelashes, rolling wetly down my cheeks. A horrible realisation sprang into awareness. A horrendous connection between past and present. "I think…you disappeared from school because of whatever is hurting you now. I think you've kept a secret all these years, and it's chewing you alive. I think you're all alone and trapped, and if I'm right, I don't know how I can ever forgive you for not turning to me. For not trusting me to be strong enough to help you. I loved you. I would've weathered any storm with you."

My tears stopped as I stared forlornly at the ceiling. "I was there for you then and you didn't want me. I'm here for you now, and this time…you don't have a choice."

Turning to press my hot, damp cheek to the door, I spoke loud enough for him to hear. "I'm not going anywhere, Gil. Not this time. So drink away your misery, hide behind this door, and take all the hours you need because when you come out, you're going to tell me. Everything."

* * * * *

My eyes flew open as something heavy tripped over me.

The gloominess of the living room gave just enough illumination as Gil opened the locked door, stumbled drunk and bleary eyed, then somersaulted over me where I lay on the floor.

He cursed as he twisted to cushion his fall, then grunted as the hard floor welcomed him with a cruel jolt.

I sat bolt upright, reaching for his sprawled body. "Sorry! I didn't mean to—"

"Kill me?" His voice once again held the heaviness of liquor and looseness. He hadn't slurred, but he definitely wasn't sober.

"I must've fallen asleep." I rubbed sleep-gritty eyes and

stared at the clock.

4:56 a.m.

Gil had been alone and drinking for almost four hours.

Sitting up on my knees, I turned to glance behind me into the room. I wanted to understand what he hid inside. To see if a blatant clue to whatever he was keeping secret lingered. But no light touched the shadows.

All I could make out was another mattress with a side table and a silver lightshade. Something hulked on the bed as if a silent figure slept beneath blankets. A faint scent of strawberry escaped, wrapping around me like a rope.

My heart rate skyrocketed as I crawled toward the threshold, determined to understand.

However, Gil beat me.

Even in his alcohol-induced wobbliness, he swooped to unsteady feet and yanked the door closed. He locked it before I could determine if the bed held a peaceful dreamer or something more sinister.

"I told you...to leave, Olin." He sniffed loudly, his eyes red-rimmed and puffy. Earth smeared his clothes, tainting him with musty undergrowth and tart evergreen.

Climbing to my feet, I touched the grime on his T-shirt. "Were you in a forest?"

He stiffened, then swatted my hand away. "I was many places." Stalking to his bedroom, he didn't make eye contact as he slipped inside.

He hadn't invited me.

He'd made it obvious I wasn't welcome.

I followed him regardless.

I waited while he kicked off his boots and yanked down his jeans. He didn't look to see if his stripping affected me. The vodka haze had given him blinders, making him focus on one thing and one thing only.

He swayed as he struggled to jerk his jeans from his feet, then grumbled as he wrestled his T-shirt over his head.

Unlike his clothing, his skin was clean from blood and mud. His muscles stood out with definition that seemed almost barbaric—as if he hadn't eaten properly in months and his body fought hard to maintain the power it had created. His biceps bunched as he buried his face in both hands and groaned as if trying to find the strength to carry on and not let his demons win.

Wading from the pile of clothing, he cut across the small room in just his boxer-briefs and tumbled face first onto his bed on the floor. His back rippled with more muscle as he hugged a pillow and gave into liquor-induced lethargy.

He hadn't looked at me.

He hadn't told me to leave or stay or showed any sign he cared either way.

I had no idea what to do.

I'd prepared for another battle. I'd fallen asleep writing scripts on how to respond to the inevitable argument. But how was I supposed to argue with someone who'd shut down and blocked me out?

I stood like a ghost at the end of his bed, studying him as he breathed slow and deep. His arms rippled with tension as he hugged the pillow as if throttling it, silencing it, doing his best to still the chaos inside him.

He might seem quiet on the outside, but his thoughts filled the room with noise. Angry, vengeful, trapped. A noise that scratched my skin and made me search the corners for a malicious enemy.

Everything about Gil spoke of a man who ought to have it all—wealth, fame, talent. Yet, something was missing in him. Something fundamental—as if his soul had been ripped from him and left him with just a wasteland filled with darkness.

I hugged myself as another wash of goosebumps found me.

What the hell was in that locked room? Was someone *in* there? What had he dealt with to be this wretched?

Questions ran riot. Anxiety lived in nervous heartbeats. I tried to formulate a question that would tell me everything. To learn in one swoop what'd happened to him so I could ease the brittle affliction wrapped tight around his heart.

But Gil had dealt with whatever hurt him by his own method. He'd tried to drown out the noise, delete the pain, and for a single breath, he looked as if he'd won a hard-earned moment of peace.

As much as I needed to know, I couldn't take that peace away from him. I couldn't ask him to step back into the storm he carried.

No matter what he'd done, run from, or was involved in, I couldn't be the cause of more agony.

Not right now.

Padding toward his mattress, I lowered to my knees and

crawled over to him.

He didn't need an inquisition. He needed silence.

A friend.

Family.

He tensed as I lay beside him. His eyes never opened, and his forehead tugged low into a harsh frown. His hand disappeared under his pillow, clutching something small and furry.

Without a word, I tugged up the edge of the pillow to see what he held.

My heart promptly bled out. No tourniquet or bandage could stop the flow.

Tears spilled from me as his face screwed up in torment, clutching the stuffed owl in his fist.

An owl.

A silly child's toy.

A toy with woodland feathers and big, soulful eyes.

Owl...for O.

"Gil..." Ripping my hand from the pillow, I cradled his cheek instead. He shivered as I bent to nuzzle his nose with mine, our faces wedged against fresh cotton, the reek of alcohol unwelcome.

"What are you hiding?" I moaned, kissing his lips with sadness. "It's killing you, can't you see? You have to tell someone."

His skin turned ashen as he pulled away from my kiss, shaking his head as if he couldn't stand the connection.

He lay on his back with an arm thrown over his eyes, erasing the outside world.

Erasing me.

But I didn't let him.

Straddling him in bed, I bowed over him and cupped his cheeks. Rolling my spine, I cradled him, giving him shelter with my body, kissing him again. I kissed him shallowly and sweetly, all while tears plopped from my cheeks to his, running along his jawline and down his throat.

He trembled worse with every heart-pound. His skin turned icy, and another noise of a wounded prey and furious predator grumbled in his chest. He shuddered the longer I kissed him, withdrawing into places I couldn't follow.

He didn't shove me away, but second by second, his unyielding tension hinted that having me on top wasn't enjoyable for him. I tasted his reluctance in the kisses he refused to return. I felt it in the snow rapidly chilling his skin.

His trembles were that of someone who would face a monster but knew the price was death if he did.

Ripping my mouth from his, I sat up and rolled off him, swiping at my tears and confusion. "I'm sorry. I didn't mean…"

His jaw worked, and he shook his head sharply.

He didn't speak as if words were too much to bear.

"God, I'm—" I sniffed and plucked at his blankets. "All I want to do is help. I want to prove you can trust me. I want you to know that, despite your secrets and my fear of what you're hiding, I'm not walking away. I want to help you, Gil, but everything I do only seems to make it worse."

His body stayed tight and unmovable.

I inched farther away from him, giving him space.

A few seconds after I shifted, he slowly came alive again. His arm slipped from his eyes, and he blinked as if disoriented. As if he didn't recognise his room, this night…me.

His green gaze met mine and, once again, that heart-breaking suspicion of tears hurt me worse than any curse or fist.

I'd never known him to show his emotions at school. I'd seen him bleeding and bruised, sleep deprived and starving, yet he'd never once looked on the brink of breaking.

Not like now.

And that drained me of my silly attempt at being his strength because if Gilbert Clark—the boy who took on the world without one whinge about injustice—could look so perfectly destroyed, something was seriously, *seriously* wrong.

"It's me, Gil. Just me." I itched to reach out and touch him, but I refrained.

The sigh that escaped him was full-bodied and from his soul. It whistled through his chest, gusted from his lips, and left his body boneless in relief.

I waited for him to ask me to leave.

For his previous commands to be obeyed.

Instead, he grabbed my wrist and pulled me down beside him. With shaky fingers, he positioned me until we lay facing each other. His eyes searched mine, fast and probing. His fingers caressed hair behind my ear. He arched closer and pressed a kiss to my forehead with such sweet-hearted tenderness my heart cried.

He still didn't speak, but his touch spoke volumes.

Stay.

Please.

I need you.

I nodded, placing my hands on his naked chest. The flutter of his heart singed my fingertips.

His lips thinned. His skin hadn't lost the ashen pallor of before. He inhaled deep, and, ever so slowly, bent to kiss me.

Our breath connected first, plaiting together with hesitation and want. Our lips met next, exquisitely soft and velvet. We stayed in that bubble of anticipation for ages. Butterflies gathered, desire quickened, the sensation of such a breakable kiss was so different to the aggressive, explosive arousal we'd shared before.

This was paper thin and precious. This wasn't two adults experienced in lovemaking, but two teenagers who'd been in love for so damn long.

His mouth whispered over mine, sending shockwaves over my lips. He never moved to increase the pressure, and I didn't want to break the intoxicating spell he'd cast over me.

Never had a kiss had the power to invoke an entire body shiver.

Never had a touch pampered me with feathery urgency, all while promising priceless rewards if we didn't rush.

He kissed me, and I kissed him back. Neither of us pushed for more, content in the delicate freedom we'd created. Our lips stayed dry and innocent against each other's, adding friction and heat. My nipples pebbled to be touched, his heart rate switched from a flutter to a steady knock against his ribs.

And still we didn't break the boundaries of virtuous. This kiss felt safe. It gave Gil exactly what I'd wanted—a place of unconditional acceptance and patience.

I sighed, melting into his control.

The moment I gave him utmost ownership over me, the tip of his tongue licked my bottom lip. Barely there, an erotic tease.

I moaned, trembling. My body liquefied and nullified—preparing for him and cancelling anything else. My fingers claimed his chest; my mouth parted with invitation.

We hovered on the precipice of a simple kiss evolving to sizzling sex.

Gil wasn't sober, but he'd successfully made my head swim with desire, so we were both inebriated and at the mercy of baser controls.

However, instead of deepening the kiss, he pulled away with a heart-wrenching groan. "I can't." His eyelids slammed over blazing, blistering green. "I'm sorry."

I trembled again, but this time with worry. "It's fine. I'm not expecting—"

"I want you, O. I want you so fucking much." His eyes snapped open again. "Turning you away tonight. Fuck." A cruel laugh shattered our safe silence. "Turning you away every time…it rips me apart."

I froze. Was this Gil talking or the vodka? Was this naked truth or embolden fibs?

"You don't need to explain—"

"Do you know what I thought when I first saw you again?" His forehead furrowed with grief. "I thought…how did I think I was living when you've had a piece of me this entire time? A piece I've been missing and could never replace."

Tugging me to him, he buried his face in the crook of my neck, preventing me from watching him. "I almost buckled to my knees when I recognised you. I fought every instinct to call you mine."

I wrapped my arms around him, hugging him hard. "I felt the same. A punch to the chest…like I came alive again and—"

"Don't say that."

"How can I not when you're—"

"You haven't heard the rest yet." His lips skated over the side of my throat, a threat rather than a caress. "I saw you, remembered you, wanted you, and then, I cursed you. I swore at motherfucking fate for putting you back in my life."

His words were scalpels slicing deep, while his voice was poison, pouring directly onto the wounds. I struggled in his embrace, trying to study his features. "Wh-what is that supposed—"

"I left for a reason bigger than you or me. I left because I had no other choice. For years, I survived without you. I lied and made myself believe I'd forgotten you. But every day, I'd see an orange or an octopus or something beginning with O, and I'd remember all over again. And I'd hate that I'd had to leave you. I'd beg for some way of explaining things—of making you understand why I left."

"Tell me now…you can—"

"No, I can't. That curse is mine to bear. I'm being punished. I deserve it for what I've done."

"You're not—"

"Punished every fucking day of my life, and I don't deserve to find small pockets of happiness whenever I'm with you. It's not fair that I have you when she—" He inhaled deep, his breath shaky and contaminated with his sins. "When I saw you again, I knew I wouldn't be able to resist you. I knew I'd take you, fuck you, and do my best to keep you. And I also knew what would happen if I did." His arms banded tighter around me, so tight he suffocated me. "I'm so sorry, Olin. So sorry for the past, the present, and the future. I'm sorry you ever fell in love with me. I'm sorry I ever fell in love with you. And I'm sorry for being so fucking weak not to push you away when I had the chance."

"Gil, let me go." I scratched at his back, doing my best to get a breath and for him to stop talking such insanity. "Stop."

His arms loosened but not enough for me to see his eyes. He sniffed, burrowing his face into my hair. "You think you're helping me...you're only making it worse. You think you're saving me...you're only condemning yourself. I'm not safe, O. I've told you that. I've tried to make you understand." He shook me as if this was all my fault. "You're not safe because of me. And even now, knowing what I know, I'm too fucking weak to push you away."

I ignored the whispers of worry in my heart and stroked his spine. "It's okay. I get that—"

"You don't get anything."

"If you stopped talking so cryptically I would—"

"No." He pushed me away, rolling me onto my other side even though I fought to stay facing him. The moment I lay with my back to him, he scooped me into his front, gathering me tight. "I'm the most selfish man alive because I don't deserve this moment with you. I don't deserve *any* moment where I get to be happy while others—" He choked, his voice turning bitter. "I hate that I have you in my arms. I hate that you've helped soothe the pain inside me. I hate that I'm greedy enough to keep wanting more, all while I know I'm not worthy. I brought this nightmare upon myself, and I can't run away from it."

His entire body wracked with violent belief of his admission. "But do you know what I hate the most? I *hate* that others are paying for my mistakes. *She* is paying for my mistakes. And I can't stop it. I can't fucking do a goddamn thing about it, and it's killing me knowing I've let her down, let so many people down. *Fuck!*"

I didn't speak, waiting for Gil to continue purging, willing him to speak and hopefully remove the festering guilt inside him.

But he didn't continue.

He didn't breathe or twitch or gather me closer.

It was as if he'd been possessed by honesty, granted a small window in which to talk, before the alcohol ripped away his coherency and shoved him face first into unconsciousness.

"Gil…" I rubbed his arm around my stomach. "Gil, talk to me."

He couldn't go to sleep. Not now. Not after so many confusing, terrible confessions.

Confessions that made no sense and only layered me with a deep-seated terror.

Who was 'she'? Was he in love with someone else? Was that why he felt guilty with me in his bed when all along he loved another? Who were paying for his mistakes? *What* mistakes?

"Gil." I pinched him.

But it was no use.

He was awake but no longer willing to narrate his secrets.

His arms banded tight and possessive. His legs hooked through mine. Our bodies plastered together, head to toe. "Go to sleep, Olin Moss. Go to sleep and forget everything I said. Forget about me. Forget you ever knew a man who would willingly put you in the face of danger all because he was too weak to say no."

"What danger have you put me in?"

He sighed. And in that sigh, too many things existed.

Too much pain.

Too much history.

Too much unknown.

"I can't answer that."

"Is it about the murdered girls? Are you involved…after all?"

He flinched behind me. "Shush. Go to sleep."

"Gil…"

"Hush." He clung to me and allowed alcohol to dull his senses.

He might have the cushion of liquor to aid his tattered heartbeats, but I didn't.

And instead of sleep, we stayed bound and entwined just as dawn arrived.

Both very aware something had happened in the dark.

That we'd broken any hope of a future.
That everything had happened too late.

Chapter Thirty-Four

Olin

-The Present-

DEATH.

Another murder.

Another girl's body painted and left in broad daylight, her camouflaged skin turning her invisible to those who sought to save her.

I stood in Gil's living room, dressed in a fresh skirt and copper blouse, ready to go to work so I didn't lose my job.

Gil had fallen asleep an hour or so ago.

I hadn't.

My thoughts had kept me far too busy—the exact opposite of counting sheep. I'd been running in my mind, and utter exhaustion made my limbs heavy as I struggled out of Gil's entrapment and slipped from his bed.

He'd stayed unconscious and in the enviable slumber of vodka while I'd flittered around dressing and making myself presentable.

I hadn't consciously decided what tomorrow would bring. I'd allowed the sunshine to warm his warehouse, content to stay in Gil's cage until he could shed light on the shadows he'd brought into my world.

But the longer he'd slept behind me, the more my fear couldn't be ignored. He'd tried to tell me something last night. He'd tried to be honest yet couldn't reveal the full story.

Was it because he himself didn't know? Or because he had a bigger role to play than I'd imagined?

Moving to his kitchen, I stole a cup of coffee, doing my best to chase away the dregs of fatigue. While sipping on bitter caffeine, I tried to unravel the knots Gil had given me, but the coffee wasn't strong enough and I didn't have enough of the pieces.

Whatever he'd told me last night was worthless unless he painted a bigger picture.

And that was why I'd decided to go to work.

I knew he wouldn't want me to. To be honest, I didn't want to go either. Being chased yesterday and having someone in my apartment had made me listen to Gil's warnings.

But I also couldn't afford to lose my job.

I had my own life to tend to, even if he was intent on destroying his.

Heading into the bathroom with my toothbrush from my overnight bag, I layered it with minty paste and began brushing. While doing the routine task, I swiped on my phone, ready to summon an Uber.

My toothbrush promptly landed in the sink in a splash of green paste.

I clutched my phone, shaking my head as I skimmed the news app that I'd downloaded a few days ago.

I'd wanted to keep track of the murdered girls. Now, I wished I'd kept my head in the sand. Articles and 'breaking news' bulletins littered my screen with alerts.

Another girl had been taken.

Another life stolen.

She'd been found in the undergrowth at Moseley Bog Nature Reserve. A small wilderness where families and walkers could explore wooden pathways and soak up the serenity of trees.

I'd walked there myself. I'd found it tranquil and picturesque.

Now, it was a cemetery where an innocent woman had died.

Nausea swiftly gathered. My heart relocated into my mouth as I read:

Another victim was found this morning thanks to a mother and son taking a stroll like they do every morning in their local park. Unlike the recent painted murders, where cleverly camouflaged girls were gagged and bound, rendered silent and trapped while they died of exposure and dehydration, this new victim was bled out at a different location while her painted corpse was hidden next to the bog with rushes and bluebells.

I swayed.

Gil had been out till late.

He'd been afraid of what tomorrow would bring.

He'd been muddy and tormented and turned to a bottle for salvation.

Salvation from what?

From murder?

From painting a cadaver?

From being a part of something I'd hoped and prayed he could never do?

My legs gave out, slamming me against the sink as my skin grew clammy with terror.

It couldn't be.

Gil had been with the police for most of the day.

He wouldn't have had the time to capture, paint, and kill. *And yet...*

He didn't come home for hours.

He acted as if his life was almost over.

He behaved like someone who'd given in to the worst kind of master.

My sickness swelled and crested, demanding fresh air and answers.

I opened another article, desperate for some hint that no matter the evidence, it couldn't have been Gil. I wanted the killer to have been apprehended and in custody.

I want all of this to be over.

With icy sweat running down my spine, I found further condemnation.

The police are still calling for help from anyone who might've seen someone suspicious last night between the hours of ten p.m. and six a.m. They are following enquires but so far have no leads. However, at least this time, a clue has been left behind. A boot print was found by the body. Size eleven Timberland with all-terrain tread. Please call your local law enforcement if you find footwear relating to this crime.

Fighting the urge to vomit, I stumbled from the bathroom and into Gil's room where he still slept like the dead. Holding my breath, I fell to my knees by his filthy boots.

The boots he'd kicked off as if he couldn't stand having

them touch him any longer.

The clothing he'd shed like someone would shed a nightmare.

My fingers burned as I hefted the heavy weight of his tan, paint-splattered Timberlands, and turned them upside down.

Please be any other size.

Please!

Size eleven.

Covered in mud.

Smeared in truth.

I bit my lip until I drew blood, scrambling to my feet as fast as I could.

No.

Spinning to face a sleeping Gil, I swallowed back rage and fear.

No.

He'd done so many things.

I'd given him so many excuses.

He was so much more than just this.

No.

My eyes fell on his boots again.

There could be another explanation.

He could've gone for a walk after his police interview.

He could've needed the silence and tranquillity only a park provided.

He could've—

No.

I could be blind.

I could be hopeful.

But I couldn't be naïve.

I couldn't trust in the past or in my useless, stupid heart.

He confessed to something…

He admitted he'd made mistakes.

He looked so innocent and harrowed, raked with hardship and sketched with despair. Whatever had happened to him had turned him into something I didn't want to see.

I didn't want to believe.

I didn't want to give up fighting for the Gil I used to love.

But…how could I refute hard evidence?

How could I ignore what my instincts had been whispering all along?

The boy I was in love with had grown into a monster.

A monster who was secretive and sly and asleep before me.
It's not him!
You've already been through this!
You've spoken to Justin.
You've asked him to his face.
So why did I back away?

Why did I grab my handbag and tiptoe through his warehouse?

Why did my instincts whisper to run, run, *run?*

I broke my promise and left when he needed me most.

Rain pummelled my clothes as I leapt from Gil's warehouse and slipped into his hatchback.

I'm sorry.
His keys allowed me to steal his car.

His scent still lingered on my skin.

I'm afraid.
I needed space to think.

To worry.

I need to be alone.

Chapter Thirty-Five

Gil

-The Past-

FUNNY HOW LIFE could promise such hope, then snatch it away so quickly.

Funny how a heart could love someone *so much* even when it could never have them.

I still loved Olin.

But she wasn't mine.

She could never be mine again.

My love for her didn't accept that, turning into a vicious, hungry thing.

It gnawed on me every day and crippled me every night.

I wanted it to stop.

I begged it to go away.

But...it only increased.

Drop by drop, I drowned in agony for what I'd lost.

School had ceased being my salvation. Now, the corridors were a tomb rather than a maze I was lost in. A tomb where my heart was condemned to die because I was no longer allowed to love Olin or had the privilege to dream of our future freedom together.

The corridors and classrooms were worse than the whorehouse I lived in. My sins echoed in the gym. My corruption painted the building's bricks.

I *despised* it.

I'd had everything taken from me.

Everything.

And still my love continued to bleed me dry.

But in my dark, dismal world, at least the woman who'd granted such loneliness stayed true to her word.

One night.

She'd used me for one night. She'd placed a photo of the girl I loved on a side table while she fucked me raw. And then…when she'd ensured I wasn't fit to touch anyone else, she'd set me free.

I'd stumbled from her hotel room at four in the morning, bruised, dehydrated, and trembling. Red marks rimmed my wrists from the handcuffs she'd used. Teeth indents tattooed me from where she'd lost control and hurt me.

I felt more exhausted than I ever had in my life, more hurt than any fist my dad could deliver, and more adrift than I ever thought possible.

When Monday rolled around, I couldn't face Olin.

I couldn't sit in a classroom with her while our teacher's scratch marks branded my body. I couldn't stop the wash of sickness each time I relived how many times Tallup had fucked me and ensured I would never be worthy of Olin again.

I'd gone to our teacher a virgin.

I'd left a monster.

And the gorgeous girl I wanted for my own was now far too good for the likes of me.

I was used and dirty.

Contaminated.

Defiled.

If that wasn't enough to keep me away, the knowledge that Tallup would ruin Olin's chances at university were the final nails in my crypt.

Seeing Olin's pinched and tear-blushed face tore out my heart and left it rotting for eternity. A few days after our ending, she chased me on the field.

Her bag fell from her body, her lips spread in a hopeful hello, she went to launch into my arms with apologies.

Apologies?

Fuck, she'd done nothing wrong.

I had.

I'd betrayed her.

Betrayed our future and our promises.

Holding up my hand, I stopped her from hugging me. My own sadness choked me until I almost broke. My teeth clenched, my stomach roiled, and I teetered on kneeling before her.

I missed her so goddamn much.

But I'd sold my soul to the devil to save her.

This nightmare was mine to endure, not hers.

I would protect her future by removing myself from it. I'd made a vow as Tallup gagged me, staring at Olin's picture on the dresser that I would never prevent the girl I loved from living the life she was meant to.

Tallup had agreed to let her go.

I'd paid the price.

But there was still a tax on that payment. A tax of silence. Not one word to the girl I would always love. Not one hint that I still cared.

The only thing I could do while Olin begged me to explain was step back, shake my head, and leave.

That was the second time that I broke Olin's heart but definitely not the last.

Every day, she sought me out, and every day, I didn't say a word. I sank deeper and deeper into ice, hoping the glaciers in my eyes would warn her to keep her distance.

In class, I studied her pretty hair while she sat in front of me.

In my mind, I apologised over and over.

In my heart, I screamed. I told her I loved her with every breath. I promised her I always would. I begged her to forgive me.

The only person enjoying my heartbreak was Tallup.

Her tiny smirk hidden beneath her teacher's tone. Her eyes smug and satisfied.

A love-killer, hope-stealer.

A total fucking succubus to the end.

* * * * *

"Gil! Please." Olin dashed toward me after school.

A few weeks had passed.

I'd lost weight. I barely slept. I welcomed the beatings my dad gave me now because it was the only way to leech out the pain.

I drove my hands deeper into my jeans pockets, striding faster.

She chased me, catching up as we rounded the corner of the street.

"Gil." Her hand landed on my arm, her eyes watering, lips thin with stress. "I can't do this anymore. I need to know why you suddenly don't want to be with me." Tears fell, sticking to white cheeks. "I'm sorry. I don't know what I did…but I love you. I miss you." She walked into me, pressing her forehead to my chest. "I miss you *so* much."

I stepped away, dislodging her hold. "Go home, Olin."

That was the worst part.

Not being able to walk her home.

Not knowing she was safe.

Not escorting her through shadows and sinners.

She followed me, her breath catching with wet tears. "Please. *Talk* to me. I don't know what's going on."

I didn't speak.

My boots thudded as she chased me down the road.

"Gil…*please!*" A sob hiccupped in her chest. "If we talk about this, we can go back to the way it was."

It was too much.

To believe we could be together again? To think I could have her, despite everything?

It hurt.

It fucking *hurt.*

I whirled on her, my nostrils flaring, temper firing. "Leave me alone, Olin. I won't tell you again."

No more nicknames starting with O.

No more togetherness after school.

It was over.

All of it.

She trembled on the sidewalk, her mouth opening and closing as if she wanted to argue but didn't know how. For a second, hate flashed in her gaze.

And it tore out what pieces I had left and threw them in the gutter.

Then she launched herself at me, her hands reaching for my cheeks, her lips seeking mine.

I didn't think.

I just reacted.

I shoved her back, making her trip and stumble.

Shit.

Shit!

I moved to support her, but I forced myself to lurch backward instead.

The last time someone had touched me, kissed me, it had been against my control. I supposed, in some way, I would have to work through that violation if I ever stood a chance at having a good relationship with affection again. But there, on that street, I couldn't stomach the thought of Olin's lips on mine.

Not after Tallup's had been there.

I wasn't *clean* anymore.

"Forget about me," I muttered, turning away from her. "Just forget I ever existed."

* * * * *

She didn't forget about me.

For weeks after, Olin tried to talk to me countless times. Cornering me in the corridor, trapping me in the classroom, chasing me over the grounds.

Tallup was there for all of it; her smugness making me sick. Her rules making me howl for this to be over.

I wanted to leave.

To run.

I'd begun having nightmares on the rare occasions I actually slept.

Dreams of being tied down, unwanted fingers on my body, hated tongues on my cock. I'd dream of Olin being violated like I had. I'd dream of both of us dying.

I'd wake in a full sweat, listening to the sounds of fucking in the next room and wished I could stop myself from ever falling in love with Olin.

Because my love for her was now twisted with what happened in that hotel room.

I hated my body.

I hated the reactions it had and the erection that'd condemned me.

I didn't care I'd been tricked into taking Viagra—it was still me who fucked my teacher, and I couldn't unscramble that from choice or command.

"Gil."

I rounded the corner by the gym, almost smashing into Olin where she waited for me. Her bag rested by her feet, her hands wrung in front of her, shadows decorated beneath sleep-tired eyes.

I sighed hard, pretending impatience and chilly disdain when really it took everything I had not to crush her to me and beg for her forgiveness.

"I love you, Gil. Doesn't that mean anything?" She reached for me, her body jerky and foolish.

Again, I just reacted. Instincts that no longer attributed affection with love lashed out and hurt the one person I never wanted to hurt.

Affection came at a cost. A cost I could no longer afford.

My hand latched around her throat, and I shoved her against the brick wall. I was tired and struggling, and I had nothing else to give.

Nothing else to offer.

I was dead.

And she deserved better. "Stop. Just stop."

She stiffened.

I froze.

Time stood still as I physically mauled her.

Bruised her just like Tallup had bruised me.

I reeled backward, ripping my touch from her, drenched with disgust and dismay.

Fuck!

Trembles hijacked my limbs as I almost tripped to the ground.

Olin stood there, shock making her eyes wide, fear making her breath fast.

And we stared at each other.

Stared with our history and our hope, knowing that this was the moment it was truly over.

She didn't say a thing.

I couldn't.

I turned and walked away from the best thing, the only thing, my forever.

* * * * *

She started dating Justin Miller a few weeks after I'd bruised her.

The first time I caught them together, I ran off school property before I did something that would end with me in jail for two crimes.

Seeing her with him?

I couldn't bear it.

I couldn't *survive* it.

I'd taken three steps toward Olin, words on my tongue full of apology. Of how much I missed her, wanted her, needed her, *craved* her. I'd taken another three with my fists curled ready to pummel Justin's face into his skull.

But somehow, in the mist of possession and pain, I stopped.

If I told Olin how much I loved her, Tallup would ruin her life and have me arrested. And if beat up Justin Miller for laughing with the girl who owned my heart, I'd be sentenced to yet another crime.

It took everything I had, but I endured the flirting, the tentative smiles, the knowledge that Justin touched her.

I deliberately picked fights with my old man when I caught them kissing behind the gym where I'd shown her my sketch book for the first time. I thought I'd die from the way my chest split in two.

But I didn't die.

And my father cracked a rib with his drunken fist.

Week after week, I had to bear witness to Olin replacing me with another. And week after week, I crumbled inside, turning into an empty shell of grief.

By the time school holidays rolled around, I was hanging on by a fucking thread.

Knowing Olin would spend most of her time with Justin during the holidays.

Wondering if she'd give him her virginity.

Imagining her kissing him, laughing with him, *touching* him.

Fuck, it made me break into a million pieces and roar with fury.

I'd have nightmares of him hurting her like Tallup had hurt me. Visions of Olin writhing in ecstasy with someone who wasn't me.

It was enough to drive me insane.

Maybe I was already insane.

Even my father started leaving me alone. His beatings weren't as often, his slurs and drunken tirades not as loud— almost as if he didn't like the way I encouraged them, accepted them, needed them.

I got a job working at a local construction company, accepting payment in cash. In return for hard labour, I earned money to repay my debts. I returned to the places I'd stolen from and left the exact dollar amount for what I'd taken—the art supply shop where I'd stolen the cans of spray paint. The stationery store where I'd nicked a sketchpad and pencils.

Once I'd paid them, I bought more supplies, returning to the freedom painting gave me.

I graffitied the ugly corners of town.

I doodled the unwanted pavements of alleyways.

I filled paper with my heartbreak.

And through it all, I never stopped watching her, protecting her, waiting on the street outside her house…making sure she was safe.

Chapter Thirty-Six

Olin

-The Present-

YESTERDAY, MY PHONE had no power to reach Gilbert Clark.

No matter how much I begged it to connect me to him, each attempt was futile.

Now, when I needed space, the damn thing wouldn't stop ringing.

I'd gone to work this morning.

I'd left Gil's hatchback parked a few blocks from my office and walked to the office without being assaulted or kidnapped. I'd pretended it was a perfectly normal day even though my nerves were fraught.

I uninstalled the news app from my phone, unable to handle the regular updates on the painted murders. I plastered on a professional smile and allowed Status Enterprises to surround me in its usual hive of employees settling in for a long day. I pretended everything was normal—that I had a boyfriend with normal secrets, that I had a love story worthy of fairy-tales.

When Shannon appeared at my cubicle at lunch, I'd apologised profusely for the mess my life had become. I'd thanked her for the opportunity of employment and promised I wouldn't let her down again.

She'd given me a hug when exhausted, screwed-up tears wobbled my voice, making me hate myself for my weakness.

For my confusion.

For my aching, breaking heart while I suspected the worst

thing anyone could suspect of another.

I couldn't stop picturing Gil's muddy size eleven boots.

I couldn't stop connecting dots from his disappearance, to the unusual vodka use, to the night-shrouded confessions.

On the inside, I was an absolute catastrophe—tangled and tired, doing my best to latch onto an answer that would make sense of the labyrinth I'd been dragged into.

On the outside, I sat in my cubicle, replied to emails, and answered calls. I was the perfect employee, doing the job she was paid to do.

I'd managed to stay busy until lunchtime.

To stay away from Google and stop conjuring stories without facts. But when I caught the elevator to the second floor café, I'd made the mistake of checking my phone.

Ten missed calls from Gil.

The first only a few minutes after I'd left him—as if he'd sensed I was no longer in his home.

I deliberated calling him back, but I had no idea what to say. He'd dumped his hardships on me last night without any concrete explanation of what it all meant. I needed time to understand—or at least try to. I needed space to clear my mind before I could handle any further conversation that I couldn't decipher.

Gil may or may not be a killer. He may or may not be blackmailed into doing things he despised. He may or may not have a tragic secret in his past that explained everything he did in his present.

The only thing that would help us move on from this mess would be honesty. Bitter, brutal honesty with nothing left out.

And I didn't think he was ready. Didn't think he had the strength to tell me what he hid in that second bedroom, where he was last night, or why he disappeared at the same time two girls went missing.

And if he wasn't ready to talk about it…I definitely wasn't ready to listen.

Just the thought of my suspicions being a tiny bit true made my stomach slither and slide into my feet.

Keeping my phone on vibrate, I'd forced myself to eat a salad sandwich. With my stomach churning, the struggle was hard even though I was lightheaded from hunger.

Avoiding fellow employee stares and unwilling to be sociable, I opened an internet browser, falling down the rabbit hole of news sites and murder investigations.

With shaking hands and racing heart, I read more details on the latest killing, skimmed hypothesises, and drank up potential descriptions from so-called witnesses.

The vague description was a man wearing a baseball hat. No distinguishing features like hair colour or tattoos. Just a masculine shadow.

Gil had never worn a baseball hat in his life.

Was it purely a disguise or was his wardrobe yet another thing I knew nothing about?

You know so little...

I gritted my teeth.

I know his heart. That doesn't change.

I sighed, tracing my thumb over the picture of the girl killed last night, following the artistic shadows and splashes of bluebells painted on her lifeless thigh.

Are you sure? Hearts can change. Hearts can camouflage into strangers.

Shaking my head, I locked my phone and slipped it into my bag. It felt a thousand times heavier than normal as I tossed out the rest of my lunch and went back to work.

* * * * *

The work day was over.

Employees slowly filtered from the building, heading home to loved ones.

I literally had nowhere to go.

My apartment wasn't safe. Gil wasn't safe. Justin couldn't be expected to babysit me.

I didn't know where to go and I still didn't have enough information.

And I needed it fast so I could make up my mind on what to trust: my heart or my mind.

My heart urged me to return to Gil and tell him how I felt. To provide a non-judgemental, totally accepting environment in which he could spill his every revelation. But my mind cursed me for being such a stupid fool. It wanted to call the police. To use the card the female officer had provided and ask outsiders for advice.

And because both options weren't practical, I had to rely on myself to make a correct, informed decision. Just as I'd had to rely on myself to cook, clean, and study when I was young. The one lesson my parents taught me well: independence was hard and lonely, but it meant you were strong no matter the situation.

As the last of the staff left for the day, my fingers flew over the keyboard.

I inputted every parameter I could. I read online articles and trawled through facts.

Gilbert Clark.

Murdered girls.

Previous Birmingham killings.

Maps of the forests and parks where the girls had been found.

Body paint supply stores.

Other body painters in England.

Bad publicity on *Total Trickery*, good press, negative reviews, glowing feedback.

I diligently did my research all while earning a chest full of frustrated heartbeats and a headache of confusion.

Nothing hinted that Gil could be involved.

The longer I stayed online, the more I hated myself for doubting.

I wanted so, *so* much to trust my heart. I wanted to be brave enough to return to Gil's and ask him point blank where he was last night. Why he'd vanished for the second time. Why he'd been traipsing around in the undergrowth. Why my instincts told me there was more to his life than he'd told me. More darkness. More pain. More sin.

But all I could think about were his muddy boots.

Size eleven.

Same as the killer.

I needed more time.

Time where no one could find me.

Using the elevator, I left work by the back entrance in case Gil waited for me in the foyer like last time. Stepping out into narrower streets, I tucked my dark blonde hair beneath a grey scarf stuffed in my purse.

Jamming hands into my blazer pockets, I weaved with end-of-day foot traffic, making my way from the work district to the more artsy side of town. Where small theatres hugged street corners and posters displaying colourful dancers decorated lampposts.

Stepping into the area where I'd practiced my art before moving to London, I struggled not to cry.

I missed dance.

I missed the smell of musty picture houses and papery playbills.

I missed Gil even while I hid from him.

Dance practice had finished for the day for full-time staff, and it seemed no after-school classes were held tonight as I slipped into the studio where I'd first been noticed by the London Dance Company. I'd sweated and cried and flown on endorphin highs in rooms that all looked similar.

Mirrored and wooden floored, a simple stage for a ballerina.

I no longer belonged here.

My accident had stolen that right.

The door clicked behind me; the heavy silence of the space hugged me tight.

Closing my eyes, I inhaled deep.

Tears sprang to my eyes as leotards and ballet slippers and sweet piano notes pirouetted on my senses.

I was safe here because no one would expect me to come. Those who used to know me had grown used to my absence, and those who didn't would never know what each dance studio—no matter where they were—meant to me.

Dropping my purse on the piano stool, I kicked off my heels and placed my silenced phone on the polished wood of the ivory-keyed instrument.

Ten more missed calls from Gil since lunch.

Ten more times I didn't answer because I had no idea what to say.

I wanted him to tell me everything.

But I was too in love with him to hear the truth.

Innocent.

Guilty.

Both came with complications I wasn't strong enough to bear.

Balancing on my toes, I spun in my stockings on the slippery wooden floor and closed my eyes. I ignored the twinge in my back where surgeries had given me the gift of mobility but taken away lithe grace. I clenched my teeth against the tightness and restriction of stolen movement. Notes of music whispered around me, and I danced...alone.

My arms rose like useless wings as I glided and spun.

My childhood found me as it so often did when I released myself from adulthood. I remembered the loneliness of having parents who didn't really care. I basked in the happiness of knowing Gil loved me enough for any missing or absentee family. My arms fanned out to hug the teenage boy who owned my soul. The music in my veins spread louder, faster, and I answered the summons.

I threw myself into the air, performing a move I'd perfected. The grand écart en l'air had been my favourite. I found it so easy. So effortless to soar from one leg to another and slice my legs into splits at the highest point.

My teacher and employer said no one could bend as much as I could in full flight.

My eyes stayed closed as I relived the sensation of being unbelievably good at something that didn't require skill or repetition—it was just a gift. My body's gift. My soul's purpose. My life's design.

But unlike so many other hundreds of times, I didn't land weightless and elegant. I didn't manage to kick and split. I didn't have that priceless gift anymore.

My ruined back seized mid-bend.

My healed bones and stitched together muscles hadn't forgotten the punishment they'd endured.

I landed with a teeth-rattling jar on my knees, bowing on the floor before mirrors that'd witnessed my failure.

And my silenced phone vibrated against the piano.

Ring.

Ring.

Ring.

Tears cascaded down my cheeks as I accepted the physical pain as well as emotional. I'd come here to torture myself deeper. To layer more agony. It might not have been intentional but the pain was double as I crawled toward the piano and grabbed my phone.

It stopped ringing; I slouched against the mirrors and stared blankly at the screen.

Gil.

I couldn't call him back.

I couldn't talk to Justin.

I couldn't turn to my old dancers.

I couldn't go home and lick my wounds.

All I could do was sit there and let my mind dance faster than my body ever could.

* * * * *

I stayed until well past dark.

Until cleaners wheeled their squeaky mop buckets, washed up shed-sweat, and tidied spaces for another day of practice tomorrow.

My stomach had quit complaining about hunger an hour or so ago, disgruntled at me for ignoring its demands. My heart had stopped grieving for my stolen abilities. My mind was exhausted from chasing thoughts and theories on Gil.

My phone was almost dead from the many internet searches and more research on the murdered painted girls.

I'd overstayed my welcome, and as much as I'd like to stay hidden, my options had drastically reduced to just one.

Regardless of Gil's involvement, I was safer with him than anyone else.

I needed to sleep, to shower, to eat.

I needed answers so I could kiss Gil goodbye if he wasn't the person I hoped or stand by his side if it was all a terrible coincidence.

Either way, answers would be given tonight.

The Master of Trickery had tricked me enough.

It was time for the truth.

Even if it killed...everything.

My phone buzzed again.

Instead of it being another call from Gil, Justin's name popped up with a message.

Justin Miller: *Your turn to disappear, huh? Can you call me and let me know you're okay. Gil is frantic. To be honest, he's scaring me a little. This morning all he wanted to do was find you so he could talk to you. Now, he's telling me to find you and keep you the hell away from him. What the hell is going on, O? Message me back, and I'll come pick you up. You're staying at my place until we figure this out.*

Before I could exit out of the message, he sent another one.

Justin Miller: *I don't know where you are but don't go see Gil alone. I don't trust him right now.*

I sighed. Just like in high-school, I was trapped between two boys. One boy was the poster child for good behaviour, helpful manners, and kind deeds. The other was the warning bulletin for bad families, harsh poverty, and dirty secrets.

I'd fallen in love with the wrong one.

I'd chosen my path.

I no longer had a choice.

I never had a choice.

Clicking reply, I typed:

Olin Moss: *I'm going to see Gil. I'm fine. I'll talk to you later.*

Locking my phone, I slung my bag onto my shoulder, took one last look at the studio that survived the death of my dreams, and slipped into the night.

Chapter Thirty-Seven

Olin

-The Present-

THE WAREHOUSE DIDN'T seem pleased to see me.

The hulking brick and graffiti held no welcome.

But at least no black van lurked down the drive and no nasty kidnappers tried to steal me as I turned off Gil's hatchback and opened the door.

I'd been a car thief. Even if I hadn't wanted to face Gil, I would've had to return his vehicle at some point.

A whip of biting wind howled down the long avenue of warehouses.

The chill made me shiver.

Wrapping arms around myself, I hugged away my trembles as best I could. My back still ached from my stupid attempt at a grand écart en l'air, and my knees held bruises from cushioning my fall.

My phone held another seven missed calls, and I braced myself for Gil's reaction when he finally found me on his doorstep.

You can do this.

I straightened my spine.

Ask him sternly but nicely.

I sucked in a deep breath.

Don't let him change the subject or argue.

My eyes fell to the pedestrian access. The door remained closed, but something white wedged in the gap between interior and exterior.

Walking toward the graffiti, I hissed at my new bruises and ducked to collect the large envelope.

I frowned as I smoothed out the blank, unaddressed mail.

Perhaps Gil didn't have a letter box? Maybe the postman always delivered correspondence this way?

Standing straight, I raised my hand to knock. To get this confrontation over with. But my eyes drifted to the envelope again and my fingers traced the unseen contents.

No name...odd.

Unsealed...strange.

Firm.

Smooth.

A clue to...something.

Breaking the law and Gil's trust, I shoved my handbag higher up my shoulder and tugged open the unstuck envelope.

Holding my breath, I pulled out a single piece of paper and a photo.

Oxygen no longer resided in my lungs.

My blood turned to sleet and my heart to lifeless stone as I read a terrifying threat. A threat addressed to The Body Painter but designed for his Living Canvas.

Me.

Her.

Tonight.

No more excuses.

Time to choose.

It's her or I steal your most precious love forever.

The simple sentences were typed in bold font and printed in morbid black. A command, not a request.

I swallowed a cry as I dropped the paper and clutched the photo.

A photo of me.

Of me leaving my office building tonight with my grey scarf hiding my hair, my steps quick and furtive.

Anxiety and fear shattered the ice crystals in my veins, sending fire into my heart. I no longer stood frozen on Gil's stoop, I reeled backward, trying to unravel this new riddle.

But the door opened.

The door opened, and Gil was there.

And our eyes met with all the sorrow in the world.

His gaze dropped to the photo in my hands.

His skin turned white.

His face slipped into torment.

He almost stumbled to one knee.

Almost.

His hand clutched at the doorframe, keeping him upright as a riot of despair and horror claimed him. His throat worked hard as if he was seconds away from vomiting. His eyes filled with tears, his head shook in denial, and his voice broke as he muttered something incomprehensible.

His utter heartbreak scared me worse than anything.

This was truth.

Here was the evidence I needed.

Gil wasn't a killer.

But he *was* involved.

Somehow.

And now…so was I.

I backed up, throwing the photo in his direction. "Don't touch me. Don't come near me."

My voice slapped away his anguish, bowing his head in defeat.

When his eyes met mine again, there were no more tears. No more torment. Just the deepest, saddest misery in his wretched green gaze. "Olin…I tried calling you."

"I needed time to think."

"I called to tell you to stay away." His voice caught with rage. "Why the fuck did you come back? You weren't supposed to come back."

"We needed to talk."

"We needed to never see each other again." He pinched the bridge of his nose as if every headache in the world crippled him at once. "I left messages. I told you…" Stepping from his warehouse, he stalked toward me. "I tried to tell you. I warned you. I—"

"Don't come any closer." My hand swooped up, forming a wall between us. A wall blocking off our teenage tragedy and fledgling broken romance. "I'm leaving."

His head shook again, sadly, slowly. "I wish you'd never come. I wouldn't have had a choice then."

"Forget I did. I'll go. Right now."

His hands opened and closed. His eyes fell to the photo on the ground. For a moment, he nodded as if he agreed. Agreed that my disappearance was the only thing to do. That he chose me over whatever consequence would follow.

But then, he buried his face into his hands and screamed. He roared with helplessness. He bellowed in whatever trap he couldn't escape.

And he didn't choose me.

He chose the alternative.

He accepted that my life was forfeited even while I fought to persuade him otherwise.

One step fell toward me as his head tipped up and desperation etched his features. "I can't let you do that."

I backed up, my heart winging with terror. "Gil...let me walk away."

"I wish I could." He chased me. Hunted me. Sad and defeated. Determined and depressed. "I'm so sorry, O. So, *so* fucking sorry."

"Why are you sorry? What have you done?"

He choked on words too horrendous to utter. He swallowed them back, along with any sign of the boy who'd protected me in our youth. "I need you to come inside now."

"I'm not going anywhere with you."

He gave a half-smile, reeking of destruction. "You don't have a choice. Not anymore."

"I *always* have a choice."

His voice dropped to a whisper. A whisper that was worse than any shout or curse. "Did you have a choice when life took away your dancing? Did you have a choice when I left you at school?"

"You can't twist this. In this, I have a choice."

"You're wrong." His hand came up to capture my cheek.

I flinched from his touch, but he kept pursuing me until his icy skin seared into my flesh. He held me tenderly but firmly. A lover's caress all while chains wrapped tight around me.

"I lost everything the moment you found me again. I thought I'd lost it all when I left you in high-school, but that pain is nothing, *nothing*, to the fucking agony now." His fingers dug into my cheekbone, seeking forgiveness, absolution. "I wanted you, but I should never have been so weak. I was selfish. So fucking selfish to keep you. This is all my fault, O. I take full blame. I will never, *ever* forgive myself."

"There's nothing to forgive. Not yet." I looked toward the street, begging for someone to fix this. To replace this terrifying, shattered version of Gilbert Clark with the protective loving one I knew.

But no one came.

We were alone.

"I've done so many things that are past forgiveness." Gil's eyes blazed with self-hatred. "Including letting you back into my life. The moment you appeared, I should've chased you away. I should've hurt you if it meant you'd never return."

"You couldn't have kept me away. I can't leave when you're—"

"I told you your goodness would get you killed." He interrupted me, his voice strange and thick, full of misery. "You've always been the one I put above everyone. I would've done anything for you, O, been anyone, fought everything…but in this, you can't come first."

"I never *asked* to come first."

"No, of course you wouldn't." His temper flared. "You'd never expect someone to love you over *everything* else. It wouldn't even cross your mind that you'd be that precious, that wanted…especially after having parents who treated you as if you were an inconvenience."

"Gil…" My heart smashed against my ribs. "Stop."

"You didn't ask to come first, but you were. *I* put you first. I never wanted you to be hurt. I did everything I could to stop people taking away what you wanted because you deserved someone to fight for you. Someone to look after you as well as you looked after everyone else."

Tears gathered. "Is that what you did? Did you leave to…protect me?"

He stiffened, his own grief glittered. "It doesn't matter."

"Don't. Don't shut down. Tell me!"

His gaze fell to the photo of me on the ground. "None of that matters now." His energy siphoned down his legs and soaked into the ground, leaving him downcast and tragic. "Time has run out. We have to go inside."

"Let me go home." My pulse pounded. "Whatever you think you have to do, you don't. Gil, please."

He sighed brokenly. "I told you, you weren't safe with me, O." He couldn't hide the heartsickness inside. "Maybe now you'll believe me."

"I won't let you do something that I know isn't you!"

He reached for me. "I wish it was that easy."

I ducked away; I spun to run.

But my back hadn't recovered from my idiotic attempt at

dance. My knees hadn't forgiven me. My broken and pieced together body wasn't limber or swift like it once was.

I moved.

He moved faster.

His hand locked around my wrist, jerking me to a halt. "I tried to stop him from having you. I truly did." His other hand cupped my throat as if we were two lovers beneath the stars. His thumb ran along the column of my neck, burning with snow and shaking with regret. "I told him I'd do whatever it took. I'd do things I'd refused to do. I'd pay any price. I'd stay in servitude for the rest of my godforsaken life. All to protect you." His forehead nudged mine as he pulled me into him. "I would've given anything to protect you, but his price is too high. I can't save you both."

"What are you talking about?" I struggled to release myself, wriggling in his hold. But he was too strong. Too focused. Too lost.

"Him. The man who owns me heart and soul."

"Who?"

"It doesn't matter."

"Stop saying that!" Anger washed through me. "I hate that reply. It *does* matter. It *matters!* Tell me. What does that bastard have over you?"

Gil dragged me into him. A hug full of menace and apology. His free hand threaded through my hair to cup the base of my skull. With a tattered sigh, he kissed my forehead with glacial lips.

A kiss that throbbed with true love. "I'm just as in love with you as I was back then...did you know that?" His breath warmed my skin before pulling away and nuzzling his nose with mine. "I've *always* been in love with you. This will end me. I might save a life by taking yours...but mine has been forfeit ever since I lost you the first time."

I closed my eyes, seeking strength. "I don't know what any of this means. I'm so *sick* of not knowing."

"It means, I love you. I always have. I always will."

My lashes soared upward, locking our gazes together. "If you love me, stop this. Come with me. We'll go to the police. They'll—"

"Lock me up for so many crimes. I deserve to be put in a cage. I've been avoiding punishment for years. But I can't be incarcerated because then I can't save her."

"Her?"

His entire body flinched.

A hitch caught in his chest.

Agony tiptoed over me. "Who is she, Gil?"

"Someone who comes first." His whisper shattered me into bleeding, gasping shards. "I'd die for her. I probably *will* die for her. And you..." His stare shredded mine. "You'll..." His voice broke. He shook his head, swallowing hard. "We'll all probably die...but I have to try."

"Don't." I fought in his embrace. "The police will listen to what you're going through. They won't lock you away without cause."

He huffed blackly. "They have cause. So many fucking causes."

"I'm sure if we *talk* to them..." My voice wavered as more tears trickled down my face. "Gil...please. You're not alone anymore. You don't have to fight this by yourself. No one...no one has to die."

"If I knew it would save both of you...I'd slit my wrists right here."

"Don't say that. What sort of world would it be if you weren't in it?" I tried to touch him gently, to shove aside my fear and hug him tight. But self-preservation howled in my blood, desperate to run, screaming to flee.

"Goddammit, Olin." He stepped back, pulling me toward the open door and the darkness beyond. "Even now, you're still so good. You still think I can be redeemed."

"You can."

"No, I can't." He jerked me closer to death. "I love you so much it's ripping my fucking heart out, but I can't stop this."

Tugging against his pressure, I scratched at his fingers. "If you love me, you'd find a way."

"There is no way. Believe me...I've tried."

"Tried what?"

"To stop him. To end him."

I shivered. "What does that *mean*? You have to give me more—"

"It means love isn't enough." He sighed painfully, stepping over the threshold and dragging me inside with him. The warehouse seemed to twist and moan with denial at what was about to happen in its walls.

"Gil. Don't." I fought. I pulled, but my struggle was nothing to him. His strength far eclipsed mine.

I wanted to scream and yell, but instead, I kept my voice low and urgent. "I love you too, Gil. I don't think I ever stopped, even when you broke my heart. Even now, when you're scaring me. So whatever you're doing, stop it. *Talk* to me. We can figure this out. Whatever is going on can be solved if we work together—like old times, remember?"

I hoped he'd listen. That he'd hug me. Kiss me. Beg for forgiveness and tell me this was a cruel joke or a massive mistake.

But he didn't.

He kept dragging me toward the stage where his finished masterpieces would stand for photos and critique. A place we'd had sex on. A place we'd bound ourselves together in more than just paint and affection. A place that now held a rope and a gag.

I struggled harder. "Gil…stop it. Stop it right now."

He stayed silent. His shoulders stooped. His body beaten. "I can't."

"Yes, you can. Just let me walk out the door. I'll…I'll vanish. I'll—" Nastiness and spite filled me, mixing with my pleas. "I'll disappear like you did all those years ago. You'll never have to see me again."

He caught my gaze as he slowed to a stop and held me prisoner by the podium. "The thought of never seeing you again shatters what's left of me."

"Then don't—"

"I don't have a choice, Olin! I *never* had a choice."

"You do! Everyone does."

"Not everyone." He pulled me into him, smothering me in another bone-crushing hug. A hug I'd wanted once upon a time but now squirmed to be free from. He kissed my temple, his entire body trembling in despair. "I love you now and always, O. You were the only one I wanted. The only one who owned me. I'm so sorry for hurting you."

Tears leaked down my cheeks. "Gil…please."

"I love you. But I can't save you." He pulled back, his own tears glittering in his gaze. "I tried, and I failed. That's how fucking pathetic I am. How useless."

"You're not useless."

"I failed everyone."

"That's not true." My gaze danced over the warehouse, looking for freedom. "Stop saying that."

"It is true. And I'm about to let you down all over again."

"Please." I reached for him. To hit him, kiss him, try to

knock some sense into him. "Why are you doing this? What the hell is so important that you'd allow that bastard to turn you into a killer?"

His eyes were endlessly sad, eternally broken. "*She* is what's important. The only thing that matters."

"Who? *Who* is important?"

"Olive."

My heart stopped beating.

Olive.

So he *was* dreaming of another O.

Another love called Olive.

Olive!

Pain I'd never felt before slithered through me. My voice was barely audible. "Who's Olive, Gil?"

He grimaced and shrugged as if he'd already hammered the nails into his own coffin. "It doesn't—"

"*It. Fucking. Matters!*" My voice resonated with more rage than I'd ever shown. "You owe me that at least. You owe me the fucking *truth*, Gilbert Clark."

He inhaled, shuddering. "Olive is..." He couldn't look at me. "Olive is my daughter."

White noise stole me.

The ground was no longer stable.

Daughter.

He has...a daughter?

A moan of pure tragedy escaped me.

"I'm so sorry, O." Dragging me into him, he kissed my forehead. A slash of liquid appeared on his cheek, entrapment wrapping him in an unwinnable nightmare. "That bastard has my daughter." His voice cracked again, his head bent. "He has my own flesh and blood. My utmost responsibility. But he'll trade...your life for hers."

Every extremity turned to stone. How did he have a daughter? When did this happen? How and who with? Questions crowded my tongue but fear made me weak. "Why didn't you tell me—"

"I couldn't."

"You could! She's your child! The police—"

"Aren't capable of helping. I'm past their help now."

"Let me go. I'll—"

"I *can't*." Another glitter of grief on his cheek. "I can't let you go. I'm so sorry, owl."

His despair turned to ruthlessness.
His love turned to coldness.
He kissed me one last time...and bent to grab the rope.

NEW YORK TIMES BESTSELLING AUTHOR

PEPPER
WINTERS

Prologue

Olin

WHEN DID KINDNESS become weakness?

When did compassion become blindness?

I believed strength, *true* strength, came from seeing past someone's actions and trusting the goodness inside them. I believed words were just words and lies were just lies and they didn't really matter, because, in the end, the truth always came out.

A person was a product of their upbringing and society's doctrine, and so, I chose to see past that creation and see the real soul hurting underneath.

I chose weakness to be kind.

I became blind to show compassion.

It made a total fool out of me...

Chapter One

Gil

-The Past-

TALLUP DISAPPEARED.

Seven months, three weeks, and eight days after that God-awful night in Motel Gardenia, Tallup vanished from school. She'd ensured my life had remained an utter misery. Her attention constantly on me. Her threats chasing me, her rules hunting me.

She'd steadily let herself go—no longer wearing tight, prim skirt-suits but hiding her small frame in loose-fitting dresses. Her face fattened, along with her waistline, and fellow teachers joked that she'd reached middle-age spread.

I didn't care she no longer looked like a soul-sucking succubus. I was glad she resembled the rotting grossness inside.

Thanks to her, I could no longer look at Olin with Justin.

I could no longer pretend life was okay.

Distance hadn't healed my heart. Love hadn't triumphed over evil.

I found it excruciatingly difficult to keep my distance, all the while far too disgusted with myself to ever talk to Olin.

Every day, it grew harder and harder to stay in town.

I only had a few months until graduation. I honestly didn't know what kept me from leaving. I knew what I wanted to be now: I was an artist. It was the cure to my insanity. And artists didn't need degrees or university accolades. Artists were talented, or not—born with the gift or refused such a skill.

I had everything I needed to succeed.

And I needed to run. Run. *Run.*

Run far away and never look back.

But Olin...

I'd lost her but at least I could still protect her. We walked the same streets. Attended the same school. Lived in the same town. That tiny piece of togetherness sustained me and imprisoned me whenever I thought of leaving.

But then...Tallup vanished.

A new teacher replaced her. Education continued on as if nothing odd had occurred. And the principal made a half-hearted attempt at explaining the switch. Tallup got a job teaching English in Japan. She'd accepted. She'd be missed. Yada yada.

For a week, I didn't trust it.

Every day, I expected Tallup to be at the front of class, ready to stare me into submission, her smirk hidden at breaking Olin and me apart.

But Monday, Tuesday, Wednesday, Thursday, Friday...she didn't return.

The next week, hope did its best to make me drunk. Instead of listening to lessons, I plotted ways to talk to Olin. To explain. To *fix* us.

But each time I tried to catch Olin's gaze, Justin was there. Making her smile through her sadness, his touch soothing her sorrows away.

By the third week of Tallup missing, I grew braver.

She'd crippled me—taken my virginity, my goodness, my strength and left me lacking in every way. But...with her gone, I was free.

Free to chase Olin and claim her back.

But...I'm not free.

Because why would Olin ever forgive me? Why would she ever love me?

She'd given her heart to someone else, and as much as that crucified me—worse than any forced sex or drunken beating—I had to honour her choice.

I left school knowing I'd lost any right to her.

I went to bed so fucking sick of being weak.

I made a pact to talk to her on Monday.

To lay the truth at her feet.

To let her judge me, hurt me, hate me.

And then...I'd kiss her.

I'd kiss her.

Beg her.

Do anything to make her mine.

And if she forgave me, I would never, *ever* let go.

* * * * *

Sunday night.

Fate decided it hadn't finished toying with me, delivering its final blow on my tragic mess of a life.

I had a script planned. Every word and apology ready for Monday morning and making Olin mine.

But then, a visitor arrived.

Not a man looking for a whore, or a drug dealer looking for his cut.

Just a petite woman with the soul of the devil.

My teacher.

Who'd been missing.

Who'd come to finish me.

I'd answered the knock thanks to my father being drunk in his bed and his current whores having fifteen minutes rest before new clients arrived.

The house was quiet, for once, and I had homework to do before I left for an evening of graffiti.

But as I wrenched open the door, my fist curled around the handle and my heart stopped beating. Tallup stood on my dirty stoop, her hair dull and eyes angry. Her cheeks pinched with age and sleeplessness.

The fury inside me exploded outward. "What the *fuck* are you doing here!?"

We weren't on school property.

No one could hear us.

I refused to be polite to this bitch.

She hoisted something higher in her arms. A bundle of fleece and blankets. "I came to find you."

"Why?" My knuckles whitened around the handle, holding tight. If I didn't, I'd hit her, strangle her, *kill* her. "Leave. I have nothing to say—"

"Here." Her arms snapped forward, shoving her swaddled package into my chest. Instinct made me take it, clutching it tight as she ripped her touch away. It fell a little before I had full control.

The bundle was warm and heavier than I expected.

And it moved.

Fuck.

My eyes shot to hers. "What is this?"

She wiped her forehead with weariness, but her gaze was

just as evil, just as cruel. "It's yours."

A small mewl sounded, ripping my eyes down and shooting me with dread.

No...

With sick urgency, I brushed aside the peach fleece and stared at the downy head of a newborn. I almost dropped it in my rush to give it back. "Take it."

Tallup shook her head. "I don't want it. I *never* wanted it." She laughed, a little crazed. "I was on the pill. This wasn't supposed to happen."

"You're saying it's *mine*?"

"That's what I said, didn't I?"

I gulped for air. "But that was months—"

"Nine months this week. It was premature. Eight days early. Guess it knew it wasn't wanted."

I turned stone cold. "How do I know it's mine?"

"Because I say it is." Her voice darkened. "It's yours."

"I don't want a kid."

"Neither do I."

"What do you expect me to do with a baby?" I narrowed my eyes at the blackened street. No neighbours spied. No one heard our dark conversation.

"I don't care." She shrugged. "I honestly don't care if you kill it."

"If you care so little for its life, why didn't you end it when—"

Her eyes snapped to mine. "I tried, believe me. I went to the clinic. I filled in the forms. I waited for a doctor to suck that nuisance straight out of me."

I couldn't hate her more than I did. A cold, oozing, insidious hate.

Her voice turned brittle. "I almost went through with it. but...I was raised better. We're Christian. Abortion is a sin."

I laughed out loud. I couldn't contain it. "And raping a student isn't?"

She stiffened. "I vividly remember you enjoying having your cock inside me."

"I vomited after each assault. Did that not hint that I couldn't stand you?"

Her face etched with fire. "You came." Her lips twisted into a nasty smile. "If you didn't, that thing wouldn't exist."

"That wasn't pleasure, you bitch. I came because you force-fed me Viagra—"

"I don't have time for childish nonsense." She looked at the starless sky, then back at the peach blanket forced upon me. "Just because I couldn't kill it doesn't mean I want it. I hate children. And the past week has proven just how much I loathe everything about them."

Instinctual protectiveness made my arm latch tight as if her words were spears. "Adopt it out then."

She rolled her eyes. "That would lead to questions about who the father is." Chilly calculation filled her face. "Do you want people to know it's yours, Gilbert? Do you want me to tell them you forced yourself on me and this is the result?"

I shook with rage. "*You* forced yourself on *me*."

"Yes, but who would they believe? Have you grown up so much you're willing to put your life on the line to prove…what? That this baby isn't yours? Because I promise you, a paternity test will undeniably show that it is."

My mouth went dry as the baby squirmed and cooed. It didn't know its very existence was being argued against. It didn't know it wasn't wanted.

Sadness filled me. Sadness for the life born from hate. A life that should never have been created.

"If you don't take it, I'll drop it off at the shelter. It can disappear into foster care. Maybe end up in a situation like yours—"

My blood ran cold. "You'd never do such a thing."

How could she? She was a teacher, for Christ's sake.

I clutched the blankets closer. "You teach kids for a living. Why can't you love your own?"

She smiled tightly. "It's *because* I teach that I don't want my own. I only teach because my mother was a teacher, and that was what was expected. I don't do it because I enjoy it. I've hated it since the moment I started."

I forced my anger to subside, doing my best…for our kid's sake. "This is yours as much as mine. Stop being such a cold-hearted witch. I know you could love—"

"Shut up, Gilbert. I'm not keeping her."

"Her?"

My insides bottomed out.

My world changed.

My priorities shifted.

Her.

A girl.

I have a daughter.

I grew up in an instant.

I was no longer a boy, but a man.

A *father.*

A father who would never be like his own. Never be a parent who didn't put their life on the line to protect his child.

I cuddled her close. So damn close.

Already in love with her and I hadn't even seen her face.

How was it possible to fall so fast? How could my heart abandon Olin and replace it with a newborn so quickly?

I didn't know how, only that it'd happened, and there was no going back.

Tallup didn't notice the change that'd happened in me. She nodded stiffly, glowering at my daughter. "It's a girl. A useless, loud, horrible little—"

"A perfect, *brilliant* little girl and you're throwing her away." I shook my head in disgust. I thought I hated this woman for what she'd done to me. I'd had daydreams of murdering her with my bare hands. I'd envisioned going to the police and having them on my side. Of explaining to O. Of winning her back and making my life right again.

But that hate was nothing, *nothing,* compared to my level of contempt now. I couldn't look at her without wanting to strike her. I couldn't stand her face, her smell, her soul. My voice vibrated with arctic snow as I looked down at the woman who didn't deserve to live. "Who the fuck are you?"

She sniffed and braced her shoulders. "I just want my life back."

I laughed darkly. "So do I."

"Oh, come on. You're still sore over losing Olin? She's a nobody."

"Don't call her that."

"I can call her whatever I want. I've accepted a job in Japan teaching English, now that this little…inconvenience is out of the way." She grinned. "My life will be my own again. But I'll still know if you've been naughty. You better not have been talking to her while I've been gone, Gilbert. Otherwise—"

"Stop."

This.

All of this.

It was stupid, pointless, *juvenile.*

Who cared about power trips and forced assaults and teenage hearts that were broken?

Who cared about right and wrong and justice?

The world didn't care.

Justice didn't care.

And I didn't care.

Not anymore.

The only thing I cared about was ensuring my daughter never had to suffer such things. She might've been born to a ruthless mother and a gullible father, but she wouldn't pay for my sins.

She deserved an empire.

She deserved stability and family.

Family.

O was once my family.

She always would be.

I would always love and care for her.

But I had someone else who needed me more.

And if her mother refused to give her the world; if her mother would rather throw her to the hounds of hell, then I would do it.

I would be there for her over my own messes.

I would fight her battles at the cost of my own.

I would *never* stop putting her first.

Above everyone.

"I'm done." I sighed, bored and no longer afraid of this sad, bitter woman. "Go away." Tucking my tiny daughter into my chest, I rocked her.

This was my legacy.

She was my reason for existing.

Tallup swallowed, watching me closely with a tilt of her head. "So...you'll keep her?"

I nodded with a stern stare.

"Will you tell anyone where she came from?" Her eyes might stay narrowed and full of threats, but her lips worried with consequence. She was afraid I'd tell everyone our story. That I'd drag my daughter through court cases, prison sentences, and foster care.

No way.

No *fucking* way.

I dropped my head and inhaled the sweet hair of my child. "I'm leaving. Tonight."

She froze. "Leaving? Where?"

"Don't know. Don't care." I looked away from her, brushing back the fleece to stare at my daughter's tiny, adorable face. She slept in my arms. Trusting me to hold her and not drop her. Believing she'd wake to warm food and unconditional love. Knowing I'd be there to keep her safe, just as I'd tried to keep Olin safe.

And I would.

Nothing would stop me from loving her.

She had me for eternity.

I'd failed O, but she had Justin now.

I wouldn't fail this new love of my life.

Tallup pointed a finger in my face. "If you say anything—"

"Enough." I just smiled. Totally unaffected and free from her wrath. "You'll never see me or my daughter again." Stepping back into the house I'd shared with drunkards and whores, I grabbed the door. "Goodbye, Jane Tallup."

I slammed the old wood in her face.

The rattle woke up my daughter.

Her eyes blinked with fuzzy sleep, her mouth opened like a tiny bird's, and her frustrated grumble made overwhelming affection and debilitating fear crest over me.

What did I know about raising a child?

What did I know about finding a place to live, a job that paid, childcare to source, food, diapers, medicine, kindergarten, and all the other things that came with a lifetime commitment to another?

I didn't have a clue.

I can't do this.

But then my daughter opened her eyes again, blinking and bold and huge.

And I knew that I could.

One day at a time.

For her.

Marching through the house, I grabbed a bag, stuffed some clothes, my art supplies, and the wad of cash my father kept from his johns into the depths.

It was the first time I'd ever stolen from him.

He'd promised to kill me if I ever did.

After tonight, he'd never find me.

Slinging the bag over my shoulder, I looked down at my daughter again, my heart fisting at her sigh of contentment.

Her big eyes were closed in slumber, quiet and safe.

She looked like a baby owl.

A big-eyed, intelligent baby owl.

Like the nickname I'd used for Olin.

Fuck, O.

My chest imploded as my heart stopped beating.

In a few short hours, I would've gotten on my knees before her and asked for a second chance. We might've found our way back to each other. We might've been happy.

But now…I'd never see her again.

I'd never be able to kiss her or beg for her forgiveness.

She would always think I'd abandoned her, turning her deeper into Justin's arms, sealing a marriage between them.

That was my only regret.

I'd leave this town, and O would never know where I'd gone.

She'd never know why I shut her out.

Never guess why I removed my love.

Never understand that the girl I held in my arms was the cause of all of it.

I'm sorry.

So fucking sorry.

With my meagre possessions and brand new baby, I slipped from the whore house, stole through the streets, and bought a train ticket to London.

I never looked back.

Chapter Two

Olin

-The Present-

"GIL…DON'T."

He gritted his teeth, wrapping the rope tighter around my wrists.

"Stop it." I wriggled and squirmed, trying to be free of him.

"Don't make this any harder than it is," he breathed, tying a knot and jerking me forward.

I fought against him, bracing against his pull.

His hand slipped on the rope, giving me a fraction of a second.

I spun and bolted.

I managed a few terrified strides before his boots thudded behind me.

He caught me so easily.

He spun me around, picked me up, and carried me to the podium. Big fat tears rolled down my cheeks, unable to believe what he'd done. In all the times he'd ever touched me, he'd restrained the power and violence he wielded so effortlessly now. He had a strength that controlled me with barely any effort whatsoever.

That alone sent my heart galloping uselessly in my chest. My back prickled with nervous sweat. My chest fluttered with anxious breath. And I moaned in disbelief as he plopped me onto the stage and kicked out my legs, forcing me to sit on the edge.

I sat with a jar, my teeth clacking together as I dared look up at the kidnapper I should've been afraid of but never suspected.

"Why do you get to decide what my life is worth?" My voice teased with a whisper but throbbed with condemnation.

He bit his bottom lip, his eyes narrowed and afflicted. "I don't."

"Yet you're playing God."

He reached for more rope. "I'm doing what's necessary."

"No, you're doing what he wants you to do." A fresh swell of tears tried to make me weak. "Don't do his dirty work, Gil. Don't—"

"I made a promise." His head hung, his hands feathering over my ankles as he wrapped the rope around them and tied an intricate knot. "I promised my daughter that I would always protect her. No matter the cost." His voice caught. "No matter the pain."

"What about *my* pain?"

His head dropped lower, his messy, tangled hair dancing with his eyelashes. "I've always caused you pain...this is no different."

"This is you taking my life, Gil. This isn't a breakup. This isn't some misunderstanding. You're tying me up to *kill* me." I tried to capture his gaze. "Listen to me. *Look* at me. Are you really prepared to kill someone who loves you? Someone you love?"

"I'm prepared to do whatever it takes to keep her safe."

Every muscle shut down. I swayed as his words fisted around my heart and squeezed its last beat.

His admission was the correct answer for a father in love with his daughter.

But his loyalties cost me so much trust. It siphoned out of me, slipped through the ropes, and puddled at my feet.

My trust in him, in *us*...was broken.

He'd just lost me.

Lost me worse than he ever did when he walked away without a goodbye.

You've lost me forever.

My heart restarted, drowning in horror.

Piece by piece.

Beat by beat.

I grew cold and empty.

Silence wrapped around us, stealing our voices, suffocating our thoughts. Quietness was easier to bear than his soul-shattering confessions, and I allowed it to hug me, trying to find comfort where there was none.

"I know you'll never forgive me," he murmured. "I know the only place I can go is hell. And I know I've destroyed any hope of a future where we could all be alive and happy. This is entirely my fault. I'm the reason Olive was taken, and I'm the reason those girls had to die. I'm the one who should forfeit his life…and who knows? Maybe that will be his next request, but while Olive is alive…I have no choice." He stood on cracking knees, towering over me. "As long as she is alive…I have to try." His misery left me stamped and branded as he turned and walked through his office to the apartment beyond.

The second he was out of viewing distance, I scrambled to undo myself. I bucked and writhed on the podium, twisting and turning, desperate to escape.

But each imprisonment stayed steadfast, and the only thing I succeeded in doing was burning through valuable energy. Energy I couldn't afford to lose.

Whatever Gil was about to do to me, I had to be smart. Had to be brave. I wouldn't give up.

I would've fought every dragon and beast by his side. I would've given him everything to keep his daughter safe…if only he'd asked. If only he hadn't taken what wasn't his to take.

A single tear rolled down my cheek, icy and alone.

I wouldn't cry again.

He wasn't worth my tears.

He isn't worth my heart.

When he came back, his eyebrows tugged low, noticing my attempt at freedom. In his hands rested a plate of peanut butter and jelly sandwiches with a tall glass of water. The only two pieces of crockery he owned that weren't chipped or plastic.

A heavy thread of strawberry followed him as he lowered to his haunches before me.

Such a simple, innocent scent.

A berry reserved for hot summers and delightful picnics. It had no place in this chilly warehouse with ropes binding me to a terrible fate.

"Open," he murmured, holding the sandwich to my lips.

I shook my head, earning peanut butter crumbs on my chin. "What are you doing?" I kept my face turned away. "Stop it."

"You're hungry. It's my turn to feed you."

My eyes widened. I resisted the urge to morbidly laugh. "You're about to kill me, but you want to feed me first?"

His entire face blanched. He wobbled on his haunches and swallowed hard as if struggling to keep his own stomach contents down. "Don't. Please don't."

"Don't what? Make you face what you're about to do to me?" I swung my knees to nudge against his, my chin high and voice sharp. "You've tied me up against my will. You're going to gift me to him. You'll allow him to do whatever he wants. The least you can do is accept the gruesome details." My anger plaited with fragility, wavering a little. "Will he kill me or you? How will it happen? Slit my wrists and bleed me out like the last girl? Paint me and leave me to die like the ones before her?"

He groaned as if I'd butchered him. With his jaw locked, he shoved the sandwich into my mouth, forcing me to chew or choke. "Just eat, O. I need you to eat."

I fought to grab air not tainted with food, but he followed my head, keeping the awful sandwich pressed tight against my mouth.

We duelled for a while. I shifted my head left and right, up and down. He employed patience and followed. Crumbs and strawberry jam smeared my face. Embarrassingly, my stomach snarled to stop fighting.

To devour the offered energy because there must be a reason he wanted me to eat. Maybe he wouldn't be the one to kill me. Maybe he wanted me to have energy to fight.

I stilled. My body relaxed. I opened my mouth politely and took a dainty bite.

Gil tensed, his eyes never unlocking from mine as I ate every inch. I swallowed it down, then waited for him to wipe my cheeks and chin free from the mess.

He did with a shaky hand, his forehead furrowed and eyes so dark they looked like crushed up jade. "I'm sorry."

"You keep saying that, but if you were sorry, you'd let me go."

"Thank you for eating." He placed the empty plate aside and picked up the glass. "Please drink."

I held my head away, my gaze searching his. "Tell me why."

He struggled to reply. The truth stayed shuttered behind his anguish, but finally, he looked at my lap and whispered, "You need to eat so you have something in your system. If you're left out there for a while...the better hydrated and fed you are...the longer you'll survive."

"That wasn't what I was asking." I'd wanted to know *why*.

Why he'd chosen the easy way out. Yes, his daughter was captive, and he'd been dealing with this alone, but surely, having me help him rather than just sacrificing me was a better option?

When he didn't answer, I sighed heavily. "You think a sandwich will keep me alive? That it will prevent me from becoming yet another dead girl in a newspaper?"

His eyes squeezed shut; a single tear rolled down his ashen face. Opening them again, he held the glass to my lips. "Please."

My heart kicked at his brokenness, even now wishing to heal him.

I locked any emotion away and opened my mouth, allowing him to pour cool water down my throat.

I drank every drop.

I will survive this.

I will.

When the glass was empty, he lowered it slowly, studying the fracturing light as a droplet danced inside. That creative spark struck a match in his gaze, turning tortured into artist. He drowned in the colour spectrum, begging the flickering rainbow to fix everything.

I was envious of him. Envious that he could still practice his talent. Jealous he had a religion that could help him, even while discussing the murder of his childhood sweetheart.

His gaze met mine, and in the green depths, he showed me how endless he truly was. How long he'd fought this battle. How I was just collateral damage in a war I could never comprehend.

And I pitied him.

Pitied the struggle that had torn away his soul. Pitied the hardships he'd had to face on his own.

But I couldn't forgive him.

I couldn't absolve him for putting a price on my life and finding it less valuable than another's. Even if it was his daughter. Even if she was...*family.*

"Justin knows I'm here." I studied him with defiance. "He'll visit soon, I'm sure."

"He won't." Gil stood and carried the empty dishes to his side table where an airgun, brushes, vials, and everything else he needed for his work waited, prepped and mixed.

I sucked in a breath, my heart once again winging. "Why won't he?"

"Because I told him not to."

"He knows something is going on with you."

Gil laughed, but nothing was jovial about it, merely black and miserable. "He should. I've been hiding this nightmare for a while."

"What's a while?"

He kept his back to me, unlocking the wheels on the trolley and rolling the supply table toward me. "Over a year."

"A year?" I squirmed on the stage, my wrists and ankles sore from the tightness of his binds. "Why didn't you go to the police? Tell them—"

"Tell them that I'm a madman's puppet? That I've tried to keep so many women from death and only succeeded if my bank account was flush?"

I stiffened. "You could have. They might have believed you."

His eyes cast back to the past, to a time I wasn't there. "They wouldn't. It's always my word against someone else's."

That statement rippled with such stark truth, I wished I could dissect it and pull free every fact, but I kept my questioning focused, determined to solve this riddle. "How many women did your money save?" I tested the ropes again, a futile attempt, but instinct demanded I keep checking.

"Not enough." He shuddered visibly, his face turning grey as a corpse. "It doesn't matter."

"Don't." My voice hissed like a python. "Don't *ever* say that to me again. Don't you think I deserve to know?" I held up my bound wrists. "You've turned me into a sacrifice, Gilbert Clark. The least you can do is—"

"You're right." His back stiffened as he pulled open a drawer and selected a pair of sharp scissors. "Ask me anything. I'll answer as honestly as I can." Coming toward me, he eyed my skirt and blouse. "I'm sorry to ruin yet another outfit of yours."

I scuttled backward, doing my best to avoid the silver flashes of his weapon. I asked again, "Ho-How many did you manage to save?"

His eyes met mine. This time he didn't deflect. "Seven. Seven girls before my finances ran dry."

"And he kept asking for more?"

He nodded as another well of rage and helplessness glossed his gaze. "I sold what I could. I worked every job possible. I gave him every penny. But it still wasn't enough."

"Enough for what?"

"To keep her safe."

"To keep Olive safe," I whispered his daughter's name.

"Yes." His fingers grabbed my ankle, pulling me back to the edge of the podium. With trembling hands, he cut my skirt along my thigh, right to the pretty faux croc-skin belt. With a snip, he cut that too, switching my skirt to a ruined piece of material now draped uselessly on his stage.

My garter belt decorated my black lace knickers; my stockings unable to shield me from the cold air.

He sniffed as if he couldn't hold back his emotion. Couldn't believe he did this to me. "Fuck, I'm so, so sorry."

"Then stop." I did my best to stay strong.

"I can't."

I flinched as he slowly cut my blouse, peeling it away from my skin. It fluttered lifelessly to join my skirt, revealing my bra.

"I need you to know." Gil cupped my chin with snowy fingertips. "I need you to understand." Tears strangled his voice. "Without Olive, I don't know what I would've become. Sh-She saved my life." His thumb stroked my cheekbone. "After I lost you, I barely survived. I was on a slippery slope of grief and heartache, but thanks to Olive...I had someone who needed me. I had someone to fight for—"

"*I* needed you!" My pain bled through my control as a sob caught in my throat. "I missed you so much. Why did you leave if you still wanted me? Why didn't you fight for me, Gil? Why don't you fight now?"

His tears flowed freely, glittering on his ghostly cheeks, tracking through his five o'clock shadow. "I had to stay away. Otherwise, she was going to destroy your life."

I struggled to breathe. "Who? Who was going to destroy my life?"

"It doesn't—"

"Gil!"

"Fine. It was Tallup." His teeth snapped the word in half, thick with disgust and heavy with loathing. "She blackmailed me." He pressed his forehead to mine, breathing hard. "I was stupid and gullible and way out of my depth. I should've told you. Should've told the authorities, but I was too afraid." He let out an agony-drenched laugh. "I was too afraid of losing you. Of being locked up. Of my life becoming a total screw-up. I thought I could protect you and fix what I'd broken. But I failed, and I lost it all anyway."

My mind scrambled to untangle the pieces. "Ms Tallup?

Jane Tallup? Our *teacher*?" I frowned. "Why would she want to hurt me?"

"Because of me."

"What? Why?"

"She went after you to get to me." His gaze shot black with hatred and unresolved torment.

"I don't understand."

"It doesn't ma—"

"Gil." I ripped my face from his touch. "I swear I'll—"

His lips crashed on mine as if he couldn't stop himself. As if the whole deranged evening was just a role-play and I'd had every choice to participate. His tongue licked at the seam of my mouth. His groan vibrated in his chest with black-edged sorrow.

I didn't kiss him back.

In that, I had a choice.

He pulled away, resting his forehead on mine as he breathed hard. "Fuck." He trembled as if he had hypothermia and only had seconds to live. He kissed me again, quick and hard, his breath catching. *"Fuck."*

Falling away from me, he punched the stage.

He punched it so hard, the vibration ricocheted beneath me and made him groan with agony. He punched it again, punishing his knuckles, ruining his painting hand all because he couldn't stand the prison we were locked in.

Part of me wanted to soothe him. To tell him it was okay. That I understood his pain.

But I *didn't* understand.

This was my life he was using to pay a debt.

This wasn't his choice to make.

"What did Tallup do to you, Gil?" My question was achingly soft after such violence.

His shoulders hunched, grief crippling him. His eyes were wet as they met mine. "She wanted me." He shrugged helplessly. "So…she took me."

"What does that—"

No.

I wanted to be sick.

A rush of heat and nausea raced up my throat.

My cheeks burned. My body throbbed with injustice. "You *slept* with her?"

He swiped at the liquid on his face and looked away.

He didn't answer as he reached for my bra and snipped it

with the scissors. Cutting the straps, he let it fall to the graveyard of my clothing before slicing up my stockings and leaving me in just my knickers. A single piece of protection against so many things I didn't know.

"You slept with her." Tears I didn't want to cry spilled over my cheeks. "Why would you do that? Why didn't you *say* something? I was waiting for you. I was *saving* myself for you. I was a virgin, Gil. I wanted you to have that. No one else. You were supposed to be my first...and my only."

His voice was dangerously low. "You think I didn't want that too?"

"I don't know what to think." My heart bruised with agony. "Did she proposition you? Why didn't you tell the principal? He would've fired her immediately for even looking at you wrong."

His jaw gritted. "Like I said...I was trapped."

"Trapped because you secretly wanted her?"

His head snapped up. *"What?"* His eyes narrowed. "Why the fuck would you ask something like that?"

"Why wouldn't I?" Anger flickered through me. "You're a guy. She was small. You could've fought her off. I mean...if you didn't want it, you wouldn't have been able to get hard—"

"Fucking hell." He swooped up, dragging hands through his hair. "I know you hate me. I know you're currently tied up and cursing the very air I breathe, but do you truly think I wanted her? Wanted her over you? Do you honestly think I went to her willingly?"

My chest rose and fell with quickened breaths. "You broke up with me in front of her. How am I supposed to know if you did that because you two were playing some twisted game—"

He bent and grabbed my face, his fingers digging into my flesh. "I deserve your doubt. I deserve you thinking the worst of me...after all, look at what I'm fucking doing. But...O, you couldn't have hurt me more if you'd tried."

My chin arched in his hold. "Well, good. I'm *glad* you're hurt. Maybe now you'll understand how I feel." Yet more cursed tears welled. "I *trusted* you, Gil. I gave you everything I had, and instead of telling me how I could help you, you went behind my back and decided for me. Twice!" I sniffed coldly. "You did it at school. And you're doing it now. We were family. We made a deal to be there for each other—"

"I was trying to keep you safe!"

"Safe by sleeping with her?"

"Yes!"

"All because she threatened my future."

"Yes, okay?! I was an idiot. I—"

"You're a walking disaster for blackmail." I wanted to laugh at the absurdity, to cry at the tragedy. "I could've handled my own future, you know! My grades were good. She couldn't have stopped me."

"You're right." He let me go, pacing in front of me. "I'm fucking pathetic. I try to do the right thing, but I always fail. She told me she'd destroy your hopes of university and dance. She said I could never talk to you again. That I had to give her my virginity and—"

"You—" I choked. "You were a virgin?"

His boots stuck to the floor as his body sagged with crippling confession. "My virginity was yours. I was waiting to make sure you were in love with me." He looked away, unable to hold my stare. "Because once I took you, there was no going back. I was going to marry you and move you away from that shitty place. I had it all planned—"

"Wait." Fury tangled with my sadness, making me tremble in my ropes. "You're telling me...that all this time...you saw a future together? You were going to *marry* me...?" A wash of tiredness crashed over me, scrambling my thoughts. I struggled to pull them back into comprehension. "You let her ruin us, all because you were too afraid to stand up to her!"

"It was my word against hers." He pinched the bridge of his nose. "There was no way I could've won."

"The *truth* would have won." I blinked back another tug of tiredness.

"The *truth* was I was the son of an alcoholic pimp who beat me. My upbringing wasn't with siblings but with whores. Tallup was a Christian teacher who lived with her mother and did charity work. Do you honestly think I stood a chance? That her word against mine wouldn't win? She could do whatever she fucking liked, and there was nothing I could do."

I swallowed hard. "And what exactly...did she do to you?"

Shutters came down over his eyes. His hands balled as pure rage dripped over him. "I already told you."

I shook my head from yet another lick of lethargy. "You slept with her."

His teeth bared. "Yes."

"How exactly? If you didn't want it, how—"

"She tricked me into taking Viagra."

"Oh…"

Time froze.

Everything stopped.

And I saw this from an outsider's point of view. I heard my judgement. I saw my dread. And I despised myself.

This isn't me.

I wasn't a woman bound and trapped by a man willing to kill me. I was just a girl, judging a boy for sexual molestation. I did what chauvinistic society did to girls who were raped. I blamed him. I believed it must've been his fault.

But it *wasn't* his fault.

And it wasn't fair to use my hurt against him.

The truth stabbed me right in the chest. "You didn't sleep with her, Gil. She raped you."

God.

She raped him and cut him off from everyone.

She—

I want to kill her.

Rip out her heart and burn it on a pyre.

My fingers turned numb along with my tongue, shutting down piece by piece. "She abused you. God, Gil, she took everything from you—"

He held up a hand, his entire frame shaking. "Don't feel sorry for me. Don't you fucking *dare* feel sorry for me. Do not be that good. Do not be that fucking kind!"

"But you were just a child. And she was our teach—"

"Stop it. I want you to hate me. You *need* to hate me." He howled at the ceiling. "I need you to resent me with everything you have. Be disgusted with me. Curse me. Fuck, please." He fell to his knees. "I can't do this if you forgive all my sins. I can't do this if you still love me…no matter what I fucking do to you."

Another lash of heaviness slithered through my brain, scattering my thoughts before realigning. I blinked back the increasing lethargy. "You dealt with that…on your own." I cried tears for the boy I'd lost. "You didn't tell me. You didn't trust me to help you. You were all alone."

He rocked with his hands clasped in prayer, bowing to me, placing me in position of a goddess. A goddess of death and destruction. An offering to a bigger, more malignant power. "I thought I could keep you safe."

"Instead, you cut me out." My voice was silk-wrapped

daggers. "You ruined both of us." I longed to touch him, to hug him. If I touched him now, I might be able to stop him from doing this. I finally knew what'd twisted him up so badly. "It's okay. It's over now."

My roped hands reached for his face to grant him absolution. To let him know, I might hate his actions tonight, but I didn't hate him—no matter how much trust he'd shattered. "Gil...it's over. Untie me. It's not just your word against hers. I'll stand beside you. We'll ask for help together. We'll save Olive some other way."

"Olin." His tears fell openly now. "Goddammit, I—"

My fingers grazed his five o'clock shadow. He reared backward, terror filling his gaze. "Don't. I'll break if you touch me. I'm breaking already."

"Let me go."

"I *can't*."

"You're not alone anymore." Another crush of exhaustion pressed into me, forcing me into haziness. My eyes unfocused on the rope around my wrists. My mind flickered on and off. I licked my lips, clawing my way back to lucidity. "I forgive you for this, Gilbert Clark. I forgive you for everything. Just let me go and..." Reality checked out for a second, my brain tiptoeing into sleep. I opened my eyes with a jerk, raising my heavy head. "What...what's going on? Why am I so tired?"

He ignored me.

"Did you...drug me?" I licked my lips, the numbness spreading.

"I can't do this anymore." Scrambling to his feet, he grabbed something from his trestle. He placed a bottle of paint beside me while holding his palm open by my face. I couldn't make sense of the small black dot in the centre. "I can't keep making you believe the worst."

I struggled to focus.

"I wasn't going to tell you this." His voice stayed low as if afraid monsters would hear. "You need to believe this is real...just like you believed the breakup at school was real."

I laughed coldly. "That *was* real. You broke up with me and never spoke to me again."

He shook his head, his hair a wild, untamed mop. "I meant to apologise that night and fix us. But you never went home, and then...I couldn't." He cleared his throat. "But this is different. I won't keep you in the dark like I did that day. I need you to know, so I have the strength to finish this."

"If the breakup wasn't real…but it ended up being true…why do you think this will be any different? You think by telling me you have a plan, it will stop me from getting killed?" My thoughts scrambled again, unable to stay cohesive. I swam in question-filled quicksand. "Wait…why did you break up with me if it wasn't real? I don't understand."

His jaw worked. "It was for her. I thought she'd back off if she saw I was no longer into you."

"Yet it only left you wide open to be pulled into her bed."

He winced. "She knew I loved you regardless that I broke your heart. It was *because* I loved you that she managed to keep me on a leash."

My eyes unfocused again. "That sounds like you're blaming me."

"Fuck no." His hands shook, still holding up the black dot. "I know I'm to blame. For all of this. I know I've broken everything between us. I know you'll never love me after—"

"I'll be dead. How can I love you?" My tongue tried to slur, battling whatever thickness swam in my blood.

"You won't be. I won't let you die." He once again shoved the dot into my vision. "This must stay secret. You can't let him know this is on you. Act as terrified and as enraged as you were before."

I couldn't keep up with his tricks. "What are you saying?"

"I'm saying I'm going to paint you, deliver you, sacrifice you, but it was never my intention to abandon you. Not again. *Never* again." He nudged my chin up with his knuckles. "I'll be with you every step, O. I'm not leaving you.

"What do you mean?"

Bending, he very gently pulled the waistband of my lacy knickers until a small gap formed between lingerie and skin. Placing the black dot against my hip, he let the tightness hug it close.

It burned my flesh with iciness.

"That's a GPS tracker. It's synced to my phone." His voice cracked again, a fresh tear trickled over thick eyelashes. "I love you, O. With all my goddamn heart. I can't bear to risk you, but I also can't leave Olive in his control. This is my last chance." He swiped at his nose with the back of his hand. "He's asked me to drop you off…painted in camouflage. I'll do what he's requested. He thinks that by taking you—by taking the only other person I love—it will make me far more obedient than I have been. But…what he doesn't get is, this has pushed me to my limit." His fists curled. "He can't have you both. He can't keep hurting those I love. This ends…tonight."

The warehouse no longer acted like steel and concrete but liquid and air, loose and floating. My mind was drunk on fatigue. My tongue twisted into knots, making conversation harder. "Wha-What are you going to do?"

He tucked a curtain of hair behind my ear. I didn't have the energy to swat him away. His lips caressed my cheek. "I'm going to kill him."

My heart picked up a panicked beat, shooing away the sleepiness. "How?"

Gil let me go, turning to his paints and brushes. Placing more on the stage around me, his mouth remained grim and resolute. "I'll follow where he takes you. He'll take you to Olive. Once I know where she is, I'll kill him."

My mouth turned dry. There were so many holes in that plan. So many things that could go wrong. "What if…he doesn't…" I blinked, fighting harder against the urge to snooze. "…take me to Olive?"

He dropped a glass jar holding sponges. It clanged on the stage, making both of us flinch. "He will." His teeth sank into his bottom lip. "He has to."

"What if he kills me first?"

"He won't."

"What if he kills us all?"

Gil unwound the hose for his airgun. "I won't let that happen."

My head was too heavy to hold up. I sagged forward, my spine rolling. "You might not have a choice."

His warmth settled into me as he sat beside me on the stage. His arm wrapped around me in both comfort and threats. "Sleep now, O. It's better that way."

Dreams dragged me down. Dreams of darkness and torment.

A single green olive in a martini glass appeared in the blackness, crystal liquid sloshing with rainbows. A cocktail stick speared the olive.

It screamed.

"Wait…" My fingers grew claws as I fought back to the surface. "I need to know something." A question danced out of reach, frolicking with sheep, begging to be counted. There was something about Olive that was important. Something about Olive that I didn't understand.

Olive...

"Hush." His lips pressed against my temple. "Don't worry. Everything will be over soon."

Tallup...

A blackboard with chalk.

A teacher with evil eyes.

Olive and Tallup.

A little girl in front of class.

A child who looked like our teacher.

His daughter!

"No!" I shot upright, blinking slow, my mind a black cloak of exhaustion. "Olive...she-she's your daughter."

Gil went statue stiff beside me, understanding the rabbit I chased. "O...don't. Please don't ask things I can't answer."

"Tallup raped you."

He trembled. "Go to sleep now, I beg you."

"Please tell me..." I forced my bowling ball of a head up, searching for his eyes. I met them. I held them. I knew. "Olive—"

"Don't." Gil's entire face cracked and crumpled. The lines around his eyes deepened. The crags in his forehead shadowed. He looked as if I'd killed him just by guessing the biggest secret he'd been hiding. The only secret that mattered. "Don't."

Our gazes tangled.

His denial blazed against my unspoken conclusion but the truth burned brighter.

Sleep tried to claim me again. "Olive...she's hers."

Gil shuddered as if he begged for any other solution than my life as currency. Any way to stop me from figuring out what he'd kept hidden. His head hung. His breath caught. He was trapped. "Olive is hers. But she's mine too. I named her...for you."

Tears beyond my control rained heavy and hard down my cheeks. I was allowed to hate him. I was meant to curse his very existence. I had no trust where he was concerned. No obligation in any form.

Yet, I cried for him and for me.

I cried for both of us because it wasn't fake breakups, molesting teachers, or blackmailing murderers who'd broken us.

It'd been the lies.

The tricks.

The shadows that'd always surrounded Gilbert Clark and the ones he retreated to rather than staying in the light with me.

No matter what happened.

No matter if I died tonight, he died, we all died, *this* had died.

Us.

There is no more us.

His arms wrapped me in a cage, his love imprisoning me.

I tried to stop crying. To put aside my grief and *wake up.*

But slowly, stealthily, finality crept over me.

My eyelids no longer opened.

My brain no longer operated.

My head lay on Gil's shoulder, needing support.

He clutched me closer as the final dregs of energy siphoned out of me. He stroked my hair and kissed my ear as I gave in to the cloud of unconsciousness. "Hopefully, by the time you wake up...this will all be over. You'll be free. You'll never have to see me again." He angled my chin, his lips claiming mine.

I tried to pull back, to stop the kiss, to study his godforsaken eyes, but he caged me closer. He pulled heat and hunger from deep within, sending me into lullabies with his taste on my lips and his grief on my tongue. "I'm so sorry, O. So sorry for ever thinking I could make you happy. You deserve so much more. I love you. I love you with every fucking part of me, but I can't stop this. At least sleep is a gift I can give you. The only thing I can give you."

Voices were far away and not of my dream world as he lowered me down until I lay on the stage. My eyelids fluttered as he turned on the air compressor and the first lick of unwanted paint landed upon my skin.

But I couldn't move.

Couldn't fight.

Gil was an artist.

Art was his drug.

The creation of beauty helped him cope in the depths of his despair. He needed art to function, to survive.

And with his talent, he stole my function.

Brush by brush, he destroyed me.

Colour by colour, he sentenced me to die.

He snuffed out my survival.

He'd poisoned me so I'd sleep.

So I wouldn't be awake when my purpose as his masterpiece was over.

Chapter Three

Gil

-The Past-

"SO...."

I looked up from my untouched beer. My eyes met Justin Miller's curious ones, and I wondered all over again what the fuck I was doing in a bar with him two weeks after the worst thing in my life had happened.

Olive had been taken from me.

Taken by someone I trusted.

I'd paid the first ransom.

The second had arrived this morning.

I'd been in my head, plotting and scheming, doing my best to figure out how to snatch Olive back when I'd bumped into my past on the street.

"So..." I gritted my teeth, tipping the pint to my lips and sipping wet froth.

Gross.

"This is random, huh?" Justin chuckled, glancing around the darkened pub that'd survived the days of witch trials, Saxon sieges, and sooty open fireplaces. The low ceilings made the dingy booths and low beams cocoon us like a cavern, while the stained glass windows refused to let twilight perk up the place.

The entire establishment matched my mood. My heart. My aching, useless soul.

I sipped again—despite my hatred of liquor—struggling to hold small talk when all I could think about was my daughter in the hands of my goddamn uncle. Why did I not see it coming? Why didn't I do something before it was too fucking late?

Goddammit, Olive.

My chest spasmed as if a grenade had exploded and shrapnel dug into my insides, poisoning me, killing me.

How could I let this happen?

Sweet little Olive who'd I'd named after Olin. Adorable little Olive who'd named herself thanks to a children's book I'd found on the bus in the first few weeks of parenthood. A dog-eared, well-loved edition of *Popeye The Sailor Man.*

I'd flicked through the pages, my heart aching at the images of Popeye in love with a feisty, perfect woman named Olive Oyl.

All he cared about was making her his.

Just like I'd done with O.

I'd read the tattered book to my nameless daughter as she'd cooed on my lap. She'd wriggled and blown bubbles each time I said Olive Oyl.

By the time the story was over, I knew what her name was.

Justin cleared his throat, dragging me back to the present. "So...are you a house painter or an artist...or something else?"

I scowled at my colour-stained hands. The clues of my trade. The signs of my failure. "Uh-huh."

"What do you paint? Houses? Canvases?"

"Doesn't matter." I shrugged, my eyes trailing to the door and the street beyond. I had twenty-four hours to come up with the second payment. I had the cash. I had more than enough. Ever since I hit success with body painting, I'd squirrelled away every penny to pave a golden path for whatever Olive wanted to do when she was older.

Those funds had been for her college, travel, or passion dreams. Not to pay a fucking bastard not to kill her.

My mind once again lashed tight to my daughter. I couldn't do much else these days apart from think about her, worry about her, stare at my goddamn ceiling at night and hate myself for failing her.

"Not very talkative, are you?" Justin chuckled, taking another sip. "How about we start with easy questions?"

I resented him for dragging me back. I hated this. I refused to live in this world where Olive wasn't with me. I'd rather live in my memories where she was safe and happy.

My memories also held moments of another girl I'd loved.

O.

I growled under my breath.

Two loves of my life.

Both stolen.

"What did you get up to after school?" Justin asked, successfully breaking me from my past.

I forced myself to sit there, to give a generic answer of ex-schoolmates. "Nothing of interest."

How could I tell him that I'd run from school and never graduated? That the weeks following my disappearance with a baby hadn't been easy. That I'd managed to find a small studio apartment by paying cash and three months' rent in advance—almost all my father's ill-gotten money gone, just like that.

I spent the next week educating myself on how to feed, burb, clean, and soothe a newborn.

I kept her alive by some crazy miracle.

"Well, I went on to get my master's in accounting. Loved math enough to make it my career."

I grimaced. "Good for you." I didn't bother pretending to be interested in my beer. Alcohol repulsed me. The taste and smell were utterly repugnant after the beatings Dad gave me thanks to the violence found in a bottle.

"So...I'm going to say you're an artist not a decorator. That fair to assume?"

"Assume away."

"Okay then...how did you start making money with your art?"

I doubted the truth would be a good answer. To admit that while Olive slept, I painted. That I created a few original pieces, while others I copied previous masters, doing my best to have something worthwhile to sell on street corners for coins. Olive had rested in the satchel I'd stolen, and I'd swallowed my morals as I used her as a tool to open the wallets of dog walkers and women with their own children.

That was how I began.

But not how I became rich.

"Lucky break."

"Yeah, I'd say." Justin grinned. "You're living the dream that most never get to achieve."

I coughed on a morbid laugh. I stifled the urge to fucking cry. "Yep, living the dream. That's me."

The worst kind of nightmare.

Olive...I'll figure this out.

Somehow.

My daughter had eclipsed everything in my life.

If something ever happened to her...

I'd die.

Plain and simple.

Her place in my life was absolute. She'd been the only reason I'd survived after walking away from O. If I didn't have her, I would've slipped so deep and dark into the shadows, I wouldn't have cared about anything.

She was the reason I was still functional as a human being.

Take her away for much longer and…*I don't know what I'll become.*

"When you left school suddenly, I figured you'd been given an opportunity you couldn't refuse." Justin clinked his beer glass to mine on the bar. "Scored a deal before even graduating, huh?"

My hands clung to my pint glass, squeezing to the point of pain.

Fuck, what am I doing?

I shouldn't be here.

I should be at my warehouse painting another commission to keep idle hands busy and broken minds out of trouble.

Then why did you say yes to a beer?

Justin must've heard my thoughts as he asked, "Look, mate, if you don't want to catch up, then why are we here?"

I stiffened.

O.

O and Justin.

I need to know.

A crest of history and heartbreak crashed over me, and honesty that I could no longer hide spilled out in a snarl. "How's Olin, Miller?"

His eyes widened, eyebrows shot up as he shifted uncomfortably on the barstool. I held his stare, not giving him any reprieve.

That was the reason I'd said yes to catching up for old time's sake.

She was the reason.

The only fucking reason.

I'd lost Olive just like I'd lost O.

The pain of that was brutal…two bleeding wounds in one.

Turned out, I enjoyed torturing myself with unfixable things.

"Olin and I…" It was his turn to swill a mouthful of beer. He was older with weathered lines and age that no longer graced us with teenage youth, but his voice stayed genuine and truthful.

"We broke up pretty much the week you vanished from school."

I froze.

Questions roared for answers. I had no right to ask. She wasn't mine. But all this time, I'd soothed my agony by convincing myself O was with a guy who would protect and love her—even if it wasn't me. All the days and nights that I gave my all being a father to a kid who would *never* have the upbringing I did, I promised myself that Olin was better off without me.

That she was happy...with Justin.

"What happened?" I swallowed hard, fighting to get my voice into some semblance of calm.

Justin rounded his shoulders. "Well, eh, I knew she still had feelings for you. I mean...that was what drew me to her. To help her get over you."

"Gee, you're a real saint, Miller. A goddamn hero."

He held up a hand. "Look, you knew what O was like. She was so sweet to everyone. So kind and helpful. She helped me once when I locked my keys, wallet, phone—all my shit basically—in my car. Everyone else had gone home, and I was stuck like an idiot. She called a locksmith and waited with me until he'd popped the lock. I offered to drive her home but she said you'd be waiting for her. That you'd make sure she was safe." He whistled under his breath. "Even then, I knew she was head over heels for you. And she deserved to be happy. Not that I understood it. The sweetest girl in school with the meanest boy?" He drank again, rolling his eyes. "Didn't get that at all. But we were friends, and I was there for her when you made her cry." His gaze flashed bright blue. "I hated you for that by the way. Thought you were a right git."

I yanked my hands off the bar, curling them into fists between my legs. "I broke her heart, but you took advantage of her. You jumped straight into her bed."

True anger highlighted his normally rational face. "Fuck you, Clark. It wasn't like that. I offered to be her friend, that's all. To be there for her, seeing as you refused to be."

My eyes narrowed. "Don't give me that bullshit. I caught you two kissing. I saw your goddamn hand up her top."

His gaze filled with calculation, doing math on our past and forming conclusions he shouldn't have. "You sound as if you're not over her."

"It was years ago." I looked away, wishing everything was different. Wishing O was mine, and Olive was safe, and I'd never made such a fucking mess of everything.

Justin muttered, "Yeah, but time doesn't matter when hearts are involved."

My eyes flickered to the exit again, weighing up the options of running. Olin wasn't with him. He couldn't provide me with any comfort knowing she was happy or safe. She was out there. Alone. Somewhere.

My back tensed. "Why did you break up? If you were such good friends, what went wrong?" My voice had way too much bite, but Justin ignored my temper, being gracious with his reply.

"She was hurting. I'm not going to deny that we kissed a few times or that I asked her out for real. I seem to like damsels in distress. It makes me feel good to help them." He shrugged. "Still does if I'm honest. I'm with a girl right now, Colleen, who I found crying at a bus stop after her twat of an ex broke up with her at the movies and drove off with her handbag. I took her home, gave her a shoulder to cry on, and asked her out the next day. I dunno how it happens. I see someone hurting, and I have to help."

"You get off on helping?"

He scowled. "It's not sexual. It just…makes me feel like I have purpose. Like life isn't all about me."

I had no reply to that. How could I respond to someone who I'd nursed a teenage hatred for? I couldn't hate him because of how genuine he was. I couldn't despise him for taking O away from me when I'd been the one who pushed her into his arms. They were similar. They were both *good people*. And I was the bad guy all over again.

I wanted to punch him in the jaw. "O was never a damsel in distress, you idiot. If you think that, then you didn't know her at all."

Justin blinked. "Yeah, you're right." He took another swig, his beer rapidly vanishing. "After we broke up, O threw herself into dance. Became obsessed with it. You know her parents weren't really in her life, and the moment school finished, she left and joined a troupe in London. I didn't see her again."

London?

Had our paths crossed when I'd lived there with my infant daughter? Had we walked the same streets and not even known it? Had I brushed past her and not realised my soul-mate had been right there?

Fuck.

The gnawing, clawing pain of missing Olive tangled with the hot poker of loss from O. I grabbed my untouched beer and shot it down my throat. Alcohol wasn't welcome in my world. But my world had become unbearable.

The nights were the hardest while I lay unable to sleep in Olive's bed, smelling her favourite strawberry body wash, hugging a pair of her small pyjamas, wondering if she'd been fed and hugged, showered and tucked into bed.

I needed something to numb that pain. To slam a door on the horrors and grant silence from the nightmares.

Maybe beer could grant that peace.

Maybe that was why alcoholics abandoned their life for the numbing prostration that liquor provided.

I struggled for something to say. Justin kept looking at me far too intently—almost as if I was his next victim in his 'gotta help someone in need' crusade.

"Well, I'm glad she followed her dreams." I pushed away my empty glass, feeling sick to my stomach. I had ransoms to pay. Daughters to save. Ex-girlfriends to forget.

I couldn't fucking afford to drink.

Justin nodded slowly. "How about you, Clark? Everything okay with you? You don't look so good."

I couldn't hold back the cold snort. *"Me?"* Fuck, what a loaded question. My life was completely out of bounds. No one must know that I'd failed my daughter. The child who was born of rape and threats.

"Yeah, what have you been up to? Getting much sleep?"

"Ah, you know." My eyes once again trailed to the exit. My legs bunched to get up and leave. He'd told me all I needed to know. He wasn't with O. He hadn't married her and given her a family in some white picketed home where she would never be lonely again.

Instead, he was with a girl called Colleen, and O was off dancing in London.

There was no connection between the three of us anymore. And I was done.

Standing, I worked out the crick in my neck. The past two weeks of no sleep, barely any food, and the stress of Olive's kidnapping had turned every fist and kick from my youth into a delayed injury. I should've been too young to suffer arthritis, but I swore every joint and muscle had crept past eighty and no longer knew how to work. "I've got to go."

"Busy night painting?"

"Something like that."

Justin stood too. "I'll walk you out." Throwing a tenner onto the bar, he waved his arm, waiting for me to stride ahead first.

Hiding my annoyance, I stalked to the exit and bowled into twilight.

Justin crossed his arms against the slight chill in the air. "Who do you paint for?"

I'd hoped he'd quit with the questions the moment we'd left the bar, but he didn't. "Myself."

"Do you have a business name?"

I narrowed my eyes. "Why?"

"I'd like to pop by sometime. See your work."

"My work is different. My canvases are…not what you're used to."

"I'd still like to come by."

"Why? To check up on me?"

"Maybe." He smirked. "What do you paint?"

I looked down the street, past the milling pedestrians and smiling shoppers, and only saw a world that didn't care that my daughter was in the hands of a monster or that I was screaming inside for goddamn help.

I couldn't enlist the police.

I couldn't go to the media.

I had no family or friends to help me make decisions.

All I had was a fat bank balance that was waiting for me to withdraw a hefty amount for ransom number two.

"Come on, tell me." He laughed. "I'm a boring accountant. O has her dance and you have your art. Both of you followed your passions, not a paycheque. Share a piece with me, so I can live vicariously through you."

I sighed, wanting this meeting to be over. "I paint women."

His eyes lit up. "Naked women?"

"Knickers on but breasts mostly bare, yes."

"Wow, that's a career choice they don't mention at school." He punched me lightly in the shoulder. "Good for you, mate."

I stepped out of his reach. "I have to go."

"Fine. But we should do this again sometime. Soon."

"Why would we bother doing this awkward attempt at conversation again?"

For a second, he paused, no doubt annoyed that I'd spoken

the truth about this farce, but then he nodded with sincerity. "Don't get mad at me, Clark, but...I think you need someone you can have an awkward attempt at conversation with every now and again."

"What the fuck does that mean?"

"It means you look half-starved and the black circles under your eyes are either from working way too many hours or worrying about way too many things. Problems are better shared, mate."

I bared my teeth. "Keep your guesswork to yourself, all right, Miller? I'm fine. I don't need you or anyone—"

"We all need company at some point in our lives." Pulling his phone from his pocket, he quickly typed in something before scrolling through lines of text that appeared. It only took him a second before looking up with a triumphant, almost pitying look. "Master of Trickery. Cool name."

"How...how did you find that?"

"I googled man who paints naked women in Birmingham. You're on the first page."

Shit.

Was Olive mentioned on there?

Was my past and what'd happened with Tallup printed for the world to see?

Snatching my phone, I did the same search, relaxing when only business-related stuff and my website popped up. Reviews of my work and chatter on Facebook feeds about my time-lapse videos cluttered the search results, but there was no mention of my personal life, who I was, and what I'd lost.

Justin put his phone away and turned to leave. "I'll be seeing ya, Clark. I'll pop by with a takeaway sometime. Make sure you're not a starving artist and eating something occasionally."

"I don't need your charity, okay? Just back the fuck—"

"Who said anything about charity?"

"I don't need you sticking your nose in at my warehouse when I—"

"Cool, you have a warehouse? Definitely popping round now."

"Don't want you there, Miller."

"Too bad. I'm a nosy git and already issued myself an invitation."

I crossed my arms. "Don't you have some other helpless stray to smother with good intentions?"

"Nope." He smiled. "Just you for now. Colleen is getting a bit annoyed with my mother hen routine, so I need someone else to bug."

"Count yourself successful."

He laughed. "I will when you've lost that tortured, haunted look."

That won't happen until I get my daughter back.

Until I can stop thinking about O.

Until I'm no longer such a fuck-up.

I backed away. "Like I said, I don't do pity. This is where this ends. Got it?"

He just smirked. "I don't call it pity. I call it being a friend. See ya next week, Clark." Waving goodbye, he vanished in a sea of tourists and pedestrians, his threat lingering on the air.

Chapter Four

Gil

-The Present-

I WAS A bastard.

I knew that.

I'd known it since I was born: a self-centred, down-to-his-core *bastard*.

But being a bastard was necessary when raising a little girl on your own. I had to suspect everyone, protect her from everything, and be on my guard at all times.

Because if I didn't treat the world as if it was my enemy, it wasn't me who would get hurt.

It was Olive Oyl.

It's almost over, little spinach.

I promise.

I stopped the car.

The engine idled as I stared into the dense blackness of Lickey Hills Country Park. Rugged and wild, the trees silent and savage. He'd brought me to this forest when he'd first taken her. It'd been the only information he'd given me—taunting me with her safety every day of my godforsaken life since she'd been stolen.

And it was all my fucking fault.

I should have stayed true to my rules.

I should never have trusted him.

The past seven years, everything I'd done was for my daughter.

I'd learned how to paint with every medium to give me the best chance at employment. I'd accepted small commissions and badly paid work to get noticed. I'd slowly gone from penniless to middle-class, earning enough to keep Olive warm and fed.

And then what had I done?

I'd failed her.

In the worst possible way a father could fail his child.

My scratchy eyes landed on my hands strangling the steering wheel. They still held colour-splatters from painting O while she'd lain unconscious in my warehouse.

I wanted to cut out my heart for drugging her.

I'd rather give up my life instead of hers.

Who knows…you might.

He'd told me to paint her with the shadows of bracken: greys and greens, blacks and browns. The perfect camouflage to make her disappear in a woodland, leaving her to die alone and unprotected.

I'd disobeyed.

Instead of nondescript concealment, I'd painted every inch of beautiful skin in a personal punishment.

Punishment for me.

I'd used the colour palette he'd requested…but the symbolism airbrushed into her skin reminded me that tonight…it all ended.

One way or another.

Turning to study O, a suffocating wave of guilt wrapped around my chest. She lay sprawled and sleeping in the back seat, her eyes closed, lips slack, her beauty even more radiant thanks to the earthy colours she wore.

She looked as if she was the queen of an olive grove. Crowned with a wreath of silvery leaves, her arms and legs entwined with the supple branches of an olive tree. Thousands of olives. Black and green, brown and purple hung heavy on the interlocking, protecting foliage that crisscrossed and hugged her chest and stomach.

It'd been the worst commission of my life.

Painting a lifeless lover with the emblem of my daughter's name, all because if I didn't have the blatant reminder of who I was doing this for…I wouldn't have the guts to go through with it.

My daughter came first.

That was how it should be.

But O…*fuck.*

The urge to vomit rose again.

The back of my throat was raw. The taste in my mouth disgusting. I hadn't eaten properly in days and couldn't keep anything down.

I was fighting for both of them…but there was a chance this might not work.

I might lose my daughter or my soul-mate.

I might lose both.

I would rather lose my own life than allow that to happen.

You're late.

Turning off the engine, I climbed achy and beaten from the shitty hatchback I'd bought after selling my expensive 4WD when the bribes kept coming and I no longer had disposal cash to pay them. I opened the back door and bent to untie the ropes around her wrists and ankles so they were looser.

Rubbing away the redness my knots had caused her, I swallowed down another avalanche of guilt as I re-tied them, looser and not nearly as imprisoning.

Hopefully, she'd be able to wriggle out of them and run if this all went to shit.

I'm sorry.

Gritting my teeth, I slipped my arms under her legs and back, pulling her from the car and into my embrace.

She remained unconscious. Her paint had dried enough not to smudge. The weight of her in my arms made me suffocate and stumble in horror.

Fuck!

I couldn't do this.

I have to do this.

Hoisting her higher into my arms, I carried her paint-naked body from the small glade I'd parked in and entered the midnight wilderness.

My boots—that had been witness to my many crimes—once again squelched through mud and forest debris. The number of hours I'd trekked through woods trying to find Olive couldn't be calculated. Days at a time, midnight to dawn…always coming home empty, drowning my sorrows in liquor—the medicinal vodka burning my throat with hypocrisy.

I'd walked the entire length of England and back, searching, searching, always searching. Hoping I could find her before the next ransom came in. Before the next murder. Before the next threat.

O stirred in my arms.

Her eyelids fluttered upward, fuzzy and hazed pupils meeting mine as I carried her through the dark.

"Gil..." She swallowed. Her face scrunched up, fighting the nitrazepam the doctor had given me for my insomnia.

Ever since Olive had been taken, I'd turned into a total insomniac. The only sleep I snatched was filled with nightmares of chasing after Olive, promising her I'd find her, protect her, save her, only to slam me back into loneliness.

I'd crushed a few into O's sandwich, knowing the punch they delivered when they kicked in.

"Shush. I got you." Tears scalded my eyes as Olin shivered.

"I'm c-cold."

"Go back to sleep. It's warmer in your dreams."

She shook her head, sluggish and slow. "I don't wan—" Her eyelids drooped closed again, sucking her back into false hibernation.

"I'm so sorry, O," I murmured while silhouettes of trees swayed around us, spectators at a funeral.

Her funeral.

My funeral.

His funeral.

Anyone's but Olive's.

I had a long walk in front of me, off the marked trail and hidden from hiker's knowledge. My heart ached with grief that I couldn't stop this. My body trembled with every step. And the rotten bastard inside me couldn't just let Olin rest peacefully in my arms.

I treated her as my confessional. A priestess who had the power to absolve me.

Looking down at her lovely face, I whispered, "I have no excuse for what I'm doing, but...I was broken when I left you, O. Damaged beyond repair. If it hadn't been for Olive—" I slipped on a wet section of decomposing leaves. "I've been such a traitor to you. The worst kind of monster. You trusted me. You tried to help me. And this is how I repay you."

She murmured sleepily; her slumbering, gentle face ripped my heart out. Lax and young, innocent and pure. Her dancing dreams had been stolen. Now, thanks to me, the rest of her life might be too.

Nausea swarmed, prickling sweat under my shirt and making sourness coat my tongue. "I won't let him have you. I promise this will all work out." I raised my arms, bringing her close enough to kiss her cheek—the softness of her painted olive grove skin. "Once you're safe and Olive is safe…I'm going to kill him. And once he's dead, I'm going to confess everything to the police. I can't live with this anymore. I deserve to be punished for what I've done." I laughed hollowly. "After all, I've always been destined to go to prison. I've avoided it longer than I expected. I was born to a pimp, whore to a teacher, and now, I'm a collector for a murderer. The first two crimes weren't my fault. But the third…I'm guilty."

My voice thickened. "I'm guilty, O. Those girl's deaths smear my hands, and I'm done. Tonight is the last time he'll ask me to kill."

Olin mumbled something in her sleep, her lips working with mysterious words.

I needed to believe she'd heard me and understood.

In reality, if she had heard, she'd condemn me to the devil and rightfully so.

My fingers feathered over her hip where her painted-lacy underwear ruined the perfection of smooth branches and tiny, silver olive leaves. Inside the seam rested the GPS tracker. I prayed to everything holy that it worked and didn't fail me.

I was placing all my faith in its accuracy.

I was gambling my daughter's life as well as O's that Jeffrey would return to his unfindable location with Olin and keep her alive long enough for me to hunt.

The small piece of technology hadn't warmed from her body; it didn't feel like a friend…merely another foe I couldn't trust.

"I'm a bastard, O, but I'm not giving up. He's bled me dry of everything. I hate what I've become. But he can't have Olive, and he can't have you. It's over. It's time for *him* to feel what it's like to die."

My hands curled into fists, tasting the black satisfaction of murdering a murderer. I had the perfect weapon to do it. It sat quiet and unassuming in my left pocket, ready to steal his life.

Once he was dead, I'd gather my daughter and soul-mate and walk back into the light.

And if he kills them before you get to him?

My rage once again became brittle with fear.

My plan was flimsy and chaotic, but it was the best I had.

I'd been backed into a corner and was willing to do whatever it took.

Including sacrificing myself if it comes to it.

My eyes continued to trace O's prettily painted face while I shifted her weight into one arm. Stopping for a moment, I pulled my phone free from my right pocket.

It was time to send plan B.

Bringing up the message I'd typed to Justin moments before O arrived at my warehouse, I fought the urge to be sick all over again.

To see what I'd become in black and white…to re-read my crimes.

Fuck.

This sort of message wasn't meant to be sent. Justin and I didn't exactly have the sort of relationship where any of this was acceptable.

We'd just bumped into each other by chance, and instead of him walking away like he should have, he'd barged into my world and refused to take no for an answer. Our 'friendship' consisted of him being far too forgiving and me being a fucking asshole.

He reminded me too much of O's kindness—constantly tormenting me with memories of them together…kissing.

But each time he'd turned up at my warehouse, his presence somehow gave me the energy to keep going. To paint another commission. To pay another bribe. To keep my secrets hidden because, despite my outward unwelcome, he'd become *needed*.

Needed to keep me human so I wasn't a total monster when I finally rescued my daughter.

I owed him so fucking much.

And this message…well, it sold me into debt that I would never be able to repay.

Miller,
I have so many things to say, but I don't know how to say any of them.
I'll begin with the simplest one.
Thank you.
You're a better man than I'll ever be. You've had my back. You've helped me book commissions. You've nodded when I've snarled at you. And you never once asked why I was such a twat.
This message should end here. It should be a simple thank you.
Unfortunately…I have a favour to ask.
I've named you executor of my estate.
Why?
Because I'm involved in the painted murders.

I've helped take lives to save a life.
The life of my daughter.
Olive.
The story of her origin isn't important, but what is important is, I will do whatever it takes to save her.
And this is the part where you'll hate me all the more.
I know you cared for O.
I love her with all my fucking heart, but…I need you to help her.
Along with this message is a link to a GPS tracker. The device is hidden on Olin. She is the next victim, and I'm doing everything I can to keep her alive.
But…if I fail.
If I die.
I need you to find her before it's too late.
Call the police. Tell them everything.
Find her, rescue her, keep her.
And…when you find her, please find my daughter too.
My heart belongs to both of them.
If I've failed…please take care of them.
I name you godfather.
Keep my loved ones as your own.
Tell O I'm sorry.
Tell my daughter that I tried.

Chapter Five

Olin

-The Present-

"YOU'RE LATE."

My eyes struggled against the heavy curtains pulling them down. A cloak of sleepiness and weighted imprisonment.

Gil's arms twitched around me, his deep rumble of a voice threatening and soothing all at once. "It's a long walk."

"Long walk or not, you took your time on this one, Gilbert. Dangerous time." The man's tone changed, speaking to someone younger and innocent. "Look who decided to join us, sweetheart. Told you he'd turn up."

I squirmed to focus on whoever he spoke to. A camping light hung in a tree, illuminating the small clearing. My eyes closed again, my muscles ignoring my commands in favour of exhaustion.

But this time, I fought back.

I fought hard.

I moaned and clawed my way to the surface.

This is important.

It was imperative I had wits and wisdom, flight and fight. I couldn't quite remember why, but...

Killers.

Painters.

I'm next.

Standing in the gloom of the false moon lashed to the tree, a man stood with a calculating grin on his face. Beside him stood a child. A girl with long sooty hair, her pretty eyes huge as a nocturnal creature better suited for darkness, not light.

"Get your fucking hands off her." Gil's entire body stiffened as his gaze landed on the child. His chest heaved against me, his heart thundering painfully. "Hey, Olive Oyl. You okay?" His voice echoed with grief and the gravity of seeing a little girl with an older man's paw resting on her shoulders in the woods.

My own stomach churned at the picture.

Olive?

Olive!

His dream, his nightmare, the love of his life.

Olive…the consequence of rape.

"Hey, Daddy…." Her face scrunched up with worry. "I missed you."

"Oh, God. I missed you too, little spinach." Gil's legs gave out, forcing him to stumble forward and place me as gently as he could on the ground. His voice cracked. "Wow…you've grown so big."

She smiled cautiously. "Uncle Jeffrey said I could come see you."

"That's great." Gil dared look at the guy holding her captive. His entire body trembled to rush forward and grab her. "You finally brought her? After a goddamn year of keeping her from me?"

"Be grateful I was feeling generous." The guy chuckled quietly, his hand waving permission to continue conversation.

Gil cleared his throat, doing his best to find strength I feared he no longer had. His eyes drank in his daughter as if he was drowning. "You okay? God, I've missed you *so* much."

Olive cried quietly. "You don't look so good. Are *you* okay?"

"I am now that I'm with you." Gil strangled a laugh. "Missing you is hard work." He forced a wink, his face twisting with relief and terror. "I haven't had anyone to help me cook spinach lately." He added wobbly humour into his tone. "Know anywhere I can get some out here? Could do with a shot of strength right about now."

Olive kicked her dirty sneaker into the earth, no longer willing to talk. "Are you not strong like Popeye anymore?"

Gil flinched. "I am now you're here."

Olive sniffed. "Daddy, I want to go home."

The love in her voice. The yearning and need. She adored Gil. Totally in love with her father just like he was in love with her.

I wanted to hate her.

I wanted something to direct my rage at Gil's molestation. Jane Tallup deserved to be publicly shamed and then shot…but her daughter? The little girl who stood in the darkness wasn't her awful mother.

She was afraid and small and trapped.

And she needed her father.

Desperately.

Another wash of tiredness tried to suck me under.

Something hurt me deep, deep inside.

My heart cried for this small family who'd been ripped apart by greed. My head pounded for freedom for all of us.

Gil's entire fight vanished; he left me lying on the bracken, raking both hands through his hair as he stood upright on exhausted legs. "I want that too. And we're going home. Tonight we're going—"

"Ah, ah, ah, making promises you can't keep again, Gilbert?"

Whatever drugs Gil had fed me fractured at the man's tone.

Him.

The black van.

The asshole who beat up Gil all because I'd used the word *us.*

Gil stiffened; his face turned black. "I'm done playing this pathetic game, Jeffery." His voice dripped with menace. No more distress, only danger. "I've given you everything I have. I have nothing left. You hear me? Nothing. You've made damn sure of that. Just let me take my daughter and—"

"Not so fast."

The little girl shot forward, spying an opportunity to run. "Daddy!" She bowled toward Gil, her arms outstretched, her face afraid. "Please—"

She didn't get very far.

Jeffrey swiped at her, catching the hood of the lemon jacket she wore. Wrenching her back, he tutted under his breath. "That's rude, sweetheart." Ducking to his haunches, he yanked the girl into the cage made by his legs. "Living with me hasn't been so bad, has it? You've enjoyed the toys I gave you. You said you did." He shook her. "Be a grateful little girl, sweetheart. Go on."

Olive sniffed back tears, nodding bravely. "Yes, Uncle

Jeffrey. Thank you for the toys."

"And?"

"And for taking care of me when Daddy couldn't."

Gil roared with fury. "Leave her the hell alone."

"There's a good girl." Jeffrey spoke to Olive before rising to his feet. "I see you brought me a gift, Gilbert." He acted as if he hadn't heard Gil bellow at him. He behaved as if this meeting in the woods was perfectly rational behaviour.

"Name your price," Gil snarled. "Any figure. I'll give it to you. A million? Ten? I'll do whatever it takes to pay you. Just let it be about the money and forget about O and Olive."

He bartered for my life.

He begged for Olive's.

My brain short-circuited, unable to accept such wrongness.

The drugs snatched me back.

My world went dark and silent.

I slipped.

Slipped from chilly forest to soft clouds.

Blackness.

Blankness.

A void.

* * * * *

I came to, being collected gently from the forest floor, only to be placed at the feet of the man who'd destroyed Gil's life.

I was cold.

The ground was prickly and painful on my bare, painted skin.

Gil's face hovered above mine as my eyes shot wide.

I was coherent and blazingly aware, if only for a moment.

His eyes held lines only old men who'd buried loved ones and survived holocausts should carry. His lips were bitten and cheeks sunken. He barely looked alive, sucked dry by the devil keeping his daughter as collateral.

"It's always been you, O. Always." He kissed me softly; his voice sullied with despair. "But…I never had a choice." His lips skated over mine again, shivering with apologetic misery.

"D-Don't…" I blinked madly, fighting the binds of tiredness, wishing my tongue worked as well as my vision.

But it was too late.

Gil placed me tenderly at the feet of a murderer.

"Now, get back." Jeffrey pointed a finger at Gil as if he was an unruly wolf. "You know what we agreed."

What did they agree?

What did I miss while I'd been sucked back into sleep?

Gil tripped backward. "Please."

I struggled to sit up, to dig my palms into the dirt and stop this madness. My mind might be awake, but my body definitely wasn't. It was loose and languid, powerless and prone.

It took every bit of energy I had to twist my head to keep Gil insight.

He looked as if he wanted to rip Jeffery into pieces all while he slowly fell to his knees and prepared to beg. He might have resorted to pleading, but there was nothing pathetic about him. Nothing useless or inadequate about a man willing to lower himself to dirt for those he loved.

He was regal, a legend, a father who knew where his loyalties lay and what love demanded.

He was the reason I was here.

His paint on my skin, and my death on his hands.

He didn't deserve my forgiveness, but he did have my understanding.

I had no choice but to understand the depths of his pain and desperation whenever he looked at his daughter. It blazed all over him like a physical entity. A power he couldn't deny.

His hands banded together in prayer as his gaze flickered from me to Olive. His throat worked as he swallowed hard, his voice strangled and dying. "Name it, Jeffrey. What do I have to do—"

"Keep delivering what we agreed."

"I have. Thousands of times over."

"Yes, but retirement is expensive."

"I'll pay your every bill and whim until the day you die, just let me take them home."

Jeffrey chuckled coldly, wrapping his fist in Olive's hair.

She cried out, flinching as he pulled her cruelly into his side. "You think I'd trust you to pay without incentive?"

"I give you my word." Gil swallowed again, his face white and strained. "You'll always be rich. I'll give everything I have—"

"Enough," Jeffrey shouted. "Get out of my sight before you humiliate yourself further."

"You can't take her again." Gil scrambled to his feet, his fists curled and shaking by his sides. "Keep your side of the bargain." He winced, looking at me bound and drugged on a bed of twigs and leaves. "Olin for Olive. I've paid your price." His hand came up, waiting for a smaller one to fit into his. "Give me my daughter."

"Popeye," Olive whimpered.

Jeffrey snickered, yanking her against his leg. "Change of plans."

Gil's face lost any sign of vulnerability. His eyes shuttered, his lips thinned. Aggression rippled over him. "Give her to me. I won't ask again."

My heart picked up, filtering the drug and granting a tiny trickle of strength to limbs tingling and tight from being tethered.

"I like how you think you're in the position to threaten me." Jeffrey snaked his arm around Olive's shoulders, hugging her close. "Maybe I'll keep both of them, tighten your leash a little more."

Olive winced, curling into herself.

Jeffrey sighed dramatically. "And you used to be so obedient."

Gil bared his teeth, his entire body vibrating with pure hatred. "A deal is a deal."

I wanted him to win.

I wanted his daughter to be saved and no longer living with a madman.

But if he won, that meant I lost.

I would die in her place, and my survival instinct wouldn't let that happen.

Flexing my fingers and toes, I willed more blood to circulate, to wash me clean, to give me power.

Slowly, my body shed the garment of lethargy, answering my commands.

Gil stormed forward, all negotiations and pleasantries over. He looked as if he'd tear Jeffrey's head right off his shoulders.

I wanted him to.

Kill him.

Save us both.

But it only took Jeffrey the smallest move to halt Gil mid-step. His hand vanished behind him, whipping forward with a gun. "Decide. Here and now." The black weapon glinted in the lamplight, morbid and menacing. He swung the muzzle to face me. "The woman you love?" Almost lazily, he tracked the weapon to wedge against Olive's temple. "Or your daughter?"

She froze like a tiny rabbit. Teeth locked on her bottom lip. Her shivers pure fear.

Gil struggled to breathe. His eyes shot black, cursing Jeffrey to purgatory for even pointing a gun at his child. "I promise you, you motherfucker, if you shoot either of them, you'll be dead a second after."

The two men's eyes locked.

A silent war passed between them.

Finally, Jeffrey nodded and waved the gun at the dense blackness just out of reach of the lamp. "I think I'll keep both alive...for now. Higher incentive for you to pad my retirement a little more, don't you think?"

"I'm not painting any more girls."

"So you don't agree with my little hobby?"

Gil couldn't hide the growl in his chest. "Killing for sport is—"

"A recognised pastime," Jeffrey sneered. "Hunters shoot deer. Humans eat animals. Anything with a heartbeat is killable." He grinned darkly. "I just happen to like the two-legged variety."

Gil spat on the ground. "I'll kill you, you son of a bitch."

"Perhaps." He laughed, way too confident and assured. "But as long as I have your daughter, you're my puppet. So...I expect you to keep dancing on your strings." He waved the gun again. "Now, run along, Mr. Popeye, and don't forget to eat some spinach. Olive Oyl is right; you aren't looking so good."

Gil didn't move.

For the longest second, he stared at me, then Olive and shook his head as if he couldn't believe the trap he'd been caught in.

He hated himself.

His self-loathing permeated the air until he choked on it.

I waited for him to walk away.

To leave both of us to our fate.

But something triggered in him. Some base instinct that didn't bow to rules or threats, not anymore. He couldn't walk away. I knew that in my bones.

I didn't know how long it'd been since he'd seen Olive.

I didn't know anything about his life anymore.

But the building outrage on his face spoke of a man who'd reached his limit. A man who would no longer kneel to another—not when those he loved were in danger and within grabbing distance—ready to be saved if he could only kill the monster in the middle.

He stalked toward Jeffrey with his gaze locked on his

daughter. "Olive, come here."

Olive squirmed and fought, kicking and scratching at Jeffrey as he struggled to hold her.

I played my part in the distraction, kicking my tied legs and wriggling on the slippery bracken.

Jeffrey witnessed his carefully choreographed meeting dissolve into anarchy.

Gil leaped forward.

One hand reached for Olive, and the other punched Jeffrey in the jaw.

The three of them tumbled in a pile of body parts while Gil tried to murder his enemy with nothing more than fists and fury.

I tried to scream. To activate a voice that stayed dormant with drugs.

But then a gunshot rang out.

A swarm of crows exploded from the treetops. Pigeons and sparrows, finches and thrushes all soaring for the sky thanks to violence.

I squirmed and gasped, trying to sit up to see. To know if the bullet had missed or...

Tears pricked as Gil fell backward, his hands high above his head in surrender, his eyes frantic as he searched Olive for injury. "You okay?" His breath caught and voice scratched with gravel. "Please tell me you're not hurt."

Thank God, he wasn't shot.

Fierce hope filled me that the rogue bullet had lodged inside Jeffrey.

Olive cried, crystal tears glittering on pretty cheeks. "I'm all right." She stayed sitting in the dirt, shoulders rolled and grief overtaking, knowing that Gil's attempt at rescue had failed, and she was about to pay the consequences.

Just like me.

With his gun high, Jeffrey clambered to his feet, brushing off leaf matter and curling his nose at the mud stain on his knee. The flutter of disgruntled birds still flapped around us.

He wasn't shot.

He wasn't defeated.

"That was stupid, Gilbert. Very, *very* stupid." He aimed the gun directly at Gil's heart. "I suggest you start walking before I change my mind."

Gil shook his head, furious despair painting his features. "I can't leave them."

"But you will if you want to live another day."

Gil looked at me, apology and uselessness blazing bright. He looked at Olive, desolation and failure crippling him.

He came to the same conclusion I did.

He didn't have a choice.

Fight now.

Die now.

Or walk away and hope to save us later.

Olive cried harder, understanding that the family reunion was about to end. "No! Take me with you. Don't—" She stood and tried to run to Gil, only to be cornered in Jeffrey's arms. "Don't go. Please!"

Gil squeezed his eyes shut, a tear licking down his cheek. "Olive. I love you. Forever and ever." His gaze opened, locking onto his flesh and blood. A family he'd created not borrowed. A little girl who idolized him. A child who believed he could fix this when he couldn't. "Please don't hate me for failing you. I'm not leaving you, okay? I'll never, *ever* leave you. I just…this is temporary. We'll be together again soon. I promise."

Olive cried harder. "*When?* When is soon?"

He shuddered. "As soon as I can. I promise we'll be together. I *promise*."

Olive somehow managed to sniff up her sadness and nod bravely. "Okay. I'll be good. Maybe Uncle Jeffrey will let me go home if I behave better."

Gil vibrated with hate toward the man holding her captive. He couldn't stop his boots crunching forward, taking him toward the gun aimed in his direction and his young daughter. "Jeffrey, please…for fuck's sake, you have O. I'll continue to paint and deliver on your demands. Just give me Olive. Let me take her home. Accept the trade."

I winced at the urgency in his voice. The utmost dedication to his child while using me as collateral.

He'd already destroyed all my trust. Now, he destroyed all my hope.

Destroyed any hope that I was as important to him as Olive was. I was only valuable if I could be traded for what he truly wanted.

Once again, I wanted to hate.

I wanted to hate him and her and the man they called uncle.

But…no matter what he'd done to me—no matter the drugs he'd fed me and the bargains he begged for, I didn't have the strength to hate.

Hate demanded such a lot. It needed energy and emotion and a deep, dark heat that *burned.* Mostly naked and shivering on the forest floor, I had no energy. I'd used up all my emotion. The only thing I felt was tired.

Tired and resigned and sad.

So, so *sad.*

I'd lost everything.

I thought I'd lost it the moment I couldn't dance anymore.

But I'd been naïve.

A tattoo couldn't fix this.

Scars couldn't repair this.

This truly was the end.

I closed my eyes, willing the drugs to whisk me away.

But they didn't. They kept me awake and at their mercy as Gil whispered, "O…I'm so fucking sorry."

My eyelashes opened, filling my vision with his misery.

"I love you." His lips turned down as he drank me in. His gaze travelled over my skin painted with his mark, my love left as his sacrifice. For the longest moment, he stared, pouring love and apology into me, and begging me to understand, all while knowing he'd lost me forever.

There was no coming back from this.

No way of repairing what was broken.

With the heaviest of nods and most reluctant acceptance, he blew Olive a kiss, gave me one last look, then turned and walked away.

He tripped as if exhausted. He stumbled as if wounded. He moved like a man who'd forfeited everything.

A cresting, debilitating wave of terror cracked my ribs, one by one. My lungs sipped air rather than inhaled it. Fear vised my skull with pressure. Grief mushroom clouded until it filled me.

I hadn't had a panic attack since the first day I'd woken and found my body restricted by pins and pain.

I couldn't afford to have one now.

Steadying my breathing, I kept my eyes locked on Gil as he slowly left us behind.

The crunch of his boots sounded as horrid as cannon fire.

The sniff of his sadness as damning as death.

As the night swallowed him, Jeffrey bent to speak to Olive, his voice just loud enough for my enjoyment too. "Daddy isn't being a good boy these days." He stroked her hair even as she squirmed to get away. "He's not a very good painter anymore." He tapped her on the nose. "You know what? I think we've had enough of boring old Popeye, don't you?"

Olive gasped, clinging to Jeffrey's arm. "He just needs some spinach—"

"No...he needs a harsher lesson." He shook her off him, standing tall. He raised his hand, pointing the gun at Gil's back.

Olive bounced on the spot, trying to grab his wrist. "No. Don't—"

"Shush, he'll hear you." Jeffrey snatched her and wrapped his free hand around her mouth. "Be quiet, sweetheart."

She moaned and mumbled behind his palm while he chuckled quietly, keeping his tone low so Gil would never know. "Let's shoot him and say bye-bye." He closed one eye, scoping out his prey. "Bye, pathetic nephew."

It happened in slow motion.

I couldn't believe he'd do it.

But then, it became real.

So unbelievably real.

No!

I opened my mouth to scream. To shout. To warn.

I jack-knifed as high as I could with rope and tiredness and yelled into the night. *"Gil!"*

But...just like before...it was too late.

The gunshot ripped my voice apart.

The bullet flashed through the dark.

Somewhere in the blackness, Gil grunted.

A vague shadow cartwheeled forward.

His arms flew backward.

Birds squawked.

Twigs snapped.

Death lodged in his spine.

Gil landed face first in the dirt.

"No!"

Oh, my God.

"No!" I rolled onto my stomach, trying to wriggle with my hands bound behind my back to get to him.

"Gil!"

I fought harder, the ropes slipping a little.

But strong fingers plucked me from the earth. Harsh breath slithered over my nape, and brute strength whipped me around to face him. "Hello again."

I had no time for him. I didn't care about him. He was nothing. *No one.*

"Gil!"

Looking over my shoulder, I willed him to be okay.

But…he didn't get up.

Didn't move.

Didn't react.

"Daddy!" Olive tried to run past Jeffrey, only to be jerked to a stop by her jacket hood again.

"You two, fuck, you have some manners to learn." Pulling a length of rope from his pocket, he managed to catch Olive's flying fists and block his ears from her terrible screams as he tied her tight.

Slapping her cheek, he snarled, "Quiet. He's dead. It's over. I'm your father now."

Olive just cried harder.

I had so many things I wanted to say.

So many curses to slur and promises to decree, but the awful, clinging sleep still hadn't freed me entirely. I opened my mouth, but only tears fell.

He shot him.

He shot him!

"Gil…*please* wake up!"

Jeffrey slapped me, just as he'd slapped Olive. "You shut up, too." Bending a little, he wedged his shoulder into my belly and hoisted me over his back. The air crushed out of my lungs. My ribcage bruised as he slung me like a carcass.

Jerking Olive forward, he looked back one last time at Gil's corpse as he stole us away. "Say goodbye to that useless body painter. You won't be seeing him again."

Chapter Six

Olin

HE'S GONE.
Gone.
Gone.
I didn't dare voice the other word. The more permanent word.
Dead.
He's dead.
He might not be.
I saw him fall.
I watched the bullet.
But I didn't see the wound.
Didn't see the blood.
Too far away to feel his pulse or check his breath.
Gone or dead...they were both the same.
The GPS tracker dug into my hip as I swung over Jeffrey's shoulder. The bones of his arm burrowed into me, compounding agony on top of agony. If Gil was alive, I was grateful. If he was dead, I was distraught.
But it didn't matter because I'd never see him again.
The GPS coordinates wouldn't save us as there was no one coming. The little blinking location on Gil's phone was utterly pointless.
Gil might still be alive.
But...I was dead.
Olive was dead.
Every heartbeat on borrowed time.
Olive hadn't stopped crying. I'd lost track of how long Jeffrey had dragged us through the dark. The paint on my skin

457

tugged the fine hairs beneath. The bite in the air dressed me in chills. And Olive's hiccups and distress sent empathy digging deep into my soul.

Her grief consumed the entire forest.

Her belief that her father was dead absolute.

I wanted to comfort her.

To tell her he might be okay. He might live. He might still come and save us.

But I had no air in my lungs from being hung upside down. I had no freedom from pounding temples or slithering tiredness that still threatened to drag me under.

Jeffrey snapped a curse, hauling Olive into a walk as she tripped mid-cry.

She'd just witnessed her father being shot, and he didn't care at all.

Numbness spread over my stomach, doing its best to protect me from the pain of being carted like a kill. My ears strained for sounds of someone chasing us. Of Gil barrelling through the darkness, healthy and very much alive.

But there was nothing.

No one.

Just my terrified thoughts jumping from topic to topic.

Of freedom.

Of fighting.

Of forgiveness.

Gil hadn't wanted to do this to me. He'd thought he could win by gambling two lives in order to save one.

But he'd lost.

Three lives in one.

His family...his true blood...his child.

A child that couldn't stop sobbing.

Jeffrey snarled again, hushing Olive so that only the hoots of owls and scratchings of foxes serenaded us as we travelled the final way.

His footsteps slowed as we reached a small clearing. I tried to see around the upside-down view of his butt but could only make out a lumbering shape in the gloom.

Olive tripped again, only to be hauled to her feet thanks to the rope around her wrists and a harsh jerk from Jeffrey. A clink of keys sounded as he shoved them at her. "Run ahead and unlock, sweetheart. You know the rules now, don't you?"

She sniffed loudly. The keys stopped singing as her fist

clutched them, and she shot forward away from Jeffrey's abuse. The rope wrapped around her wrists slithered after her in the bracken like a venomous snake.

She moved as if she knew this place well. As if this was her home, all while Gil had done his best to save her. Jeffrey chuckled as he jostled me higher, carrying me to where Olive sniffed and struggled to unzip a large tent.

Bending his knees, my captor groaned as he slid me from his shoulder and plonked me onto the forest floor. For a moment, I couldn't breathe. The release of pressure from my ribcage was too much, and my lungs no longer knew how to operate.

My head pounded as blood whooshed from my ears and back into my legs. Grey and black spots danced over my vision as I shook my head, doing my best to clear the remaining fogginess.

Whatever this place was, I couldn't afford to stay a victim. Jeffrey had shot Gil after telling him he'd keep us alive for better motivation. He'd ended his retirement pay-out by shooting him, so why would he need to keep us breathing?

We were merely a nuisance now and not an incentive.

Time was running out.

Jeffrey checked the rope around my wrists and ankles, re-tightened the knots Gil had done around my wrists, undid the ones around my legs, and hauled me to my feet.

He grunted as I wobbled. "For fuck's sake, I've carried you for long enough. Walk the final distance." Shoving me forward, he chuckled as I plummeted to my knees. With my hands tied and balance still compromised, I face-planted into a rotten pile of leaves and muck.

"Don't know what he saw in you." He nudged me with his boot as I pushed up and did my best to stand. His gentle kick was enough to land me in the dirt again. "Come on, Bambi, don't have all day."

I threw him a glower over my shoulder. "Stop it."

"Stop what?"

"This. Whatever you're doing. Let us go."

I fought for the child of the woman who'd ruined Gil's life. A child of her creation. But Olive was Gil's, not Tallup's.

And this bastard shot him.

My heart squeezed, allowing the word 'death' to sink past my fortress. I didn't have time to grieve.

Sticking my chin up, I forced myself to picture Gil alive. I stood, working out the tightness in my muscles as my body came alive after being hung like drying meat, and focused on freeing myself and Olive.

Jeffrey grinned. "Didn't learn your lesson from last time, huh? You're still using that dangerous little word." His face shot close to mine. "Us."

"Fine. Release Olive and me."

"Nope." He laughed. "Why would I do a stupid thing like that?"

"You shot Gil. What other use do you have with us if he's not around to pay your demands?"

"Oh, I have other ideas." He tapped his nose with airs and graces of a secret. "He did a good job padding my retirement. He kept his mouth shut and his wallet open. It'll be sad not to have such a lucrative nephew, but…" His hand shot out, arching my chin up with his knuckle, bringing the whiff of old cigarettes. "You two can fetch me a pretty penny in other ways."

I wanted to spit in his face. "We're not for sale."

"Sweetheart, everything is for sale." He smirked coldly. "Gilbert knew that lesson very well."

My teeth clenched together, hate rolling over me like a wave.

Jeffrey pulled me through the tent's entrance, revealing it wasn't a tent but an awning attached to a caravan. A three-seater couch sat beneath an outdoor heater along with a coffee table, TV, and two plastic boxes of household supplies. A threadbare rug covered most of the bracken and twigs, creating the illusion that this was a cheery cabin in some safe woodland. The caravan door hung open, spilling light into the awning.

"Gil was born to whores and became a whore. Their shelf life isn't the longest—just like any merchandise." Jeffrey looked me up and down, licking his lips. "He was at the end of his use-by-date. But you…you're just getting started. I'll probably sample you before I sell you. Write a review for prospective buyers— that'll be a laugh. Are you worth one star or five?" He snickered to himself, dragging me up the caravan steps.

Olive whimpered as we entered the cramped space. She huddled against a window, wedged between a long table with bench seats on either side. She pulled her legs up, scrunching them against her chest. She hugged herself tight, while her chin rested on her knees.

Colouring books scattered the narrow table, revealing vibrant doodles and designs outside of the printed mandalas. She was Gil's daughter all right: she had his talent with colour.

I gave her a smile. A smile that I hoped said I was there for her and I wouldn't let anything happen to her. A smile that most likely said the same things her face did: that we were screwed and all on our own.

She gave me a watery smile back, tears still falling silently down her cheeks.

Jeffrey pushed me until I slammed into a bench seat opposite Olive. My bound wrists throbbed as they smashed against the table. Pencils jumped at the impact.

Jeffrey rolled his eyes as if I couldn't do anything right. Closing the caravan door, he locked it, then marched to the kitchen and fridge in the middle of the tiny home. Ripping open the door, he pulled out a beer. Twisting off the cap, he drank the entire thing in one go.

I supposed shooting his nephew and kidnapping was thirsty work.

Gil.

He's dead.

My heart skipped a beat.

You don't know that.

He tied me up and left me to die.

Stop it.

My hands balled as I focused on Olive.

Her eyes skated away from mine, wet and full of sadness. I studied her cute button nose and petite forehead—two features that came from Tallup. I traced the thick unruly dark hair and cutting cheekbones—two inheritances that came from Gil.

She was a beautiful child.

Dainty and delicate, long-legged and sweet.

She looked as if she'd been born to these woods. As if she'd had a fawn for a father and a fairy for a mother.

Her eyes met mine again.

Grey.

Not green. Not blue. Not brown.

Grey.

Gil doesn't have grey eyes.

Didn't *have grey eyes.*

Stop that.

He's alive.

My stomach clenched as I fought off black thoughts, recognising the identical stare of the woman who'd been our teacher.

Years existed between that time and this yet, watching Olive, I saw similarities. The quick movements as Olive swiped at her damp cheeks. The intelligent gaze as she glanced at Jeffrey.

She had a lot of Gil running in her blood, but she also had a lot of her mother.

My heart fissured with hurt.

The pang of jealousy didn't make sense.

The rush of confusion and pain was a luxury I couldn't afford.

The GPS tracker in my underwear pinched against my side, giving false promise that someone would find us before unspeakable things happened, but all I could do was stare at the sweetest girl born from assault on a teenage boy.

A boy who'd given up all his dreams to love and protect her.

Another tiptoe of tiredness hit me.

I didn't want to think or worry or hurt anymore.

I wanted to sleep.

And then wake from this nightmare.

Olive sucked in a shaky breath, her tears still flowing. Looking at her uncle, she whispered brokenly, "Ca-Can we go back?"

Jeffrey tossed the empty beer bottle into the sink. "Go back where?"

"To see Daddy. He was hurt." Her fists curled. "You hurt him."

With a threatening swoop, Jeffrey squeezed onto the bench beside Olive and crowded her against the wall. Her shoulder bumped the lacy tieback on the cream curtains. She didn't whimper when he gathered her into his side and wrapped a reptilian arm around her fragile shoulders. She had courage. She'd lived with this monster a while.

"I didn't hurt him," Jeffrey muttered. "He hurt himself by not being a good boy and following the rules." He tapped her on the nose. "Unlike you, sweetheart. You're very obedient, aren't you?"

I squirmed on my side of the table, my body writhing in denial of this grotesque human being tormenting a young girl. "Don't touch her."

Jeffrey chuckled, cuddling Olive closer to spite me. "You,

meanwhile, have a lot to learn."

Olive's cheek squished against his chest, her eyes closed while evermore tears fell. I didn't know how such a young girl could be so brave and quiet.

It hurt me to see her so manhandled and alone.

Ignoring Jeffrey, I spoke to the little girl who desperately needed a friend. "Olive...I'm Olin. Our names are so similar. So...that means I like you straight away."

Olive stiffened, her eyes flashing to mine.

Grey as a winter's day. Endless as infinity.

Her grief over Gil's shooting twisted into shock. "You're...you're Olin, too?"

It was my turn to stiffen. I didn't like the way she looked at me. As if she knew me. As if we hadn't just met and she knew my deepest, darkest secrets.

Jeffrey narrowed his eyes, waiting for me to reply. I hated that he shared in this conversation but at least it bought me time to figure out how to escape. "I am. Do you know another?"

Olive sniffed, wriggling in Jeffrey's hold to rub her nose with the back of her hand. "Daddy has an owl called Olin." Her eyes filled with more liquid. "I bought it for him with my pocket money."

My heart slowed and raced at the same time. "A nice name for an owl."

She cried quietly, her sorrow consuming her. "He told me he had an owl as a friend when he was younger. It was called Olin. It was my favourite story. He always seemed sad, so I bought him a stuffed one to try to make him happy."

Something hot stabbed me in the chest. "That was very nice of you."

My mind raced back to the second night Gil was drunk. When we kissed in his bed and he clutched a fluffy owl beneath his pillow. An owl that represented me, given to him by his daughter.

Tears welled and overflowed. I couldn't stop them.

The secrets.

The pain.

It hurt too much, firing through my insides, leaving a vast, aching emptiness behind.

"He's a good liar, my nephew," Jeffrey said. "Promised there was no connection between you two. Yet I find out that you were the one telling the truth. There was an 'us'." He smiled cruelly. "Although…not anymore."

I swallowed back my hate and tears. "You're a bastard."

He chuckled. "No swearing in front of the kid."

"Age doesn't stop her from knowing exactly what you are."

Jeffrey soared upright. The caravan wobbled from his momentum, shuddering like an earthquake. His fist connected with Olive's colouring books, scattering pencils.

Olive quickly snatched them before they rolled to the floor. Scooping them into a pile, she nursed them as if they were alive and in need of soothing.

Leaning toward me, he growled. "You're lucky you're worth more to me alive. Otherwise, you'd be tied to a fucking tree, dying." Without looking at Olive, his tone switched to syrup. "Sweetheart, can you tell our guest what happens if you speak out of turn?"

Olive gulped. Grabbing a sky blue pencil, she coloured furiously, keeping her gaze on the paper. "You don't get any food for a full day and have to sleep tied to a tree outside in only your nightie." She licked her lips, obviously reliving a similar sentence. "It's scary and cold, and you don't sleep much. And then, in the morning, you have to wash your mouth out with the dishwashing brush while Uncle Jeffrey helps clean your dirty tongue with vinegar."

"Thank you, Olive. You remembered your lesson very well."

She shivered and switched her blue pencil for a red one, digging the pigment into the paper all while tears dripped onto her design.

I held back my own shiver and kept my spine locked. "You think you're special for torturing a child? You're nothing more than a mons—"

His hand lashed out, all five fingers squeezing tight around my throat. The smear of paint on my skin felt oily against his touch, all while dried parts flaked away.

My roped wrists swooped up, trying to scratch him for breath. But he merely caught the rope and kept my hands away.

I held his stare, doing my best not to panic or struggle.

He smirked, leaning into me to whisper in my ear. At least he had the decency to keep diabolical plans for adult ears only. "Listen up, Olin Moss. And yes, I know who you are. I know about you and Gil at high-school. I know about your failed dancing. I know everything there is to know about your pathetic little life."

His fingers relaxed a little, granting a much-needed gush of air. His nose tickled my throat as he dragged his lips along my painted skin. "You want to know what's going to happen? I'll tell you. We're about to hit the road. I've had a long day. I wanted to sleep before we began our long journey, but you're just so eager to get started that I'll be a good host and do what you want."

His sour breath sent goosebumps all over me. He angled my head toward Olive, his thumb pressing hard on my pulse. "And that little girl is going to come for the ride. We're heading to Italy. There's a market there in a few weeks. A market for men who want exclusive, pretty things. That gives me plenty of time to train you up for whoever is stupid enough to buy you. And it gives you time to stare at that cute kid and know what her fate will be. Every time she plays, you'll know that in a few short days she'll belong to some man who will pay a fortune to fuck a child. You'll know that her time of innocence and freedom is ticking away, hour by hour, and there is nothing, *nothing* you can do about it."

Bringing his lips to mine, he forced words into my mouth even as I struggled to get away. "You'll do your best not to get attached to her. You'll try to save her. To be her friend. To promise her you'll both get free. But you can't stop what's going to happen. You'll hope that each day will bring rescue, and each day it won't happen. That's what will kill you. Not the fact that this rope will never leave your wrists. Not the fact that you'll be chained to this caravan until your new master takes control. Not the fact that I will fuck you daily until some other bastard pays for the privilege."

He kissed me harshly, pulling away with a feral gleam in his eyes. "The thing that will kill you, Olin Moss, is hope. Idiotic hope that this is all a crazy mistake and will be over soon."

Letting me go, he stepped out from the bench seat and towered over me. "Do you know what I loved about letting dehydration and exposure kill those painted girls?" He sighed with contentment. "I never got my hands dirty—apart from the last one—but the thrill was just the same as if I'd been the one to snuff out their lives."

I couldn't unlock my jaw to be human and speak words. If I opened my mouth now, I'd snarl and spit and howl like a trapped animal that held nothing but loathing for its captor.

"It was the anticipation. The journey of watching them fight; their eyes bright with hope and expectation of being found in time. Then slowly, minute by minute, that hope vanished all while their bodies gave out."

Olive bit her bottom lip, acting as if she couldn't hear her uncle talk about murder.

He clapped his hands. "Olive. What time is it?"

Olive leaped to her feet, scurried around him, and bolted to the bunk beds at the other end of the caravan. In a flash, she dove beneath covers with pink ponies on them and stared back at us with big, grey eyes. The obedience and quickness in which she moved broke something inside me. She didn't smile or seek reward for her good behaviour. She didn't obey him out of respect.

Just fear.

"Bedtime, Uncle Jeffrey."

He beamed like a proud gorilla. "Good girl. You stay there until I come get you."

Snatching me, Jeffrey unlocked the caravan door and hauled me from the couch. His fingers wrapped around the rope on my wrists.

Light-headedness made me sway while I blinked back residual drugs.

"We're going for some private time."

Stark fear clogged my veins. "No."

He didn't reply, just dragged me down the caravan steps and into the chilly awning. His yellow teeth glistened in the hanging lantern by the boxes of belongings. Wrapping his arm around my waist, he pressed himself against me, rolling his hips into mine, revealing the horrid hardness in his dirty jeans. "Time to learn what my nephew saw in you."

"Take your fucking hands off me." I squirmed and tried to knee him in the balls, but his hold was too tight. My wrists burned as I fought to get free. My heart raced faster than it ever had before.

Jeffrey let me wriggle, unfazed and gloating, knowing he'd won. "Let's see why he never got over you, shall we?" Throwing me onto the threadbare couch, he cupped my jaw and held me down. His knee landed on my belly, pinning me onto my back. "I'm telling you now, I'm more experienced than my nephew. I also have different needs." His rancid lips landed on mine. "You'll find that out soon enough."

I bit his bottom lip, spitting onto the floor as metallic copper hinted I'd broken his skin.

I braced for a fist or retaliation. However, he just chuckled as if my rage was mere melodramatics. His hand landed on my naked, painted breast and squeezed so hard white light exploded behind my eyes.

I gasped and bucked, trying to run from the painful whip of hot agony.

He stopped.

He shoved my arms up and looped my roped wrists around a hook holding the metal framework of the awning.

My shoulders screamed for release.

My soul bellowed for salvation.

Jeffrey climbed off me and pulled the gun he'd shot Gil with from his waistband. He stroked it as if it were alive and a very good friend of his. "I didn't like guns before tonight, did you know that?" He placed the heavy weapon onto the chipped coffee table reverently. "I'm more of a fist and blade kinda guy." He smiled. "That's changed. I'd rather enjoy another excuse to use it, so by all means, fight. I'm sure whoever bids on you won't mind an extra hole somewhere on your body."

"You're deranged."

"Maybe." He unbuckled his trousers, his belt buckle dangling as he winked. "Deranged or not…you're mine now. And I'm ready to play."

Chapter Seven

Gil

I'D WITNESSED MANY things children shouldn't see.

Things *any* person—young or old—shouldn't see.

I'd watched men beat whores. I'd heard whores scream behind walls. I'd lived in hell where the devil constantly drank and slurred and punched his only son.

I'd dealt with all of it.

I'd blocked out what I couldn't process and focused on a future that he could never touch.

Before Tallup put her claws in me, before I lost O, before Olive was stolen, I still believed in hope.

But now, I didn't have much left.

My boots crunched and tripped as I followed the flashing dot on my cell phone. My vision faded around the edges, my breath shallow, my blood decorating the forest floor like a cookie crumb trail back to freedom.

The pain had become unbearable.

The urge to drop to the ground and die a sinister whisper in my veins.

Keep fighting.

I texted Justin, willing my fingers to move over the tiny screen.

Call police. I fucked up.

I could barely see to send it, falling to my knees as another lick of agony lashed down my back.

With a groan, I climbed to my feet.

And kept going.

* * * * *

I was too late.

O would never forgive me.

Not for any of my sins.

Especially this one.

I couldn't see my daughter, but I knew she was here.

The camouflaged painted caravan and its long-stay awning was where that bastard had kept her from me.

I would've killed him for that alone.

But watching him tear off his shirt and unbuckle his jeans added a whole new homicidal rage to my already flaming hate.

O lay trapped on her back on the couch, glowering at him, her lips pulled back in a snarl. She didn't beg or reason; she just waited for his attack as if ready to fight until death rather than let him touch her.

My vision flickered again as my hand slipped into my jeans pocket where my weapon of choice still waited. The violence that I'd always pushed aside roared through me. It heated my blood and deleted my agony.

I stepped silently into the awning.

The darkness kept me hidden. The lantern too weak to throw illumination my way. O fought my uncle as he grabbed her thighs and tried to spread them.

Both of them preoccupied.

Both of them unaware as I sneaked on shaky legs.

My fingers ached to steal his gun, discarded and lonely on the coffee table. To point it at his head and pull the trigger like he'd done to me. He deserved to feel the fire it left behind. The punch. The shove. The heat.

But he also deserved to feel how his victims had felt.

The helplessness.

The awful, terrible sensation of dying from passing time.

Pulling the syringe from my pocket, I carefully uncapped the needle while O screamed a curse and Jeffrey threw himself on top of her.

The deadly sharpness of the needle made my heart pound.

I couldn't fuck this up.

If I did…

O's gaze wrenched to mine as I took the final step toward my uncle.

Her mouth fell open, her fight vanished, disbelief pinning her to the couch.

Jeffrey froze, twisting on top of her to look behind him.

I couldn't let him grab his gun.

I couldn't second-guess.

Without a word, I lunged forward and jabbed the needle into his naked ass.

The entire length vanished into him, earning a howl and violent fist swinging in my direction.

But it was too late.

My thumb pressed on the plunger, and I shot the entire contents into him. I didn't know if it would work, not going directly into a vein, but I had to hope.

He roared upright just as I stumbled backward and snatched his gun from the coffee table. My back roared from his previous bullet. My vision grey and black. I levelled the muzzle at his chest. "Don't move."

His boxer-briefs clung to the top of his thighs. His disgusting erection made me want to vomit.

If I'd been any longer...

O squirmed and kicked on the couch, doing her best to remove her binds. I would've given anything to free her, but it wasn't over yet.

Soon.

Soon it would be and I could rest.

Wedging one arm against my bleeding side, I struggled to keep the gun raised and ready. "Pull your pants up, you fucking bastard. Don't want to die with them around your ankles, do you?"

His lips pulled into a snarl as he hoisted the material up. "Die? The only person dying here is you, my boy."

I shook my head. "Not tonight."

That might be a lie or the truth. I couldn't tell anymore.

I was mentally and physically exhausted.

The trek through the forest. The worry over what I'd done. The warm blood cascading down my legs.

My body didn't feel right anymore.

Pieces of it shutting down.

I didn't have much time.

Jeffrey lunged toward me. I feathered my finger on the trigger. I'd put a bullet in his face if need be. I wouldn't hesitate. But he was already dead. He just didn't know it yet.

"Daddy?" Olive appeared at the door of the caravan. She had a blanket around her shoulders and her long hair static from a pillow.

"Hey, little spinach." I grimaced, doing my best to smile.

"Stay in the caravan, okay?"

"You're alive!" She leaped down the three steps and launched toward me. "I knew you were okay. I knew—"

Jeffrey grabbed her, yanking her by the hair and jerking her into his side. "He's a ghost, sweetheart. A dead man walking."

"No!" She struggled, her cheeks wet with tears.

"Let her go!" O kicked the air and cursed.

And I just smiled at my daughter, relief slowly overtaking my panic. I'd kept my promise. I'd found her. "It's okay. Don't struggle."

Tears spilled down her cheeks. "You're here to take me home, right?"

"Right." I nodded, the gun growing heavy in my hand. My arm shuddered with the weight as another wash of lacerating agony slashed at my back.

Jeffrey's hand curled around Olive's throat. She went deathly still. "Give me the gun and I won't kill your daughter."

Just like I'd been over the dramatics and threats with Tallup, I was over this too.

I let my arm fall. The gun clattered to the leaf-strewn carpet.

Olive whimpered, thinking I'd given up.

I hadn't.

I'd won.

Jeffrey coughed and stumbled.

Olive squeaked as he pulled her with him. I shadowed them, ready to grab Olive the moment he dropped.

It wouldn't take long.

His eyes widened as things started dying in his body.

"Wha-What did you give me?"

My voice was cold as stone. "Succinylcholine."

He swallowed hard, his throat blocking breath. "What the fuck is that?"

"It's as close as I could get to showing you how your victims felt."

His knees gave out, plummeting him to the floor. Olive cried as he clutched her for support. But I was done letting that monster control my daughter.

My side snarled as I leaped forward and scooped Olive out of his grip. He didn't fight me. He couldn't. His muscles and bones no longer obeyed him.

Already his eyes struggled to stay open. His mouth hung lax. He tumbled onto his side, bound in a prison of his own making.

Olive clung to me as Jeffrey drooled. I kissed the top of her head and let her stay plastered to me while I skirted Jeffrey and unhooked O's rope.

She glared unforgivingly as I grabbed a knife from my back pocket and sliced through the final restraint.

She rubbed the rawness on her skin, embracing freedom. She looked me up and down, no sign of trust or affection, just relief that I wasn't dead. "You're alive."

"I'm alive." I bowed my head, unable to stomach the blood ringing her wrists from where she'd struggled against the rope.

Fuck, I'd let her down so much.

Backing away, understanding she wouldn't want me close to her, I twisted Olive around so her face pressed into my stomach. I didn't worry that her arms would get sticky with my blood. I didn't have any idea how much this would traumatise her or how I could ever make it up to her.

Olive moved with me as I crouched beside him. His eyes stayed half-hooded and crazed with confusion.

I murmured, "You're dying, Jeffrey. The drug is used to paralyse. It's part of what surgeons use in local anaesthesia. Administered like this with no breathing apparatus or doctors nearby, it's fatal." I sighed, reliving the utter despair I'd felt one night. The inability to sleep. The failure of losing Olive. The destitution at paying blackmail. I'd walked the streets, seeking help.

I didn't know what I wanted. I wasn't weak enough to kill myself, but I was weak enough to dabble with the idea of forgetting for a night.

The drug dealer I'd spoken to had a range of pharmaceuticals. His sister was a nurse. Underpaid and overworked, she helped stock his street store with things otherwise impossible to get hold of.

He'd described the deadly drug with a strange kind of fondness. Said he'd watched a *Forensic Files* from America and how it'd been used in a killing where the murderer got away as the drug left no trace behind.

He'd told me the method of death.

How the nervous system shut down, followed by respiratory failure, and every other pump and flow that kept us humans alive. The victim suffocated to death, all while their body lay paralysed. Unable to scream. Unable to move. Locked inside a form that no longer belonged to them.

I didn't know why I'd bought it.

I used up money I didn't have.

But I was angry.

I was broken-hearted for the girls who'd lived such similar fates, tied to trees and hidden under bushes, bound by ropes and silenced by gags.

Jeffrey deserved to feel a fraction of what they went through.

And even though I'd researched it—read studies on other killings involving the drug that said science and forensics had gotten too advanced to no longer be the invisible killer—I didn't care.

I would go to prison for murder.

But so what?

I'd been avoiding jail my entire life.

I'd managed to stay out of the system even though my childhood was primed for me to become a pickpocket and delinquent. I'd managed to raise a daughter on my own after a teacher molested me and threatened to have me thrown in jail for rape.

Jail for me was always a shadow, stalking me, waiting for me, playing roulette with which crime I'd be imprisoned for.

At least this one was justified.

Patting Jeffrey's cheek, I said, "Thank you for teaching me the most important lesson of all, uncle. Thank you for showing me that trust isn't something I can afford. I'll make sure to teach my daughter, so she's never as gullible as me."

His lips didn't move even though his eyes begged for breath. His stare was full of panic and pleas, desperate to live. He didn't even have the luxury of gasping for air or thrashing around for help.

He was silent.

Still.

A corpse already.

He'd taught me how to use my painting talent. He'd also taught me that I'd come from a lineage of bastards.

I was the last one left.

And who knew, maybe I'd die with him tonight.

The adrenaline keeping me awake finally gave way under an icy cloak of shock. The blood that'd steadily been pumping down my legs was no longer warm but chilly.

I was cold.

And very, very tired.

My eyes met O's as she hugged herself, dabbled in painted olives, crowned in silver-leafed twigs, she was so beautiful she could pass as the angel that would guide me to heaven.

But I didn't deserve heaven.

I knew where I was heading, and I clung to my daughter one last time.

"I'm sorry, Olive Oyl. So, so sorry." Her hair smelled wrong. No scent of strawberry or home. She felt bigger than last year. Her arms stronger and hair longer. I'd missed her growing. I'd failed her for far too long.

She wriggled closer as my head swam and I no longer had the strength to fight.

Olive was free.

O was safe.

That was all that mattered.

I fell to the floor and blacked out.

Chapter Eight

Olin

THE AWNING HAD become a tomb.

My hands were soaked in Gil's blood from trying to stem his bleeding. Olive had helped me grab kitchen scissors and cut up one of Jeffrey's shirts to wrap around his wounded waist.

We'd both tried to revive him, yelling, touching, even throwing a glass of cold water on his face.

I couldn't carry him out of here on my own and I had no idea where we were.

My skin had turned to frost from the bitter night and Olive couldn't stop whimpering beside her unconscious father. My gaze kept crawling to Jeffrey, open-eyed and slack mouthed, dead and silent on the floor.

Forcing myself to stay focused and not give in to shock, I patted Gil's pockets, searching for a phone. I cringed against the tackiness caused by his cooling blood, refusing to look at the red pool beneath him.

I couldn't carry him to help. Therefore, help would have to come to him.

I cried out in relief as I found his mobile.

Olive huddled close to me as I swiped it on. No password, which was good. A black screen with a red dot and a dark forest glowed. The GPS had worked.

Gil had chased us.

He hadn't given up.

I won't give up on him either.

Typing in the emergency number, I pressed connect, only for the device to leap in my hands with an incoming call, interrupting the outbound attempt.

I recognised the name.

I answered with a shockwave of relief.

"Justin." My voice cracked. Heat flashed up my spine.

I sticky-taped my emotions together for Olive and Gil's sake.

"O? Oh, my God. Is that you?" Justin's panic filled the awning, cutting through Olive's fresh sobs. Poor girl had witnessed her dad being shot and had his blood all over her innocent hands. And now she shared space with a cadaver. What sort of psychological issues would she battle?

"Yes, it's me, but I'll have to talk to you later. I need to call the police."

His voice lowered with authority. "I already did. I called them forty minutes ago when Gil sent his second message. What the fuck is going on, O? Where's Gil? Are you okay?"

I looked down at the taupes, silvers, and blacks decorating my mostly naked body. I couldn't make out what foliage pattern he'd covered me with, but I had no injuries of my own—just Gil's blood painting me in a morbid hue.

"He...he said he has a daughter. Is she...with you?" Justin's tone held disbelief. "Tell me what the hell is happening."

I looked at Olive. She curled beside Gil, nuzzling into his side, crying softly for him to wake up. Inching closer, I stroked her back, doing my best to offer comfort when I had none to give.

"Yes, she's with me. We're fine. But Gil's been shot. He needs medical attention urgently."

Something rustled outside. Twigs snapped. Leaves crunched. My skin pebbled with fear as I stood and braced for yet more predators.

Jeffrey had been a predator and had been put down for his violent tendencies. What new evil had found us?

"The police shouldn't be too far away. They'll be able—"

"Police! Don't move." A bright spotlight suddenly shone from the deep darkness beyond the awning. I raised one arm, keeping the phone by my ear with the other. "They're already here." My eyes squinted against the brightness, shivering in the cold.

"Hands up!" More boots, more footsteps, more officers.

Letting the phone fall to the floor, I raised both arms and stood as close as I could to Olive and Gil. Nudging him with my toe, I wished he'd wake up and tell them exactly what'd happened.

But he stayed unconscious. His blood was a dark stain on the dirty carpet. Three officers flooded into the awning, their shrewd gazes bouncing from my painted nakedness, Olive's tears, Gil's blood, and Jeffrey's corpse.

A cop ducked to Gil's side, tending to him, checking for a pulse.

A wave of utter exhaustion swept through me. Most likely from the drugs but also from the chaos that would come from this. The fear of Gil's survival. The worry over Olive's trauma. The total upheaval of my own life going forward.

Tomorrow lurked largely with the unknown.

If Gil died…my future would unfold one way.

If he didn't…it would unfold another.

Either way, I would never be the same.

A young male cop with a black beanie and bright blue eyes came toward me. "You can put your arms down, miss."

I nodded, lowering them gratefully. They automatically wrapped around myself, seeking warmth after being naked for so long.

Another officer with a matching black beanie and grey beard appeared behind me after checking the coast was clear in the caravan. He draped a woollen blanket over me from one of the bunk beds.

I gave him a weak smile, tugging the scratchy material closer, glancing at the officer still checking on Gil.

A female agent with her blonde hair wrapped in a knot at the base of her nape went toward Olive. "Hey, you okay? Not hurt anywhere?"

Olive scrambled to her feet, Gil's blood all over her from where she'd hugged and pleaded with him. "It's my dad. Please help him."

The woman nodded. "We'll take care of him. But right now, I need you to come with me. All right?"

Olive scowled. "No. Dad needs me." Tears wobbled on her bottom lashes. A tantrum made up of horror and heartbreak quickly scrunched up her face.

I scooted next to her, wrapping half my blanket around her tiny shoulders. "It's okay, officer. I'll stay with her."

Olive looked up, her huge eyes blinking and distrustful. "Do you know how to fix Dad?"

Shaking my head, I whispered, "No, but these nice people

do. They need to take him in an ambulance to the hospital. The doctors there will help."

Olive bit her lip. "I don't want him to leave. He can't leave me again."

How many fears would she have to overcome after the tragic year she'd suffered? The separation and threats?

Two officers squatted by Jeffrey's body, their voices low while checking vitals. Finding none, they spoke curtly into a walkie-talkie, hinting they'd just elevated this crime scene from worried caller to homicide.

A young male agent asked me, "What happened here?" He gaze travelled over my painted legs poking from the bottom of the blanket.

Where did I begin?

What could I say?

I would never be able to lie, but I also couldn't tell the truth.

Gil killed him.

I wanted him to do it.

Another wave of tiredness caught me, making me wobble. I overacted the effects, purely to get out of unanswerable questions.

An older man appeared. He'd taken his beanie off and his dark hair stood up in disarray. He spoke into a walkie-talkie stuck on his shoulder. "Three for an ambulance. One critical." Giving me a smile, he said, "Questions will come later. For now, let's get you help."

Chapter Nine

Gil

"YOU GOOD FOR nothing son of a bitch!"

I ducked my father's swing, missing the full brunt of his fist. I wanted to shout back that he would know. Only he knew which of his whores I'd been born to, seeing as when I asked them, they never answered me. Never hinted who I belonged to.

But even at seven years old, I knew better than to answer back.

Dad chased me, quick for a man drowning in booze.

I bolted from the lounge and into the dingy kitchen. "Come here, you little runt."

Breathing fast, I tried to charge around the table piled high with dirty dishes, only to be yanked back with his fist in my hair. He threw me to the ground. He loomed over me like a bear. He kicked me so hard in the side, I almost blacked out.

The world went slow and sluggish as pain overtook every perception.

I curled around the dull throb from his boot, swallowing back silent tears, refusing to let them fall.

"There. That's your punishment for not picking up my pack of smokes like I told you to."

The pain didn't diminish.

It only spread.

When I didn't get up and scurry away like I normally did when he beat me, he crouched and nudged me with his cigarette-stained finger. "Winded, boy?"

I gritted my teeth and didn't move.

I couldn't move.

The agony in my lower back stole everything.

Bored of my injuries, he stood and chuckled. "Ah well, learned ya lesson. Next time do what I tell you and you won't get hurt."

He strolled from the kitchen with a drunken whistle, leaving me to watch daylight switch to midnight. Whores came in and stepped over me.

Paying customers rolled their eyes as they chose which woman to use.
And I waited until I felt better again.

* * * * *

I woke to heaviness.

To false numbness.

To terrifying strangeness.

My limbs were connected to my body, but they were stretched and knotted, utterly useless against the softness I lay upon. Just like so many times in my youth, I lay still, waiting to heal so I could be free from overwhelming agony.

My throat was the first thing to trigger an avalanche of pain. I swallowed, trying to push away the sensation of underwater sluggishness, but it seemed to give permission for every injury to roar alive, every cell determined to destroy me first.

I gasped, crashing fully awake, wishing I could reverse the process and fall back into the numbing blackness once again.

The heart-rate monitor attached to my chest beeped as my pulse increased. A door opened and closed, delivering a middle-age female with brown hair and silver-framed glasses to my bedside. Her blue slacks were covered with a white coat and the pink sneakers she wore squeaked a little on the linoleum. "You're awake."

Turning a few dials on the machine beside me, she stayed busy for a moment, administering something with a push of a button. "I've just given you another dose of morphine. It will take the edge off."

I didn't have chance to thank her before the door opened and another visitor arrived. Not a white coat of medical personal but a stern uniform with important buttons and emblems.

Police.

He marched to the bottom of my bed, his arms crossed and face cold. "You're under arrest, Gilbert Clark, for the murder of Jeffrey Clark and accessory before the fact in four other cases."

I winced as a flare of heat lashed around my back.

So this was what it felt like to finally be held accountable for your crimes.

His chin arched, delivering the rest of my fate. "While in the care of Birmingham Medical, you are not to leave this room under any circumstance. You are allowed an attorney and have the right to remain silent—"

"Can't that spiel wait?" The female doctor scowled. "He's just woken up from surgery. He won't be walking anywhere."

I swallowed again against the wildfire in my throat. I didn't care about me. I was irrelevant. "My daughter. Where's Olive?"

The doctor patted my hand, careful not to bump the IV line disappearing into my vein. "Your daughter is fine. She was kept overnight for observation. You can see her later."

"No visitors." The cop frowned.

"He can see his daughter, for crying out loud. She's screaming blue murder to make sure he's okay. If you won't let him see her for his sake, then do it for the child's. She's been through enough."

I didn't know who this woman was, but I liked her immensely.

A flood of gratefulness and fresh agony gushed through me. "Is...is Olin Moss okay?"

The woman nodded. "Fine. Both are fine."

I had so many questions, but they scattered the moment I tried to move and my side felt like hungry wolves shredding my innards. "Holy—"

"Ah, yes. Don't move if you don't have to." She lowered her voice, shooting a look at the lurking cop before focusing on me. "You sustained a gunshot wound to the back. The bullet didn't cause excessive damage, going in clean and causing a large but manageable puncture wound upon exit. The good news is, it didn't hit anything vital. Far enough away from your organs to go clean through you."

I blinked. "I bled a lot."

"You did. You needed a transfusion." Turning to the cop, she snipped. "Can my patient have some privacy please?"

His eyes narrowed. "He's under arrest. He doesn't get privacy."

"What happened to innocent until proven guilty?"

"He's guilty of murder."

I flinched.

Before, I'd been willing to pay the price, but now sick worry filled me.

Will they take Olive away?

How could I be such a fucking idiot not to think of that?

Fear landed like a landslide on my chest.

I'd only just gotten her back.

I wouldn't survive losing her again.

Losing Olin again.

You lost O a long time ago.

The doctor's tone softened as she did her best to ignore the unwanted visitor in the room. "Do you remember arriving in the emergency room? We did a CT scan before surgery to ensure there were no internal injuries."

I frowned. "I don't remember."

"That's okay." She smiled. "The complicated jargon can wait. For now, the abbreviated version is, you'll live. You've been stitched up and responded well to treatment. You'll be in a fair amount of pain for a few days, but then it will ease, and healing will accelerate."

Days?

I didn't want to be in here for days.

I wanted to be with Olive.

I needed to talk to O.

You leave this bed, and you're in prison.

Either way, I would be kept away from the people I needed the most.

Shit.

A lash of agony ripped up my back. I sucked in a breath, shifting on the bed.

"We'll leave you to rest." The doctor patted my hand again. "Sleep. Heal. I'll answer any questions you may have when you're a little more comfortable."

I resisted the urge to capture her wrist, asking, "Can I see my daughter?" I needed to see her with my own eyes. To touch her. Kiss her. To never let her go again.

"Soon." She backed away from the bed, eyeballing the cop to leave too. "Rest first. I'll bring her to you in a bit."

I wanted to argue, but sudden tiredness hung off my eyelashes, dragging them down. I felt cold and strange—as if the foreign blood in my veins poisoned me from the inside out.

I couldn't fight the sinking.

I lost the fight.

I slept.

* * * * *

"No! I want to see him. I need to make sure he's okay. Daddy! Dad! Popeye!"

My eyes wrenched open, my heart galloping at the sound of Olive's shout. Jack-knifing upright, I forgot too late about my stitched together side.

I groaned in pain as I lay back down, a prickle of sweat breaking out all over me.

The heart-rate monitor went berserk, and the sounds of angry officers threaded with the melodic calm of O's gentle tone. I couldn't hear what she said, but after a minute of whispered argument, the door cracked open and Olive bowled inside.

"Dad!"

I braced myself for her hug. Ready to hide my agony from her at all costs. My arms spread as she launched against the bed, her face landing on my stomach and arms around my hips. "You're alive!"

It fucking hurt.

Everything fucking hurt.

My body screamed to push her away, but my heart would never do such a thing. My heart hurt worse than any physical form.

I'd failed this perfect creature.

I could never fix what'd happened.

I clutched her so damn close, suffocating her into me. I stroked her soft, silky hair, squeezing my eyes from suspicious, stupid tears.

The luxury of touching her.

The privilege of having her back in my embrace.

Fuck.

I didn't care I was bankrupt, full of holes, and other people's blood.

I didn't even care I wasn't a free man anymore.

All that mattered was Olive was safe.

Finally.

Swallowing back heavy gratitude, I pulled her away so I could see her pretty face. "Hey, Olive Oyl. You okay?" Nudging her chin up, I smiled as her huge, gorgeous grey eyes met mine. I'd long ago stopped comparing her eyes to her mother's. In Jane Tallup, the grey had been evil and flat. In Olive, the colour was pure and wholesome. I loved the soft shade. I loved how serene and endless they were.

The greyness suddenly glossed with tears. Her mouth wobbled, and she pressed her cheek into my palm as I raised my hand to touch her. "You were lying in the forest. Not moving."

"I know. I'm sorry I scared you."

"I wanted to come back to get you. But Uncle Jeffrey wouldn't let me."

"It's not your fault, little spinach. None of this is your fault."

She bit her lip, doing her best to stem her sadness. "I missed you so much."

"I missed you more."

She threw herself onto me again. Her face pressing into the blankets covering my wounded side. I hid my pain, wrapping my arm around her fragile back.

I didn't think about the future.

I didn't worry about how much time I had with her.

I just closed my eyes and hugged my daughter.

Chapter Ten

Olin

STARING AT MYSELF in the hospital bathroom mirror, I did my best to clutch to the resolve I'd made last night. The oath I had no choice but to follow.

I didn't like hospitals—they reminded me too much of what I'd lost after my accident. I hadn't wanted to come back.

But I had to see Gil.

To convince myself he would be okay…before I left.

You know what you promised, O.

I pointed a finger in my face, waggling it at my reflection.

Stand by it.

I nodded.

Today, my skin was its normal colour. My hair clean and brushed. My pink jumper and tight jeans my only decoration. I was just a simple girl visiting an old friend from school.

Yesterday had been a different matter.

I'd showered at the hospital so they could apply creams to my rope-burned wrists and ankles and check me over. They'd given me a hospital gown to dress into and guided me to a room to wash. I'd closed the door on the nurse helping me and seen my painted flesh for the first time.

I hadn't known what Gil had painted me with.

But there, standing under the bright neon, I found out.

Olives.

Thousands and thousands of olives.

He'd cried while forcing me to eat a sandwich laced with sleeping tablets. He'd apologised while he'd carried me deep into the forest. And he'd painted me in the namesake of the only girl who would ever own his heart.

That had been the moment.

The moment.

Where all my misery and patience just…stopped.

It was like a switch flicked from forgiving to done.

Gilbert Clark had been through a lot. He'd dealt with things no one should have to deal with. He'd never had anyone to rely on and kept far too much sorrow to himself. He'd pushed me away out of some broken chivalry to protect me.

And by trying to protect me, he'd forced me to face his demons and risk being sold by his uncle.

I'd believed I could save him with kindness. I'd hoped compassion could set him free.

It's time to stop being so idealistic and blind.

He'd broken my trust while painting me that night.

He'd saved my life by killing Jeffrey before collapsing at my feet.

The wrongdoing he'd done by sacrificing me was paid in full by stopping a terrible fate. I could forgive him for what he'd done. I forgave him for everything he'd put me through.

But…that was where my tolerance ended.

He might have had a rough upbringing and allowed society to carve him into something he wasn't, but I'd had my own share of nightmares.

I'd coped with a lonely childhood, a life-changing accident, and loving a boy who would always grant more pain than happiness. I'd endured trials and sacrifices and managed to retain the goodness that I valued over anything.

That was where we differed.

I fought for what hid beneath the lies.

Gil pushed away what was in front of him.

And…it was over.

I would be nice and gentle. I would be his friend.

But I would also pick me from now on because I'd given him everything I had.

I'm leaving.

Starting afresh.

I had to.

As I'd stepped into the shower, a calm sense of relief filled me. Relief to finally have a decision that felt binding. I would always be Gil's friend. I would answer his calls and accept his messages if he wanted to stay in touch, but that was where my loyalty had to end. Where I had to choose not to be the tragic wallflower, wilting in a sad little vase, waiting for him to choose me.

He could never choose me because he'd chosen Olive.

As it should be.

That night, I'd done my best to sleep in an uncomfortable hospital bed, tossing and turning, knowing Gil was in surgery and his daughter was in the care of strangers.

I'd been released in the morning and gone home to my apartment.

Everything had felt in a different dimension. A strange new planet.

My key still fit in my lock. My kitchen still held my dishes. My bed still smelled of me. But none of it seemed real anymore. I'd distanced myself from it and needed to leave.

To leave and start again…for me.

Shannon had called from Status Enterprises, and I'd apologised yet again for not turning up for work. She assured me it was fine. She'd heard the news about what'd happened. That the company would give me two weeks fully paid to recover before returning.

I hadn't had the heart to tell her I no longer wanted to live in my home city.

I didn't have the courage to go online and read the news articles about what'd happened.

Instead, I dressed and ate a muesli bar before catching public transport back to the hospital.

To say goodbye.

My hand dropped. My reflection showed a girl far older than she was. Dark circles painted under my eyes; my lips permanently sad.

I didn't want to be that girl anymore.

I wanted more.

I deserved more.

You deserve to be happy.

I nodded at the mirror, brushed a few stray hairs from my forehead, and left the bathroom.

* * * * *

I stood outside Gil's room, listening to the low rumble of his voice and the high-pitched tone of Olive's. The two cops guarding his door stared at me with annoyance. Pissed off that I'd stood up to them when they'd tried to deny Olive from seeing her dad.

487

It'd been serendipitous timing.

I'd arrived at the barricaded room just as Olive came flying down the corridor, no longer willing to wait for a nurse to take her to her father.

I'd argued on her behalf.

I'd won her entry.

And now, I wanted to give them time to say hello, before I said goodbye.

Focusing on the older cop with his handlebar moustache, I asked, "Why are you guarding Gil's door?"

His eyebrows drew together. "He's a prisoner."

My heart kicked, not wanting to accept that Gil's problems weren't over. "For what?"

"For killing Jeffrey Clark."

I scowled. "But Jeffrey kidnapped us and murdered at least four women. He took me and would've raped and killed me if Gil hadn't—"

"Murder is murder, miss." He crossed his arms. "And Gilbert Clark was involved."

My temper rose. "He didn't kill those girls."

"He was an accessory. Caught with his hands dirty."

I gritted my teeth, unwilling to argue the painted murders but needing to justify Jeffrey's. "Did you not hear me? Jeffrey Clark was seconds away from raping me. Gil killed him in my defense. He killed him because he kept his daughter for over a year. He was *justified*."

The cop didn't react.

It wasn't fair.

Gil had done many wrong things, but killing his uncle was not one of them. I still didn't understand if they were related or if it was just a term of speech, but his death was the only good thing to come out of all of this.

Footsteps sounded on the bleached linoleum. Wrenching my head up, I expected to see a doctor. Instead, the air in my lungs vanished as Justin spotted me and increased his speed until his arms wrapped tight around me. "O. Thank God, you're okay."

I squeezed him back, drinking in the familiarity, no longer cringing against it. "Thanks to you."

He pulled away, shaking his head. "Thanks to Gil." He glanced at the cops watching us closely and cupped my elbow to guide me away. Keeping his voice low, he said, "He told me he's involved in the painted murders. Is that why the police are outside his room?"

My heart turned to stone. "He told you that? How…how is he involved?"

He painted them…didn't he?

He painted them for his uncle.

He has their blood on his hands.

I didn't want to believe it, but the thought had been growing ever since I'd seen my photo wedged in his door.

He frowned. "He said….you know what? It doesn't matter. We'll talk about it later." His gaze flashed with pain. "I need to see the bastard. To see with my own eyes he's still alive. That text he sent sounded too full of death for my liking."

I arched my chin back at the two police. "We can ask to see him, but I'm not holding my breath. They barely let Olive in."

"Olive…his daughter?"

I nodded.

"Did you know he had a daughter?"

"Not until recently."

"Who's the mother?"

Looking away, I whispered, "You'll have to ask him that."

"Fine. I will." Straightening his spine, he took my hand and led me back to the law enforcers. "We want to see our friend."

The guy shook his head. "No visitors."

"He has his daughter in there right now."

The younger cop with his sleek dark hair glowered at me. "Only because someone wouldn't accept no for an answer."

Justin narrowed his gaze. "Just like I won't accept no for an answer." He sighed. "Look, the bloke isn't going anywhere. He's in a hospital, for God's sake."

The older cop sighed, his resolve weakening.

I jumped in. "Please let us in. I'm leaving and want to say goodbye before I do."

Justin froze beside me, blue eyes trapping mine. "What? You're leaving? Since when?"

I shrugged. "Since I decided."

"Because of Gil?"

"Because of me." I didn't want to discuss this in front of uniforms. Smiling at the older officer, I did my best to appease him. "We'll only be fifteen minutes. I just really need to say goodbye before…"

His hand rested on his baton before he sighed again, heavy

and annoyed. "Fine. Fifteen minutes. But no longer." Turning the doorknob, he opened it enough for me to slip through.

Justin followed, pushing the door closed behind him.

Olive looked up from where she stood beside Gil's bed hugging him. Her eyes were red and cheeks damp but she smiled for the first time since I met her. "Hi, Olin. Thanks for helping me sneak in to see my dad."

I nodded with a soft smile. "You're welcome."

My gaze travelled to Gil.

The world once again stopped and spun in the opposite direction.

He looked wrung out and pale. His hair a diabolical mess, his body cocooned in white blankets while a needle punctured the back of his hand and fed necessary antibiotics and painkillers.

His mouth opened to speak.

My heart begged to retreat.

And Justin broke the tense connection, striding in front of me to embrace his friend. "Good to see you're still alive."

Gil winced, his gaze struggling to leave mine as he focused on Justin. "At least I get to say thank you in person now."

Justin nodded. "You owe me. Owe me huge."

Gil nodded, his tone deadly serious. "I know I do. And I'll pay you back somehow. Some day."

"You do know I expect to be told everything." Justin's eyes narrowed. "And I do mean everything, Clark. You can't leave anything out."

"I know."

Olive's attention danced between her dad and the man she'd never met. Her curiosity practically burst out of her. The scared girl from the caravan gave way to a feisty little thing, almost as if having her father back erased the badness of before. She drank strength from him. She trusted that things were okay now—that the past year of entrapment was over because she was with her dad and the world was righted.

She's the bravest little thing I've ever seen.

I envied her ability to ignore history and live purely in the present.

It made me feel weak for wanting to leave, guilty for choosing myself over Gil when he lay sore in a hospital bed.

I should stay.

I should help.

But how much is enough?

After everything...when was it okay to say no more?

My heart beat strangely, confused and afraid as I stayed on the outskirts of their conversation.

Gil cleared his throat, smiling at his friend. "Justin, I'd like you to meet Olive. My daughter." His body melted as he looked at Olive, his eyes so proud and grateful. "Spinach, I want you to meet your godfather, Justin."

"Yeah, about the godfather thing." Justin coughed quietly. "You do know I have no experience with kids right, Clark?"

Gil nodded. "I know. And it's not fair of me to nominate you without telling you, but for now...while I deal with this aftermath, do you think—" His eyes caught mine, wincing. He seemed almost apologetic, as if he didn't know if he should've asked me if I wanted that role instead.

I approved of his choice.

Justin was stable.

I was not.

Justin was staying.

I'm...not.

"It's fine." Justin grinned. "All good. You know that."

"I know you're a goddamn saint, and it pisses me off no end," Gil muttered wryly. "But it also makes me a lucky SOB to have a mate like you."

"Aww, I'm blushing." Justin laughed. "Seems getting shot took that stick out of your arse."

Gil's gaze narrowed. "Don't use bad language in front of—"

"What's a godfather?" Olive's nose wrinkled, her eyes volleying between the two men as they spoke.

Gil seemed different. Lighter, even while heavier. Happier, even while hurt. Just like Olive, he took support and strength from his bond with her, drinking the same medicine she did just from being around him.

They couldn't survive without each other. Couldn't be whole while apart. The true sense of connection and family.

I rubbed at the ache in my chest as Justin bent to Olive's level, offering his hand in polite introduction. "A godfather means I get to keep you if your dad here ever has enough."

I cringed.

Justin meant it in a relaxed, soothing way, but after a year of forced custody with her uncle—

Olive looked at him warily, obviously thinking the same thing I did. "I don't want anyone to keep me who isn't my dad."

Justin dropped his hand, noticing his mistake. "Of course. I only meant that—"

"You can trust him, Olive," Gil gruffed. "He's not like Jeffrey."

"You were wrong to trust him, Daddy." Olive stuck out her bottom lip. "I told you something wasn't right about him, didn't I?"

Gil flinched but nodded. "You were right. He was a bad man."

"He was mean." She scuffed her blue sneaker into the floor. "I-I'm glad he's not alive anymore."

"Me too." Gil squeezed his eyes shut for a second before opening them again. "I agree that Uncle Jeffrey was bad, but Justin is one of the good guys. Look at him. You'll see."

Olive pursed her lips suspiciously, eyeing up Justin. "I dunno." She traced his face, his chest, his legs, and back to his eyes. Her head cocked as if deliberating. "I don't think I want you as my weird godfather, but you can be my friend…I guess."

Justin chuckled. "Gee, thanks." He bent down again, whispering, "I promise I'll be a trustworthy friend who doesn't kidnap you."

"You better not." Her fist shot up in a laughable but totally serious threat. "I only want to live with Daddy from now on."

Gil froze in bed. His gaze lost the pride and adoration, filling with torture and the familiar unhappiness of before. He pinched the bridge of his nose with a hiss, doing his best to shove aside whatever had terrified him before Olive noticed.

His head turned, his gaze caught mine.

The electrical current that refused to be cut hummed with honesty.

He's afraid.

Afraid of being arrested and imprisoned.

Afraid of having Olive taken from him.

My chest filled with painful pressure. He'd only just been reunited with his daughter. They deserved their happily ever after, but this was just an intermission. A brief, sweet interlude before real-life wedged between them again.

Gil had promised Olive that it was all over.

He'd lied.

It's only just beginning.

"O…" Gil's eyes tightened, pain etching into his skin. "Can…can we talk?"

Justin twisted to look at me, his eyes narrowing. He rocked his head in a come-hither gesture, moving away from Gil's beside. "Here, take my spot."

I couldn't move.

Talking was too dangerous.

I'd made my decision.

I couldn't take it back.

No matter if Gil might face prison and Olive's future was uncertain. No matter if this little family was once again split up.

They weren't mine to care for or worry over. I shouldn't fear what would happen to the tiny girl I'd just met, or the boy I would never forget. I should pick me.

I will pick me.

I will walk away.

I will say goodbye.

Gil's energy wrapped around mine as physical as a hug, as brutal as a fist, as sharp as claws. We didn't need words to talk. We communicated right there, in our silence.

He shouted apologies.

I shielded my intentions.

He begged me to move closer.

I stood my ground.

This was safe.

Distance was safe.

Gil's forehead furrowed, accepting the mess between us, and knowing, without a shadow of a doubt, that whatever we'd been, whatever we'd had, whatever we could have been…was over.

The tension between us thickened with clouds, a rumble of thunder was the sounds of hearts breaking.

Justin shifted by Gil, his hand skating on the bedspread.

Olive immediately pushed him away, her voice high and worried. "Don't hurt him. He has a hole in his tummy. Things might fall out."

Justin coughed. "A hole?"

I fought my smile, amazed that I found Gil's injury humorous thanks to his adorable child.

Gil groaned, struggling with his own grim grin. "I told you, little spinach. It's not a hole anymore. Things won't fall out of me."

"But I saw it. Back at Uncle Jeffrey's. Blood fell out of you. Lots and lots of blood." She looked as if she fought tears and a tiny bit of rage. "You said that if I ever hurt myself that bleeding wasn't good, and I should get help straight away. But you were sleeping and didn't get help, so you still have a hole where blood can slip out."

Gil twisted in bed, swallowed his grunt of pain, and scooped his daughter into a side hug. Pressing his lips to her hair, he murmured, "I love you so, *so* much." His smile glowed with affection. "You're very sweet to worry about me, but I did get help. I'm in the hospital, and the doctors sewed up the hole inside me. I'm all better now. See?" He raised his arm, showing no blood stained the white sheets around him. "No more bleeding."

"I dunno." Olive wrinkled her nose in distrust. "Are you sure you're okay?"

"Never better."

"But you said it hurt when I hugged you there." She pointed at his side. "You shouldn't be in pain. I don't want you in pain. If the doctors can't fix you, I can. I know I can." She wriggled in Gil's embrace. "Tell me what to do, and I'll do it."

Gil kissed her nose before letting her go and reclining against the pillows. "You do make it better. Just having you here takes all my pain away."

Olive pouted. "No, it doesn't. I'm not magic, you know."

Justin chuckled, catching Gil's eye, sharing the vibrancy of the little girl willing to stand up to agony for daring to hurt her father.

Gil gave me a quick look, his face unguarded for the first time since I'd answered his job advertisement. No hidden secrets, no diabolical blackmails, just him in a hospital bed with his daughter from another woman fussing over him, and my heart healed a little. It let go of its own pain and sense of betrayal, repairing a tiny piece of friendship.

My feet drifted toward Gil without my permission. I joined their group, not in touching distance, but no longer ready to bolt out the door.

Gil sighed heavily, his gaze tangling with mine. His head tipped down in a silent thank you.

My voice scratched as I asked, "Are you sure you're all right?"

He grimaced. "I should be the one asking you that." His eyes flashed. "O...God, I'm so sorry."

"It's fine."

"It's not fine. And it won't ever be, but I need you to know how grateful I am. I took far more than you were willing to give. I'll never forgive myself, but you're the reason I found Olive—"

"Don't." I held up my hand. "I understand."

Justin cleared his throat, moving away a little, giving us privacy.

This wasn't the place to discuss.

Not with Gil fresh out of surgery, cops barricading the door, and his daughter who listened to every word.

"But how can you stand there and—"

"Because it's my choice what to forgive and what not to. It's over." I sighed, signalling an end to airing dirty laundry. "It's okay, Gil. Truly."

He snorted as if he couldn't believe me. His mouth opened as if to argue but I shot my attention to Olive instead. "You're wrong, you know."

Olive pinned me with her grey stare. "Wrong? About what?"

"About not being magic."

"I don't get it."

I nudged my chin at Gil, smiling gently. "You do take his pain away. I knew your dad before you existed, and I knew him while he was searching for you, and I can say you are definitely magic. Want to know how I know?"

Olive licked her lips, her gaze so eager to learn. "How?"

"You make him happy." I looked at Gil, unable to ignore the pull. To ignore the truth of what I said. "You make him whole. You take away all his pain, internal and external." I dropped my attention back to her. "You truly are magic...to him."

"Am I, Popeye? Do I really do that?" Olive sidled closer to Gil.

He wrapped an arm around her tiny shoulders. "Definitely. All the time. Without you, there's something missing deep inside me."

"Me too." She pressed her face into his chest. When she pulled away, tears shone on her cherub cheeks. "I'll make sure I make extra magic, so you can get better super-fast and can come home with me."

"Sounds like a great plan."

Justin's phone beeped. "Sorry, guys." Pulling it from his pocket, he withdrew from the tender family moment and went to stand by the window, typing quickly on his phone.

Gil caught my eyes over Olive's embrace.

A vortex sucked us into the same undeniable depth we'd always shared. Tension appeared from nowhere. The air became heavy. The possibilities of so many futures and fates waiting for us to decide.

Gil broke the unbearable quietness. "I know it isn't worth much, and for some reason you don't want to hear it, but I truly am sorry, O. From the depths of my soul. I'm forever in your debt."

"Enough."

But he didn't stop. "I need you to know I will *always* love you. I will always adore you for what you've done for me—both willingly and unwillingly. I don't expect to ever hear you love me back. I know that's something I lost and the price I had to pay."

I dared meet his green gaze; my spine threaded with steel.

He wasn't supposed to talk of love.

He wasn't supposed to be so open or genuine.

I wasn't protected against this new Gilbert Clark. This honest, hurting, hopeful version who no longer believed in silence but in truth.

How could I tell him I'd come for closure? That I'd emptied my hope of ever having more with this man and now only wanted a farewell?

"I had to see you…one last time."

His body stiffened, fear licked into his eyes. "One last time?"

"I'm very glad you're okay. That you survived…for Olive's sake."

And for mine.

I might not be able to be with him but I didn't want him dead.

Gil was sweet with a heart full of affection and protection to give. He'd just never really been given the opportunity without monsters tearing that heart to pieces.

In a way, I was failing him at the worst possible time.

But time never did play fair when it came to us.

"He…he didn't hurt you, did he?" He swallowed hard. "Please tell me I arrived before he—" His voice cut off, unable to verbalize what could've happened if he'd been five minutes longer.

I wouldn't have just had rope-burned wrists to treat but a

whole host of other ailments. Rape kits and counselling. Stopping those thoughts, I shook my head. "He didn't hurt me."

"He yelled at her," Olive said, popping into the conversation. "And then he whispered some things that made her go all white and strange-looking, like she'd be sick."

I winced, studying Olive and what Jeffrey had threatened. How he'd planned on selling both of us. How Gil might never have known the fate his daughter was sold to. "He wasn't a nice man, was he?"

Olive narrowed her eyes. "Nope. Not one bit."

I smiled, shaking away that night all over again. "But you're with your dad now and things will be better."

Gil flinched, knowing as well as I did that things might be about to get worse.

"Yep. I'm never leaving him again," Olive vowed. "Ever, ever, ever."

"I'm glad. He needs you."

"What aren't you saying, O?" Gil asked gently, his eyes roving over my face. "Are you truly all right?"

Bracing myself, I prepared to say the hardest thing. "I'm fine. And I came...I came to see you because..." I sighed, forcing myself to finish. "I came to say goodbye."

The flash of agony glowed and fired in his eyes. He cleared his throat, nodding fast, accepting there was no other choice. "I understand."

"I'm moving."

His body twitched on the bed. "Where?"

"I don't know yet. I-I guess I'll figure that out when I'm there."

"You'll travel?" His voice gruffed and thickened.

"Perhaps. I'm not sure."

Our awful conversation petered out. There was *so* much to say, but it wouldn't make a damn bit of difference to the way we'd ended.

Olive reached out to take my hand, her shoulders still wrapped up in Gil's embrace. By accepting her touch, she united us. An unlikely trio all bound in complicated ways. My skin tingled as I allowed her hold, a similar curse to what her father made me feel.

There was something about this girl that snatched me around the heart just as much as Gil did. Probably because she was half his. Half his blood. Half his soul.

And my soul reacted to both of them.

"You can't leave." Her pretty face cast upward to look at me. Her plea reached into my chest and squeezed. "I don't want you to go."

"O has a destiny to follow, Olive Oyl. We can't stop her from being happy." Gil pulled her closer to him, doing his best to dislodge her hold on me. "She has to go."

He smiled at me, but his eyes didn't look happy. They looked sad and lonely and breaking. "Don't let her guilt trip you, O. She's mastered the art of that unfortunately."

I laughed quietly, feeling endlessly sad. "I'll do my best."

"But you *can't* go." Pinpricks of colour highlighted Olive's cheeks. "You're the owl from the stories. You're his friend. Friends don't leave."

Gil groaned. "God, did she tell you about the owl?" He blushed like his daughter. "I'd run out of bedtime stories and was sick of reading *Popeye The Sailor Man*. I told her about a dancer who—"

"Turned into an owl at night and danced with feathers in the moonlight." Olive nodded furiously. "The owl was called Olin—which is a crazy weird name—but was kinda cool too. And you're called Olin, so you *have* to stay."

I struggled with how to reply.

Justin re-joined us, tucking his phone into his pocket. "What did I miss?"

Gil shot his friend a grim look while I tried to untangle my hand from Olive's. "Not much."

Olive let her hand fall, her shoulders slouching as if the past year had caught up to her. "Can we go home yet, Dad? I want to sleep in my room." Her face shadowed, showing signs of the trauma that would take a while to cure. "I miss my room. I didn't like sleeping in Uncle Jeffrey's caravan."

"Yes, we can go home—" Gil froze, halting his lie. His eyes rose to mine, pleading for a way to break the news to her. That he couldn't go home until he'd healed. And even then…it might not happen.

"Your dad has to stay here another couple of nights." I reached out and stroked her dark, glossy hair. "The doctors are magic too, and they're making him better."

"But…what about me? Where do I sleep then? Will you take me back home and stay with me?"

My heart flipped at the thought of returning to the

warehouse where Gil had drugged and painted me.

Gil jumped in. "You'll have to stay here with me in the hospital, little spinach. Just for a couple of days." He looked at Justin. "They allow that, right? Single parents are allowed to have their kid stay?"

Justin shrugged. "I can find out."

Olive stuck out her tongue as if she was gagging. "I don't want to stay here. It stinks and I don't like sick people."

"I know," Gil muttered. "I don't want to stay either, but—"

The door opened with no knock or request for entry.

Two women entered, stern and prim. Their matching black suits strict with discipline and an official-looking badge over their breasts.

"This is a private meeting," Justin said, striding forward to intercept them. "You can't just barge in—"

"Mr. Clark?" The younger of the two with red hair in a sleek ponytail held up a piece of paper. "We're here to discuss the accommodation and care of your only offspring, Olive Clark."

Justin continued acting as bodyguard. "And you are?"

"Child Protective Services."

I sucked in a huge breath.

Oh, no.

Tension in the room wound tight.

I moved closer to Olive, shielding her.

The woman cast her stare on all of us, saying, "The police informed us of the incapacitation of Mr. Clark, along with the impending trial for the events over the past few months. We were asked to arrange appropriate care for Olive Clark, and to discuss the fact that she hasn't been attending school for over a year. As far as we're concerned, it's in the best interest of the child that she be placed with a foster family who will ensure her wellbeing and education is—"

"You are not taking my daughter." Gil sat straight up in bed, his face blanching with agony. "No way."

The redhead bypassed Justin, coming far too close for comfort. "Do you have relatives who could take the child?"

"The child's name is Olive," Gil snarled. "And she's standing right in front of you."

Olive kept her shoulders squared, her little body brave but trembling. "I don't want to leave my dad."

"I know," the other CPS agent said, coming toward us with her satchel swinging by her side. "But you need structure, sweetie. You need a family who—"

"Don't call me sweetie!" Olive slammed hands over her ears. "Uncle Jeffrey called me sweetheart and I *hated* it!" She turned into me, and my arms automatically wrapped around her.

"I think you better leave," I snapped.

"Get out." Gil tried to climb free from the tight bed sheets, but the monitors beeped and accused him of movement not recommended for someone in his wounded state.

Justin came to my side, forming a barrier, a family unit where all of us stood up to the law. "I'm Olive's godfather. She can stay with me while Gil is in the hospital."

The redhead scowled. "Have you had experience with children before? Will you ensure she attends school, seeing as Mr. Clark failed on that account?"

"She was fucking kidnapped," Gil snarled, finally ripping off the sheet even though his face shone with sweat and a bloom of red appeared on his side. "I've been trying to find her for a year. Do you honestly think the kidnapper would take her to goddamn school?"

I reached out, resting my hand on his quaking arm. "Calm down, they're only here for Olive's best interest."

I did my best to stay rational, even though I wanted nothing more than to dump the carafe of water on their head and kick them out the door.

"Thank you." The woman with dark hair sniffed in my direction. "Like your friend said, Mr. Clark, we're only here for the best interest of—"

"Her best interest is to stay with her father." Gil panted, raking a hand through his hair and dislodging my hold. "I have no intention of letting her out of my sight again."

"You're in a hospital. She can't stay—"

"I can take her to my place," Justin interrupted. "I'll care for her."

Olive scrunched up her face. "No, I want to stay with Dad!"

The agents looked triumphant. "It seems you are unsuitable. We believe the child needs to undergo extensive therapy after her ordeal. She needs to be placed with a family capable of nurturing troubled—"

"She's not troubled," Gil roared. "She's loved and she's back home with me. You're not having her." His finger soared to the door. "Leave. Before I do something I'll regret."

The redhead stood up to his temper. "You're about to go

through a lengthy trial for your involvement in the painted murders, Mr. Clark. Do you really believe you're in a position to care for a child who needs psychological—"

"Get out!" Gil tripped from the bed, his IV line catching on the railing. Justin swooped toward him, supporting his weight as his legs gave out. More blood saturated the side of his hospital gown.

Olive began to cry, silent and sorrowful.

It broke my heart.

All of this...

It broke my stupid, foolish heart.

"I can look after her."

Everyone froze. All eyes locked on me.

I trapped a lock of Olive's hair and pulled gently. "Would that be okay? Would you be all right staying with me while your dad heals?"

Olive blinked, her eyelashes dewy with tears. "Stay? With...you?"

I nodded, bending to her level. "You don't have to. You're the bravest girl I've ever met, so I know you can face anything, but while your dad gets better, you can stay with me...if you want."

Gil made a noise in his chest.

A noise that wrapped around me and made tears prick my own eyes. Even now, I wasn't immune to him. Even after everything.

"You don't have to do that, O," Gil strangled. "You're leaving, remember?"

"I know."

I wasn't a martyr or a sacrifice.

But I was a person who tried her best to be good.

This offer wasn't for him.

It was for her.

This little girl who'd captured me from the moment I'd seen her blinking like a woodland creature in the dark.

Olive's shoulders fell, her hand slipped into mine. She held onto me while she turned and faced her father. "Can't I stay here with you?"

Gil's throat worked hard as he swallowed. "I wish you could, little spinach, but it seems that option has been taken away." He threw a glower at the women. His gaze tracked to mine with a shake of his head. "You don't have to do this, O.

Truly. I'm not trapping you into yet another mess of mine."

"I can help," Justin murmured. "I don't mind."

Gil shot him a grateful look even as pain blended. He'd only just found his daughter, yet he had to relinquish her all over again. To watch others care for her the way he wanted. "Do you think you could stay with her at my warehouse? Instead of taking her to yours?" His voice lowered. "I don't want her to think she's been kidnapped twice."

Olive sniffed, her energy levels quickly slipping into sadness, knowing her happily-ever-after of going home with her father wouldn't come true. "I don't want to go home with him. I want to go home with *you*." Her grey eyes snapped fiercely to Gil, her hand squeezing hard around mine.

Gil sighed sadly. "And I want to go home with you. And we will." His attention shot to the CPS agents watching us with suspicion. He dared them to refute his claim about going home.

Gil might've saved Olive but he'd lost any right to keep her.

I thought he'd have more time before they tried to take her away from him.

It wasn't fair.

What would happen now?

Who would have custody while he was arrested and put on trial for a murder that he *did* commit? A murder that would come with prison time.

I froze as the future unravelled before me. Gil in jail. Olive with foster parents. A lifetime of broken families. We weren't just talking about a few days here; we were talking about Olive's entire livelihood.

She can't be allowed to leave with them.

Justin followed the same path I did. His harsh inhale wrenched everyone's attention to him. He looked at Olive with a pained expression, wanting to talk frankly but aware that word selection had to be careful.

"Clark..." He cleared his throat. "Um, seeing as your hospital stay might be longer than a few days..." His hand shook as he rubbed his mouth. "And we all know how slow doctors can be..." He looked at me, seeking support, refusing to look at the agents. "Perhaps we should arrange a longer-term arrangement for Olive than just a few days."

The agents crossed their arms, tapping their feet.

Olive narrowed her eyes, trying to follow the cryptic conversation.

I deciphered it and my heart sank further. *Seeing as you're arrested and we all know how slow court dates and hearings can take, Olive needs a caregiver for the next few weeks at least. And longer if you're convicted. These CPS agents can't be allowed to take her. Who knows if you'll ever get her back.*

Gil's whitewashed face turned a greenish hue. He rested on the edge of the bed as he buried his hands in his hair, tugging hard as the ramifications crashed into him. "Oh, God." He looked as if he'd be sick.

I wanted to go to him. To rub his back. To assure him he wouldn't lose her for the second time.

But if I did, I'd fall into the same pattern.

The pattern I was trying to break.

The pattern you're stuck in now that you've offered to care for Olive.

"What? What is it?" Olive asked.

I pulled her into my side. "Nothing. Your father is just sad he can't come home with you for a while." Turning her to face me, I added, giving her options, giving myself options where I could still leave and not be linked to Gil, "Justin has the coolest place, and you can stay with him for a bit. It's probably best if you stay with him." I smiled as wide as I could. "He's your godfather, after all. He's kind of like an angel who will look after you. It will be fun. A little holiday."

Olive's eyes welled with fresh tears. "But I don't want a holiday. I want to go home."

"How about I come stay at your place then?" Justin offered. "It will be a holiday for me, instead."

She cried harder. "I just want to go home with my dad."

I hugged her close, my heart a bleeding ruin.

Gil looked into me, his stare piercing and full of so many troubled, hurting things. He nodded in thanks while I rocked his most precious belonging.

My stomach knotted.

My heart pounded in answer to his gratefulness, his sorrow.

God, what a mess.

"Look, we can discuss the fine print in a few days when emotions aren't running so high." The redhead tried to pry Olive out of my arms. "Just give us Olive, and we'll ensure she's well taken care of—"

"No!" Olive's little hand slipped into mine again, deepening the bond between us that'd formed from dark forests and her father's blood. "I'm not going anywhere with you!"

I stood, keeping Olive's hand tight in mine. "I think it's best if you come back later."

"We can't leave until we're sure Olive's living arrangements are satisfactory."

"Can...can you look after me?"

I looked down as Olive tugged on my hand. Her face seemed older, alive with understanding that I was the lesser of the evils. She couldn't have her father. She didn't want Justin. She definitely didn't want to be given to strangers.

She'd chosen me.

And her choice sentenced me to yet another cycle of not being able to say no.

"Can you? Please? Can you come stay until Daddy can come home?"

Justin stiffened.

Gil groaned, putting my welfare above Olive's in a way that made me feel both cherished and utterly guilty. "No, little spinach. Let her go. O has already done far too much. She's going away—"

"Please?" Olive looked up, her fingers so perfect and trusting in mine. "I'll be good, I promise." She practically climbed up my body with her panic. "I'll go to bed when you tell me. You won't have to tie me to a tree outside for being naughty. I'll be super quiet and good, you'll see."

My eyes flew to the CPS agents.

Shit.

The dark-haired one narrowed her eyes, hearing what I did. That Olive had been subject to abuse that needed to be repaired. Abuse that I wasn't qualified to deal with.

Gil made a broken noise, forgetting our unwanted audience. "God, he tied you to a tree?" His hands curled. "What else did he—"

"Gil." I flashed him a warning look. "Now is not the time."

He choked, his face white and hospital gown bright red. A crimson trickle ran down his naked calf, licking through leg hair and plopping onto the disinfected floor.

He shouldn't be vertical. He shouldn't be fighting such fear.

This wasn't fair on either father or daughter, and I'd had enough.

No wonder I despised hospitals.

They were the steppingstone to hell.

A stopping place where those injured had to get better and

those waiting had to hope their loved ones returned. It was purgatory and I wouldn't let them suffer anymore.

I looked down at a little girl who'd somehow replaced my desire to run with unbreakable loyalty.

Olive's tears were fast and fat, heavy with hurt. "Please! I don't want to go with them—"

"You're not going anywhere." My vow hissed with promise. "Ever."

She burrowed into me, trusting me. She trembled; the brave, curious girl who I thought was resilient to what she'd gone through buckled in my arms. She was fragile beneath her courageous exterior. She was hurting beneath her spirited exterior.

She's like Gil.

A perfect chameleon, hiding her true feelings until she couldn't hide them anymore.

This promise would break me all over again.

But I also couldn't deny her.

Glaring at the agents, I clipped, "I'll take care of Olive. She can stay at my apartment with me until Gilbert Clark is released from hospital. I'll ensure she attends school and any other requirements you have. I'll fill in any reports and do what you ask as long as you don't take her away from her father."

I could care for her in my home, as long as she didn't want to return to the warehouse.

I couldn't go back there.

Not yet.

"And when he goes on trial?" The redhead crossed her arms. "Who's going to look after her then?"

"I will." Justin puffed up his chest. "We all will. We'll make it work."

"She has family," I said. "She doesn't need strangers."

"O," Gil groaned, his voice deepening. He couldn't stop looking at me, his body rigid. Love that he could no longer hide poured from his gaze, wrapping around me, drowning me. "O, you don't have to—"

"I do." My voice was bold and determined. "I am." Wrenching my gaze from his, I focused on his daughter. The daughter I'd been sacrificed to find. The daughter who'd been the reason Gil had left me.

Her creation drove us apart.

Her desperation kept us together.

There was no other option but to protect her like Gil had.

Pausing all my plans, allowing love to trap me further, and kindness to make me powerless, I arched my chin at the agents. "Is that satisfactory enough for you?"

The redhead pursed her lips, looking at her colleague. "I suppose that would be okay, for now. We will monitor the situation."

"Fine." I nodded. "Now, please leave."

In a tense standoff, the women looked one last time at all of us, turned around, and vanished out the door.

The moment they'd gone, Gil almost crashed off the bed.

The monitors screamed.

A doctor flew in.

The chaos that followed ensured everyone focused on Gil's recovery and not the future where he might have wished he'd died in that forest instead.

I wished I could stop what was coming for him.

I wished I had the capacity to slay monsters and defeat court dates and stop murder trials, because it wouldn't be a disgruntled, greedy family member who would tear him apart this time, but the law.

A monster no one could win against.

Chapter Eleven

Olin

POLICE RELEASED A statement today, assuring the public that the killer responsible for the body painting murderers has been arrested. Currently, it is believed there were two men involved. Jeffrey Clark was killed the night a fifth girl went missing. Olin Moss was to be the next victim and was already painted before the police found them. The second man, Gilbert Clark, is in hospital. The families of the deceased are demanding swift and severe justice for their loved ones and have taken to online petitions and GoFundMe requests to ensure Gilbert Clark receives life imprisonment. More details to come.

I trembled on my couch, phone in hand, internet searches giving me nightmares.

Darkness rained all around me, hissing with horrors, while Olive was in my room, asleep.

It'd been a long day.

After leaving the hospital, Justin kindly dropped Olive and me off at my place. He'd offered to stay, to run errands with us. But Olive had withdrawn and I sensed female company would be better for her fragile state. Once Justin had gone, I'd shown her around, changed the sheets on my bed, then taken her grocery shopping.

She'd perked up toward the end, asking if I could take her to Gil's warehouse to grab her things as she literally had nothing. No toothbrush, no nightie, no clothes.

But I'd rather use the money from Status Enterprises that'd been earmarked for rent and bills to replace her things rather than go back to the warehouse so soon. I bought her what she needed, doing my best to buy her happiness as well as staples.

The strawberry scent I'd caught in Gil's apartment now laced mine from her shower. The sweet pull of maple syrup and pancakes lingered from the unhealthy dinner I'd made, cooking Olive pancakes like I'd once cooked for her father, hoping it would fix her troubles and knowing nothing had that much power.

Exhaustion had sat on my shoulders all day—a whisper in my ear to fall asleep and hide, but I waited until Olive collapsed beside me watching Netflix before carrying her into my bed and returning to the little nest of blankets and pillow I'd made on the couch.

I got comfy.

I closed my eyes.

And images of paintbrushes and caravans and blood, blood, blood surrounded me.

Gil followed on such gruesome thoughts, fisting my heart and making me fear he'd died after all. That the blood he'd lost at the hospital would push him the final way into a grave.

He won't die.

He can't.

Even though his future was bleak, he had to stay alive for Olive's sake.

Heart winging, I sat up, peering into the darkness. I checked the door was locked for the third time, and grabbed a glass of water from the kitchen.

My pulse stayed too high to rest, so I made the terrible decision of googling information on the most recent body painting murder case.

I hated that my name was printed for everyone to see.

I hated that Gil sounded like a blood-thirsty beast.

They hadn't given any facts, just vague accusations that would lead to a witch hunt.

Returning to the page results, I braced myself all over again and clicked on a link for a petition set up by the parents of Moira Jonston, one of the murdered girls.

Sign the petition below to ensure this doesn't happen to any other English girls.
Gilbert Clark, the renowned body painting artist and owner of the company Master of Trickery, used his stature as an artist to lure unsuspecting women into his lair to kill them.

He is a despicable human being and we boycott all his work.
We want Facebook to delete his Master of Trickery page.
We want the police to provide clear justice.
We want compensation for the families he's torn apart.
We want him to pay to the highest degree.
Sign now to ensure he doesn't get away with it.
#deathsentenceforthebodypainter

I tossed my phone away, closing my eyes from the screen's glare.

Could they do that? Could they take away his business and force the law to lock him away indefinitely? There was no mention of his arrest for killing his uncle. But they'd pinned the girl's murders on him instead.

Gil hadn't killed them.

He might have painted them, but he didn't actively kill them.

Jeffrey had gloated that he'd done that.

Their deaths coated his hands, and Jeffrey's demise coated Gil's.

He'd done the world a favour by removing him from society, yet he might end up serving a life sentence because of the power of social media and the pressure of people with a voice.

And Olive…what will happen to Olive?

I rubbed my eyes.

God, this is such a catastrophe.

My phone illuminated the gloom as it vibrated across the couch. An unknown number flashed across the screen.

Who the hell is calling me at two in the morning?

My heart kicked.

Gil?

Could he call me from his room in the hospital? Had something worse happened?

Scooping up the phone, I answered with a whisper, doing my best not to wake up Olive. "Hello?"

"Olin, is that you?"

I stiffened against the cushions. "Mum. Wow, hi." I hadn't heard from my parents in months. The last time was via email because phone data was expensive and international calling daylight robbery according to my father.

"We just heard the news. Are you okay? What on earth is

going on?"

"I'm fine."

What could I tell them? We'd never had a close relationship, and I'd never learned the art of assuring them I was happy and healthy while hiding things I didn't want them to know.

"Did someone try to *kill* you?" my father bellowed. "Are you in protective services? I hope you're taking this seriously and listening to authorities."

I sat taller, scrambling for things I could admit while censoring so many others. "It's all over. I'm safe. The murderer is dead and—"

"He's not dead. He's in hospital. He could get out at any moment and come and finish the job." My mother lamented.

Dad jumped in. "We'll send you a plane ticket. Come join us in Argentina. Get away from that place until he's in a cell and some inmate with big arms and lots of tattoos rips him into pieces."

The mental image of Gil being abused and killed in prison made me rub the sudden ache in my chest.

God, I hadn't even thought about that.

What if he was killed behind bars?

What if he was found guilty and—

Gil can't go to jail.

His personality wouldn't survive. He'd either shut down and give up or he'd join the ranks of merciless criminals and never look back.

Or he'll die.

I swallowed away my parent-induced panic. "I'm fine here, Dad. I don't need to fly—"

"Are you traumatised?" Mum asked.

"No, I'm good."

"You don't sound good."

"Well, I don't know how I'm supposed to sound at two in the morning."

"Why are you up so early?"

I held back my frustrated laugh. "You called me. Remember?"

"Humph." Mum huffed. "Well, are you working? You're not dancing, so where are you working?"

I gritted my teeth. They knew about my accident, but they hadn't really understood, nor cared what the lack of dancing did to my soul. It was an open wound, and this phone call was not the time to tell them how callous such comments made me feel. "I got an admin job. It's enough to get by."

"Do you need more money?" Dad asked.

I balled my hands. I'd never taken money from them. Not once. Not even when I'd been in hospital with my surgery. They'd offered. Fairly regularly in fact. The guilt probably made them offer me at least something. They couldn't provide love or companionship but they could provide cash.

"No, it's fine. I can manage."

"It's not about managing, Olin; it's about being honest if you need help," Dad snipped. "I'll send you something anyway. In case you're not up for work with what happened. Shock can be delayed, you know. Don't want you to end up homeless."

I slouched into the couch, drained beyond belief. I was grateful for the money. Of course, I was. But I was also devalued and left with a sour taste in my mouth. "You don't have to do that, Dad."

"Already done." He snorted down the line as if he'd fixed world peace. "Anything else we need to know?"

A two-minute conversation and they were ready to go back to their lives. They'd been good parents and checked on their offspring who hadn't been murdered, they were free again.

I shook my head. "No, everything is fine."

Fine.

Fine.

That word echoed around empty and meaningless.

"You guys all good?" I added, being the dutiful daughter.

Mum mumbled something in the background while Dad replied, "Brilliant, honey. Time of our lives."

"I'm glad you're having such a great adventure."

"You too, honey," Mum said as if completely forgetting the circumstances of why they'd called me in the first place. "Love you."

"Love you guys, too."

Kisses were blown down the line before they hung up, and I clutched dead air and a cell phone that judged me.

Throwing it away for the second time, I slid sideways onto the couch and closed my eyes.

Chapter Twelve

Gil

SEVEN DAYS PASSED excruciatingly slowly.

I might not have been in prison yet, but I was trapped against my will. I wasn't allowed to leave my room. I couldn't care for my daughter. I had police watching my every move and listening to every doctor's visit.

The only spots of happiness in my long, lonely days of healing were when O brought Olive to visit. Without fail, the woman who'd I'd treated so badly and done so many unforgivable things to, arrived at lunchtime with my daughter.

The first day, Olive looked tired and timid. She'd clung to O's hand as if sleeping in a strange bed in a strange apartment had regressed her to living with Jeffrey. I'd held her close, kissed her glossy hair as she admitted that O had made her pancakes. I'd told her how jealous I was after sharing my gross hospital lunch with her, all while O made an excuse to go to the gift shop to buy me a book so boredom didn't kill me.

I did my best to stay light-hearted and normal, asking Olive lots of questions to assess her mental health. Overall, she seemed resilient. The same adorable kid I'd been lucky enough to share my life with until a year ago.

She was older.

A little more cynical, a lot more distrusting, and wise beyond her young years, but she wasn't too messed up from her year-long ordeal.

Thank God.

Despite her seemingly okay exterior, I did my best to pry what'd happened without asking directly, trying to determine if she truly *was* okay or if a psychiatrist was needed.

Olive was too like me. Too clever at hiding her real

emotions behind fake ones.

If I hadn't killed Jeffrey, I would kill him all over again for what he'd done.

Each day, I was grateful to O for bringing my child and the time alone she gave us, but I hated that, once again, I was adding more stress on her.

I wanted to talk to her.

To tell her she should leave and forget about me.

That I didn't deserve her help.

And it fucking tore me up that she was *still* helping me.

After everything I'd done.

I was draining her, breaking her, taking things I wasn't allowed to take.

It didn't matter that I loved her.

That now I had Olive safe, my heart no longer felt guilty for wanting her. All I could think about was the closeness we'd once shared, the ease between us, and the intensity of connection.

I'd always loved her.

I would *continue* to love her.

And that was why she had to get as far away from me as she could because I couldn't offer her what she deserved. Olive and I were just another accident that O had to heal from and move onto better things.

By the end of the week and seven visits of O and Olive, my body had healed enough that the painkillers had been reduced. My stitched together side no longer stabbed me each time I took a breath, and my desire to escape the hospital became undeniable.

I still hadn't been able to talk to O alone. Olive was always by my side, listening to every word O and I said to one another. My desire to set O free dwindled with every hour we spent together because how was I supposed to say goodbye to her? How was I supposed to face what I was about to face without her?

But how could I keep her after everything that I'd done?

My heart waged war against itself, wanting to be selfish all while knowing it had to do the right thing.

O had kindly brought a sketchpad and watercolours two days ago, along with magazines and a fully stocked e-reader. However, the distractions weren't enough to stop me from watching the news and seeing how many people wanted my head on a spike for the girls my uncle had killed.

My future was undetermined.

My freedom no longer guaranteed.

And it all came to an end at eleven a.m. on the eighth day in hospital.

I looked up as the door opened, a smile already on my face in anticipation of my favourite visitors popping by. My heart pounded harder just at the thought of seeing O. My arms empty to hug both of them, even though O never came in touching distance.

But my smile fell as the kind doctor came in, her professional nod and gentle eyes familiar now. "How you feeling today?"

Sitting in the chair by the window, I sat taller. I didn't hiss in pain anymore. Considering they'd stitched a big chunk of my side back together again, my body was miraculous with fast healing. The black threads holding my flesh together no longer looked morbid. My skin no longer swollen or infected. "Better."

"That's good."

She read something on her iPad, skimming my notes and updates. "Your blood work looks fine and you're healing better than I expected." She looked up and smiled. "The good news is you'll be fine. No long-term complications. Just listen to your body as you continue healing, and you should have no issues."

"Okay, will do."

Her face fell as she looked at the door then back to me. "Unfortunately, I do have some bad news."

My pulse quickened. "They're sick of waiting?"

She clutched the iPad to her chest. "Yes."

"When?"

"Today. Now."

My heart rate exploded. "Shit."

I still accepted the consequences of my actions. I would be honest and take whatever punishment they deemed fit. But it didn't stop the rush of panic or cold sweat at the thought of never having a private conversation with O again. Of never kissing my daughter or tucking her into bed.

Of never being free.

I wasn't under any illusion that I was a saint. My chances of having a light sentence were slim…especially with the hate threats online and screams for justice on the news.

The doctor came closer. "If you tell me you're not feeling well, I can ask to keep you here for another few days."

I half-smiled. "I'm grateful, and believe me, I'm extremely tempted. I don't want to go to jail, but I also can't sit in limbo. I might as well get it over with."

"Fine, but we'll need to see you for check-ups every other day for the next week, so they'll have to bring you back. And if you go home, please take it easy. Don't ruin your progress by overdoing it."

I thought of Olive and O. I thought about my warehouse that I'd sold to pay yet another ransom. I thought about paying rent on something I used to own and the mess I'd left my paint supplies in.

I thought about all of it in a terror-coloured blur.

Would I be released to sort out my life before I was jailed? Or was this it?

Maybe I should feign sickness to stay a little longer.

My thoughts blackened as she backed toward the door. "I guess there's nothing left to do apart from say you're ready."

Bracing myself on the armchair, I stood.

My body stayed upright. My pain stayed low.

I'd lived through worse.

I'd survived worse.

I'll survive this.

"Thanks for fixing me," I said, smiling gratefully as she reached the door.

She stared into me, stern and worried. "Good luck, Mr. Clark. For the record, I believe you're a good person and not what they're painting you out to be online." Turning the handle, she gave me one last look before slipping into the corridor just as two uniformed officers barged in.

Their legs spread, their arms crossed, their pleasure in finally arresting me glowed bright. "Mr. Clark. Please come with us."

"Give me two minutes." Grabbing the bag that Justin had brought me from my warehouse with a pair of jeans, a t-shirt, and boxer-briefs, I stepped into the bathroom. Slipping from the god-awful hospital gown, I dressed slowly, favouring my right side. I cleaned my teeth and stared into the mirror, trying to come to terms with no longer being a free man.

When I returned to the room, the police looked me up and down, then moved aside to the now open door. "After you."

"Can I call my daughter? She's only eight. I can't just—"

"That will be sorted later."

"I can't be locked up without figuring out her safety." My

voice vibrated with anger. "She's my responsibility—"

"Should've thought of that before you committed a crime."

My hands balled. "I killed Jeffrey Clark because he'd kidnapped her. I did what I could to save her."

"And your excuse for killing those other girls?" The older one glowered.

"I didn't kill them."

He chuckled. "How about you hold off on your unbelievable explanations until you have a lawyer present."

"But my daughter—"

"Can wait," the younger clean-shaven one said. "Now, do you need a wheelchair?"

Temper raged through me, but I managed to stay controlled. Just. "No. I'm fine."

"Good."

The older one narrowed his eyes. He pulled out a pair of handcuffs.

I stiffened.

He chewed his cheek, eyeballing me. "Do I need to handcuff you?"

"No." I held his stare. "I won't run. And even if I did, I wouldn't get far. All I care about is ensuring my daughter has someone to—"

"Fine. Don't have time for this." He pursed his lips. "Let's go. All that nonsense can be taken care of at the station."

My anger flared hotter. "You're calling my daughter nonsense?"

"I'm calling you thinking you have any special privileges nonsense." The older one rubbed his nose and cocked his head toward the exit. "No cuffs is your one and only privilege. Now, no more delays. Out."

The younger officer moved first, expecting me to follow.

Swallowing back my rage, I fell into line and did my best not to shiver as the older one positioned himself behind me.

A sandwich of law and criminal.

I wished I'd been able to call O and tell her.

I didn't want her to come here with Olive and find me missing.

I couldn't expect her to figure out Olive's living arrangements.

She was only supposed to look after my daughter until I was released from hospital.

But now my custody included police instead of doctors.

This whole fucking mess was on me.

No one spoke as I did the walk of shame through the hospital, down the elevator, and out into the bright sunshine. England looked practically cheerful even though my freedom was ending.

The older officer stayed with me, his hand resting on my elbow while his partner went to collect the patrol car.

No lights, no sirens, just a smooth glide to the curb and a door opening wide to welcome me.

I winced, holding my side as pain flashed. Ducking to climb inside wasn't as easy as I hoped. The internal pain of healing organs and stitched together muscle grumbled at the movement.

The second I was inside, the door locked me in, and the older officer joined his colleague in the front. They drove me away from the hospital just as I spotted O walking from the visitor's car park, holding Olive's hand.

Her gaze caught mine.

A brief, violent moment.

Our connection snapped tight.

My heart crashed hard.

I twisted to keep both girls in my sights as the car turned the corner and she vanished.

* * * * *

"Mr. Clark. You've been arrested for the murder of Jeffrey Clark by use of succinylcholine." The judge read the file on her desk, her half-moon glasses sliding down her nose. "You've also been charged with accessory before the fact and second-degree manslaughter for the four women who lost their lives while covered in the same pigment found in your paint supplies."

She pinned me to the spot, her brown stare severe and unyielding. "How do you plead?"

"Guilty for the murder of Jeffrey Clark. Not guilty for the women, your honour." My voice stayed stable, but my heart was a fucking mess.

"You don't have a lawyer present. Are you sure you'd like to submit those pleas?"

I nodded.

The sooner this was over, the better.

The past few hours had been mayhem.

Thanks to the eight days I'd already technically served being arrested in my hospital room, the moment I'd arrived at the station, they booked me, fingerprinted me, asked for any personal items, which I did not have, and placed me in a holding cell with a few other men who looked as shell-shocked as I did.

I didn't know how the justice system worked and figured the cell I was in was the cell I'd be living and sleeping in for the next unknown while. However, a few hours later, an officer appeared, called my name, and hurried me down a concrete corridor and into a room with heavy wood panelling.

The judge eyed me up and down. "Murder charges are serious, Mr. Clark. Ordinarily, I would hold you without bail until your trial." Her gaze went to my pale blue t-shirt and the small bloodstain that'd appeared from my stitches. I'd twisted too far in the squad car, trying to see Olive and O. I'd ruptured something.

"As you've come here directly from hospital and still have at least a month of recovery, I will permit you to post bail with the strictest instructions not to leave Birmingham or even the street where you live. You will wear an ankle bracelet at all times. Do you understand?"

I nodded again. "Yes, your honour."

Bail sounded great. I could go home. I could be a father. I could cram in as much normalcy as humanly possible before I couldn't anymore.

But I had zero equity. I had no cash. No assets to use as collateral.

It didn't matter if bail was ten pounds or a million, I couldn't afford it.

My shoulders rounded, my pain level magnifying as she muttered, "Bail is set at two hundred thousand pounds, and your hearing date will be advised." Her gavel smashed down with finality, and the next unlucky schmuck was shuffled forward.

I had no time to question or let shock trickle through my bloodstream.

I'd been processed.

It was done.

I was guided to a small room where more paperwork was presented and signed, a monitoring anklet was locked around my leg, and the terms and conditions of my bail advised even though I had no way of taking them up on their offer.

With the condemning device strapped to my ankle, the guard guided me back to the holding cell. This time, the icy depressing space was empty.

"In." The officer pushed me forward.

I hissed as my wound twinged. I sat on the metal bench and rested my head in my hands.

Now what?

If I couldn't post bail, would I have to stay here until my trial?

Would they at least give me a blanket because I was fucking cold?

Would they let me see my doctor tomorrow like she requested?

I didn't even know O's cell phone number to call and tell her what happened. To make arrangements for Olive. To advise her that Justin would once again have to pick up my fucking pieces so O could run far away from the mess I'd caused.

Fuck, poor Olive.

She wouldn't understand.

She'd hate me for failing her all over again.

My grey sneakers would soon be traded for prison shoes. My jeans would become a jumpsuit. My business no longer operational. I would never paint again. Never watch TV with Olive again. Never tell O every answer to her every biting question.

It's over.

I couldn't catch a proper breath as I accepted that fate had once again fucked me over.

I'd lost my freedom, daughter, and the love of my life all over again.

And this time, I only had myself to blame.

＊ ＊ ＊ ＊ ＊

"Clark, you made bail." A guard banged his hand on the bars, wrenching my eyes open.

I hissed between my teeth as I moved too fast, hurting my side. I would kill Jeffrey all over again for some painkillers and a hoodie.

The guard opened the cell, waiting for me to exit.

The prison vanished for a moment as my blood pressure dropped. The goosebumps that had permanently decorated my skin increased as my bones complained of being so cold.

I hauled myself to my feet, fighting a body that craved rest.

I'd been stupid to think I was cured.

I wasn't nearly as healed as I'd hoped.

Clearing my throat, I moved into the corridor and waited

for the guard to lock up. "Who paid my bail?"

He shrugged. "No one tells me nothing." Striding forward, he looked back at me. "Come on. I don't have all night."

Following him as fast as I could, I kept my hand on my wound as we entered the foyer of the precinct and I signed yet more paperwork that they shoved under my nose.

My back prickled as someone came up behind me.

Someone I knew.

Someone I owed more than I could ever repay.

Turning slowly, I held out my hand to shake Justin's. Half of me wanted to punch him while the other wanted to bow in defeat. "You didn't have to do that."

"I know." He nodded, his dark blond hair neat and body encased in a suit from work. "But I couldn't let you rot in there awaiting trial. Besides, I know you won't run, so it's not like I'm going to lose my investment in you."

We broke contact. "I won't cost you bail." I frowned. "How did you find out about it? No way should you have had to part with two hundred grand for my sorry arse."

He smiled, heading toward the exit and waiting until I fell into step with him. "You've listed me as next of kin. They called and asked if I wanted to post your bail or knew of someone who would."

"Why did you do it?"

"It's either free your sorry arse or become surrogate father to your child."

"I wouldn't expect you to do that." I winced. "I've already asked so fucking much of you."

"So you're okay with O looking after your kid?"

"O needs to be free of me. I've already hurt her too much."

"So your plan is to let O run away and Olive to be packed into foster care?"

My heart stopped beating. "Fuck, no. But I refuse to put my fuck-ups on others anymore. None of you deserve this. I should've handled the situation better. I should've—"

"Look, I'm going to be black and white here, all right?" His eyes flashed. "You don't have a choice. You need us, mate. Me and O. You need our help. There is nothing wrong with that. It doesn't make you weak. It doesn't make us hate you for asking for help. But it does get old when you constantly fight the help we're trying to give you."

I had no reply. I stared at him dumbfounded.

The first time Justin had shown a spark of temper and he'd put me in my place like a kick to a barking dog.

He sighed, shrugging. "Sorry, but that's the reality of the situation. You have no choice but to lean on us, all right? The other shit? It doesn't matter. It's all in the past." His long legs ate up the pavement, his back ramrod straight. "Just focus on getting better. The rest we'll figure out."

I wanted to argue. To tell him I would figure this out without him, but fresh air licked over my skin as we strode through the door and into the night sky, and reality smashed me in the face.

I was lucky.

So fucking lucky to have people who hadn't given up on me, no matter what sort of bastard I'd been.

Relief tried to worm under my overwhelming guilt.

I would never take freedom for granted. I would forever be in Justin's debt. But I also couldn't justify his sacrifice.

Why had he put so much on the line after only a troubled year of friendship?

Who did that?

Who was that selfless?

O.

O is that selfless…and so is Justin.

Two similar people who'd been lumped with the unlucky job of looking after me.

My teeth ground as self-hatred wormed through my chest. "You've given me time, Miller, and for that I'm terribly grateful. I will cherish every moment I have with Olive, I'll do my best to repair what I did to O, and I'll figure out a way to pay you back, but you can't keep doing this. I'm not your responsibility. I know I listed you as Olive's godfather but I don't expect you to adopt her if this all turns to shit. Don't feel like you're trapped just because I am."

He closed the gap between him and his parked car. Resting his hand on the roof, he scowled. "You're a friend, Gil. Friends help out."

"There's helping out and then there's being too fucking generous."

"Look, I put myself in your shoes. I thought about how shit I'd feel being locked up when my daughter is too young to take care of herself. I don't know a hell of a lot of what you've been going through, but I know it hasn't been easy." He unlocked the black sedan, cracking open the door. "I'm still waiting for that explanation, by the way. But in the meantime, just accept it for what it is. Despite all your efforts, you actually have two friends who care about you. You should be with them until..." His eyes flickered away.

"Until I'm sentenced."

"Pretty much. Yeah." He waited until we'd both slipped inside, and I'd puffed with pain to fasten my seatbelt.

He asked softly, "Do you know when they'll call you to court?"

I shook my head. "They didn't say."

He started the car and shoved it into gear. "It can sometimes take months for a hearing."

Staring out the window, I didn't reply as my gaze landed on a small group of people with placards walking down the road to the police station in the dark. Streetlights highlighted a banner linked between the two women walking in front.

A banner that said, *'Gilbert Clark deserves the death sentence.'*

My heart stopped beating.

The placards all depicted paint splashes and pictures of the girls who'd worn my colours and who'd died because of it.

The family of the murdered.

"Shit," Justin muttered as he stomped on the accelerator and shot in the opposite direction.

Yep, shit.

The world was out for blood.

And I was at their mercy.

Chapter Thirteen

Olin

UNKNOWN NUMBER: *O, it's Gil. I've typed, deleted, and retyped so many messages to you, but none of them sound right. No amount of apologies will be enough. No number of thank yous will ever come close. So...I'll keep it simple. I'm back home. I saw you arrive at the hospital today with Olive as I was driven away by the police. I tried to get in touch but was refused. I don't know what the staff told you, but I was officially arrested, booked, and granted bail. Anyway, I just wanted to say, you're free to travel now. I can look after Olive and figure out another scenario for her before my court date. I'm desperate to see her. Tomorrow, I can pick her up or you can drop her off. Either way, I'm extremely grateful to you for looking after her.*

I re-read Gil's message ten times, sipping on a glass of cheap supermarket wine, glancing at my bedroom door to make sure Olive stayed asleep and none the wiser.

I'd never had a message from Gil before.

The novelty sent shivers down my spine.

A teenage reaction to flirting and fun when neither of those options was real.

The wine was to settle my fear over what'd happened to him. After seeing him being driven away in a police car and being turned away at the hospital because he'd been discharged, I'd hid my own concern to protect Olive. I'd taken her to the library and checked out whatever books she wanted—mainly sketching and painting workbooks—and done what I could to distract her.

After a week of living with her, I'd grown used to her triggers.

Her bravery was sometimes far too good. She could laugh

and joke and seem like any normal child her age. However, there'd be a moment. A fleeting second when her guard would drop and I'd see the truth. The worry over being in public if I'd gotten too far away from her. The bitten lip if a man walked toward us on the street. The jumpiness if someone came up behind us unannounced.

The fact she could hide her true fears as well as Gil drained me because my instincts took over—just like they had when doing my best to help Gil through his secrets.

My brain told me to give her space—to watch but not hover, to accept that time would heal her from the worst of being held hostage—but my heart wasn't interested in giving her space or letting time heal her. My heart wanted to cure her. It wanted her laughter to be true and not some carbon copy of joy. It wanted her to be able to stroll down a supermarket aisle and not freeze in panic if I wasn't there.

I sighed.

Poor thing.

But at least, she had her father back.

She could go home now.

She could bask in normalcy until Gil was summoned for trial.

Saving his number into my phone, I typed a reply.

Olin: *I'm glad you're back at home. Did everything go okay with the police? I can drop Olive off tomorrow around mid-morning if that works. She'll be beyond happy to be home with you. She's really missing you.*

I inhaled sharply as I pressed send. I didn't want to go to his warehouse. I still wasn't prepared to enter the place where Gil had painted me. But I equally didn't want him in my space, either.

Dropping Olive off was the best choice because I could leave straight away. If he came here, he might stay...he might try to talk.

Gil: *Okay, great. Thanks. By the way, don't feel like you can't keep using my car if it makes your life easier. I'll figure out an alternative.*

Olin: *It was kind of you to let me borrow it to drive Olive around, but it's yours. I'll just catch the bus back after I've driven her to you.*

He took a long time to reply, as if he was once again typing and deleting multiple responses. My heart flurried as words flashed over my screen.

Gil: *I know it's over between us but...if you want answers, I can give them to you. I'm done with lies and hiding. I'll tell you all of it...if you ask.*

My eyes flashed to my bedroom door as it cracked open. Olive rubbed her eyes sleepily, her forehead furrowed with exhaustion. "Oh, good. You're still there."

I tossed my phone onto the couch, climbing to my feet and going to her. She walked into my embrace, squishing her face into my chest. "Of course, I'm still here. I told you I'd keep you safe."

She pulled away, looking up at me. "You're the best, O. My second favourite person after my daddy."

"Wow, that's a great honour." I smiled, pressing a kiss to her forehead. "And you're the greatest little girl I know." Holding her shoulders, I pushed her away until I could study her face clearly. "What woke you? Another nightmare?"

She dug her barefoot into the carpet. "I thought I heard something. A man."

"Nope. Just us."

"That's good."

She'd grown used to Justin but not to the degree of our bond. Justin had come over a couple of times with pizza and Thai takeaway. He told kid jokes, brought dessert, and braved through a Netflix program for little girls. He was allowed to touch her shoulder in goodbye and take her dishes into the kitchen, but that was where her comfort level ended.

If Gil did get sentenced, who would care for her? Who would step up to be the parent she needed—the protector, the artist, and the disciplinarian?

"Want to know something awesome?" I made my voice bubbly and light.

Her eyes widened in excitement. "What?"

My phone vibrated on the couch behind me, signalling a new message had been delivered.

Gil.

God, why couldn't we have messaged each other before? It would've made a lot of his secrets easier to share via a faceless text.

"You're going home tomorrow. Your dad healed enough to leave the hospital. How freaking cool is that?"

Olive froze, then pure joy rippled through her. She clapped her hands and spun in place with the biggest grin. "Oh, wow, really?!" She bounced on the spot. "Yay! Yay!"

I pointed at my bedroom door. "It's going to be super fun tomorrow, so you better get some sleep. You don't want to be tired, do you?"

She turned deadly serious. "You're right. I don't want to be tired. I get cranky when I'm tired."

"Yeah, me too. Should we go to sleep, and when we wake up, we'll go see your father?"

She threw herself at me, planting a wet kiss on my cheek. "Yes, please!" Pulling away, a frown stole her smile. "Wait...you'll stay with us, right? You'll come live at the warehouse?"

I stiffened. "That's your home. This is mine."

"But I like living with you."

"You'll love living with your dad more."

Her face fell. "But...I'll miss you."

I hid the dagger she stabbed me with. The dagger of kindness and affection. After living a lonely life, being told you're wanted was the worst kind of drug because you could swiftly become addicted to it.

Smiling broadly, I turned her around and marched her back into my bedroom. "You won't miss me, silly. You won't even notice I'm not there the moment you're back with your dad. Now, go to sleep so you have lots of energy tomorrow."

Closing the door, I returned to the couch and let out the tangled breath I'd been holding.

What was it about Gil and his daughter that turned me inside out? How did both of them have the power to reach inside my chest and claim what wasn't theirs to claim?

The sooner I leave, the better.

My phone revealed the newest message that'd come in, flashing in warning as I clicked on it.

Gil: *I have no right to say this after what I've done, but I love you, O. I always have. I always will. I know I don't stand a chance to fix what I've broken, and I'm not asking you to forgive me. I guess...I just wanted to be honest. To finally be honest how it's always been you. I was in love with you for two years before we even officially talked. I was in love with you the entire time we were apart. And I'm still in love with you, even though I know I will never deserve you. I guess that's my true punishment. I won't bring it up again. I won't make you uncomfortable. But I had to say it.*

Anyway, goodnight.

Thank you from the bottom of my heart for looking after my daughter. If I know her as well as I think I do, I know she'll miss you. She'll ask you to move in with us. She'll be as in love with you as am I.

And I don't blame her.

I slouched against the pillow, my heart racing, my blood gushing. Tears glazed my vision as I read and re-read his message. A text like that had the power to drop my guard and give me permission to forgive anything and everything.

It reeked of a promise of love and togetherness and home.

It made me want to type that I loved him too. That I always had and probably always would. To accept his proposal to become a part of his life, to possibly become his wife, and mother to his child.

I could have my very own family.

No.

Stop it.

You can't.

Our foundations were rotten and full of holes.

Our walls were riddled with secrets and lies.

Our trust was torn apart.

There is no us anymore.

And it's for the best.

Swiping away a tear, I clung to my resolution of being stronger this time. Of not letting my need for company and closeness belittle my own self-worth. Gil had taken and taken from me.

The small part that was left had to remain mine.

Olin: *Goodnight, Gil. I'll see you tomorrow.*

My hands shook as I sent the polite message back.

A message that didn't just give a generic goodbye but an entire fistful of honesty.

An ending hidden behind the simple phrase.

It's too little.

It's too late.

We're friends.

And nothing more.

Chapter Fourteen

Olin

"IT LOOKS WEIRD," Olive muttered as I parked the car in front of warehouse twenty-five. The Master of Trickery graffiti and gravel frontage hissed with memories of Gil being beaten by his uncle, of Jeffrey trying to drag me into his van, of Gil pulling me inside to paint and deliver me.

I swallowed hard, scolding my pounding heart.

I could do this.

It's just a building.

He's just a man.

It's all in the past.

"How did it used to look?" I unbuckled my seatbelt, climbing from the car as Olive hurled herself outside.

She squinted in the watery sunlight. "Not sure. It's just...different."

"Maybe the paint has faded since you last saw it? It has been a year."

"Maybe." She didn't look convinced. Slamming the passenger door, she skipped eagerly to the pedestrian access in the large roller door. "Dad? Daddy?" Her tiny fist rapped on the metal, echoing down the driveway of warehouses.

I flinched.

Needing to stay occupied, I reached into the backseat for Olive's backpack full of newly purchased clothes and toiletries. I didn't need them anymore.

She was home.

Hopefully indefinitely.

The door swung wide, and Gil appeared. His face

immediately turned lighter, younger, *happy*. The seriousness in his gaze became playful. The worry in his jaw relaxed. I'd never seen him so enamoured and carefree. "Spinach!" He bent down and swung her into his arms.

Immediately, he groaned and plopped her back on her feet. "Sorry, kiddo. I forgot I still have a few weeks of healing until I can lift you. You've gotten big."

She pouted but buried her face in his belly, wrapping her arms tight around him. "It's okay. I can wait." She jiggled in his embrace, her joy at finally being home overflowing as she looked up. "Can I go see my room? I missed this place so much!"

Gil nodded, sidestepping out of the way so she could bolt inside. "Of course. Go ahead and get reacquainted." He chuckled as she took off, vanishing into the cavernous warehouse.

His head tipped up, his gaze caught mine, and instantly the dreary English day became alive with electricity. My skin sparked as I clutched her backpack closer, forcing myself to delete the distance between us. "Hello."

He wiped his mouth with a rough hand. "Hello." His green gaze once again became weapons. Only this time, they weren't weapons of annihilation—determined to scare me away and hurt me—but pools of regret and love.

Love...the most terrible weapon of all.

He didn't try to hide it.

He didn't care his guard was down.

He acted as if showing his true colours was a relief after a lifetime of hiding.

"Thanks so much for looking after her, O."

"Not a problem." I held out the backpack. "Here, this is hers. I bought her a few things."

"I'll pay you back."

"It's fine." I backed away. I'd completed my task. I'd delivered his daughter and returned his borrowed hatchback. I was free now. Free to pack up my life and run far, far away like a coward.

"Will you come in? Olive will want to say goodbye."

"Um, I might go if—"

"Daaaaaad!" Olive's high-pitched voice travelled through the space and erupted outside.

Gil looked over his shoulder, his body already turning to go to her. He grimaced. "Look, don't go. I have to...I better go check on her." Striding deeper into the warehouse, he waved for me to follow. "Please, O. Stay…for a moment."

I really didn't want to, but some invisible force tugged me.

Stepping inside, I braced myself as my attention fell on the podium where I'd eaten a drugged sandwich, found out about Gil's past, and fallen asleep while he'd painted me.

He'd tidied up the equipment and hidden away the brushes, but goosebumps spread over my arms. I hugged myself, keeping my chin high and spine straight.

I wasn't afraid of this place.

I wasn't afraid of him.

I was just wary of falling into the same trap of being caught up in the pain of others. Of wanting to fix what I couldn't fix and believing I could be happy if I could make others happy.

I'd learned a valuable lesson that giving too much of yourself never ended well. Generosity with feelings was a must in a relationship, but endless forgiving was a recipe for disaster.

Gil made his way to the office leading toward the small apartment. Olive bowled right into his arms from the opposite direction. Her eyes wide and mouth parted as she pointed around the space suspiciously. "Where is everything?"

Gil hid his wince, his hand pressing to his wounded side as he steadied her. "What do you mean?"

He let her go as she darted toward me, pointing like a crazy thing at the empty walls, cupboards, and floor. "The paintings, the furniture. It's all gone." She spun to face her father with a helpless shrug. "Where'd it go?"

Gil looked at me, fibs forming in his eyes. Fibs to protect her from the truth. But almost as if he didn't have the strength to tell another lie, or because he valued his daughter far too much to keep things from her, he said, "I sold most of it."

"Sold your *paintings*?" She soared around and shoved her finger toward the sky where a bare hook hung between two windows. "Even that one? The one we did together?" Olive marched toward me, stealing my hand as if this was very important. "I liked that painting. It wasn't all that nice 'cause I wasn't as good as I am now, but I liked the turtle. It was huge and scaly and its shell had lots and lots of little creatures painted on it." She nudged her chin at Gil. "Daddy did the smaller animals. He also had the turtle eating spinach 'cause apparently they like that and said it would always be a joke that I'm so fast and speedy, but the giant turtle ate me."

Gil came toward us, looking at the blank spot on the wall.

"Someone paid big money for your turtle, Olive Oyl. It's gone to a good home."

"But it belongs here."

"You belong here more."

"I don't get it."

Gil bent forward, bringing his stare in line with hers. "I sold things to get you back. Some things I didn't want to get rid of, but I wanted you more, so I found them new homes." He cupped her cheek with a soft smile. "And it worked because you're back here. We can paint together again. We can go shopping and replace what I sold. It will be fun. You'll see."

Her eyes lit up, already her mourning for missing things replaced by the idea of new. "Can you take me to Kohls…like before? Is it still there?" She looked up at me, pinpricks of excitement on her cheeks. "Daddy used to take me to Kohls once a week if I did my chores and helped him tidy up his paints after he worked. He let me buy one thing each visit. Last time, I bought a pencil case to keep my crayons in." She frowned, facing her father with a strict expression. "You didn't sell my pencil case too, did you?"

Gil chuckled. "No, that I kept. Go and see for yourself."

Olive sniffed, flashed him a grin, and bolted back through the office. A second later, she called, "My room is locked! Why is my room locked?"

Gil groaned. "I forgot what a little tornado she is."

"She's definitely bouncy." I smiled, sucked into Olive's purity and infectious energy.

"She's always kept me on my toes."

"You probably need it." I scanned the sparse place, trying to see it from Olive's point of view. Imagining it full of artwork and couches and chairs and *life*. I'd been so used to Gil's melancholy and his unattachment to physical items that the bareness of his home didn't ring alarm bells. However, in the short interactions I'd watched him with Olive, I uncovered a totally different version of him.

A man who found peace in the chaos of parenthood.

A man who decorated and nested because his little daughter demanded vibrancy and colour.

His lies fell apart while standing in that barren room, the truth blazing hotly in the emptiness, the forlornness. The plastic cups in the cupboards weren't for his painting but his daughter. The room he kept locked a shrine to the little girl he'd lost.

He'd been dying day by day, pushing me away for my safety and jerking me back for his next breath. My soul wanted to chase that path, to vindicate him and give me permission to give in, but my mind focused on something trivial but vitally important.

He takes her to Kohls.

My heart squeezed, condemning myself for my spat of jealousy in the Kohls changing room. The huge store where we'd fought and my jealousy had reached critical, and Gil had turned me green (in more ways than one) to match their logo.

He'd seemed uncomfortable talking about visiting the place when I'd called him out on his familiarity. I'd assumed it was because he didn't want to admit he'd taken prior girlfriends.

Now, a whole new meaning arose.

"You took her to Kohls. It was her you were talking about when you said you went there often. Not with other women."

He massaged the back of his neck, embarrassment etching his cheeks. "I wanted to tell you then about her. I wanted to tell you so many times. But…it wasn't as if I could say… 'oh, by the way. I have a daughter. Want to meet her?' She was a product of a night that should never have happened, and I'd failed to protect her from being taken. The guilt just wouldn't allow me to tell you."

I nodded. "I understand."

"Do you?" His forehead furrowed. "*Do* you understand, or are you just being nice again?"

My back straightened; my temper bristled. "I'm done being nice when it's not deserved."

"Good. I'm glad."

"And I do understand. I know why you kept her secret. I follow your reasoning. I just don't agree with it."

"So you would've enlisted the police and told everyone what a fuck-up you were?"

"No. I would've enlisted the help of those I trusted and asked for their advice."

"What if you'd never had anyone to trust and those you *did* trust turned out to be the worst?"

I frowned. "You're saying I'm the worst?"

"Fuck no." His face darkened with horror. "I'm saying my uncle was."

My temper refused to be pacified. "Well, regardless, I'm not just anyone, Gil."

"No, you're *everything*."

"And you destroyed any trust between us by—"

"Dad. Hey, *Dad!*" Olive came bowling out, grabbing Gil's hands and yanking. "Key. Is there a key? Why can't I get into my room?"

Gil wrenched his gaze from mine, the heat from our almost-argument hissing with hope of a bigger blow-up.

I hadn't noticed it before.

I hadn't allowed myself to feel it.

But now I did.

Now I felt the burn to shout, the urge to yell, the undeniable need to tell him exactly what I thought about everything.

That was what was missing.

A fight.

A cleansing, healing good-old-fashioned *fight*.

But the luxury of frank conversation—of raised voices and angry shouts couldn't happen in front of a girl who'd already been through so much.

I knew it.

Gil knew it.

We allowed the moment to ease and the tension to fade between us.

Gil sighed, his skin a little whiter than usual thanks to his healing side. He stroked Olive's hair as he pushed her back the way she came. "I've got the key. Come on." Following her into the apartment, he fished out a key ring and selected the right one. Inserting it into the door, he stepped back as it cracked open.

The door that'd always been barricaded next to his in the graffiti rainforest wall. The room he'd consumed a lonely bottle of vodka in, the room I'd glimpsed inside and began to wonder if Gil wasn't as safe as I thought.

Olive ran in.

Curiosity got the better of me, and I drifted forward until her room came into view. Olive bounced from her pillow-stocked bed to the rattan rocking chair to the wardrobe to the pink tallboy. Touching everything, examining anything, getting reacquainted with her old belongings.

Her face glowed with relief. "You didn't sell anything in here."

Gil slouched against the doorframe, his hand touching his wounded side as if pain snuck up on him. "This room was off-limits. It's yours."

Olive threw herself at him, squishing him in a hug. "I love

you, Popeye."

He tripped backward, deep pain and endless gratitude radiating in his eyes. He crushed her close, bowing over to press a kiss to the top of her silken hair. "I love you too. More than you'll ever know."

"Oh, I know." She grinned up at him. "I know you love me loads and loads."

He nodded, releasing her with a grimace. "I do."

"And I know you love Olin loads and loads, too." She gave me a sneaky look. "You told me so in the stories."

Gil groaned, trying to laugh but tangling up a tortured noise instead. "Sometimes stories don't have happy endings."

"Ours does," she said with utmost conviction.

His skin turned ashen. "Ours will, eventually. However, just like other stories, there will be new trials ahead."

My heart skipped a beat.

He's trying to prepare her for the possibility of him going to jail.

"Nothing bad will happen now we're together, silly." Olive patted his waist, still smiling at me. "And nothing bad could ever happen if O moves in with us. We can be safe together."

I coughed, shaking my head. "You guys have each other. You don't need me."

"Yes, we do. I don't want you to go." Her voice slipped into a plea. "Please...can you stay?"

"O has her own life, little spinach. Don't make her sad by asking for things that can't come true."

Her shoulders fell. "I didn't mean to make anyone sad."

I held out my hand. She immediately flew to my side and took it, blinking huge grey eyes, wrapping her little spell around my soul all over again. She made it sound so easy—nullifying a lifetime of complication into one stupidly simple conclusion.

Love had the power to heal, start afresh, move on.

Pity I didn't have the strength to do such things.

"I'll always be your friend, just like I'm your dad's friend. We've been friends for ages."

"Can you be our friend while living with us?"

I chuckled. "Stubborn little thing, aren't you?"

"Yep. Dad said I'm worse than a donkey."

"A donkey?"

"A stubborn arse." Gil chuckled. "I shouldn't call her an arse, but...if the description fits." He smiled, slightly embarrassed, mostly proud.

"I'm an arse." Olive snickered, alive and happy as if she'd been asleep for the past year and just woken up to her father's protective kiss.

"The prettiest arse I've ever seen." I pressed her nose.

She wrinkled it, tossing her head. "I want to draw a donkey now. Wait here." Dashing away, she barrelled to her dresser, ripping open drawers and finding stationery and pencils.

I smiled, entranced by her innocence and total faith that in this moment, nothing could be more perfect.

Gil came toward me, sucking all the air from my lungs.

He stopped within touching distance, his eyes firing, lips parted. For the longest moment, he stared at me. His intensity was bright and fierce. His shields fell, revealing every emotion I'd never been allowed to see. "I shouldn't have messaged you what I did last night. I shouldn't have told you I've always been in love with you. That even now I want you, all while knowing I've ensured I'll never have you."

I shivered, needing to back away, unable to move. "It's fine."

His hand came up, cupping my cheek as if he couldn't control himself. "Fuck, I'm so fucking sorry."

My skin blistered beneath his touch. My stomach bottomed out. My heart cried. I backed up, forcing his hand to drop and my skin to scream in denial.

"Don't." I did my best to keep my stupid heart in its iron-clad box.

This was one promise I wouldn't break.

He'd broken my faith.

My confidence.

Me.

And with that came a distance I wasn't prepared to cross.

I was struggling, I would admit.

I came here offering condolences and concern but nothing more.

But standing there? *God*, every part of me wanted to be touched. Every cell wanted to combust with lust and lunacy. I wanted to scratch him, scar him, and show him just what he'd thrown away. But I shook my head, forbidding both of us from thinking there was any chance to repair this.

He sighed and raked a hand through his hair. The strands were unkempt and wild, as usual. "I'm so deeply indebted to you...for everything."

"You don't need to keep saying that, Gil. You don't have to repay me…for anything."

He licked his lips. "Are you sure? There's nothing I can do to fix this?"

Kiss me.

Fight for me.

Prove that I'm wrong to leave.

It was time to go.

Time to walk out of Olive's life after falling headfirst into it the past week. Loss kicked me in the stomach. I would miss her. I would miss watching her come alive again.

I could understand why she'd helped Gil so much. She was a natural cure to the hardships of life.

"I…I better go."

He tried to hide his flinch but wasn't successful. "Of course."

"Will…will you be okay? Do you have arrangements made for Olive if you're…"

He swallowed. "I'll figure it out. It's my problem, not yours."

"If you need help…"

"I'll manage. You've done far too much already." His face twisted. "I'll never be able to apologise enough for what I did."

"Stop. Honestly, you don't have to mention it again." I tripped backward, instincts ordering me to leave now, before more memories of murdered girls and body painting sprang anew. "You killed your uncle…for that I'm grateful. But…"

I couldn't ask.

I couldn't *not* ask.

My voice abandoned me.

"What? What do you want to know?" His eyebrows tugged over his gaze, shadowing him. "I'll answer anything you want."

My heart raced. "What part of this did you play, Gil? Did you…did you hurt those girls?" My question fell like unexploded dynamite, dangerous and volatile.

Silence stole the carnage before Gil shifted and sucked in a breath. His stare smoked with apology. "I painted them." He shrugged, holding up his palms. "It was my paint on their skin."

I trembled. "I don't want to believe that."

"It's true."

"I can't believe you could paint someone knowing they would die."

His face fell. "I painted you."

Silence fell.

Truth fell.

Despair fell.

My insides collapsed into one another.

He'd painted me in olives. He'd prepared to sacrifice me.

If he could do that to someone who'd been in his bed and in his heart...what made strangers any different?

The chilly warehouse prickled my arms. "Those people online and the ones on the street...they want you dead."

"I know." He no longer glittered with the ice he'd used to keep me at bay but wore a cape of desolation. Of acceptance that everything had gone wrong and the only thing he could do now was pay the price. "I'm aware that I've fucked everything up all over again. And Olive will pay the most."

"What if they put you away for decades?"

"I'll find her a family worthy of having her love before it's too late."

"And you? What will you do?"

He gave me the saddest, rawest smile. "I'll tell the truth. I'm done hiding, O. When they come for me, I'm going to tell them...everything."

Chapter Fifteen

Olin

"THANK YOU FOR seeing us, Miss Moss."

I nodded, cupping my warm cup of tea with icy hands. "You're welcome."

They weren't welcome, but it wasn't like I had a choice. I'd woken to a rude knock at seven a.m. I'd made the mistake of opening it. I now stood in my pyjamas and dressing gown in an apartment that felt even more lonely and oppressive now that Olive had gone home, and did my best to shake away the nightmares.

Nightmares of Gil being given the death sentence. Of him being fried in an electric chair. Of Olive going to live in a whorehouse with a backpack stained in dumpster dirt. Of Ms Tallup selling her off to the highest bidder.

It'd been three days since I'd dropped Olive off.

And I was going out of my mind.

I needed to do something.

Go somewhere.

Figure out what the hell I should do from here.

"Are you okay? Healthwise?" Two new officers interrogated me today. Two women. One plump with her uniform neatly pressed and her name tag, Gloria, proudly pinned to her breast, and the other as skinny as a pen with her hair tied tight at the base of her nape.

"I'm fine. I wasn't hurt."

"You were found naked in a forest, on a cold evening in England. It's lucky you didn't have hypothermia."

"The adrenaline kept me warm." I stared into my milky tea,

wishing I'd never opened my door. What did they want? What could I tell them that would benefit anyone?

Almost as if they sensed my unwillingness, they jumped straight to their point. "Can you tell us, in your own words, what happened the night Gilbert Clark painted you and took you into Lickey Hills Country Park?"

I looked up. "I already told the officers who found me."

"Yes, but we'd like to hear it again."

"There isn't anything to add."

Gloria scowled. "Just in your own words, please give us an account of the evening in question."

I paused, going over the facts and wondering if lies were necessary to protect Gil. A fabrication to perhaps grant a shorter sentence. But lies hadn't saved him, and lies wouldn't save me. The truth was the only option.

My voice stayed monotone as I gave as much information as I could in as few sentences as possible. "Gilbert Clark painted me at his warehouse, drugged me so I'd stay asleep, planted a GPS tracker on me so he could follow, and took me to the location his uncle had advised. The plan was to trade me for his daughter and then chase after me and set me free. He was shot in the back after his uncle decided to keep both me and Gilbert's daughter. Jeffrey then took both of us deeper into the forest where he'd been living for a while in a camouflaged caravan. He said he planned on selling us into the sex trade. He took me outside to rape me, Gilbert arrived just in time, he passed out once Jeffrey was dead. That's it."

The skinny officer looked up from scribbling notes. "You said he put a GPS tracker on you? So he had hope that you wouldn't die?"

"Of course. His intention was always to keep both of us alive…if he could achieve it."

"Yet he painted those other women and allowed them to be murdered?"

I still couldn't believe he'd been guilty of that.

I looked into my tea again, wishing it had the answers.

"Do you think Gilbert Clark is a good person?" Gloria asked, pen poised over paper.

I nodded fiercely. "Yes. He's a good person."

"Is he a killer?"

I don't know.

"I don't believe so."

"But he did paint them?"

I swallowed hard. I didn't want to answer because Gil had told me the truth. The same truth he'd provide in court. I stood taller. "Yes. He painted them."

Flicking back through her notes, Gloria asked, "In your previous statement, when you first called the police about the attempted kidnapping outside Gilbert Clark's warehouse, you said the van used was white with blue stripes. Do you still wish to stand by that statement?"

I slouched, knowing I'd been caught in that fib. "I lied to protect Gil. It was a black van."

The skinny cop sniffed. "Do you think, if you'd told the truth about the van, we might've been able to prevent what happened to you and ensured both Gilbert and Jeffrey were in prison?"

"I have thought about it, and I agree that lying prevented Jeffrey from being found. However, I lied because Gil asked me to, and I would lie again, knowing what I know now."

"And what is that?"

"Olive would've died in that caravan if Jeffrey had been caught. She wouldn't have been found until it was too late."

"And the life of one girl is worth the lives of others?"

I tipped my tea down the sink. "I can't answer that." Striding to the door, I opened it. "I need to go to work. I'm sorry, but I have to ask you to leave."

They stood, tucked their notebooks away and walked in heavy boots across my threshold. "We'll be in touch, Miss Moss."

I nodded, smiled goodbye, then closed the door in their faces.

The moment their boots sounded on the staircase, I grabbed my phone and called Shannon at Status Enterprises.

"Hello?"

"Shannon, I've had enough time off. I'm ready to return to work."

"Oh, that's great! We're short-staffed so we'd super appreciate it. You can come in tomorrow."

"Today? I'm free today."

"Today is great! See you soon."

I hung up and padded toward my bathroom and the shower.

I couldn't save Gil from what was coming for him.

I couldn't protect Olive from having her family torn apart.

I couldn't figure out what I needed to do to put this behind me.

But I couldn't sit at home anymore.

I had to do something productive.

Before I did something wrong.

Something like catching a bus to Gil's and demanding the entire sordid story so I knew what he would face in court, so I knew how long he would be imprisoned, so I knew how this sorry tale would end.

Chapter Sixteen

Gil

I UPLOADED ANOTHER time-lapse video of a girl I'd transformed from human into a lush, dew-misted strawberry last year. My Facebook page no longer acted as a positive beacon for my business. Instead, it granted a platform for people to comment on how vile I was, how they wished I was dead, how they planned on killing me if I wasn't dealt life imprisonment.

My star rating had plummeted from five stars to one, effectively blacklisting me from any future commissions.

I'd done my best to keep uploading previous videos and pieces of art, hoping my inbox would fill with a request for work rather than death threats. But no company contacted me for ad work. No campaign or business dared hire me with the bad press surrounding my name.

It fucking sucked because yes, I was involved, and yes, I had taken a life, but no one knew the full story, and they'd stolen my livelihood. I only had a finite amount of time to pay off my debts, squirrel away enough cash for Olive, and figure out a way to keep her happy and safe before the police summoned me to trial.

I even considered getting a job as a house painter or some other labourer, but I couldn't leave Olive. I knew I should enrol her back into school and set up a routine so she had something familiar and trustworthy in her life, but I wasn't prepared to miss out on huge chunks of time together.

Not now.

Not when every moment was precious and our time together unknown.

Two weeks had passed since I'd seen O.

Two weeks since I'd had my daughter back and pretended things were normal. I'd taken her to Kohls and bought her a new outfit to replace the ones she no longer fitted. I'd sold my car so I had some disposable cash for food and incidentals. And Justin had become a regular dinner guest. Some nights we ordered in. Some nights I cooked. Most times he fucking paid.

My guilt and self-hatred at him picking up the bill and delivering groceries because I couldn't leave ensured I diligently kept note of what I owed him. I had a little notebook now, full of numbers, the tally growing bigger and my debt growing heavier each time he popped round.

I'd warned him that he wasn't welcome if he continued to bring small gifts for Olive and found some unsubtle way of ensuring we ate. He'd jokingly said 'I'll put it on your tab' when I'd tried to force the entire three-thousand-pound pay-out I got for my car into his hand.

He'd been kidding.

I hadn't.

I took it literally, and my notebook had become my tab.

One that I had every intention of wiping clean one day.

I wanted to banish him from popping around so much, but yet again, I was fucking selfish.

I knew why he made the effort after a long day in the office to swing by my place and watch TV with Olive. Why he learned the names of silly cartoon characters and sat on the floor and submitted himself to a painting lesson that ended up speckling his suit with colours.

I'd catch his eye mid stupid joke with Olive and my heart would squeeze in agony.

This bloke, who'd been more like a brother to me than any other family, went out of his way to make sure Olive was comfortable with him. To prove to her that he was trustworthy. To prove to himself, and to me, that when the day came for me to be locked up, he could cope being a godfather and Olive could cope being raised by yet another man who wasn't her dad.

Fuck.

Slamming my laptop closed, I eyed it. Perhaps I should sell it too. After all, the uploaded content didn't seem to be resurrecting my career, and I didn't need the expensive Photoshop software to edit my painted canvases.

My career was dead.

The public had officially murdered any chance I had of

climbing my way out of the hole I was in. Not to mention, O hadn't messaged me or emailed or attempted to get in touch in any way.

I checked my phone for the billionth time today.

She'd gone from coming around when she wasn't invited to avoiding me at all costs.

The amount of times I'd stared at her number on my phone, willing myself to call her, even while knowing I never could was pathetic.

In her mind, we were over.

In my mind, I couldn't allow us to be.

Not like this.

Not without confessing everything.

"Hey, mate."

I jolted as Justin appeared behind me, slapping a hand on my shoulder and eyeing my phone. O's contact details blazed on my screen, condemning me to a life I'd totally destroyed.

"Still not got the balls to call her, huh?" He tutted under his breath. "Two weeks is a long time. She might've moved out and flown overseas for all you know."

I stood, shoving my phone into my pocket and marching past all my paint supplies that no longer had a purpose and into the small apartment.

"Hey, Dad." Olive waved with her tiny paintbrush as I brushed past her and planted a kiss on her crown.

"Wow, that's amazing, little spinach."

And I wasn't just saying that.

My daughter was fucking talented.

Her eye for shading. Her patience with detail. Her skill at intricacies. I'd like to think she inherited all that talent from me, but the reality was, she got some from Jeffrey too.

God rot his soul.

"It's a toucan to go in the rainforest." She pointed behind her at the rainforest graffiti on the wall. "It needs more animals in there."

"Good idea. Perhaps do an otter next."

The word turned to ash on my tongue.

Otter.

O.

Fucking hell.

I couldn't stop thinking about her.

I'd always carried her in my heart since I'd walked away

from school, but now the memories of her, the thoughts of her, were a hundred times stronger.

I couldn't stop them. I had no peace from them. Every part of me craved to see her. To touch her. Kiss her. Slip inside her and erase all the badness between us.

Carrying on into the kitchen, I tore open the pantry and grabbed a box of risotto. Tonight, I'd cook creamy mushroom risotto because it was filling and cheap and the leftovers could make a pasta bake tomorrow night.

I'd make every penny stretch as much as I could, so Olive at least had some cash to take with her when I was incarcerated.

Justin unbuttoned his blazer and sat on the wooden barstool. His hands rested on the same counter where O had cornered me, stolen my vodka bottle, and I'd consumed her instead of alcohol.

My gaze fell to the floor where I'd thrust inside her for the first time. The rush of lust and the cloak of shame at being so rough with her after only wanting to be gentle. My healing side twinged a little, jerking me back to the present.

"You're thinking about her again," Justin muttered under his breath. "Why don't you do what I said and *talk* to her?"

"Shut up." Opening the fridge, I pulled out an IPA and shoved the cold bottle at him. "Here. Sip your beverage, let me cook, and then you're leaving."

Unscrewing the lid, he smirked. "How about I'll drink my beer and harass you while you cook? I like that plan better."

"I just won't listen to you." I tapped my ears. "Selective hearing, Miller. And tonight, I don't want to hear what you say every fucking time you come here."

"What? That I think you're giving her too much space and should go over there before it's too late?"

My heart kicked. "You keep threatening me that she might have gone. But...has she left yet?"

"No, but that's beside the point. The longer you leave it, the harder it will be."

Hard, definitely.

Hard emotionally and physically.

My body tortured me on a daily basis. I almost had a fucking wet dream the other night. I woke to an orgasm threatening to crash over me, her scent in my nose and her touch on my skin. I'd finished myself off in the dark, drowning in the fantasy that I hadn't destroyed us.

"I'm honouring her wishes, Miller. She wants nothing more to do with me. And I can't fucking blame her."

Justin swigged his beer, settling in to give me the lecture he'd given almost every night he'd visited. "Yes, you fucked up. Yes, you used her to find Olive. You didn't tell her—or me, I might add—what you were going through. You pretended you hated her, when really, you've always loved her. You sent out so many mixed signals and made up so many lies that she has no idea what part of you is real."

"Exactly. That's exactly why she wants nothing to do with me." I dumped the risotto into a pan and scooped some butter into it.

"So...why don't you go and tell her the truth? Why don't you show her what part is real so she knows for sure that leaving is the right choice."

"She deserves better."

"Ugh, don't start this martyr bullshit again, Clark. You know as well as I do that if she'd truly been afraid of you, if she truly never wanted to see you again, she would've booked a ticket anywhere in the world to run away from you. She would've vanished by now." He pinned me with a stare. "But she hasn't. She's still here. She's waiting for closure or hope—just as much as you are. So...you should go to her."

"She probably wouldn't even open the door if I knocked on it."

"Don't you owe it to both of you to find that out instead of making up bullshit excuses?"

I scowled. "Just stay out of it."

He looked over his shoulder at Olive still engrossed in her painting. "Answer me one question. If the answer is honest, I won't bring this up again." He drew an x over his chest. "Cross my heart."

I rolled my eyes, ignoring the itch of healing from my wound. "No chance."

He lowered his voice, not giving me an option. "That teacher bitch you told me about. She took your virginity, right?"

Tearing open vegetable stock and pouring it over the risotto was suddenly fascinating. I kept my gaze well away from Justin's. I'd told him where Olive had come from a week ago. I'd skimmed the details but gave enough that he looked even more fondly at Olive. As if being abandoned by her mother after raping her father made her even more worthy of being protected at all costs.

It so happened I agreed with him.

Olive didn't have an evil bone in her body. She was my little firecracker. My tiny tornado angel. The fact that I'd soon be torn away from her brought as many sleepless nights as I'd suffered when she'd been torn away from me.

Life could stop being a bastard.

I just wanted simple.

A job, some money, and freedom to keep my daughter happy.

If I could have O to fix my broken heart, then that would be a dream come true, but if I couldn't, I'd always been satisfied to put my needs aside and focus on Olive's.

"Answer me, Clark," Justin muttered. "It's the first and last time I'll bring this up."

Spinning to face him, I closed the distance between us so I could keep my voice as low as possible. Olive didn't know about her mother.

I'd lied on that front.

Again.

I'd told her her mother had given her to me because she was sick and loved Olive far too much to put her at risk. That she'd moved to Japan to get treatment and could never come back.

In a roundabout way, it wasn't a lie. Jane Tallup had been sick...in the head. And she had gone to Japan for treatment...teaching other kids. Who I hoped to fucking God she hadn't molested.

"Fine, I'll answer you. Yes, she took my virginity. What's the problem?"

He shook his head, asking me another question. "And have you been with any other women since her?"

I froze.

Where was he going with this?

What was the point?

"Just answer it, douche-bag." He raised an eyebrow. "Any other women between you being raped as a kid and then falling into bed with the love of your life?"

My hands balled.

There'd been one other girl.

Not that it could be classified as sex.

I'd been lonely.

Olive had been about three years old.

Her tiny hugs kept my pieces together, but one night, it wasn't enough. I'd missed O with every fucking fibre. I'd gone to a bar. I'd watched men and women drink while I'd stayed stone-cold sober. A tipsy chick flirted with me. She touched me. She laughed with me. She asked me back to her place.

I went.

I tried to be with her.

I really fucking did.

But I just...couldn't. It wasn't the fact she was tipsy—by the time we fooled around she was coherent and fully aware of her choices. It wasn't the fact that I didn't trust my babysitter to keep Olive safe—I'd used my elderly neighbour before when I'd stayed up all night painting.

I just couldn't move past being forced by Tallup.

I couldn't stop thinking about O.

I sighed, my shoulders slouching. "What's your fucking point, Miller?"

Justin smirked, the beer bottle dangling from his fingers as he took a smug sip. "My point, Gilbert Clark, is you're fucked if you don't go and at least try to talk to O. You fell in love with her before the bullshit with your teacher. You don't associate her with forced assault. You *trust* her. You don't stand a chance with anyone else but her."

The stock started to boil, overflowing the pan.

Giving him the finger, I returned to my job as chef, doing my best to ignore his twisted logic. I didn't necessarily believe in the phenomenon of soul-mates. But I did believe that O was the only woman who fixed me. The only woman I could ever adore with all my being.

But if I couldn't have her, a life of celibacy and singledom was fine.

I had Olive.

I'd live through her.

She would grow, fall in love, and have a family of her own.

And I'd be there, on the outskirts, a desperate father begging for scraps of attention, pleading for them to come round for Christmases and holidays, slipping further alone as the years wedged us apart.

Or you'll just be in jail.

A sad old convict with no one.

Goddammit.

Justin chuckled. "Once Olive's in bed, I'll stay and catch up on a bit of work while you go and see if you can fix at least one thing before you're thrown in jail."

He meant it as encouragement.

But it only made me hyperaware that even if I told O everything. Even if she forgave me. Even if we could *somehow* make it work, I would still let her down the moment I was sentenced and locked away.

The monitor bracelet around my ankle said I couldn't leave the street where I lived.

The promise of fixing what I'd broken with O overrode the consequences.

I should ignore Justin's advice.

I should let O continue to live without me.

But I'd never been very good at doing the right thing.

Chapter Seventeen

Olin

TWO WEEKS HAD passed.

By day, I returned to work and kept to myself.

By night, I went home to an empty apartment and surfed the internet for news about the upcoming trial.

Justin had popped round a few times to check on me, delivering little notes and paintings that Olive had done. She still wanted me to move in with them. Her hints with her drawings of happy owl families made that totally obvious.

I missed her.

I missed Gil.

But he kept his distance.

He respected my need for space, even though I tormented myself each night with thoughts and dreams of him. It didn't help that each day there was a new article or slur about him. A new claim that he'd killed a hundred women. That he'd killed puppies and kittens and even had his eye on children.

Two new GoFundMe campaigns had sprung up asking for money to hire a hitman to kill him before the justice system gave too soft a punishment.

The amount of hate was insane.

It sickened me.

It worried me.

Social media had so many positive applications, but where Gil was concerned, it was worse than a witch hunt. They didn't care about the true story, only about blood. They didn't want facts, only carnage.

Even Gil's Facebook page dripped with venom. The hostility in the comments on his posts gave me nightmares that he truly might be hurt before he could face trial and the truth could protect him.

He needed to address it.

He needed to douse the flames of malevolence with honesty before it got dangerous.

I shivered and pulled the fake-mink blanket tighter around my shoulders. The TV mumbled in the background, and a library book of the best places to live in the world rested on my lap. The edition was from the 1990s so I was sceptical about some of the claims like Australia's cheap housing and Thailand's low taxes. If I had skills in finances or trades, I could've travelled and found it relatively easy to relocate overseas, but with nothing more than menial labour and a failed dancing career, I doubted I could settle anywhere long-term.

And I didn't know if I had the gumption to waitress in foreign places or live in backpackers with travellers far younger than me.

Why couldn't I make a decision?

Why couldn't I just book something?

Why couldn't I stop researching Gil and worrying about his future?

Because you're a sucker, that's why.

A spineless, stupid fool who still wants the boy she shouldn't have.

A fist hammered on my door, wrenching my head up.

Who on earth?

I cuddled deeper into my blankets. I hated unannounced visitors, especially late at night. Justin had made a habit of popping by, and I'd grown used to it, but tonight, I wasn't in the mood.

It might be those awful police again.

The knock came a second time.

Dammit.

Hauling myself from the couch, I placed the heavy book on the coffee table and padded across the small apartment to open the door. I didn't have a peephole, so risked unlocking and opening it a crack.

"Gil." My heart hammered against my ribs. "Wh-What are you doing here?"

He rubbed his face with a shaky hand. "I'm not here to hurt you." The tormented vow in his voice made my stomach squeeze.

"I know you won't hurt me."

"I'll stay out here if you're more comfortable."

"You don't have to do that." I opened the door wider. "I know you won't hurt me now that you have Olive back. Is she okay? Do you need anything?"

He grimaced. "You're still so kind, even after everything I've put you through."

My fingers latched tighter around the handle. "It's not kindness, Gil. It's concern. How are you…and her? You guys safe?"

"Safe?" He scowled. "Why wouldn't we be safe? Jeffrey is dead."

"I mean the online stuff. I don't know if you've looked, but it's getting scary. For me at least."

His green gaze searched mine. "You've been reading up about me?" His tone stayed carefully neutral.

I'd never been one to play games or pretend I didn't care when I did. I knew I should tell him to leave, close my door, and book that damn plane ticket out of here. Instead, I fell into old patterns and backed into my apartment in invitation. "We haven't been in touch. I research a little at night to see if you've been granted a court date."

His black sneakers crept over my threshold as if he couldn't believe I'd invited him in. Where were his paint-spattered timberlands? Had the police confiscated them as evidence?

Most likely, yes.

They were the same size as those found by the body of the last girl.

A clue to the crimes committed.

"I haven't heard when I'll go to trial."

"I can imagine the not knowing is driving you crazy." I closed the door. "Have you got things arranged…for Olive?"

He shrugged helplessly. "How can I have another home ready when I can't bear the thought of not being the one to take care of her?"

I nodded, backing away for my sanity.

It was so, *so* hard not to reach out and comfort him. Not to honour old promises to always be there in times of trouble.

I was his friend.

But that friendship now came with uncrossable boundaries and restrictions. "I'm so sorry, Gil."

He sighed, raking a hand through his messy hair. "It's nothing I don't deserve." His head tipped down as he followed me into the kitchen. His teeth sank into his bottom lip before he blurted, "I shouldn't have fucking come. I know that. I've done my best not to contact you, even though I think about you every damn day. I know I have no right to be here…but I need to talk to you. I can't end it like this."

Goosebumps exploded all over me. "End it like what?"

"Like this." He spread his arms as if incorporating our twisted, tangled lives. "Not able to have an honest conversation because Olive is there. Not able to be truthful and finally have the guts to give you answers to your questions." He held up his hands in surrender, looking healthier than the last time I'd seen him. His colour was back and his wound no longer draining his energy. He looked ready to tear open his secrets and purge.

And as much as I wanted to finally understand, I didn't trust what I'd do if I finally knew.

I shook my head, pulling the blanket that still caped my shoulders tighter around me. "It's fine. We don't need to—"

"We do." He stormed right into me, shoving me back and pressing me against the countertop. His hands clamped on my hips, his forehead nudged mine, and my entire world combusted in a rain of comets.

I couldn't swallow.

Couldn't breathe.

Couldn't blink.

"Gil…"

His fingers dug harder into my hipbones in denial of touching me. His nose brushed mine, his eyes closed, his lips came so, so close to kissing me.

We stood like that for an endless trembling second.

A second where our hearts *pounded* against each other. Where cymbals and castanets replaced my ribcage and stomach. Where we fought fate and battled with decorum.

"I can't stop myself," he groaned. "Not anymore." With a belly twisting growl, he stumbled away from me, shaking out his hands, no doubt suffering the same surge of heat and chemistry I did. "Fuck."

I shuddered, desperate for him to deliver on his threat, but grateful that he'd pulled away before he did.

My blanket lay abandoned on the floor.

My hands shook and body quaked, and I tripped to the fridge for something to do.

With my back facing him, he confessed, "I can't sleep at

night with wanting you, O. I'm fucking hard just at a single memory of you. I feel sick that I'm so goddamn hungry for you, because what sort of monster thinks about sex after he willingly betrayed your trust and prepared to trade your life for another?"

He laughed coldly. "I don't know why you haven't tried to shoot me yourself. Why you're still standing there, listening to my bullshit, when you should call the police and have me arrested for intruding on your life all over again."

Grabbing the cheap supermarket wine that was my guilty pleasure, I poured two generous glasses. "I know that's the logical reaction. And I know I'm being stupid by not doing those things. But…I've asked myself the same questions, and I don't have any answers. Why can't I move on after what you did? Why can't I just forget about you? God only knows, I should."

Gil shook his head gently as I tried to pass him the glass. "I can't drink alcohol." He pointed at his stitched-up side with a self-conscious sigh. "Not while I'm healing. And now I have Olive back, I doubt I'll ever turn to liquor again. It didn't solve my problems; it only made them worse." His eyes shadowed. "If I hadn't been drinking that night, I would never have fucked you on my living room floor, and we might not be in this mess."

My insides clenched at the crudeness. And the barbarity and the fact that my heart might be bruised and my common-sense in tatters, but my body most definitely had its priorities.

And it wanted rough.

It wanted anger, violence, passion.

It still craved a fight.

A rough, dirty, hot-as-hell fight.

Swallowing a big mouthful of tart courage, I whispered, "Maybe that was the only honest thing we did."

"What?" His voice turned dangerous. His body went loose and rigid all at once. "What do you mean?"

My skin blazed with fire. I didn't recognise myself. I didn't know this demoness who thirsted at the thought of tearing at his body, scratching his scars, and taking from him like he'd taken from me.

I was hungry.

Hungry, hungry, hungry for the blunt, basic truth that came from wild inhibited sex.

"You let down your walls that night. You gave in to the years of build-up between us. Maybe you should get drunk again and see what else happens."

He made a strangled noise. "If I got drunk again, I'd probably have you spread-eagled on the floor and so far deep inside you we'd both die of pleasure."

I shivered. I grew wet. "Do it then."

He choked. "Do what?"

"Fuck me."

He groaned long and low. "O…what are you doing?"

"I'm avoiding facing what has to happen."

"What? What has to happen?" He stepped toward me almost unwillingly. His hands opening and closing, his body tight and predatory.

"We need to walk away. There is no future for us. There can't be. Not after everything that's happened." I drank back the rest of my wine, welcoming the buzz, the lightheaded recklessness. "Words can only do so much. Conversation can grant sentences and paragraphs and finish this mess with a full stop, but only sex can grant us an ending."

"You want us to end?"

My heart wanted to shake its head.

My soul screamed for him to call me out on my lies.

I nodded instead. "Yes."

He crowded me against the countertop again, bringing fire and regret and the deliciousness of the forbidden. His eyes blazed with lust and love. "I came here trying to prevent an end."

This was wrong.

This was dangerous.

But I was through being good and safe.

I *wanted* this.

I wanted a clean, corruptible goodbye.

"It's inevitable."

"It's salvageable." His hand cupped my chin, jerking my head to the side so his mouth could latch onto my throat. His teeth unsheathed and sank into my skin, sharp and unforgiving; his tongue lapped at me a second later, soft and pleading. "It has to be."

I moaned and puddled into his chest, wanting my brain to turn off and my body to take full control. I wanted to be used, abused, and then I wanted him gone.

I wanted him gone for my sake and for his.

We were toxic to one another.

He'd always screw up and I'd always forgive him.

He's going to jail.

Even if I did agree to try, our futures had already been decided.

"Shut up and kiss me." I arched for his mouth, desperate to stop talking.

"Don't command me, O." He bit me again, yanking at my cotton pyjama top, popping the buttons holding the cute pink umbrella fabric together. My bare breasts ached to be bitten, squeezed, claimed. "Don't force me to do something I don't want to do." His voice rippled with history. Of another time when sex had been used against him.

A flush of guilt made me lucid, but then vindictiveness made me nasty.

Perhaps, by using Gil's demons against him, I could sever this infernal link between us. Maybe by pushing him too far, I could push him into admitting that we just couldn't work.

I could break us both so we could finally walk away without constantly looking back.

"God, you taste amazing." His tongue lashed against my throat, his arms banded tight around me.

For someone saying no, his body screamed yes.

I wriggled against him, rocking my hips into his. "You know as well as I do that we're powerless against each other."

He groaned, his hips answering mine with a slow, heavy grind that sent heat and wetness between my legs. "I'll always be powerless when it comes to you."

"That's why we're not good for one another."

"You're the best thing to ever happen to me." His fingers latched onto my hipbones, jerking me harder against his erection. He winced a little from his still tender wound. "I've never wanted anyone else but you. Never loved anyone else—"

"Stop." I cupped his cheeks, yanking his lips down to mine.

He growled low in his throat as I kissed him, stealing from him, all while offering him to take. This was war. This was a white flag of surrender even while I desperately tried to survive.

His tongue plunged deep; his body crowded mine. We rocked and clawed, slipping down the slippery slope of foggy desire.

Our lips crashed, teeth clacked, tongues danced a fiery battle.

Our bodies understood the goal, rocking and thrusting, seeking space to join.

I was too far gone to care.

Too drunk on lust to worry about consequences.

Too stressed and spiteful to stop trying to hurt both of us, all because I wasn't strong enough to admit that there would never be anyone else like him, never be another boy I loved so deeply.

"Fuck me, Gil." I kissed and licked him. "I need you."

"Don't do this, O." He growled again, ripping his lips away and ducking to suck my nipple into his mouth. "I want to talk. This isn't what I came here for."

His voice said no. His touch already agreed.

My head fell back as he branded me with his teeth.

I clutched his head to my chest, crying out as he bit harder; he suckled, making wetness gush between my legs. "Finish it, Gil. We need to finish this."

"I want to *save* this." His hand dove between my legs, finding me drenched. "Goddammit, O. We can figure out a way to fix this."

Yes, my heart screamed.

No, my mind cautioned.

I embraced sex to protect myself.

"It's over, Gil. It has to be."

"Don't fucking say that. It's not." Even as he begged, he shoved my night shorts down and plunged two fingers inside me. "Don't ask me to give you up."

"God." I buckled in his arms, my hips thrusting forward unashamedly.

"Fuck, you're driving me insane." His fingers pulsed inside me; his gaze shot black with need. "You're pushing me too far." His eyes closed tight, his brow furrowed and lips thin. "I'm losing control. I won't be responsible for—"

"For fucking me?" I licked my lips, moaning as his fingers dove deeper. "I want you to. I *need* you to."

"And I need to earn your forgiveness. Not fuck you like you mean nothing."

That sounded delicious to my current delirious state.

I didn't want sonnets or softness.

I wanted fast and brutal.

I need this over.

"Do it. Please." I clawed at his shoulders, not caring I was naked and he was fully dressed. My eyes hazed as my hands dropped down his front and unbuckled his jeans. "Gil…"

"O." He snarled as I shoved the denim down along with his

boxer-briefs. "Fuck, stop."

His cock leapt out and I pumped him.

His back bowed. His legs buckled. He drove his fingers deep inside me. "Goddammit." His forehead crushed on mine, both of us stroking the other, punishing the other. "I'll never be free of you." He thrust into my hand as his fingers rocked against my G-spot.

"Me either." I trembled, moaning, "And that's the problem."

"That's our curse."

I arched up to kiss him. "I don't have the strength anymore."

His lips slammed down to kiss me. "I never had the strength."

Our tongues knotted.

Our bodies battled.

And he lost.

I lost.

We destroyed each other with a violent kind of lust that incinerated right and wrong, past and present.

All I wanted was him.

All he needed was me.

Sex.

The rawest link that could come with the strongest of love or the most painful of hate.

Gil had suffered both.

His body had been used against him. My heart had been used against me.

I was in the wrong to do this, but he followed me into despair because that was all our future held. Despair and complication.

Our kiss turned far too hungry.

Our patience snapped.

"Fuck, O." Breathing hard, he tore his fingers out of me. "You're trying to make me hate you. But you're only making me want you more." He hauled me up, imprisoning me against the cupboards. "You're it for me. Always were." The tip of his cock nudged my entrance.

I sucked in a breath as he swallowed a curse. Pain etched his features, his healing side adding another element of torture.

Our eyes locked and held.

Glowing and wild. Hungry and hurting.

"You're mine. You always will be." His voice sucked shadows from the room, a vow of irrefutable possessiveness.

And then, he thrust.

One.

Thick.

Long.

Blistering *thrust.*

One second, we were separate, the next, we were joined.

We froze.

Panting and moaning, stripped to our most basic core.

We looked at each other as if we couldn't quite believe what'd happened. Shaking against the crack of our hearts and the thunder of our souls.

Every joining felt like this.

Like the earth shattered and the skies cried and the only place we belonged was with each other.

He was right.

We are a curse.

Softness slipped between our passion, covering me with goosebumps and the poems I hadn't wanted. His gaze whispered that he would never let me go, even though he would always do what I asked. His cock throbbed with fury that I belonged to him, even while he accepted that he'd lost me.

All of that emotion. All of that pain.

It punched us in the chest and we buckled beneath it.

His hips rocked.

He broke the spell.

And I was immensely grateful.

Clinging to his shoulders, I bowed into his control.

And he began to move.

To fuck me.

To eradicate the agonising moment we'd shared.

His mouth captured mine, his hands held me prisoner, his hips were the polar opposite of his lovesick gaze, punishing me, pistoning quick and deep inside.

Wordlessly, he fucked me exactly like I wanted.

He ignored his injury and showed no mercy.

He treated me with no kindness.

The countertop wedged into my spine.

My breasts bounced.

My core clenched.

And an orgasm spindled out of nowhere.

I kissed him violently.

He kissed me brokenly.

We rode each other as if the world would end in twenty-eight heartbeats.

I didn't try to slow it down.

I didn't nurse the idea that this was it.

That I'd made this happen because I wasn't strong enough to hear his secrets after weeks of begging to know.

I was weak.

But this made me strong.

This is goodbye.

"More. Gil, more. More!" I dug my nails into his neck, riding him as he rode me, our skin slicked with sweat. Pain radiated in his eyes. Agony lived in his kisses. And the finality of farewell added a sharper, sinister flavour to our release.

Thrust.

Thrust.

Thrust.

I exploded.

My insides ricocheted with broken bliss.

He roared into my mouth with fractured feeling.

We shivered and convulsed in each other's arms.

And then, his phone rang.

Ring.

Ring.

Ring.

A sense of déjà vu struck me. Whenever something momentous happened between us, the phone always managed to ruin it.

At least this time, there was nothing to ruin.

I'd done that.

And it was over.

Gil winced as he pulled out of me, his cock glistening and angry. Hoisting his jeans up, he pressed a hand against his injured side, and ripped his phone from his back pocket. Breathing hard, his face lined with fear. "Shit." Pressing accept, he held it to his ear, his eyes locking onto mine. "Justin. What's up?" His breathing was tattered and torn.

The faint voice of Justin echoed in the silence.

Gil's cum trickled down my inner thigh.

I made no move to dress. No move to hide.

"Okay, I'll rush back straight away. Tell her I'm coming. I'll be as fast as I can." Gil hung up, shoving his phone where it belonged and buckling his belt. "I have to go."

"I understand."

"Olive woke up. She expected to see me but found Justin instead. She's broken down and barricaded herself in her room crying." He backed toward the door. "I'm so sorry."

"It's fine. Go to her. I hope she's okay."

"Will *you* be okay?" His eyes cast down my nakedness, focusing on the remnants of the explosive, hurried sex we'd shared.

I nodded, forcing a smile. "I'll be fine."

Unlocking the door, he paused as he opened it. "I don't feel right leaving you like this."

"You don't have a choice."

"But…this. What happened between us—"

"Was closure."

He winced. "Closure? That wasn't fucking closure, O. That was…I don't know what that was." He raked a hand through his hair. "Most of it was way too fast and sudden, and I feel guilty as fuck for taking you when we should've talked, but it's far from over. We're not done here. Not by a long shot."

"We are. We have to be."

He stalked toward me, his hands fisting by his sides. "And if I don't want this to be over?"

I hugged my breasts, cursing the goosebumps covering me. "It's already happened."

"It hasn't. Nothing's happened apart from the realisation that I was wrong to stay away. I thought I was doing the right thing letting you walk out of my life, but fuck, it was totally the *wrong* thing. I'll do whatever you need to make you trust in this, trust in me. I'm not going to quit, O. I'm going to fight to keep you—"

"I don't belong to you, Gil." I rested my hand on the door handle, growing weaker by the second.

This was what I wanted.

This was what I *needed*.

I needed him to fight for me.

To prove he cared above everything.

Above court dates and murder trials and a life he might have to abandon.

But just because I was cruel to need his undying declarations didn't mean they'd throw me back into his arms.

He wasn't mine.

He was Olive's.

And soon he'd be locked out of my reach.

If we didn't choose for this to end now, his prison sentence would do it for us.

His face waged battle between calm and furious. "I'll come back. We'll talk about this. Talk about everything."

"No." I locked my knees from trembling. His body still summoned mine. The crackle of electricity, the sharp serenade of desire. Even though we'd just had sex, the lust between us never died.

And that was why this had to end.

Now.

Here.

Forever.

Because…I couldn't be his friend.

And I couldn't be his lover.

Because I would give everything, over and over again, and I would never have enough left over for me.

He backed over the threshold. "I'll come back. Once Olive is settled, I'll come back and we can try this again."

"I think it's best if you didn't."

Frustration etched his face. "This isn't over."

"It has to be."

"Stop saying that. It doesn't have to be. If you feel anything for me then we can talk and—"

"I do feel something for you." I allowed brutal truth to break us. "I love you, Gil."

His eyes flared, he moved to touch me. "Then let me fucking fix this."

I held up a hand, praying my voice stayed steady. "I love you, but I can't be with you."

"But—"

"Please…don't make this any harder than it is." I clutched the door, ready to close it. "It's done. It's over. We just ended it."

"So…that's it? You don't want to know? You no longer care?"

I shook my head, fighting the sudden tsunami of tears. "I no longer want to know. I no longer care."

Pain that I'd never witnessed burned deep in his gaze. "What the hell is that supposed to mean? For weeks you wouldn't stop badgering me to tell you what I kept hidden, and now that I'm finally free to tell you everything, you suddenly have no interest to hear me out?"

I locked my fingers together, keeping my curiosity buried.

I wanted to know.

I wanted to know *all of it.*

But…if I knew, I wouldn't have the power to put myself first. I would risk everything because I wouldn't have the strength to walk away.

"I wanted to know so I could protect you." I shrugged sadly. "Now, I don't want to know to protect myself."

Our gaze caught.

My heart hiccupped.

He froze as he finally heard what I said. Finally accepted what I wanted. "You truly mean it, don't you?" His voice roughened. "You've had enough of me."

"I've had enough of lies and deceit and feeling as if I'm cheating myself out of happiness by being too weak."

"You were never weak."

"*You* make me weak."

He swayed on my doorstep. Anger and hurt blazed in his green gaze.

A loud beeping noise came from his ankle, dragging his attention to his foot.

He growled like a beast.

He nodded.

He stared at me one last time, trying to figure out a way to stop my stubbornness.

His ankle beeped again.

His shoulders fell. "If that's what you want." Looking at me one last time, he whispered, Goodbye, O."

He turned and vanished down the staircase.

Chapter Eighteen

Olin

A WEEK PASSED.

Every day, I struggled not to hand in my notice at work.

Every night, I struggled to sleep.

Every time I went into the kitchen, I stared at the spot where we'd had sex, and a wash of regret and relief filled me.

The regret was the hardest—full of tears and heartache and the overwhelming sensation that I'd made a massive mistake.

The relief was a gentle balm—doing its best to heal me and remind me I did the right thing.

I'd done the *only* thing.

No matter how hard it'd been.

But it did mean I could no longer stay here and postpone my decision.

The money my parents had deposited into my bank account remained untouched, even though my salary wasn't enough to carry my weekly bills and pay off the debt I'd accumulated while looking after Olive.

I didn't want to owe them anything, even though their funds would be greatly appreciated right about now.

They'd tried calling again two days ago. I'd ignored it, unable to discuss the latest news articles and the ever-growing unrest about Gil's involvement in the body painting murders.

Maybe I'd go visit them on their travels.

Maybe I'd vanish like they had.

Either way, tonight, I had a plan.

Placing a spinach and feta pizza into the oven—unable to stop my mind from thinking of Gil calling Olive his little spinach—I carried my decrepit laptop to the dining room table and turned it on.

This time, I wasn't looking at job sites.

Clicking on the website I'd found last week that compared international airfares and found the cheapest, I hovered my fingers over the keyboard.

Birmingham to...

I bit my lip.

Hong Kong?

Vietnam?

New Zealand?

America?

Where could I find a fresh start?

Where could my mind find peace from Gil?

I deliberated while my pizza cooked and made a list of pros and cons while I ate.

I finished two glasses of wine—very aware I had the potential of becoming an alcoholic if I kept up my alone-time drinking—and decided to let fate choose for me.

Fate had messed up my life, so perhaps, it could fix it too.

Clicking on the icon that listed last-minute sales, I held my breath as one for Brisbane, Australia popped up. Warm, friendly, lots of beaches, and tanned locals. They spoke English so I could get a job. The temperate weather would be good for my ruined back, and it was too far to rush home if I feared I'd made yet another mistake.

I inputted the parameters, chose a date two weeks in the future to give me time to end my lease, hand in my notice, and sell my few pieces of furniture, and pulled my tired and battered credit card from my purse.

I peered at the faded number.

My phone vibrated across the table.

Not again.

No.

I refused to let a phone destroy every big moment of my life.

I locked my attention back onto entering my credit card details.

It vibrated again.

And again.

God!

How was I supposed to move on if so many things kept

yanking me back?

Snatching my phone, I swiped it on.

Justin: *When was the last time you saw Gil?*

I sighed heavily, remembering all over again what we'd done when we'd last seen each other. The way he'd been inside me. The way he'd grown angry when denied a second chance. The way I couldn't stop thinking about him even though I made a vow to move on.

Me: *A week ago. Why?*

Justin: *He was attacked two nights ago.*

My heart crawled into my throat.

Me: *Attacked? How?*

Justin: *Two men who knew one of the murdered girls. They waited for him outside his warehouse. Beat him up pretty good.*

Me: *Was Olive there?*

Justin: *She was inside. Gil called me before she found him. Got most of the blood off but he's stiff. I've just been with him for a check-up to make sure they didn't injure his side or rupture anything internally.*

Why didn't he contact me?

You ended it, remember?

I'd given no room for negotiation, even when Gil had begged for a single conversation.

Guilt slithered through me.

Worry followed on its tail.

I'd been so *selfish.*

I'd chosen myself over him.

I'd acted as if I had the worst deal just because he'd lied and tied me up and carried me unconscious into the woods.

He was facing prison.

His life was threatened thanks to a mob of enraged people.

His daughter had a high possibility of growing up without having him as her father.

Oh, God.

What had I been thinking?

Me: *Thanks for being a good friend, Justin. He's lucky to have you. I haven't exactly been there for him lately.*

Justin: *Yeah, he's been pretty low ever since I loaned him my car and offered to babysit so he could come talk to you. He didn't tell me what happened between you guys, but I'm guessing it wasn't anything good.*

I didn't know how to respond. Admit that I'd forced him to find closure through sex or pretend things were a work-in-progress?

Before I could fib or confess, Justin messaged again.

Justin: *O…I have another piece of news that I don't know how to tell you. I'm not expecting anything. I'm not asking for something you can't give it. I'm just…telling you.*

I went ice cold.

Me: *What is it?*

Justin: *Gil sold his warehouse to pay the blackmail on Olive a few months ago. He's been renting it back from the new owner ever since.*

I waited for him to continue, terrified of the conclusion.

Justin: *The owner has just given Gil notice. With all the shit happening online, he doesn't want a murderer living there. He's given him five days to move out.*

Me: *Oh, no.*

Oh, God.

Justin: *I've offered him to move in with me, but Olive hasn't gotten over what happened last week. She's relapsing. Doesn't want to be near other men apart from Gil. I know he'd never ask this himself but…is there any way you can put them up for a night or two? While I figure something out? Gil has to stay in Birmingham so he doesn't void his bail agreement—he already got in trouble going to see you. If they think he's a flight risk, they'll revoke his bail, and Olive isn't ready to cope with that shit.*

I sat frozen in my chair.

Why hadn't Gil told me he'd get in trouble for visiting me?

Why had he put his freedom on the line, knowing there'd be repercussions when the cops figured out he'd left his home?

I stared at my phone.

My blood raced in my veins.

The last time Gil had stayed the night in my apartment, we'd been in a much better place than our current one. Even with his secrets, I could handle him being near. We'd had Thai and I'd woken to him talking to his uncle, agreeing to yet another blackmail to protect Olive. He'd unsettled and confused me but at least we'd been civil.

I'd gladly let Olive stay again.

She'd been a perfect little house guest but my apartment was too small for the three of us.

Far too small for the tension and complications that would curdle.

You don't have a choice.

Could you honestly turn him away when the entire world is turning its back on him?

Olive was too important and sweet to let her suffer.

And Gil…well, Gil was also far too important.

I was fighting an unwinnable battle. I was lying to myself and only causing pain.

I couldn't abandon Gil while he faced incarceration. Just like I couldn't abandon Olive.

I should've known I could never be so self-centred not to put anyone else first.

I can't leave.

Not yet.

No matter how much I needed to.

Once I knew how his trial went, maybe then I'd be free to move on.

Once I knew Olive was safe, hopefully then I could leave and never look back.

Until that happened, I was stuck in limbo.

We all were.

Me: *Of course. Goes without saying.*

Justin: *You're a saint, Olin Moss. I know how hard this is going to be for you. I also know how worthless Gil is going to feel being such an imposition.*

Me: *It's fine. We'll work it out.*

Somehow.

Justin: *I wish it could've been different for you guys. I really do.*

Tears rushed up my spine.

Yeah…me too.

Justin: *I'll help him pack and see you in a couple of days with your new tenants.*

Chapter Nineteen

Gil

"I CAN'T FUCKING move into her space, Miller. Goddammit, stop trying to be a fairy fucking godmother. I can figure this shit out on my own."

"First, I'm a godfather, not a mother. And second, excuse me for doing what any good godfather would do and think of Olive's livelihood instead of her stubborn mule of a relative."

"You're taking your role as her guardian far too fucking seriously."

His face tensed. He marched closer so Olive, who was packing the final things into her backpack in her room, didn't overhear. "Aren't you glad about that? I didn't ask to be a dad, Clark. But you assigned that possibility to me and then went and got arrested. For *murder.*" His eyes narrowed. "I don't know how it's going to work. She tolerates me, but she's still uncomfortable around me. She had that crazy meltdown that's left me totally wary of what other crap might happen. And if you're called to trial tomorrow, what then, huh? Isn't her protection better than your sorry excuses of why you can't couch surf at O's for a few days?"

I rubbed my face, wanting to punch him but knowing he was right. "I can't impose—"

"It's either my place or O's. Unless you have some money you want to tell me about and you're planning on staying at the four fucking seasons?"

My temper blazed. "You're really getting on my nerves, Miller."

"Yeah, well. You too."

I blinked. "I'm sorry my shitty life is ruining yours. I didn't ask you to take over. I'm perfectly capable of arranging accommodation for myself and my daughter. I've done it many times before you barged in."

Justin crossed his arms. "Yeah, but have you done it while healing from a bullet wound, suffering a mild concussion from being beaten up, and an anklet that reports your every fucking move to the cops?"

I froze, breathing hard.

He had a point.

I'd had a visit the morning after sleeping with O from two uniforms. They'd given me a warning: leave a pre-approved location again and my freedom would be replaced with bars until I faced court.

After dealing with a broken heart from O kicking me out, worry over Olive breaking down just because Justin had babysat, and now being served notice that my home had been snatched away...I didn't know what problem to tackle first.

I wanted to see O. I *needed* to see her. But I'd been blocked from visiting. A phone call or text wouldn't cut it. I didn't know how to say what I needed to without seeing her face. And now, Justin expected clearance from the cops for me to couch surf and Olive's mental health to cope with being homeless, all while the goddamn bruises on my body reminded me all over again that I sucked at life.

I rubbed my face, trying to get my anger under control. "Look, I'll figure something out. You're not responsible for us. Just let me deal with this."

Justin rolled his eyes. "Do you honestly expect me to just let you be kicked out onto the street?" His voice lowered. "Come on, mate. Don't be such a stubborn ass. Let me help."

"I'm not accepting charity."

"For the last fucking time, it's not charity. It's what friends do."

"And you've already done far too much. So has O. Where does it end, huh? How many favours do you both have to give before enough is enough?"

Justin shrugged. "Until you're back on your feet."

"And if I'm never back on my feet?"

"Then we figure it out."

"No. *I'll* figure it out. This is on me. Not you."

"You made it personal when you said I was her damn godfather, Clark! Just accept it and stop being a twat, all right?"

I wanted to tell him to get the hell out but…I couldn't.

He had every right to yell at me.

Had every concern about how I'd fix this shitty situation.

I'd sold my warehouse and in turn ran the risk of renting.

I'd put Olive's future at risk all because I hadn't kept her safe to begin with.

I had no money for a hotel.

No other friends to impose on.

I couldn't stay at Justin's 'cause I didn't want to risk Olive having another meltdown so soon—which only added to the stress of who would look after her if I was imprisoned if she never got over her fear.

And just because no commissions had come in didn't mean I wasn't actively trying to find work. Temporary, menial—I'd accept anything if it meant I could at least leave something for Olive.

My temper faded. "O doesn't want to see me again. Even if I was okay with imposing, *yet again*, I can't."

Olive appeared from her bedroom. Her backpack slung over her shoulder.

The past four days had been an awful whirlwind of trying to explain that we could no longer live in our home, that the few pieces of furniture we had left had to be sold, and I didn't entirely know what the future held.

Olive had hugged me tight and whispered she didn't care where we lived, as long as we were together.

I'd been both proud and horrified.

Proud that she was such a brave little thing not to worry about material things. And horrified that I was about to fail her all over again when the summons came.

"Eep, are we moving into O's?" she asked, her eyes sparkling with hope. "Yay! I miss her. I sent her notes and drawings asking her to visit, but now we get to visit her!" She spun in front of me. "Her bed is super comfy. Do you think she'll share with me, or I'll have to share the couch with you, Dad?"

I choked. The thought of being in O's space, of wanting her, craving her, only for her to look at me in that dead-eyed, all-hope-ended way was unthinkable.

I'd gone to her place hoping to explain myself. To finally share the secrets she'd begged to know. Only for her to push me until I'd pinned her against the kitchen bench and taken her fast and ruthlessly. I hadn't wanted to do that. I'd never wanted to touch her so violently. Yet, each time we slept together, softness wasn't part of the equation.

She'd made me take her, use her, and then she'd told me goodbye.

My heart fisted at the thought of living through that torture, day after day.

"Can we go now? I want to see her." Olive took my hand, tugging me toward the exit. Not caring this would be the last time she'd be allowed in this place.

I held her back, stopping her momentum. "O is too busy to have us stay right now, little spinach. We can visit her, though. You guys could have lunch next week."

"But Justin said we're staying."

"Justin was mistaken."

"Justin already cleared it with O, and she's agreed," Justin interrupted.

"You what?" I spun on him. "What the fu—" I cut myself off, not wanting to swear in front of Olive.

"I asked her a few days ago. She said no problem."

"Of *course,* she said no problem." I raked a hand through my hair. "She's the sweetest person on the goddamn *planet.*"

"It's only for a few days, Gil. Until we can sort something else—"

"A few days is too long, don't you see?" I wanted to punch him. How dare he fucking meddle? My still healing side twinged. My insides felt hollow. Pain lashed through me. "I can't expect her to do this."

"It's already done." He strode past me, heading to his sedan and the meagre amount of belongings I'd packed. I wasn't attached to clothes, and with a totally different living arrangement in my future, I hadn't bothered keeping crockery and other life requirements. I'd sold everything in a flash sale, earned another few thousand pounds, and budgeted each penny to its maximum.

The only items I couldn't sell had been my paint supplies. Boxes of brushes, sponges, and airbrush attachments would travel with me. The bottles of pigments would also come. Along with rhinestones, metallics, and a few prosthetics that made fantasy into reality.

One day, I would use those mediums to make another fortune.

Until then, I had to pay the taxes on my life choices.

Jeffrey popped into my head. He'd fucked me over while he was alive, and he still fucked me over even when he was dead. Would I choose differently if I could redo the night I killed him?

I'd asked myself that question a lot.

And the answer was…complicated.

I would've spared his life if it meant I didn't have to let Olive down by going to jail.

I would've still killed him because he deserved to know what those girls felt as he watched them fade into death.

There was no right or wrong answer.

Unlike now.

It was wrong to go to O's. Wrong to encroach on her space. Wrong to not honour her wish to end things permanently between us.

But what other choice do you have?

"Come on, Popeye." Olive pulled her hand from mine, skipping after Justin as he continued stomping through the warehouse to the pedestrian access. "Time to go see, O."

* * * * *

"O!" Olive bowled through the door the moment it cracked open. "Hi! Yay, I'm so happy to see you. Did you get my notes? Did Justin give you my drawings?" She squished her face into O's chest, hugging her fiercely. "I missed you!"

O froze in almost comical shock. Unprepared for a hurricane to smother her with conversation and cuddles. Her eyes met mine, then skated away almost immediately. "Hi, Justin. Hi, Gil."

"Olin." I nodded.

The moment polite greetings were done, O dropped her arms and squeezed Olive back with just as much affection. "Hi, little Olive Pip. Man, I swear you've grown since I last saw you." She pressed her hand on Olive's glossy dark hair. "Yep, you've definitely sprouted another inch at least."

Olive Pip?

O had given my daughter a nickname?

Yet another fist reached into my chest and punched a bigger hole into my heart. If I wasn't careful, the hole would soon be big enough to bleed me dry.

Olive snickered. "Probably been eating too much spinach. Dad makes sure we eat lots of veggies."

"That'll do it for sure. You'll be taller than him soon."

"Eww, no." She wrinkled her nose. "I don't want to be that tall. I want to be dainty, like you." Looking past her, she asked, "Can we come in? We don't have much stuff. We promise not to take up too much room."

O backed up, welcoming us. "Of course. Come in. It seems my home is now your home."

"Only for tonight." I cleared my throat. "I won't put you out any longer than that."

O nodded. "One night, one week. It's fine." Her smile was genuine, but her eyes remained guarded. She'd returned to the sympathetic sweet friend who always put others first. No sign of the explosive heat from the week before. No hint of the heart-breaking farewell.

Goddammit, the agony was more than I could bear.

My back prickled as Justin practically shoved me inside, moving to give O a kiss on the cheek. "Olin. You're looking gorgeous as always." He winked, making her chuckle.

"Yeah, jeans and old t-shirt totally deserve compliments like that."

"They do if they fit you that well."

"If you like them so much, you wear them. Let's see if the t-shirt becomes a bra on you or a crop top."

Justin laughed. "God, no one wants to see that."

"Seriously, no one." O smiled.

Their friendship was no longer stilted with history but smooth with familiarity.

For the first time, I wondered.

Wondered if Justin still had feelings for O. If O still had feelings for him.

I shut those thoughts off straight away. There was only so much torture I could tolerate.

"Come in. Come in." O backed up, catching my eye again with a hurried glance. The second we locked gazes, the world faded, noise silenced, and that damn connection that would destroy me until my dying day hissed like wildfire.

I couldn't take my eyes off the girl I'd loved since I was a teenager. I couldn't stop looking at the smudges under her pretty hazel eyes or the tense strain I'd put there. The strain of being a good friend while never wanting to see me again.

Justin pushed past, breaking our moment.

I followed, lugging in the two duffels of paint and work equipment. O's apartment wasn't exactly big enough to expect her to store my shit as well as put us up as house guests, but I couldn't exist without the ability to paint.

Just like when I was younger, it was the only thing that cured me of the constant chatter in my head. The worries, the guesses, the failures.

Moving forward, my arm brushed against O's.

She stiffened and backed away. That slight movement was as sharp and as deadly as a blade to my chest. My shoulders sank. "Can't get rid of me, huh."

"Seems as though destiny has other plans."

"Destiny can take a hike. She only seems to screw things up."

Her nose wrinkled. "Or it's just us who does the screwing."

My heart pounded the longer we stared. Images of screwing her in her kitchen exploded in my mind. It'd happened so fast. It'd been explosive and raw. It'd also been the last time I would ever be with her.

She blushed, no doubt thinking the same thing as me. "Anyway...like I said, it's fine for you guys to stay." She closed and locked the door.

Ignoring my heated stare, she moved forward, pointing at the new additions in her small space. "Gil, you'll have the couch. It's not much, but I bought a new pillow and washed the blankets. Olive, you'll have the blow-up mattress behind the couch. Again, it's not much, but I got you a cute flower comforter and hot water bottle in case you're cold." She sighed, shrugging. "I'm sorry I can't offer you your own rooms. It's frustratingly small this place."

Olive zoomed to the mattress behind the couch. Back there she had privacy and her own little world.

"You kidding? This is awesome!" Olive threw herself on the air mattress, only to bounce far higher than I expected. "Wow, it's like a trampoline."

Justin chuckled. "I don't think the manufacturers were going for that. But hey...looks fun."

"It's better than any of the hard bunk beds in Jeffrey's nasty caravan." Olive sat cross-legged in contentment. "Thank you so much, O."

"You're very welcome."

I cleared my throat. "Seriously, Olin. This is better than any five-star hotel. You shouldn't have gone to so much trouble."

She smiled self-consciously. "It's not luxury, but that's nice of you to say."

Our eyes locked all over again, imprisoning each other—two elements that always joined whenever close.

I couldn't break the spell, and neither could she.

Justin cleared his throat. "Look, I...eh, I'm gonna get going. Have to go back to the office. You guys all good?"

Shivering at the overwhelming need to touch O—to pull her into me and drop down all my barriers, I forced myself to look at my friend. A friend who sometimes I wanted to kill but a friend I trusted to look after my daughter when I couldn't.

"Thanks, Miller." I held out my hand. "Thanks for the lift over here and for arranging this."

O came closer, smiling gently. "You're a good man, Justin Miller."

Justin actually blushed, backing toward the door as if he couldn't wait to run from honest compliments. "Just don't kill each other, okay?" He pinned me with a stare. "I'll call tomorrow. Maybe you guys should go out for dinner. The three of you. Celebrate your new living arrangements."

Any tender thoughts toward him evaporated.

Dinner?

Fuck, I would rather inject myself with succinylcholine than go out for dinner. To a restaurant with the woman I loved and the daughter I'd do anything to protect. To eat food that O would have to pay for because I couldn't afford it.

No way.

No fucking way.

O deserved so, *so* much. I owed far too much to ever pay back.

I wouldn't add yet more debt to my pile of worthlessness.

My pride was bruised.

My ego destroyed.

If I let O pay for dinner—when I knew how tight her own finances were—I'd never forgive myself.

And I couldn't go out anyway.

The move here had been cleared with the police, but that was as far as my new boundaries went according to my anklet.

"That won't be necessary. I brought the rest of my groceries. I'll cook something," I muttered. I couldn't take her out, but I could at least prepare something. "A tiny thank you for having us."

"Sure, that sounds nice." She gave me a wary smile.

"Appreciate it."

"Dad makes a yummy pasta," Olive piped up from the bouncy bed, her hands already rummaging in her backpack for crayons and paper.

O grinned, forcing lightness into her face when only heaviness existed between us. "Look forward to it then."

My thoughts tripped backward to a time when O had made me lunch. When she'd pulled me into her house and made me fall head over heels for her.

Pancakes and syrup.

We'd vowed to be each other's family.

I doubted a simple bolognese could reinstate family bonds that were long gone.

"Okay, guys, have fun playing happy families." Justin waved, opening the door. "See ya soon."

The door closed.

The apartment seemed to shrink around us.

O made an excuse to disappear into her bedroom.

And I stood like an idiot in her living room, so fucking aware of everything that I'd lost.

Chapter Twenty

Gil

I COULDN'T SLEEP.

The ceiling offered no salvation from reliving the most awkward evening of my life.

I'd cooked in O's tiny kitchen while Olive and her played scrabble at the coffee table.

We'd eaten in relative ease, both of us using Olive as the ice breaker. Talking to her instead of each other, overly attentive to her every need.

O's smiles had been reserved and her voice measured whenever she'd had to speak to me directly. Her eyes hid so many things. She was angry with me. Annoyed. Pissed off. All of the above. So many painful things bubbled beneath the surface, and the longer we spent together, the more the tension increased.

I shook while doing the dishes.

I fought with ways of ending this nightmarish situation.

But then, O retired early with the excuse of a headache, and Olive and I stayed up a little longer watching TV on low.

By the time Olive passed out on her mattress and I slipped beneath the blankets on the couch, my entire system felt jacked up and on edge.

We needed to talk.

O and me.

Truly, *really* talk.

No sex.

No swearing.

Just frank conversation that might have some chance at clearing the air.

But O had made it obvious she wasn't open to speaking.

That she'd pulled away from me—accepting my presence while waiting until I was out of her life for good. She didn't need to tell me she'd locked her heart to me.

I felt it.

I felt the emptiness when she looked at me.

I tasted the sourness of obligation.

This was goodbye in a terribly drawn-out way.

Checking my phone, I cursed under my breath.

Two a.m. and I was fucking wired.

I couldn't stay here.

I needed to expel some of my tension before I marched into O's bedroom and demanded she listen to me. Listen to my apologies, explanations, and every dark, dirty confession I'd collected over the years.

Hauling my arse from the covers—ignoring the stiffness and new bruises from being beaten up a few days ago—I pulled on a pair of tatty jeans and t-shirt from my packed duffel. The one saving grace of having to sell off your possessions for blackmail meant when you got kicked out of home you didn't have much to pack. Another blessing in disguise was being kicked out of the place where angry society knew you lived and planned an attack when you stepped out the damn door.

Even if we hadn't been evicted, Olive wouldn't have been safe to stay there.

Because of me.

It's always because of fucking me.

At least thanks to the punishment I'd received, the police had approved my address change. Allowing me to travel and stay at O's without revoking my bail.

Checking on Olive and finding her fast asleep, I slipped from the door and jogged down the communal stairs.

With the stars and crescent moon for company, I stood outside O's building and watched night turn to dawn.

I couldn't walk away because of my anklet.

I couldn't prowl the alleyways and find salvation in graffiti.

I couldn't head back inside and slip into O's bed and delete this awfulness between us.

All I could do was watch the world wake up and count down the moments I had left.

Chapter Twenty-One

Olin

"OH, WOW, I love that."

I spun around, holding the towel tighter around myself. Olive stood in my doorway; her gaze transfixed on my tattoo-covered scars.

I'd just had a shower after being unable to sleep. Dawn crested ten minutes ago and I figured I'd get ready for work early, so I could sneak out and not have to deal with Gil this morning.

However, when I'd tiptoed to the bathroom, there'd been no sign of him sleeping on the couch. Olive had been tucked up in bed, but I guessed the creaky pipes and running water had woken her.

I shivered a little as my damp hair clung to my shoulders. I craved clothing for both protection and warmth, but Olive drifted into my room, her hand up as if to touch my back.

Turning to face her, I said gently, "You should still be sleeping."

"I woke up and I'm not tired anymore." She skirted around me, looking at my ink again. "That's so cool. Is it a tattoo? It doesn't look real."

I caught a glimpse of what she saw in my wardrobe mirror. The huge geometric owl bleeding into realism. The many animals beginning with O hidden in its feathers. "Yes, it's a tattoo. And no, you can't have one." I laughed. "I don't think Gil would ever forgive me if I'm the reason you get ink before you're eighteen."

Her nose wrinkled. "It's my body. I can draw on it if I want."

"Your dad called it scribbling when he first saw it."

"It's not scribbling. It's amazing!" Her tiny hand reached out, stroking the ridges and ugliness of my patched together wounds. "Did it hurt?"

I guessed she asked about the ink rather than the injury hidden beneath. Unless you knew what to look for, the tattoo did what I intended and camouflaged the mess.

Striding away, I turned my back on her and pulled on a sports bra and black blouse. "No, it wasn't too bad."

"Do you have any more?"

"No." Feeling strange dressing in front of her, I stepped into a pair of knickers before dropping my towel and wriggling into a skirt. "That piece is enough."

And you can't tattoo over emotional wounds, so I'll just have to cope.

Making my way to my small dressing table by the window, I grabbed my hairbrush. Olive followed me, her cute hummingbird pyjamas revealing Gil didn't worry about masculinity when he obviously doted and bought his daughter the most girlish, prettiest things.

"Are you going somewhere?" Her happiness level dropped. "Can I come?"

Quickly taming my dark blonde hair, I smiled. "I have to go to work. Believe me, you don't want to come. It's boring being in an office all day."

"But you didn't work when I stayed here with you last time. It was so awesome spending the entire day with you." She leapt onto my bed. "I wanted to go to that park again and the library and that place you took me to that sells those yummy muffins."

Adding a lashing of mascara and some peach lip-gloss, I looked at her in the mirror. "I'd love that too, but I need to work to pay the bills. Being an adult sucks sometimes." Placing my makeup down, I spun to face her. "But you don't need to spend the day with me. You have your dad. You guys will have a great day together. Maybe paint or—"

"He won't have time. He's trying to get work too." She pouted, plucking at my bedspread. "I want him to paint those women canvases again instead of being stressed about money. At least at the warehouse, I could watch him work. I helped him clean up when I wasn't at school."

"Do you miss school?"

She shrugged. "Kinda. But not really 'cause I missed my dad more and all my friends won't care about me anymore."

"They will care." I sat on my haunches in front of her, grabbing her ankles as she kicked her legs off the edge of my bed. "They'll have missed going to school with you."

"But I won't even be with them in class. Won't I be held back a year? Seeing as Uncle Jeffrey kept me out of school for so long?"

Damn.

Gil had been held back because a teacher had her own diabolical reasons.

Olive might be held back because of her uncle's.

Life truly isn't fair.

"Maybe you can be in the same grade and just have some extra coaching at home, so you can catch up fast. I'm guessing you're a very fast learner."

She perked up. "I am. I love books and things. I don't want to be with younger kids."

"Okay then, well if we enrol you back in school, I'll do my best to find you a good tutor."

We enrol you?

What are you saying, O?

You can't promise such things. You won't be in her life. You're leaving, remember?

"Could *you* teach me?" Her grey eyes searched mine. "That would be so much fun."

Standing, I shook my head. "I don't know enough to teach you, Olive Pip, but I have no doubt you'll be the smartest girl in class."

The front door opened and closed, wrenching both our attentions to it.

Gil appeared in the living room, his eyes catching mine and then Olive's. Lines etched around his mouth, and his hair was once again messy from being outside, but he looked calmer than last night.

Moving slowly toward us, he cleared the gravel in his throat. "Seems everyone is up early this morning."

"Daddy!" Olive leaped off my bed and ran straight into his arms.

Gil dropped to one knee, wrapping her tight in his embrace. "Morning, tiny spinach. How did you sleep?"

"Fine. The mattress was super comfy. But then I woke up, and you weren't here." Her head tilted. "Where'd you go?"

Gil gave me a guilty glance, climbing back to his feet. "I

watched the sun rise."

Raking a hand through his hair, he looked my office attire up and down. "Heading in this early?"

I nodded. "Duty calls."

"It always does."

His face filled with love, ruining me all over again. I wasn't used to this respectful version of him. The one who accepted my boundaries and didn't scale my fences to talk to me.

I didn't know if I liked it. If I was honest, I hated the distance between us even while we stood so close.

"O...I—" Raking a hand through his hair, he sighed. "Thank you for letting us stay the night."

"You're welcome." Something lodged in my throat, a stone heavy with hurt and honesty.

Olive piped up, "Have you seen Olin's tattoo? It's amazing! Like amazing, amazing. Can I have one, Dad?"

The tension evaporated as Gil snapped into father mode. His eyes gleamed with strictness even as his lips quirked in a grin. "Any drawings you do, missy, are to end up on paper only."

"What about on people? Can I paint naked people?"

"When you're older, fine."

"So when I'm older, I can get a tattoo like O's?"

"No. Absolutely not."

Olive pouted, hanging on Gil's hand. "I'll make you say yes. I always make you say yes."

Gil chuckled painfully. "That's entirely true." He looked at me, his eyes clear and smile simple. A simple smile of frustration and pride for his child. "She's a master at getting anything she wants."

I laughed quietly. "Maybe you're just a soft touch."

His simpleness vanished under a cloak of awareness. "Maybe I am. Maybe I'm being too soft on you, too."

My heart pattered quickly. "What do you mean?"

"I mean...I still want to talk." Patting Olive on the butt, he said kindly, "You. Shower. Now."

"Aww, but I don't—"

"Shower and I'll cook you pancakes for breakfast, and then, we'll spend the day together. Just you and me."

Olive's adorable face lit up. "All day? Really?" She wriggled in place. "No job searching? No working?"

"Nope. Just you." He bowed to kiss her, covering her with unconditional love. "I want to spend the day with my favourite girl. Job hunting can wait. Maybe we'll go apartment searching instead, so we don't impose on O any longer than we have to."

"I like living with O, but I can't wait to spend the day together. Yay!" Olive sped toward the bathroom, throwing a wave in my direction. "Bye, O. Have a good day working."

"See ya." I waved to a closed bathroom door, laughing quietly. "She certainly adores the ground you walk on."

"And I can't imagine my life without her." His tone slipped into despair. "Shit, I can't leave." He scowled at his ankle. "I'm under house arrest. Is it okay if I hang here with her? I'll do my best to find alternative arrangements online."

My heart squeezed. I'd opened my home to him because it was the right thing to do, yet I couldn't deny I'd been selfish too. Selfish and dishonest because as much as I didn't have the strength to deal with the mess between us, I wasn't ready to never see him again.

"Of course."

He rubbed the back of his nape. "You must think I'm pathetic. Unemployed. Locked in one place. A single dad who can't do anything right."

I stepped toward him. "I don't think you're pathetic, Gil. I never have."

"But you've had enough of dealing with my nonsense."

"No. I just..." I held up my hands in surrender. "I don't know anymore. I don't know about anything. I don't know about you or me or what I should do...it's terrifying."

He stormed toward me, grabbing my cheeks and holding me firm. "All of this is fucking terrifying. Knowing I've lost you. Knowing I'm about to lose Olive. My freedom. My future." His thumbs ran over my cheekbones, his hands shaking. "Knowing I'm one of the reasons you're afraid." His forehead pressed against mine. "It fucking butchers me, O. I never meant to hurt you. I'll never forgive myself for painting you, drugging you. I could apologise every damn day of my life, but...it's not going to change anything."

I swayed in his touch, suffering heat and hunger.

The same violence that clawed for a fight returned, and I didn't entirely know why. Gil had apologised. I'd forgiven him. We should be able to move on.

And yet...we couldn't.

We kept clinging to each other in unhealthy ways, making us weak and wanting.

My lips throbbed for his.

His body stepped into mine until no space existed between us and his head tipped down. His mouth descended, and we both jerked at the connection.

Hot.

Painful.

Unforgiving.

I sighed.

He groaned.

His hands fell from my cheeks to wrap around my hips, pulling me into him, making my stomach flip.

The kiss wasn't planned.

Our confessions messy and dangerous.

But as his tongue touched mine, and we began a dance that twisted me up and made me fly, I didn't care.

I hugged him back.

I kissed him back.

And then it was over as he pulled away.

The early morning sunshine shone through the window, highlighting a shadowy bruise on his jaw and the discolouration under his eye, reminding me violence had found him once again.

That his troubles weren't over.

"Are you okay?" My question was breathy, my heart out of control.

He chuckled darkly. "No, I'm not fucking okay. I miss you, O. I've missed you my entire goddamn life."

My knees wobbled. "I meant your incident with whoever hurt you."

"Oh, that." His forehead furrowed. The connection between us faltered as he took a step back. "Yeah, I'm fine."

His departure wrenched deep inside me but my question had done what I'd intended. I'd popped the bubble we'd been in. The bubble we had a habit of creating. The precious, perfect moment where it was just us and kisses and nothing else mattered.

If we could live in that illusion, we could be happy.

But we couldn't because real life wasn't that easy.

"Justin said a few men surprised you outside your warehouse. That they were friends and family of one of the painted girls."

Gil stroked his jaw where a bruise hinted he'd been punched pretty hard. "They got a few strikes in, but I didn't let them use me as a punching bag like I did my uncle, if that's what you're worried about. I fought back."

"I'm just worried that society is lynching you."

"They don't know I didn't kill those girls."

"No, but vigilante justice is dangerous."

He shrugged. "Nothing I don't deserve."

"Don't. Don't keep saying that."

He didn't argue. Instead, he stared at me the way he'd stared at Olive. With undying affection and unconditional love. "Feel free to throw a punch too, O. A fist would hurt far less than you cutting me out of your heart."

Tension once again detonated around us.

My heart flurried.

My stomach knotted.

I couldn't look away from him.

This was another blistering moment.

A moment that could fix all other moments.

A fragile moment where we could break the ice, talk, and find happier ground than this precarious plateau we currently navigated.

But I didn't know how.

Gil raised his hand as if to touch me. He licked his lips as my name fell with a whisper, "O...I—"

I shook my head. I backed away.

Gil honoured my wishes.

Barely.

His body bristled with explosive need. The sudden softness of before vanished as he clipped, "If you don't leave to go to work now, I won't be responsible for what I'll do. I won't care my daughter is the bathroom. I won't care that I hurt you beyond anything. I'll grab you and fuck you, and I won't let you out of bed until you forgive me."

I stood rooted to the spot.

Unable to move.

Unable to stay.

It was my turn to struggle with a sentence. "Gil...I—"

He pinched the bridge of his nose, his hand trembling. "Go, O. I don't want to hurt you any more than I have." He looked up, his eyes blazing emerald desire. "And I will hurt you. That's why you're keeping your distance, isn't it? Because you know that soon I'm going away. And no one knows for how long. I could be an old man before they let me out. I might die in there. What sort of bastard would I be to fight for you to love me, only to abandon you all over again?"

He gave me the saddest smile. "Fuck, I wish I'd never let you go when we were younger."

I tripped backward.

I'd waited so, *so* long to hear that.

It sucker-punched me in the chest. It ripped out my soul. It brought tears to my eyes.

Olive darted from the bathroom with toothpaste dripping all over her pyjamas and her toothbrush in her hand. "Dad, I don't like O's toothpaste. Do you have the stuff we use?"

And just like that, another moment was gone.

Again.

I sucked in a breath, jittery and lost.

Gil swallowed back the hurt between us and ducked to scoop his dirty daughter from the floor. "Sure, it's in my bag."

Life once again carried us in different directions as he performed fatherly duties, and I grabbed my handbag, looked at him one last time, and slipped out the door.

I was two hours early for work.

I was trembling like a fool.

I was in so much more trouble than I feared.

Chapter Twenty-Two

Gil

I LASTED THREE days.

Three long, terribly excruciating days of loving O, wanting O, knowing I couldn't have O.

We'd both come to the same painful conclusion.

This was all we could afford.

This tentative friendship.

This tense flatmate arrangement.

After that first day when O went to work and I did my best to come to terms with letting her go, I looked for apartments so I didn't have to destroy any more of her life.

But the market held no decent rentals and the ones viable required a one-year lease. I had no idea when I'd be called to trial, and frankly, I couldn't fucking afford anywhere anyway.

Not with my business in ruin and hate still vicious online.

I had to accept that for now, I had no choice.

No choice but to stop cursing Justin for his charity and stop hating myself for taking O's generosity. This was my life right now…no matter how I wished it wasn't.

Life slipped into a routine.

O would go to the office, and I'd spend the day with Olive, all while doing my best to find work. I allowed the necessity of earning money and the needs of life to drive me, but I also permitted myself space to enjoy my daughter. To make up for lost time. To learn all about her and the growth she'd done in the year that I hadn't been part of her life.

I did it for her.

I did it for me.

We made memories that hopefully would sustain me

through whatever was coming.

By the time O returned in the evenings, I'd already have dinner cooking and conversation carefully stayed on Olive and her increasing excitement of returning to school.

O's idea of a tutor was great but just added yet another financial strain.

I made a note to see about taking out a loan, so I could make Olive's hopes a reality. Not that I held my breath with my current shitty situation.

When bedtime came around, O would vanish into her room, and I would lie on her couch doing my best not to get hard or burst through her door and force her to listen to me. To tell her I was wrong in staying away. That I needed her to fight beside me...like she always had.

I missed her.

I wanted her.

But I wouldn't do that to her.

At least having Olive between us gave us safe harbour and prevented any chance of breaking our strange, brittle truce.

Our voices had to stay light and civil for innocent ears. Our interactions had to be upbeat and chipper, all while we acted our arses off for my daughter's sake.

It physically crippled me watching O laugh with Olive and Olive fall in love with O. They'd been thrown together by a mad man—two, including me—and that bond only grew stronger the longer we stayed in O's tiny apartment.

I knew I couldn't let them get any closer. I was only setting Olive up for yet more heartbreak if I did. O was leaving on a jet plane, and Olive would soon have to face my disappearance for a second time. Plus, O couldn't be expected to share her heart with a child created by our old teacher and me.

But knowing all that didn't mean I could stop the inevitable connection they shared. The sweetness when Olive showed O how to blend watercolours, and the pride when O showed Olive how to dance.

Fuck, it would've been so perfect if O was mine.

We could've been a family.

A true, happy, *perfect* family.

Instead of this pretend pocket of time, both of just waiting for it to end, preparing how to tell Olive that life wasn't fucking fair and her hardships weren't over yet.

"Dad....*Dad!* You're not painting."

I snapped out of my thoughts, slamming back into the present where I hung with Olive across the street from O's apartment. I hoped the distance from the approved flat and this park wouldn't set off the sensor in my anklet.

Poor Olive had cabin fever.

We'd come to the tiny square between four busy roads to paint the fountain splashing over marble swans and lilypads.

I'd carried my portable easel, a selection of paints, and a packed strawberry jam sandwich—her favourite—and spent the afternoon while O was at work painting the sun-glittering structure with my daughter.

"Sorry." I held up my paintbrush. To be fair, I wasn't doing much. The sketch and slowly-coming-to-life painting was all Olive's, and once again, I was blown away by her young talent.

She had the scale nailed. The shadows perfected. The bend of the swan's neck lifelike.

"What'cha thinking about?" she asked.

I smiled, nudging her small shoulder with mine. I didn't have chairs, so we'd set the easel low so we could sprawl on a blanket. "Nothing much. Just how talented you are."

"Nah, I'm not nearly as good as you."

"You're getting close." I eyed up the way she blended white, blue, and black to make a shade of grey so similar to her eyes. "I'm very proud of you."

She blushed. "You're a good teacher."

"Nope. It's all you, kiddo."

Her tongue stuck between her teeth as she shaded the swan's neck. "O said she was proud of me too. She showed me another dance move this morning while you were still sleeping."

"She did?"

How the hell did I not hear them?

"Yep. In her room. She said I have good balance."

I pretended to shove her, jerking her back into place before she fell. "You do. Look how stable you are."

She snickered. "Do you think we can stay with O? I really like living with her. She's super nice." Her sweet gaze met mine. "I like her and you like her. I know you do. You more than like her. But you're sad too." Her head cocked, sending shiny hair over her shoulder. "Why are you sad? Don't you like living with O and me? Do you want to go back to the warehouse?"

I swallowed the sudden obstruction in my throat. I'd long ago learned not to be shocked at the intuition of children and their perception of the truth, but it still punched me in the chest. "I'm not sad. I'm so happy we're together again." Dropping my paintbrush into the water jar, I added, "And you know we can't stay with O for much longer, right? This is only temporary. She has her own life to live, little spinach. And we're not part of it."

"We could be. She likes you too, even though she's mad at you right now."

I froze. "How do you know she's mad at me?"

Had O talked to her?

She wouldn't.

Would she?

Our drama was our own fault—*my* fault—and shouldn't be dumped on a kid.

Olive scowled as if I was an idiot—which I was, so I couldn't argue. "I know the way she talks to you. She really likes you, but you did something, and she's mad." She pinned me with a ruthless stare. "Whatever you did, you should apologise and then we can all move into a bigger place where we all have bedrooms and can be happy forever and ever."

Shit.

This was getting bad.

Olive had attached herself way too much to O.

I should've taken her to Justin's so she could bond to him instead. How the hell was I supposed to dump her on him when I got sentenced and expect her to be comfortable living with yet another strange man?

Fuck.

My phone rang, vibrating in my pocket.

I didn't want to answer it.

Nothing good ever came from answering my goddamn phone, but I pulled it out and climbed to my feet. "I'll be a sec, okay?"

Olive nodded, pinning all her attention on her painting again. "Okey-dokey."

Pressing accept, I walked away, answering the unknown number suspiciously. "Hello?"

"Gilbert Clark?"

"Who's this?"

"This is Brad Scott from Scott, Smith, and Grampton. I'm calling to inform you that a court date has been set, and you're expected to be at the crown court in six days' time at nine a.m. sharp. Please be presentable and prepared. I request we meet tomorrow to go over your testimony and explain in detail what to expect."

Shit.

Shit.

Shit.

"Six days?" My heart sank to my toes. "That soon?"

"They've hurried your trial. These things happen with high-profile murder cases, especially when pressure is put on the system by the public."

I rubbed my mouth, spinning to face Olive who sat innocently on the blanket. "How long with the trial take?"

"Not sure. Depends how much evidence there is to present. You'll be subjected to a jury trial. Your verdict might be given that day or it might take a week or a month, who knows. I'll be able to advise more once we've sat down, and you've answered my questions."

"Questions?"

"We'll run through a fake trial. I'll pretend to examine you, you answer, we get our ducks in a row, and you'll be prepared for the real thing. Sitting in a courtroom can be scary business, Mr. Clark. It's my job to ensure you're ready and nothing goes wrong."

I couldn't stop looking at my daughter.

I wanted to be fucking sick.

"What if I'm found guilty? Will I be sent to prison straight away?"

Brad made a noise; paper shuffled in the background. "I'm afraid so. It's best to get your affairs in order and prepare your family, just in case."

Pacing the soft grass, blanketed by warm sun, I asked as quietly as my nerves would allow. "Do you think I have a chance of walking out of there?"

After a long pause, Brad muttered, "You killed a man, Mr. Clark. It might've been in defense of Olin Moss being assaulted, but the fact remains, you took a life."

"He held my daughter hostage for over a year."

"He was your family."

"He was a liar and a traitor."

"So you say."

My hands curled. "What are you implying?"

"I'm implying nothing. Just showing you how the court will be. No one will be on your side, Mr. Clark. Except me."

"So you believe I deserve to go to jail?"

He sighed with exasperation, as if he'd had this conversation with so many criminals. "It's not about what I believe. It's about what the facts prove. I'll do my best to ensure they work in your favour. But you confessed to the murder. You are being lynched online. The possibility of this all blowing over and you remaining a free man are slim to none."

Silence filled in the gaps.

I had nothing more to say.

He cleared his throat. "Tomorrow at my office. We'll go through everything and I'll make sure you're prepared. Until then, enjoy today, Mr. Clark. Enjoy all your days because you might only have six free ones left."

He hung up.

I stared at the traffic surrounding us.

I tripped back to Olive and collapsed beside my daughter just as a stopwatch started a countdown to the end.

Tick.

Tock.

It's over.

Chapter Twenty-Three

Olin

I DIDN'T KNOW how much longer I could take it.

Seeing Gil every day.

Having him in my house.

Watching the incredible way he loved his daughter.

Suffering a stupid heart that still wanted what it couldn't have.

It was too much.

I needed space.

Time alone.

I needed to rein in my rapidly fraying life before I was left with tattered pieces and no hope of ever sewing myself back together again.

The civility between us was worse than fighting.

The fakeness between us far more draining than being honest.

But we couldn't have a fight, and we couldn't be honest because Olive was there.

Every night.

Every meal.

Every morning.

That sweet, adorable little girl who watched me and Gil with far too much understanding in her grey gaze. She saw what we were trying to hide. She heard what we weren't saying. And it worried me because the longer we skirted around each other, pretending we could be friends when it was obvious that we couldn't, the more Olive watched with a plan gleaming in her eyes.

A plan that little girls make up when they think they can play matchmaker to two people who are stubborn and broken and successfully ruining any chance of happiness.

I couldn't let her do that.

I had made my choice.

I've made it.

I have.

I won't fall into the same patterns.

Not this time.

Yes, being a supportive friend and offering free accommodation was harder than I thought. Yes, being kind wasn't nearly as rewarding as it used to be. But at least I had my work. I could lose myself in the repetitive routine and find salvation from an unsolvable complication until five p.m.

Unfortunately, the moment I climbed on the bus and travelled home, all those jumpy, itchy needs swarmed me, and by the time I walked in the door, I was exhausted, frustrated, and just plain twisted up with barbwire-filled knots.

Tonight, I honestly didn't know if I could walk through the door and do it all over again. To smile and laugh and let Gil cook me and his daughter a simple but tasty dinner.

It was far too domesticated.

Way too dangerous for my heart.

Sighing, I fished my keys from my handbag and sucked in a deep breath.

Unlocking the door, I braced myself, schooled my features from tortured to serene, and stepped into my apartment.

"Oh, hi." I stopped on the threshold, finding more people than I expected.

Justin immediately got to his feet where he sat at the dining room table with Gil and Olive. A tower of pizza boxes rested in the middle of the table, along with wedges and garlic bread. "Great, you're back. We've been staring at this food like slobbering hyenas for twenty minutes but didn't want to start until you were here."

Olive giggled. "I wasn't slobbering."

"You were too." Justin stuck out his tongue at her. "I saw drool on your chin and your tiny fangs."

"Did not." She crossed her arms, a cross between a smirk and a pout on her face.

Gil just sprawled in his chair, his gaze once again pinned on me, his body wound tight despite his relaxed pose. I didn't know how I knew, but something had happened today.

Something bad.

I read it in the way he studied me as if he'd never see me again.

I felt it in the electrified air between us.

I grew wet despite myself.

I grew angry because my body kept betraying me.

Ripping my gaze from his, I kissed Justin on the cheek as he kissed me. Gil stiffened in his chair.

I smiled. "You could've started without me, you know."

"Nah, that wouldn't be fair." Justin took my handbag, tossed it on the couch, then escorted me to the table. "Gil called and asked me round. Hope you don't mind me imposing." Sitting down, he divided up the boxes and opened them.

A punch of cheese, barbecue sauce, and grease filled my nose.

"I don't mind. You're welcome anytime."

"I bought pizza as a guest tax." Justin grabbed a piece of veggie-something-or-other and plopped it onto Olive's plate. "After you, tiny one."

Olive plucked a piece of onion off, then took a dainty bite. "Yummy."

"Great. I'm glad it's approved." Justin chuckled, placing a piece onto my plate then onto his. He didn't serve Gil, just shoved the box his way. "All yours, mate."

"Cheers." Gil took one and ate quietly. Once again, that intensity, that wrongness scratched down my spine.

What'd happened?

Why was Justin here?

How could I ask when it wasn't my place?

Conversation was few and far between as we ate unhealthy but delicious takeout. Olive managed two pieces and a handful of wedges. I ate three pieces. And the guys managed to devour almost an entire pizza each.

By the time everyone had their fill, Olive looked ready to pass out and threw herself on the couch amongst Gil's blankets and turned on the TV.

Justin passed out napkins for greasy fingers.

Gil raised an eyebrow, catching Justin's attention.

"Yeah, yeah." He grinned, hiding the scary urgency in his tone. "Prove to her I'm trustworthy before it's too late."

"Appreciate it." Gil sat forward in his chair as Justin went to Olive and struck up a conversation about whatever show she'd selected. He perched next to her on the couch, his gaze on the screen but his attention entirely on her.

"What are you watching?" he asked gently.

"Dunno. What do you want to watch?"

Justin grinned. "Anything you want to watch." The strain in his shoulders relaxed. He'd successfully proven not to be the monster she'd feared just a few weeks ago.

Once again prickles shot down my back, suddenly understanding why Justin was here. Gil had invited him to bond with Olive. To ensure they could live harmoniously when the time came.

Oh, no.

My eyes shot to his. "Did something happen today?" My pulse pounded in worry.

Gil stiffened and stood from the table. "Can I talk to you, please?"

I looked up, frowning. "Sure...please tell me—"

"Not here." He arched his chin at my bedroom. "In there."

I instantly shook my head.

Him and me in a room with a closed door?

No way.

I wouldn't have the strength to stop whatever would happen.

And it would happen.

Each stare was a touch.

Each word was a lick.

Living together and not acknowledging the flying, raging need between us had ensured we'd been pouring gunpowder directly onto open wounds. If we had a single opportunity to even say a fraction of something that wasn't controlled and civil, I didn't know what would happen.

You do know.

You know exactly what would happen.

The rough, quick sex we'd had in my kitchen would be *nothing* compared to the explosive aggression we'd indulge in.

"It's probably best if we stay—"

"It's important." His head tipped down, shadowing his gaze. "Please?"

Olive giggled at something Justin said.

He beamed as if he'd solved complex math.

Just because Olive was distracted didn't mean we were free to become animals behind my bedroom door. The walls were paper thin. Justin was right there. There was safety in that—knowing we still had boundaries and rules in place.

"Okay." Brushing off pizza crumbs, I didn't say a word as I followed Gil through the small living room and entered my bedroom.

The moment we were inside, he closed the door.

He took a deep breath.

I spun to face him, crossing my arms, doing my best to hold myself together. "What is it? What's happened?"

He rubbed his face with both hands, the mask he'd kept in place the past few days slipping to the floor. "Fuck, do you know how hard it is not to kiss you? It's all I ever fucking think about." He moved toward me, only to pace away before he could touch me. "Fuck, if I kiss you, I won't be able to stop."

He headed to my window, raking hands through his hair. "Night after night, I battle myself not to come in here and take you. To see if there's any way we can fix us. To stop our inevitable separation."

"Gil, don't—"

He held up a hand. "It's okay, O. I'm not going to force myself on you. I'm not going to kiss you. I'm not going to do anything apart from say…it's all too fucking late."

The hair on the back of my neck stood up. I stepped toward him instead of away. "What do you mean, too late?"

"I had a phone call today."

"From who?"

"The lawyer who's been put in charge of my case." He pinched the bridge of his nose before looking up. "I'll be sentenced in six days."

My heart stopped beating. "*What?* That's so soon. How can they—?"

"Six days before I have to say goodbye to Olive for who knows how long. Six days to make sure she's comfortable with living with Justin, even though she's fallen madly in love with you. Six fucking days to find some way of making even the smallest amount of money so she's not destitute like me." His voice cracked with rage and impotency. "Fuck!"

His shout was heartfelt and passionate, but also quiet, staying below the decibel guaranteed to reach Olive's small ears.

I didn't know what to say or how to comfort him.

I was petrified for him. I couldn't imagine how it would feel to know your freedom was about to be stolen, and there was nothing you could do about it.

He'd committed the crime.

He wouldn't run.

He wouldn't lie.

Whatever sentence he was given would be served with honour, and his daughter would miss him every day of her life without him.

The urge to hug him overwhelmed me. I moved toward him. "What can I do?"

He held up his hand, his eyes flashing with a mixture of helplessness and violence. "Don't touch me, O. Not when I'm like this." His voice turned dangerously dark. "You touch me and I'm inside you. I won't be able to stop myself."

I stopped.

Pain crashed over his features.

"Tell me what you need," I whispered.

"I owe you so much already."

"Tell me what you need, Gil."

He glowered at my carpet, unable to meet my eyes. "I need money. To pay you for the days we've stayed here. To pay Justin for Olive's upkeep. To give Olive some pocket money for while I'm gone."

"I don't see how I can—"

His head tipped up, the heat and hardness back in his stare. "Be my canvas. Let me paint you...one last time."

I stumbled backward. "Excuse me?"

What about the petitions online chanting for his business closure and death?

What about the absolute hate bleeding through the keyboard?

"I know my business is dead. No one wants to be associated with a murderer. My visibility and ratings are in the gutter. I have no new content to share, which means algorithms aren't delivering to new people." He paced again, driving yet another hand into his hair. "I'm aware it probably won't work. I know what I'm asking. It's a huge gamble that any commissions will arrive in time before my court date, but...I have to try."

He chuckled blackly. "I've really fucked up this time, O. I should never have killed him. I should've let the police deal with him. But...I did it and I won't apologise for it nor regret it; he needed to die. I'm okay paying that price. I just don't want Olive to pay with me."

Old habits were so hard to break.

I wanted to grab him close and tell him that yes, I would be his canvas. That I had the strength to help him all over again after I'd used up every ounce of help I had to give.

I was so close to doing exactly that.

So reckless to touch him, knowing what would happen if I did.

His warning was real.

The desire rampant between us.

One touch would lead to him attacking me, taking me, destroying the final weak pieces of me.

I was prepared to do all that...but one thing stopped me.

A single memory.

A tiny piece of the past.

I swallowed hard and prepared to say the hardest thing in my life. "I can't help you, Gil. I'm so sorry."

He locked in place. His urgency slipped into despondency. His need into acceptance. "I understand."

"I'll help you find money some other way, but...I can't let you paint me again."

He froze. His nostrils flared. He slouched with self-hatred. "Of course. What a fucking arsehole thing to even ask." He paced again, shaking his head as if he could punch himself for being so clueless. "The last time I painted you, I drugged you and—"

"I know what you did." I held up my hand, trying to figure out how to say what was needed. "Gil, the fact that you're asking for help is...healing. You didn't lock things inside this time and make mistakes because it." I licked my lips, stalling for a second. "I don't want you to take my refusal as a sign to never ask for help again. You should be able to trust that sharing your burdens with others is beneficial...for everyone involved. I'm honoured. Truly. I'm grateful you came to me. And I'm eternally sorry that I have to say no."

His hands fisted by his sides, struggling to control whatever he felt. With jerky steps, he came toward me.

I stiffened and sucked in a breath as he placed a chaste kiss on my cheek. "Don't ever apologise to me, O. Ever." His lips trailed to my mouth, hovering over me in punishment and prayer.

I swayed into him, swept up and unable to fight.

But he closed his eyes and backed up, physically putting

space between us while emotional space was that much harder. "I was wrong to ask. Wrong to stay here. Wrong about so many fucking things."

Shivering, I hugged myself. Whatever fragile moment we'd shared was ending and I had to know. Had to ask. "When you face the courtroom...what are you going to tell them?"

He smiled sadly. "The only thing I can. The only thing I have left." He strode to the door and wrapped his hand around the handle. "I'm going to tell the truth. I'm sick of lying. I'm done running. I'll tell the truth and accept the consequences."

A tear escaped my control as he stepped through the door and went to sit on the couch with his friend and daughter.

Scooping Olive up, he dragged her onto his lap, rocked into her, and pressed a kiss to her hair.

He didn't say a word.

But all around them echoed goodbye.

Chapter Twenty-Four

Gil

WHILE O WAS at work, I moved my daughter and meagre belongings into Justin's place.

I didn't tell O we were leaving. I didn't give any hint that we wouldn't be there when she returned home. Once Olive was settled, I would visit O one last time to explain, to thank her, to apologise, to say…goodbye.

I'd called the cops and asked for yet another address change, gaining permission to travel between the two locations. They gave me twenty-four hours to complete the move before warning I'd be under house arrest again.

Justin took the day off from the office and spent every moment with us. He showed Olive the spare bedroom, which used to be sterile and bland but now held purple curtains, lacy pink pillows, and a massive artwork of a field filled with wildflowers on the wall.

I'd caught his eye as Olive shot to the bed, the white desk, and the cute little dresser he'd arranged.

Fuck, I owed this man a lot.

Bumping into him on the street after so many years had been one of the best things to happen to me. He hadn't been a curious sod—only there while times had been normal. He hadn't bailed when I finally accepted his help and kept requesting more.

He'd proven himself to be loyal and generous, and I would be grateful for the rest of my godforsaken life.

After Olive explored her new space, still suspicious about why she got a room and I got the couch, I whispered into her ear to hug Justin. To push them together and create that trusting bond so I could be locked away next week and not worry that

Olive would have a breakdown, that Justin could handle her, and that there was no chance of this falling apart.

No one knew how long I'd be in jail for.

A year, a decade, forever?

Justin was taking on so fucking much without asking for anything in return.

There is something *you can give him.*

The thought appeared and ran away, as if too scared to stick around and find out how I truly felt about offering him something that meant more to me than my own life.

But as Olive tentatively shuffled to Justin and hugged him at my request, I balled my hands and made a promise.

Once I knew my punishment.

Once Olive was no longer mine to care for.

I would tell him what I was willing to sacrifice for all his support.

* * * * *

"You sure you got this?" I muttered as Justin grabbed a beer from the fridge and I stacked the dishwasher from the plates we'd used with Thai takeout.

"I'm sure." He twisted off the cap and tossed it into the bin. "If Olive and I can't hang out on our own for a few hours, then I don't see how living together is going to work out. You need to do this, and we need time alone to figure out the ground rules." He patted me on the shoulder, leaving the kitchen and returning to the living room where his black couches faced the TV and Olive sat snuggled in one watching Disney's *Mulan.*

Drying my hands on a dishtowel, I followed and kept my distance while he collapsed next to her and tapped his beer bottle to her glass of apple juice. "What are we watching, tiny pipsqueak?"

She grinned. "I'm not a pipsqueak."

Justin smirked. "See, to me, you're smaller than a pipsqueak. You look like a mouse. An itty-bitty, teensy-weensy mouse. So pipsqueak fits you well."

"Well, you're just a…a…you're a hippopotamus."

"You calling me fat?" Justin scowled dramatically. "Is it because I had two beef curries?"

"Yep!" Olive giggled, sipping her juice as her attention fell back on the TV.

Justin gave me a wink. "All good, mate. I got this."

Nodding, I made my way to the exit. "Olive? I'm heading

out for a few hours. Justin will keep you company."

I didn't ask if she was okay with that.

I didn't make her doubt her comfort level.

She didn't really have a choice in the matter anymore.

She nibbled on her bottom lip. "Will you be back in time to say goodnight?"

I braced myself. "Probably not. But Justin can help, and I'll be back later. I'll definitely see you in the morning, though, okay?" Unable to leave without touching her, I strode over and bent to kiss her forehead. Keeping my lips on her sweet-smelling skin, I murmured, "You're safe with him, little spinach. Jeffrey is gone. You were right that he was bad, but Justin isn't. I need you to be okay with having him as your friend, all right?"

She gave a side-eye to Justin before nodding slowly. "I like him as a friend. We can hang out."

"Great. Good girl."

"But I miss O. Can we go back to see her tomorrow?"

"Maybe." Backing away, I imprinted the image of my friend watching cartoons with my daughter then turned around and walked out the door. I'd keep that image safe. I'd pull it up when I got sentenced and I was alone in some goddamn cell, missing Olive with every fucking fibre of my being.

Not for the first time, the urge to pick up my daughter and run hijacked my nervous system.

I wanted to fly away and hide on some secluded island where I would never have to be torn away from her again.

But that was selfish.

That would backfire on Olive as she got older.

I meant what I told O.

I was done running.

I'd been running since Tallup blackmailed me into sleeping with her—always wondering when I'd be arrested for sexual assault.

Well, I wouldn't have to wonder anymore.

Consequences were almost here.

I'd done what I could to protect Olive from the worst of it.

But tonight…tonight I *was* going to be selfish. So fucking selfish.

Tonight was for me.

My last shred of happiness.

Tonight…O was mine.

Chapter Twenty-Five

Olin

"WHAT ON EARTH?" I froze on the threshold, confused. Did I walk into the wrong apartment?

Where my couch and dining table used to be, a black sheet now hung from the window and draped on the floor, creating a void of darkness, a backdrop to nothingness.

"You're later than I planned."

My attention shot to the kitchen where Gil stood, mixing paints. He'd lined his bottles and tools up neatly, pigments from gold and taupe right through to aqua and obsidian waited to be used. He tested the airbrush, wiping the nozzle with a paper towel all while I gawked like an idiot.

"Eh…" Closing the door behind me, I slung my handbag onto the floor, kicked off my heels, and padded toward him. "What are you doing?"

"I came to say thank you." His green eyes met mine. "And to say goodbye."

My heart fisted tight. "What do you mean?"

"I mean Olive and I moved out today. I thought you'd be home before I could come back but you weren't…and…" He looked at the black sheet and his takeover of my place, adding. "I had some spare time on my hands."

"You moved out? Without telling me?"

"It was for the best." He gave a sad smile. "My daughter is attached to you. She needs to bond with Justin, so she's comfortable for when I—" He groaned low, cutting himself off.

I nodded, hating the way my chest squeezed. "That makes sense."

He cleared his throat. "I hope you don't mind me, eh,

redecorating."

Grasping at the change of subject and latching onto a less painful conversation, I said, "Depends what you're planning on doing." I crossed my arms, keeping the breakfast bar and my body language between us. "Do you have a canvas coming here to be painted? Did you get a commission?"

Gil winced, shaking his head. "No...no canvas." Placing the airgun down, he pinned me with his stare. "Only you."

Goosebumps scattered over my arms. "Gil...I told you I can't be painted again. Not yet."

"I know." He stared hard, his gaze deep and deliberate. "But I can't accept no for an answer, O."

I backed up, goosebumps turning into trembles. "Why are you looking at me like that?"

"Like what?" He tipped his head down, watching me beneath shadowed eyes.

"Like you don't care if I give consent or not."

He shrugged. "I love you. I want you. And now...you're here."

I gulped, grasping to say something normal and not laced in lust.

I failed.

I swallowed.

Gil placed his palms on either side of the sink, bracing against the countertop. The same countertop where we'd had a furious quickie. Where we'd chased fast pleasure. Where our hearts had once again become tangled.

His voice was decadent and dangerous as he murmured, "I've had a lot of time to decide if I should do this or not."

"Do what?"

"Take something from you that you undoubtedly don't want to give."

I swallowed again. Hard. "I don't know what you mean."

"You do know." His gaze turned brittle. "You know exactly what I mean. Leaving me alone for so long wasn't a good idea, O. It's not been good for my self-control." He looked down at his ankle where the monitoring device kept him leashed. "This is the last time I can be here. I've changed my address with the authorities to Justin's apartment. I won't be able to come and see you before I go to court." His fingers clutched against the counter. "This is the last time I'll have you alone. And I'm done."

"You're done?"

He nodded once. "I'm done. Done pretending I can cope without you in my life. Done lying to myself that I don't need you. Done accepting your choice to break my fucking heart."

Heat filled my cheeks as his gaze travelled over my cream blouse and pinstripe skirt. "You should probably strip, O. I don't want to ruin any more of your clothes."

I coughed. "Excuse me?"

"Have you eaten? Are you hungry?" His voice stayed smoky and deep, even though he'd just sent me into a free-fall.

"Hungry? No, I'm…"

"Okay then." Pushing off from the countertop, he exited the kitchen and stalked me. He stopped within touching distance but kept his hands fisted by his sides. His energy wrapped around me. Energy that used to match mine. A synergy of auras and souls.

Tonight, his energy was treacherous, precarious.

I shivered with premonition. "Gil…what are you doing?"

"I'm going to paint you."

"But I told you—"

"That it brings bad memories." He nodded. "I understand. But it doesn't change the fact that tonight, my brush is touching your body and my paint is staining your skin."

"It does if I don't say yes."

His brow tugged over turbulent eyes. "But you will."

"Why? Why would I agree to let you paint me after the last time?"

"Because this is the last time we'll ever have."

"When you painted and drugged me and prepared to sacrifice me for Olive, I believed *that* was the last time we'd ever have. That I was about to die because of you."

"I was never going to kill you." His body twitched with pain. "I would've killed myself before he was able to do what he threatened. You have to know that."

"You almost *did* die, remember?" My temper crackled into awareness, remembering that night, the fear of him dead on the forest floor, the promise from Jeffrey of sex slavery and child molestation. "You left us both unprotected, all because you didn't ask anyone for help."

"You're right. Just like you were right last night. I asked for help too late and I paid for it. Who knows how our lives would've turned out if I'd told you back at school what Tallup threatened me with. We might be married. We might have our own family. But...I didn't ask. And I lost you. Twice."

His hand cupped my cheek, digging the pads of his fingers into my softness as I tried to back away. "Tonight, I'm not asking anymore. I'm *telling* you what I need. I'm being honest for the first time in my godforsaken life. I'm about to be locked up like an animal, O. I've done my best to ensure Olive will be okay, I've accepted way too much support from Justin, and I've stayed in your home without telling you exactly how I feel. I should walk out that door. I should pay you the pittance I have for the days you let us stay, and I should accept that I will never see you again."

His arm slithered around my waist, jerking me into him. "But I don't accept. I *can't* accept. And tonight, I'm done doing what I *think* I should. Everything I do is wrong. My natural instincts are fucked. So...I'm ignoring them. I'm ignoring the fact that you're trembling and want me to back the fuck off. I'm ignoring the part that this is yet another assault. For once, I'm going to be selfish."

"Gil...stop."

His hand left my cheek and captured the back of my head. His other arm crushed me to him, bending me, imprisoning me. "I can't stop."

My palms smacked against his chest, fighting his control. "Let me go."

"No." His lips smashed on mine. His tongue broke into my mouth. And the ferocity of his kiss was precisely what he said.

This was an assault.

Unwanted. Unprovoked. Assault.

His lips were warm and wonderful.

His body felt like home.

Every part of me screamed to give in. To rock with him, dance with him, explode with him.

But a final shred of common-sense made me squirm in his embrace.

You can't do this.

You're not strong enough.

My fingernails dug into his chest. I wriggled and fought to get free.

But he kept kissing me, holding me, forcing me to take what he gave.

He'd never been coldblooded before. Icy and impenetrable. Explosive and stubborn. But never violent against my wishes.

Never tried to take something that wasn't his.

He groaned into my mouth, his tongue withdrawing, his lips leaving mine.

Our eyes locked and he showed me everything. The fear. The apology. The pain.

"Be my canvas."

"It's too late," I whispered.

His forehead pressed against mine. "It *is* too late. Everything is too fucking late. I'm too late to make any money. Too late to fix my business. Too late to save my daughter. Too late to repair everything broken between us. But it's not too late to say goodbye."

My heart jackhammered as he clutched my hair and tugged, forcing my neck back, kissing his way along the column of my exposed throat. "I'm running out of control. I'll ask one last time before I won't ask anymore. Be my canvas, O. Let me paint you, fuck you. I need to remember you for always."

I shivered at the naked beg in his voice. "I can't."

"You can." His lips were cool, but his tongue hot as he captured me in another kiss. He breathed against my mouth, "Fuck me one last time, O. You said your goodbyes the other night. You used me for closure. I pleaded with you not to make me do it. I begged you to stop. But you didn't. You took from me. And now, I'm taking from you."

I tried to push him away again, cursing how my blood bubbled and wetness gathered between my legs. "I didn't rape you, Gil. Don't you *dare* insinuate I'm anything like that bitch who—"

"You're not." Capturing my wrist, he jerked my hand down and pressed it over his erection. "I wouldn't be hard if I didn't want you. I've never been with anyone else. It's always been you. It will *always* be you. You'll move on after this. You'll travel the world and find a perfect ending, all while I rot in my jail cell. The only thing that will keep me going is my memories of you."

He rocked his hardness into my palm. "Let me have you, one last time. Let me paint you, love you, fuck you, imprint you." His lips trailed along my jaw until he found my mouth again, kissing me long and slow.

I did my best not to respond. Not to kiss him back. But a low moan echoed unwillingly in my throat.

"Let me try to forget you, Olin Moss, even though I know that's impossible." Stepping back, he let me go.

My hand fell from touching him. My lips tingled from his kiss. And we stood facing each other as if drawing the battle lines for war.

He acted as if he'd force me against my will, and I actually believed he would do it. But I also knew, he'd hate himself the entire time. He'd use me, but he'd ultimately suffer.

He was right.

We'd run out of time.

Everything was too late.

The end was here, and there was no right or wrong anymore.

I couldn't be with him. I shouldn't do this. But...it was all over anyway.

Another night together wouldn't change that.

Gil shuddered, his eyes dark. His erection wedged against his paint-splattered work jeans while the black hoodie he always wore in his time-lapse videos held colours from other canvases.

I might be the last one he ever painted.

All the rage inside me vanished.

He's losing everything.

Not just his freedom but also his art.

He'd stood in my apartment a few months ago and asked how I'd tolerated losing dance. He'd genuinely seemed perplexed that I'd survived having such an integral part of me stolen.

He'd told me he wouldn't survive if he couldn't paint.

I'd believed him then.

I believe him now.

Jail wasn't just an institution where he would be captive. It was the accident, the car, the restaurant window. Jail was going to strip him of his ability to paint. Possibly forever.

I sighed heavily, allowing my body to shed its terror and embrace lust.

Deep, deadly, unhealthy lust.

"Will Olive be okay if you're gone for a while?"

Gil stayed frozen, his hands balled by his sides. "She's with Justin. It's best they have time to figure their shit out before I can't be there."

"What happens after?"

His throat worked as he swallowed. "I walk away."

"And if this destroys us even more?"

"Then we're destroyed."

"This won't change anything."

He nodded. "I know."

"I can't be in love with you anymore, Gilbert Clark."

"I'm not asking you to be."

"I should curse you. I should hate you."

"You should."

Tears erupted out of frustration. "*So why can't I?*"

He stepped into me, cupping my cheeks with quaking hands. "Because I can't stop loving you either."

I couldn't *feel* anymore.

I didn't have the strength.

But I also couldn't *lie* anymore.

I didn't have the power.

"You're a walking gift of pain, Gilbert Clark."

"And you're the ultimate gift of redemption, Olin Moss." Brushing his thumbs over my cheekbones, he let me go to flip his black hood up and over his messy hair.

His mask in place. His face obscured.

I flinched. "You're going to record this?"

"Yes."

"Will you post it?"

"Yes."

"Why?"

He captured me again. "Because I deserve a lifetime of agony for what I did. This video will always be there. It will be waiting for me on the day that I'm free. It will be a constant reminder of my one and only canvas—my true work of art that I did nothing but try to destroy. You."

"I don't want to see it."

"Then you won't."

"I don't want to see you."

"But you're the only one who does."

I shuddered.

I didn't want to love him, need him, miss him.

The Master of Trickery.

The Wizard of Paint.

The Love Executioner.

But my head tipped up.

His tipped down.

We kissed.

And our denials were over.

Chapter Twenty-Six

Gil

O STOOD ON the centre of the black sheet.

Her breasts bare.

Her pussy covered by her black G-string.

Watching her strip had almost stolen everything I had left. My cock threatened to snap off. The tension between us hissed and crackled. And my lungs refused to deliver more than a few sips of oxygen.

I'd meant what I said.

Waiting for her to come home had given me far too much time to imagine what it would feel like to be with her one last time. If she hadn't agreed…I honestly didn't know what I would've done.

I'd like to think I would've had the strength to walk out the door.

But…

This was O.

This was the only woman I could be with without reliving the night Olive was created.

This was the other piece of my heart, and I couldn't go to jail without feeling whole one last time.

Keeping my distance, I brought my paints onto the sheet by her feet. I arranged my brushes and sponges, positioned my airbrush, and drank in every inch of her.

We didn't speak while I prepared.

Our silence only added pain to the quietness already torturing us.

With shaking hands, I turned on the small video camera I used to capture my creations. I muted it so no sound was captured. I angled it so O took centre stage. And I made sure my hood tugged low over my face so I remained anonymous, even though mug shots and newspapers had shown the world who I was.

I wasn't a talented artist.

I was a murderer.

Forever and for always.

Moving toward O, I sucked in a useless breath as she trembled. I couldn't tear my eyes off her perfection. Off the scars on her back. Off the ink on her skin. Off her strength and femininity and broken dancer's grace.

"You've always been the most beautiful creature in the world to me." I ducked to my haunches, unscrewing a midnight blue vial, already diluted and ready for my airgun.

She bit her lip, keeping her gaze on the wall beyond. I hadn't asked her to hold a pose. She didn't need to. Just the way she stood echoed with angelic poise. Her wrists always delicate. Her fingers always curved. Her neck arched with royalty.

She looked as if she'd once had wings, weightless and balletic before a car crash stripped them from her, leaving her to the mercy of monsters like me.

"Wh-What design are you going to do?" her voice remained just above a whisper.

"I don't know yet."

"You don't have a concept?"

"I have a feeling."

"A feeling?" Her gaze snapped to mine, despite herself.

I loved watching her study me, bowed at her feet.

I wanted her to remember me like this, worshiping her, wanting her.

"Secrets."

She frowned. "Secrets?"

"The piece will be called Secrets."

Her eyes leapt from mine, fully aware of the connection binding us exquisitely tight together. I felt it. She felt it. Fate fucking felt it.

Her eyes glossed. "Secrets are always drenched in pain."

I nodded, testing the spray before standing in front of her. "They are. That's what you are." I kissed her softly. "Love painted in pain."

She swayed as I pulled back and pressed the button on my airgun. The spray of midnight shot from the muzzle, instantly changing skin to canvas.

I didn't normally cover a girl in one shade.

I didn't usually allow creativity to control me.

But this wasn't a commission.

This wasn't prepaid and scripted.

This was just us.

A canvas and a body painter.

Both in love.

Both in agony.

Both fighting goodbye.

Time slipped between the silence, blending the two until the world no longer existed. All I saw was O. All she felt was my paint. Slowly, I covered her from head to toe in deep, distressing blue.

The longer I painted, the tighter her muscles became. Her face strained and eyes full of memory. She was back in my warehouse the night I'd drugged and kidnapped her. She was back to cursing my existence.

"Jeffrey was my real uncle...did you know that?"

My voice snapped her from the past and did exactly what I hoped. Her eyes narrowed, locking onto me as I shaded the inside of her thigh. "What?"

"Jeffrey...I know you would've heard Olive call him uncle." I wiped the excess off, leaning in to spray again. "He was her great uncle. My father's brother."

"What are you doing?" She shifted a little, breaking the position she'd chosen.

Wrapping my hand around her ankle, I shook my head slowly. "Don't move."

She locked in place all while her voice rained from above. "Why are you telling me about Jeffrey? Why bring his name into this...when you're painting me?"

"To distract you."

"Distract me."

"To talk to you."

"To confess."

I nodded. "To confess."

She shivered as I added a final lashing over her kneecap and reared back. The whites of her eyes and teeth popped from the darkness of her face, body, and hair. She wasn't O anymore. She was a faceless secret with no substance. A white lie that hadn't been told yet.

As I added more depth and detail, the lie would grow, the secret would swell, and the damage it reaped would magnify.

I no longer had frost around my heart. No icicles in my blood or snow within my voice. I was done freezing O out from my truth.

I wanted her to ask.

To know.

Unscrewing the empty vial from my airbrush, I reached for quicksilver.

She swayed as I added a splattering of stars on her leg. A twinkling galaxy over her stomach. The admission that secrets didn't just affect a single planet but the cosmos.

"Why did you sleep with her? You had to have known people would have helped you?" The question strangled in her throat. "Why did you throw us away?"

Finally.

Finally a question.

A question shooting a dagger straight into the heart of all our problems.

I looked up as I dipped a fine-tipped brush into blood-red pigment. "If we do this...no more secrets."

She held my stare, trembling beneath my colours. "No more secrets."

"Okay then." I cleared my throat again. "I threw us away because I was a fucking idiot. Tallup threatened your future. I kept it to myself because I was afraid." I drew a line over the top of her hipbone, tracing what felt right, but unsure what it would become. "I wanted to protect you, not ruin you."

"You ruined yourself."

I continued painting, half in the otherworld of creation where noise was muted and reality dulled and half with her in a dreamlike state of confession. "I was young and stupid."

"You were targeted and molested."

"I should've trusted someone." I drew my brush down her leg. "I should've trusted you."

She shivered as I continued staining midnight with blood. "Instead you broke up with me."

"I kept my distance because even though I'd done what she'd asked, my freedom came with consequences."

Her stomach tensed as I swapped red for black. Soaking up the ink, I sponged sinister shadows above her G-string and along her belly.

She breathed, "Consequences?"

"One of her conditions was that I could never talk to you or any other girl in school."

She gasped as I left her skin and pressed my sponge right between her legs. Hard. Hard enough to squeeze black paint and watch it dribble over her knickers-covered core.

"Why?"

"Because she knew I loved you."

"But why didn't you come to me when she left school? She wasn't there to terrorize you anymore."

I fought back the lashes of regret as I traded black for magenta. "I was going to."

"What?" She froze, her eyes locking onto mine.

"I had a plan. I waited to be sure she'd gone for good. I made up a script so I could talk to you without blurting nonsense. I had full intentions of finding you on Monday and begging your forgiveness."

Her face twisted; her eyes glazed with wetness. "But you ran away."

"Tallup visited me." I painted faster, my brush becoming an extension of my pain, using my secrets as its colour. "She brought Olive."

Silence once again whispered in as O stood still.

"The moment I saw her, O…I couldn't stop it. I fell in love." I painted harder, cursing the design that only now I recognised. "I fell in love and I knew, without a shadow of a doubt, that her life came before mine. I didn't have a choice."

O continued to shiver silently, giving me far too much space to fill. "I stole from my old man that night, and ran away. I didn't say goodbye. I made it work in London for a bit. Made enough cash with painting and selling my work to get by. Then I earned a few bigger jobs. I was hired to graffiti a local hostel and its dorm rooms with images of downtown. While Olive grew, I tried to find a more reliable income. However, time passed. Olive went to preschool. Then kindergarten. And I kept painting."

I looked up.

I ignored the scene I'd painted on her thigh.

A scene of a boy holding a fleece blanket, the blanket trying to escape on a kite string, hiding something priceless. "I'd already given you up, O. I couldn't give up my art too."

She trembled again. Her stomach fluttering as I once again traded brushes for the airgun. I didn't have control anymore. My body bypassed my mind and painted purely from my heart. Whatever masterpiece O became tonight would have no input from me, just instinct, just hope, just pain.

"But you became the Master of Trickery."

"I did." My voice sounded rough, strangled. "Thanks to Jeffrey."

"What?"

"He appeared one night, knocking on my one-bedroom apartment. Olive was asleep. He claimed to be my dad's brother. He'd been looking for me and heard my name at a local market where a wholesaler sold my paintings."

"Why had he been looking for you?"

I continued painting, switching methods and mediums, trading pigment and metallic. "Dad died. Alcohol poisoning. He told me the whores left town, and the bank seized the house and sold it. Jeffrey was the one listed as next of kin."

"So…he came to give you an inheritance?" She sucked in a breath as I took her hand, painting a row of dying blackbirds up her arm.

"No. He'd already spent what pittance he got from the foreclosure." I swallowed, bowing my head over her shoulder as I traded birds for feathers, mimicking her tattoo, dressing her in a cape of them. "He tracked me down 'cause he thought I might have more money."

Her body swayed as I went behind her, tracing my brush over her scars, adding another picture to her ink. "He blackmailed you right from the start?"

My heart hurt. I didn't want to tell this part of my tale. It once again showed how gullible I was. How stupid. "No. To begin with, he was the perfect uncle. It took a very long time for me to drop my guard. To stop throwing the door in his face or walking across the street if he tried to talk to me. I kept Olive away from him at all costs. I told him to leave me alone."

I bent my knees, and my eyes became level with her gorgeous arse. The muscle definition and sexiness of her grace fogged my thoughts, conjuring more explicit designs. It was easier to tell her this way. Where she couldn't see me. Judge me. "A year passed, and he still stuck around. My resolve to continue hating him just because he was my father's brother faded a little. I let him buy me lunch. I actually listened to what he had to say. I began to *trust*."

My lips pulled back in a snarl. My brush slipped down her

crack with temper.

She flinched and went to move away, but I grabbed her hipbone, smudging my previous work. "Don't. Don't move."

It took a few heartbeats until I could uncurl my hand and continue. "I learned we were more similar than I wanted to admit. He painted cars for a living. Doing decals and pinstripe, special one-of-a-kind commissions on boy racer's wet dreams."

I made my way around to her side again, drawing a tiny car on her foot. "He let me set up an easel in the back. I painted there while Olive was at school. It was…nice."

My voice once again slipped into unbridled rage. "He was the one who taught me to paint other things than walls and paper. He showed me how to do bold lines on the panels of a jeep and airbrush wings on a Ferrari. Anything was paintable. Cups and plates. Glass and fabric."

"Women," O murmured.

I nodded. "Women."

"Is that how you got into painting girls?"

"Yes." I moved onto her calf, not caring what I painted just that I did. That I bled out the pain in purple and blue and grey. "He joked about it, showing me other artists who'd transformed human into landscape and animal. The moment I saw the pictures, I knew what I wanted to do. I wanted to create magic. To twist reality. To form an illusion just like others had."

I forced myself to chuckle rather than fucking cry. "The first few I did were terrible. The next were passable. Woman after woman. Night after night. I dabbled with camouflage and shadow. Olive was kept safe with a babysitter. I told myself I did this for our future. So I could afford to buy any dream she desired. I grew better. My skills improved. Until one night, I nailed the perfect illusion." I let my brush hypnotise me for a moment, needing a break.

O waited for several heartbeats before asking, "What illusion?"

"I made a girl vanish into a backdrop of vineyards and wine barrels. A huge movie poster for some rom-com that had been thrown out." I swallowed hard, chasing back the acid in my mouth. "Jeffrey congratulated me. Took me out. Praised me. And I let down my fucking guard. I told him about Olive. I offered to let him meet her. I invited him into our lives."

O stayed quiet but tangled up enough in my story to ask, "If he spent all that time helping you, why did he start hurting you?"

I shrugged. "Jealousy? Hatred? I never found out."
Changing to my airbrush again, I went to her other side, allowing
the vibrant aqua to highlight her skin. "Thanks to him, I started
painting women all the time. Most of them for free, salvaging
paints from second-hand suppliers, begging for finished tubes to
do as much as I could on the cheap. One girl brought her friends
to watch. They filmed me painting, and put it up on social media.
The rest...is history."

I looked up for the first time in a while. I needed to see her
now. "The post went viral. I can't even remember what I'd
painted. But a few weeks later, I had a business profile, email
account, and companies asking me to paint for them."

Rocking back on my heels, I shrugged again, helpless
beneath the truth. "The money they offered, O? It was ten,
twenty, forty, a *thousand* times more than what I could get for a
hanging canvas. I accepted every gig. I gave half of everything I
made to Jeffrey to say thank you. I introduced him to Olive,
believing I'd finally found someone I could trust."

I dropped my eyes, unable to hold her stare. "I was lonely.
I'd done my best to raise her as a single dad, but I knew I was
lacking. I didn't know shit. I wasn't enough. She needed a bigger
network to rely on so she didn't turn out like me."

"What happened?" she whispered.

"For a year or so, things were fine. He came round for
dinners. He helped me source the warehouse. I offered to let him
move in with us. But then, one day, I got a gig worth a fortune.
Almost a hundred thousand pounds to do three girls
camouflaged into a peacock. It took twenty-four hours, but it
was one of my best pieces. Jeffrey popped by after his shift to
see, and something switched in him. I felt it. I didn't know what
it meant, but by the next week, he asked for a substantial loan."

I wiped my mouth with the back of my painted hand. "I
gave it to him. Of course, I did. I was nothing without him. But
the week after, he asked for more. And again, I gave it to him. I
wanted to share everything because he was the reason I had such
success."

"You were very generous."

"I was looking after family." I threw myself back into
painting, my eyes glazed and colours finding homes upon her
flesh. "I couldn't look after you, so I was determined to look
after those I could."

I shook my head, rushing now, needing this over. "One

night, he asked for everything I'd made on a recent commission. I'd already put it into a savings account for Olive's education and I couldn't withdraw it due to the terms of the account. He left in a rage. Came back drunk. I kicked him out and told him to return sober and tell me why he needed the money, then we'd talk."

Scowling at O's foot, I hunched into myself, finding it unbearable to admit. "The next day, he took Olive."

O sucked in a breath. "He took her because you refused to give him what you'd saved for her?"

I nodded, painting furiously up her leg, bringing to life little fishes of truth, swimming bright in a sea of secrets. I hadn't gone to the police because I didn't want them to know Olive's origins and risk having her taken from me. I'd stupidly thought I could handle it.

That this family spat would resolve itself without a fight.

I'd slowly fallen further and further.

Bankrupt.

Broken.

Until finally, an accessory for murder.

"How did blackmail turn into killing four young girls?" Olive asked, tears smudging her midnight cheeks.

I dared look up, embracing the agony. My hood cut out my peripheral, keeping my attention locked on her. "He was always a psychopath. I found out later that my father's whores hadn't left...he'd killed them. Jeffrey constantly moved because he couldn't restrain his thirst for death. And I introduced that fucking animal to my daughter."

"That's why you let him beat you up."

"Anything to keep his temper away from Olive."

"That's why you gave him every penny."

"Anything to keep her alive."

"That's why you were filthy the nights I came over."

"I was out looking for Olive, trying to stop another girl getting hurt."

O cried openly now. "And that's why you drank."

"To try to forget what I'd caused." My voice cracked. "It was my fault he took her in the first place."

Her entire body shuddered.

She collapsed to her knees beside me.

We were kissing before I realised a fucking tear ran down my cheek.

Chapter Twenty-Seven

Olin

HIS BODY CRASHED into mine.

His hands flew up, grabbing my cheeks and holding me firm. He didn't care about the paint, the art, or the confessions he'd strewn around my feet. He kissed me hard, tilting his head and licking me with twisted desire.

Dragging me closer, we bowed to each other, his body still towering over mine. We kissed savage and unforgiving. Gentle and tender weren't welcome here.

I'd had my dose of violence, and this was his. This was him doing his best to destroy me and remember me all at once.

This was a punishment.

Punishment for himself and the future he faced.

My hands shot to his face, skimming into his hair and pushing away the black hood. I tore off his mask, revealing the tortured painter, the broken lover, the boy I would always miss.

His teeth clacked on mine as he kissed me deeper, pushing me down until I sprawled on the black sheet on the floor. Bottles of paint spilled, oozing their vibrant contents into the fabric. A tub of rhinestones tipped over, scattering brilliant sparkles and sticking to my skin.

We didn't care about any of it.

He pressed himself on top of me the moment I lay on my back. His hand cupped my breast, squeezing and claiming, making them heavy and throbbing.

His touch smeared his art without a thought.

I arched my back, demanding more.

Needing more.

I moaned as he spread my legs and settled between them.

Once again, he was fully clothed and I was gowned in just his creation. No words were exchanged. No soul-stealing stares. Just the urgency to connect.

He kissed me deeper, stealing our final shreds of sanity.

His taste erased everything. His touch deleted the outside world. It was just us. How it should've been. How it could never be.

His hand skated down my breast and over my waist to my hip. Tugging at the knickers he'd painted and pressed a black dripping sponge against my clit. With a savage kiss, he pulled them down until I kicked them away.

The minute I was bare, a slim piece of virgin skin amongst the colours he'd transformed me with, he fumbled with his belt.

I helped him, pushing his hand away and unbuckling the leather. He shuddered as I unbuttoned and unzipped his jeans, then arched his hips as I pushed down the barrier between us.

He groaned as he settled back between my legs. The warmth of his cock, belly, and thighs made me shiver with pleasure. He was heat and hope all at once.

"Fuck," he grunted as my fingers dived between our shared warmth and wrapped around his length. His teeth clamped on my bottom lip, sucking it into his mouth before kissing me roughly. Our lips never unlocked. We kissed violently but also slowly, devouring each other with ruthless determination. The glide of his tongue almost distracted me from the feather of his fingers over my core.

My back bowed as the feather became penetration.

I cried out as he drove two fingers deep.

He groaned as he found me wet.

His thumb rocked on my clit as his five o'clock shadow punished my skin; his kiss so deep, he smashed my head against the floor.

His fingers withdrew.

The soft nudge of his cock replaced them.

I froze in his arms, teetering on the precious knife-edge of anticipation.

His tongue swept into my mouth.

His cock thrust swift and thick into me.

God.

I was totally at his mercy.

Totally with him.

Totally his.

The final barrier Gil had always hid behind shattered. I felt everything he did. I felt his regret, his worry, his love. I felt his teeth and tongue as they left me hollow. I felt his thrusting hips and pounding cock as he stole me from any other thoughts.

He invaded me.

Consumed me.

Made sure that I would never, ever forget him.

"Please, Gil." I didn't know what I asked for. But he gave it to me. He thrust deeper, kissed harder. Grabbing the back of his nape, I forced our mouths together. I spread my legs shamelessly, granting him space to sink further, drive faster.

My body flushed with wetness and want.

"Shit you feel..." His forehead crashed on mine. He clutched the floor beside my ears, pulling himself up and into me, pinning me to the floor with his hips. "You're mine, O."

I didn't know how to reply.

I wasn't his.

I couldn't be.

But I nodded as his thrusts increased. His hips rolled. And his thumb found my clit again.

Fever sprang through my blood. Hot and hungry for the release he conjured. I purred, throwing my head back, scratching my nails on his hoodie.

Once again we fucked in the middle of blues and purples. Other paint bottles tipped over thanks to the sheet tangling beneath us.

We grew wild and furious.

The sensation of having him on top.

The hardness of him inside me.

The way his eyes sank into mine, begging access to my heart all while his body conquered my soul.

His paint had the magic to lie, hide sins, and camouflage flaws. He could create a masterpiece from imperfection. Too bad that tonight, our masterpiece was over, and the magic had to die.

"I love you, O." His voice resembled a colour, a dark broody copper. Something that had dulled with reality but could sparkle once again if polished.

Our eyes locked.

Gil paused inside me.

The moment stretched for far too long, turning this from goodbye to something unbearably complicated.

"Gil...I—"

"Don't." He shook his head. "Don't."

With our gazes still locked, he pushed harder, rocked deeper. He thrust so hard, I cried out, squirming under him. The pinching, consuming pressure of him. The delicious discomfort that followed.

My core rippled around him, welcoming and rebelling against his thrusts.

This was dangerous.

So, so dangerous.

Already I felt the crack in my heart, the tiny hairline fracture that would keep growing, continue to spread until it just tinkled apart.

I clutched him closer.

Our foreheads pressed together as he rode me with awe and dismay.

He kissed me again, joining our mouths as well as our bodies. Carnal and crude, pleasure spiralled from every cell.

We both became lost to it.

Lost to the cresting, lusting release.

I rocked my hips up, grinding myself onto his thick cock, seeking solace from the overbearing connection we shared. This wasn't fucking. This was something so much worse.

This was raw and bare. And it pushed me to the brink.

I wanted to surrender to him.

I wanted to give in to my heart and forgive and forget and promise I'd be there no matter what happened.

But then he shoved away the rawness, pulled curtains over the tenderness, and rutted into me. He deliberately shut down any feelings between us because feelings would ruin us.

His thumb rocked with single-minded determination to make me come.

My mind scrambled with the primitive instinct to mate.

I held onto his hoodie, throwing my head back and giving him utmost control.

Fireworks crackled in my blood.

I opened my legs wider, taking more of him. He sucked in a loud breath, stretching me, taking me. Our rhythm became wilder, brutally deep.

"Fuck, O. I need you to come." His hips rocked against me; his thumb pressed with pain.

Fireworks became comets.

Comets became a supernova.

My neck arched, rising off the sheet. "God—" Searing pleasure split me in two as he drove as hard as he could. My core squeezed around him, over and over and *over.*

I came and it brought a whole suitcase of fears.

I cried out as another wave caught me by surprise.

And Gil lost it.

His lips descended on mine, hips surged upward, and he fucked me with mind-numbing need.

He gave up part of his humanity. He traded decorum for death. The death of love between us. The sheet crashed down from the wall where it'd been pinned, floating over us as his hips slapped against mine.

I couldn't breathe. I couldn't think.

All I could do was hold onto him as he broke.

His heart thundered against mine.

He seemed possessed, entranced, utterly broken.

Another wave of paradise shot up my spine, hinting that one orgasm wasn't enough.

He felt it.

His green eyes gleamed, and his hips pounded unforgivingly into mine, punishing me all over again, dragging me up the mountain with him, coiling me, tightening me.

His cock grew bigger inside me, hardening, thickening.

And then, there was nowhere else to go.

We plummeted together.

Giving in to the rapture of release, knowing the minute it was over...we were too.

Chapter Twenty-Eight

Olin

I WOKE TO heart pangs and belly pain.

My core was bruised from the rough lovemaking we'd indulged in.

My skin still held stars and feathers and a school of fish swimming up my leg.

Smudges ruined perfection and fingerprints smeared crisp lines, I didn't need physical reminders that we'd had sex…my body shouted the truth in its painted defilement.

Along with my skin, my apartment had a paint-spattered sheet on the floor and evidence of emotional carnage.

But Gil had gone.

Along with his box of brushes, colours, and tricks.

We'd said physically what we couldn't say verbally, and he'd left the moment we'd untangled ourselves and our futures, then said a faint farewell at the door.

If I let myself think about him, agony was a sharp arrow waiting to stab me in the chest and deliver a bolt of poison. So, I did my best to keep him on the outskirts of my mind. To stretch out the kink in my spine and climb into the shower. To wash away the final body paint I would ever wear.

It didn't help that I stopped in front of the mirror before sluicing his art down the drain. Or that I traced the many images hidden upon my skin. Of a peach blanket with a baby tied to a kite string. Of a boy holding a bunch of wildflowers outside a house he couldn't enter. Of a man watching a woman through a window he couldn't open.

Of so many things that Gil treasured and couldn't have.

Other images were ruined beyond recognition, bruised from

reality to muddy memory.

But through the smears, I noticed dead girls painted and hushed upon my thigh. Tombstones decorated my hipbones. A prison cell glowed beneath my ribs. And through it all, a calligraphy stroke of letters looped around my belly like jewellery.

Love is misery. Lust is loss. Family is my failure.

Tears fell and mixed with hot water as I stumbled into the shower.

I cried all over again for things I could no longer differentiate. Every incident had blended into one painful despair.

I did my best to stop my tears as I finished washing away Gil's confessions. I tried to reset my scattered thoughts and focus on the monotonous and uninspiring task of heading to work.

Once dressed, I straightened up my place, folded the ruined sheet, realigned the furniture, and found my phone abandoned on the kitchen bench.

It flashed with a message.

A dangerous, deadly message.

And I made the stupid mistake of clicking on it.

Gil: *O, I have so much to say about last night. So much that it's literally killing me that I no longer have the luxury of talking to you. I asked for closure. I got it. I have to be happy with what happened. I know you said you didn't want to see the video of me painting you, but it's attached below...just in case. And don't worry, I deleted the part where we slept together before uploading to a public internet page.*

The good news? The video garnered a few positive comments before the haters turned up, and I received an email about a commission. Obviously, it's too late to do, but it gives me hope that I might be able to resurrect my business when I'm free again.

I love you.

Thank you.

For everything.

Tears welled and spilled as I clicked on the video.

The emotion I'd been hiding from found me, slipping through my ribs with its tiny pitchforks of agony.

It's over.

How could it be over?

My tears ran faster.

I didn't have the strength to watch what we did last night. To witness Gil hood-obscured and in his element of painting while I stood stiff and vulnerable as his canvas.

But I also couldn't turn it off.

My knees gave out, buckling me into a chair as the video skipped forward, increasing minutes into a blur of brushes and colour.

I swiftly transformed from normal human to some midnight, galaxy wearing goddess with power over birds, fishes, and every other symbol of secrecy that Gil adorned me with. I popped against the black background, giving the watcher no hint of where we were.

We were in a black hole, utterly alone and unfindable.

My heart stopped beating as the video suddenly slowed to normal speed, and Gil kissed me.

I watched as I kissed him back. I couldn't tear my eyes away from my hands as I pushed off his hood, revealing the Master of Trickery to the world.

He looked regal.

He looked ruined.

Truth blazed with its own colour on the video. Vicious and vibrant, a hue far too bright to ignore.

How could I make anyone believe I wasn't in love with him—that I wouldn't do anything in my power still to help him—when the evidence bled from the screen?

It was so blisteringly obvious.

So painfully real.

No lie could hide it.

No paint could camouflage it.

I was in love with him.

He was in love with me.

There was no end or over for that kind of bond.

Gil had let me walk away because he didn't have a choice. In a couple of days, he was stepping into a courtroom and might not walk out as a free man for decades. He'd let me go because he felt it was the best thing for me, even with blatant evidence that we were made for each other.

That our bodies weren't the only thing joining last night.

That our souls had found each other as kids and had been claimed ever since.

I was an idiot.

A stupid, *stupid* fool to think I could find happiness overseas with new people, new places, new me.

Gil would always be the key to my happiness, no matter what he'd done.

And the fact that he'd set me free showed just how deeply he cared.

Showed that my happiness meant more to him than his own.

Showed that Gilbert Clark had grown up and shattered the ice that'd protected him since his childhood.

More tears rolled as our video kiss hissed with passion and heartbreak.

Everything we'd done last night replayed in crystal detail.

The pain.

The ecstasy.

The *realness*.

It hadn't been sex. It'd been a testament to soul-mates, consuming two hearts, knitting two bodies into one.

I trembled as Gil entered me.

Last night, it'd felt raw and violent. A claiming plunge that wrenched my back off the sheet and made me cling to him.

Now, I knew the truth.

I paused the video.

I froze time as Gil's body joined with mine, and our eyes locked onto each other's.

The way he mounted me *was* raw and violent, but it was also achingly vulnerable and intense. The way he curled over me in protection. The way he kissed me with devotion. The way his body worshipped mine with every apology and sweetness he could.

We'd made love last night.

We'd made promises we hadn't been aware of.

Promises that couldn't be broken.

Chapter Twenty-Nine

Gil

WALKING INTO THE courtroom seemed simple enough. Shoes on feet and suit on body, striding into a room just like any other day.

But it wasn't any other day.

It was judgement day, and I was fucking terrified.

For the rest of the week, after I'd painted O, I'd avoided all thoughts of her and focused entirely on my daughter.

O and I…we were over.

And soon, I would have to say goodbye to my child too.

Olive sensed my urgency for her to accept Justin's care. Her suspicious little nature turned into clingy need, wanting to be near me in ways she'd never done before.

And to be fair, I clung back.

I held on for all I was worth because I knew this day was coming.

My days were entirely Olive's. I did whatever she wanted. I set up a contract with Justin that I would pay back whatever he spent on Olive's care while I was gone. I even had an enquiry for a commission or two, thanks to the video I'd shared of painting O. I'd told her the truth that I hadn't shared the part where we'd had sex.

But I had shared the part where she pushed down my hood, revealing me to the online world, and the exquisite agony of our first kiss.

I wanted to show the people who wanted me dead that I was human too.

That yes, I'd made mistakes.

A fucking lot of mistakes.

And I would continue to make them, just like them.

But I was prepared to answer for those mistakes without needing death threats and pure hate.

"You all good?"

I looked across at my lawyer. Brad Scott was a typical lifer in a suit. I'd met him twice now, being open and honest in his office, learning his lesson on how I'd be torn to shreds on the stand. For a crown appointed counsel, he gave me confidence that I wasn't just another schmuck to half-heartedly fight for.

His face had switched from trying not to judge me for killing four women to curiosity in how it'd all fallen into place.

He trusted that I hadn't been the one to murder innocence and now had a thin vein of pride that I'd killed the bastard who'd done it.

I was under no illusion that today would not have a happy ending for me, but I hoped he could convince the jury that what I said was the truth.

I had no intention of lying, embellishing, or using tricks to avoid my punishment.

I just didn't want to have to pay more than what I owed.

"Yeah, I'm okay." My voice was rough and eyes gritty from refusing to break in front of Olive. Saying goodbye had bled my heart dry. I hadn't recovered from ending it with O. I'd fallen to my knees losing her, and now I'd collapsed into hell losing my daughter.

"You have things in place like we talked about?"

I nodded. "I filed my will—not that there's anything to bequeath—and signed that contract with my friend who is officially Olive's caregiver while I'm gone. Child Protective Services have been dealt with and are happy with the arrangement. I did what you said."

"Good."

Silence fell between us again.

I'd made Justin swear to stay away from court. To spend the day with Olive and focus on taking her to school for re-orientation. She'd officially start back next week, once my fate was decided.

Justin had once again proven to be a friend who deserved a seat on the council of heaven. He was so selfless that it sometimes seemed sinister. I caught myself searching for an ulterior motive, some sign he was evil and running a long game like my uncle.

I almost wanted him to turn out to be a bad guy because I

couldn't accept that there were people as good as him. As good as O. They were the same. Two generous, loyal people who shouldn't have to put up with the likes of me.

"Does your kid know what's happening?" Brad asked, shuffling his legal pad and pen into orderly fashion on the desk. We sat in court, waiting for everything to begin.

I cleared my throat. "I told her I would still be close and that she can visit but that I won't be living with her for a while."

"How did it go?"

I laughed painfully. "Awful."

"Always is." He gave me a pitiful look. "Just remember, nothing lasts forever. Good, bad, terrible—it all passes in the end."

I didn't reply.

Last night, while hugging Olive, I'd done my best not to suffocate her, knowing my allotment of hugs had come to an end. Justin had given us privacy, vowing he'd guard her while I could not.

I'd never felt more destitute as I had in that moment. Asking another man to look after my own flesh and blood. I didn't have shit in my bank account, and I didn't have shit in my human worth to ever pay him back.

My heart pounded as more people trickled into the courtroom. Brad Scott had fought many cases, representing low-level criminals and white-collar, but I doubted he'd dealt with a case where the public stood outside the courthouse, demanding justice by cutting off my hands so I could never paint and then tying me to a tree to bleed out.

The family of the girls who'd been killed sat silently on the benches, waiting to hear my fate. A few journalists with pens poised over notepads and recording devices also waited for the show. It wasn't a big audience—probably court requested so emotions didn't get out of hand—but I had no support or friends in the sea of people who wanted me to die.

Justin was elsewise occupied.

And I hadn't told O what time I would face judgement.

I didn't want her to see my end.

My gaze danced around the space, not making eye contact with anyone. The overall atmosphere was of death and decay, ready to send me to a coffin rather than a cell.

The jury hadn't come in yet. I didn't know how courts worked or what I was in for.

I would learn as it unfolded and then suffer the consequences.

"How will this go?" I linked my hands together, thinking of the paint supplies and boxes that I'd put into storage that Justin had in his apartment building. I thought about Olive and her pretty smile and not being able to tuck her into bed tonight. I thought about the waste of a life all because I'd always been so fucking naïve and too proud to ask for help.

I wanted help today.

But I didn't know how to ask for it.

"Well, you're slightly different. The public have put pressure on the system which is why your court date has been rushed. You'll be judged by a twelve-person jury. Once they're sworn in, the prosecution will present the evidence. Call a few witnesses if they have any. Maybe call you to the stand. And then, it's my turn. The judge has already read the case files but we'll give our side of the story as candidly and as truthfully as you did when we rehearsed the other day. Okay?"

I nodded even though nausea ran through me. "Okay."

"Good." He brushed lint off his navy suit. "Once everything has been presented, the jury will deliberate, and the judge will oversee the verdict."

"And then I go to prison."

"Maybe."

"But the chances of me going home tonight are nil."

His eyes narrowed, not sugar-coating or making false promises. "You committed murder, Mr. Clark. You admitted to it. Unless a miracle happens today, you're serving time. The question is how much and in what form."

I settled back in the hard chair as more people dribbled in. Time took on a strange nightmare quality. My body felt as if quicksand sucked at me, sinking into the floor.

A loud clang sounded behind me as the double doors of the crown court were closed. An official clerk asked us to rise for the honourable judge, and the selected jury trickled in from the backroom to be sworn in to assess me fairly but harshly.

By the time the judge pinned me with her icy blue eyes, her age wearing lines around her lips and white wig sitting perfectly on her head, I'd died, revived, and waited for death all over again.

Shifting in the chair, I pulled out a picture of Olive that I'd tucked inside my wallet. A printed piece of normal paper where the colours were wish-wash and paper creased, the image snapped on my phone and printed on Justin's printer.

It was us two nights ago while we'd sat at Justin's dining room table with the views over the Birmingham skyline while I taught her yet another technique of bending paint to her will. She was so smart. So talented. She could scale any goal and crush any dream.

She'd survived a year without me.

She could survive more, especially now that she had Justin looking out for her.

My thumb traced over her lovely face as the prosecution began presenting the evidence. I didn't listen. I already knew what happened to the girls as they'd slipped into drawn-out death. I already knew how Jeffery took his last breath.

I just kept my eyes on my daughter and waited for my turn to tell a story.

* * * * *

"Mr. Clark, as you're aware, today has been a long day and we've seen and heard some disturbing things. It's public knowledge that the family of the deceased want you to pay for what happened to their daughters, as they should—as anyone should when a loved one is stolen from them." Brad Scott paused, walking around with his hands in his suit pockets, looking at the jury, judge, and audience. "I'm an upstander of justice, and I'm also sworn to represent you to the best of my ability. Since taking you on as a client, I've had emails and phone calls, death threats and curses if I get you off what you deserve."

I swallowed, risking a quick look at the jury. They sat stone-faced and already resolute on their verdict, thanks to the overwhelming evidence presented by the prosecution. Sitting in the box in front of court was a terrifying place to be. I was on display. I had nowhere to hide. No way to stop the inevitable.

For four hours, they'd thrown every fact and grotesque incident that'd happened, sticking it entirely to me. Even I couldn't deny the facts—the man who orchestrated those poor girls' deaths was a monster and deserved to rot in hell.

Only problem was, I was only half that monster.

Brad continued, "Now that we've heard the evidence, I want to hear your version of events because it's not as black and white as the prosecution suggests."

I swallowed again, preparing to be honest about my life for the first time. When Brad had walked me through how things were going to go and what he expected me to say, I'd been against it. Why did they need to know my past? What did my high-school years have to do with now? But he'd insisted and...I'd agreed.

Scanning the sea of angry, judging faces, I did my best to stay unaffected. To deliver what was needed and accept the consequences.

O.

I froze.

I did a double take.

Olin Moss sat in the middle of the audience.

My gaze snagged with hers.

I locked in place and was owned entirely by her.

Fuck, seeing her here.

What...what is she doing here?

She bit her lip, her eyes wide and worried. How long had she sat there, obscured by the crowd? Why had she come?

She shouldn't be here supporting me. I'd set her free, goddammit.

"Mr. Clark? Can you inform the court who Jeffrey Clark was and why you killed him?"

A murmur went around the silent jury, tearing my gaze from O's. I had so much to admit. Why had it been easier confessing to total strangers than it did to someone I loved?

My eyes sought hers again, and I found strength that I should've found years ago.

She was here.

She hadn't left me.

Fuck, I loved her.

Sitting taller, I balled my hands and prepared to answer.

To admit...everything.

"Jeffrey Clark was my father's brother. I'd never met him until a few years ago. He came looking for me when my father died."

"Your father who died of alcohol poisoning and raised you in a whore house?"

I didn't flinch. "Yes."

"And Jeffrey gained your trust?"

"Unfortunately."

"Why did he go out of his way to make you trust him if his sole intention was to kill women?"

"At the time, I thought it was because he was family. I didn't know he was a psychopath who killed my father's whores.

I didn't know who he truly was and wanted to believe not all my family was bad."

"But what he told you turned out to be a lie, correct?"

"Not everything. He said he was a car painter and detailer—that was true. He said he shared my drive to create art—that was also true. But everything else was just a ploy to take my money—money I only started earning because of his tutoring and pushing me into a business idea that I would never have had on my own."

"And what business was that?"

I avoided looking at O, feeling suddenly seedy. "Painting mostly naked women for large advertising campaigns."

"Why didn't Jeffrey just do that himself?"

I shrugged. "Not sure. He had the talent to do it. He painted the fourth girl, after all."

An electrified murmur shot around the court. Brad held up his hand for quiet, continuing his line of questioning.

I added before he could speak, "When my business became successful, he wanted what I had. What he didn't realise was I would've shared it all with him. I was unbelievably grateful for his guidance. He didn't have to take it by force."

"How did Jeffrey Clark take it by force, even when you ran out of income?"

"He kidnapped my daughter and blackmailed me."

"Why didn't you go to the police?"

"Because I didn't want them to know Olive's origins."

"Why not?"

"Because I didn't want them tracking down her birth mother and forcing me to give up custody."

O flinched. But she never looked away. Never left me hanging or alone.

Brad consulted his notes for a second, asking, "The mother of your child is called Jane Tallup, correct?"

"Yes."

"And who is Jane Tallup to you?"

"Your honour, what is the point in dragging up the past?" The prosecution's lawyer interrupted. "This isn't relevant to the case."

"I beg to differ, your honour. It has everything to do with the case." Brad scowled.

The female judge peered at both lawyers then me before finally nodding, "Carry on, Mr. Clark."

I cleared my throat. "Jane Tallup was my teacher at high-school."

"And she's the mother of your daughter."

I nodded again, annoyed at his repetitive question but aware of why he did it. To add more power to the punch line.

The court moved restlessly, no doubt thinking I'd forced myself onto her.

That I was a rapist as well as a killer.

Brad paused, then said, "She raped you when you were a teenager, correct? She alienated you from your friends, forbid you contact with the girl you were in love with, and molested you."

I curled my hands. "I was a stupid kid who should've spoken out but didn't."

"That sounds like you're blaming yourself for what happened."

"I'm blaming myself for the consequences of not telling people when I had the chance."

"Hurry it along," the judge muttered. "Get to the point."

The jury shifted on their chairs, their attention fully on me. My eyes stayed on O's hazel ones, safe as long as I just focused on her. I wanted to do this. I needed to be honest. To finally purge the rot inside me, to eradicate the poison I'd carried alone for so long, but it didn't mean it was easy.

My life was full of regrets.

Today would not be one of them.

"So, not only were you raped in your youth, but your teacher—an adult in a position of power—stripped you of safety and dumped a baby on you...all because she didn't want it?"

I nodded but then shook my head, unable to let Olive be talked about as if she wasn't wanted. "Olive might not have been wanted by her mother, and I might have been a vulnerable son of a bitch, but the moment I held her, I knew I loved her. She was wanted by me with all my heart, I just didn't know it until I met her."

My lawyer strolled calmly around the courtroom, nodding as if what I said made perfect sense. "Once you met your daughter, you left your home and family behind."

"I did."

"Why?"

"Because I didn't want anything to jeopardise Olive's future. My father wasn't a good role model; my family environment was abusive and unstructured. The only good thing in my life was my girlfriend who I'd hurt when I'd tried to do the right thing by breaking up with her. I was prepared to walk away so Olive had things I never did. Safety and good food and a father who cared about her."

"Very noble," the prosecution lawyer muttered.

I glared at him. "I just did what any father would do."

"Not every father." Brad pinned me to the chair. "Tell the court what happened the night you confronted Jeffrey with Olin Moss as his next victim."

A rise of energy swept around the jury as I admitted, "He shot me in the back, leaving me for dead."

"So your uncle tries to kill you and your father regularly used you as a punching bag." Brad peered at the jury. "I'd say family hasn't been kind to you, yet you did everything humanly possible to protect and claim back your daughter."

"Of course. I would never stop fighting for her."

"Would you kill another to protect her?"

He'd warned me he'd start sweet and swiftly divert into dark. I'd been waiting for the hard questions but it still made my heart skip. "I think anyone would if it was justified."

"Did you kill those innocent girls?"

I sat taller, keeping my hands on my thighs. "No, I did not. My uncle, Jeffrey Clark, did."

"The same Jeffrey Clark you killed?"

I nodded. "I ended his life for killing those girls as well as hurting Olin Moss and kidnapping my daughter."

My eyes searched out O's. Her skin had turned white and lips bitten with nervousness.

"So you admit that you *are* a murderer."

"Of a man who'd murdered girls, blackmailed me, and threatened rape to the only woman I've ever loved, yes. I am. I killed him."

A buzz of energy came from the jury again.

Brad ignored them. "But you didn't kill the other girls?"

"No."

His eyes narrowed. "Then why was the same brand and batch number of your paint found on their skin?"

I braced myself. "Because I painted them."

The buzz of energy became a tidal wave of tension.

I stayed focused on my lawyer, trusting him to navigate through the next chaos.

"How is it that you painted them and didn't stop them from

being killed? If you painted them for your uncle to murder, you knew what their fate was. That makes you an accessory. You had a moral and civil obligation to report the crime."

"I didn't know."

My lawyer scoffed before the jury could. Such a weak and useless answer. But it was the truth, regardless. "You didn't know? How did you not know? You painted them to match the undergrowth where they were killed."

"He did that."

"You're saying he staged each murder depending on how the girls were painted?"

"Yes."

"You do realise how this sounds? That you're asking the jury to believe in an unbelievable excuse that you didn't …know?"

This was where he wanted me to play my trump card.

I'd rehearsed my paragraph. I had my truth. It wouldn't set me free, but it would grant some resemblance of peace.

Looking again at O, I said, "I've done many commissions over the past few years. Some are garish and bright, some are fantastical and mythical, others are natural and pure. Those are the jobs I love the most. The ones where I get to use nature as my palette. The designs where foliage and shadow, flora and fauna consume the model and make her a part of their world."

Some of the jurors rolled their eyes. Others stared at me with doubt. Only a few kept judgement from showing.

"The girls were painted because of me. I can show you the invoices and emails requesting that sort of camouflage. I can show you where the photo shoot was taken and even present a couple of magazines where the photos were used. What I can't show you is the location of where Jeffrey Clark put them because if you look very closely, they weren't designed to go with that body paint."

"So they were canvases you'd hired?"

"Yes." I nodded. "If you look at their bank accounts, you'll see payment for the time we spent together."

"How did your uncle grab them before they'd showered off their paint?"

I pinched the bridge of my nose, cursing once again for being an idiot. "The number of canvases who ask if they can keep the paint on to show loved ones before washing is extremely high. I always offer them a shower before they leave.

Some take it, but most don't. I'm not responsible for them when they walk out the door."

"No, but you are responsible if they get killed."

I hung my head. "I'll always feel guilty for playing even a small part in their demise. I'm guilty for a great many things. But I didn't kill them. I didn't know they'd been targeted until it was too late. When the ransom demands came in, I always paid. I paid countless times and he held off killing—or at least, I hope he did. When the girls started showing up, I didn't know it was my paint they wore. After all, Jeffrey taught me. He was just as capable of the artwork as I was."

"But you had a suspicion?"

"By the second girl, yes...I worried."

"And why didn't you go to the police then? When you knew lives were being taken?"

"I honestly can't answer that." I sighed. "I was still afraid of Olive being taken away from me, but she'd already been taken so that wasn't such a big restriction. I guess, I knew I was in too deep. And if I was arrested, how could I keep working and paying him? How could I prevent him from killing Olive if I was in jail? She would die."

"So you kept paying him, hoping you could stop him yourself?"

"Yes. I paid until I was bankrupt. I sold my warehouse, my furniture, everything I could. On the nights when the demands came in, I'd trawl the streets until dawn, looking for him, searching for Olive, for a girl he might have taken. I walked up and down the length of England. I explored countless forests and estates. I kept trying, but I always failed."

"Is that why your footprints were found at the location of the fourth girl?"

"Yes. Jeffrey gave me her location. I hadn't painted anyone in camouflage that week and hoped...I hoped she'd still be alive to save." My head hung. "But he hadn't waited for nature to kill her. He'd done it himself somewhere else, then painted her to match the bluebells where he dumped her body."

"And you didn't report this?"

I winced, accepting how it sounded. "No."

More noise in the court. More hate.

Hearing it out loud was worse. Everything I'd done, I'd done for Olive. I'd sacrificed everything I could—my fortune, my freedom, my very fucking soul. But it wasn't up to me to play

God and let those girls die.

I *had* killed them. I'd played executioner just by keeping silent.

That was my true crime.

Staying silent when a teacher took advantage of me, staying silent when O came back into my life, staying silent when my daughter was taken.

Fuck.

Silence was my mistake.

For everything.

Brad paced for a moment, working up to his next question. "How many girls did you save by paying his ransoms?" He stopped and looked at me. "Do you know?"

I shook my head. "I can only go by what he told me. But he was a killer before he took Olive. I don't know how many lives he took while he had her."

"Just a guess is fine."

"Seven, eight? Enough to know at least my money saved a few girls, even if I couldn't save my daughter."

"And when you found him that night, when he went back on his word to trade the woman you loved for your daughter, you decided enough was enough?"

Temper curled through me. My mind shot back to the night in question. The guilt in my veins. The self-disgust in my heart. "Yes. It was pre-emptive."

"How so?"

"I bought succinylcholine, also known as sux, on the black market. It's a drug they use in anaesthesia."

"And you injected him?"

"Yes."

"But you almost died before you could."

"I did." I rubbed my side, poking at the soreness that still lingered. "I almost lost the two people I love most in the world with my idiotic behaviour. I thought I could fix what I'd caused. I tried to do the right thing."

"By killing someone."

"By killing a monster who'd already taken far too many lives."

Brad nodded and turned to face the jury. He spread his arms and delivered his closing statement. "Gilbert Clark is a boy from a bad neighbourhood, born to an abusive father, and someone who prefers to suffer in silence than ask for help. He's admitted to the crime he did. He's willing to pay for taking a life of a man who murdered an unknown number of innocents and kidnapped his daughter for over a year. A man who took every penny he had and left him homeless because he didn't want to involve the police in case his daughter was taken away for the second time by the courts. He's also a man who dedicated his time teaching art part-time at his daughter's school—even though his childhood was traumatised by a teacher who raped him. Living through these traumas has had profound psychological effects. He's now bankrupt after a year of failing to protect his daughter. Overall, Gilbert Clark is not a bad man. He's just one who fell into bad situations and didn't ask for help. Thank you."

Nodding at the judge, he added, "That's all, your honour." To me, he said, "You may leave the stand."

I stood, searched for O in the crowd one last time, then returned to my seat for sentencing.

Chapter Thirty

Olin

"ALL RISE FOR Honourable Judge Hoft."

I stood with the crowd, gritty-eyed and heart-racing, staring at Gil's back.

I hadn't slept at all last night.

I doubted he did either.

I worried that I hadn't been called to testify. If that was a good or a bad thing.

I worried about so many, many things.

After his time on the stand yesterday, the judge adjourned for the next day, giving the jury time to mull it over and for any other evidence to be presented when it wasn't so late in the day. I'd waited for the police to pop by again—prepared to battle on his behalf.

But no one knocked on my door, and I'd forced myself to stay away from Justin's, even though I basically had to chain myself to my apartment not to intrude on Gil and Olive's final night together. He hadn't expected the extra night. And I wouldn't get in the middle of an already excruciating goodbye with his daughter.

Instead, Justin had text me and filled me in. How Gil had told Olive the truth about what he faced today. About how jail worked and why he was going away. He said Olive had taken it okay but he feared how things would go when Gil didn't go home.

I'd tried to drown out my worry about Gil with concern about my own life. I hated my job. I despised my apartment. I was done living here alone and doing my best to settle for things

I didn't want.

Gil was almost out of my reach.

Justin and Olive would become close.

I wasn't needed in their future anymore.

But that didn't stop me from returning to the crown court the next day. It didn't prevent me from sitting stiff with goosebumps as Gil and his lawyer returned in suits that didn't have a speck of paint on them.

He'd never looked so presentable or so tragic.

His hair was tamed off his face as he sat in front of the audience. His hands remained balled on the table even when his lawyer scooted closer to talk to him.

The aura of the court was hushed and waiting.

Judge Holt glanced over the jury as she settled on her podium. Smoothing her gown, she asked, "Is there any other evidence or closing statements from either party?"

Sweat rolled down my spine as both lawyers shook their heads.

She nodded and turned to the jury. "In that case, do you have a verdict?"

A slim woman with a blonde plait nodded. "We do, your honour."

"And?"

The woman opened an envelope.

Everyone held their breath.

I couldn't take my eyes off Gil as he stiffened and braced himself.

The woman locked eyes with him and read in crisp firm voice. "We find the defendant, Gilbert Clark, guilty for the murder of Jeffrey Clark."

The judge scribbled something down before looking up. "And the four painted girls?"

Tears prickled my eyes.

I wanted so much to hug Gil. To tell him I'd changed my mind. That I did have the strength to be his…if he still wanted me.

"Not guilty," the woman announced.

Gil's spine rolled. His hands dove into his hair, his elbows wedged on the table.

His lawyer patted his back with a rough slap.

The judge waited for the murmurs of the court to die down before rapping her gavel loudly. Her steely gaze caught Gil's.

"Mr. Clark. After your testimony and the evidence presented yesterday, I can say you are not a threat to society. You killed out of self-defense of those you loved, and, although your paint obscured the girls who were killed, you aren't directly responsible. However, you did take a life, and for that, you must pay. Taking the law into your own hands always comes with consequences. If you'd spoken up about what had happened, those four young women might still be alive today."

She shuffled a few pieces of paper. "The court demands you pay a fine to the families of the deceased of four hundred thousand pounds, one hundred thousand per family. You will not be charged with accessory before the act which carries up to fifteen years and instead will serve five years with one hundred hours of community service upon release."

Her gavel slammed down.

It was done.

My ears rang with the sentencing.

Five years?

Five years?

Such a long time, but really…incredibly short for murder.

He'd been lucky.

Life had finally been kind.

"Bailiff, please escort Mr. Clark to his new home. Thank you, jury, for your help in delivering justice today." The judge stood. "Court dismissed."

People sprang from their seats, journalists crammed to listen to what Gil's lawyer said to him, and I wriggled my way through the crowd to say goodbye.

All over again.

Gil seemed to sense my closeness, turning to catch me from the crowd before he was ushered out and into places I couldn't go.

I searched his eyes for panic or pain, but I only saw relief.

"You okay?" I asked softly, barely audible above the hum of other conversation.

He nodded. "I don't want to leave Olive. But I'm okay with serving what I owe."

"Five years is a long time."

"It is. But if it helps rid some of my guilt, then I'll do it without complaint." His eyes dropped to my lips. "My one huge regret in this is that I hurt you so much, O. There's no punishment that can take that guilt away."

My mouth went dry.

I ached with so many things.

Justin and Olive should be here.

They should be allowed to hug him, so he wasn't shuffled off without knowing he was loved.

Words crowded on my tongue.

Promises and commitments that I wanted so much to give to him.

But the bailiff pushed Gil forward, breaking our connection, ending the time we had.

"I'll come visit you." I walked with him on the opposite side of the rail, getting caught up in journalists and tape recorders shoved in Gil's direction.

He smiled softly. "I don't expect it." He held my eyes as the guard opened a side door and ushered him through. "Be happy, O. Find a new dream and forget me."

The door shut.

Gil was gone.

Chapter Thirty-One

Olin

MY APARTMENT WAS terrifyingly lonely.

After having Gil and Olive share it, after being painted and made love to, after all the sleepless nights thinking about him, the walls were ever more depressing. The sparse furnishing and lack of home—the aching loneliness...everything was a disease.

A disease I couldn't suffer anymore.

It hurt.

It stung.

I can't stay here.

All I could think about was Gil locked up for five years, his hardship of figuring out how to pay such a massive fine, and the knowledge that even when he was released, his punishment wasn't over.

I was being so selfish. So what if my flat made me claustrophobic with the need to run? Gil didn't have the luxury of his own place anymore and he *couldn't* run, no matter how much he wanted to.

God.

I hugged myself, unable to stop thinking about Gil in prison. Gil being shoved into inmate population. Gil dying inside a cell.

What about his art?

What about his need to create?

What about Olive?

I...I can't do this.

I needed to leave.

Immediately.

Grabbing my handbag, I swept out of my flat in the same cream blouse and black skirt I'd worn to court. Fighting tears, I summoned an Uber to take me to Justin's.

He answered the door before I could even knock, yanking me into his arms, his nose buried in my hair, his body tight and tall. "You holding up okay?"

I nodded, breathing him in, finding some resemblance of strength. "How's Olive?"

Pulling away, Justin closed the door and led me into his minimalist bachelor pad. The two-bedroom apartment had epic views over the Birmingham business district and the twinkling lights looked too merry for my liking.

Apart from the colouring pencils on his breakfast bar and a small purple hoodie thrown on his couch, it still looked like he lived alone.

Now, he lived with a little girl.

A little girl he was godfather to for a friend serving time for murder.

"She's about as expected." He cocked his head to the spare room which had become hers.

"Do you mind if I see her?"

"Not at all." He let his arm slip from around my shoulders. "She'd love that. She's learned to trust me but she still doesn't like living alone with me. She's going to take it hard. If I'm honest, I'm kind of terrified that I'm going to set her back. That I should find a good therapist so she has someone she can talk to when it all becomes too much."

I didn't really have an answer for that. "You're already doing a great job, Justin. You've got this."

"Not so sure about that." He squeezed the back of his neck. "Go on. Go see her."

Giving him a slight smile, I headed down the corridor and knocked on Olive's door. "Olive, it's me? Can I come in?"

Her tears were my answer.

I turned the handle and entered. Moving swiftly to her bed, I sat beside her as she cried with her face buried into a pillow. My hand rested between her tiny shoulder blades, rubbing soft circles. "It's okay. Everything is going to be okay."

She didn't look up, just cried harder. "*How?* Daddy's in prison. You're going away. And Justin works all the time, and I don't like the babysitter." Her cheeks glowed red as she looked up, anger and agony in her grey gaze. "I don't want this. I want to go home with Dad. I want him to come home with me. I miss him." Her tears became sobs as I pulled her into my arms. "I miss him *sooooo* much. How much longer do we have to live apart?"

I rocked her, kissing the top of her head. "Not long. Once this is over, you'll both be free to live the rest of your life together if you want."

Olive sniffed. "But five years is *forever.*"

It is.

It's so, so long.

"It will go by fast if you stay busy." I said that for her benefit but also reminded myself too. "You're going back to school. You'll make new friends and learn more skills. And when he's out, you can paint together all the time. A true family business."

"But it's so *long.*" Her shoulders drooped, more tears splashing. "I don't think I can do it."

"You can. You will." I kissed her head again. "It's a long time, but Justin is here. He'll take care of you and you can still see your dad. You can go visit him."

"Wait...I can?" Her eyes lit up instantly. "Can we go now?"

I didn't know what prison protocol was but I guessed they'd need him to settle into his new home before visitation. I stroked her glossy hair with a gentle smile. "I'll find out when you can."

"Can you come too?" She threw her arms around me, squeezing me tighter than I expected. *"Please?"*

Justin appeared in the door frame, his lips twisted into a half-smile, his body reclining against the wall.

I held his gaze as I squeezed Olive back. "Of course, I'll come for however long I'm in town."

My promise to leave tasted like ash in my mouth.

Could I leave?

Where would I go?

Why would I go when this poor little girl needed care?

She has Justin.

Gil set you free.

You have to leave.

If I stood any chance of finding who I truly was, I had to open my wings.

But...

What if I don't want to fly away? What if what I want is right here?

"I don't want you to go. All the people I love leave me."

Olive pulled away, her face deadly serious and determined even as crystal tears rained. "Move in with us. Don't go away. Please, *please* don't go."

I froze.

Justin stiffened.

Olive arched her chin, defiant and ready to fight. "I like Justin. He's way nicer than Uncle Jeffrey, but…I don't want to be alone without my dad. I liked staying at your place. If you won't move in here, can I come live with you instead?"

Oh, no.

I tried to apologise silently to Justin over Olive's head. I didn't mean to destabilise her new home with him. I didn't want to ruin their fragile bond.

But Justin shrugged, saying quietly, "There's plenty of room if you want to join us, O."

My heart crashed blindly. "But I have an apartment."

"An apartment where your lease is almost up and you weren't going to renew it."

Damn for confiding in him.

"You know I'm planning on travelling."

"You need time to save and decide where to go. You could save more by moving in here."

"I wouldn't live here for free, Justin. I'd pay rent, same as any other place."

He nodded, appeasing me. "That's fine. But you have to admit, it makes logical sense."

I tried to think up another excuse why moving in with Gil's only friend and his lonely daughter was a bad idea. The truth was, it was a *terrible* idea because it kept me in Gil's stratosphere.

Justin seemed to sense my thoughts. "He let you go that night…didn't he?"

I jerked. "How do you know about that?"

"I didn't until now." He sighed. "When I saw him the next morning, he seemed different. Sad, definitely, but relieved too. Relieved that he'd set you free and wouldn't mess up your life any more than he already had."

"Isn't it up to me if I want him to mess it up or not?"

He chuckled. "I suppose." His eyes glowed with questions. "So…are you? Going to wait for him?" He looked at Olive. "Are you really thinking of putting your life on hold for five years?"

Olive watched us, cheeks glistening, chest heaving from her sobs. But she didn't interrupt, almost as if she knew this was one of the most important conversations of my life.

Justin was forcing me to answer a question I didn't know how. Asking me if I would wait for the boy I'd been waiting for my entire existence.

Could I wait?

Should I?

Why would I when there was so much that'd gone wrong between us?

I wanted to move on.

I *needed* to move on.

I wouldn't survive five years pining after him.

And yet...

The thought of walking away, of finding him via a job advertisement, then just leaving?

God.

I knew what it was like to miss Gil.

I'd learned that lesson many, many times in the years we'd spent apart.

But that was yet another reason I *should* go.

Before it was too late.

Because missing him was too painful and living in limbo too great a toll.

I slouched, running my hand through Olive's hair. "I honestly don't know."

He gave me a half-smile. "You don't have to decide right now. That's the beauty of this situation. Gil isn't going anywhere."

I tried to laugh—to find humour in hardship. Instead, I cuddled Olive close and kissed her crown.

"So...?" Olive blinked. "Are you staying? You can move into my room with me. Can't she, Justin?" She looked at her godfather.

"She could." He nodded. "But she can also have my room, and I can take the couch."

I scowled. "I'm not kicking you out of your bedroom, Justin."

"Ah, so you are thinking about it?"

I shrugged again. "I don't know what to do anymore."

"But you haven't made any decisions on flying away yet."

"No...I've been looking at flights, but every time I go to book, something happens."

He chuckled quietly. "Could be a sign that you're meant to

stay here."

"And here is just as complicated as there."

He sighed. "Isn't that the bitch."

I placed my hands over Olive's dainty ears. "Language, Mr. Miller."

Olive smiled through her sadness. "Dad swears far worse than that. I know all the swear words. Uncle Jeffrey said a lot of them too."

I tried to be stern. "Well, just because you know them doesn't mean you can use them."

"I know." She pouted, plucking at the comforter. "I miss Dad. Are you sure we can't go see him yet?"

"In a few days, pipsqueak," Justin said gently. "They'll need time to settle him into his new home."

"It's not a home. It's a jail." Her eyes flashed. "He should be here, with me."

"He should." Justin came in, squatting to his haunches by the bed and staring up at Olive. "But you know why he had to go away. We talked about it last night, remember? He stopped Uncle Jeffrey from doing bad things to other girls. He did the right thing by stopping him, but the rules of society means he has to pay for taking the law into his own hands."

"That's just stupid." Olive stuck out her bottom lip. "He should be given a gold sticker like they used to at school when you did good things."

I smiled, hugging her close. "How about we give him a gold sticker when we visit him."

"Can we?" She turned in my arms, her grey gaze so intelligent and fierce. "Can we go together all the time and let him know that we don't think he's bad."

My heart squeezed. "Of course."

Justin stood, looking down at both of us, his gaze pensive. "Stay at least tonight, O. You'd be doing me a huge favour." Lowering his voice, he added, "I'm not entirely sure I'm equipped to help if Olive has a panic attack tonight."

The thought of returning to an empty apartment and my chaotic thoughts was definitely not appealing. But staying would feel like a betrayal to Gil—agreeing to play families with Justin and Olive, all while he rotted in a cell.

Justin was my friend.

Platonic and sweet.

And I liked him.

But I didn't know if I could live with him.

"Is that a yes?" he asked gently.

I looked away, unable to keep his stare. "It's a maybe."

"No." Tears fell swift, Olive clung to me. Her chest rose and fell, faster and faster, her grief finding her all over again. "Don't go. *Please* don't go." Her arms were wiry and tight, locking around me.

And I did something stupid.

I let her keep me.

"Hey, don't cry." I wriggled a little in her embrace and brushed back her hair.

Her eyes met mine.

My heart pounded.

And I said, "I'll stay…for a little while."

Chapter Thirty-Two

Olin

"HELLO, GIL."

Gil stood beside the metal table in the visitation area, his love for me evident in his gaze.

My heart kicked, responded, replied.

It'd been eight days since I'd seen him.

Eight days since I'd listened to his sentencing.

Eight days since I'd come to the realisation that I was still stupidly in love with him and still stupidly unable to make a decision about my life.

I'd been a fool to think I could walk away.

I'd been an idiot to think I could stay.

Limbo was where I'd existed the past few years since my accident, and I couldn't seem to get free. Especially now that Gil had stolen the final pieces of my soul and became untouchable.

"O...hi." His voice licked around me with velveteen love. His affection no longer buried beneath ice. He seemed different. He was a ward of the crown, yet...he seemed freer than I'd ever seen. "It's so nice to see you."

The urge to hug him was agony.

But we'd been told hugging wasn't permitted. At least he'd been placed in a low security prison where face-to-face visitation was allowed and not maximum security where glass and phone was the only way to communicate.

That would've been an extra level of hell for Olive.

This was already unbearable.

I wanted to tell him what the last week had entailed.

How my lease ended in a month and I didn't know what I

should do.

How Olive had begged me to sleep in her room at Justin's four out of the past eight nights, because she couldn't cope knowing he was gone.

How Justin had offered again for me to move in, and I didn't know what my answer should be.

My tongue tied.

Desperate to tell him everything. To ask him what he wanted. To hear him say he could never let me go, and that I should stay.

And wait.

But Olive barrelled past me, stealing Gil's attention.

"Olive Oyl." His entire body softened as he fell to one knee. His arms opened wide, looking like a proud father, starving man, and pained protector all at once.

"You can't hug—"

Too late.

Olive launched into his embrace, and Gil trapped her close. He buried his face against her sweet, strawberry smelling hair, and Olive clung to him like a baby spider monkey.

They didn't obey the rules as fresh tears rolled down Olive's cheek as she leaned back to kiss Gil's five o'clock shadow.

He kissed her back before pushing her painfully away and standing. A guard caught our gaze in warning, shaking his head at our affection.

Gil cleared his throat and pinned his attention back on Olive. "Wow, little spinach. You better stop growing because I swear you're already bigger than last week."

Olive smiled but didn't laugh. Her bubbliness had faded somewhat. But her joy at being with Gil was evident. "I'll stop growing. I promise I won't grow another inch until you're home."

"Nah, you can't do that. Ignore me. You have to grow into a gorgeous creature who will kill me on a daily basis with how awesome she is."

She blushed.

Now our reunion was over, the rest of the world came back into focus. Other families chatted with loved ones, the visiting room buzzing with relief and regret at seeing each other but still torn apart.

We stood in the corner; our own private oasis.

Olive's gaze skipped over other parents with their kids,

grateful prisoners, stern guards, and doting wives and girlfriends.

The scene was sweet with so much affection but raw with so much loss.

I hoped she wouldn't have a nightmare tonight.

She'd suffered pretty bad since Gil had gone. She'd wake up screaming and only my touch could snap her out of it. If Justin tried to soothe her, he just made it worse.

On the nights that I hadn't stayed, he'd called in the early hours of the morning, begging me to talk to her. To help her know she was safe, that Jeffrey was dead, and Justin wasn't her uncle.

Child Protective Services had also called, checking in on Olive's living arrangements and providing the name of a therapist with skills in helping children overcome traumatic events. At least they were happy that Olive's best interests were upheld and allowed us to keep temporary custody.

We were all tired.

And confused on how best to make our new realities work.

Cupping Olive's cheek, Gil earned a scowl from a nearby guard. He reluctantly let her go and motioned to the metal chairs bolted to the floor. "Sit. Hang out with me."

Olive took one while Gil and I took the others.

Reaching across the table, Olive grabbed his hand and didn't let go. Even when another guard moved toward us and Gil dropped their grip beneath the table out of sight.

I waited to see if he'd be reprimanded, but the guard just narrowed his eyes and returned to his post, allowing a small kindness between father and daughter.

"Are you okay? No one is being mean?" Olive sniffed back tears.

Gil smiled and shook his head. "No, everyone has been very welcoming."

His eyes slid to mine, hiding the truth.

I doubted everyone had been welcoming. Shadows marked his jaw, and he'd sat stiffly—all signs I recognised of him being bruised from a fist.

I shivered, hating that he was locked in there and unable to escape brutality. Hating that I couldn't have a frank conversation with him because of innocent ears.

Was he truly okay? Was it true that men shed their human skins and became monsters in jail? That beatings and rapings were just a part of prison life, or was that merely conspiracies and gossip, designed to scare you into staying straight?

"Are you painting?" Olive asked, swiping her nose with the back of her hand and blinking away more tears, as if she knew her grief was hard on her father.

"No. I don't have much inspiration. My muses are all back at home." His eyes flashed to mine again, holding my stare with a need so rich and deep, if it was a colour, it would've been a decadent red.

"Will you teach other prisoners how to paint?" Olive looked around at the bland beige walls. "Maybe you can graffiti in here like our rainforest wall. It's ugly."

Gil chuckled. "That would be an improvement to the place. I agree."

I leaned back, allowing the small family to have their conversations and privacy. I'd come as chaperone to Olive as Justin was working, and I'd been given the afternoon off. Shannon wasn't as friendly these days, and the mystery of me being used as a pawn in the painted murders had worn off. No one in the office liked me because I didn't make an effort to mingle.

I didn't go there to find company. I went there to earn money, and frankly, I didn't know how much longer I could stay.

It was yet another hurdle I had to jump.

Quit my job and have no income.

Give up my lease and have no home.

Walk away from everything and have no Gil or Olive.

I couldn't deny that watching Gil with his daughter made me more alive than I had been in days. I fell deeper into him, seeing such a tender side. My shattered trust stitched itself back together, witnessing a guy who wasn't the scared, icy boy anymore but a man who wore his mistakes with pride.

It punched me in the heart with hypocrisy.

I loved Gil.

I probably always would.

And now…when there were no more secrets keeping us apart, I was the one who hid the truth. Who didn't know if she was brave enough to admit that *this* was what she wanted.

Him.

Her.

A ready-made family who I'd fallen head over heels for.

Five years was an eternity.

But it was nothing in the term of a lifetime.

I sat stewing in my thoughts as Olive chattered and drank in her father. Gil smiled dotingly and gave her every scrap of attention.

Fifteen minutes later, a buzzer sounded, announcing the end of visitation.

Olive's eyes immediately filled with tears again. "No. I don't want to go. Dad, come home with us."

Gil cupped her cheek, sadness creating grooves in his forehead and deep brackets around his mouth. "I'd love nothing more than to go home with you, little spinach, but I can't. Not yet."

"Can I move in here with you then?" She stood and hugged him while he still sat in the chair. He squeezed her, even as a guard cleared his throat, encroaching with his rules. "This isn't a nice place for little Olive Oyls."

"Then where can we go to be together?"

Gil pushed her toward me, a plea in his gaze.

I stood, understanding what he needed. I opened my arms to catch her, to prevent her from clinging to Gil. It felt wrong to separate them. So, so cruel. "We just have to be patient, Olive. He'll—"

"No!"

I clutched her close, bending down to kiss her temple. "Remember what we talked about? How Dad will be home soon? And then you'll be together forever. This is the last time you guys have to be apart, okay? But you have to be strong."

Olive sniffed. "I don't want to be strong. I just want him to come home."

Gil swallowed back agony as another buzzer went. "I'll come home soon, Olive Oyl. I promise." Kissing her cheek, he looked at me with every weight of the world. "Thank you for coming, O. I'm sorry we didn't have a chance to talk."

He went to touch me.

A guard came toward him.

He sighed and followed the other prisoners through the door.

His gaze never left us until he was gone.

Chapter Thirty-Three

Gil

"JUSTIN...IT'S ME."

Justin swallowed a mouthful of food, surprise in his voice. "How are you calling me, Clark? It's in the middle of the day."

"Prison allows phone calls." I'd deliberately called during the week, and on his office line. This was a conversation just for us, and I couldn't afford to be weak and not do what I should've done a long time ago.

In reality, I'd already made this offer.

In a text while walking through a forest with an unconscious O in my arms.

"True, yeah. Cool. Hey, do you want me to get Olive? She's in the empty office next to me, drawing. She wasn't quite up for school today, but she's going tomorrow. She promised."

Fuck.

Poor thing.

So many things to adapt to and accept.

Me gone. Justin her guardian. Returning to school after so long away.

I worried that she'd be picked on and held back. That a teacher would touch her like one had touched me. Familiar rage and fear crested through me, and I couldn't swallow it back.

I just had to hope Justin was vigilant and wouldn't accept her silence for an answer if she started to shut down.

"Don't get her. This is just a quick call."

"Okay...what's up?" His voice turned serious. "Everything going okay in there? You safe?"

I nodded, even though he couldn't see me. "Yeah, it's fine."

"You don't sound fine."

"All good." I sidestepped the question. It wasn't that I didn't want to be honest, but he didn't need to know about the beatings I'd already taken or the threats. Other inmates didn't believe I wasn't involved with the girls' murders and dished out their own punishment.

I'd held my own.

I'd find my rank in the hierarchy.

Eventually.

"I didn't call to talk about me."

"Okay...what did you call to talk about?" His voice changed, turning wary.

As he should.

I couldn't seem to stop asking this guy for goddamn favours. "First, how *is* Olive? She all right?"

Justin cleared his throat. "As well as can be expected. She's still guarded around me at night, when it's just us. I don't push her, though. She's much better when O stays over."

My heart stopped beating. "She what?"

"Yeah, sorry, mate. I wanted to tell you but didn't know how. I wasn't coping the first few nights with Olive's nightmares. O seems to have a magic touch and agreed to help Olive adjust." He cleared his throat, pausing for a second. "Look, you should know that I asked O to move in with me." He rushed as if terrified that I'd throttle him through the phone line. "Her lease is almost up, she hates her job, and she's at a total crossroads on what to do with her life. While she figures out that shit, I invited her to stay with Olive and me. To help ease everyone into this new routine, you know?" He kept talking, not giving me a chance to interrupt. "You know O is thinking of travelling. At least this way she can save up some money before she goes. And...I can keep an eye on her for you. I know you'll worry about her, and if she does move in with me for a little while, you can relax knowing I have both of your girls safe."

He stopped.

The line crackled.

He asked cautiously, "Eh, Gil...you still there?"

I rubbed my face. "Yeah, I'm here."

"You...okay with what I just said."

"I'm okay as long as my daughter is happy. O doesn't belong to me anymore. She can stay wherever she wants."

"Okay...great."

I sighed heavily. I'd sounded like a bastard. I sounded as if I was jealous. Justin had just proven why this phone call was the best choice for all of us. He'd already taken the step toward the future I was willing to give up in gratitude for his help.

Squeezing the back of my neck, I asked softly, "Is there anything I can do?"

As if I could do anything trapped inside here, but I had to offer. Had to try.

Justin sighed. "Honestly, mate. Just get out early on good behaviour. Come back to your kid as fast as you can."

"I'll do my best, believe me." I was still shocked I'd only received five years. It felt like an eternity but also didn't feel long enough. I knew that was the guilt talking, but still...life had finally been kind to me and I didn't know how to accept it.

Looking at the dirty clock, fully aware that my phone privileges were running out, I said as firmly and as genuinely as I could, "Look, I'm glad you asked O to move in with you. You're a good bloke, Miller. And...your offer makes why I called easier." I laughed under my breath. "It's not fucking easy. It's the hardest thing I'll ever do, but...it seems fate is one step ahead of me."

"Oh?" He cleared his throat. "What are you trying to say?"

"I have another favour to ask." I groaned, leaning against the wall where the bank of telephones hung. "The last one I hope, but it's still another bloody favour."

Justin chuckled. "You don't need to feel so bad about asking, Clark. That's what friendship is."

I didn't want to argue again about friendship and how one-sided ours had always been. I didn't have the luxury of not asking, even though it would tear out my heart once and for all.

It wasn't really a favour.

It was an offer.

Fucking permission even though neither of them needed it.

It was just my way of coming to terms with everything.

Accepting my future.

"If O does travel, then I'm glad. I want her to be happy and won't stand in her way."

"And if she doesn't? If she stays in town?" Justin's suspicion bled through the phone line.

This was it.

No going back.

My knuckles tightened around the phone. "If she doesn't, if she moves in with you and finds happiness under your roof with you and my daughter…then…I give you my blessing to love her. Make her yours. Be together. Get married. Just…be happy."

Justin choked before coughing and blurting, "You're giving me *permission* to date Olin. To *marry* O?" His tone turned cool. "I don't need your permission, Clark."

My temper fired, but I kept it locked away. "I know. I just didn't want you to hold back if there came a moment where you two could be happy together."

"If O knew you'd said this to me, she'd be right pissed. You're acting as if she doesn't have a mind of her own."

"She does. Her heart is big and desperate to love, but she's also kind to a fault and far too generous to even consider being more than just friends with you out of fairness to me and our past."

"I think you should talk to O."

"I don't want to mess her up any more than I already have."

"Look, you're tired and missing home and thinking you'll never be happy again. I get it. Having your freedom taken away can't be easy, but, Gil, stay focused on the future. You will get out of there. You will have Olive back and raise her into a wonderful young woman. And who knows, maybe O will wait for you, and you'll all ride off into the sunset with your paintbrushes. Just focus on the possibility of—"

"Times up!" a guard shouted, waving his finger in the air and stabbing at the watch on his wrist.

"Shit, I've got to go." I turned my back on the guard, swallowing hard. "Just…just be open to the idea, Miller. If you still have feelings for her. If you want her, and she wants you. Don't worry about me. I just want her to have the best. And that isn't me. It never was. It's always been you. You guys are the same, Miller. Like should stick with like. Anyway, thanks for looking after my daughter. I promise one day, I'll find a way to pay you back."

I hung up before he could protest.

I walked back to my cell with images of O kissing Justin when he told her he still had feelings for her. Of her moving into Justin's bedroom and becoming a surrogate mother to my child.

They would move on.

They would live in domestic bliss.

I would remain here in limbo.

A prisoner with nothing and no one.

And I was okay with that.

I was *happy* with that if it meant the two girls I loved more than anything were protected and cared for by a man I trusted with my life.

Chapter Thirty-Four

Olin

GILBERT CLARK, the body painter from Birmingham responsible for killing the man who murdered at least four girls, with possibilities of countless more, has been incarcerated for the past six months.
Served five years for his role in the Painted Murders, the online community who demanded the death penalty and did their best to destroy his business has now faded into white noise on the web.
For such a prolific painter, Gilbert Clark refused to touch a paintbrush for five months where he's currently serving his sentence. However, just last week, three canvases have been placed up for auction by the prison itself, donated by Gilbert Clark who, according to our sources, has returned to painting and now teaches a class to fellow inmates.
This past year, the prison has been working on the education offered to its prisoners, along with rehabilitation programs. Painting has been proven to have a positive impact on both psychological issues and stress levels.
The canvases on sale depict scenes from inside the jail. One shows the cafeteria where the inmates eat, another the barbwire-enclosed field where exercise is encouraged, and the last of a cell itself—complete with sketches of Gilbert Clark's daughter, the woman he loves, and the friend who stuck by his side, blue-tacked to the cell walls.
If you wish to bid on one of these limited-edition canvases, please head to the prison website and click on the link provided.

I locked my phone as I entered Justin's building.

I'd finished work early and surfed the news on the bus.

I'd stumbled upon the article about Gil's return to painting.

My heart hurried in hope, grateful he'd finally embraced his gift again. I knew what it was like to live without such an outlet. To no longer be able to dance. To no longer be allowed to paint.

Thank goodness he'd been permitted to indulge his gift inside, and how brilliant that the prison had accepted his donations to sell. Hopefully, they could put the profits toward providing better programs for the inmates.

For six months, I'd stayed in town.

For six months, I hadn't told Gil that I loved him.

For six long months, I still hadn't made up my mind.

Stay.

Go.

Commit.

Fly free.

Sighing, I unlocked the letterbox and pulled out new mail.

Two letters.

One addressed to me and one to Justin.

And one magazine from Kohls showing their new line.

Instantly, my breath caught as I traced the glossy magazine covered in cellophane.

Thanks to reading the news article about Gil, his presence already wrapped around me.

But now...I almost felt his touch.

Felt his brush upon my skin.

His paint upon my body.

Tearing open the magazine, I stared at myself.

At the green camouflage transforming me from human to department store logo. Along with the mannequins in the fellow letters, it punched the shopper with a unique offering. A symbolic advertisement that said if you bought things from them, you too could become anything you wanted.

I sighed, my heart hurting as I relived the changing room jealousy, the tension while painting, the awfulness of watching the police steal him away.

I should've known then that Gil's freedom was running out even though, at the time, it had been mine.

We'd both been victims of circumstances outside our control, and as I stood in Justin's apartment stairwell, clutching a magazine where my naked body was hidden beneath my lover's talent, I finally knew what I would do.

Finally knew the answer to the question I'd been too afraid to ask.

Where do I belong?

Easy.

With him.

With the man who'd terrified me, sacrificed me, almost died for me.

With the boy who'd claimed me, loved me, protected me.

With the body painter who saw past my colours and painted his own upon my heart.

NINETEEN MONTHS LATER

Chapter Thirty-Five

Gil

TIME HAD DIFFERENT speeds.

For the circumstances you couldn't accept, it went slow—tormenting and giving plenty of opportunity to either rebel against the current situation or finally accept the unacceptable.

For the events you *could* accept—the ones where joy was the main ingredient and life was good, time sped up, as if hurtling you toward the next catastrophe.

Prison had consisted of two versions of time.

The beginning was slow and miserable with no end in sight.

O kept chaperoning Olive for her weekly visits, and we stuck entirely to conversation about my daughter, her progress at school, and the life I was no longer a part of. The fifteen minutes always went far too fast, and the urge to grab O and demand she tell me what she wasn't saying built and built until I'd tremble in my cell at night, desperate to know.

At no point did she advise when she was leaving and to where. At no time did she put me out of misery and say she'd fallen in love with Justin.

And I was too gutless to ask.

The subject of her vanishing one day slowly buried beneath all the other topics we didn't discuss.

It fucking killed me to think that the past had repeated itself and Justin had claimed the love of my life, but if it meant she was happy, I would hide my pain forever.

All I could hope for was that every week, she'd turn up. And every week, she'd still be there.

As my friend.

As my family.

Their visits got me through the first few months of claustrophobia. The only bright speck in cell time, yard exercise, and prison monotony. I returned to sketching to keep boredom at bay, sending fortnightly letters to Olive, enclosed with drawings and renders of things created from memory, from my previous freedom.

Justin visited too.

His upbeat convo and antidotes of Olive helped keep me a little sane. He tactfully avoided the subject of O and their home life, and out of respect—to show him I meant what I'd said on the phone—I kept my questions silent.

By the time routine set in, and I accepted my new temporary home, minutes no longer made me suffer such long days. I agreed to lead a painting class for fellow inmates, using broken down easels and painted over canvases. The stock of paints ranged from dry oils to old acrylics, but I never complained.

They were colour.

They were small tubes of freedom into my craft.

I returned to painting normal canvases and not O's perfect skin.

I didn't care that some of the inmates would rather flick paint at fellow cellmates than follow my instruction. I didn't mind that the results of the class were worse than any kindergarten finger painting. It was nice to have a task and a relief to create.

It was also rewarding to conjure a scene that others might see outside of these walls and gave me purpose again when the warden said they'd hold an auction and use the proceeds to buy more supplies for my newly established painting school.

I painted a canvas for Olive, full of owls and ballerinas.

I painted a canvas for O, drawing her tattoo from memory.

Inmates took note of the skill it took to turn lines and shadow into recognisable things and my class attendance switched from taking the piss to dedicated.

I became a teacher.

I thought about Jane Tallup, our daughter, and O.

And through the medium that had always helped calm my thoughts, I somehow helped others too. Fellow prisoners relaxed around me. The stress in their eyes faded while focusing on pigment rather than regrets. I gained more freedom within the new world I inhabited, and I unofficially became someone they could talk to.

I didn't know how it happened, but the prisoners who took my painting classes seemed more centred and not nearly as violent.

The warden noticed.

He gave us more supplies.

Gave us more opportunities to use our passion for paint in other areas.

When a renovation budget was announced, we put up our hands to help refresh the jail. We painted it from top to bottom—grey walls and white windowsills.

Along with painting, I continued to volunteer for odd jobs and handyman tasks. The yards were redesigned. The gym equipment upgraded. The kitchen supplied with better facilities.

I had every intention of learning new skills, so when I was freed, I could be a reliable father to Olive. I had no idea if my Master of Trickery business would resurrect. I couldn't check my website or emails. I'd filed for bankruptcy and had nothing left apart from my wonderful daughter.

When I got out, I had no intention of being a failure to society. I planned on finding work straight away because I had no intention of making Olive feel anything but pride.

I wasn't a convict who had accepted his uselessness.

I was a man who'd paid the price of his mistakes and now was free to move on.

I was the person I always wanted to be.

* * * * *

One day, eighteen months into my term, the warden called me into his office.

I'd had my monthly meeting with the in-house shrink, and my results were glowingly positive. The monthly conclusion was always the same: I wasn't likely to offend again.

My murderous tendencies were not a repeating occurrence.

I wasn't a danger to society.

The warden read my file with a frown etched deep into his forehead. He told me the prison was at full capacity, and he'd been instructed to select inmates he felt were rehabilitated enough to be released on good behaviour.

I would be monitored if released early. I would be expected to fulfil my community service.

But there was a chance…a small, small chance, I could go home.

I daren't let my hope explode.

I nodded calmly and agreed to yet more interviews and assessments.

After a week of talking to people in suits, I was advised they'd be in touch.

I didn't tell O or Justin about the possibility of being released early. I didn't want to promise Olive something that I couldn't guarantee.

A month later, when I was called to see the warden, I refused to be hopeful. The chances of being told that serving nineteen months of a five-year sentence was enough to be freed were slim.

However, fate once again treated me kindly.

Within a week, I'd signed the paperwork, been advised of my parole officer and community service liaison, and given a date.

O and Olive were due to visit me three days after my freedom was reinstated.

I had the choice of telling them the good news.

I mulled over the options of sharing the celebration now—when I was penniless, unsure of my future, and homeless...or wait.

To keep one last secret so I could get back on my feet and prove to them that my past was behind me. I didn't know how O would take it. Would she be mad that I kept silent and didn't ask for help, or proud that I hadn't given up?

It was Olive who made the choice for me.

I called the night I was due to leave and asked how school was going. How things with Justin and O were. She'd said things were good, but she missed me and couldn't wait until we lived together again.

I'd promised it would happen sooner than we figured. The news of my parole itched to be said, but if I told her, I would break a promise because she couldn't live with me if I didn't have anywhere to keep her safe.

A halfway house for reformed felons was not ideal.

And so, I kept quiet.

One last time.

I told her I was coming down with something and to avoid me for a week because I didn't want her to get sick. I slept one last night in prison, traded my uniform for civilian clothes, and stepped from the gates far sooner than I'd hoped.

The guard signing me out asked if I had family to call or a

pick-up arranged.

I just shook my head and strolled from the jail, destitute and in the same clothes I'd faced court in. I'd asked for too many favours of too many people. I would stand on my own feet from now on.

Otherwise, I really didn't deserve my daughter.

As I'd slinked back into society, I used the change in my pockets to rent a computer in a downtown Wi-Fi café and checked my business accounts.

My emails had dried up.

No commissions had waited nineteen months for a reply.

But at least my Facebook page was still up.

The visibility was obsolete and content buried with no traffic, but the photos and videos were still there. Emblems of my past. Reminders of a talent I once had.

Clicking on the last video I'd uploaded of me painting Olin in her flat that night, I tortured myself with our kiss.

I relived the connection we'd shared.

The goodbye I'd done my best to honour.

My finger hovered over the mouse.

I wanted to delete the video. To put aside those heart pangs for a girl who might be in love with my best friend by now.

But I left it.

I left it as yet another reminder not to ruin her happiness, and used the many videos and photos saved in my cloud to add new content. Previous commissions. Accolades from advertisement companies. Images of magazines and billboards and the many places where my creations had ended up.

I even uploaded a picture of Olive painting a kid from her school while dressed in her hockey uniform. The poor kid had ended up looking like some squashed marshmallow but both she and Olive had had a great time.

It showed in their smiles and splashed paint.

An image of powerful joy.

Once I'd scheduled and arranged a few posts that hopefully would get exposure, I updated my business description.

Experienced Body Painter willing to work for free.
Ex-convict, single-father, determined.
You supply the paint, canvas, and location.
I'll do the rest.

I was willing to start from the ground up again.

I'd brush the cobwebs off my fingers, raise my business

from the ashes, and be worthy of all the wonderful people in my life.

And this time, there would be no one to blackmail or bleed me dry.

No uncle to steal my daughter.

No teacher to send me to jail for rape.

No secrets to make me lose my soul-mate.

People knew the truth.

It was time I accepted that I no longer had to look over my shoulder.

It was time to live.

* * * * *

That'd been four weeks ago.

I'd called Olive once a week—like I used to from jail—assuring her I was fine and not to come and see me. That I couldn't quite shake the flu and didn't want her to catch it. A few fake coughs and sneezes, and she agreed to be patient.

I hated lying.

I worried about keeping silent.

I was *desperate* to see her.

I barely slept with the need to ensure she was safe—to assure myself she was free and no longer prisoner like I had been.

But unlike the panic that'd filled me when searching for her, I could temper my desperation with the knowledge she was happy with Justin and O. She had everything she could ever want. She was loved and protected.

And if I stood any chance of providing for her half as well as Justin and O did…then I needed time to make myself a better man.

To ensure I could be the father she deserved.

And besides…I had a plan.

Four weeks had already given me enough time to paint and get the word out that I was back.

Thanks to the prison selling some of my work, my reputation had been patched up with the underdog tale of a guy incarcerated for putting a psychopath down.

People no longer hated me, and it wasn't the battle I'd feared to get noticed.

I did three free commissions.

One for a woman on her thirtieth birthday who wanted to wear her 'birthday suit' with paint embellishments.

Two for a small pet shop who helped rehome shelter animals and wanted two women painted as one stray looking for a home.

And three for an up-and-coming band with no cash who wanted their drummer to be covered in their logo for their banner and next week's show.

For each one, I uploaded the time-lapse video of creation, and each one got more and more traction online.

By the fourth one—a law firm who wanted a woman painted as a judge—I deleted the promise of free work and accepted my first paid gig in almost two years.

I slashed my usual rate for the right to share.

The second gig, I increased it.

And by the fifth, I was confident in my skills again.

Confident enough to charge higher prices, invest my new funds into fresh brushes, bottles, and sponges, and dared hope that I could step back into my role as Master of Trickery.

There'd been no hate directly into my inbox.

No beatings or awkward moments when I went to paint.

It was as if everyone had moved on. As if they no longer cared about something that happened so long ago, even if it was scandal and murder.

I didn't question the luck I had.

I scooped it up as fast as I could, focusing on my goal of a home for Olive and money to pay Justin for caring for my daughter.

I worked every hour I could.

Day and night.

I didn't rest, even when I had enough for a down payment on a rental only a block away from Justin's place. My parole officer helped vouch for me and acted as referee on my rental request. Luckily, the landlord took a chance and I signed the lease with a chest-full of relief.

The place came fully furnished, and the first night I slept there and not the halfway house provided for ex-prisoners, I knew I could do this.

I was done taking the scraps life threw at me.

I would make a success of myself and not feel guilty or undeserving.

There was also another reason for staying busy.

Each time my thoughts strayed to O, my heart would buck and writhe. I'd lost her. I'd let her go. And that was the biggest punishment of all.

Not jail time.

Not fighting from the ground up.

Just the knowledge that I'd grown the fuck up finally, I'd let down my guards, and it didn't matter.

Because the chance of a happily ever after was too late.

Chapter Thirty-Six

Gil

SCHOOL LET OUT in a gush of same-dressed students.

Nerves raced down my spine. Sweat broke out on my palms.

I waited until Olive spilled out with her satchel bashing against her side and her smile wide and confident.

She'd grown a lot in the past year.

She was no longer the tiny girl with hurricane love but a timid heart. She was closing in on ten years old and resembled the young woman she'd become.

Wiping sweaty palms on my jeans, I checked that my grey t-shirt was presentable and my new boots—that already held specks of paint—were tied, then crossed the road to surprise my daughter.

"Olive Oyl."

She slammed to a stop. Her bag swinging and mouth falling open. "Dad...*dad?*" Then she was running, bolting into my arms and leaping into me.

I swept her from the pavement and hugged her close. Her hair still smelled of strawberries. Her body still felt like her. She'd changed but was also so familiar.

"How? How are you here?" She squirmed in my embrace. "I thought you were sick! And...in jail."

I put her down, unable to stop grinning. "I wanted to surprise you."

"Did you break out?" Her voice lowered to a harsh whisper. "Are they gonna come arrest you for escaping?"

I laughed hard. "No. I didn't break out. I was released."

Her forehead furrowed. "But…it's not time yet. O and I have a calendar at home that shows when you'll be free, and it's not for ages."

I fought the urge to touch her ponytail. To cup her cheek. "I got lucky."

"So…you mean, you're out for real? Like forever?" Hope exploded in her pretty grey gaze.

I nodded.

She squealed and launched herself back into my arms.

Chuckling, I held her while she nuzzled into my neck, her legs kicking my knees in excitement. "This is *amazing*! This is so good. Yay!" Pulling away, seriousness bled through her joy. "So…are you moving in with Justin and O and me? We'll need to get a bigger place. There isn't another bedroom."

O had told me she'd moved in with Justin a while ago.

But I hadn't pried for more.

I battled the awful question. The question I couldn't run away from.

Were O and Justin sharing a bedroom?

Were they a true family, raising my daughter as their own?

I swallowed it back, shaking my head and that nasty thought away.

So what if they were?

I had to be happy for their happiness.

I would not ruin it just because I was out early and suddenly desperate to see if I could salvage the wreckage of O and I.

"I have my own place. Not far from Justin's."

She looked around; searching for the guards she'd grown used to tolerating whenever she came to visit me. "So…does that mean you don't want to live with us?" Her forehead wrinkled. "You don't want to live with me?"

I ducked to one knee, looking into her pretty eyes. "Of *course* I want to live with you. I was hoping…well, I hoped you'd come live with me in my new place. I got it for us." I brushed a lock of dark hair from her cheek, then captured her hand. "But I can see how that's rude of me to expect you to change your life so much. So…if you don't want to live with me, that's totally okay too."

My heart hurt.

I didn't like the stares of other parents or the high-pitched chatter of other kids.

I cursed myself for being so forward when I should've known Olive would grow attached to Justin and O. Why did I expect her to leap back into my arms when she had a great thing going with them?

She licked her lips. "It's not that. It's just…um…" She kicked a pebble with her patent black school shoe. "I just have to ask them if that's okay."

"Completely understand." I stood, glancing around at the mayhem of parents picking up children. I probably looked totally suspicious. Stepping back a little, I stared down a young woman who looked at me as if I was some paedophile.

Olive took my hand, tugging me gently. "I know. We can ask them right now!"

"Wait…what?" My eyes fell to hers, my body yanked into movement thanks to her tenacity.

Pulling me across the street, she grinned. "They're here. They pick me up."

"They do?"

"Yep." She skipped beside me. "Sometimes it's just O and sometimes Justin. But lately, they've both come to get me."

Lately.

I swallowed hard.

Was that a sign of true love finding separation excruciating?

She pointed up ahead. "That's O's car."

My legs suddenly turned into pillars of concrete. I stopped without thinking; fear a tangible thing in my blood.

O lounged against her car, waiting for my daughter. Her gorgeous face was framed by long dark blonde hair. Her smile was carefree and genuine.

And beside her was Justin.

My chest crumbled as he shoved her, mid-laugh, as if she'd ribbed him and he'd retaliated. Their body language was loose and happy, smiles full of affection.

I'd given Justin permission to chase her if she'd wanted to be chased.

I wouldn't stand in their way if they got married or wanted nothing to do with me now I was free, but I couldn't deny that my heart fell into a blender and sliced to pieces. A salsa of pain. A rain of ruin.

"Come on." Olive tugged my hand, yanking me toward the two people who meant so much to me in different ways. Doing my best to keep my face neutral and ordering my arms not to reach out and snatch O, I smiled the best I could as Justin's gaze met mine.

He froze.

O looked to where his eyes had locked.

She froze too.

For a second, guilt flashed over her face before a huge grin split her lips and she charged toward me. "Gil!"

I braced myself for her hug, unable to fight the urge to bury my face in the crook of her neck. She felt so warm and soft and right.

She felt like home.

Justin came over, pulling me into an embrace after O let me go. "Mate, how the hell are you here? Why didn't you tell us you were out?" He slapped me on the shoulder. "Did you just get released? We could've picked you up."

I hugged him back, gratefulness a warm Band-Aid over my bleeding heart. "Don't get mad but I got out a few weeks ago."

Olive's face scrunched up, dragging my eyes down to her level. "You didn't come see us straight away?"

Us.

Not me.

Us.

Like it or not, she'd made a family with O and Justin. Whatever our joint future held, I would share Olive with them. I wouldn't take her away. Not after nineteen months of them being together.

I kept my voice neutral of pain. "I wanted to have a home before I came to you, little spinach. I can still call you that, right?"

She frowned. "Yeah, but I don't know why you didn't come find us sooner. You wasted all that time when we could've been together."

"I didn't waste it. I used it to get my painting back on track and fix what I'd broken."

"Huh." She crossed her arms, still annoyed. "I still think you should've told us."

Her firecracker temper made me chuckle, but I swallowed it back, staying serious. "I agree. It was wrong. Can you forgive me?"

Her lips twitched. "I suppose so."

"Phew." My eyes trailed to O as understanding glowed on

her face.

"You've been painting," she said softly. "I haven't been online lately...I should've checked your page."

"I wanted it to be a surprise."

"It is. A great surprise." She smiled. "So...you're working?"

I nodded. "A few commissions."

O's hazel eyes warmed with a thousand different things. "That's wonderful." She understood why I needed to repair myself on my own terms. She got why it was important that I came to them whole and not ask for more hand-outs.

"That's great, Clark." Justin patted me on the back. "Guess you'll be slammed with work again. No rest for the wicked."

"He's not wicked," Olive piped up. "He might've been sent to prison, but he isn't wicked." She stepped closer, and I wound my arm around her delicate shoulders.

"Thanks for having my back."

"Anytime." She winked, filling my chest with love.

O watched us, the same kindness and gentleness that'd always drawn me to her spilling from her soul. "Olive's missed you. We all have."

I couldn't look away from her. "I've missed you." Clearing my throat, I added, "All of you. I missed everyone."

O tucked flyaway hair behind her ear. "Do you...do you need somewhere to sleep? You're welcome to come home with us."

Two words that left literary power and became physical as knives.

Us and home.

So they were together, and they shared a home.

"Yeah, mate." Justin shoved his hands into his suit pockets. "You're welcome anytime. You know that. The couch is super comfy. I can vouch for it."

Justin only had a two-bedroom place.

Olive had one.

O most likely had the other.

And if Justin wasn't couch surfing anymore...that meant he and O shared a room.

And a bed.

Fuck.

I hadn't wanted to jump to conclusions, but it became impossible not to.

"That's very kind of you, guys, but..." I let Olive go, my

feet backing up and putting distance between us. "I have my own place."

Stop being an ungrateful prick.

This was the price I'd been willing to pay.

So pay it.

"Besides, I've already been far too much of an imposition."

"You've never be an imposition, Gil." O's eyes burned. "You know that."

I didn't know what to say or how to deal with the wave of emotion emitting from her. My skin prickled, my heart begged, life felt empty knowing I'd lost her.

But it *wasn't* empty.

It was full because I'd paid my sins, my conscience was clear, and for the first time, I had everything to look forward to.

Olive was safe.

I was free to protect her the way she deserved.

Free to spoil her, raise her, and love her until she became an adult in her own right.

That was what I focused on.

That was what I was grateful for.

I forced another grin. "I better let you guys go—"

"But you just got here." Olive pouted. "I want longer than the stupid fifteen minutes in prison."

"Yeah, Clark. You can't go yet." Justin smoothed his suit. "Tell you what, we need to celebrate! Let's go out. Have a drink. Catch up. All of us."

Olive bounced on the spot. "Yay! Let's go."

O sucked in a breath.

My every cell was attuned to her. She flinched as if going out to eat with me wasn't tolerable. "I don't know. You probably have a million and one things to do—"

"Nope. Done for the day," Justin interrupted. "Let's go to dinner."

"Dinner is hours away, silly." Olive wrinkled her nose. "I've only just finished school."

Justin held out his hand, letting Olive slap it as if he deserved being told off. "Okay, smartypants, call it a late lunch or pre-dinner. How about a lunner? Does that work? You know…like breakfast and lunch are combined to make brunch? Lunner."

He shrugged as O groaned, rolling her eyes. "What? It's a legitimate question."

"You're so weird." Olive giggled.

"Takes one to know one."

O laughed. "Both of you are weird."

"You're weirder," Justin shot back.

"I have to be to put up with you two." O's gaze sparkled with contentment.

The trio of togetherness while I watched in envy.

The ease between them.

The connection that'd grown while I'd been locked away.

I stood quietly, not sure how to untangle myself from this family. Not sure how to claim back my daughter when she'd found something so special. And most of all, unsure how I could cope after losing both girls of my heart to a guy who deserved to be loved as much as he was.

Justin cleared his throat, noticing my stiffness. He tapped the top of the bronze sedan beside him. "Everyone pile in. Let's move this party to somewhere cooler than a pavement."

O inched toward me, hesitating before threading her arm through mine.

The second she touched me, my body reacted.

My heart pounded.

My blood gushed.

The chemistry and electricity that always punished us sprang into full force.

I shuddered. I couldn't breathe.

O murmured, "You'll come eat with us…won't you, Gil?"

There was that word again.

Once upon a time, I'd fought against such a promise. I'd told her there could never be an us because I was hiding so many goddamn things.

Now that word belonged to them, not me.

Shit.

Olive hugged me from the other side, putting me in the centre of an affection sandwich. I couldn't stand much more before I broke, so I untangled myself and said the simplest thing. The thing guaranteed to avoid an argument but also destined to destroy me. "Sure. Dinner would be nice."

And it would be.

Dinner out in the real world with my child and friends would be better than nice.

I just had to rein in my heart and force it to get the memo that O was off-limits.

"Great." O smiled.

My nervous system disagreed as O strolled to the car. Returned to Justin. Left me.

I drank in the way she moved. The dancer's grace that still ran in her blood. The kindness that was visible around her, a softness that made her ever more stunning.

I fell deeper into love with her when I should've been schooling myself into platonic boundaries.

Justin opened the door for Olive as she hopped in the back. O went to sit in the back with her but I leaped into action and ripped open the front door. "Please. I'll take the back."

"You sure?"

"Yeah. It'll be fun hanging with, what did Justin call her? The pipsqueak?"

Olive piped up from inside the car. "I'm not a pipsqueak anymore. I grew."

O chuckled and slipped into the car. "She has many nicknames these days. Pest being a favourite one."

"You're the pest." Olive stuck out her tongue. "The best pest."

O laughed again and I hid my gratefulness of their care and the agony of what I'd missed out on. Falling into the car, I forced a grin at my daughter. "I can see pest suiting you."

"You know nothing." She arched her chin, flicking her hair smugly.

I know some things, little spinach.

I know that I love you.

And O.

And you've both moved on.

And I know I'll do whatever it takes to not jeopardize the happiness you've found.

Justin turned the car on and switched into gear. "All in? Let's go."

Chapter Thirty-Seven

Olin

HOW COULD DOING something as mundane as going to a restaurant be equally strenuous and enjoyable?

I couldn't stop looking at Gil.

Couldn't stop pinching myself that he was out and free and back.

Nineteen months served.

An eternity for all of us.

Yet…it felt like yesterday that he'd painted me and we'd slept together and I'd vowed that I'd never turn my back on him.

Each time I'd visited him with Olive, I'd wanted to tell him that I would wait. That we weren't over. That I'd forgiven him and accepted that whatever madness we shared was worth fighting for.

That I finally knew I belonged to him, with him, and always had.

I wouldn't give that up.

For anything.

But each visit, I kept my secret.

Until one day, I no longer knew if he even wanted me in that way anymore. He'd given me no sign that he hungered for me. His smiles were warm but reserved. His animation and energy given to Olive while I was just his daughter's chaperone.

I appreciated why he'd pulled away.

In his mind, we'd said goodbye that night in my apartment.

And I'd moved in with Justin.

"What did they feed you in jail?" Olive asked, sucking on the paper straw in her raspberry coke.

Gil raked a hand through his hair, looking ruggedly

handsome. His messy dark locks were just as wild. His eyes just as piercing. He ought to have looked older thanks to almost two years in prison, yet whatever demons had hounded him had gone.

He no longer looked wary of the world or on guard to everyone around him.

He looked like the boy I'd fallen in love with.

"Bland, boring things mainly." He twisted in his chair, facing his adorable daughter. "They need a proper chef."

"I can cook okay." Olive stirred her straw. "O taught me how to bake banana muffins the other day."

"You did?" Gil's gaze caught mine.

My heart fluttered.

"I can't take the credit. The cookbook did all the work. We just followed the recipe."

"They were pretty tasty, though," Justin said, sipping an ice-cold pint. "Ten out of ten."

"Yeah, and you ate them all." Olive pretended to frown. "You didn't leave any for me."

"You're forgetting you ate three, you glutton. I only had two."

"Oh yeah? I think you should go back to school and learn how to count." Olive giggled.

"I'm an accountant, little pest. I know how to count. And you had three." Justin winked at Gil. "That's why she's grown so much. She's a piggy."

Gil laughed, sounding strained, almost as if he wished like hell he'd had the stupid volley match with Olive.

I worried we'd overstepped. Feared Gil would think we'd replaced him just because we bantered a lot.

In the months we'd all lived together, I'd come to love Olive to the point of disaster. If her father held my soul, she held my heart undoubtedly. I was unbelievably happy Gil was back, but if I was honest, I was also terrified.

Terrified of losing Olive.

Of losing the family Justin, she, and I had created.

I hadn't been lonely with them.

I hadn't been lost.

Gil would always be a missing piece of me but I'd found enough to be happy. That was another reason I hadn't needed to travel. I'd found contentment in the very same city where all my dreams had shattered.

"I'll bake you some, Dad." Olive touched Gil's forearm on the table. "And you can have all of them. Justin gets none."

"Meanie." Justin wiped a fake tear from his cheek. "I get it. Now your dad's back, I'm forgotten." He laughed, but it held the same thread of fear I felt.

We both struggled.

Both ecstatic that Gil was home.

Both afraid that Gil was home.

Olive blew a kiss to Justin across the table. "I won't forget about you. Ever."

"Ah, shucks." Justin smiled, deeply genuine and relieved. "I'm going to hold you to that. I expect weekly hangouts. And daily updates."

"Wait…are-are you kicking me out?" Olive squeaked.

Justin glanced at me, panic in his eyes. "Of course not. I just figured with your dad back you'd want to—"

"Olive wanted to check with you guys first," Gil cut in. "I have my own place. I'm earning an income." He swallowed hard, taking a sip of his lemonade and avoiding my stare.

His abhorrence for alcohol hadn't changed in prison then. He still hated liquor. I doubted I'd ever catch him drunk again.

Gil rushed, "But I don't expect Olive to move out if you're not comfortable with that. If you guys are happy, then…I'm happy for her to keep living with you."

Everything in my chest ached.

He was once again willing to sacrifice the most important person in his world. He'd sacrificed me. He'd sacrificed Olive. He did it out of love, but I worried Olive might take it as if he didn't want her enough to fight for her.

Justin leaned forward, the green velvet bench seat we shared creaking under his weight. He looked seriously at Olive, asking her as an adult for her decision. "What do *you* want, Olive Oyl? You have three grown-ups wrapped around your little finger, so you get to choose."

She bit her lip, her gaze dancing from Gil to me to Justin and back again.

The ancient pub where we sat hugged us with smoke and stale beer. The low beams and dark walls cocooned us, making it seem like it was midnight and not late afternoon.

This was one of the few places still open and serving food at three-thirty in the afternoon. And in a way, it was fitting. A pub this old held so many secrets. Lives had changed, and friendships were tested, all hidden within its protection.

Just like now.

"Um…" Olive's eyes widened, feeling the pressure.

She loved Justin.

She loved me.

Those two facts I knew without a doubt.

But she would never love anyone as much as she loved her father, and that was exactly how it should be.

"It's okay, Olive. You don't need to rush. And you don't need to decide right away. Everything will work out, you'll see." I nodded in encouragement. "We're all family. Always will be."

Gil sucked in a breath.

Olive relaxed a little.

Justin picked up his beer and held it out for a toast. "To family."

Gil clinked his lemonade, Olive tapped her raspberry coke, and I raised my wine glass. "Family."

We all drank, sharing a tentative smile, all of us wondering what the future held.

Justin broke the tension by asking Gil, "So, you've been out for a few weeks, got your business back on track, and found a place. What else have you been up to?"

Gil slouched in his chair, comfortable with the easier topic. "I started my community service two weeks ago. I go every other day for a few hours."

"Oh yeah? What do they have you doing?"

"Last week, I helped out at a cattery. The week before that I helped move heavy furniture around a Salvation Army store. I think next week I'll be on food prep somewhere downtown at a shelter."

"Enjoying it?"

Gil nodded. "Actually, yeah. Seeing things I wouldn't necessarily see has been great for creative inspiration. It sucks to witness the hardships of others, but watching the other side of society has been beneficial. It's been almost healing to paint their sadness."

"I get that." Justin swigged back his beer. "Bet it's nice to be painting again. And not teaching untalented convicts."

He smiled. "It was actually kind of rewarding teaching. A lot of inmates found it calming. Teaching the class was probably a reason I was allowed out so early on good behaviour. Rehabilitation comes in many forms."

Gil's gaze caught mine, trapping me in the green icy depths like only he could. "It didn't escape me that I actually started to enjoy it, after despising teachers all my life. Ironic that I found satisfaction in being the one thing I hated."

Hated one teacher in particular.

Jane Tallup who did her best to ruin him.

I'd stalked her online.

I'd found her still teaching English in Japan. A few months after Gil's imprisonment, I'd requested local authorities to file an arrest for her if she ever came back to England. To get justice for what she did to Gil.

Maybe one day I'd tell him, but not now.

Not when the past had been dealt with and the future beckoned bright.

God, I'd missed him.

I wanted to talk to him, but I didn't know what to say. How to say things. How he'd take them.

Almost as if he sensed my reluctance to share, Gil asked, "O...you still working at that place...Status?"

"Status Enterprises." I shook my head. "No. I quit not long after you were—"

"Incarcerated. I get it." His tone held no malice or meanness, but he couldn't hide the ache of loneliness. "Where do you work now then?"

I swallowed a mouthful of white wine. "Well, after giving up my lease and moving in with Justin and Olive...I still planned on travelling. I just couldn't stand going back to that office though. So...Justin had an opening for a personal assistant and...offered it to me."

Gil coughed. "You live and work together?"

Justin winced. "Yeah, O's become rather fundamental to our office. She basically runs my life and the other partner's."

"That's great." Gil looked as if he'd lost something all over again. "Sounds like a perfect fit."

I rubbed at the lacerating lightning inside my chest. I felt guilty all over again. Upset for upsetting Gil. Confused as to why he looked at me as if he wanted to stab himself through the heart.

He was the one who acted as if we were over.

He was the one who told Justin he could be with me—just like high-school.

Justin hadn't wanted to tell me what'd happened on the

phone a fortnight or so into Gil's sentence. He'd come home steely-eyed and tense, hiding the truth until I kept bugging him for answers.

I'd been pissed off that Gil thought I would jump into Justin's bed the moment he was gone. Furious that he'd given his 'permission'.

What happened between Justin and I was our business and ours alone.

Silence became strained, growing tighter as a waitress came over with big bowls of fries, onion rings, and a basket of fish bites.

Olive stuck her hand into the onion rings straight away, oblivious to the stress between adults. "Yum."

This is stupid.

I wouldn't let tension ruin the celebration of having Gil back.

Reaching over the table, I placed my hand on Gil's, squeezing the heat and strength of him. "We missed you so much."

I.

I missed you.

He flinched but turned his hand up so we linked fingers. "I missed you guys too."

You.

I missed *you*.

Olive put her head on his shoulder. "But we never have to be apart again so that's the good thing."

Gil tugged his hand from mine.

I couldn't breathe through the pain still alive between us.

He grabbed a fry and grinned as wide as he could. "Exactly. We'll be together. Always."

Justin chewed a fish bite. "And that brings us back to living arrangements." He held up his hand when I went to remind him that we didn't need to rush, adding, "Decisions don't need to be made now. But…if Gil is okay with it. How about we head over to his place, check it out, and go from there." He smiled at Olive. "What do you say?"

Olive tapped her fingers against her mouth, thinking deeply. "Sure. That sounds good." She looked at Gil. "That okay, Dad? Can we go see your place?"

Gil nodded quickly. "Of course, that's okay. More than okay."

"Great." Justin wiped salt off his fingers. "It's a plan."

Gil went still, his gaze shifting from Justin to me, pinning us to the velvet bench. "Just so we're clear, I'm not going to demand or expect anything. Olive is yours as much as mine. I'm happy if you want to keep her, and I'll see her when you're free. Or vice versa."

The thought of not seeing Olive every day. Of not making pancakes with her or experimenting with other cooking with her. Of not watching her laugh and scream at the TV with Justin when he watched football. We didn't own Olive. We hadn't created her. But we had grown into something that meant a great deal to all of us.

"Of course." I nodded. "We're together now. That means all of us."

Us.

That pesky, damning word.

Gil's green stare shot right into my heart. "I love you." His cheeks pinked as he hugged his daughter and glanced at Justin. "All of you. We're family."

Those three little words wouldn't stop colliding in my chest.

I love you.

I

love

you.

I love you too.

Chapter Thirty-Eight

Olin

"WOW, THIS IS super cool." Olive drifted forward, inspecting Gil's new apartment.

Tiny in size but cosy.

Newer than my old apartment, the walls were a fresh white and the floors bamboo planks.

Gil's paints rested in a big box on the dining room table, reminding me that he still had a bunch of belongings in storage at Justin's.

The kitchen was modern with nice pendant lights, the bathroom with a shower over the bath, and two bedrooms: one with a queen bed, black sheets, and Gil's signature scent of citrus and paint, and a second with a king single, rainbow bedspread, and a huge stuffed owl waiting in a rattan chair by the wardrobe.

I moved toward the quaint lounge.

Olive would be very happy here. Happier than anywhere because she'd be with her father. Justin and I had been a temporary fix. We'd been there to nurse her nightmares and help her feel safe again, but there'd always been something missing, something we could never be.

"Did you want to stay the night here, Olive?" I asked softly. "We can go back to Justin's and pack a bag if you want?"

Olive paused, yet another huge decision for such a young girl to make. I hated putting her on the spot and I hated that all our lives would have to change from this point on, but I also refused to keep daughter and father away from each other.

"It's the weekend tomorrow." She frowned. "I have dance practice."

Gil's head snapped up. "You dance?"

Olive nodded proudly. "O showed me a few moves when we stayed with her before you went to prison, remember? I was too busy with school to learn more, but last month she taught me a few new steps. But now I go to a fancy place because she said I have talent."

Gil looked at me, disbelief and awe in his gaze. "Are you dancing again?"

I blushed, hoping he didn't mind that I'd added an afterschool activity to Olive's life. I would continue paying for the lessons. Now I worked for Justin, I'd been able to squirrel money away. He overpaid me really but I was good at my job and worked hard.

We both did.

It was probably rare that we could live together, raise a child that wasn't ours, and work together without trying to kill each other.

Guilt squeezed me again, but I kept pushing it away. I had nothing to feel guilty about. Nothing.

"No but we had fun playing one night. She's a natural." I beamed, forgetting as I sometimes did, that Olive wasn't mine. That her skill at dancing didn't come from me but someone else. Maybe someone in Jane Tallup's family tree had been a dancer, lithe and limber like I used to be. "I was going to tell you…we wanted it to be a surprise next time we came to visit you." I smiled. "But you visited us instead."

Gil's gaze caught mine, holding for long enough to make my heart skip a beat. The green shone with gratefulness and pride.

He cleared his throat, saying, "She's always been quick to learn." Turning to grin at his daughter, he added, "You'll have to show me a few of your moves."

Olive's face lit up. "Why don't you come to my practice tomorrow? I'm still new there, but you can watch." Her eyes dipped with shyness. "Then maybe I could have a sleepover here…with you."

Gil's face turned serious and intense. "I'd love that. I've love that very much."

"Great." Olive spun in place, her arms flying out in a messy pirouette. "It's a date."

Gil looked at me again.

That hissing, licking need that always consumed me around him raced down my spine.

It'd been almost two years since we'd talked in private.

Two years where his daughter hadn't been there—a sweet distraction from our honesty.

If Olive moved back in with Gil tomorrow, I'd lose my chance to be truthful.

To tell him exactly how I felt.

To tell him honestly what'd happened between Justin and me.

I owed him that.

I owed him transparency because he was home now, and we were family.

And family didn't keep secrets.

While Gil drifted off and made plans with Olive for tomorrow, I made plans to return tonight and fight for our future.

Chapter Thirty-Nine

Gil

I SAT AT the dining room table doing what I did best. Painting.

The sketch I'd done of a ballerina with musical notes dancing around her, signified both O and my daughter. Olive had been taking dancing lessons. What else had I missed while being in jail?

Everything.

Dipping my brush into the water glass, I opted for a fuchsia watercolour, highlighting the ballerina's slippers.

I'd missed O and Justin getting close. I'd missed joking and arguing with Olive. I'd missed restaurants and moonlight strolls.

But at least the things I'd missed had given me redemption. They'd wiped my future clean, so I was at peace to enjoy those things. *Deserved* to enjoy those things.

Looking up, I studied Olive's bedroom. The apartment was small and both bedrooms entered straight onto the living area. The decoration I'd purchased and prepared, the hope I'd nursed, all sat hushed and waiting.

Tomorrow, I would get to see Olive dance. I'd no doubt suffer reliving a past where I'd watched another girl dance for me, and then I'd say goodbye to O and Justin and bring Olive home.

We'd start slow.

One night to see if she still loved me enough to live with me.

Another night if she wanted to stay.

Then possibly, *hopefully*, a whole week, where I'd be privileged enough to take her to school, cook her dinner, and help with her homework.

Swirling the brush in water again, I swiped the thin, soft bristles in aquamarine to decorate the dancing notes and threads of music ribbon.

A knock resonated through my front door, wrenching my head up.

My eyes narrowed. Suspicion that'd saved me from a few beatings in prison made my instincts prickle. Who the hell would visit me at eleven in the evening?

The knock came again.

I stood and strode across the small lounge. With muscles tense for confrontation, I unlocked the door and ripped it wide.

O flinched, her hand flying to her chest. "God, you scared me."

I froze. "*I* scared *you*? You're the one on my stoop at almost midnight."

"Sorry, I—" She blushed; her tongue licked her bottom lip. "I admit it's a little late. I didn't wake you, did I?" Her skin glowed as if imagining me in bed made her hot.

Suspicion bled into lust in a single heartbeat.

She couldn't be here.

I didn't have the strength.

My hand curled around the door handle as I fought the urge to slam it in her face. Better that than snatching her wrist and jerking her into a kiss.

And not just any kiss but a full-blown nuclear meltdown of a kiss.

"You need to leave." I braced myself, inching the door to its closed position.

Her hazel gaze widened. Her mouth parted. "You're kicking me out without even inviting me in?"

The way she looked at me.

The way her entire body invited me to take.

I swallowed hard. "You can't come in, O. Not tonight."

Her face fell. "Why?" Her question was soft...almost a whisper, but it ricocheted through my blood.

I went to lie.

To tell her it didn't matter. That my reasons were my own.

But...I'd made a promise to stop staying silent.

Truth was the only way forward.

Every muscle locked in place as I muttered, "Because I'm recently released from prison. I haven't been with anyone in a very long time. The last person was you. And you've always been *my* person." I cleared my throat, my voice growing raspy and harsh. "But you're not my person anymore. And I respect that, so I need you to respect my request for you to go."

Her arms wrapped around herself. "Wow, I wasn't expecting honesty."

"Yeah, well. That's what you'll get from now on." I raked a shaky hand through my hair. My self-restraint had frayed so much around the edges, and I was hanging on by a fucking thread. "Please, O. Go home. Go back to Justin."

O ducked her head, her eyes skating down my body with fire. "Not yet. I came to talk to you. It's important that we talk."

"Talking isn't going to be my strong suit tonight." I angled my hips away, doing my best to hide just how much my body *didn't* want to talk.

I was so hard, it hurt.

"I've been wanting to talk to you for almost two years, Gil. At least give me ten minutes." Her eyes met mine, emotion bleeding through her calmness. "If you don't like what I have to say, then I'll go. No questions asked. At least...at least I'll know I tried and can put it behind me."

Didn't she get it?

I let her into this flat and talking would swiftly end up beneath the clothes I'd rip from her body. I swallowed a groan as images of her naked and me inside her exploded in my mind.

Goddammit, I wanted her so fucking much.

"O, please don't ask me to let you in here." I dropped my head, glaring at her beneath my brow. "I don't have the best self-control, and I don't trust myself around you."

She stepped forward, placing her hand on the doorjamb. "Ten minutes, Gil." Her voice turned smoky and loose. "You won't do anything. I know you and your honour."

In a split second, my fist curled around her wrist, my arm yanked her inside, and the door slammed closed. My entire body burned as I pressed against her, wedging her against the wall.

She sucked in a heady breath, her eyes sparkling with need.

"I have no honour left. I have *nothing* left. And it's fucking liberating because I can start anew. I *have* started anew. Whatever I make is fresh and untainted by all the shit I did wrong." My hand cupped her cheek, holding her still. "And you were my biggest mistake, O. Just like it was your mistake to come here."

I already regretted my actions.

I already cursed what I couldn't stop.

But my lips ignored my loyalty to Justin and sought hers. They crushed over her mouth. Her taste exploded onto my tongue. My knees wobbled. My breath stopped. And I shoved myself away from her as fast as I could.

"Shit." Pacing with my hands buried in my hair, I growled. "Please, go. I won't betray Justin. Not after everything he's done for me."

O stood plastered to the wall, her gorgeous eyes tracking me. "Gil, please...calm down."

"I won't fucking calm down. I can't be around you, O. You're not mine anymore. You're *his.*"

"I'm not though." Her hands balled. "If you just listen to what I have to say, you'd—"

"Wha-what did you say?" My feet glued to the floor. My hands fell from my hair.

Her chin arched. "I'm not his."

"But...you live together."

"We do."

"You share a bedroom."

She smiled, laughing quietly. "No, we don't."

"What?"

"I share with Olive."

My heart hammered. "How...how is that possible?"

"We have two singles. We're roommates."

"Why would you bunk with a child?"

O sighed gently, infuriatingly patient. "Because that child had nightmares for months after you were locked up. She still has them occasionally. It made sense for me to be right there when she woke up screaming rather than have no one to soothe her."

"Fuck." I wrapped hands in my hair, overwhelmed all over again at the selflessness of this woman. "You truly are the kindest person I know."

"No...I'm not." Her face fell. "If I was kind, I would've told you this a long time ago. Instead of keeping a secret that's literally been chewing me alive."

I dropped my hands; a shiver ran down my spine. "What secret?" I shook my head, still unable to believe she wasn't with Justin after all the time they'd lived together, worked together, been together. "The secret that you're in love with Justin?"

She rolled her eyes. "No, dammit."

"Look, you don't have to lie to protect me. I'm happy for you. I'm glad you're both—"

She sighed dramatically. "Oh, my God, will you just listen? And you're happy? Really, Gil? Honestly, how would you feel if I stood here and told you that yes, Justin and I *were* together. That yes, we sleep with each other every night. That yes, I'm madly in love with him and plan to marry him next week." She planted hands on her hips, her temper appearing. "Tell me, Gil. How does that make you feel?"

How did that make me feel?

Fuck.

I'd tell her.

She wanted to know so badly?

Fine.

Honesty was a disease because once you'd started, you couldn't fucking stop.

"I feel as if my heart has cracked into pieces and turned to dust. I feel guilty because I shouldn't want you and angry that I still do. I hate that I have my freedom and Olive is safe and I'm still not fucking satisfied. That I'll never be satisfied until I have you. Until we're together...just like we should've been since school. And I'm fucking furious that Justin gets to touch you, kiss you, love you when all along it should've been me."

"There." Her hands slipped from her hips. "Was that so hard?"

I groaned. "Don't ask me what's hard, O."

Her lips twitched with dark humour, her gaze trailing to my jeans.

My need was evident. Grotesquely eager after being caged for so long.

"It's a relief to finally hear you say it."

"Say what?"

"That you love me."

I stiffened. "I told you before. I told you so many—"

"You told me while tying me up to paint and sacrifice me. You told me when we were saying goodbye." O pushed off from the wall, coming toward me in the middle of the lounge. "You told me in texts and whispers, you told me...but you didn't make me believe you."

I trembled. "How was I supposed to do that? It was the honest to God truth. Still is."

"I believe you now."

"Why, what changed?"

"The fact that *you* believe that you love me. Your jealousy makes yourself believe."

Anger rippled through me. "You're saying I didn't love you even when I told you I did?"

"I don't think you trusted you had the *right* to love me. You wanted me, but you wouldn't have kept me if you thought I deserved better."

"Of course, I wouldn't. I was the puppet of a psychopath and then facing jail. Why would I trap you into a relationship with someone like me?"

"Because I love you, too. I never stopped."

The world screeched to a halt. Words stuck in the back of my throat. "You love me? Still?"

She smiled. "It seems it's a lifetime affliction."

"But…we agreed it was over. You didn't contradict me."

"I needed time. I needed to come to terms with the truth."

"What truth?"

"That I've always loved you, even when I shouldn't. That I always put you first, even when some might call that weak. That I believe we're meant to be together, no matter what nonsense life throws in our way." Her voice lowered, softened. "I've wanted to tell you for ages. Every time I came to visit you, I wanted to say I was waiting for you. Every time we said goodbye, I wanted to hug you and say it wasn't really goodbye. That you were it for me. For always."

My heart tripped and stumbled. "Then…why didn't you?"

I didn't dare believe her.

Couldn't figure out what this meant.

"Because Olive was there, and she took first priority. Our visits were for her. To assure her you were okay, even if you were trapped for a little while. I wouldn't take that away from her—"

She sighed, shaking her head slightly. "You know what? That's a lie too. I had plenty of opportunity to talk to you. I could've told you in a letter. I could've visited on my own. I could've just called you and told you that I was waiting, worried, and completely unable to get over you."

I swallowed, trembling. "You didn't tell me because you didn't want it to be real. You might've still been in love with me, but you didn't want to be."

She nodded, spearing a harpoon through my chest. "You're right," she said quietly. "And that's why I didn't tell you. That's the honest truth."

Truth had always been brutal, but now it cleaved me into pieces. "Look, O, if you came here to tell me you don't want to love me anymore, that's fine. I get it. But we can work out Olive's schedule without—"

"Stop." Placing her hand over my pounding, aching heart, she murmured, "Not telling you I was still in love with you was my one selfish choice. I wanted to feel no obligation or expectation by announcing that I would wait. I wanted to wait…for *me*, not you. I wanted the freedom to change my mind. I needed the space to choose you without feeling trapped." Her lips tipped into a shy smile. "You know…that's the first time I've been honest with myself too. I always made up excuses about why I hadn't told you. That I didn't know if you felt the same way anymore. That it wasn't the right time or place. That our complicated past meant our future could never work. But none of that matters because…it's always been you."

I shivered. "But…what about Justin?"

O spread her hands with a shrug. "What about him? I love Justin. He's one of the kindest, sweetest, most uncomplicated people I know. He's been so good to me, Olive, and you. Yes, I moved in with him because it made financial sense and because Olive was more comfortable having both of us there. But at no point has there ever been a romantic entanglement—even when we were kids. He always knew how I felt about you. He knew there was never anyone else for me."

A bright smile lit up her face. "You can ask him. He started dating a woman called Chloe a few months ago. She's super nice. Don't think it's going to last the distance, as she's a little too independent for a guy like Justin who just wants to dote, but it's nice to see him with someone."

She sighed again. "So…you see, I'm not with Justin. And you don't have to feel guilty for wanting me. You have me. You've *always* had me and—"

I didn't let her finish.

I grabbed her, wrapped her in my arms and kissed her.

Her spine melted.

Her body liquefied in my embrace. And her mouth opened, welcoming me to kiss her deeper, harder, forever.

Heads dancing. Tongues licking.

I couldn't get enough.

The chains around my heart broke away. Padlocks shattered.

Ropes unbound. All the restrictions I'd placed on myself vanished the longer we kissed.

There was something special about this kiss.

Something new and honest and true.

This was real.

Real and promising eternity.

Her heart pounded against mine as I tripped backward, needing every part of her.

Immediately.

Now.

Unable to keep kissing her and navigating my new place, I scooped her into my arms, and stormed into my bedroom.

O shivered as I placed her onto the bed.

A bed.

We'd connected in so many erotic ways. With paint smearing us and cameras recording us, but we'd never done it somewhere that promised romance as well as sex. Somewhere that gave us the freedom to fall into each other, rather than drown out the love with the noise of why we couldn't.

Her hands landed on my chest, her fingernails scraping down my belly. Her touch ran over the scar from Jeffrey shooting me, and banished the last remaining bad memories. Maybe I'd get a tattoo like hers—colour and design that was already a part of me to cover up the ugly scars and mistakes of my past.

But then again, those mistakes had made me worthy.

Worthy of my soul-mate.

My mouth crushed hers again.

I kissed her.

And kissed her.

I kissed her with the softness I'd always wanted to treat her with. The respect, the worship, the undying affection where every touch bled with permanence.

I'd never experienced softness.

Never allowed myself to relax or trust enough to give myself entirely to another.

The sensation of falling into her and out of me, of creating something new together, wrapped around my heart and squeezed. It squeezed with joy and euphoria and a crushing amount of regret.

Regret at not experiencing this overwhelming closeness before.

Of not realising just how special our connection was when we were younger—before I almost ruined everything.

My pulse pounded as our kiss took on another dimension.

Of longing and longevity.

I would kiss this woman for the rest of my life and never get tired of her, never stop wanting her or being so fucking grateful that she waited.

That she had an endless well of forgiveness and strength to put up with all my mistakes.

She moaned as my fingers trailed to her belly, lifting her white t-shirt over her head and breaking our kiss. Hating the distance, I unzipped her jeans and shimmied them down her legs before kissing her again.

Our lips never stopped touching as I removed her bra, socks, and underwear.

Only once she was naked, did I stop.

I pulled away, looking down at her hair tousled on my bed, her perfect breasts rising and falling with erratic breath, and her lips red and swollen from mine.

She was the most perfect thing I'd ever seen.

And she belonged to me as surely as I belonged to her.

It wasn't a matter of possession.

It was a matter of undeniability.

Of two souls being one.

"My turn," she breathed. Arching up, she tugged my t-shirt over my head and unbuckled my belt.

I shuddered as her touch skimmed over my bare flesh.

I'd never get over how reactive I was to her. How much I craved her. How much I fucking loved her.

Her hands looked so delicate as she pushed aside my jeans, and I shifted to shove them down my legs. No boots, no socks, they slipped off the bed, leaving me in my boxer-briefs.

Her fingers wrapped around my erection, her skin hot even through the cotton.

"Wait." I clutched her wrist, my heart racing.

Her eyes flared. "Why?"

The urge to rock into her hand made me grit my teeth. I squeezed my eyes closed, doing my best to scrape together the last remnants of my self-control. "We do this, and there is no going back. Until death do us part, O."

Her hand fisted me, fierce and possessive. "No more secrets. No more sacrifices."

I bared my teeth. "No more being apart."

"I'm okay with that." Her grin was light-hearted even while everything about me was heavy. My blood was heavy. My desire heavy. My promise to always protect her heavy with utmost honesty.

I kissed her again, shuddering as she shoved down my boxer-briefs, and our skin connected bare to bare.

Heat. Softness. Overwhelming need.

Her hand found my cock again, this time without cotton separating us. She squeezed me, stroking up and down. My head tipped forward as I lay on top of her, trapping her arm between us, smothering her with my weight.

Our eyes locked. My heart overflowed. The past meant nothing because this was where I earned everything I ever wanted. Olive was safe. My soul was healed. And O still loved me.

Despite everything.

"I need you, Gil." She rubbed against me, her touch tightening in command.

My own hand slipped between her legs, finding her wet and wanting.

She cried out as I pierced two fingers inside her, claiming her, tormenting her.

I kissed her, harsh and dominating as her hips worked up and into my control. My own hips worked into her hand, both desperate to connect, impatient and hungry.

I wanted to take my time.

To touch every part of her, suck her nipples, grant her orgasm after orgasm, but…there was time for that. We had a lifetime to make up for the fast moments. We had forever to explore and experiment.

For now, this was a hello.

A long-awaited hi.

Withdrawing my fingers, I nudged away her hand and settled between her thighs.

She spread wider, her smile bright and blinding.

I couldn't help it.

I had to kiss her again.

Deeply, deliciously *kiss* her.

Her tongue danced with mine as my cock found her entrance.

She gasped into my mouth as I slowly pushed inside.

I went slow, tantalisingly slow. This wasn't sex. This was so, so much more. This was us no longer fighting destiny.

We quaked as I finally slid the final inch and sheathed myself completely within her. Her body radiated heat and I struggled with the need to thrust. To push us both to the release just out of reach.

Instead, I paused.

I looked down at her, nestled beneath me, her lips still red, eyes liquid with love, and for the first time in my life...I trusted.

Truly, unquestionably *trusted.*

This woman was mine.

She always had been, always would be.

I would never doubt that again.

I pumped into her.

She moaned and dug her fingernails into my lower back, rocking with me.

My thrusts turned faster, deeper, plunging as far as I could.

And O demanded more.

We traded the slow rhythm for a primitive one. Chasing love and lust in its rawest form.

Our lips collided, quick and out of control.

Need galloped around my blood and an orgasm wrapped around the base of my spine.

O shuddered, her mouth parting as pleasure rippled through her. The bands of her release squeezed my cock. I grew harder, thrust faster.

"Fuck..." I groaned.

She cried out as I drove into her, burying my face into her neck and biting her as I lost control.

I came harder than I ever had before.

My stomach hollowed out. My muscles locked. I poured into her, giving her every part of me.

Over and over I came until I trembled and slowly returned from paradise to earth.

For the first time, I wondered about birth control. I'd slept with O without protection. We'd never discussed if she was on the pill. We should probably chat about our future dreams and goals regarding family, but for now, I was open to anything.

I didn't care if I spent the rest of my life loving O and Olive or if we'd add to our brood.

Either way, we were family.

Now and forever after.

* * * * *

"Good morning." I smiled as O appeared from my bedroom.

Her answering smile was almost sheepish, her hair tangled and body loose. "Good morning."

"Coffee?" I poured a fresh cup for her.

"Please." Padding over to me in bare feet, I couldn't stop staring at her. Couldn't stop believing this was real. That I got this fucking lucky.

Passing her the mug, I couldn't stop myself from hugging her close and kissing her.

It was meant to be a short kiss.

It turned out to be a long, heated hello.

By the time I let her go, I was hard again and cursing the clock for not having enough time to get her back into bed.

Justin had text and congratulated me. He said he knew why O hadn't gone home last night and was glad I'd finally come to my senses. He also said to meet him and Olive at her dance practice downtown and not to be late.

My grin was stupidly big as O sipped the drink I'd made her and practically swooned. "How is it that life feels so much brighter? This coffee tastes better than any other coffee. The sun is prettier than any other sun. It's as if—"

"We've come alive again," I murmured.

"Yes, exactly." Her eyes snagged mine and once again my heart skipped a beat.

Without looking away, I pulled the small piece of paper from my pocket. "Here."

I hadn't planned on giving it to her so soon. But...this moment was perfect. This moment was just us, before we returned to reality.

"What is it?" Placing her coffee on the bench, she grinned.

"Read it."

Her eyes left mine, skimming the newly-penned job advertisement. If she accepted the job, there would be no terminations or quitting.

The position was for life.

Must be brave, stubborn, and impervious to the tempers of loved ones. Hours are endless, pay is non-existence, quitting absolutely forbidden. Able to function on no sleep, refrain from running when times get hard, and be more than just a living canvas but a lover...a mother.

Other attributes required: forgiving, opinionated, and not afraid to tell me when I'm wrong. Must also enjoy being touched and kissed at any time of my choosing.

Call or email 'YOUR HEART, HIS SOUL' if interested in applying.

Her head whipped up the moment she'd finished, her gaze searching mine. "What is this?"

I fought the weakness in my knees, going to her and cupping her cheek. "It's exactly what it looks like."

I'd written it an hour ago as dawn arrived. I'd dared to dream I could have everything.

"What are you saying?"

"I'm saying that I want you in my life. My business is back in full work, and I only want to paint one canvas for the rest of my days. I want you there to scold me when I'm being an arse. I want you to continue loving Olive like you do. I want to share everything I have and am with you...forever."

"Gil, I—"

"You don't have to say yes...not straight away. I can wait."

"And if I say yes now?"

"Then it's binding. A contract for eternity."

She blushed. "Eternity is a long time."

"It's far too short." Gathering her in my arms, I kissed her gently. "I will never be as good as Justin. I accept that. I accept that I will never be as selfless as either of you and acknowledge that I will probably let you down at some point, but, O...I don't want any other canvas. I don't want any other mother for Olive. I want to share art with you. I want to paint and dance together. I want *you*."

She trembled under my touch. "I...I don't know what to say."

"Say you'll marry me."

Her lips parted. She gasped. "Are you serious?"

Instead of answering, I dropped to one knee. "Marry me, Olin Moss. It's always been you. It will always be you. I don't know how to survive without you."

O tugged at my hands, trying to bring me to my feet.

I fought her, waiting for a reply.

I would stay on my knee for weeks if that was what it took.

Slowly, a tear ran from the corner of her eyes. "Yes."

"Yes?"

She bit her lip, nodding. "Yes. Yes, I'll marry you."

And suddenly, I was that kid falling in love with a girl in a school corridor.

Possibilities were endless.

Love guaranteed.

She was my family.

Finally.

Epilogue

Gil

IT TOOK A year to pay off the fine and the donations to the victim's families.

I technically didn't have to pay. I'd filed for bankruptcy in prison and all debts against my name were null and void.

But...I wanted to.

I *needed* to.

I might not have killed those girls but my silence gave Jeffrey the freedom in which to take their lives.

I also paid Justin for his time and cost of looking after Olive in his home.

He tried to give it back.

Said it was insulting.

But I wrapped his hand around the thick envelope and begged him to take it.

Money was crass and not worth nearly what he'd done for me, but I needed to even the scorecard between us. Until he had a kid of his own that O and I could babysit, I didn't want anything outstanding between us.

I didn't want him to feel like I didn't appreciate what he'd done when he was as important to me as my daughter and wife-to-be.

It took another year to save enough for a new home for the three of us—four counting our regular guest, Justin.

Business was good.

Commissions were piling up.

O was my canvas every day.

She ran my page, liaised with companies, and ensured my notoriety went global.

Without her, I would never have reached the levels I had. She ruled me and my creativity with her capable, wonderful kindness.

Working with her, living with her, I was aware I'd replaced Justin in both those roles. But at no point was there animosity between any of us. Justin hung out almost on a nightly basis—unless he had a date, and then he'd vanish for a week or so, figuring out if this new girl was worthy to join our extended family.

Once O and I had saved enough to buy a home, all of us went house hunting. We started in the city, looking for large warehouses like I had before. We investigated the suburbs next, traipsing through derelict homes and abandoned corner shops that could be renovated into the next location for our business.

In the end, we went into the country, door knocking on old farms with large barns, asking local villagers if they knew of estates coming up for sale.

And we found nothing suitable.

The hunt had been fun before it became frustrating.

I wanted a large studio with its own shower and lots of storage.

O wanted lots of sunshine and big windows.

Olive wanted a huge bedroom with a painting corner and chalkboard walls.

Justin wanted a guest suite with its own sitting room so he could come stay with us for days at a time and work away from the office.

Our hopes dwindled as we struggled to find anything remotely perfect.

Until...we finally found it.

A 1600s barn that had been converted into a four-bedroom, three bathroom home with modern editions of glass and steel. The ceilings soared above us with exposed centuries-old timber. Sun streamed in from big skylights and our wish list was complete with a private studio and guest suite dotted around the hobby farm.

Olive got a conservatory and O got her sunshine. Justin got his guest wing and I got a large studio for my business.

Life was good.

Better than good.

Life was perfect.

And I was so fucking grateful.

"Hey!" I chuckled as Olive dashed past me, stealing my paintbrush.

"You're too slow." She waggled it, dropping ochre splashes on the polished concrete floor. I didn't care about the paint spots, this entire place would be covered when I started working. That was the beauty of paint. It belonged on the tools and walls as much as it did on the canvas.

I chased her, grabbing her around the middle and flipping her upside down. A couple of pennies fell out of her pockets along with a blue pencil and scrunched up piece of paper.

"Put me down!"

"Do you promise not to be annoying?"

"*You're* annoying." She giggled.

"You're the most annoying." I spun her the right way up and plonked her onto her feet. "The most annoying of annoying."

She stuck out her tongue, swiping the paintbrush over my cheek. "No. *You* are."

"Oh, now you're gonna get it." I launched at her, only to miss as she barrelled around O and tucked herself against the wall.

"Nu-huh. You will!" She laughed as I bear-hugged both of them, squishing O against me and Olive against the wall. "O will protect me!"

To be able to joke like this. To be stupid like this.

Fuck.

O rolled her eyes and laughed softly. "You two need to grow up."

"Tell him that." Olive stuck her tongue out again. "He's not painting. He's just standing there with a dopey look on his face."

O looked over her shoulder, kissing the tip of my nose. "I like that dopey look."

"And I like you," I murmured, placing my mouth over hers for a quick kiss.

I would never get used to that privilege, that sense of completeness. I was home. In every sense of the word. We'd found our dream house, but without O to share my heart and Olive to take care of, it would be meaningless and empty.

"Eww, you two are so gross." Olive wriggled out, returning to the huge mural we'd started this morning as a family.

Part graffiti, part geometric, part realism.

I'd taken inspiration from O's tattoo. The owl with its

hidden animals beginning with O. This time, it was a design that incorporated all of us, and took up the entire two-story wall at the end of the studio, showcasing the art of paint and the master of shadow.

O had agreed to help paint the simple stuff—outlines and bold block colours—saying she didn't have enough talent to do more. Olive had exceeded all my hopes of her following in my footsteps, and her talent with a brush sometimes made me sit back in serious awe.

We returned to work, colours flowing harmoniously.

O glanced at the clock, her stomach rumbling. "In another thirty minutes, I'll put dinner on."

"Don't forget I have a dance lesson tonight," Olive said. "The teacher is coming here."

"And don't forget I asked for a lesson for me after." I chuckled. "Thought we could practice outside by the pond."

O spun to face me. "You asked for a dance lesson?"

"Yep."

"Why?"

Why? Because dancing had been torn from her life like Olive had been torn from mine. I'd been lucky enough to reclaim Olive, but O…she wasn't under false illusions that her body would always be a slightly bit broken.

I didn't want her to go through life without soul food.

So…I'd arranged ballroom dancing for us. Salsa and jive. I sucked and my coordination was laughable, but I would embarrass myself every night if O danced with me.

Because when she danced, the music whispered through her veins, and she glowed.

Glowed like the angel I always knew she was.

"I need the exercise."

She chuckled. "You work out every morning." She walked into my embrace, her lips seeking mine. Her eyes said she knew exactly my intentions. "You're so good to me, Gilbert Clark."

"I love you, Olin Moss."

She kissed me harder and I smiled around a secret.

I meant what I said about giving her what she needed, but I also had an ulterior motive for the dance lessons.

I was going to marry this woman.

Now my debts were settled and bank account flush, I was happy knowing I had enough to protect her for life. That I could afford to make her mine.

In two months' time, we would get hitched and our family would be official.

And after I made this wonderful woman mine, I would spin her and dip her and waltz her into our future.

Forever.

Epilogue Two

Olin

"QUIT MOVING." Gil's fingers latched on my hipbone, his voice strict and chilly like it did when his art stole his concentration.

"Quit tickling me then."

"Quit making me want to skip the wedding and go straight to the consummate part."

I swatted his ear, my gaze skimming over to Olive who stood in the bathroom fixing a final flower into her hair. I doubted she'd heard, but still. "Your daughter is right there."

"*Our* daughter." His eyes caught mine and my heart melted just like always. I would always be weak where he was concerned. Always have no future or home unless he was there.

I accepted that.

Embraced that.

I smiled as he dropped his attention and airbrushed crème and ivory over my skin. "I'm marrying both of you."

"And no divorce shall be given," he growled threateningly, but it ached with need.

I chuckled, loving all over again how carefree he was. How different he'd become now he actually communicated his hardships and shared his troubles. "You know you're not supposed to see the bride on her wedding day."

He bit his lip, angling the airgun to follow the shadows along my leg. "Not many husbands help dress the bride."

"You're not my husband."

His head tipped up, his eyes flashing. "Not yet. But in ten minutes, I will be."

I bent in half to kiss him, keeping my bouquet of white

roses away from the perfection on my skin. All I wore was two pasties, a skin-coloured G-string, and his paint. I was about to walk down an aisle in front of my family, mostly naked, and I couldn't wait.

Couldn't wait to show them the talent of my husband-to-be.

After all, our relationship had started this way—our second chance. It was fitting that it would finish this way—marrying us for eternity.

"I love you, Gilbert Clark."

"And I love you, soon-to-be Mrs Olin Clark." He pressed a kiss right over my underwear before adding the finishing touches of my untraditional wedding gown. Only once my skin wore ice, alabaster, and snow did Gil put away his brushes, wipe his paint streaked hands on a rag, and slip into his tux jacket.

He frowned as his gaze slid over me, judging his creation, assessing if I was perfect.

"Oh, wow." Olive's mouth fell open as she came toward us. "That's...you look amazing, O." Her grey eyes, so intelligent and gentle sparked with love.

My own eyes prickled with overwhelming affection. She might not be mine by blood but she was my daughter through and through. "Thanks, lovely." Things grew hot and melty in my chest again. "I can't take credit. It's all this body painter's work."

"Helps that the canvas is beautiful to begin with," Gil muttered, adding a last-minute flourish.

More tears built.

Olive shook her finger at me. "Don't you start crying, O. You'll ruin Dad's art." She giggled. "And you know how much trouble you'll be in."

"He'd probably divorce me." I chuckled, sniffing back liquid that wasn't allowed to fall.

"He has to marry you first." Olive snickered.

"I married her the moment she made me pancakes when I was a teenager," Gil said. "She just didn't know it."

I wanted to laugh but kept my face composed so I didn't ruin the rhinestones Gil had embellished my eyebrows with.

Today was already perfect, and we'd only just dressed.

"So...are you done?" Olive asked her dad, moving forward to help close up the paint and box the bottles where they belonged. "Justin text me before. He said they're almost ready."

"Yeah, I'm done." Gil raked a hand through his hair, leaving behind a streak of white in his otherwise dark unruly mess. I didn't tell him. I liked the roguish imperfection.

"I'll go and see if he needs any help," Olive said, blowing me an air kiss. "Don't be too long! It's not raining but we don't want to push it."

Gil chuckled, his face soft and full of affection as Olive smoothed down her pretty grey bridesmaid dress and slipped from the guest apartment.

I had no doubt in five minutes, Olive would have everyone sat in the white wooden chairs, the music would be playing, and our small neighbourhood would be ready to witness our nuptials.

Together, we would walk through the studio to the manicured garden at the back. To the pond twinkling in the sunshine and over grass that looked like perfect green carpet. We would become betrothed beneath a small alter made from twisted old branches and flowers.

Justin would stand beside Gil as best man and Olive would stand beside me, and tonight, I hoped Justin might pop the question to his year-long girlfriend, Monique. A year wasn't a very long time, but when you met the right one, you only needed a day.

One day to understand that you could like others, love others, even marry others, but unless that person was approved by fate and your perfect other half, then it wasn't entirely your destiny.

Gil was my destiny.

Even though I'd tried to fight it.

Even though he'd tried to kill it and I'd walked away from it...the undeniability of us had won.

Gil moved toward me, keeping his hands to himself with a groan. "I'd give anything to smudge you. To grab and kiss you."

I blushed. "You can kiss me but you can't touch."

He groaned again. "I can't kiss you. I painted your lips too. If I do, they'll smear."

"Guess you're going to have to wait until the official kiss then."

"You're determined to kill me."

I smiled. "Determined to marry you." Spreading my arms, I added, "Thank you, Gil. For giving me such a wonderful gown."

Leaning in, he pressed his lips to my ear. "I'm far from done with you, O. I have another artwork in mind for the honeymoon."

I shivered in anticipation. Kissing his cheek, I pushed him

away so I didn't leap into his arms. "Shoo. It's time for me to finish getting ready. You can't see this next part. It's a surprise."

Olive and I had put it together.

I wore Gil's paint, but I needed something that moved with me. Something that would dance around my legs and arms. Together, we'd sourced panels of sheer lace and organza, designing a dress that hung like a kimono, open down my chest and tied at the waist with a simple silver sash with the sides split, revealing my lace-painted legs and body paint.

The fabric would frame the masterpiece Gil had done.

He chuckled as Olive darted back into the room. "Everyone's ready. You guys coming?"

Gil brushed past her, giving her a quick kiss on her hair. "You're gorgeous, little spinach. A perfect wedding planner."

She blushed. "The wedding won't work if the bride and groom are late."

He laughed again. "Fine, I'm going." He looked back at me, drinking in his colours and creation but only seeing me beneath it. Loving me despite everything.

My heart swelled and spilled over.

An affliction of love that would happen every day for the rest of my life because I was so unbelievably lucky to marry my soul-mate.

Gil winced as if he couldn't bear to say goodbye. "Guess I'll see you both soon."

"You will." I smiled softly.

"I'll be the guy waiting at the altar."

"I'll be the woman walking up the aisle."

"Don't make me wait too long." He drank me in one last time. Smiled at his daughter. And then, he left.

He left behind all the mess between us.

He walked into the future where all our dreams came true. And I followed him.

THE END

Fable of Happiness
Coming 2021

BOOK ONE

fable
of
happiness

New York Times & USA Today Bestselling Author
PEPPER WINTERS

It's the start of something huge

From New York Times Bestseller, Pepper Winters, comes a new Dark Romance full of decadent angst, monstrous heroes, and pages chock-full of lust.

A house hidden in the middle of nowhere.
A man who's lived alone for a decade.
A woman who trespasses on his solitude.
A love full of hate as well as hunger.

The thing about my life is...I was never in control of it.
I just I thought I was.
I thought I had everything figured out—a good career, fun hobbies, a bright future, but everything changed when I found an ivy-cloaked house, tucked in a forgotten valley, hiding a man who corrupted my world forever.
I thought I was successful, until he showed me fortune and happiness could be snatched away in an instant.
I believed I was blessed, but really, I was cursed.
Cursed to become a plaything for a monster.
Cursed to become a prisoner just because I trespassed.
Now, I know nothing.
I am nothing.
I'm just his.

Please note this is a dark romance and not suitable for people who have triggers. Content included can be hard to read and only recommended for people who like dark romance.

Made in United States
Troutdale, OR
10/31/2024

24321794R00434